REUNION

THOMAS ANTHONY

ELLIS

REUNION

For her. . .

First published in Great Britain in 2012 by The Derby Books Publishing Company Limited, 3 The Parker Centre, Derby, DE21 4SZ.

This paperback edition published in Great Britain in 2013 by DB Publishing, an imprint of JMD Media Ltd

ISBN 978-1-78091-160-1

Printed and bound in the UK by Copytech (UK) Ltd Peterborough

Chapter 1

Even though he would never know of it, today Padraig Skelly was about to capture a moment that would begin one of Orplow's finest tragedies. Known as Parti to his friends, the man was nothing if not conservative. Having lived in the small town of Orplow for his entire life, he prided himself on his ignorance of the world outside. Even his very first memory was that of his late father, proud and stiff in stature, walking him through the wild flowered meadows and telling him that everything that he would ever need could be found within the tranquil confines of the town walls. The memory always brought back the sweet medicinal scent of the wild blue flowers cast upon the sea front breeze that salted his face as he had looked out onto the coast from the meadow's head. His father had held his hand tightly that day as they stood bearing witness to the commanding tide of the Irish Sea – as if to anchor his son to the very earth on which he stood.

Sixty years on and Parti had not moved a muscle. Time had relaxed his once sporting physique and now offered the sight of an elderly gentleman bent almost completely double. Entirely flat-backed, Parti had to raise his neck up to its very limit just to look ahead of himself. Through school-ground whispers and sniggers, the local children had cruelly dubbed him 'Farty Parti', but never to his face, regardless of how constantly constipated he looked. The steady strain upon his back had forced Parti to adopt a permanent scowl and toothy grimace and, whenever he would waddle by, even the parents would joke that one of the gargoyles from the local church had sprung to life.

However, unbeknown to Parti, this was to be the final day of his life. Later this evening, a fatal seizure would grip him while he was saying his nightly prayers. Yet, this morning was about new beginnings, and it held an activity that had become somewhat of an annual task for Parti. Coming from a wealthy family, Parti had been passed his late father's pride and joy; his Daguerreotype camera. It was the envy of every household in the town. Now looking tired from almost 40 years of service, the leathered accordion like camera was being prepared for what would be its final picture.

Leaving his cottage, Parti locked the front door to his resting place and set about town. A small wooden placard with the legend 'Dunromin' clunked against the door as it closed. Adjusting his stance, Parti could feel the weight of the camera resting heavily in its satchel. Slumped over Parti's retiring shoulders, his back tabled the satchel while both of his hands grasped its thick leather strap. He could feel the contents of the bag digging into his side; the roll of filter paper, cleaning cloth and the polished sheet of silver on which the image would be developed, all clunked into his ribs. However, there was no room for the tripod. Awkwardly, this found its place under Parti's right armpit and across his chest – the top of which occasionally blasted Parti in the face whenever he was to over-step his staggered stride.

Thankfully, the walk into town was a casual one and not too far. Finding his feet upon the first road from his cottage, Parti waddled past the grand Darby estate. This country manor was home to Raegan Darby, the town's wealthiest landowner and descendant of a protestant family of English tenant farmers. With an astute sense for business, Raegan Darby had seized on the opportunities afforded by capitalist farming and the arrival of enclosure. Watching his lesser-shrewd peers outlive their leases on their farms – Raegan Darby offered them a self-nourishing lifeline. Having bought the land from right under their noses, he gifted the onetime landowners the chance to work the land as an employee of the Darby Empire. Today he could be seen sat next to his handsome wife Fiona on the porch of their manor house, while three bounding great danes enjoyed the lush and lavish land before them.

The Darby land itself reached far and wide, grasping the pebbled shores of Lake Doriend. Dutifully, the sun seemed to rise and set upon this great lake. Each compulsive season of the year brought with it a timely frame to the shores. And Parti had enjoyed them all. The spirited spring brought life to the lake as woodland creatures gathered and bathed. In summer, the bright dandelions burst from their buds, crowning the lake gloriously. In turn the roaring autumn winds would appear but a breeze upon the still lake's surface, while the harsh screaming winters froze the land and glazed the lake with a lick of frost.

This day was a surprisingly warm September morning. The dirt tracks into town had a spring-full bounce to them. The dust from the tracks completely masked Parti's scurrying feet, giving the impression that he was being carried into town on a tiny sandstorm. Occasionally, he would stop and rest up the sturdy stone walls that framed the fields of the town.

Looking up, or straight ahead for most people, Parti could see the church spire. It pierced the horizon, stretching towards the sky without a single cloud to shroud it. The church was the centrepiece to the town, and stood as such to the many lives that passed through it. Parti himself had been baptised, christened and confirmed in the church of St Peter. He had also married and buried his late wife in the church grounds, some 50 years between. And despite the death that the walls housed, the church remained the heartbeat of Orplow. Every Sunday, the people would flock to hear the teachings of Father Daniel; forever grateful to Lord for their salvation.

But salvation always carried a cost. The great famine, or the fungus famine as the townspeople called it, lasted three hopeless harvests from 1845 to 1848. Orplow had prided itself on being self-sufficient, but even the occupants of this town felt the famine's fatal effects. Forced to live on subsistence, people grew accustom to the face of hunger. However, for those few who were wretchedly poor and already etching out a living before the famine struck, it was sadly more than just the apples of the earth that were soon rotting within the fruitless ground.

Now, stood at the church gates, Parti could practically feel the pulse of the town. The bells on the bicycles of early morning commuters jingled; friendly voices combined into one indecipherable chorus; while children could be heard laughing and at play. Parti had always loved this town and, through his photographs, Parti had always strived to capture the beauty of it. His sole function was to show how Orplow worked; to illustrate how the people of

Orplow lived, and what threaded their lives together. His favourite time of the day was the dawn. For him, the mornings brought with them a thrust of life; the earliest opportunity for fates to collide and paths to be taken. And yet, despite years of trying, Parti had never found that one moment that would capture this. That is, not until today. He had always been a believer that a caged bird could never be seen to fly, and so felt his pictures were always doomed to fail. But today was a day for new beginnings, and fate was set to detain the detail that Parti had always desired. Yet, he would never live to know just how doomed the detail was.

The laughter of children was Parti's compass today for he was heading to the local primary school. This was named after the local church of St Peter, but was commonly referred to as Eden. This was mainly down to Father Daniel's proud proclamation that it was within the walls of the school that every child gets their first bite at the apple of Catholicism. Befittingly, the part of the dogged snake was played by the school's own Ms Flannery Ryann. Her core principle was that it was only through sin that people could then go boldly from it. Therefore, her shrewd eye for discipline was sharp if not original.

Being the headmistress to the only dual religion school in the county, Ms Flannery Ryann had quite a juggling act on her harsh hands. With the small population of Protestants in Orplow failing to even fill a single class – let alone justify a whole school – Eden had encouraged their enrolment into the town's Roman Catholic School. Only a mere tenth of the school's pupils were protestant, but it still made national headlines, as the school was seen to be trying to bridge the gap between the divide.

Originally constructed in 1845, the school had been greatly expanded in 1885. This was largely funded by the charitable Raegan Darby when his first child took to the school. The extension allowed the population of pupils to rise to 220; nearly the entire child population of the town. However, with free education not due to hit London until 1891, families still had to find the means to pay for the weekly tuition. Unfortunately, as a slave to its remoteness, Orplow would not enjoy free education for a further 10 years after that of England's capital. Remarkably, Raegan Darby kindly agreed to cover the cost of every child that came from the family of one of his employees. However, he flatly refused to fund those who were outside of his provincial grasp.

But today, the school was in someone else's grip. With crimson hair pulled so tight it looked almost raven black, Ms Flannery Ryann cut a lean, sharp figure. She moved like violence and her half rimmed glasses rested precariously on the tip of her sharp Roman nose. Her eyes were always tunnelled, and if they were to ever lock onto you it felt like the reckoning itself had arrived. Or so the children were made to feel. For among the adults, there was a more intriguing eye cast upon this teacher. It was rumoured that Ms Ryann – though stern and cold in her public display – was once quite the firecracker in the bedroom. However, no known male had stepped forward to confirm this just yet.

Away from the anecdotal adults, today Ms Ryann was putting the children through their paces. The class of 1894 had already shown that they were going to be a handful; the young girls skipped and giggled together, keeping their distance from the boys who huddled and plotted behind them.

'Come on children, get together,' said Ms Ryann. Her voice was shrill and piercing. Her order greeted with abiding silence. The playground froze for a second before the rushing of feet flocked towards what called them. Each child raced as if to come last was rewarded by nothing more than an unimaginable torture. And quite rightly, it was.

Ms Ryann's long stretched, pale fingers clipped the ear of the young chubby brown haired boy who was last to pass her. His ear throbbed as he walked down the line to stand at the back of the boy's queue. Both sexes were in single file and stood either side of Ms Ryann as she now led her little militia through the playground. Both the boys and girls were ordered to stare straight ahead and march towards the school gates. A single word from either would be met with the sharpest scowl you could possibly imagine, swiftly chased by a decree of complete silence for the remainder of the day.

'Right this way, children. Not a peep, please.' Ms Ryann marched ahead. Her shoulders were stiff and her arms swung like fierce pendulums. The girls were uniformed, mirroring her movements exactly. However, the boys were not so precise. One freckled faced boy in particular was turning to the chubby boy with the red ear in an attempt to make his soon-to-be best friend laugh. Embellishing the movements of his mentor, he swung his shoulders in a way to seductively shake his imaginary bosom. Yet, it had not gone unnoticed, and he was to spend the next week nursing his spanked cheeks while cleaning the chalkboard during every break time.

Apart from the sprog-march, the school was still today. The dusty red-bricked building was calm and settled inside. It was a tradition to open the school a day early for the first year infants; it allowed them to become familiar with the surroundings. It also allowed for the school to go through the formalities of registration and of course the famed school picture.

The tight corridors of Eden were adorned with dozens of these pictures; all framed magnificently as every child sat proudly and faced the front. Each picture was flawless in its duplicity and consistency – each year mirroring the last if not for the different faces within them. Often parents would whisper of the irksome feeling of a thousand bright eyes following them as they passed through the school corridors. Today was to be no exception. The class of 1894 were about to have their very first school picture taken. And it was to be the pride and joy of all visiting parents throughout the years. Given the welcoming nature of Eden, the school portrait depicted a class pure in its diversity – as children from various backgrounds were seen sat side-by-side. Sadly for some, it was the only time that every child was seen as equal in the town of Orplow.

The class divide within the town was as clear as day and night, and every child soon took their place within it once their education was complete. Very few would ever get a chance to break through the class barrier and change their fortune. If seen to from the lower tier, then even the brightest of brains would be put to work as soon as their hands were strong enough, while those of the upper tier would fill the positions forged for them by their fathers.

However, today was different. Today was a time for equality. Every boy had on their uniform – reminiscent of the Eton suit, with broad white collared shirts, grey cotton short pants and stunted jackets known scornfully as bum-freezers. Every girl, on the other hand, had on a white blouse topped by an ironing board like grey pinafore. And both sexes had knee high white socks and dark sandals.

Positioned directly in front of the main doors, the class was finally in place. Arched above their heads, engraved into the stone were the words 'St Peter's Roman Catholic School'. The letters appeared more golden today as the sun beamed proudly on the school's face. Beneath the bright light, the children squinted as they faced their mistress.

Scuttling behind her, Ms Ryann heard Parti approaching before she saw him. Riding through the gates on a miniature blanket of sand, his curses and 'fecks' were thankfully muffled by the clattering of the tripod in his arms. She had always had a soft spot for the man. His outlook had conflicted with hers so drastically that she adored him for it. She was regimented and in order, while he appeared to just fumble through life and somehow make a success of it. A true perfectionist at heart, she had always taken little pleasure in anything other than greatness. Yet, her piercing eyes had grown green when she realised that, unadorned by scepticism, Parti could find great pleasure in the little things that life afforded. However, despite her knowing her feelings to be true, it was more likely that the heel of her shoe would meet with the cheeks of his behind before their two hearts would ever entwine. Parti was a widower after all, and he was loudly committed to his late wife. Ms Ryann on the other hand had never married nor enjoyed the pleasures of a married man, despite the whisperings of the townspeople. And so, she guessed that it would simply be put down to one of the town's many tragedies.

'Morning Ms,' shouted Parti breathlessly. 'Where do you want me?'

If a wry smile crossed her face, Parti didn't see it. Instead, he stood facing his boots; his right-hand outstretched, propping him up against the school gates. The satchel weighed heavy in his committed hand – as the strap began to slip through his sweaty palm. He pushed himself from the wall and grasped the strap with both hands as his legs steadied beneath him. Staggering slightly, Parti eventually made his way towards Ms Ryann. She was after all his biggest distraction in life since the passing of his wife. And on the brief occasions when they had met, Parti had always wanted to tell her how he had felt. But his commitment to the church, and his love for his late wife, had always stolen his tongue.

'Over here please, Mr Skelly,' said Ms Ryann. 'By my side, please'. Her tone of authority always put life into his old legs and Parti forced himself forward.

Stepping forward, he did not know whether it was the blinding pain or the crippling embarrassment that he felt first, as his overzealous stride had brought the tip of the tripod he carried to crash directly into his forlorn face. Like a man bent over in the stocks, he had to embrace the impact totally and suffer the subsequent jitters of the crowd.

The giggles of the children were allowed to play out for an extended second for even Ms Ryann needed a moment to compose herself and stifle her laughter before turning and silencing her class with a single signature stare. Meanwhile, Parti's face was flush and his cheek numb and swollen. He placed his satchel on the ground and turned his back to the children to save his humiliation further. His posture, however, proved too inviting and the boy with freckles doubled his punishment by pursing his lips and blowing a silence shattering raspberry. Even his mother-melting puppy-dog eyes could not thaw Ms Ryann, and her frosty fury was as blistering as Parti's cracked cheek. Whipping out her arm, her sharp cold hand snapped in the air and left a bright red print on the boy's exposed legs. The second slap that had contacted with his buttocks had now made it unbearable to sit still.

With the sun beating down, the heavens began to shine their glory upon the school. The white light was brighter than any Parti could ever remember seeing before. He felt like he had just walked out of the darkest depths of a cave and straight into daylight, as his eyes struggled to adjust to it. He tried in vain to block the blur by squinting. Blinkered, he began to set up his camera. Fortunately, he could do this blindfolded and in the dark, having memorised every component by heart. Having cleaned them over a thousand times, Parti could identify each part by weight if not by shape alone. Once in position, he cleaned the lens once more with his dust cloth and removed the silver plate from the satchel. The sunlight skimmed across the silver plate.

Turning the camera towards the children, Parti saw the usual response. On any other occasion many would become more animated at the sight of this contraption. And the rest would just become more reserved. However, every child in Orplow had been told of the importance of this very moment since the first instance that they could listen. Well versed and over rehearsed, they knew their role and would play their part perfectly. For if not, then Ms Ryann was in place to orchestrate. Overlooking her class, she stood by Parti's side.

'Sit up straight; backs arched; hands on laps.' She barked orders as she observed the class for a final time, before taking her position in the front row at the centre of the children. Boys were sitting straight to her right, and the girls sat neatly to her left. Confident they were all in order, Ms Ryann trusted Parti completely to ensure that they would not move or falter. He had been the only school photographer since the school had first opened and had always gotten it right. His photographs had become as much a part of the institution as the walls themselves. To many, they were the very keystone to the building itself.

Parti held his breath. He had gotten it right countless times before; every picture had been flawless in its design. However, today something felt different. Parti could not see properly. The sunlight was bouncing off his lens brighter than ever and he struggled to make out every child that it framed. Due to its design, the camera only afforded one chance to take the picture, and Parti prided himself on his accuracy. Yet at this precise moment, holding the trigger blindly, he prayed that Ms Ryann had got it right. Filling his shallow lungs and steadying his shaking arm, Padraig Skelly clicked the button and took his final ever picture.

It would not be until later that evening – once the picture had been developed – that Parti would find that every child befitted the tradition. Every child, that is, except two. Across the class, two children gazed into each other's eyes for the very first time; framed for an eternity and already breaking the rules in their very first encounter. The names of these children were Michael and Grace.

Chapter 2

The most beautiful day in 1889 proved to be the worst day of Abigail Alpin's life. While the spring sun sprinkled the far fields of Orplow, Abigail Alpin, hormonal and three months pregnant, was to become a widow. Her childhood sweetheart, and father to her unborn child, was soon to be found hanging from the thick willow tree that shaded their lakeside cottage.

Abigail could still remember the first day she saw Ferris. His chocolate brown hair kinked at the ends as the summer rain soaked his linen shirt to his strong broad chest. He was 14 at the time, but years of working the field with his father had granted him the physique of a man. His arms were thick and his shoulders bulged as he tightly held the handles of his horse drawn plough. All the local girls had begun to talk about Ferris Alpin. He came from a family of labourers who were sadly way down the food chain of the Orplow hierarchy. Nevertheless, it was still this young man who was the local dish of fancy, especially for the younger female population of the town.

Never regarded for his intellect, Ferris always worked until his body could not give anymore. He had a fine eye for the line of the plough, and used it as precisely as a surgeon would their scalpel. The fields he tended were dissected into intricate rows, each proving to be a vital lifeline, feeding the very heart of the town like great earthy arteries. Despite his intense focus, Ferris always enjoyed the distraction of the young fair skinned girl that came to watch him as he worked. Her hair was as black as night and her eyes as radiant as the stars that punctured the winter sky. Whenever exhausted by his labour, he would remember the first time his hand had ever touched hers. His heart had instantly invited him to love something other than the only thing he had ever known. And love her he did. Right up until his dying day.

The day Ferris had proposed to Abigail he had not even needed to utter the words. Spread out upon a tartan blanket, overlooking the great lake, she had felt his steady hand begin to shake in hers. His heart raged within his chest as the sun began to rise from underneath the lake's long mantel. Looking into her eyes his breathing steadied and, as his thick lips pursed to break the silence, Abigail had whispered 'Yes'.

The years that followed had been a struggle but a worthy one. Among the hunger and workload the couple remained strong and united. Nobody in the town could vouch for ever hearing a bad word uttered between the two and, while private in their personal lives, their love was as public and as obvious as the days were bright. From the very first moment their worlds collided, both Abigail and Ferris knew without hesitation that they were loved by the other. The few family members present at their modest wedding ceremony had all discussed how even the heavens had shed a tear that day; the cloudless sky offered a gentle shower that washed over the church just as the couple began to say their vows.

Eternally grateful for her blessings, Abigail thanked the Lord every day and so could always be found praying in the church during her scarce spare moments. However, these visits grew more often as the struggles and demands of life forced the couple apart for hours that began to feel longer than days. To make ends meet, Ferris had taken more work on the farm. Unable to ignore the man's potential, Raegan Darby had begrudgingly appointed him as the head farmer for the Darby estate. For, despite his natural credentials, Ferris had never been favoured by the forever envious Raegan. Determined to be branded as its saviour, Raegan strived for the town's admiration. He hungered for the recognition he believed his wealth deserved. However, it would be Ferris that the townspeople took time to speak with. Charmed by the man's honesty and integrity, they saw that it was Ferris' toil rather than the spoils of Raegan that truly nourished the town.

The greater workload inevitably meant less time together for Abigail and Ferris. But it was within the few moments that they shared together that life was completely savoured. Lying together during the warm hours of the night, Ferris prayed for Abigail's head to rest on his chest forever. Yearning for comfort and protection, her head would slip and fit perfectly into the nook of his arm. It was in these moments that he was completely at peace. It was these moments that he worked so hard for.

In the final few months, without enough hours in the day, Ferris had abandoned the church. As the townspeople would filter past on a great tide towards St Peter's, Ferris' Sunday mornings were greeted by further graft and labour. On the first Sunday that he had been forced to work, Abigail had stirred and woken to see her husband taking his thick sheepskin coat off the door. He was creeping out of the cottage when she spoke.

'Good morning, my love.'

Stopping dead in his tracks, Ferris turned and looked at his beautiful wife – her eyes scrunched up in a tight ball as they adjusted to the daylight that beamed through the open doorway.

'Pray for me,' said Ferris before stopping her heart with his signature smile, and then leaving the cottage.

And so they would play out this exchange every Sunday for their final few months together. Ferris, ignoring his fatigue, would work on the town's day of rest, while Abigail knelt in the church and prayed tirelessly for her husband. Unbeknown to them both, everyone else in the church – aware of the couple's plight – were praying for them too.

Grateful for the life she had led, Abigail had not lived with many regrets. However, it would haunt her remaining days that Ferris met with death before being greeted with the news that he was to become a father. Her world had come crashing down as hard and as fast as her knees had hit the earth when she first saw her husband hanging. His final face had etched into her mind and flashed before her with every blink of her eyes. What cut her the most was that the expression was not one of fear or anguish; it was one of sadness. His eyes were solemn and his mouth drooped. It destroyed her that, her rock of a partner, was now wilted in defeat.

Ferris' funeral had brought the entire town to a standstill. The church service was the first time anyone had seen Abigail since the news broke of her loss. Many had noted how her once milky skin had become ashen – having grown accustom to the darkness of her blacked out cottage. Despite Raegan Darby's offer of funding an extravagant service, the ceremony was humble and low rent. Abigail knew her husband was a simple man of simple pleasures. Therefore, she was insistent that his farewell would befit the man, more than the moment.

Stood by the graveside, tears streamed down her cheeks as Father Daniel said his blessings. Her small shaking hands clasped firmly the rosary beads that Ferris had bought her. She was to never be seen without them from that day forth.

***

Five years on and Abigail could once again be found grasping what Ferris had left behind. With time, she had regained the soft natural tone to her face. For now, she had Michael. A true son to his father, he already enjoyed a strong head of thick wavy dark hair. He had his mother's piercing eyes, and a roguish temperament he had gathered from both of his parents. More playful than hurtful, Michael was always active and his curly hair would often suffer further entanglement from every townsman who seemed determined to ruffle his head as he passed. Never truly knowing the deep effect it had on his mother, Michael always smiled. It was the same heart-stopping smile worn by his father, and it would strengthen and break his mother's heart every time that she saw it.

Today, Abigail had brought Michael along with her to church. Father Daniel was holding his Easter sermon and, as usual, the church was full. Father Daniel had not seemed to age a moment since the first day Abigail had seen him. His cotton-topped head was as white as paper and his nose as bulbous as the town's local drunk. Not ever seen to drink in public, it was rumoured that the priest's wine was not always reserved for communion alone. However, the townspeople were known to enjoy the sour wine of the grapevine a little too much. And it could be said that almost every house were a little guilty of stoking the fires of the rumour mill.

Placed at the centre of Orplow, the church itself was the most beautiful structure the town had, and would ever see. Having stood for nearly 300 years, the church of St Peter was as strong as ever. Every Sunday morning families filled the aisles, each grouping together on the dark varnished oak benches. The central aisle was robed in a crimson red carpet that poured out towards a grand altar that was overseen by a large looming crucifix. Abigail had not looked at the church's statue of Christ on the cross for some time; she found the sorrowful look on the statue to be too reminiscent of her saddest hour.

Despite its ability to constantly remind Abigail of her loss, the church was now alive with people. Mother's whispered and updated each other on the successes and trials of their families, while fathers sat back and politely tipped their hats to one another. As usual, one father in particular was making his customary effort to be seen by all. Dressed in his finest hunter tweed jacket, Raegan Darby was accompanied by his handsome wife Fiona, who wore her pale blue bustle that appeared to be moulded to her fine frame. Mother's bitched how the heavy corsetry armour complimented the cemented expression of detachment upon her face. Walking slow enough to be seen, they were closely followed by their three daughters. The eldest, at 14 years old, was Cara. She stood tall for her age and was known by all to be a calm, sweet girl. Naturally maternal, today she was holding her infant sister Imogen. Barely a few months old, no-one could ever recall seeing Fiona Darby holding her newborn daughter about the town. There seemed to be a distance between them that nobody could really understand. And lastly, walking out of line, was Grace. The middle child of the Darby family had eyes as wide as the moon. She skipped and hummed at the back of the procession as she rubbed roughly at her button nose. All three daughters were dressed in fancy floral dresses and soon took their places alongside their mother on the front stool. As a show of his kind nature, Raegan Darby stood, allowing his family to get seated before facing the congregation, gently nodding, and eventually taking his place in the space nearest to the aisle.

Sitting next to her father, Grace had chosen to kneel on her stool and face the back of the church. Without turning to face his daughter, Raegan tugged firmly at Grace's dress, issuing the firm instruction for her to sit still and face the front. Cara's lips curled into a slight smile as she saw her sister flick her tongue out to her father before taking her seat.

Michael was now staring at the back of Grace's head. He was three stools behind her, and had giggled when he saw her get a telling look by her father. Sat by his mother, Michael held her right hand tightly. She was clothed as he had always remembered; in her dark dress of mourning, with her left hand clutching her rosary beads. She held them to her mouth as she whispered softly into them. Michael noted that, every time that she did this, his mother would always look down, and never up. Sat near to the aisle, Michael left his mother to her whisperings and looked about the church.

The great stained glass window flooded the building with a cacophony of light. Streams of broken colour filtered over one side of the congregation. Michael thought to alert his mother to the old man whose face had turned bright green through the windows glare, but he could still hear his mother muttering and decided to leave her to it.

The ceremony proceeded as routinely as ever. Befitting the season, Father Daniel read a passage from the gospel according to Mark. The passage detailed Jesus' final trip into Jerusalem, where the disciples were in awe of Christ as he explained exactly what was about to happen to each of them. Despite the accuracy in the Lord's account, the concept of fate failed to resonate with Michael. He was too busy rustling through the song-book while looking at the tiled numbers above the church piano. He loved to sing, and it was one of the few times that his mother's sweet voice lost its trace of sadness.

And so, with the reading of the passage completed, they came to sing. Passionate in their devotion, the congregation belted out hymn after hymn after hymn. Michael nudged his mother and flicked his head backwards to point out the tone-deaf old man and his portly overzealous wife behind them. Together they sounded like a wheezy old camel. Not wanting to make his observation obvious, Michael faced the front. He could see that Grace was shouting. She threw her head from side-to-side, and her arms gesticulated at the all wrong moments: infuriating her father. His anger was cold and obvious in his stillness. Even his shoulders were tense, shaking slightly like a kettle on the brink of boiling over. Stood by his side, Fiona Darby, forever the wall-flower, appeared as still as the statue of the Virgin Mary that decorated the wall next to her.

Then the singing ceased. Exhausted, the church pianist slumped over his ivory keys. The clatter of chords brought a blunt stop to the proceedings. Father Daniel walked over to the pianist, and gently lifted his shoulder. He was sound asleep; his breath ringing with the scent of rum. Blessing the dreamer, Father Daniel broke the cold silence.

'Let us pray,' said Father Daniel.

The jingle of bells rang out from the side of the altar boy and the congregation knelt. The tiles of the floor were like ice. The congregation muttered and droned out the prayers as many fussed and fidgeted. Abigail did not falter for a second. With her eyes fixed upon the floor, her voice ran like an ocean's undercurrent; hidden from the surface but with an irrepressible power and conviction like no other.

With a flick of his wrist, the altar boy sounded out the bells to raise the church to its feet. Father Daniel was preparing communion. He blessed the bread and wine, lifting them both to the heavens. The church began to shift and shuffle. Michael was certain he could hear the crack of the old man's knees behind him, inbetween the exasperated breathing of his well-fed wife.

Then as if the damns had burst open, the rows flowed out into the central aisle. Staring forwards, the people queued for their communion in two separate lines. The left side of the church headed towards Father Daniel; the right side towards the altar boy. Both carried a bowl full of slim, white wafers, which represented an offering of Christ's body sacrificed by him for his church. At the head of the left line was Raegan Darby.

'Body of Christ,' said Father Daniel, placing a piece of wafer onto Raegan's tongue.

'Amen,' said Raegan, as he moved to the left and looked to his right. Stood behind him was Grace. Her arms were outstretched, and her palms were crossed, facing the skies. She gestured for an offering from Father Daniel. Her eyes were as wide as an angel's wings, and Father Daniel smiled and began to kneel to explain that she would have to wait for her First Communion until she could receive the Eucharist. However, before his kind words could be given, Grace's palm met with a sharp crack as her father slapped her hands down and dragged her off to the side.

The church did not seem to flinch for a moment. Raegan had his reputation and appeared to enjoy it. But Michael noticed. He looked to his mother for a reaction but she was still deep in prayer. She didn't even feel her child's grasp tighten. Soon, both Michael and his mother were stood in the aisle. One by one the queue shortened towards Father Daniel.

'Body of Christ,'

'Amen.'

'Body of Christ,'

'Amen.'

They were three people away from the front now. Michael tugged at his mother's dress. It took three tugs for her to look at him. He opened his arms for her to pick him up. Abigail finally looked at her son, her face showing the slightest trace of bemusement.

'What do you want?' Abigail whispered.

'Raise me up mother', declared Michael. His arms were wider now, his left arm accidentally slapping the buttocks of a lady in the right aisle.

In fear of further embarrassment, Abigail did as her son wished and picked him up. He was five years old now and weighed heavy in her arms, but he helped by holding onto his mother tightly.

'Thanks Ma,' Michael whispered into her shoulder as his head was tucked away.

'Body of Christ,' the priest continued.

'Amen.'

His mother was next. Raising his head from her shoulder, Michael faced Father Daniel. The priest smiled with suspicion, then looked down and picked up a single slice of the white wafer with his left hand. He motioned the offering towards Abigail, his arm stretching forward and his eyes firmly on her.

'Body of Christ,' said Father Daniel. Placing the wafer on her tongue the priest stared at her for a second. He noticed that she always looked down in church.

'Amen,' said Abigail.

Michael took his opportunity. Looking at his mother, his right arm flashed out and plucked a single wafer from the priest's bowl. It went completely unnoticed. Michael smiled and nodded to the priest as his mother carried him away and back to their seat. She knelt for a moment in prayer. This time silently. These prayers were her own. She made the sign of the cross on her chest and raised herself back up onto the stool next to her son. Michael patted his left hand on his mother's lap and smiled directly at her. The smile she gave back to him made the dimples in his cheeks burst with joy.

After a set of more prayers and passages the mass came to an end. Father Daniel sent the church out in peace and offered his blessings. The pianist stirred and jumped up in his seat. His face startled for a second before breaking naturally into a tune for the procession.

The rows broke once more from the front as the people left their stools and made their way down the aisle. This time heading for the exit, Raegan Darby was once more at the front and was followed in uniformed fashion by his family. Still seated and by the aisle, Michael watched as Raegan passed, followed by Cara with Imogen, and then Fiona. Somehow Grace had moved down the line, away from her father. He was still on the boil and his face flushed, with cheeks as red as the carpet he walked on. His nostrils flared as if they were to consume his great moustache in one foul snort.

Grace was behind her mother. Her expression was glum; her eyes were full of tears and her arms hanged by her side. Blindly, Fiona faced forwards towards her husband. Meanwhile, Michael saw that his mother was still whispering into her brown wooden beads; the silver crucifix hung down from them and brushed gently on her wrist. He looked around him. People were busy in their movements. Nobody noticed him as he rummaged through the pockets of his shorts. Swiftly, he removed his white cotton handkerchief. It was neatly folded into a thick cushioned square.

Timing it just right, Michael waited for Grace to pass. Her eyes were still wet and her cheeks damp as she rubbed at her nose with the left sleeve of her dress. Her right arm hanged down by her side. Seizing the moment, he reached out for her hand. It was just the lightest of touches but enough to place the handkerchief firmly in her palm. Taken aback, Grace looked at Michael. While her legs still carried her away, her eyes were fixed on him. His chin was sunk into his chest as he peered up from under his brow. She was about to smile when suddenly her arm was taken by her mother and she was dragged away. Raegan had plans after all and the family were not to fall behind.

Outside, Raegan Darby was already seated in his carriage. The leather hood was up to hide his anger from the public, but Grace could still see his hands simmering on his lap. The landau carriage itself was a fine vehicle. With two stunning, majestic, black Friesian stallions at its front, the carriage was set to take the Darby family back to their estate. Last inside, Grace took a seat by the window. She looked away from her father, desperately trying to not let him see her tears.

Dabbing at her eyes with the white cotton handkerchief she felt the brittle edge of something give and break a little inside. Cupping the cloth to her chest, she opened it up. Inside was a brittle white wafer. Grace quickly popped this into her mouth before her family could see. The wafer dampened and toughened on her tongue. She smiled and uttered 'Amen'.

Chapter 3

By law, every parish had to look after their roads. Men were meant to be put to work for a minimum of six days a year in order to maintain and repair them. However, very few travelled, and the occupants of Orplow were not particularly interested in the prospect of leaving. This tended to make the Darby's trip home from church an unpleasant and bumpy one. The carriage rocked and burped over every ditch and divot. To make sure his grip did not falter, the coachman would always wear his best leather gloves.

Inside, sat upon the fine leather upholstered seats, the Darby family were deafly quiet. The tension within the carriage was an unwelcome distraction from the silence. It was clear to all that their father was struggling to keep his public mask on. His eyes were his traitor and always ratted him out. They would shift from side to side; always failing to land on the object of his anger. This afternoon, it was Grace that avoided his stare.

Raegan was already furious with his daughter for ruining the school photograph; he felt humiliated when it was seen to be his daughter that had broken the tradition, and he had demanded that another picture be taken. However, the townspeople unanimously disagreed. Many argued that it would be an insult to remove the last photograph taken by the late Padraig Skelly. Others just liked to see Raegan Darby knocked down a peg or two.

And today, once again, Grace had played the deviant. Arguably his prettiest daughter, she was by no means his most obedient. Always quiet about her feelings, she never spoke much. But her actions were always loud and clear. She simply could not take the orders of her father.

The carriage was now pulling up to the tall-standing gates of their manor house. The gatekeeper had already pulled them open on seeing the carriage approach. He was wise to recall how he was given this job after the last gatekeeper had kept Raegan Darby waiting for the briefest of moments. As the carriage passed, the gatekeeper could see that Raegan was unhappy and with Fiona as expressionless as ever, it had always plagued the staff just where the children got their smiles from.

Rolling up the lengthy driveway, the carriage began its ascent. One of the hired help was out walking the family dogs. Allowed off the leash, the three blue great danes bounded towards the carriage. Excited by movement, they ran alongside their master as the afternoon sun flickered on their steely grey coats. Their mouths jostled and swayed while their ears remained upright and rigid. Raegan had insisted that their ears be snipped as puppies to ensure that they remained upright.

The carriage rolled to a slow stop. The excited dogs circled the carriage and made their way to its side. They sat obediently as their master stepped down onto the pebbled sandstone. His 18th-century Georgian manor stood before him. The bays were decorated with the remaining flowers of spring, and evergreen ivy crept up the grey walls towards the children's bedroom windows. The housemaids, butler, footmen and hall-boy all lined up outside in a guard of honour as the Darby family walked past.

At the tip of the line was Connell Locran. Having sat at the right hand of Raegan Darby for almost twenty years, Connell was his most trusted friend and servant. Ruthless in his management of the help, Connell enjoyed brandishing his masters iron fist a little too much. Stout in figure and dressed all in black, his muddied hands appeared large as they burst from his shadowy sleeves. He was as strong as an ox, and his firm palm print could be frequently found on the faces of the female staff. For the male staff, he preferred a clenched fist to the ribs. Hearing the crack of bone beneath his hands always brought a vulgar smile to Connell's face.

'Welcome back, sir,' said Connell. 'How was the *lord* today?'

'Too forgiving Connell,' spat Raegan. 'Follow me to my study; I need a drink.'

'Very well sir,' replied Connell. 'Come now, staff. Help the fair lady and her children to the house'. His hands joined in one triggering clap. The staff took up their roles, helping the family with their bags and coats while Connell made use of his great stride to catch up his hasty master.

Walking through the entrance hall, passing the series of fine art that filled the walls, Connell made his way into the study. Raegan was already draining a decanter of its brief brandy tenant. Coughing slightly, he poured another as Connell joined him.

'Did the communion wine whet your whistle sir?' asked Connell.

'I'm always bloody thirsty Connell. You know that,' replied Raegan.

They both flashed another drink down their throats before pouring a larger measure and taking a seat in front of the fireplace. Raegan placed his glass on the small table to his side as he rustled in his jacket for his favourite briar smoking pipe. Lighting it, he let the fishtail mouthpiece hang in his mouth as he gathered the glass once more.

'I have three daughters, Connell. And believe me, one is enough of a cross to bear for any man' said Raegan as he slumped into his chair. The leather creaked as he did so.

'Ha!' cackled Connell. 'Count your blessings sir. If you had just a single son, who was anything like his father, then I promise you, you would have more than three daughters to worry about – and their fathers on top of that!'

'Quite right. At least I can eventually ship mine out. Let them trouble some other wealthy baron as I enjoy the spoils of his land in exchange.' His face had no hint of amusement.

They chinked glasses before draining them. Both of them knew that this bottle of brandy was to be emptied that night, so they sat back and let the liquor break its way into their veins; warming the chest and clouding the mind. Tonight, they would drink until the early morning, and face the world with all their scorn and heavy head tomorrow.

'To the fruits of families', said Connell raising his glass in the air.

'To a father's seed', toasted Raegan. Both laughed heartily as another draft fired their bellies.

In the hallway, the children were not happy to hear the laughter of their father. This meant most definitely that he was drinking. And also, that someone was to suffer. Surveyed by their mother, Fiona could see the look of concern creep across their sweet faces. Taking Imogen from Cara, Fiona held her tightly to her chest. She knew that she was in for a tireless and torrid night.

Her husband, fired by the brandy would be frivolous and lustful. However, like an apple-tree branch at the peak of winter, it would prove entirely fruitless. His every thrust would only serve to annoy himself further, as his body remained limp under the influence of drink. Inevitably, his pent up anger would be rained down upon his wife, and her body would be shelled in bruises. The only reason she dressed so well, was to cover the markings of her lover's bite.

Fiona took Imogen to her room. It was time for her afternoon rest and Fiona would sit by her side the whole time. Cara and Grace, meanwhile, had run up the stairwell to their shared bedroom. The room itself housed huge hulking wardrobes, brimming with clothing that neither child was ever allowed to choose from. Instead, they would always be dressed as their father desired.

Usually both girls would leap onto their beds, but today they had cause to stop themselves. Laid across the crisp white sheets of their beds were two open violin cases. Encased within each was a freshly varnished violin. Neither girl knew how to play a single note, but – unbeknown to them – their father had now arranged for a tutor to attend every evening after school to teach them. Raegan hoped that the discipline found within music would harness the children's gaping creativity. They were, after all, to live to their father's hymn-sheet; it was time they all began to sing in tune.

Grace put the violin on the floor and began to jump on her bed. Being the elder, Cara instead chose to sit. They both ignored their new gifts. Totally engrossed, Cara flicked at a book of fairy tales. The tale of *Sleeping Beauty* was her favourite. She must have read this a thousand times, and every time her heart would flutter at the adventures of the brave prince. Most nights, she would sit and read the book to Grace, but Grace would often be fast asleep before the best part. Nevertheless, Cara always continued to read the story to its heroic and romantic end. Distracted by the dance Grace had begun, Cara watched her sister with one eye as the other glanced at the beautiful illustrations in her book.

'Come on Grace, behave,' said Cara. Her voice more pleading than demanding.

'Sorry sis,' said Grace taking a seat on the edge of the bed. Her body still bounced slightly with gentle excitement. She looked at Cara straight in the eye.

'What is it?' said Cara knowing Grace wanted to say something.

'I ate Jesus today,' she said proudly as she stared at the white handkerchief in her lap.

'What are you rattling on about? You do play the fool sometimes.' Cara shook her head and laughed into her chest. She was concentrating on her book now.

'My saviour… I ate him,' said Grace. 'He was a little mouldy.'

'You do baffle me Grace' replied Cara. 'Come here and sit on my lap, I'll read you a story.'

'No thank you. I don't have time for stories,' said Grace. 'It's almost candle-lighting… and I want to play.'

And for the following few hours that is exactly what they both did. Cara sat peacefully and read while Grace tirelessly ran around her room playing every game that her room contained. By the time the bells rang for dinner, the bedroom floor was more toys than carpet. For the last half an hour, Grace had been camped under her bed sheets. Torn from her book, Cara had briefly helped Grace to build a castle at the base of her bed. As the dinner bells rang out for a second time, Grace crept out from under her white-cotton fort.

Skipping down the spiralling staircase that led down into the hallway, Cara held Grace's hand. The girls were just in time. Leaping onto their chairs as maids pulled them from the table, Grace hit her cushion a little too enthusiastically. Bouncing straight off her chair, Grace disappeared under the table as her hands slapped the table cloth, causing her cutlery to leap into the air. Cara could not stifle her laugh as Grace appeared from under the table; her smirk as wide and bright as her rosy cheeks.

Fortunately, the clatter was not heard by Raegan. He was yet to join his family at the dining table and there was a sense of relief from all members. However, the room fell silent as his laugh bellowed from the corridor. Accompanied by Connell, the lord of the manor finally graced the hall. His step was staggered and his face was flush. Sharing a knowing laugh with Connell, Raegan took his seat, knocking back the maid's arm who had tried to direct him into his chair. She was dressed as all the maids were, in a white mob-cap and apron, but she now wore a scowl as tight as the bunch in her hair. It was noted by Connell, and he would deliver her penance later.

'Let us eat', said Raegan sat at the head of the table.

Raegan did not wait for grace to be said and instead began to dine. The table was lined with rich cuts of meat, seasonal vegetables and bottles of both red and white wine. Each child had a decanter full of ice-cold water in front of them. A thickly sliced piece of lemon bobbed through the icy surface of the jug. Grace went to help herself, but was beaten to it by the grubby hands of Connell. He greedily gulped directly from the jug itself, before slamming it back upon the table with a loud thud. Grace looked at him with a furrowed brow, but he was too busy shovelling his dinner into his sharp, thick mouth to notice.

✲✲✲

Bloated and tiring, Connell eventually set about returning to his chamber, via the staff quarters. As they sat discussing the world with one another, Connell bounded in and slammed the leftover meat onto the wooden table. The dull sound of this brought a blunt silence to the room. Usually used as a currency to curry favour from the young female staff, very rarely did Connell leave the leftovers for all to share. Yet, today it would serve as a distraction to the fortunate, as not all of the staff were to get their share of the spoils. One maid in particular was to bear the full brunt of Connell's rage.

Seeing the kitchen maid that had scowled at his master, Connell brought his wide open palm crashing down across her left cheek. The crack popped in the air and filled the ear drums of all those watching. Some male members stepped an inch forward and then stopped. None would dare challenge their manager. As the maid brought her left hand up to her cheek, Connell took hold of her dainty wrist and dragged her to his chamber.

Slamming the door behind them, Connell turned and faced his prize. The maid was stood up with her back to the door when Connell tore at her blouse with both of his hands. The cotton top ripped open and her youthful bosom peered out from tears of the shredded garment. She was not fully mature yet, and the firmness of her body suggested that she had not had a child. Her cheeks dampened with tears as Connell threw her onto his rigid bed. He lay on top of her, allowing his weight to push her legs wide open. Her muffled screams could still be heard from outside.

Meanwhile, upstairs in the master bedroom, Fiona Darby was also stifling her breath. Her chest ached and her ribs felt like they had been cracked completely. Battered and bruised, she breathed as shallow as possible, praying that none of her cries would stir and wake her now sleeping husband.

Chapter 4

Springtime was full of life in Orplow. The townspeople always seemed more cheerful, and the fields held more colour than during any other season. Bursts of yellows, blues and whites rained over the lush green of the land, as the morning sun beamed down upon the town, breaking every shadow and drowning out the tired night. Sat along the town's border, Lake Doriend glistened lazily, its surface distorting the sun and firing back a reflection as bright as a candle's flame. Down at the shore, gentle waves lapped at the sands that greeted the Irish Sea. The brief coast enjoyed by the town gaped into a wondrous cove. The rocks within the cove stood firm as the waters broke fiercely upon them. The frothy whites of the waves seeped down and dried upon the rock before they had the chance to rejoin the sea. Clubs of seals sunbathed on the rocks with their cubs, their skin oiled and sleek with the sea water. Gulls circled overhead, swooping every so often and piercing the seas surface. The fortunate ones would emerge with a beak brimming with fish. But it was not only the gulls that broke the surface of the waters. Occasionally, the thin fins of the dolphins would cut across the horizon, raising and dipping as gently as the waves.

From a great waterfall, Lake Doriend fed the ocean. Its stream led into the sea and separated the sand directly through its centre. Two beaches, encased by the rocks of the land, now rested either side of this watery vein. It was one of Michael's favourite sights. He would always enjoy his walks to the beach with his mother, and especially in the springtime. Then the sun would kiss his mother's face softly and he would hold her hand as firmly as he could. He loved his mother completely, and all he knew of his father was that his mother was now somehow saddened by the mere mention of his name. Michael was still too young to be told the truth. Instead, Abigail would explain that his father was taken from them both, and that they would have to pray every day to get him back.

A staunch catholic, Abigail knew the full repercussions of suicide. The thought of Ferris' soul trapped in limbo haunted her every waking thought. It was for this reason alone that she gave every spare minute of her life to the church. She prayed fiercely and lived in hope that her sacrifice would grant her one true love his redemption.

He still lived inside of her. His touch still resonated on her as she slept. Every night she struggled trying to arrange her pillows in a way to replicate his flawless chest and the cradling nook of his arm. It was now seven years since Ferris had left her, and still she could find no comfort at night.

Having woken Michael earlier than usual, she wanted to take him on one final supervised stroll before allowing him to go and play freely with his friends. Until now she had always been with him. But she knew Michael's soul ran free and she was in no mind to hold him back. He needed to get his hands dirty and enjoy the scruffy spoils of being a child. However, she knew that this freedom would not be long lived as he would soon be put to work once his education came to an end. That was one of the agreements she had settled on with Raegan Darby; Michael was to run the land as his father had done.

Michael had not stirred when she had woken him early. He was always delighted to see his mother, and it was always a relief to get out of his hard stiff bed. Stretching and cracking his back, Michael hopped off his mattress and chucked on his clothes that his mother had placed on the wooden bedside chair. Today he would be wearing his flat peaked cap, white cotton shirt and grey shorts with braces. He was tugging on the shorts when his mother walked in.

'Ready for an adventure angel?' said Abigail. Her voice was soft and raised by the smile she was wearing.

'Always,' yawned Michael. 'Where are we going?'

'I thought we could walk to the cove and then you can go and play with your friends. It is beautiful outside,' said Abigail.

'Fine' agreed Michael. 'Are we going to see Oscar later?' Oscar was the son of Abigail's closest friend Margaret Sterrin.

'Ay son,' said Abigail. 'I thought you and Oscar could go and play together while his mother and I caught up.'

'On our own?' said Michael, barely managing to hide his excitement.

'I am sure you will be fine without me son', replied Abigail with mock reassurance.

After a hearty breakfast of oats and a thick slice of soda bread, Michael and his mother made their way through town. The cottage in which they lived was on the very edge of the Darby estate. Three vast fields separated the Darby's from the Alpin's, and it was only by chance that their lives, outside of the church and school, would pass. Walking by the old willow tree that shaded their home, Michael saw his mother stroke the bark as they passed. Her hand remained there until her body carried her fingertips out of reach. The morning was as glorious as his mother had described. The land was vibrant and birds held a chorus to the break of day.

Because he lived in the rural side of Orplow, there were very few opportunities for Michael to go into the marketplace. During his walks with his mother he noticed how the soft spongy soil would gradually be replaced with the cold cobbled paths of town. Here the air felt thinner as people were packed into rows of houses and shops that faced each other along a narrow corridor of pavement. But still, everyone smiled. Young gentleman would wink and tip their hats to his mother, only to have the older men whisper vigorously in their ear. Their once charming smile now became a blank nod. They all knew that nobody would come close to her late husband and – therefore – no male would get close to Abigail Alpin.

Despite the early hour, the town was full of people. Shopkeepers equipped their stalls with their finest goods, as traders lined up crate after crate of everything from fresh vegetables to polished ornaments. Walking among the people, Michael always looked up and met their faces with his chocolate brown eyes. Any eye-contact was always greeted by Michael's signature smile. Strolling among the bustling scene of preparation, the bells of the church rang out six single chimes. The first brought with it the fluttering of the birds that had nested on the ledge of the bell tower. They flew overhead and landed directly outside the baker's store. Taking an interest in the sacks of grain laid up along the wall, the birds began to peck at the seams. The baker, busy amongst his morning chores, burst from his doorway with a large long handled straw broom.

'Feck off, you fecking flying rats!' The baker swung his huge broom. His chest expanded proudly as the broom swatted at least two of the birds into the air. However, it soon sagged and his shoulders sank as he saw the alarm on Abigail's face. It almost entirely masked the beaming smile worn by her son.

'I am so sorry', said the embarrassed baker. He offered a coy grin and looked up through a low discomfited brow.

'It's quite alright sir' said Abigail as she nodded her head.

'Feck off!' shouted Michael without any understanding of the meaning. His head jerking sharply to the side as his mother clipped him to his ear. The pain simply confirmed to Michael that he had just inherited a new wicked word. He sniggered as his mother looked away.

Passing through the town, they came to the meadow that surrounded one side of Lake Doriend. There were not many trees in Orplow. Once cloaked in a rich tapestry of junipers, birch, hazels and even Scots pine, the land now boasted little more than countless, endless fields. The deforestation of the land nearly two hundred years ago had unlocked the horizon completely. Land was wrenched open to accommodate the boom in agriculture, as well as to rid the countless rebels of their favoured hiding spots. Today only a few of the vast hills remained crowned by mighty oak trees that splintered the skyline. The landscape stretched as wide as the eye could travel, and to an outsider the many fields would blend into one, blurring any bearings they may have gathered. However, to residents of Orplow the story was much different. As crafted by nature's many hands, each field had its own signature, its own intricate feature that identified it clearly from its neighbours.

Abigail would always highlight these to Michael. Whether it be a small dip in the land, or the slightest man-worn pathway, Michael would need to remember them all if he were to ever know the land like his father. The field they now strolled within was the closest to the cove. Juxtaposed with the blue waters of the lake, the green of the field fell like a gown of grass at its side. Michael ran his fingers through the fern and wild furze. The edge of the cliff's face stood at the foot of the field. Michael could feel the land toughen beneath his feet. At the very brink of the field the soil turned to rock and the horizon came crashing forward. Below, the curt partitioned beach held back the Irish Sea at low tide, while the lake held onto the ocean by the loose thread of water that streamed through the shore.

The waterfall itself pounded into a small dense pool. The jaws of which held sharp, jagged rocks that allowed the water to seep out into the stream. Michael had always wanted to take the plunge. However, his mother would always hold his hand tightly as Michael would lean over to take a look. The sprays of the falling waters would mist before him and tease the skin of his face. Today he opened his mouth as he always did, certain that he could taste the water as he breathed in deeply.

Looking out to the ocean, Abigail and her son stood silently for a moment. Michael was aware of the silence every time. It made him uneasy, like he ought to know something. His mother would breathe deeply, timing her breathes to the gentle tide. Her lungs filled as the waters were dragged from the rocks, and then she would breathe out in a gentle blow as the waves came crashing back. This would only last for a minute or two, but it always unnerved Michael, like his mother shared a great secret with the waves.

The moment ended like it always did. Abigail shook her head slightly, hummed as if to connect herself back to this world and smiled at Michael.

'This is where it ends Michael,' whispered Abigail. 'You don't need me by your side all the time. You're free to go wherever you choose.'

'But I don't want to,' said Michael. 'I want to stay with you.' His voice was as childlike as his years.

'I know son. But all I am giving you is the chance to be free for a while. Go and enjoy yourself. Play with your friends, and enjoy life. I want you to be happy.' The waves seemed to crash louder as his mother said this.

'Just be aware Michael, that I am always here for you. But I don't need to be with you all the time. You are a young boy and need to have a good time. You don't need your grouchy mother looking over you.'

'I know', said Michael. It surprised him that he had wanted this for so long but now that it was here the news made him sad. It was only free time to go and play after all, but Michael could not remember a time outside of school that he had not been by his mother's side.

'Look, go and have some fun. Your tea will be ready at the usual time. I'm off to Margaret's now. You don't have to come with me.' Abigail smiled.

Knowing that his mother would prefer the company, Michael followed her. Walking by her side through the lush grass of the fields, Michael could hear the waters break softly behind him. He skipped ahead as it dawned on him that he could now take the plunge. With his hands firmly in the pockets of his shorts, Abigail watched Michael skip in front of her. Both her hands grasped her rosary beads tightly.

✿✿✿

The Sterrin's household was a stringent one. Margaret ran the household while her husband Maik worked ungodly hours at the shipping yard. The lord had blessed them with a son and they had chosen to call him Oscar after his late grandfather. Margaret was a buxom woman and full of figure. Her face was flush and would redden at even the simplest of tasks. In her late twenties, she had already taken on-board the teachings of her mother. She ran a ship as tight as a door mouse's nostril, and could often be heard barking her orders to the long suffering Maik.

With her house being the middle terrace on the main road of the town, Margaret greatly enjoyed sitting at the engine room to the town's infamous rumour mill. Presently, she was fitting up tea and cakes for the arrival of her good friend Abigail. They had met at the church of St Peter's, or rather Margaret had ambushed Abigail on the church steps. At the time, Abigail was a heavily pregnant widow and the talk of the town. Margaret had offered Abigail her shoulder to cry on, and her itchy ear to inform. Not a soul could reason as to why the beloved Ferris Alpin would have taken his own life, and it saddened Margaret to her very core when she found that Abigail could not reason it either. The poor girl had wept solidly for hours in Margaret's house that day, and Margaret was still to see the sorrow leave her eyes.

Upstairs, she could hear the rumbling of feet. Oscar was eagerly awaiting his friend Michael. It was with a hard and harsh word that Margaret had used to convince Abigail to let her son play freely with Oscar. The boy needed to learn the laws of the land by his own hand and not while in that of his mother's. Maik and the stale scent of fish would be out of the house for the afternoon, so it was an ideal time to let the boys play while Margaret treated Abigail to the juiciest berry from the gossip grapevine.

Trundling down the stairs, Oscar was openly excited. Underneath his sailor boy hat, his fat face scrunched up into a ball of flesh as he smiled. Contemporary fashion was very much focused on the freedom of movement, and befittingly Oscar wore his open collared shirt and buttoned trousers. His belly bulged at the seams, as his mother was insistent that he tucked his shirt in. Sweating slightly, Oscar scoffed down the breakfast his mother had provided for him.

Only looking up once his plate was empty, Oscar gulped down his water and readied himself for the day ahead.

His timing was pin point for the scraping of his plate was muffled by three gentle raps on the door. Dusting the crumbs of her son's chest, Margaret scanned the room to make sure her house was in order.

'Come in', she hollered, straightening Oscar's hat.

The door opened gingerly and Abigail popped her head around the splintered sheet of oak. Her hand was taken by Margaret's as she was spun and plonked into a tableside chair. Behind her skipped young Michael. He looked at Margaret first, smiling and nodding mid-stride before walking and standing by Oscar's side. Oscar grabbed his hand and was about to run out of the door before Margaret leaned her heavy hand across it. The door slammed with a blunt thud.

'Listen here boys. Your mothers have worked damn hard to make sure that you come from a family of sound repute' said Margaret, her outstretched finger swaying like a sausage before the noses of both boys. 'So don't you go and bleeding well run our names through the muck.'

'We won't miss, I promise', said Michael his voice soft and sincere. He looked at his mother for her to say her part.

'Go ahead children, have fun,' said Abigail.

With this Oscar charged for the door, dragging Michael behind him. With the ease and grace of a matador, Margaret whisked the door open and set the young bulls free into the unsuspecting street. Their laughter could be heard above their thunderous footsteps as they ran down the road into the town.

Pouring a cup of tea and then filling the fine cup sat in front of Abigail, Margaret slid into her chair and passed Abigail a plate of her freshly made cakes. Margaret was renowned for her baking and played testament to the old adage that little pickers wore bigger knickers. Above the warm scent of the tea, the cakes smelled delicious. Selecting one and raising it to her mouth, Abigail took her first bite as Margaret leaned forward.

'You'll never guess who's been sampling the butcher's meat' she said. Abigail almost choked.

***

The world seemed bigger to Michael. The houses reached for the highest clouds, and the skies above were wider than he had ever seen. With his senses livened, the cheer, smell and feel of the town seemed louder, thicker and stronger. Away from his mother's side, Michael felt less imposing. But he felt freer with it. The weight of staring eyes did not rest on his shoulders as much as they had done, and he felt he could pass by without a trace. He filled his lungs and let out a happy sigh. Oscar meanwhile was panting from his brief sprint, his hands firmly on his knees, and his belly folded over his lap.

'So, what do you want to do?' said Oscar, ending each word with a quick pant of breath. He stood up straight but kept his hands planted on his sides like a chubby sugar bowl.

'I just want to see everything,' replied Michael as he scoped out the streets. The traders had begun their trade. Women stood before them nodding approvingly to the deceiving descriptions being offered. Michael wanted to rush over and warn the women not to be fooled, but this was his first afternoon alone and he did not desire the company of another woman so soon.

'Nowhere you fancy going to?' Oscar's face slumped into a grumpy scowl.

There was one place, but that was Michael's and he was not about to give it up to anyone. He wanted to take the plunge when he was ready, and the truth be known Oscar was a friend out of convenience more than one of choice. Their mothers got on, and so in turn they had to make do.

Wracking his brain, Michael could not think of a single place to go. So he decided to let Oscar lead the way.

Walking aimlessly, the boys strolled into town. Outside the church, they saw a young woman holding her infant child. She clutched at a wedge of bread – tearing chunks off with her free hand and tossing it to the birds that clothed the steps. They swarmed and quarrelled over each morsel of bread. One tried greedily to carry a large chunk away from the flock – but the chunk dropped to the ground and was devoured among a burst of frantic feathers. Oscar headed over to the woman. She looked more occupied with her child than feeding the birds.

'Here, miss. I'll help you with that bread if you like,' said Oscar, stretching out his chubby hand. The lady handed the remains of the wedge over and Oscar palmed it between his clammy hands. He picked at the bread with pinched fingers. Plucking the tiniest piece of the doughy white bread, he flicked it to the birds. He watched the lady walk into the church through the corner of his eye. As she entered the doors, Oscar plunged his right hand deep into the loaf, scooping out a palm brimming with bread and dunked his doughy fist straight into his mouth. It looked to Michael like he was hand feeding his stomach directly. His puffy cheeks seemed to devour his arm almost to the elbow.

'Phaaa! It's stale!' Oscar spat the bread out onto the floor and trod it into the ground. He tossed the remains upon a lawn behind him, ignoring the fact that the birds were all in front of him.

As Oscar turned and stomped away, Michael followed at a single pace behind. Passing the bread he quickly swept it with his foot towards the birds upon the church steps. Quickening his step, he caught up with Oscar.

Continuing their stroll, they soon came to the open fields. The blistering sun bore down upon the land, and the boys were starting to feel its punch a little. They headed for a rare row of trees and basked in the shade provided by the leafy branches. Sat upright at the base of the tree, Oscar plucked at the petals of a flower. He looked locked in his own thoughts.

'I don't think Ms Ryann likes me', said Oscar as he looked down at the torn flower in his hands. He spun the remains of the flower by its stork.

'Why do you think that?' replied Michael. He was lying on his back now, rubbing his bare feet upon the soft grass.

'She always hits me… before I get home I have to pull my hat over my ears every day,' sulked Oscar. 'If my Ma was to see how red they were, she would go at Ms Ryann full chisel.'

'Ha!... that would show Ms Ryann alright' giggled Michael, imagining the full frame of Margaret Sterrin – rolling pin in hand – blasting through the front gates of Eden.

'Anyway…' continued Oscar. 'The other day, I heard my Ma saying that she didn't know what all the fuss was about with Ms Ryann.'

'What fuss?' said Michael rolling onto his belly and turning to face his friend.

'I'm not sure… but me Ma said that she was no Norma Stockers' declared Oscar.

'Who's that?' asked Michael.

'No idea. But she's got bigger apples than Ms Ryann according to my Ma'.

'Apples? Well she is pretty thin I guess,' said Michael in sweet ignorance, 'You must have big apples!' He prodded his friend's belly.

The boys chuckled together in their unknowing. Oscar chucked the remains of the flower at Michael, causing him to get to his feet and set himself ready to pounce on Oscar. His knees were bent and his arms spread wide like a battle ready gladiator.

'Hold on,' wheezed Oscar 'that gives me an idea.'

Chapter 5

Having been up since the early dawn, Aidan Adams had one last chore to complete to earn his daily bread. With only his own mouth to feed, Aidan had chosen to gather work from the biggest toad in the puddle. Aidan had worked for the Darby family for the past ten years and now was the proud single occupant of a small cottage that overlooked the largest orchard in Orplow. Boasting a wide range of apples from widow's whelps to angel's bites, the Darby estate made fine use of the fruit for trade. The core of the business fed the local grog shops to produce the sharpest cider in the market. Aidan himself had been partial to this local tipple, and for years had displayed the bright strawberry cheeks of a proud drinker.

It was early in the afternoon, and Aidan was to attend the orchard and remove any of the crops that had gone rotten. It was springtime after all, and the apples were not ready to fall until autumn. Nevertheless, Aidan had a fine eye for the apples that were not going to make the cut. So throughout the seasons he would attend the orchard and pluck those he deemed bad. Doing this prevented the rotten fruit from spreading to the rest and ensured that the Darby stock remained as good as its reputation. With his apple basket to hand, Aidan made his way to the orchard. Made from mellow willow and with a fine hessian lining, the basket swung in Aidan's rugged hand as he strolled through the fields.

Although he was enjoying the middle years of his life, Aiden looked older. The years spent on the Darby estate had aged his body faster than mother-nature had first intended. However, the rapid ageing process had been given somewhat of a helping hand. On more than one occasion Aidan had felt the full fury of Connell Locran. As savage as a meat axe, Connell had frequently beaten Aidan and not always with his master's orders. These beatings had recently stopped, but his body still housed the splintered ribs from his younger years. It was for this reason more than most that Aidan was happy in his lodgings. The orchard was a long dirt-track and steep hill away from the Darby manor, and as long as his work was done to the best of his ability there would be no need for his master's axe to fall so far. And so, as he did throughout the seasons, Aidan took pride in his work and checked on the fruits of his labour.

The orchard was the largest in the county. While neighbouring regions had an average of twenty trees per orchard, the Darby estate whistled to the sweet tune of almost threefold that figure. Despite the size of the orchard, Aidan knew that the fruit was only young and one basket should suffice to carry those plucked today. The sun was baking the ground and Aidan had begun to regret the sweet allure of the cider from the night before. His head felt like a sandbag, and his eyes were heavy.

Once among the orchard, Aidan began his final errand. He was thorough in his work, and would part the branches and delve right amongst the leaves to locate any of the flawed fruit. To do this he needed both of his strong hands, as one – shaking from the evenings drink – held back the branches and allowed the other to reach in and snare the chosen apple. Freeing his hands, Aidan placed his basket on the dusty ground behind him. Knowing every inch of the orchard instinctively, he blindly tossed the apples behind him, each landing directly into the basket. The basket was filling quite nicely, and this began to concern Aidan. Raegan Darby hated any of his crops to be deemed rotten and tended to blame those handling them rather than the hidden failings of the land that bore them. Aidan knew he could be in for a tough time if his master was to learn of such bad stock.

Hidden from the baking sun and the rosy cheeked man pulling at the apple trees, Michael and Oscar lay in waiting under a thick laurel hedge. The man was presently at the other end of the orchard and was preoccupied within his duties. With their chins to the ground, the boys whispered through muffled breath.

'What did I say', panted Oscar. 'I told you, didn't I? Apples as far as the eye can see.'

'I know', replied Michael. 'I've never seen so many in all my life. So what now? Shall we ask the man for one? I'm sure he'll hand us one if we ask nicely.'

'Are you joking?' screeched Oscar before quickly regulating his tone back into a whisper. 'Those apples belong to Reagan Darby. He'd rather burn the apple than give it to you for nothing. We'll have to steal them.'

'You're tugging on my ankle right?' declared Michael. 'Our ma's would kill us if they found out. Why do we need them anyway?'

'Because...' answered Oscar. 'Remember what my mother said? Ms Ryann is a nobody because she doesn't have any apples. We need apples to get recognised. Don't you want to be someone Michael?'

'I'm quite happy being invisible for now' replied Michael with one eye focused on the frustrated man pulling at the bushes.

'You're right… we'll need to be if we want to get those apples. Follow me.' And with that, Oscar began to crawl towards the man. Hidden by thick foliage, Michael followed cautiously behind. The man seemed angry and Michael could not let Oscar get caught. He knew how easily Oscar bruised, and a sound clip from this man would soon put an end to any future adventures if Margaret were to see the result.

A few feet separated them now. The boys could hear the man whispering angrily to himself. He did not seem pleased with something, and was now tearing at the bushes rather than gently plucking the fruit from within. Apple after apple, the basket began to fill as each fruit was thrown with more force than the last. A few had been thrown too hard and had rolled out onto the dusty ground. Once the basket was full to its brim, the man stopped a second and removed a handkerchief from the back pocket of his trousers. He dabbed at his forehead, as the handkerchief grew damp in his palm. He closed his eyes as he dried his face and raised his chin to the sun. His back arched slightly as he filled his lungs and steadied himself.

Lying beside Michael, Oscar leapt to his feet and dashed for the basket. Michael had never seen his friend move so quickly before. But it was not fast enough. Moments before Oscar reached the basket the man turned around to face it. Opening his eyes to the blistering sun, he took a moment to adjust, giving Oscar the exact time he needed to roll under the nearest row of apple trees. He now lay facing Michael in the opposite row of trees, and gestured with his chubby hand for Michael to come over.

'Are you mental?' mouthed Michael.

Again, Oscar gestured for Michael to come over. The man was heading to the basket and Michael knew he did not stand a chance of getting hold of the apples. Then he realised exactly what Oscar was fretting about. The man had already gathered the fruit from the row of trees that Oscar was lying in, and next he would be heading directly to where Michael was hiding. Michael knew he needed to make a move, but he could not see how. Then, as the man reached his basket he looked about him and shook his head disappointedly, spotting the fruit that had fallen out of the basket. He tiredly bent down and began to gather them – using the bottom of his shirt as a pouch.

Michael saw his chance. The man had turned away from him and was clutching at his shirt and grabbing the apples on the floor with his spare hand. Before he knew it, Michael was stood at the basket. He had two choices; he could run by and meet with Oscar, or take his chances with the fruit. Making up his mind, Michael grabbed at the basket. It felt heavy in his hands. Michael grunted slightly as he raised it up and straightened his back. This was enough to alert the man. He turned and faced Michael directly. Michael's eyes widened as his whole body froze for the longest second he had ever experienced.

Aidan could not believe his eyes. Stood before him was a young boy, no older than seven, who had the audacity and stupidity to try and take what belonged to Raegan Darby. He even had the foolishness to try and steal something that was worthless. The fruit was not fit for anything other than destroying. Nevertheless, Aidan could not afford for any of the bad fruit to reach Raegan. However, before he could try and reason with the young boy, the ruffian turned, glanced to his right and then darted off in the opposite direction.

Michael had turned to see that Oscar had disappeared. Now his feet beat at the earth, hoping to help its rotation and push the man further away behind him. He ran like the rough waters of a rapid – each step followed fluidly by the next. The basket clattered in his hands as his knees struck the bottom of it. Dark, mushy fruit bounced and kicked up in front of him. His hands gripped the handles tightly as he pressed on, never once pausing to look back.

'B'hoy, Get back here!' screamed Aidan. 'I'll fix your friggin' flint if you don't!'

Michael heard the man screaming behind him. The voice was getting louder and Michael knew the man was gaining on him. His hands began to sweat and loosen his grip. Michael turned and headed out of the orchard. A dirt path lay ahead. Running up to the top of the hill, the dusty road was his only route out of there. The path was closed in by rock walls and Michael could not leap them with the basket still in his hands. Behind him the blunt thud of footsteps grew thunderous. With a flash of thought and as smart as a steel trap, Michael tilted the basket forward – pouring a stream of fleshy fruit down behind him.

Aidan was gaining on the small boy. He had stupidly run out onto the enclosed road and was heading uphill. The boy had not let go of the basket and would soon slow down. Aidan begged that his unsteady legs would not fail him. Beyond the brink of the hill lay a straight downward run to the Darby manor. Gravity would take the boy away from Aidan, and already the cider from last night was tiring his legs. His lungs burned and his breathing became sharp in his throat. But he did not worry as the young boy was just out of his reach. A few more strides and he would have him by the scruff of his shirt. The hill had slowed him down as expected, and the boy appeared to lean forward tiredly.

Aidan was too close to see the rotten apples that pebbled the road beneath him. They squished beneath his heavy strides and flicked his feet backward as his body came crashing forward. Several more clattered and plopped into Aidan's flattened face as he lay winded on the floor. The boy did not look back as he made his way out of reach and onto the peak of the hill.

Michael could no longer hear the dry breath of the man behind him. It had all stopped a few paces back with a large clatter and a wheezy cry. But Michael could not risk looking back. His legs were on fire. Acid poured into every muscle and his legs began to weaken beneath him. His arms felt numb and the basket hung heavier. Stood at the very top of the hill, Michael gave himself a single moment to get some air. He breathed deeply and his mouth hung open like an exhausted dog. He was panting louder than he thought. Stood outside the gates to a hill-top cottage, Michael felt a hand land on his shoulder. His back froze and his fingers dropped the basket in front of him. From the corner of his eye, Michael saw a bright white glove. He had only seen two gloves like this before and they had both been on either hand of the local member of the Royal Irish Constabulary. The three large golden chevrons that blazed on his sleeve confirmed it was Sergeant Ende.

'What in heaven's name is the rush boy?' asked Sergeant Ende. His voice muted into an inquisitive 'hmmm' as he spotted the basket of apples.

Michael saw the shadow of the officer darken the path in front of him, the head of which leant enquiringly to the side. He could feel the officer peering at the apples – reasoning the situation. Michael stood staring at them himself. On the very peak of the bundle lay a rare ripe Irish peach. It must have been in the basket before the man had filled it at the orchard. Breaking from the officer's hand, Michael made a dash past the basket. His hand flashed out and grabbed the peach in one swift swipe.

'I say, what the devil are you doing?' Sergeant Ende reached for his rattle and whistle.

Michael saw that the officer had leant his bicycle up against the stone wall. Straddling the central bar, Michael put the peach between his teeth and placed his free hands on the handle bars. With his feet tip-toeing at the floor, Michael pushed off on the bicycle. He leapt up onto the seat as the bike leaned forward over the peak of the hill. A fresh dark green lawn lay in front of him.

The bicycle rattled and raced off down the hill. The handlebars shuddered in Michael's hands as his feet spread out wide in front of him. His teeth gritted and bit into the peach – releasing its sweet juice onto his dry tongue. If he had time to concentrate it would have been like nectar down his throat, but the wind was forcing his eyes shut – the blindness tightening his grip. Behind him, Michael could hear the clucking of a rattle and the shrill cry of a tin whistle. He held on with all his might as the wheels of the bike bumped and jolted over mounds of earth. Michael opened his eyes just in time to steer the bicycle past a grand willow tree that graced the lawn.

Passing through the shade of the tree, Michael saw three thick shadows break away and follow him. The pedals whirred beneath him and Michael kept his legs spread open to stop them from being lacerated. Kicking his feet out, Michael's right foot met with a fleshy thump that brought a loud whelp from one of the three Great Danes that were running alongside the bicycle. Michael screamed as they bounded beside him, their mouths open with excitement. There was one on either side and a winded one directly behind him. Like a gang of sheepdogs they seemed to guide Michael down the hill and towards the manor house. He could no longer steer to either side as he would now clatter into one of the huge dogs, nor could he brake.

His teeth met with the wooden seed of the peach as he made his final descent. Followed in the distance by Sergeant Ende, and channelled by three humongous dogs, the bicycle reached the home straight. The land settled into a flatter, straight run. However, Michael's momentum was set and there was no stopping him. Screaming forwards, the bicycle carried Michael through the main gardens of the manor. The thin wheels ploughed a delicate trail in the lawn, tearing through the first layer of grass and kicking up the dirt behind it. Still with his fingers fastened to the handles, Michael let out an almighty cry as the front wheel met with the base of the garden wall – the force tossing Michael past the handle bars and over the wall completely.

The three Great Danes and Sergeant Ende stood still for a moment as the young boy disappeared from out of sight – the snapping sound of a body flung through branches did its best to drown out the clattering of the bicycle against the wall.

***

Earlier that morning, Grace had been woken by her sister Cara. It was the beginning of the weekend and there was no need for school. Instead, their father had hired the help of the local musician Francis Morgan. Raegan was hell-bent on getting his children refined and deemed that music would be the best option. Francis Morgan had come highly recommended – known throughout Orplow as the only man to master any instrument you lay before him – he orchestrated all the major functions and town balls. Seen as a child prodigy in his early years, the townspeople had seen him leave the county and travel around Europe to display his fine talent. However, he had always vouched to return to his homeland and Orplow was once more his home.

Still only in his forties, Francis had never chosen to marry. His chosen wife was his music and he had treated relationships as his fruitful, yet fleeting mistress. Handsome and still sporting the browned skin of the European sun, Francis was not without his admirers. Nevertheless, his gentile manner and staunch passion for his craft had distanced him from the tales of the bored housewives. There had never been so much as a rumour about Francis for his openness towards his true love had eclipsed any doubt or spited speculation. Now back home in his boyhood town Francis wanted to give his passion to those that he held dearest. He wanted music to guide the hearts of his townspeople.

Today his task was to pass on this zeal to the young minds of Cara and Grace. Raegan Darby had employed him as a tutor, stating that he wanted his young girls to be as continentally commercial as they could be. As music held no language barriers, Raegan believed that to have his daughters well versed would increase their stock amongst international suitors. Francis scoffed at such tripe but would not deny anyone the chance to play their favourite tune. All that he insisted was that it be by their own hand, and not that of any other's.

Stood in the entrance hall of the Darby manor, Francis played witness to Raegan's firmest handshake.

'Welcome my good man. Welcome!' Raegan's grip tightened around Francis' delicate fingers. 'My girls lie in wait for your marvellous bounty Mr Morgan.'

'Please Sir, call me Francis' he replied as he slipped his fingers from out of the grasp of his newest employer. 'I hope the girls have an open mind. I have a lot to teach them. Is there any specific instrument you wish me to tutor them on?'

'Well… Francis, I was rather hoping the violin. It is an instrument enjoyed throughout Europe after all.' Raegan tweaked the tip of his moustache.

'Well, I must say that from what I've seen, it is not the person that picks the instrument, but the instrument that picks the person' answered Francis. 'The girls may find themselves drawn to other forms of music sir, and I would gladly guide them to where their natural passions fall.'

'No' said Raegan bluntly – his chin raised slightly. 'The girls will learn the violin and that is all for now.'

'As you wish' said Francis. 'But rest assured. As talented as I am, even I will not be able to make a person play to the beat of another man's device.'

With this Francis made his own way upstairs. He did not carry any instrument but rather preferred to tutor his students using their own. He was pretty sure that two fine, brand new violins would be awaiting him upstairs. However, whether two violinists did was a different matter entirely.

Strangely, for the first time in his life he prayed that there did not. Despite his fervour for the fruits of music and song, he never wanted to tune a person's heart to a different tone. Instead he wanted to harness the opera from within the person themselves. He believed that each person had their own song sheet by which to live from, and not one person should or could be able to change a single note of it.

The first time he saw the two girls his heart lifted. The elder of the two was already sat on her stool, violin in hand and facing a song sheet. The other, to Francis' delight, was not. Instead she had emptied the violin case and was now scattering the petals of flowers within it. The violin itself was tossed to the side, resting on its face at the foot of the bed.

'Hello Mr Morgan' said the eldest girl. 'I am Cara Darby'.

'But of course you are my dear' replied Francis. 'But please, call me Francis. This must be Grace I assume?'

'Yes… Francis' said Cara with a childish giggle. She felt quite mischievous calling an older man by his first name. 'You will soon find that Grace has quite the rambunctious spirit.'

'Fantastic' replied Francis. 'Would not life be but a dull drum if we were all the same.' He sat on the edge of the bed and spoke to the youngest girl directly. 'Hello Grace, I'm here to teach you music. You do not have to like it but it would be a blessing to me if you tried.'

'Of course' said Grace as she lifted her head up. Her eyes were as brown and polished as the wood of the violin itself. 'Will you teach me?'

'I promise to try' said Francis taking Grace by the hand and leading her to the stool next to her sister.

Knowing that they would not have played a single note before, Francis took his time to tell the girls just how a violin worked. He explained every component and its importance to the next. He detailed the enchanting power felt when knowing that the gentlest switch of the wrist can bring with it a wondrous melody. He expressed how the instrument could capture every mood and reflect every aspect and emotion of the human heart. Francis showed that it was within these strings, and these emotions that every person was bound to the next. The animation in his description enchanted the young girls. They smiled and gawped with wide eyes as their heads were flooded by his message.

Reaching a state of fever, Francis clutched at Grace's violin and played the most beautiful song. Unbeknown to the girls, he played the freshest violin concerto of Camille Saint-Saens – a tune that had never graced the emerald isle before this very moment. Francis had studied under Saint-Saens for five years in Paris and was forever grateful for his style. For since those years, Francis had created his music through his fingers and wrists rather than his arms. And now both Cara and Grace could see that, while almost perfectly still before them, a great song came from Francis' fingertips.

The rest of the morning was spent watching Francis drain every drop of emphasis from the appeal of the violin. As the early afternoon sun broke though the grand windows and shrouded Francis, Grace was forced to squint, allowing her to see nothing more than the image of flailing lines of shadow among the sunlight. As the shadow became still and silent, it was now time for the girls to try out their new gifts. Turning firstly to Cara, Francis stood behind her and held her wrists as he guided the bow across the strings. He did this three times before letting go and leaving Cara to the gentle chiming of an A minor.

Grace was thumbing at her bow as Francis made his way over to her. The violin did not rest in the nook of her small neck so easily and she was having difficulty keeping hold of it. Dropping the instrument into her lap, she looked up with a protruding bottom lip and saw Francis smile at her. His head tilted slightly to the side as he gazed at her for a moment. Suddenly, before he could convince Grace to try one last time, a large commotion could be heard outside. The rattling of rickety metal, followed by a number of dogs barking, filtered through the windows.

Rushing to see what was happening, Grace dropped her violin and propped herself up onto the windowsill. Looking out from the grand window, Grace could see her father's dogs sprinting across the lawn, followed distantly by an old man in a dark uniform. They both seemed to be chasing a young boy on a bicycle.

Grace laughed as she recognised Michael. His legs were spread out wide and his face was more terrified than she had ever seen. He bounced in the seat of the bicycle as it buckled and blundered its way through the gardens. Following Michael's descent, she smiled at the sight of him. She did not take her eyes off of him for a moment, not until the very last. It was then that the bicycle struck the garden wall and the young boy took flight. Everyone behind him stood completely still, but Grace had a clear view of the hill beyond the wall and could see Michael rolling down it. He came to a sudden stop as his body lunged forwards and wedged him deep into a juniper bush. Only his legs could be seen, and they lay slumped and still.

Leaping down from the windowsill, Grace ran out of her room. She brushed passed her sister Cara and tutor Francis.

'Sorry' she shouted behind her as she left the bedroom.

Rushing down the stairs, her arm was grabbed by her father.

Chapter 6

When Michael opened his eyes he was not on the leafy bed of the bush as he had expected. Instead, he was on the softest mattress his back had ever felt. The comfort was almost enough for him to ignore the blinding pain that beat at his crown. He could only see through his right eye – his left was firmly shut. Every so often his head would rock and a sharp pinch would be soon followed by a swift tug near his left brow. Through his right eye, he could see Grace sat at the end of the bed. She was staring at him and held a wet flannel inside a bowl of warm water. She seemed perfectly still, while Michael's heart raced inside his chest.

Distractingly, his left eye was able to open for a slight moment. It was enough to see what was happening. An elderly man was threading a needle through Michael's left brow. A droplet of blood ran from the wound and closed Michael's eye. As it did, Grace leaned forward and dabbed at his face with her cloth. The warm water drained into Michael's eye.

'Don't worry, I'm here for you' said Grace gently as she rested her hand on his.

Grace and the man with the red hot needle were not the only people in the room. Michael could see that he was surrounded. Behind Fiona Darby, Connell Locran, and an olive skinned man, stood Raegan Darby. His face looked like a damn on the brink of bursting – his pumped cheeks seemingly brimming with the fruit from his acid tongue. His lips were contorted into a tight knot of blood drained flesh – his arms firmly planted across his chest.

From his blind side, Michael could hear the sound of footsteps rushing through the door. They came to a halt at his side, and soon he heard the soft cry of his mother. Her hand touched his left hand, grasping it gently.

'Are you alright son?' Abigail leaned forward and kissed his cheek. He was lay out upon a bed with a ragged, deep gash sprawled across his left temple. The doctor was pulling the torn skin together as close as he could. A dark black stitch had been threaded across Michael's ripped flesh. Once the minor surgery was complete, Michael was encouraged to sit up.

'What were you thinking?' asked Abigail. She wanted to brand his behind but was more relieved to find that her son was not badly injured. Back at the Sterrin's house, while Margaret had been relaying a sordid fable fresh from the street, Oscar had burst through the door declaring that Michael was in serious trouble. He was not able to give Abigail any-more detail other than a location before she had rushed out of the cottage and headed for the Darby manor. She knew she shouldn't have let Michael out of her sight, and she hated herself for letting it happen. She kept telling herself that he would have been fine if she had just kept an eye on him.

'He is very fortunate that the authorities are not involved Ms Alpin' said Raegan from the rear of the room. 'Your angelic b'hoy was found apple scrunching before stealing, and subsequently destroying, a police officer's bicycle. I have also overlooked the damage caused to my lawn and garden wall, but I insist that you punish the young man. As for the damages, I am sure we can come to some sort of laboured arrangement to pay me back. We shall have the boy taken out of school after this term and he can begin to work the fields.'

'Yes Mr Darby' said Abigail, her eyes not flinching for a moment from her son.

'I mean, good lord!' announced Raegan. 'He must be suicidal like his late father. Doesn't the young boy know any better? You've already been abandoned by one of your loved ones. I'd have thought Michael would have been in no rush to follow in his father's cowardly footsteps.'

These words cut Abigail like a knife. Michael could see the pain in his mother's face as her knees gave a little. She had not wanted her son to find out the truth about his father like this – especially not from the mouth of someone as cruel and callous as Raegan. Michael had been taught all about heaven and hell, and was well versed from school about the repercussions of suicide. The thought of his father choosing eternal darkness over the light of his mother tore at his brain. The unknown now became hatred, as his father stood for everything that had ever brought misery to his kind mother.

The room became hushed by a muted gasp. The air grew thicker, and Michael's jaw clenched as his teeth gritted together tightly. Getting to his feet he launched himself towards Raegan. His mother had been humiliated enough, and this creature could not be allowed to punish her further. The soft cushions of the bed hindered Michael's leap and he hit the ground way short of Raegan. His right side was then met by a clattering thud as Connell brought his corpulent clenched fist crashing down across Michael's temple. The young boy lost his footing almost as soon as he lost consciousness.

Abigail screamed and tore at Connell's shirt. The metal cross on her rosary beads dug into his skin and punctured his greasy chest. He grabbed at her hands, holding her firmly by the wrists.

'Calm down woman' spat Connell. 'Your boy will be fine. It's nice to see that his old dear has a bit of fight in her, unlike his dear old pa!'

Abigail's eyes flooded and the anguish locked in her chest burst open. She flailed for a moment but felt an entire room of eyes set on her. Two maids had lifted Michael back up onto the bed. His was still unconscious, and one of the maids opened his mouth to check that he had not swallowed his tongue. Grace looked at her father for him to do something. She wanted him to punish Connell, to cast him out.

'Now everyone' said Raegan. 'It has been quite the testing day for all of us. This boy here needs some rest. We'll let him sleep here for a few hours and when he wakes he can return home to his mother. Abigail, I suggest you go home and get yourself together. I will not have any member of my staff behave in such a manner again, do you understand?'

Abigail did not reply. Instead she went to the bedside of Michael and kissed his head tenderly. Francis took her arm and led her outside. All the time she looked behind, gazing at her wounded son. She knew the impact of today would not even itself out for some time. Michael had always asked about his father, and it always added one more prayer to her list every time she failed to tell him the truth.

Reaching the main doorway to the manor house, Abigail turned and offered a subservient smile to Francis. His eyes showed no flicker of anything other than sincere sympathy. He nodded as she turned and walked slowly away, clutching at her bloodied beads with both hands.

Back in the room, Michael lay fast asleep. There was not a single dream inside his head. Instead his mind was clouded and dark. His head swirled and the darkness grew heavy. He fell into a deep state of unconsciousness. Fiery anger burned its way into his brain and forged a bitter seed of resentment for the most important man outside of his life. Michael would soon awaken and never be the same again.

The crowd that had stood around him had begun to disperse. The staff tended to their chores, and Fiona had marshalled her daughters swiftly out of the room. Raegan held the door for all to pass as only he and Connell remained inside. Raegan glanced to Connell and then to the boy. Catching his master's eye, Connell approached the bedside.

'Look at him sleep' said Connell. 'This one could sleep on a rope.'

'Just like his father' sneered Raegan.

Connell gazed at the craftsmanship of the doctor that had stitched up Michael's temple. The cut would now heal into a fine slit of a scar, barely noticeable and almost pretty in its precision. Removing his lock knife from inside his long jacket, Connell stroked the blade across Michael's face. The sharp steel sliced through the cotton stitches like a breeze among the grass. Raegan patted Connell firmly on the back as the two men left the room. The ragged scar was left open on Michael's temple. Fresh blood dripped down his face.

✷✷✷

Michael woke a little later. The pillow beneath his head felt dank and soft. Sitting up he leaned and turned to his right. He saw that a glass of water had been left by his bedside. Picking up the glass, he raised it to his mouth. After taking a long draw of water, he brought the glass down to his side. He felt droplets slowly sprinkle his forearm. Patting at his mouth, Michael checked that he had not spilled any of the water. His head was still a little hazy and he was not entirely out of his slumber. But the drops continued. Glancing at his arm, Michael saw the crimson red flecks of blood that stained his skin.

Not knowing what to do, Michael clutched at the flannel left by Grace. He held it to his temple and stood up from the bed. Taking one final gulp of water and draining the glass, Michael tested his footing upon the solid oak floor. His feet stood firm as his head swayed a little. He walked to the door and leaned out. No one was around or tending to him anymore, so he decided to go home. The evening had only just begun and the sun was setting across the fields. Without looking as to who was around him, Michael staggered slightly as he walked through the entrance hall and out of the manor house.

Orplow was preparing itself for the cover of night. Birds burst into the sky and savoured the final rays of light from the day. The cold breeze filtered through the long grass of the meadows as the sun sank softly into the horizon. A brief tinge of orange paved the land before resting beneath the dark cloak of the evening. Michael felt the warm glow of the sun pour down his side as he walked home.

The soothing sunset was soon replaced by the coldness of night. Michael shook as the winds held him. Walking through the long grassed meadow, Michael began to feel his way home. With the cloth still pressed to his head, he held out his right hand and let the tips of the grass flicker through his fingers. He read the land like a blind man read Braille. His senses filled his head, mapping out the landscape perfectly. He closed his eyes and let his feet carry him through. With each step he knew he was getting closer to home. The long grass dipped from his fingertips, guiding him into the final field from his home. The sweet scent of the rapeseed crops filled his nostrils.

As this passed, Michel opened up his eyes. Oil lanterns flickered in the windowsills of the cottage. The soft silhouette of his mother swayed within one. Opening the door, Michael saw that his mother had tears drying on her cheeks. She rushed to him, knelt and held him tightly.

'I'm so sorry' she whispered into his ear.

Michael felt the strength from him drain into the arms of his mother. Her muscles clenched with one final embrace before pulling away and holding him at arm's length. Her smile was one from a loving mother slightly amused at her roguish child. Her smile warmed him – he held back his tears. With the cloth still in his hand, Michael brought it down from his face. The bleeding had stopped, and the gash was lined with clotted, dry blood. Abigail took the cloth from Michael's hand, dabbed the tip on her tongue and gently wiped the blood from her son's face. She saw that the cut would leave a scar. The edges were jagged as it curved around Michael's left brow. His once soft, smooth skin had been given the rough character of life.

'I never told you the truth about your father, Michael' said Abigail. 'I'm truly sorry about that. But the real truth is that I don't know much either. All the stories I told you of the love we shared are true. Even now I still love him as much as my heart will allow me. Yet he chose to leave me, and with all my heart I do not know why. But you must know he did not leave you, he never knew you were coming. Maybe that would have changed things, but I was never given the chance to tell him. That is why we must pray for him Michael, so that one day we both may know him. You see, he already knows you through me Michael. Every day I tell him about you.'

'How did he die?' asked Michael. The light of the lamp flickered on his mother's face. Her eyes were shaded as they looked towards the floor.

'I found him' replied Abigail. 'He had hanged himself on the willow tree outside our cottage. He looked so sad. In all my time here, I shall never forget that moment, of how my world changed forever. But, you see, I can't be angry with him because he brought me you Michael. He brought me the son that he truly deserved, and I see him in you every day.'

'I can't forgive him mother' snarled Michael.

'Leave that to me' said Abigail reassuringly. 'I have enough prayers for the both of us. God will deliver him to us one day, I promise. But until that day, I must teach you how to lead. You're heir to a great reputation Michael, and I know you have the heart to exceed even the highest of expectations.'

'I will not be my father' said Michael. 'But I'll always be here for you mother, and I'll provide as best I can.'

'You don't have to be yet son. Learn the spoils and joys of life first. Here, let us put some music in those sturdy legs of yours.' Abigail held out an extended hand. 'Stand on my feet, I'll show you how to lead a lady.'

Abigail encouraged Michael to bow as she curtsied gracefully. Tentatively, he removed his shoes and stepped onto his mother's feet. She wore rough, coarse sandals that locked Michael's bare feet in place. She held out her arms and showed Michael the leading stance. He smiled up at her as she had the posture of a princess. And as she hummed the sweetest song, Abigail danced. Her feet raised with ease as Michael learned the steps that carried him.

'Do you like the song I'm humming' asked Abigail as she continued to sway Michael around the cottage. 'It's a song by Turlough O'Carolan. You know, he was blinded at a young age

Michael but still went on to create such beauty.' She saw the sadness in her son's gaze. 'Please don't let today cloud your eyes.'

Michael stared at his mother. His feet were already growing accustom to the soft waltz, and his ears filled with the wonderful rhythms of O'Carolan's *Butterfly* and *Dream*. He had never loved his mother more than in this moment. He had never seen her move so freely, and the smile she wore was one of true distanced peace. They danced for hours until the final drop of oil in the lanterns dried. Stepping down, Michael held out his mother's hand and bowed. She curtsied and looked outside. The shade of the old willow tree was masked by the night. She was ready for bed.

'I need to go out mother' said Michael. 'I shan't be long. It has been a long day and I do not want to sleep with the thoughts that are in my head. My dreams would give me no rest.'

'Fine,' said Abigail. 'Just be careful.'

Watching his mother knelt by her bed, Michael left the cottage, passed the willow tree and let his feet carry him through the shade to his most favourite place.

***

Raegan Darby had been drinking heavily. Two empty thick crystal glasses rested on the table in front of him. He ran his thumb across the jagged contours of the glass as Connell gathered another bottle of brandy. Finding the bottle of choice, Connell returned to the table, placed the bottle down and poured two thick measures into the glasses. The liquid lapped at the glass as Raegan swirled it in his tense hand. Fiona was tending to the children upstairs and Connell had ordered the help to give his master some privacy for the evening. His daughters had been distressed at the events of the afternoon and Grace especially had not uttered a word since.

The fire roared in the background. The flames reached and sprawled upwards towards the exceptional marble mantle-piece. Held in a garish gold plated frame, a large family portrait hung above. There was no other light in the room other than that from the fire and, sat among the shadows, Raegan pondered the events of the day. Firstly, he would have to punish Aiden Adams for his incompetence. He lamented on the man's audacity in bringing attention to any of the Darby's flawed fruit, and while the man had not let him down before, an example must be made.

'I need you to pay a visit to Aiden tomorrow' said Raegan. 'He needs to sample a little bit of the sharp sting from the humiliation that I endured today.'

'Very well master' replied Connell. 'The apples will not be ready until the autumn so I'll make sure his hands will have healed by then.'

'Good. Just break every finger in his left hand. He will still need to tend to the crops in the meantime, and I do not want to hinder my stock too much.'

They both drained their glasses and refilled them just as swiftly. The heat from the fire had made the air dry, and Raegan found that he could not quench his rampant thirst. His mouth felt like the parched sandy shores at low tide. He sat with Connell as they lay set to finish the entire bottle of brandy. Connell sat back and unwound. He could already hear the sweet sound of the cartilage crack and pop in Aiden Adams' hand.

Upstairs, Grace was being comforted by her mother. She had sprinted out of the room once she saw that her father was not going to punish the brute Connell for striking Michael. She could not bear the sight of him hurt and had remained in her bedroom all day. She had wanted to call out to him as she watched him leave just before nightfall, watching him disappear among the meadows as the night crept over the land. Now she lay in bed with her mother by her side.

'Don't worry about today' said Fiona. 'That young boy will be fine. He was just a little stupid to try and test your father like that. We all know how he is when he doesn't get his way. It insults him'. She held her bruised side as she whispered her words.

'I don't care for father's pride' snorted Grace.

Fiona attempted to assure her daughter that her father had her finer interests at heart, but was interrupted by a clatter at the door. Raegan was stood at the doorway to the bedroom – smashed glass lay at his feet.

'Fiona' slurred Raegan. 'It's time for bed. Leave the children and come with me.'

He held out his hand. It appeared heavy on the end of his lean arm as he struggled to keep it outstretched. Fiona patted Grace's arm and stood up. She walked over to her husband. He turned and gestured for her to follow when she was near to him.

He staggered into their master bedroom and leant up the wall. He was pulling at his cravat, undoing the knot and dragging the material through his hand. His eyes were glazed and he appeared to be on the very edge of consciousness.

Fiona hoped that the drink took him before he tried to take her. She hesitated to get undressed. She did not want to tempt him to remain awake. He lingered, leaning against the wall for a moment. He raised his foot and pulled at his boot. The laces were tightly fastened and the boot refused to come off.

'Come now, Fiona' spluttered Raegan. 'Come to your keeper.'

His breath reeked of brandy as he leaned in to kiss her. His broad moustache felt like a wet slug on her lips as he brought it crashing forwards. Fiona grimaced as their lips met. Leaning back from her, Raegan saw his wife's distress. It sobered him instantly. What was once limp now stood rigid. Raegan brought his hands up to his wife's face, clasping her cheeks in his palms as he kissed her ferociously. He pushed her face into his as he kissed her – his teeth grinding behind his bloodless lips.

Struggling for breath, Fiona pushed at his chest. Raegan stood firm. Still locking his lips onto hers, he swept his foot between hers – opening Fiona's legs up to receive him. She staggered back and caught Raegan off balance. He lost his grip and stumbled forwards. He was panting heavier now and frowned as he faced his wife. Dropping his right hand down to his belt he whipped it up and smacked the back of his hand across Fiona's face. She fell to the ground as Raegan stood over her loosening his belt. Folding the thick leather strap in half he held the belt by the thick buckle. Fiona curled her legs into her chest and covered her face as her husband brought the belt down onto her side. Vehemently, he whipped at her legs. She could feel the warm trickle of blood on her calves. Closing her eyes, she bit her lip, praying not to scream and awaken her children.

But Grace could not sleep. She felt guilty for being so blunt with her mother earlier. After-all it was her father that she was mad at. Through his silence he had practically applauded Connell's vicious act. She climbed out of bed. Sliding her feet into her slippers she tiptoed out of the bedroom. She crept past Cara who lay sleeping with her book of fairy tales pressed tightly to her chest. The night air was cold so Grace picked up her coat from the bedside chair. It was the coat she wore to church in the winter. Thick and big buttoned, it hung heavy over her nightdress.

Pushing the bedroom door open slowly, Grace crept onto the landing. The huge spiral staircase lay in front of her. Only the sound of the house sleeping could be heard. Steps creaked and branches stroked the windows as the building breathed wearily. Grace made her way to the master bedroom. She was fully aware that this was off limits, but she saw the state her father was in and hoped that he was fast asleep. Her mother was a light sleeper, and Grace would often see her at the children's bedroom door watching them as they slept. Grace always pretended to be sleeping so not to embarrass or catch her mother off guard.

The door to the master bedroom was slightly ajar. Grace could see a streak of stale yellow light flickering through onto the landing. Holding her breath, she approached the door. She held her coat closed so the buttons did not tap at the banister. Coming to the door she peered inside.

Her father was standing above her mother. He was beating her with his belt. The cracks were muffled by her mother's dress but the tears still flooded her face. Grace gawped. Her father was relentless; each thrust of the belt became heavier and harder than the last. His legs were wide apart, giving him more thrust in his assault. The savageness of the attack was only equalled by the eerie silence of it. Grace could not believe how skilled her father was at removing the sound from the situation.

The sight repulsed Grace. She wanted to cry out for her mother. Her chest pounded with the combination of terror and anger. Instead she took flight. Rushing back to her room she looked around for what she might need. There was nothing that she could think of. She ran from the room – not looking back as she knocked the book from Cara's hands as she brushed past.

Grace crept hurriedly down the stairs, desperately trying not to alert anyone. Her hand swept the spiralling banister as her eyes took a moment to adjust to the darkness again. The main door was locked tight. Using a satin cushioned footstool as her aid, Grace pulled herself up onto the window ledge and opened the window widely. She dropped out the other side onto the cold sandstone driveway, turned and ran away.

Cara watched through her bedroom window as her younger sister ran from the house. She had woken as Grace had knocked into her moments earlier. Looking at her sweet young sister now, Cara allowed her to feel free for a while. She wanted Grace to get away but knew that she could never allow her to come to harm. Giving her sister a minute to enjoy her release, Cara woke the household.

Grace ran with all her might. Her chest was pounding as the long grass whipped at her legs. The earth dipped and heaved in front of her. The cold of the night smacked at her face. She felt the bitter air fill her lungs as she pressed on. The field lay out far and wide. She was completely lost. Every patch of grass looked like the last under the nights light. All she knew was that she was running straight ahead and farther away from her father. Tripping on a tree's raised root, she fell to the ground. The soil felt dry and chalky in her hands. She clambered to her feet and looked behind her. The manor house was awake now. The windows glared with light as the softest trace of sound and life could be heard upon the roaming winds. Without a single plan in mind, Grace pressed on.

The Darby manor was stuck in a whirlwind of panic. Every member of staff had been woken and were now being handed burning torches and gas lanterns. Raegan had regained his footing and was barking orders at everyone. Led by Connell, they all poured out onto the grounds of the manor like a thick swarm of fireflies. The ground before them lit up as if greeted by the morning sun itself. They pushed forward towards the fields – spreading quickly across the land.

Upstairs, Fiona could not move after Raegan's attack and remained beaten on the floor. She had barricaded herself inside her bedroom in case anyone came and found her in this state. She wept with worry as the blinding pain in her chest crippled her cries. Cara was left to take care of Imogen. With Imogen asleep nestled into her lap, Cara sat by her windowsill and overlooked the action. She opened up her book of fairy tales and began to read to her sister. She smiled as the book fell open onto the tale of Sleeping Beauty.

Seeing the light from behind her bounce off the fields in front, Grace ran into the darkness. Keeping away from the light, she came to the shore of Lake Doriend. The waters skipped in the moonlight, as small bubbles climbed from the lake's bed and rippled on the surface. Grace was exhausted. She had never been this far away from home without someone with her. She suddenly became scared. The trees began to transform into hideous monsters – their dangly fingers stretched out wide. She stood still, hoping not to get caught.

Motionless by the lakeside, she could see two swans upon the water – they nestled in together upon the moon's rippled reflection. It was then that Grace decided to remain still and let her father find her. She was lost and too exhausted to return by herself. Sat still by the shore, Grace heard the flicker of footsteps approaching.

'Grace?' said the soft voice. 'Are you alright, what are you doing out here in the cold?'

Turning to see her companion, Grace saw Michael stood before her. His hands were spread out by his side and his eyes were wide open. Her heart lifted at the sight of him. He smiled at her and offered his hand for her to stand. She shook her head and nodded in the direction behind her. Upon the crest of the meadow came a burning hoard of light. Dots of fire bobbed and weaved among each other but grew increasingly closer. Michael turned to Grace.

'Are you in trouble? Do you need my help?'

'I was running away, but I am completely lost.'

'Running eh?' said Michael. 'Well, if you must, then run this way.'

He took Grace by the hand and led her away from the torchlight. The hill became steep and a full moon lay directly in front of them. Grace felt like Michael was going to launch her into the night sky itself. The lake rested to their left. Soon the waters started to surge by their side. The soil beneath their feet had turned to hard, slippery rock.

Suddenly, the path in front of them ceased. Stood at the edge of the land, Grace looked out onto the most beautiful setting she had ever seen. The cove was clothed in moonlight and the stars danced off the ocean's surface. The waters of the lake broke over the land and descended through a glistening mist – straight into a thick pool of dark water. The rocks surrounding the pool bit and chewed at the waters as they broke upon them.

Looking behind her, Grace could see that the torches had already reached the spot where Michael had found her. The swans on the lake had retreated from the mob and could no longer be seen. Michael was smiling at her side. She could feel his eyes burning into her cheek as he watched her take in the view. She felt a sense of panic. She thought he was going to help her escape, but Michael had only taken her to a dead end. There was only one way back and that led to her father and his loyal henchman.

'So what now?' They stood toe to toe.

'We fall' said Michael. 'Hold my hand tightly.'

Following Michael's lead, Grace took several steps back from the cliff's edge, raced forward and leapt high into the air. Her hand tightened around Michael's as they began to fall. They tore through the air – the wind gushing around them. The sense of pure freedom lasted for a few seconds before they met with the frosty waters below.

Crashing through the surface, they stayed hand in hand. The cold waters surrounded them, shaking them to their senses. Acting on impulse alone they thrashed out their legs and headed for the moonlight. The waters were still and Michael held Grace as he swam backwards to the rock's face. She felt heavy in her coat. Above them they could see the flicker of light pause at the edge of the cliff before it turned and disappeared.

Clambering onto the rocks, they sat silently and watched the waterfall beat at the pool. Grace was dithering and her hands shook in the hope to grasp some warmth from the night. Getting to his feet Michael took Grace's coat from her. He drained it and rested it on the rocks closest to the cliff face.

'Come with me' said Michael. 'Let's see what's behind the waterfall.'

Hand in hand, they crept around the side of the water as it raged and fell before them. The mist sprayed at their feet as they stepped inside the cavern that lay behind. A wide and high room of mountainous rock was inside. It was not deep and the far wall was only a few feet away. The only entrance was the one that both Grace and Michael had come through. Together, they were completely alone.

Without a word shared to one another Michael wrapped his arms around Grace as they lay on the dry rock. The air behind the waterfall was warm and locked in tight by the curtain of falling water. Completely at peace, they both fell asleep — their chests breathing in time to the gentle waves breaking upon the rocks.

✲✲✲

The breaking of the dawn woke Grace as the rainbow of light burst through the falling waters. Flashes of reds, greens and yellows painted the cavern. Michael was out by the rocks picking up Grace's coat. The cold night air had dried it out, and the morning sun began to warm its thick material. Michael walked over to Grace and put the coat around her shoulders. He took Grace's hand in his and with his finger drew out a single cross. He smiled as she looked up at him deeply.

'Good morning' said Michael. 'Let's get you home. I reckon your parents will be more worried than mad now.'

'I don't want to go back.' Grace yawned. 'Can't I stay here with you?'

'Ha! I don't live here. I usually just come and look out at the waters. It frees me a little.'

'But I don't want to go home' said Grace as she rubbed at her eyes. Images of her mother lying beaten on the ground filled the darkness. 'Tell me something nice.' Grace offered a warm smile.

'I'm not too good with words miss. But if I can, I promise to show you something nice each time we meet. Anyway, If you don't go now, then you'll never be able to come back here will you?' His sweet smile creased the flesh of his cheeks, and his scar beamed above his brow. He lifted Grace up and buttoned her coat. Placing his hands on her shoulders, he looked her in the eye and spoke.

'Come on.'

They walked bare foot upon the damp shores of Orplow. The sand bulged between their bare toes. They held their boots in their free hand, as they walked hand in hand back to the town, their feet pressing gentle puddles in the sand. The morning breeze was clean and crisp. Gulls flew overhead and cried and croaked above the sound of the waters lapping at the shore. Michael and Grace's footprints were the first to break the sand that morning, leaving a delicate trail back to the cove. This trail would gradually become swallowed as the waters gently washed over them.

It did not take Michael long to guide Grace back to her home. He had taken a shortcut off the beaten track through a field that passed a single house. Michael watched the interest grow on Grace's face as he told her the story that surrounded this solitary cottage. It had been rumoured that many years ago, while the husband had been on his travels, the house had been broken into while the wife lay fast asleep. The shock of the ordeal had caused the woman to have sleeping fits every night until her husband returned. Now, every night he sits by her bedside in a chair that faces the window – surveying the land. Not once does he share her bed with her, but takes his comfort in seeing her rest. Both Michael and Grace had wondered if the man had sat watching them as they passed.

Stood at the edge of the final field before the Darby manor, Michael watched as Grace made her way back home. He watched as she rapped gently on the large doors, and he watched her turn back and look at him before disappearing inside. The heavy doors closed with a thud behind her. He did not know that this would be the last time he saw Grace for almost thirteen years.

Smiling to himself, Michael walked home. He had never had such an affinity with someone before – a connection where words were unnecessary and emotions so clear. All he wanted to do was protect her from that day forth. Returning home, he found his mother still fast asleep. Creeping into his bed, Michael made the sign of the cross, held his hand in prayer and whispered 'Thank you'.

He fell back to sleep – his head holding images that would craft the most beautiful of dreams.

Chapter 7

The year of 1899 saw the laying of the foundation stone at Belfast's St Anne's Cathedral by the Countess of Shaftsbury, it witnessed the Ireland Rugby Union team set sail for their tour of Canada, and Britain readying itself for the second Boer War – where 180,000 men were soon to be sent to scorch the earth of South Africa. It would also be another ten years before Michael saw Grace again. After she returned home from running away, her father had immediately taken her out of Eden and set about having her tutored at home. The Darby family no longer graced the church with their presence and Michael was instructed not to come past the high walls of the closest field to the Darby manor. For months on end, at the same time each night, Michael had waited by the water where he had met her that evening. Grace had never come back.

The turn of the century afforded Raegan the opportunity to hold the grandest of balls. Like his own commercial chess board, Raegan would arrange the function to manoeuvre his political pieces as he wished. Commissioners from the Council of the Agriculture and Technical Instruction Act would mingle with the war generals of the British Empire, each affording Raegan the opportunity to extend his mighty estate. All that was left to him was to decide which would satisfy his greed the most. The councils could allow him to extend his land as well as avoiding taxation through the registration as a congested county, while the generals would soon be stretching the British Empire across the African continent, wherein their sons could lay claim to the captured land. After all, Raegan was well aware that his eldest daughter was at the fruitful age of nineteen and ripe for a suitor. If all went to plan, Raegan would see that the ball provided more than one lasting and rewarding partnership.

With the birth of the century just a few weeks away, the Darby family had some preparing to do. It was early December and Cara was being tutored by Francis Morgan. They were under strict orders to be ready to perform at the ball and Cara was proving to be something of a natural. Her supple dainty wrists seemed motionless as the bow coursed up and down the strings. She was still missing a few notes, but Francis was confident that his young protégée would be ready. She had already mastered the concertos of Bach, Mozart and Beethoven and was now moving onto Francis Morgan's personal showstopper.

When studying under the great Camille Saint-Saens, Francis was asked to play for his mentor every afternoon. Saint-Saens had grown tired of playing himself, believing that when he did he was feeling the music rather than listening to it. And so it was through Francis that Saint-Saens strived to listen. By listening to the young boy play, Camille Saint-Saens would again recognise the delight enjoyed in his passion for music. It was under this appreciative ear that Francis discovered his showpiece. On a cold winter morning, Francis had gone to visit his mentor. Saint-Saens was sat in his favourite chair facing a single music stand and a stool that had a violin perched upon it. Francis recalls asking as to why he needed a music sheet at all – he knew almost every song by memory alone. It was only when Francis stood before the music stand that he saw that the music sheet was completely blank of any music. Not a single note or hint of a tune was upon it. Instead a short inscription had been made by his mentor's hand that simply read '*Play as your soul decides*'. It was here that Francis would learn that he was to perform not from his memory but from his heart.

Seeing the penny drop on the young boy's bright face, Camille Saint-Saens opened his hand to invite Francis to begin. He sat back, closed his eyes and listened to find where Francis' soul stood. Hailed as the very first romantic symphony, Francis began with Mozart's symphony in G minor. He played this flawlessly – his chest beating to the rhythm as if it was the very first time it had ever been played. He followed this with an entire rendition of Mendelssohn's violin concerto in E minor. His passionate start was joined by the beautiful dream that is found in the sonata allegro. Saint-Saens smiled as the two symphonies merged and passed each other like two hands meeting in a solitary clap.

The young boy played on as his piece met with an anxious cloud of sad notes – sounding out from his monologue cadenza. Saint-Saens could feel the boy's body slow down as his head began to rule his heart. However, Francis cleared his mind and seized a passionate finale in the allegro molto vivace as he finished on notes of pure energy and sparkle.

It was the finest arrangement Saint-Saens had ever heard. Technically, he had played better, but he struggled to remember a time when he had played with such honesty and spirit. It was within this moment that Francis Morgan had committed himself completely to his music.

Nearly thirty years on and it was now Francis who sat and listened. He listened as Cara played the song that had once enraptured and captured him. As she stood by her windowsill, with the window wide open, she played as she looked out across the fields. The meadows were crystallized under a carpet of thick white snow. The high hills, scattered boulders and staggered rocks now shared the same powdered blanket of winter. And yet, despite this heavenly sight, Cara played with a natural sadness that was colder than the season itself. The music sounded crisp and beautiful, and the melody was caged in a sinuous rhythm, but Francis recognised that Cara's true nature was more visible whenever she played the sad, slower notes. Like a lover without someone to love, Cara's passion was without an aim. Francis wondered whether he had asked his student to do too much. It was, after all, a symphony from the strings of his heart and not Cara's. Maybe he had asked the impossible when he had asked someone to play and feel what only he had felt. He knew that freedom of expression could not be replicated, rehearsed or ordered, and never before had he felt so egotistical and rotten. If it was not for the beauty of the music itself, Francis would have asked Cara to stop immediately.

'Bravo, Bravo!' said Raegan as he walked into the bedroom. He was applauding slowly and firmly. The slow, hard rhythm of his hands caused Cara to miss a key and stop playing. Raegan was dressed finely as always, and was making his way over to Francis as he nonchalantly lit his pipe.

'So, are we all on course?' He blew a puff of smoke into Francis's face. 'The ball is only just under a month away, and I am attracting quite a crowd. We'll need Cara to be at her best. There will be plenty of young bucks present and I have the whiff of a hunt in my nostrils.'

'Your daughter is wonderful Mr Darby' spluttered Francis. 'She has the poise and passion of a true dreamer. She will make you proud, I guarantee it.'

'Well, she better' stressed Raegan. 'There is a hell of a lot riding on this ball going to plan, and Cara is my most pivotal piece. Make her desirable if nothing else. Oh, and I hope the arrangement is continental. We have a broad range of people attending from all over Europe and I'd rather not alienate any of them.'

'Rest assured that the piece is universal' said Francis. 'There are no borders in music Mr Darby. Only those that feel and those that have cause to listen.'

'Very good' scoffed Raegan. 'Well you better listen to me. I hired you because you had the best reputation, and I hope you will be so kind to ensure that mine remains intact also.'

'Believe me Mr Darby, your impact on your children will be clear for all to see when Cara plays.'

'And what with young Grace?' He looked at the young girl who was stood by the windowsill, scoping the land outside. She was laughing as she watched two young boys racing horses across the snow-capped meadow.

'I meant to talk with you about Grace' replied Francis. 'She is not skilled in the art of music. She has no sense of the rhythm within it. The only thing I'm trying to work out is whether it's because she's not interested or because she doesn't feel it. There just seems to be no response whatsoever, and the more I try to teach her the more she shows that she wants to do her own thing. The girl's a free spirit; her heart doesn't sit within music.'

'Well, make her' said Reagan. 'Firstly, we shall see how much of a benefit it is for Cara at the ball. If it works then Grace will have to do as she is told when her time comes.'

Francis could see the intense intent in Raegan's eyes. The brown of his iris' were so dark they appeared jet black – like two empty chasms. Raegan took a long draw on his pipe and turned to where Grace was standing.

'Grace, come here' barked Raegan. 'I want you to explain yourself.' Grace just stood there ignoring her call. Her eyes were set on the boys outside.

'I said, come here at once little girl!' Raegan's face was flush and the blood rushed to the surface of his skin. Grace still did not come. Reaching the end of his infamously short temperament, Raegan rushed over to his daughter and took her by the arm. She continued to look towards the window as her father dragged her in front of Francis. Francis regretted his comment of Grace being a free bird. He was fully aware that nothing can be truly free if shackled by their family.

'Now Grace, tell me and Francis why you refuse to play.' Raegan bent down and stared directly into her face. His head filled her sight and she could not look elsewhere. She did not answer.

'With all respect sir' interrupted Francis. 'It's not a case that she has refused. She has tried to play what I have asked her to, she just has not taken to it completely. Maybe a little more time with Grace and I can uncover a hidden talent from her.'

'Maybe' Grace whispered.

'What was that?' scoffed Raegan. 'There are no maybes in this household. Either you do as you are told or you will do nothing at all. There is no middle ground with me little girl, do you hear me? If you don't do as I design then you will not become anything other than a tragedy. The opportunities in front of you are clear for all to see, and if you don't want to make the most of them then you can rot away alone.'

A gentle tear softened Grace's stubborn cheek. Seeing this before her father did, Francis took Raegan by the arm and led him away from Grace. Standing by the door, Francis uttered the first lie of his life.

'Please, do not worry Mr Darby' said Francis pleadingly. 'I shall get Grace to listen.' He patted Raegan on the back as his stormed out of the room. Turning back to the girls, Francis felt like he had betrayed them. Music was about expression, and both girls could not be clearer. Cara was a gentle dreamer and Grace was a wingless bird. It would be his greatest challenge of all to engineer a way for these girls to be free. If music held the key, then Francis was the only locksmith they could trust.

***

Down in the fields, Joseph Eagles was preparing the horses. Today he would be joined by the two newest workers on the land and wanted them to become familiar with his animals. The Darby estate had a stable of fine Andalusian horses. Regarded as the most beautiful breed in Europe, it was Joseph's task to keep them that way. The horses themselves had been tirelessly handpicked by Joseph from the very best stud farms in Spain, the main criteria being to ensure that there was a strong bocado bloodline within them. This would allow Joseph to breed and raise horses with true beauty, nobility and above all movement. In truth, Ragan's use of the horses broke his heart. They were viewed as merely ornamental to him, and while nature had built them to dance and perform as the showcase to any dressage arena, they had proved to be mere aesthetic objects to their materialistic owner. Their keeper felt differently though. Joseph had insisted that an authentic ménage be made for the horses to train in. He wanted to give them at least some form of expression.

Stood in the ménage, Joseph shovelled the snow off the top of the frosty surface. The sand underneath was still hard and Joseph worried that the surface may be too hazardous for the horses. These were extremely expensive animals after all – but only if all their legs remained in working order. A single fracture or break meant that the horse would have to be put down. Joseph knew that he could not afford for that to happen. These animals were precious to him, and he had raised them like they were his own family.

He looked across the long grassed meadow and felt the light winter wind flow over him. The air was soft and clean. The sun was breaking through the clouds and the snow was beginning to thaw. Using a garden fork to split and twist the hard ground, he went to work on the surface. With his graft and endeavour, and partnered by the blazing sun, Joseph broke up the sand into a layer of soft, cushioned earth.

Nearby, walking through the fields, alongside the fencing were Joseph's two new labourers. They were still too young to work the plough or any heavy equipment, so the two boys would be put to work in the stables. There were new colts to be raised and tended to, and Joseph would have the boys familiarise themselves with the horses right away. Coming closer, Joseph could see that the boys were wrapped up for the winter, with thick heavy clothing encasing them. The thinner boy walked with good posture and was not reacting to the bite of the cold. The chubbier boy seemed to be dithering and held himself as tight as a shy butterfly.

Standing before him now, Joseph watched as the thinner boy seemed to be looking past him towards the manor house. His eyes scanned the walls but did not seem to lock onto anything.

He now looked at Joseph who was stood straight in front of him. He leaned on his huge garden fork.

'Sorry, I'm half asleep' the thin boy lied. 'I'm Michael Alpin sir.' He held out his hand.

'It's a pleasure to meet you son' replied Joseph. 'I had the honour of knowing your father.'

'I didn't,' said Michael without a hint of sadness. 'But I'm told he was a good man.'

'He was, son' said Joseph as he rested his hand on Michael's shoulder. 'He was a noble and honest man. It saddened the town to hear what happened to him.' He knew he needed to drop the fork and stop digging. 'Anyway, who else do we have here?'

'Oh, forgive me.' Michael opened his arm. 'Hiding under all those clothes I think you'll find my friend Oscar Sterrin. He seems to suffer through every season sir. It's either too warm or too cold,' laughed Michael. 'If he has a middle ground, I've not found it yet.'

'Well, I'm Joseph Eagles, and it is my pleasurable task of having you look after the new colts.' He noticed how much older Michael appeared to his friend. He spoke with the confidence of an adult, and held himself straight and tall. 'Have you ever dealt with horses before boys?'

'That I haven't sir. And I don't think we eat them here, so Oscar won't have met with one either,' said Michael as he poked his friend in the stomach. A slight puffy, muffled groin could be heard under the set of thick scarves around Oscar's face.

'Very well,' said Joseph. 'After today you'll be able to tell everyone that not only have you dealt with horses, but that you have dealt with the finest horses that Europe can provide. We have two young colts that I'll ask you to look after. Let's go and get them.'

Walking the young boys over to the stables, Joseph noticed how neither of them were really watching where they were going. Oscar seemed too occupied in his own cold hands, as he rubbed them feverishly together. Michael on the other hand stood by Joseph's side and matched his stride exactly, but again his eyes had wandered unblinkingly to the front doors of the manor.

As the stable opened up, the mixed smell of sawdust and livestock filled the air. Two jet black Friesian stallions stood regally in their stables, their chins raised and their feet firmly set in the ground. Michael marvelled at the sheer size of these beasts. One snorted out a stream of hot air as Oscar passed, making him nearly jump out of his skin. Michael laughed loudly at his cowardly friend.

At the very end of the stable stood two of the most beautiful creatures Michael had ever seen. The two colts were stood side by side, looking almost identical to one another. Their dark grey, almost black colouring was magnificent.

'So, here they are boys.' Joseph patted and stroked both horses. They responded to his delicate touch – their noses following and tracing Joseph's hands. 'This one here on my left is called Paco. And his fine friend to my right is called Amador. Paco, Amador… say hello to your new keepers.' The horses shook their heads and tapped their front hooves in a slight dance.

Michael looked at both the horses in wonder. Their energy was enchanting and Michael was already in love with them. Despite them being near mirror images of the next, Michael could not help feeling himself drawn to one of the horses in particular.

'Can I look after Amador?' asked Michael. The request surprised Joseph. He felt an urgent and unexpected sense of pride. He turned and smiled widely at the boy.

'Of course you can. But be warned, this one is full of surprises.' Joseph gave a knowing smile to Michael.

'Hold out your hand.' Michael walked over to Joseph and held out his right hand. Joseph raised his above the boys palm and poured a fist grain into it. Without invitation, Michael placed the grain to the mouth of Amador. He flinched slightly as the horse parted his wide lips and bared his gnashing teeth. But Michael kept his hand in place, and could soon feel the dry, leathery tongue of the horse eating from his hand.

'Well, my oh my, you two are practically friends already,' boasted Joseph. 'I've never seen such young horses take to strangers like that. They usually get very nervous. I'm starting to think your task might be easier than I first thought.' He turned to the dithering boy. 'Now Oscar, that leaves you with Paco. He's one stubborn colt, but be patient with him and you'll have yourself a worthy beast.'

Joseph smiled as Oscar walked over to his horse. The young boy seemed hesitant and only stroked the colt through his thick gloves. Joseph poured a similar amount of grain into the boys palm and invited him to feed Paco. Oscar's hand shook as he held it out in front of him – he covered his eyes with his spare hand. There was very little grain left for Paco to eat by the time the horse noticed the boys shaking palm. Almost aware of the humour in the moment, Paco lowered his great head into Oscar's palm. His thick tongue layered Oscar's trembling palm and in one swift motion whipped the glove straight off the boy's hand.

'Sweet Jesus!' yelped Oscar. He snatched his hand back to his chest as he watched Paco chew on his thick glove.

'Now, now' laughed Michael. 'Don't go distracting the good lord. He's got more worthy people to attend to than you pal!'

Soon, out in the ménage, the young horses were putting the boys through their paces. Joseph would tell the boys of their more arduous unromantic tasks later, but first he just wanted them to see the beauty in the beasts. For starters, he had instructed them to just walk the horses around the edges of the pen. The surface was too hazardous for anything more than a soft canter, and these colts were only five years old. Both had plenty of adventures left in front of them and Joseph was concerned about taking any unnecessary risks. Nevertheless, he was aware of the sad truth that only one of them would be picked to stud, leaving the other open for auction if not a fate far worse. Only one fully grown stud could be allowed in the stables, as the competition for breeding would become a huge problem as the young colts meet their mares. Therefore, there would be a day where one of these horses would be picked, and the other deserted. But that day was some years away, and Joseph was hell-bent on enjoying every second with them until then.

Watching the young boys, Joseph could not help but marvel at how Michael had taken to Amador. Like a star to the night, he shone as he led the colt around the ménage. Their eyes were locked together as gentle snowflakes fell upon their backs. The contrast of colour was alive upon the horse, and Michael could feel the young colt's heart racing beneath its thick black chest. Frosty clouds burst from the animal's nostrils as he grew colder with each lap. Oscar was lagging behind with Paco as the colt jumped and leapt around. It appeared as if the horse was leading the boy rather than the other way around. Oscar was breathing heavy and he gripped the reigns tightly with both his hands.

'Well boys, keep that up' shouted Joseph as he was walking away from the pen. 'I've got to feed the other horses so just keep on with getting to know them for a while. I'll be back soon.'

'What?' Oscar cried. He spun on his feet to face Joseph but Paco kept on cantering forward. Determined not to let go of the reigns Oscar fell backwards, his cold buttocks thumping onto the ground with a hard bump. Paco bounded forwards, dragging Oscar behind him. His stomach jolted and bounced as he was dragged along the ground for almost half a lap before Michael spotted that his friend was in trouble. Letting go of Amador, he ran over to Oscar and leapt on top of him, grabbing his flailing heels and pinning him to the ground. The sharp pull made the reigns snap out of Oscar's hands, causing him to scream almost as loud as Michael's laughter.

'The crazy god-damn bastard animal!' screamed Oscar.

'Easy there boy' said Michael grinning. 'You heard the man. We have to give these horses a bit of time. Anyway, yours seems the livelier one. I bet you breakfast he's faster than mine.'

'I don't care if he is faster than yours. Have you seen my bloody hand?' Oscar raised his gloveless right palm. The skin was stark red in the cold and a bright white blister hand begun to develop.

'Ah, get over it. It's still attached, and it'll heal' smiled Michael. 'Your hands have always been too soft anyway. Come on Oscar let's race them. They're freezing in this weather, and it'll do them good. And, besides, it'll warm you up too.'

'You must be insane Mike. I can hardly walk with mine. He's possessed.'

'Come on…' insisted Michael. 'Fields are made for working on and horses are made for riding. As we can't do the one we may as well take advantage of the other. Joseph will not be back for some time. Did you see the size of those horses? They'll be eating for hours.'

Oscar accepted his friend's pleas and tentatively made his way over to Paco. Michael found Amador exactly where he had left him – his legs were straight and he was as still as a statue. Both the horses were without saddles. All the boys had for a grip were the loose reigns that they had led the horses around with. The ménage had a two barred fence surrounding it. The gate was near to Michael and unlatching it he swung it wide open. Seeing the open gate, the horses suddenly became animated. They could see the open fields before them, and they steadied themselves as if preparing to explode with energy. Bizarrely, Paco had calmed a little, as if he had recognised Oscar's intent. His best behaviour applauded the boy's decision to free the horses, if only for a while. Both colts stood as still as their excited legs would allow them as the young boys clambered up onto the ménage fence. The wood was slightly frozen over, and Michael's feet met with a slippery surface. He planted his hands onto Amador as he regained his footing, and leapt onto the horse's side. Oscar followed suit, and after some jumbled readjustment both boys were sat astride their colts.

'Now what?' offered Oscar in a hushed tone. He still did not want to alert Joseph and was scared to make too much noise.

'I have no idea' Michael chuckled. 'Let's leave it to the horses, shall we?' And with that Michael lightly tugged on his reigns, locked his legs down tight and held his breath.

Amador responded and headed for the gate, bursting into a gallop the instance they had passed through the fencing. Seeing Amador run free, Paco followed suit. The thrust in Paco's legs threatened to throw Oscar completely from him, and so Oscar wrapped his arms tightly around the horse's thick neck.

Together, the horses galloped across the meadows. The tips of the long grass lashed at Michael's legs as the winter air filled his lungs. He felt like he was falling, as the whistling winds wrapped around him. The sound of roaming hooves clattered on the ground as the soft white snow kicked up around them. Amador was well in front now and ran beautifully. His heart was pounding beneath Michael, and thick veins pulsated on his face. Without missing a single stride, Amador leapt over a small rock wall and broke into the next field. Snow-capped crops pierced the ground firmly like a glistening bed of glass arrows. A herd of Red Deer starburst across the field, freeing the land up for the horses to pass through without any obstacle.

Sat high above the hills, the sun shone brightly upon the boys. Paco was following the trail of pressed crops set by Amador, and neither horse faltered for a moment. Their hooves flicked and skimmed upon the surface, while the freshly pressed snow thawed under their feverous feet. As slaves only to their nature, nothing else was going to stop them.

Michael had only felt this sensation once before in his life, and the thick snowfall chilled his body like the cold waters of that fateful night many moons ago. But his heart was once again on fire, and nothing would make him let go of this feeling. He steered Amador back towards the manor house. Facing the building, Michael could not believe how far they had travelled. It was no longer the fortress it had appeared up close, but a mere dot upon the hillside. Fearing that he may have angered Joseph, Michael decided to head back. Unaware that they were returning to the shackles of their stables, the colts continued to gallop at full pelt.

Returning from his chores, Joseph's jaw nearly broke the ground. The ménage gate was wide open and there was no trace of either the boys or their colts. He could see thick prints ploughed the deep snow and reasoned that the boys had headed out into the meadow. He was now panicking. The ground was too slippery and firm for the colts to be running and even the slightest slip could be life threatening to both the horse and its rider.

The field in front of him began to break. Two dots in the distance bobbed and weaved as the ground around them flattened. The sight stopped Joseph in his tracks. He could see Michael on Amador as the colt leapt high and over the stone wall separating the fields. Joseph's heart almost filled his throat as they took flight. He braced himself for the landing, and his stomach jumped to the roof of his chest. Nothing but the sweet scent of relief washed over him as Amador landed beautifully – his rider sat on top with near perfect posture. Through all the concern and anger, Joseph wanted to believe his eyes. Buried inside his worry was a shining trace of appreciation. Not in all his years had he seen any of the horses gallop like they did in this moment. The image was the most wonderful thing he had ever seen, and he knew he had Michael's roguish temperament to thank for it.

The two horses slowed and approached the stables in a gentle canter. Oscar looked terrified astride his horse, as his arms continued to choke Paco. Sat high atop Amador, Michael's smile was humble. His heart was galloping within his chest, threatening to break free with every beat. But he knew he had broken a man's trust. Despite his own emotions and connection to the animal, Michael knew it was not his to enjoy freely. Nevertheless, he would do everything in his power to stay with it. Michael dropped his head slightly, sinking his chin into his chest. Joseph had no idea what expression his face displayed. On one side he was terrified and enraged by the children's actions. On the other, he felt a warmth that he had always longed for. His body had radiated at the sight of these horses doing what they were created for – he knew he could not be angry at anything embracing its nature, especially one as beautiful as this. He sighed deeply and tried to collect himself.

'B'hoys. . .' said Joseph as he shook his head. 'That was one of the most foolish things I've ever seen. If you cared for these horses, you need to recognise just how delicate they are. You can't just run away with them. They need a cautious care and anything else could be their undoing. Do you understand?'

'Yes, sir' sighed Michael. 'I'm forever sorry. I would do nothing to harm them. I just let my emotions get the better of me. I'll try to control them, I promise.'

'Well you bloody better!' Joseph feigned his anger.

He helped the boys down from the horses and guided them back into the stables. Their mucking out lesson was now long overdue. Walking next to Michael, Joseph let Oscar pass before holding onto Michael's jacket. As the boy turned and looked up at him, Joseph could not help but see the wild heart of Ferris colouring his face.

'For what it's worth son...' said Joseph. '...Thank you.'

Chapter 8

Christmas in Orplow was always a joyous occasion. There had not been a winter season for twenty years where it had not snowed. Families excitedly prepared for the celebrations ahead, whilst young couples were always grateful for their company. Romance warmed the town and a greater sense of love and cherishment could always be felt. Father Daniel held countless masses to an always heaving church, while everything about the town just seemed to be more pleasurable. The choir sang with more conviction, the people wore smiles that had no need to be forced or feigned, and a day's work was never so easy to do. Exhausted in their enthusiasm, folk would sleep with fuller dreams, brimming with plans and desires. It was a season for love and nothing else.

On the eve of this great occasion, Michael had finished his labours at the stables. He had fed all the horses, mucked out the paddocks and because of his efforts had been rewarded with a brief ride on Amador. Joseph could not deny the boy his pleasure. They had a bond that he just could not fail to acknowledge. It was, after all, somewhat of a selfish gesture; Joseph took almost as much pleasure as Michael did in seeing the stunning colt gallop at full pelt. Because of his unreasonable anger, they had always made sure that Raegan had been away from the estate and unable to witness Michael's pleasure.

Before Michael had joined Joseph at the stables, Raegan had instructed him to exhaust the boy. He appeared to hold the boy in deep contempt, and wanted him to suffer dearly through his labour. It pleased Joseph endlessly that Michael enjoyed every exertion put upon him. In time, his body grew with the workload, and all his passion were completely satisfied in his one reward. The boy was as free as the earth would allow when he was riding his colt. When they were joined as one, they became a force of such beauty that no man could dare deny them.

Parting from his colt, Michael whispered his thanks into the ear of Amador. He stroked his strong hand along the horse's body and left the stables. Oscar had already left for the evening as he did not care much for riding Paco. It had terrified him too much. Making his own way home, Michael had one stop-off that he needed to attend to.

At the church, his mother would be found there praying as Father Daniel held his last sermon of the evening. She had been there all day, not shifting once as she called on the lord to watch over her husband. She always spoke to Ferris through the church rather than at his graveside, as it broke her heart to see how a single piece of marble could reduce her husband into a mere hyphen between two dates – the latter being seen as too soon to complete a man such as her Ferris. For Abigail, he rested in her heart and not the ground, and her heart was now in the church. She whispered for hours into her rosary beads, telling Ferris of her love for him and hoping that the lord would eventually overhear and intervene. Every prayer was for his redemption. She knew that it would not be until her judgement that she would know if her efforts were rewarded, and so it would be until that moment that Abigail would continue her labour of love.

Trotting up the steps, Michael waited by the church doors. He had not been inside since the day he found out about the fate of his father. The red mist would descend each time he saw the heartache that his mother endured because of that man's selfish act. Because Michael loved his mother, he in turn hated his father. Even his prayers were altered by it. Each night, he would only mouth the words to the *Our Father* as he prayed before his bedtime, and had recently replaced it by repeating the *Hail Mary* twice. Aside from his deep desires and passions, Michael had chosen to live for his mother. She had given up her days for the man who had abandoned her – an act Michael swore to his soul that he would never mirror.

Abigail genuflected, made the sign of the cross and bid goodnight to her lord. She found Michael outside – his face slightly scrunched up like a pug dog. She knew his feelings about the church, but also knew that he was always pleased to see her. His face soon thawed at the sight of her and he walked over and took her hand. Despite being inside the church all day, Abigail's hand was the colder of the two. They both looked out onto the town as they reached the bottom of the church steps. It was alive as candles and lanterns streaked the streets. A warm yellow glow radiated between the snow-fall and hopped off the faces of everyone that passed through. The town was getting ready for the annual Christmas Dance.

Every year the townspeople would assemble and erect a huge marquee in the very heart of the town. Inside there would be a celebration fit for any man, woman or child. The musicians of Orplow would gather and play through the night as the people danced and drank until their hearts burst. The sweetly sharp cider of the town would fuel the fires as the music stoked the flames. Countless folk songs would be played and a wealth of festive dances performed. Michael prayed that his mother would be going. He loved to see her dance and was eager to learn more from her. They had been dancing for most nights together now, and Michael was starting to grasp the basics. However, his feet had always moved to the enchanting sound of his mother, and he was yet to dance to live music.

'Are we going to the dance tonight Ma?' He tried to sound casual and fleeting.

'Maybe Michael' replied Abigail. 'I said I would pay a visit to Margaret first. We'll see if we have time after that.'

***

Entering the Sterrin household, Abigail and Michael saw that Margaret was deep in conversation with her exhausted husband Maik.

'... And underneath her, he was as cold as a wagon's tyre!' Margaret laughed raucously as she delivered her punch line to Maik. Shrugging his shoulders he could not have looked less interested. He took a long draw of the cider from his tankard.

'Oh, sod you then' barked Margaret 'Abigail! Welcome, take a seat next to me. You'll never guess what happened when old Reece Staple went to bed with his young mistress?'

'I think I can guess Maggie' replied Abigail as she smiled and sat down. Margaret poured her friend a full cup of freshly brewed tea. Steam danced through the air as the liquid filled the delicate cup.

The house had a lively feel to it. The room was over lit with candles and not a single shadow could be seen. Near to the door, Oscar was greeting Michael like an old man would his fellow workmen. His face was held in an expression much too old for his boyish cheeks and his nod only made his sailor boy hat seem even the more unfitting. He offered to take Michael's coat, but Michael just laughed and patted his foolish friend on the back. Oscar had always tried to adopt a more mature stance in front of his mother. Michael had two friends in Oscar and it amused him endlessly to try and work out which of them was the more inane.

An understood, almost prepared silence entered the room as both Abigail and Margaret starred at their sons. Abigail smiled widely and glanced at Margaret.

'We'll be having dinner tonight here boys' said Margaret. 'I have a fresh broth all warmed and ready for devouring. So who wants the first bowl?'

Abigail could see the deflated look on her son's face. She knew he would remain polite throughout the evening, despite having his heart set on the dance. She winked at Margaret.

'Come, now Michael' declared Margaret. 'If you don't fill your belly, how are ever going to have the energy to dance tonight?'

His face beamed with delight. Michael looked from his mother to Margaret and back again. He could see that they were both smiling with him. Maik shakily raised his tankard in the air as a slurred gesture of celebration. Oscar was already sat at the table and close to emptying his first bowl of broth. He held it to his mouth with both hands as Michael took his seat next to him – plonking it down on the table as Margaret dished out Michael's helping. He could see Oscar eyeing up his bowl in the corner of his eye. Too excited to eat, Michael passed the bowl over to his friend. The spoon filled his greedy mouth before he could even say 'thank you'.

The walk to the marquee was Michael's favourite walk through the town to date. The snow scrunched beneath his feet as he walked aside Oscar, as Margaret and Abigail walked in front, flanked by the staggering Maik. On approach, the tent appeared as though it had swallowed the town entirely. The great canvases were taught and held tight to the ground by huge anchored ropes. Michael stood before the entrance and let the sound of the music fill his ears. He could feel it deep within every fibre of him. A warm glow emanated from inside and Michael could feel the vibrations of life draw him from the cold. Walking through the open canopy, Michael saw exactly what he had wished for.

There were a series of tables spread out sparingly, as the central focus was on the dance itself. Tankards, weighted with cider, held the tables to the ground as the music lifted everyone onto their feet. At the far end of the marquee was a host of musicians playing their drums and fiddles with all their muster. Nobody inside was still. Standing became toe tapping, walking became lively skips and dancing became a religion. An open layer of ground dominated the centre of the room, and upon it moved the masses of the town.

Michael could not have been happier. His mother was wearing her most radiant smile and gripped his hand excitedly. Tonight she wore a delicate white silk slip with violet trimmings and flowers. Margaret was being dragged by Maik to the dance floor as he skipped and bounced forwards. She looked back and waved her hands over to Abigail for her to join them. Michael scanned the room to find Oscar but could not see him. He had already darted for one of the tables and was now looking over his shoulder cautiously as he raised a brimming tankard to his licked lips. The boy greedily drank the cider down as the sharp liquid tore at his gentle throat. The tankard was held up to his face as a dancer bumped into Oscar causing him to empty the whole jug into his startled face. The liquid stung his eyes and Oscar walked blindly into the crowd.

Michael led his mother onto the dance floor. He turned to her and looked down at her feet. Abigail stepped backwards purposefully, causing Michael to look up inquisitively.

'I think you are ready to lead Michael' smiled Abigail. She curtsied and held out her hand. Michael could not tell what was beating at his chest, whether it was excitement or nerves – but he seized it regardless. He took his mother's hand and bowed before adopting the lead stance.

Despite the amount of people surrounding them, Michael and Abigail moved freely amongst the crowd. The dancers shifted and accommodated everyone around them. Michael felt the ground beneath his feet as he glided effortlessly across it. He looked like a small man rather than a tender boy as he danced, although he would occasionally switch between looking at his feet to his mother as he still feared that he may trip.

The music was sweeping and soft as they danced their first dance. Abigail burst with pride as her son beamed with joy. She loved him more than anything and had always seen how big a heart he had. In everything he did, Michael gave his all. She hoped that he had the strength to cope with such emotions. If it were not for his zest for his surroundings, Abigail would worry that Michael's heart would be the death of him.

The music paused for a beat as the rhythm shifted. The sound was now one of true Irish Folk as the six piece band and their spirited caller began to ring out. Michael could see that his mother was now raising her knees as she danced. The energy had increased, and sweeping movements had become near to jumping. People bounced and cavorted around the room. Partners began to change and revert back to their first. People swung each other by the arms propelling them towards an expectant other. The party was alive and Michael watched his mother as he whizzed across the floor after an old farmer had taken his arm. The men beamed around his mother; she was an angel as she floated through the hoard.

The lanterns licked at the last drops of oil as the dance came to its close. Margaret was propping up Maik with one arm as she carried an exhausted Oscar with the other. Everyone was heading home. Dozens of tankards had been emptied and music had drained the energy from the town's legs. Abigail and Michael broke from the road and headed through the far fields back to their cottage. Masked by the night, Michael closed his eyes and let his senses lead them home. He was now completely literate in the lay of the land and walked confidently among the long swaying grass. The wind carried the singing of the town across the fields, and Abigail hummed gently as her son led her home. It was Christmas morning and the birds were preparing their own song as the day began to break across the horizon. However, Michael and Abigail were thankful for the remaining shadow of the dawn. For Abigail, it allowed her to hide the warm tears that cascaded across her raised and smiling cheeks. As for Michael, he did not want his mother to see that his eyes were closed. They had given him several years to learn the land before setting him to work it forever, and he was not ready to leave his mother just yet.

✳✳✳

As always, the Darby household was ready for Christmas, and the day's customary procedure was well underway. Cara, Grace and Imogen were all sat by the fireplace as the family exchanged their gifts. Fiona was stood by the side of Raegan's chair as he sat and watched his daughters enjoy the bounty he had blessed them with. He patted his wife's hand as he held a crystal glass heavy with brandy in the other. Apart from their great financial worth, there was nothing of any specific sentimental value among the gifts. Each child was grateful for their presents but found the exchange of gifts between themselves almost redundant as they merely swapped the same garments of differing sizes between one another. Raegan had yet not allowed his children to pick their gifts and had relied on the town's finest tailor to dictate their fancy. With the fine clothes rested by her feet, Grace instead enjoyed the sweet taste of the tangerine that had filled the foot of her stocking. The bitter blast of juice on her tongue made her flinch slightly as she shuddered and rode out the sharp taste. Meanwhile, Cara was using a new nutcracker to crack a variety of festive nuts before feeding them to her younger sister Imogen, who would hold each one with both hands and nibble on it like a nervous squirrel.

As the fire roared before them, Fiona began to softly sing a song of good tidings. Her voice was fair and fine and the children listened to the first verse before joining their mother on the chorus. True to form, Grace sang louder than anyone. Her voice was almost on the brink of shouting as she rocked her head from side to side. Her eyes were wide open and her smile drew close to the tiny lobes of her tone deaf ears. Both Imogen and Cara smiled at Grace as she threw herself into song. Fiona rested her hand on Raegan's shoulder as his frustration simmered at his unwieldy daughter. It infuriated him that she had the physical beauty and fire of a red breasted robin but carried the dull elegance of a puffin. She had been tutored at home for several years now and while her academic mind was on course, her creative one failed to blossom. Francis had told Raegan how he regarded Grace as the music without the musician – she had it within her but not the means to set it free.

The children had finished with their gifts now and Fiona was coming to the end of her carol. Floors beneath the peaceful family, the staff were preparing a feast capable of satisfying the entire town. Maids, servants and chefs rustled and bustled in the kitchen like clockwork. The organised chaos came together in one fruitful chorus as the feast was beginning to take shape. At the heart of it all, Connell played the part of the cruel conductor. He swung his meaty fist in the air as a blunt, grizzly guide to the choir. His rumbling voice fused with the slamming of heavy oven doors, clattering of cutlery and clanking dishes. Everything had to pass his approval, and he tore at the remains of any carcasses that were ready for disposal. His chin gleamed with the grease of fresh meat and his tongue lashed out chunks of cooked flesh as he spat out his orders.

'Hurry up. Master wants his dinner set within the hour. There is plenty of room on the spit for the lazy, so crack on!'

He was drinking as usual. For months now he could not recall how his head felt without it being basted in booze. He had become increasingly violent towards his staff and many a young maid had felt the vile thrust of his frustration. Recently he had begged Raegan to bring Abigail Alpin in from the fields and into the kitchen. Connell had lusted after her for some time, but always found her somewhat guarded by his master. For months, Connell had begun to watch her work as she tended to the lighter crops in the early morn. Not once had she come within the confines of the grounds of the manor, and yet he was well aware of how well regarded she was inside of it. Like a fruit ripe for dessert she had only been pricked once, and Connell felt she was ready for a true needling.

The staff swarmed around him. Several gentlemen wheezed past as the youngest of maids wore their collars high to hide the bruises from his black kiss. The final touches of the banquet were being tended to, and the food was laid out in front of Connell on a huge array of serving carts. He was ravenous, and – in particular – the sweet cherry of the young maid that was glazing the ham took his fancy. However, he would save that for his midnight treat after the feast had finished.

'Merry Christmas to you all' blurted Connell as he thrust his tankard in the air. His eyes were locked on what he craved, and his thick tongue licked his greasy, glistening lip.

Sat around the grand dining table, the Darby family were giving thanks. The feast was spread out widely in front of them, and Grace could barely see Cara above the large glazed ham that filled the table. Stood at the table's head, Raegan sloppily carved the first cut from the huge, roasted turkey. His hand was unsteady as the brandy begun to flood his cold veins. Defeated by the task, he slumped into his chair, allowing the head chef to cut the rest and cater to his family.

There was very little conversation over dinner. The children felt separated by the sheer size of the table and Fiona seemed to have the appetite of a field mouse as she picked at the slither of meat on her plate. The clunking and short screeching of cutlery on the china plates filled the pregnant pauses between Raegan's heavy breathing.

'I take it everything is ready for the grand ball?' posed Raegan as he geared his head towards Cara. 'Francis tells me that you have almost mastered a piece that is sure to show the town your full emotions.'

'Yes father,' replied Cara. 'The music is truly beautiful. It is Mr Morgan's favourite arrangement, and I pray I make him proud.'

'Balderdash' yelled Raegan as he held his cutlery upright, with his fists planted on the table. 'Your aim is to make your family proud. Not some travelling musician. He is a hired hand and nothing more. You will play for your family that evening, in view of making one for yourself. There will be plenty of suitors amongst the guests and you my dear will be the object of their attention.'

'You mean affection, surely dear' said Fiona.

'I know what I mean dearest' Raegan sneered. 'Cara is of the age now to marry and bring two families together. With the turn of the century coming up, we have a great opportunity to take our estate forward. Ireland has been kind to us and Orplow a good nest for our young. But the world is widening and we need to move with it.'

'Our daughters are not cattle to be drove around continents' replied Fiona. She stared down at her plate as her chest expanded. Her breathing was heavy and her pulse had quickened. She already knew the reward that lay in wait for her that night. Raegan had turned a shade of scarlet and had risen from his chair. He stormed down the side of the table, jamming his knife into the large cut of beef as he passed. Light bounced off the handle as it shook atop the punctured meat. Standing by the side of his wife, Raegan pointed his furious finger straight into her down turned face.

'Don't you ever…'

'Stop father!' interrupted Grace. It was the first time she had spoken to him since the night she had ran away. For a moment her plea had worked. But it proved only to deflect his wrath. Turning, Raegan walked towards his middle child. Her frown was firm and crowned her furiously beautiful eyes.

'So, she finally speaks' snarled Raegan. 'I think the silence may have made you forget your place, little one. I make the orders around here. I'm the man of the house and you'll all do as I command.' He raised his hand above his head now, with his open palm facing Grace.

'You're a monster' cried Grace. Her tears burned her soft cheeks. She was terrified of her father and knew exactly what he was capable of.

'Would a monster want the very best for you!' shouted Raegan. His face was flush and his lips sprayed globs of saliva as he bellowed. 'Would I not be a father if I did not wish the best for my children? I live for it. One day you will all look back and see that I gave you everything in this blasted world!'

It felt more like hell, thought Grace. She had sunken her head into her chest and held her hands in her lap. She was hoping that if she did not look at her father then he would go away. Meanwhile, Cara and Imogen stared blankly ahead of themselves, watching as their father stormed out of the room, clutching a fresh bottle of brandy from the table.

***

Once the night had arrived, Connell decided to venture outside. A tireless fire had been set inside his belly, and the noise of the house was stifling his thoughts. Thoughts that were mainly of one particular person – Abigail Alpin. Her skin was as fresh and white as morning milk and how he longed to devour her. Deciding that he would take his time with her and drag out his ferocity, he had etched out exactly how he would take her. He could already see the sweet anguish scream across her face with every thrust of his hard body. Having planned it for years, Connell knew he would give her a night to remember, and a lifetime to get over it. Sat out on the manor steps, Connell looked out over the fields. The dark shade of the willow tree was nothing more than a dark blot on the dusty, orange-drenched land. As the day drew to its close, Connell sat pondering his opportunity. Watching the small fireflies dance in the dark, he decided that the ball would be it.

Chapter 9

Major Irwin was in agreement with Raegan Darby. His latest correspondence from the battlefields of South Africa read as if Raegan had written it by his own hand. It had detailed the contract that agreed that Major Irwin would offer his son David's hand in marriage to Cara if Raegan would in turn provide fifty men from the town for immediate conscription into the army. It was a highly illegal and immoral agreement, but in the eyes of Raegan it was the quickest and most promising contract he had ever signed. He could provide almost the entire number required from his staff and regional farmers. The women could tend to the duties left open and their children would be removed from school and put to work. For Raegan there did not appear to be a cost for him at all. His land remained well managed and his daughter held claim to whatever land David Irwin inherited.

David Irwin was already on his travels to Orplow for the ball. He would meet Cara after her performance – a performance, according to her mentor Francis Morgan, sure to melt even the most battle hardened of hearts. Cara had been rehearsing tirelessly with every spare hour of each day, and could now play the piece entirely from memory, which allowed her to throw her body and soul into her performance. When reading from the sheet, Francis had found that she remained completely still. It was only until he removed it that Cara moved freely within her music.

Up in her room, with one day away from the big event, Cara practised for the last time. She was unaware of her father's arrangement and was already dreaming of her very own Prince Charming entering the hall. As she played, she pictured the noble prince whisking her off her feet and carrying her out into the night – his arms firm and bulging as he gripped her. Her head floated as her heart fluttered at the thought. She smiled at Grace who was sat watching her. Grace could see the happiness in her sister's face, and it was only when Cara smiled that she looked her true tender age. Straight faced she carried an older, almost war worn appearance, but as she smiled the light of youth burst in her eyes, with only a sparkle of naivety.

'What does he look like?' asked Grace as she saw her sister finish her piece.

'Who?' replied Cara, a slight blush appearing on her face.

'The man you were dreaming of?' Her grin reached from cheek to cheek.

'Ha!... that obvious eh?' laughed Cara. 'You'll be best advised not to dream dear sister. Dreams bring expectations that life only fails to reach. No desires, no surprises, that's my motto.'

'Do you think father will have arranged as many suitors as he says? Maybe I can run off with one!'

'All in due time Grace' said Cara, admiring her younger sister. 'I'm sure father has a plan for each of us. If there is a suitor coming tomorrow night then I can only pray he is to my fancy and not fathers.'

'Eww.. You'll be kissing Connell by midnight' scoffed Grace, as she pursed her lips and pretended to hug a huge figure in front of her.

'Sweet Grace' laughed Cara. 'I would rather starve to death than feast on that man.'

The girls burst out laughing at the devilish thought of Connell Locran and his ghastly appearance. Though the girls would never entertain hell's invitation, they believed that the devil's owb henchman would be cut from the same cloth as Connell. His lumbering swagger, meaty fists and protruding brow assured the young girls that he was not of this world – a world that they felt held such beauty and promise.

Downstairs, the devil's mould was helping Raegan in supervising the decorations. Dozens of staff were swarming around the great hall with flowers, lanterns, candle stands, and great streams of white cloth to cascade across each side of the room. Raegan had arranged for an extensive amount of fireworks to be imported from the Far East, and huge crates of the explosive decoration lined the many windows outside. Connell had already tested each type of rocket out in the fields – startling the horses as they exploded in the air. There were those that burst and scratched a golden trail into the sky, ones that shot a jet of glittered fire from the earth and those that flashed and cracked like an exploding star. They had all been lined up outside every window that looked out from the hall. Connell would have them triggered at midnight to bring in the new century with a bright and memorable burst of light.

'Sir, everything is set' said Connell. 'I have marked out where each rocket needs to be and we will set them hours before the ball.'

'Good work' said Raegan appraisingly. 'This will be a night envied by all that did not attend to see it.'

'What with that firepower outside sir, I'm pretty certain the entire continent will be witness to it' boasted Connell.

'Well it's about time a little light was brought to this dank town' replied Raegan. 'Has young David arrived yet?'

'Not that I am aware sir' said Connell as he tasked a member of staff to go and check. 'I have arranged for him to stay in the guest house to prevent Cara from seeing him.'

'Good' said Raegan. 'He is the most important person at this ball after all, and we need to make sure his every appetite is satisfied. If he's anything like his father, Major Irwin, David will be a hot blooded male with a pallet for the port. So make sure his legs are full of liquor before his belly fills with lust. We know what the young maids are like with a new man around. Their virtues are lost almost as quickly as their undergarments.'

'I can vouch for that sir' said Connell as he licked his thick lips. His teeth looked sharp as he smiled.

'I don't doubt that for a moment my good man. But do me a good turn and keep David drunk, and the young girls distracted for tonight at least. I need this arrangement to go as planned.' Raegan snapped his fingers at a maid who walked past carrying a great bouquet of wild flowers. He pointed as to where he wanted her to put them without a word of instruction. She dutifully obliged.

***

Raegan Darby need not have worried. David Irwin did not arrive until the late afternoon. His arrival was modest – bringing only one aid to carry his bags from his carriage. Appearance wise, he was unlike his father. His skin was fair and his wispy hair was a damp blonde. Despite never being in any form of battle, David, by order of his father, wore a formal British uniform. His left breast was decorated with the medals of his fore fathers and his blazer was a bold, battle shy blue. Having been arranged for him to arrive the day before, David had purposefully held up his travels a little. He always hated a fuss being made and was well aware of the seedy reputation his father had planted in his name. For some unclear reason altogether, Major Irwin wanted his son regarded as somewhat of a cad, and his travels were now forever preceded by tales of debauchery and lust. As a shadow to his colourful reputation, David feared the day a real woman would put his fierce reputation to the test.

The weather was clear. The crisp snow crunched beneath his feet as David made his way into the guesthouse. Able to house an entire family of five, his lodgings were more than necessary for the single night that he was intending on staying. A large hamper had been prepared for him and left on the kitchen table, and a large measure of port had already been poured for him. Another fable from his father, David did not even touch the drink. He emptied the glass out of the window and rested his hands on the windowsill. His father had briefed him on the reason for his visit to Orplow and despite his lack of choice on the matter he did not seem to mind the arrangement. Forever in the shadows and false light of his father's fibs, David had grown altogether lonely. He no longer knew anybody who knew the real him. Instead, he was met with those who were drunk from the grapevine wine and saw nothing but his father's son.

From his window, David could see the many hands put to work on the ball. A dozen people were bustling around by the walls planting an overwhelming number of rockets. A ragged, dirty looking man was in control of them as he barked his orders. The ball was only a few hours away and David could feel the prickly arrival of nerves. Half excited and half anxious, David sat and examined his hamper.

By the time David attended the ball it was in its full and harmonious flow. Victorian society was on its very best behaviour. The rules of the ballroom were regulated according to the strictest code of good stock and breeding, and every guest had mastered the indispensable etiquette of the event. A refreshment room, with the finest teas, ices, cracker–bonbons and cold tongues, had been arranged. During the main feast, asking nothing of the high-end guests, nothing on the table had required carving. All the fowls were cut up and held together tightly by bright red ribbons.

The grand hall was filled with the gathering of societies finest. Standing back from the crowd, David admired just how beautiful the scene was. Huge drapes loomed from every wall as wild flowers cascaded down around them. He had turned down the offer of dining with the Darby's, apologising that he had failed to pack his hearty appetite along with him on his travels. The truth was simply that he could not eat a bite. The nerves had grown in the pit of his stomach and filled his small trembling belly. His palms had become sweaty and he shook slightly beneath his fine uniform.

'David Irwin... a very warm welcome to you sir' boomed Raegan. He stood from his table and held out his hand. David could see that only two young girls sat at this table. Cara must be elsewhere. However, having never seen he could not be entirely sure. The music was playing out and guests had left their seats and began to dance. Despite the sound of the band filling the hall, David had no trouble hearing Raegan.

'I hope everything at the guest house was to your liking' said Raegan. 'Come, sit with us. We can put the world to rights before we lay claim to it!'

David took his seat next to Raegan, and was soon joined by the man he had seen earlier in the gardens.

'David, this is my family. My fine wife Fiona, my daughters Imogen and Grace, and my most trusted fellow Connell Locran.' Raegan rolled his arm through the air in the general direction of those he named.

'It's an absolute pleasure to meet you all' said David. His voice was a little rough as he realised it was the first words he had uttered for some hours. He took a glass of water to soothe his dry throat.

'Water?' questioned Raegan. 'Nonsense. Connell pour this man a hearty measure of brandy. He has a night of celebration in front of him and we must start as we intend to go on. Now, my daughter Cara will be with us shortly, and I must say she is a handsome girl who will make you a very proud man. You have my guarantee on that.'

'I have no doubts about that sir' David lied. 'I can only promise to try and make her as happy as she can be.' He took a drink from his glass and felt the brandy rip at his throat. The liquid fused with the whirlpool of nervous acid in his stomach and made David feel instantly nauseous. Looking around the table, he took the time to view his future family. Fiona was dressed in a moiré of white silk, properly trimmed with tulle and flowers. She also had on a single golden bracelet, despite having no intention on dancing. Next to her, Raegan was suitably attired. He wore a black superfine dress coat, well fitting pants and a black vest, all cut from the best cloth available. His new and glossy waistcoat was low and showed off an ample shirt front, crowned by a white cravat. His low heeled patent leather boots squeaked as he walked, and his white kid gloves and white linen handkerchief finished off his outfit perfectly.

'So, to the arrangement' said Raegan with no hint of haste or decorum. 'Your father is out in the battlefields is he not?'

'That he is sir. Though, I've not heard directly from him for some time. But I am assured his plans are playing out perfectly.'

'Wonderful' toasted Raegan. 'I hear whispers of a scorched earth policy. That will teach those damn settlers eh!'

'Possibly' sighed David. 'But it does baffle me as to why we must spitefully destroy a land we wish to take over. The independent republicans will not give it up without a fight. The whole matter promises to be a bloody one, and the rest of the world is not glowing in admiration for our empire at the minute.'

'Damn jealousy' declared Raegan. 'In life the world is criticised by its losers young David. That is why tonight, we rejoice!' He raised his glass and implored David to drink with him.

Connell was acting as the floor manager for the evening and made his order for the orchestra to commence. A trumpet sounded abruptly, and people took their places. David stood by as he watched the gentlemen join the promenade. Their first duty was to procure a program for their lady and then introduce her to their friends, who in turn placed their names on her card for their chance to dance with her. David was well aware that a lady could not refuse the invitation of a gentleman, unless of course she had already accepted that of another, and to be found guilty of incivility was practically a one way ticket to the dusty shelf of wives passed over. David smiled as he saw women obey their duty with guarded resentment. Each showing reserve at all times, never showing a trace of preference for a particular gentleman. Having been one of life's spectators, David understood the game more than those that played it.

As master of the house, Raegan saw to it that every lady danced. Noting the line of shy wall flowers who gathered at the darkened side of the hall, Raegan approached the spare gentlemen and instructed them to invite the ladies to dance. These men were ready to accede to Raegan's wish and even appeared pleased at dancing with the lady recommended. Each man asked in the same fashion. Stood at a proper distance, they bent their body forward and accompanied this by a hint of motion with the right hand in front. They looked at their ladies amicably, keeping the assumed position until the lady signified her acceptance.

As Raegan intended, the floor was soon filled and the orchestra led the people around the room. Partners changed and dances continued. The conversations held between near strangers were cautious at best. Once the dance was complete, the gentleman held out their right arm as they led the lady back to her chair, never allowing himself to sit by her side unless they were on the unlikely level of early intimacy.

With the New Year closing in, David was still alone. Connell had thrust several more drinks down him and David was now starting to feel a heavy head. His legs felt planted to the side of the floor as he watched the guests dance to the wonderful music, until it slowly came to halt.

Then he saw Cara. Dressed in a rich, brilliant green tarlatan dress she stood tall as a simple chaplet sat atop her strong, thick hair. To David she was an absolute picture. She stood on the stage in front of the orchestra and raised a violin to her shoulder.

The music she played moved David. With his eyes fixed on her, he was unaware that his legs carried him across the floor and closer to her. She swayed as she played, filling David's eyes with a swirl of colour. He could not have painted her more perfectly. Looking up as she continued to play, Cara saw David and knew him instantly. Her face burst a crimson red as the blood rushed to fill her smiling cheeks. Behind her the first of the fireworks were ignited outside. Streams of glittered fire burst from the earth and gripped the air. The windows surrounding the hall teemed with light. David's entire body radiated within the moment. His heavy head had lifted as Cara continued to sweep him from his feet.

The guests all looked on from the side of the floor. Many stood in awe of the fireworks outside while the rest were captivated by the first meeting of Cara and David. As the music played out, Cara raised her violin triumphantly to the air as the remaining tonnes of fireworks were unleashed. The skies lit up as the rockets competed for their place amongst the stars. The new century had begun, and with it a love between two strangers.

The crowd rejoiced as the new year arrived. Francis Morgan stood at the front of the orchestra and played on. He smiled as Cara stood down from the stage. She stood before David who had assumed the position of a hopeful dancer. Her intentions were clear as she firmly took his hand. He led her around the floor with ease as the music carried them.

'I'm David' he whispered.

'Cara' she replied.

They faced each other, and their faces tensed as they both resisted their wish to kiss. Instead they held the eye of all the guests as they danced with no one else for the entire night. With Imogen sat on her lap, Grace smiled widely as her elder sister continued to fall in love. Grace recognised her expression; it was the same she made each time she played her music. Cara was daring to dream and had found the man to her fancy.

As the song came to a close, David guided his lady back to her table. She sat by her mother's side as David remained standing. His eyes never left Cara's for a moment. With an impish smile, Cara kicked out the chair by her side and nodded for David to sit. Before he had time to blush, David felt the heavy hand of Raegan on his shoulder, practically slapping him into the chair.

'Bravo boy!' declared Raegan, his breath dashed with rum and brandy. His nose was rosy and his hand remained on David's shoulder as much for balance as it was for affection. 'I say, she put on a good show, did she not?'

'The finest I've ever seen' replied David as he looked at Cara. She was smiling and gripping his hand tightly.

'Then tonight has been a complete success.' Raegan smiled across the table and looked upon his family. He did not even realise that his wife had not left her seat all night. 'Once the ball ends, let us all drink to the new year and new beginnings. I have some of the finest champagne on ice in the refreshments room especially, just for the two of you. Now, take a good look at her David for she'll be whisked away after tonight until your wedding day.'

The declaration startled Cara somewhat. She looked at David as he shyly and awkwardly looked back her. She could feel the magic drain away. The romance began to abandon her, and was replaced by images of her father and David plotting. Her hand left David's as she ran from the room.

Following her into the night, David found Cara stood by the ornamental wall that cased the stone stairway leading into the main garden. He could see that her cheeks were wet and that her nose reddened slightly. Her eyes were damp and puffy as she looked at him.

'I feel a fool' said Cara. 'In there all I felt was you and I. Yet now all I can see is you and him.' She turned away. 'My father designs everything.'

'Cara' said David softly. He took her hands in his and squeezed at her fingers tenderly. 'Our fathers are far from selfless, I know. But no man can instruct me to feel what I felt when I first saw you. I came here under the pretence of finding a partner, and in turn I found a match. I don't know exactly what it is I am feeling right now, but I implore you to let me find out.'

And with that David kissed her. His lips trembled slightly as they met with hers. His nerves began to calm as he found that she was responding with as much passion as he could have asked for. She sighed softly as he backed away from her.

'I'll let you find out' smiled Cara. She walked back into the hall, turning briefly to look at her match one last time before disappearing into the manor house. He was as charming as she had hoped for.

David remained by the wall looking out onto the gardens. The remaining rockets cracked in the night sky, and laughter filled the air from the droves of guests that had poured out into the gardens. David looked across the land as the fires flashed light across the fields. He had never seen grass so green in all his life.

Amid the many that had filled the gardens was Connell. With a single lantern in hand, he walked through the dark fields that surrounded the manor house. From the great hall he looked like a lost firefly as his torch bobbed and bounced across the land beneath the sparkling skies. The night was cold but the brandy had fuelled the fire in his lustful legs.

He had hoped that all members of staff would have some part to play in the ball tonight, but it would appear that one member especially had failed to accept the invitation extended. Nevertheless, Connell was sure she would play her part. Protected only by her young sprat, Abigail was his for the taking. Knowing that all the eyes of the town would be resting on the manor house, at a function that he was a manager to, he had the perfect alibi. Drunk or not, nearly three hundred people cannot be wrong in placing him at the ball.

Connell was thankful for his torch. He did not know the land too well this far from the estate and needed the light to find his way. Passing through the rapeseed plants, he was sure that the cottage was not far. The looming shadow of the willow tree grew ever closer with each step.

Branches snapped beneath his feet as Connell continued forward. He was wrapped up warmly from the cold but his licked lips began to chap and dry in the air. Taking a deep gulp of air through his wide nose, Connell let out a curdling sigh through his ragged throat. If it were not for the blood pumping ferociously at his loins, Connell may have turned back. However, Abigail's soft skin and firm thighs were too much of a prize to turn away.

Picturing the impending moment, there was something inside Connell that wanted her to put up a fight. He wanted her to thrash and beat at him, to grit her teeth as he forced himself inside her. He wanted to see her pained expression as he filled her.

The cottage was now before him. He cleared his throat and spat heavily on the willow tree as he passed it. His heart was thumping, and his hands greased his leather gloves. He was already growing hard with the thought of what lay ahead of him. He tugged at his pants slightly as he approached the cottage and peered through the window.

✲✲✲

Michael was away in the fields when he saw the fireworks break upon the sky. He was sat by the lake where he had first met Grace. Each night he would sit and wait in the same place, reliving the feeling he had when they ran from the fire that approached them. He had not shared the cove with anyone since that day – not even his mother. Instead he would go and look out over it each night and say a single prayer that one day they may meet again.

The moon shone weakly upon the lake this evening and not even the swans were enticed by its light. Standing by the lakeside, Michael picked up a flat stone from the ground. He dusted off the light snow that weighted it and then skimmed the stone across the water's surface. He watched as the stone bounced four times before disappearing in one smooth splash. Soft ripples reached from where the stone rested and almost touched the shore. Michael knew she would not come. He knew that she would be elsewhere, occupied by her busy life and without a thought for what they had once shared.

He was almost at the point of feeling sorry for himself when he saw the fire. Upon the hill top, just before the horizon, a bolt of flame burned brightly and upright. Michael knew that it was near to his mother's cottage. Like a ship making use of the light tower, Michael tore towards the flames. His legs pounded the earth and his arms danced in front of him as he leapt over fences and stone walls. The thought of his mother trapped inside burned into his brain. He could see her screaming inside among the flames, beating at the windows and falling to her knees. His breathing was deep and heavy and the cold air tugged at his lungs. But still he ran towards the fire.

Having never dealt with a fire before, Michael did not let the thought of unknowing cloud his mind or slow his feet. He had no idea of how to fight one but prayed that he would find the means to save his mother. He would let the fires burn forever, as long as he mother was safe.

He was one field away now. The fire had only broke moments ago and already Michael was almost upon it. He could see how the thick yellow and orange flames pushed out a copious, compact trail of black smoke into the sky. Gaining on the fire, Michael saw that the flames, though high and wide, did not seem to have covered the whole cottage. He saw flickers of shadows at the fire's base, thrashing about it, trying to stem the flames. He saw his mother.

Abigail was knelt at the base of the willow tree crying heavily. Michael could see Margaret comforting her, whilst Maik and Oscar were throwing whatever they could towards the burning tree. Clumps of snow melted in the air before they even reached the flames. Pounds of dirt were being shovelled on by Maik who was drenched in the sweat of heat and toil.

'Mother' screamed Michael. 'Are you ok? What happened?'

'She's fine' said Margaret. 'She's just a little bit shaken. She saw a man peering through the window as we sat around the table. Then we hear a huge crash and the tree is alight'.

'Who was it?' asked Michael. 'Who did this?'

'We didn't get to see Michael' replied Margaret, her arms wrapped around the weeping Abigail. 'We heard the crash, saw the flames and then a shadow scorched through the bushes back towards the Darby estate'.

'Watch over my mother' begged Michael as he kissed her head softly and turned, running into the night.

Michael ran towards the shadows – deep into the fields that led back to the manor house. His eyes struggled as they adjusted from the bright flames to the smoky darkness before him. Hot water began to burn at his eyes slightly. He closed them firmly and held out his hands. The land felt different tonight. A trail of broken branches and torn crops paved a way in front of him. Michael followed this path carefully but swiftly. He knew the bastard that had terrified his mother could be found at the end of it.

Connell could not see a thing. Instead he ripped at the crops and plants in front of him and headed for the lights of the manor house on the hill. He could not believe that Abigail had company. He was well prepared to beat the little blighter of a son she had, but when he saw her sat with that robust gossip monger Margaret and the thumb-printed husband of hers, his body raged with unspent lust. Without a thought he had tossed his lantern at the willow tree. The lantern was heavy with oil and, partnered by the dry night, the tree exploded into flames. Connell had enjoyed the briefest of moments watching it burn as the hanging place of Ferris Alpin quickly turned to ash. That fool was never good enough for Abigail and now there would be nothing for her to remember him by. That tree had hung over that cottage for far too long and deserved to join its once swinging occupant in the tired earth.

As the ground became more downhill and steeper, Connell struggled to keep a quick pace. His knees buckled slightly as his short heeled shoes slipped, failing to gather any grip from the damp soil. Sprawling, he used his heavy hands to grab at anything that would support him. Mounds of earth were torn with each pull as crop by crop were ripped from the ground. Darkness still rested on the tip of his bulbous nose and apart from the distant lights, Connell was blinded. He needed to get back to the ball quickly so to have him placed among the crowd before news of the fire reached them. It was highly likely that they would not be able to see the fire among the thunderous fireworks. However, Connell could not take that chance and did not want any interrogation to ruin whatever opportunities towards Abigail the future allowed.

He could hear the scampering of footsteps gaining on him from behind. It sounded like a wild boar was chasing him as the breathing was beastly and sharp. Fearing what it may be, Connell lay on the floor and rolled towards a bush that rested against a stone wall. He cowered beneath the foliage as the dark figure passed by and came to a sudden stop.

The trail had ended. Michael stood almost breathless as his lungs wheezed and spluttered. He knew where he was but could not feel anymore breaks in the grass or crops. Whoever he was following was nearby. He held his breath and listened for the sound of another man panting. His blood was pumping too fast, and the silence was only filled by the beating of his pulse across his brow. Michael held out his hands to feel for any clues. The moonlight shone behind him and cast an enormous shadow upon the wall. Seeing the wall Michael tip toed towards it. He fingered the wall as he pressed at the roots of the bush with his feet. He grabbed a loose, sharp rock from the top of the wall when his feet met with a layer of flattened grass.

Looking up from beneath the bush, Connell could not make out what stood before him. Moments ago the beast stood outstretched like a huge bear before turning and searching at the wall. His tiny, almost cloven feet stood before him now, and Connell shook as the cold and fear grasped at him. Connell knew there was no fight in him if he were to remain on the ground, so he took flight.

Leaping to his feet, Connell tried to make himself look as big as he could. However, the animal was upon him and in one clumping swoop, it lashed at Connell with his mighty jagged claw. The impact smashed Connell's nose and blood burst brightly from his nostrils. He toppled onto one knee, howling in pain and expecting to feel the finishing blow crash into his crown. But it did not come. The moment's pause gave Connell the chance to making a dash for it into the darkness. It was so black and Connell could no longer feel his feet. Numb and dizzy, he had no idea whether he was conscious or not.

The rock was still in Michael's hand. The thick, warm blood had splattered up his arm as he struck the coward in the bush. Michael could not tell who the man was, and had paused to ask him before the man had ran off. His hand was trembling slightly and Michael did not trust the adrenaline that was coursing through his veins. He wanted to chase the man but had soon seen that he was twice his size and as angry as a hungry wolf.

Michael's thoughts now turned to his mother. He had already chosen not to tell her about his chance meeting with the man, and instead would offer her comfort by sitting by her bedside all night. Watching out in the direction of the manor house, Michael walked the first hundred yards home backwards. He was sure that the man would not return tonight, but wanted to be certain.

Walking past the lake Michael tossed the large rock into the waters. A deep and full splash could be heard as the lake pulled the leaping water back down to its bed. Michael paused for a moment and looked back towards the manor house. It concerned him greatly that the man he had just met was heading back towards Grace. He prayed for her safety before returning back to his mother, who he found knelt by the smouldering remains of the willow tree. The cottage had been untouched by the fire but the tree was caped in soot. The flames had finished their lethal licks upon the wood and feint smouldering smoke encircled the tree. Abigail held her rosary beads tightly to her mouth as she rested one hand on the earth.

'Don't worry mother' said Michael. 'I'm here for you.'

Chapter 10

The wedding between David Irwin and Cara Darby was a wondrous occasion. Four months into the year and the date had been set. Since the turn of the century, David and Cara had been inseparable. David had only planned to stay for the night and then return once all the wedding arrangements had been made. However, like lovebirds in spring, he could not tear himself away from his Cara. And why would he want to, he thought. Nothing waited for him back in England. His mother had died giving birth to him and his father was off fighting in some foreign continent. David did not have any brothers or sisters, or surrounding family for that matter. All his friends were built solely on the reputation granted by his father, and David had never really liked them anyway. So instead, he remained in Ireland with Cara.

The church of St Peter's had been chosen for the ceremony. David had been granted four months to get acquainted with the venue and its evergreen patron Father Daniel. Every Sunday, David had returned to the church to hear the preaching's of the passionate priest. He was soon part of the community and after a substantial offering to the church, Father Daniel accepted the couples application gratefully.

Always after an audience, Raegan had invited the entire town to the event. Everyone except those tasked to work the fields, that is. Having honoured his part of the arrangement, Raegan had sent nearly fifty of his male staff to fight alongside Major Irwin in South Africa. The men had initially been against the proposition but were soon brought around by a mixture of heavy bribes, blackmail and threats to their loved ones. Many went to the war knowing that they would face death unnecessarily just so that their families could remain living back in Ireland.

The ceremony was as beautiful as everyone had anticipated. The springtime sun scoured the sky, lifting everyone's spirits to the heavens. Families filled the aisles on both sides as they were all keen to get a glimpse at the blushing bride. Rumours were rife that she was pregnant and that the ceremony was being pushed through to accommodate this. There was, however, no truth in the matter. Despite being inseparable from her partner, Cara was always heavily chaperoned and could not even steal a kiss with David. Nevertheless, the rumour-mill rolled along and churned out any grain of gossip it could gather, tending to bring stale news rather than the hottest and freshest truths of the town.

Sat anxiously at the front of the church was David. He wore a three piece suit with a top hat and tails. With his hat resting on his lap, he tugged on the knot of the golden silk cravat that capped his bright white shirt. Sat beside him and in charge of the rings was Connell. Given David's difficulty in finding a best man, Raegan had insisted that Connell would do the honours. He sat beside the nervous groom, looking ridiculous in his attire. Like a shire horse in a pony's clothing, his body bulged at the seams, as his matted hair looked even worse now some design had been attempted with it. As the room continued to fill and Francis Morgan took his place by the organ, the groom and his best man shared not a single word.

'May we all stand' issued Father Daniel.

The congregation stood with the shuffling of feet as many turned to see the approaching bride. Perched next to the altar, Francis Morgan rained down the wedding march as beautifully as it had ever been played. Streaks of light broke through from outside and pierced the crimson carpet that ran down the aisle, pinning it to the ground like heavenly daggers holding a guard of honour for its glorious guest.

Grace and Imogen walked down the aisle first. They held small wicker baskets full of golden and yellow rose leaves. They scattered them in front as they walked the entire length of the aisle, taking their places next to their mother Fiona on the opposite side of the aisle to David. Refusing to be upstaged by anyone, she was wearing a fine s-bend dress with a lace bertha collar. They draped on her slight shoulders like a great matador's epaulettes. Thankfully her bullish husband was not braced for battle.

The music continued as Cara entered the church. Despite promising himself he would not look, David could not stop himself from turning and facing his bride. She shone as she stood at the church doors with her father. He was dressed to match David and had vigorously groomed his thick moustache, lacquering it tight so that the tips sat like sharp horns upon his lip. With his arm entwined with hers, Raegan held his daughter almost as proudly as David was to receive her.

She wore a bustle wedding gown with a long cathedral train that was layered and trimmed by a balayeuse. The colour was a radiant mixture of ivory and champagne. The form fitting bodice was fastened and drawn at the front through deep eyelets, and the veil reached from the back of her thick hair down to the very tip of the dresses train. In her hands she carried a bouquet of freshly plucked yellow roses bunched and bowed together by golden ribbon.

David felt under dressed to receive such an angel. He squinted slightly as Cara broke from her father and joined him at the altar. Light from the doorway flashed into his eyes. He wanted to speak but could not find the words. Instead he hoped that the way he made her feel would tell her everything. He held her hand as tightly as he did the tears that welled behind his eyes. He had never been happier in his entire life and was now forever indebted to his woman.

The joining of David and Cara went by in the usual fashion and unsurprisingly a great reception was held back at the Darby estate. Having already delivered on his side of the contract, Raegan had very few staff left available, and so he had chosen to invite Abigail Alpin to lend a hand at the dinner. Even Michael's workload had tripled. With Aidan Adams and Joseph Eagles doing battle in South Africa, Michael was tasked with tending to the fields, the horses and the orchard. A workload that delighted Raegan, who secretly hoped the exertion would break the boy.

Potting a fine bouquet of roses in the centre of one of the tables, Abigail was putting the finishing touches to the arrangements when the hoard of guests arrived back from the church. It had grieved her somewhat that she was unable to attend the church to pray on the morning but was at least grateful that it was spared for the joining of a loving couple. She had seen

David in church over the past few months and she had noted that all he spoke about was Cara. It warmed Abigail's heart to see young love within the town and she always saved an extra prayer for both of them each night. David was always polite to her and was handsome in his meekness. She noted that while he was not full of figure, he held the soft, petite features of a young boy. It proved impossible for any mother not to love him.

The crowd swarmed in and took their place as ordered by a large wall display. Families were bunched together while other tables were filled with couples and singletons. The round tables were draped in a fine white cloth and pebbled the floor in front of the main table. A small box of sugared almonds rested aside each guest's plate as well as a single imported bar of Hershey's milk chocolate. Raegan had felt that the sweet treat added a certain level of cheek to the quaint service and also boasted his vast international trading connections.

The dinner and speeches were over quickly. Abigail had stifled a rare laugh when she heard Connell's disastrous speech. It was clear that he knew nothing of David and struggled to read the small pointer cards his master had designed for him. His body shook with a suppressed anger as he failed to deliver a single joke correctly. This ironically brought a greater level of laughter as anticipated – albeit the tone a different one to that of an applauding crowd. Abigail realised that she had not seen Connell for several months now and was surprised to see that his nose was horridly out of joint. Such news, she thought, would have travelled quickly to Margaret at the very least. But then really who would notice if Connell grew uglier? Like throwing a stone through a broken window, it was near impossible to spot any fresh damage.

Sitting at the main table, Grace had seen Abigail and had excitedly looked around for her son Michael. She had not spoken with the boy for years, but still held him firmly in her memory. Every night she would look out of her window towards the lake where they had first met. Beings though he had worked on the land ever since, she had been able to steal a sight of him every night as he tended to the horses. She would smile as she watched him steal off into the night sat astride his young colt. However, despite the thousand times he had, she had never seen him once look up towards her window. Cooped up in her room, she remembered the gesture he once made to her, and every time she thought of him she traced a single cross in the palm of her hand.

Sitting flummoxed in his chair, Connell was humiliated. He was not a public speaker by trade and had felt forced into making a fool of himself in front of the entire hall. What was the point? Even the night before, David had spurned his invitation to go and entertain several of the maids in the staff quarters. Regardless of his rejections, Connell had still gone ahead and savoured his own invitation, despite it not being a purely coessential arrangement from the maid's perspective. She caved eventually though. He had refrained from his usual line of 'I can see us having sex tonight, not because I'm charming, but because I'm stronger', and opted for a more straight to the point endeavour. His groin still chaffed a little from how dry the girl had been.

Never satisfied within his spent lust, Connell had then been excited about the prospect of seeing Abigail. But having just embarrassed himself greatly in front of her, he doubted that her affections towards him would have altered. Nevertheless, he had no intentions of romancing the whore, but still he despised offering his prey a chance to mock him. After all, the hawk simply takes his prey – he does not entertain or play the fool to it.

Retiring to his room, Connell clutched at two bottles of champagne and slammed the door behind him. Letting the bubbles burst upon his dusty tongue, he would drink to forget the day entirely.

Having bid farewell to their guests and thanked Raegan for his hosting of such a glorious day, David and Cara went to their bridal suite. David had arranged for the four poster bed to be pattered with white petals and for a series of candles to have been scattered and lit about the floor. On entering the room, the light flickered and danced off the walls. Looking at her sweet husband, Cara could see that David was nervous. She had heard the rumours about his exploits, but saw them not to be true the moment she first set eyes on him. His soft gentle features betrayed the image of philanderer, and taking his hand she led David to stand beside the bed. She undressed herself as he looked on – his eyes widening at the sight of her milky skin. She teasingly bit her lip, allowing the blood to rush to the surface and colour her fuller mouth a crimson red. She brushed her long nails down the side of David's neck, and his back arched with excitement.

Stood before David, Cara was completely naked. Soft wavering light coated her, as she walked towards him and slowly took off his clothing. The formal clothing fell around their bare feet, like the shaken leaves of autumn. She kissed his shallow mouth deeply and rested him on his back atop the soft, full mattress. He held his trembling breath as his bride sat astride him and took him deep inside her. Rocking gently, she brought herself down on top of him and kissed his quivering mouth once more. Her breathing was unsteady as he grew harder and more confident.

Feeling her husband respond to her touch, she flung her hair back and writhed on top of him, rolling her eyes feverishly. On the tip of exploding, David closed his eyes and let his whole body feel the soft caress of his wife as she longingly made love to him. Joined as one, and climaxing at the very same time as each other, Cara and David enjoyed the pure ecstasy of the sweetest union.

✵✵✵

Loyal to the most important woman in his life, Michael had arranged to meet his mother by the closest field to the manor house. Making a habit of protecting her, he had still not told his mother about meeting the monster months before, and how he feared he would return. Instead, Michael had lied to his mother, claiming that his final daily chore brought him close to the estate each day and so he would walk home with her each night. The truth was that Michael walked the full stretch of the fields after his last labour just to make sure he was there for her. Never ignorant of a man's endeavours, she could see how tired he looked as he leaned heavily against the stone wall like a discarded broom, his muscles bulging from exertion. Michael was strengthened by his daily toil, and he looked just like his father.

Abigail recalled once seeing Ferris waiting for her after work. His body was broad with the labours of his day, and his thick arms were crossed tightly across his chest. He was her weakness, and she fell in love with him every time she laid eyes on him. This was partially because whenever he left her side she feared never seeing him again. The fear of losing him to some unforeseen circumstance, even threatened to cause her to end the relationship in its early stages – as she feared her emotions were too much too soon. She remembers almost writing a letter to call off their romance before her heart was not her own anymore. But she could not put pen to paper. Each time she saw him she not only knew that she loved him completely, she felt it entirely.

Ferris' smile flashed across Michael's face as he greeted his mother. He was doing his best not to look exhausted, but the task of covering a man's labour threefold was almost too much for the boy. Learning a trick his father had once enjoyed, Michael kept his strength up by constantly eating off the fruits of the land. The many berries he devoured could have coloured his blood a deeper purple if they wanted. Revived by the sight of his mother, his weary legs could not fail him as he walked towards his mother.

'Good evening mother' said Michael as he held out his right arm. 'How was your day?'

'Long, my dear boy…' replied Abigail, '…Long'. She put her arm around him. 'The wedding looked beautiful, I must say. It was a shame we couldn't attend.'

'I wouldn't have gone even if invited' snapped Michael. He felt tired but he meant the venom in his voice. Knowing of his father's fate, Michael had severed his ties with the church. He was confused as to who was damaging his mother the most – the memory of a coward or the condemning church that separated her from him. Without a firm answer, and without a single thing on which to position his blame, Michael chose to despise them both.

'Well, for what it's worth they all looked beautiful' said Abigail. 'Young Grace was there.'

Michael could not hide his flinch. 'Did you speak with her?' he asked pleadingly.

'No son, she was busy with her family. You'll see her again someday I am sure of it… just don't do anything stupid this time. It'll only keep you apart from her once more. I mean, fancy running away like that.'

Michael's eyes opened almost as wide as the moon. 'You knew about that?' asked Michael. He had never mentioned it to his mother before.

'Of course.' Abigail flashed a backwards nod towards the manor house. 'She told her sister, who in turn told another and soon it reached her father. It won't come as a surprise when I tell you that he had some firm words to say about the matter. He even instructed me not to let you come within a stone's throw of the house for some time.'

'Why didn't you tell me?'

'Ha! I could never tell you what to do my son.' She bent down and kissed her son's cheek. 'Your heart is too strong and loud for you to ever listen to my wise words. And a stone's throw? With those arms? You'd have to stand on the shore all day.'

'You fill my heart, Ma. Completely.' Michael embraced his mother tightly. He did not want to tell her about the small place in his heart he had saved for the sweetest girl he had ever seen.

✿✿✿

Sat once more in her room, young Grace looked out of her window. It was the first night that she would not share her room with her sister Cara. Now, the room itself felt wider and taller, and she would have felt completely alone if it were not for the sight of Michael standing by the stone wall. He always raised an excitement within her whenever she saw him. He had looked tired and beaten as he rested a while. Grace was well aware of what her father was tasking his staff with these days, and had no doubt that Michael would be feeling the full thrust of her father's demands.

However, never far from her father's reach, Grace was under the strictest orders herself. She was not to fraternise with anyone outside of the family unless in the presence of her father or mother, and only if by appointment through the house. Free from any social obligations, it allowed for her to be tutored throughout the day and to endure the countless attempts of Francis to find her an instrument. By now, they had tried almost everything, and still she could master neither a song nor the slightest hint of a tune. Though it was not an issue of toning – as she heard the music beautifully – she just could not find it in herself to create it. The only beat she could truly muster was that of her heart every time she saw Michael. Without fail, her belly would flutter incessantly, as though she had feasted only on a thousand butterflies. Seeing his sunken face, Grace was determined to make him smile. She clenched her fist ready to beat at the window, when suddenly his expression changed.

The smile that stretched across his face was one of pure delight, and one reserved only for his mother. From out of the shadows of the grounds, Abigail had walked towards her son. Rejuvenated by the sight of her, he stood up straight and greeted her as a gentleman would his partner. Grace watched as they walked hand in hand through the fields, and her deep hazel eyes began to hold the boldest hint of green.

Enviously looking out of her window, she saw the silhouettes of a woman and a young boy joined in a tender embrace. Having seen the shadows merge, Grace turned and threw herself onto her bed, her dampened eyes scanning the room for something to distract her from the distance she shared with Michael.

Alone in her darkened room, all she could see was the closed book of fairy tales settled upon the empty bed of her sister Cara.

Chapter 11

Sitting on his broad stone porch, Raegan was proudly patting his Great Danes, who stood statuesque beneath their master's touch. The day was damp and slightly overcast for the season. But a little rain did not hurt the crops. With the heaven's drizzle upon the land, Raegan was determined that he would have his stock in order for any impending opportunities.

Cara and David Irwin now resided in the luxurious guest house. They had been living there for nearly two years, after David had explained to his new father-in-law that there was very little waiting for them in London, and that they would be best placed to settle for now within the confines of this bountiful town. Raegan was loathed to agree to the arrangement but saw it as merely temporary until Major Irwin returned triumphant from the war.

They had gathered news that in May 1902 Lord Roberts had successfully led a British offensive to relieve the sieges at Colenso, Magersfontein and Spion Kop. By the 31st May the British Empire was triumphant if not internationally popular, and Raegan knew that it was a matter of time before the news of his extended land would reach his estate.

He had designed that it would be best for Cara and David to live in the seized new land, and he would in turn utilise David; educating him in the ways of running a profitable and efficient estate. The whole arrangement appeared the perfect stepping stone to take the Darby Empire to a new continental level. Granted it would carry the name of Irwin but he had already formulated a trading contract that would join both family names as one unified corporation. Always a few selfish steps ahead of himself, Raegan had decided that initially he would explore the land thoroughly, identifying any keen crops with which to trade.

Sat plotting his profit, Raegan heard the approaching motor vehicle before he saw it bounce upon the dusty road. It was a ten-horse powered Panhard with a bonneted front engine and shaky rear drive. Two large brass light fittings were fixed to the front, and a golden horn and spare wheel clutched at the car's side. Its body was jet black, and the leather hood was up, shading the passengers but leaving the driver completely exposed to the elements. Raegan watched quietly as the dust kicked up from the road, peppering the hulking wheels and their strong spidery wooden spokes. Coming to a loud, rattling halt, the vehicle parked in front of Raegan and two elderly men stepped down from the passenger carriage. They were dressed in full military uniform, and their faces were spared of any emotion.

✳✳✳

Waking next to his wife had become a tireless treat for David. Each morning he stole a moment to watch her wake as he lay by her side. Her face was fresh; naked from the makeup of the day. Cara had always hated knowing that David saw her unmasked, but he always reassured her that it was in these moments that she looked her most wonderful. He hated the trappings and coats that society rested upon people and loved nothing more than the simple sight of his wife in the morning. Her tired eyes offered stark contrast to her lively smile and he was well aware that they would make love before they greeted the day entirely.

Outside, a gentle breeze carried a damp drizzle of rain upon the windows. The day was grey and the land looked lazy as the crops slumped achingly towards the earth. With the tingle of ecstasy yet to leave his legs, David watched the workers toil in the land as Cara prepared their belated breakfast. They sat and ate in silence as they held each other's hand and looked out from their home.

Despite the temporary arrangement, everything felt like it was finally in place for David. For as long as he could remember he had never felt completely at home in any of the countless towns he had stayed. Even as a child, his father was little more than a passing ship, and David was often tended to by maids with strange faces. It dawned on him that he did not really know his father and in turn was not known by him. It pained him to think that the rumours his father fuelled could be honest insights into the son his father had truly desired. The distance was, therefore, a gift to both father and son — as the father would never get to know the son he did not want.

Cara and David had not taken a honeymoon on the advice of Raegan. Like a coiled serpent, he was braced, certain that the war could be won at any moment, and he wanted the couple to be ready to uproot and head for their new land as soon as the news broke. David had not heard much correspondence from his father since the first few months but was well aware that the war had been won and that his father would return with the spoils soon. Despite the distance his father and he enjoyed, David could not wait to show off his bride. The fact he was now married could allow him to get to know his father in an honest light — to show his father the true man that he was through his loyalty towards his dearest Cara. David was determined to earn that reputation more than any of those that his father had offered for him.

Unbeknown to Raegan, Cara and David were keen on raising a large family, and they had been trying for a child for the past few months. The task of making love to his wife had been the most enjoyable labour intensive activity of David's life. His angelic wife was somewhat of a devil within the witching hour, and loved nothing more than to enjoy the saintly sins of the flesh. David offered a knowing stare at his wife as she smiled coyly and gripped his hand tighter. He leaned across the table to kiss her passionately but was interrupted by a loud rap at the door. On the cusp of kissing his wife, David was unable to stand to greet anyone in his current excited state and asked Cara to do the honours. Sitting, with his legs lodged beneath the table, David saw young Grace at the door. She had grown taller over the years and her long brown hair was fuller and held with a gentle wave.

'Dear sister' she said. 'Father has asked for you and David to meet him in the study. There are two gentlemen with him and I think they bring news from the war.'

'Oh my, of course. Thank you sister' replied Cara. 'We are not yet dressed for the day but we'll be over as soon as we can. Could you pass the message on to father that we'll be with him shortly'.

'Of course' said Grace as she offered a cheeky glance between the two lovers. She saw that her sister was flushed and skipped back merrily and hurriedly towards the manor.

'What do you think it is?' Cara turned to see her husband scurrying about the ground for his clothing. He tugged up his trousers and slapped the braces across his shoulders.

'I have no idea. I'd take a life with you anywhere Cara, you know that, but I was really getting used to this place. And anyway, we may not know whether you're fit to travel just yet.' He said patting tenderly at his wife's stomach. She smiled broadly and held his hand there for a moment. If it not for her pressing engagement with her father she would have taken David where he stood.

As always, Raegan Darby was playing the honourable host. He had offered his esteemed guests a drink, cigar and had complimented them richly on their motor vehicle. He was at odds whether to get one himself but was not too trusting of the foreign hands that had made the one that rested by his porch. Despite his offerings, the gentlemen had not offered Raegan a single nugget of information, and his appetite for knowledge remained whet. The only information they had so far passed was that the letter they carried was addressed to Master Irwin and none other. Raegan had explained how David and he were practically related, but the taller of the two men – and the one in possession of the letter – had smiled insincerely and encouraged his impatient host to wait.

David appeared flustered as he entered the room accompanied by his wife. He did not recognise the two men that stood before him and was pretty certain he had never met them before in his life. However, it did not surprise him to hear that they knew his father. Bracing himself for lengthy discussions about battles he had no understanding of, and talk of settlements that far outreached his local ambitions, David took a seat by the fire and encouraged his guests to do the same. They remained standing.

They were both fashioned in pristine British military uniform and held a battle hardened stare. They held their hats by their sides, as the older, and shorter, of the pair spoke first.

'Master Irwin' his voice was slightly nasal and high. 'We bring you news of your father, Major Irwin. My colleague here has a letter addressed for you and you alone. He can read it to you or leave it for you to read if you so wish.'

David could see the excited and expectant expression etched across Raegan's face. There was a nervous tint in the air that David could feel and the hairs on his arms pricked slightly. Raegan remained oblivious, while Cara stood behind David's chair and rested her hands on his shoulders. She could feel her husband grow tense to her touch.

'Please,' said David coughing slightly. 'Whatever news you have for me is news for my family also. Please tell us all, so that I'm not to get it wrong if asked of me once you have gone.'

The tall man spoke now.

'Master Irwin, in January 1900, I had the great pleasure of fighting alongside your father Major Irwin. Under the orders of General Buller and in a bid to relieve Ladysmith, your father's regiment were ordered to cross the Tulega River that lay west of Colenso.'

The man stopped to clear his throat. David noted the date and was wondering why this man was set to give him a two year breakdown of the war. He was after all detailing the month that David had begun his courting of Cara, and admittedly had been a little distracted from the news reels covering the war at the time. Thinking back on that blissful time, David found himself completely unaware of any of the developments of the war at all. The tall man continued.

'Your father and Major General Warren were successful in their crossing but were faced by a fresh defensive position centred on a prominent hill known as Spion Kop. In the resulting battle, your father captured the summit by a surprise attack in the early hours of January 24th.'

'Hurrah!' Raegan punched the air. He was already picturing his hill top fortress with the thick rich vein of river running at its side. He visualised holding annual celebrations and balls to commemorate the great victory, where they captured such a fine land. With baited breath he paused and allowed the taller gentleman to enlighten him of his capital.

'Master Irwin, I must tell you that on the morning of the same day, as the early fog lifted, it was soon realised that the summit was overlooked by heavy Boer gun emplacements on the surrounding hills. It proved a massacre. Your father fought bravely and died a true hero. Master Irwin, I'm eternally sorry for your loss.'

David's world collapsed around him as the words crashed against his ears. He could not feel the tender touch of Cara as she pulled at his shoulders. He did not remember the men leaving as they placed the letter in his hands. All he had acknowledged was that his father had been dead for over two years. That and the ghastly mournful expression that held Raegan's gawping face.

⁂

For the many months that passed, David struggled to come to terms with his loss. He had retreated into his guest house and rarely took to the long walks he had once often shared with his wife. True to her vows, Cara had become his rock and had supported him throughout his turmoil. Not a very talkative man at best, David would go for days without uttering a word, and the few words that did cross his thin lips were always those of gratitude towards his serving wife. Despite his search for a remedy, David had not given in to the intoxicating allure of the drink, nor had he held anyone unaccountably responsible for his loss. Instead he chose to revel in the love that Cara offered. She was his opium, and her touch never failed to cloud his mind, and numb his pain.

The loss of his father had hit him harder than he thought it ever could. David had no great desires to travel and – if never informed of his father's historical demise – would have happily lain his feet to rest in Orplow with his dear Cara until his final days. Having seen them pass by several times, he had grown to love the intensity of the seasons. Each tried to outdo the last in their splendour and battled to offer the perfect postcard frame. Not that David had anyone to send one to. Instead, he satisfied his need to express himself by writing his feelings down for only Cara to read. He was not shy in saying the words themselves, but felt that they would not be lost upon the wind if sealed forever on paper. Each letter read like a diary of gratitude to no one else but his wife. He adored her completely, and made it as clear as crystal that he wanted to bring a child into the world with her.

'I'm sorry' David said on a brisk autumn afternoon. He and Cara were out walking in the town. The pavement was wrapped by fallen leaves.

'For what?' Cara's voice had forever softened since the day she felt her husband's loss.

''For testing you. I never meant to burden you with my loss and I can only imagine how much of a task it's been to keep me upright. I just love you, with every inch of my fibre. When I lost my father, I didn't lose the man who made me... I lost all the times I could proudly show him the woman that caused me to be. I lost the selfish pleasure of blunting his lying tongue, as I so wanted to show him that I loved just one woman, and that it was the love of this one, and no other, that filled my world.'

'Then I in turn am sorry' said Cara. 'If I wasn't so blasted brilliant then you wouldn't have much to mourn at all.' She hesitated to smile until David's raucous laughter penetrated the pause.

Entwined, they walked home. The afternoon was still to be spent but they had decided to retire for the day. David would watch as his wife played her violin to the land, and he savoured the life that was in her performance, silently praying that he could bring a shared life into their world. He sat in wonder at the freedom in which Cara played. Often he would just sit and let her play in the background as he read countless stories to her. David had an impressive array of romantic novels and poetry, and Cara would play with delight as he read them aloud to her. His voice was intoxicating to her, and relaxed her every tension. In turn, she had played for him every day, and not once had he tired of listening. It was a complete assault on his senses and, even when he closed his eyes to listen intently, his mind was wrapped in her image.

The night eventually drew in. The dark, crisp brown leaves – that carpeted the ground around the trees – were swallowed within the deep mouth of the night. David sat and watched his wife as she slept by his side. Her breathing was full and slow. He saw her chest rise and fall like the oceans steady, dependable tide. Holding his breath, he wished that the world would freeze and let him live encased within this moment forever.

The same set of months had treated Raegan Darby differently. As far as he was concerned the contract between Major Irwin and himself was severed. Despite his demise, Major Irwin had received his troops and in turn the empire had their victory. But this left Raegan with nothing. He had hoped to offload his daughter and her feeble and frail excuse for a husband into the Irwin family. He wanted them to build a bridge on which his trade would travel, handpicking Major Irwin because of his late wife and only son. This left very little manoeuvrability in terms of inheritance and whatever David held claim to, so would he. Raegan had no doubt that he could con David into handing over ownership of all that he had, but now he had nothing to give. David's proudest object was Cara and Raegan had no need to get her back.

Therefore, David's loss was ultimately Raegan's loss. His grand design was too dependent on others and soon Raegan grew to hate the land that had brought him such stature. He resented Orplow for all its trappings, and hated how it appeared as a beautiful boastful town to its visitors, but had failed to deliver to its most loyal occupant. Like a husband to a whore, the loyal were overlooked for a more passing trade.

Raegan believed that, more than any other man, he had pumped life into this land, and in return had been rewarded by the empty promises of a stolen and soiled earth. He had wanted nothing more than to be held as a saviour to this once dank puddle, this once pitiful excuse for a town. Throughout his time, he had brought life to the fields, filled the farmers' hands with grain and brought supper to the plates of nearly every family. And in return he was gifted with nothing but an endless cycle of tireless, seasonal demands.

A prisoner to his ambition, Raegan plotted as best he could. Fuelled partially by the brandy he had begun to beat his wife more often, and damned her for her daughter-spilling seed. He needed a son, and if she was not to grant him one then he would endeavour to capture one belonging to another.

Next in line for his design was his little tyrant Grace. It would be sometime before he could marry her off to a gentleman, but at least it gave him time to turn her into the dutiful daughter her elder sister had proved to be. Pondering his approach, Raegan smiled as he admired his devilish image within the family portrait that blazed above the fireplace. By the time he was done with his dearest Grace, he knew he would have the finest crop with which to barter at the market.

Chapter 12

The following years passed by as planned for Raegan. He continued to hold a firm grip over the trade and industry in Orplow, and had mastered the demands of every season. After five years into his selfish grooming of Grace, Raegan was having her master another art form. He had employed none other than Ms Flannery Ryann to be Grace's full time tutor, and she was set the task of teaching Grace the beauty of the written word. Haunted by the memory of her beloved Padraig, Ms Ryann had left Eden several terms after his passing. Officially, she had called time on her illustrious career so that she could concentrate on her writing, but the truth was that she had not written a single word since. Unable to cope with seeing the photographs that lined the corridors of the school, Ms Ryann quit and turned her back on her loved-one's legacy. Each picture now represented a missed opportunity in which to tell him how she felt – another year that had passed without him by her side.

Today she worked only with Grace and was hell bent on getting the girl to master her second passion – literature. The half of the large bedroom that Cara had once inhabited had now been converted into a miniature classroom. A heavy chalk board hung on the wall facing a single table and chair. It was on this chair that Grace now sat. She swung her feet sweetly and stared out of the window as Ms Ryann entered the room. Grace's hands were planted to her desk aside a fresh notepad and a large wooden pencil. She had grown out of chewing the ends of these for some years, and now presented herself with all the tools she would need to learn.

Ms Ryann looked exactly as Grace remembered. She still wore her hair in the same tight way that pulled her eyebrows up her face an inch or two. It gave her a permanent scowl, or startled expression depending on what angle you were viewing her from. Her clothes were pristine, dark in colour and tight to her slight frame. She started with wiping the board clean of the work from the previous day. She had tested Grace at the end of yesterday's lesson and she was confident that the young girl had mastered the content. In fact, Ms Ryann had been very impressed by the intellect of young Grace. When her father had asked for her help, he had reported Grace to be somewhat of a person with slow learning capabilities. However, Ms Ryann's experience suggested the contrary as Grace was an expert reader for her age and was quite the writer too. She recited every text perfectly, if not with a slight cute lisp, and was able to write down what was recited to her in return. What only concerned Ms Ryann was not Grace's ability but more of her interest. She had not yet found a text or subject in which Grace had been enraptured by. She had observed the many plays of Shakespeare and had just finished reading Sheridan's *The Rivals* – while appearing amused at the foolishness of the characters, especially the aspiringly pretentious Mrs Malaprop – nothing real fired her up.

Today, determined to stoke the flames, Ms Ryann was going to introduce Grace to the works of John Donne. He was one of Ms Ryann's favoured poets and she simply adored his work. She hoped that her own passion would be realised and grasped by Grace.

'Grace' said Ms Ryann as she grabbed the young girl's attention from the window.

'Today we will be taking a look at one of my favourite poets.' She turned to the chalk board and picked up a long, fresh white piece of chalk. 'John Donne was a fantastic poet from the late 16th to early 17th century.'

She wrote his name in thick chalk on the board and drew a huge egg shaped ring around it.

'He was deeply religious and fully aware of the attendant dangers and difficulties in being a Roman Catholic in his time. Throughout his life he deeply repented the excesses of his youth, and was always preoccupied by his mortality.' Grace was listening as Ms Ryann drew a line from his name to the word Roman Catholic.

'What we must acknowledge is that he was the archetypal metaphysical poet' she hesitated as she spelled the phrase out in her head before committing it to the board. 'He was great because of his style. It provided the framework...' she wrote down framework '...for him to display the force of his emotions and the vividness and immediacy in his expression.'

Grace was scribbling away trying to keep up with the frantic notes of Ms Ryann.

'He was at his very least original. He worked within the Elizabethan era – a time where the poetry was largely based on Petrarch and Spenser.' Grace remembered the lessons covering Spenser and began to sing *The Faerie Queen*.

'Exactly' declared Ms Ryann excitedly. 'Their works were mostly written to be sung. They were rhetorical pieces... entirely artificial if you ask me. They had no dance or movement within them. But Donne, his verse is colloquial' she was near to the nub of her chalk as she scratched this word onto the board. 'His style moves in its freedom from elaboration. And, my dear child, it is in his love poems that we will understand his works completely.' Ms Ryann was excited. She held Grace's full attention and the girl was mirroring her notes, no longer passive in her listening.

'John Donne's love poems analyse and observe every aspect of the relationships of love – pleasing or punishing. Today we are going to start with *The Sunne Rising* and his *Song for Sweetest love*.' Ms Ryann handed Grace her book of poems. The corners had been creased back to indicate which pages she wished Grace to read from.

Grace stood at the front of the feigned classroom. She glanced out of the window, but could not see anyone in the nearest field, sighing silently as she opened the book at the first folded page. The book looked large in her tiny hands, and she rested them on her chest. Her hands were clasped as if in a gentle prayer.

'Busie old foole, unruly Sunne...' she began. She continued to read the verse perfectly. Her voice was raised and plosive at the right moments. Ms Ryann felt the trickle of goose-bumps rise on her skin as the young girl continued to read, grasping the poem perfectly. Ms Ryann mimed the words silently as she saw them bounce from Grace's tongue.

'...This bed thy centre is, these walls, thy spheare.' Grace ended. She looked up from the text book and stared towards the opposite end of her room. Her bedroom was in place – her bed tightly made. She waited a second before remembering that she was not alone in the room. She shook her head slightly and smiled to her tutor.

'That was wonderful Miss Darby' uttered Ms Ryann. Her throat felt blocked and locked with emotion. 'So, tell me. What are your thoughts on that poem?'

The truth was Grace did not know how she felt about the piece, as she had never encountered the emotion contained within it. Fearing that she would get the thoughts from her heart wrong, she offered a criticism, in the hope that her teacher may be impressed by her acknowledgement of the fault. 'He could work on his spelling a little' smiled Grace.

Ms Ryann could have shaken her. She wanted to grab the girl by the arms and rattle the feeling from her like draining water from a wet towel. She knew that Grace felt what the poem intended, but was for some reason reluctant to realise it.

'John Donne is cursing the sun. He is mocking it for all its glory, and comparing it to the beauty that lies beside him' said Ms Ryann sharply. 'He is declaring that he has all the wealth of the world next to him and could make the sun redundant by simply closing his eyes.' She shifted out of her chair. 'But doing so would make him lose sight of her.' Ms Ryann stared at Grace hoping to see the recognition in her eyes.

Grace knew exactly what the poet was declaring. She had often looked out onto the sun – onto how it warmed and greeted the land. But unlike the poet, Grace did not have everything she desired within the confines of her room. Her father, on the other hand, was insistent that she had everything catered for between these four walls. What he hadn't realised was that her prison had a view – an immoveable glass ceiling that taunted her heart's ambitions. So she understood the poet alright, she just envied him entirely.

'Grace...' said Ms Ryann noticing that the young girl's eyes had glazed over.

'We have another poem that I'd like you to read. I believe it is on page seven.'

Grace did not need to count the pages. The top corner was unnecessarily folded as the pages naturally fell open upon the cracked and broken spine of the book. Grace cleared her throat and began to read aloud.

'Sweetest love, I do not goe...' said Grace. Her voice was softer as it was carried through this poem of two lovers separated. She could feel the strain on the heart endured by the distance between them. She could feel the sorrow in the words of the man who had to leave his loved one. But, ultimately, she saw that through love they remained in the company of the other. '...They who one another keepe alive, ne'er parted bee'.

Both ladies were dreaming now. Miss Ryann had cupped a small handkerchief to her eyes as she cried a little, while Grace stood smitten by the words. She read the poem again to herself silently, and still the words had the impact that volume had given to them. She felt exhausted and exhilarated by them, confused but also consumed by the text. The poet's message made her miss something she did not know she had ever lost. It caused her to dream of a love that she did not realise could exist. It packed meaning into the emptiness that she had been feeling for so many years. And though she smiled widely, her eyes poured with tears, and in the company of such beauty, she had never felt so alone.

'That concludes the lesson for today I think' said Ms Ryann.

✻✻✻

Carmel Rhodes loved to watch Michael work. Her mother worked in the fields with Abigail Alpin, and it was on one autumn morning when she had broken her daily routine to meet her mother out in the fields that she first saw Michael. He was playfully teasing his mother by eating the fruit that she had picked and put into her basket. She would turn and slap his hand each time, but it was always too slow and his mouth bulged with fresh fruit. Despite his full cheeks, and the juice dripping from his chin, Carmel had never seen a boy so handsome. Her mother had often spoken of Michael and how he was the image of his late father. But Carmel's mother was forever playing the match maker, and Carmel had learned not to take her referrals too seriously. The reputation of Ferris Alpin still lived within the whispers of the town, but Carmel had to hand it to her mother – Michael was quite the young man. While gaining his father's physique from his daily toil in the fields, he had kept the soft skin and complexion of his mother. His skin, although kissed by the sun, did not look rough or ragged. His hair was thick and as dark as the ocean's depth. A gentle cow lick gave a slight wave to the front of it, and he wore the rags of the workman better than any other she had seen before. The open-necked shirt hung on his broad shoulders and his tight pants encased his powerful legs. Although she was more than two years his senior, Carmel lusted for the young man like a smitten, little schoolgirl.

That once break from routine had now become routine itself. Each day Carmel would find an excuse to visit one of the fields that Michael worked. If she was forced to pick then she would have to say that she favoured the times she saw him tend to the horses. He looked powerful and calming in charge of such beasts. They kicked and bucked wildly until they felt the soothing touch of his hand. He would grab at their great heads and rest his brow on theirs affectionately. The animals loved him. The ménage was often visited also by the three Great Danes from the Darby gardens. They bounced and leapt up at the fences, making the horses feel tense. But Michael would simply pay the dogs the attention they craved, before sending them on their way, and reassuring the horses through softly whispered words.

Michael could feel that he was being watched. He sometimes played to the fact – pouring fresh buckets of water over his head to drench his clothes and have them cling to his skin, before running his thick hands through his soaking hair. And though it gave his audience a sight on which to feast their fancy, it was often an exercise of necessity rather than vanity as the sweltering heat of the meadows bore down upon him. On the brink of burning, the cold water would shake him from the searing slumber.

The girl was watching him again today. He had never talked to her but knew her name to be Carmel. She was quite the talk of the town – a truly handsome girl with long wavy hair that framed her face like wildfire. She looked all-knowing and worldly wise to Michael, yet he had not met a man who boasted of taking her virtue. Her face was always taught in a sultry smile that told Michael that her sweet eyes hid quite the filthy mind. Her body was generously formed, and her milky bosom heaved at her blouse.

Because she had not made her affections known to Michael, he had not announced them to his friends. Michael knew that Oscar would have immediately told his mother and before tea time Michael would be held guilty of servicing the girl in every acre of the land, bending each blade of grass with their bouncing backs. So he decided to keep the attention to himself, and today planned to finally introduce himself to her. But she beat him to it.

'Michael Alpin...' her voice was slightly raspy and husky. 'My name is Carmel Rhodes. Our mothers are good friends.' She smiled a wicked smile and used the bright sun to disguise a wink. She held her hand across her brow to shade her eyes so that she could see him clearly. It pleased her to see that he was smiling and rubbing his hands nervously.

'Carmel Rhodes...' said Michael, raising his eyes from the ground. 'It is a pleasure to meet with you, finally'. His smile was just as wicked. He licked at one of his wisdom teeth that were breaking through. 'I have just this field to tend to, but will be free after if you care to walk with me?'

'I find two hands get the job done quicker. Maybe I can help you?' she was already climbing over the fence before Michael could answer. The truth was that he had very little left to do, but had planned to string it out a little. He glanced back at the Darby manor. The windows appeared like dark slits in the grey walls.

'So...' issued Carmel, 'Where do you want me?' she planted her hands on her hips and let one side kick out a little. Her bosom jiggled slightly and grabbed young Michael's attention. Despite his broken allegiance with the church, he knew his thoughts were unholy. His loins ached a little and his face became flushed.

'Erm...' Michael struggled to concentrate. 'If I'm honest, I only have to carry these baskets of grain down to the stables. They're quite heavy so it would probably be best if...'

He did not finish before she hauled a huge basket into her arms and stood with a straight back. He felt a complete arse.

'...Great. Well I'll grab these two and we'll head back then'. If it would not have tripped him and make him more the fool, Michael would have kicked himself. He knew that she was older than him and probably used to men bigger and stronger than he, and yet there was he declaring something to be heavy that she lifted as easy as she would an empty sack.

Despite the fact he looked cute when he was embarrassed, Carmel was glad that Michael walked ahead of her. The basket was seriously weighty and the handles had begun to cut into her hands. What a fool she was – trying to impress a lad more than two years younger than her by a show of strength. His shoulders were thickly set and he walked effortlessly in front of her with one basket heaving on top of the other. She did not mind her view though. The baskets had caused Michael to straighten his back up and tighten his buttocks. She smiled to herself as she watched the young man walk.

They eventually reached the stables. Carmel dropped her basket slightly short of where Michael had and he turned and gathered it from the floor. He took the baskets into the stables, and she remained outside wafting at her face to try and cool herself. The task had left her near exhausted.

Inside the stables, Michael found David Irwin. The guest house he lived in with his wife Cara looked out over the stables and he and Michael had become acquainted on a daily basis. Michael found David to be a polite and calm man - a man with very little to say but every moment to listen. Michael had often bent the man's ears with the labours of his day, always asking after his wife in the slight hope of grabbing any scrap of information about the elusive Grace.

'Good evening Michael' said David. He was petting Amador and Paco. 'Does Raegan know you keep a white horse in here?' David's question was one issued with a wry smile rather than interrogation.

'I believe he does not' said Michael.

It had turned out that Joseph Eagles had been quite the deviant. He had not returned from the Boer War and no news of his fate had reached them still. However, it was clear to Michael that Joseph made no mistake when picking Amador from the Spanish stables. The horse was a traditional Blanco. Although born as black as night, his coat had gradually become the brightest of whites. It was common in the colts to be born black and turn out this way and Joseph would have known this when seeing the horse's bloodline and skin tone. It seemed he had picked this horse to fool his master and break his tradition of purely black stock.

'He was black to begin with' said Michael. 'I just think he was too pure to remain in the shadows though' he patted the horse. It was almost fully grown now and was the most beautiful in the stable. Paco stood nearby remaining a sooty shade. So far Michael had hidden Amador from Raegan. He was certain that the horse would be sold the second that his master found out and it would be the unruly Paco that would be left to stud.

'He is a wonderful creature' said David. He had in his time seen a series of military horses through his father but none had been as stunning as Amador. 'What will Raegan do if he were to find out?'

'He can't see past the colour of the coat' said Michael sadly. 'If not to Raegan's uniform, then I guess he'll put the horse to auction.'

'The blind bastard.' David patted Amador. 'How does he ride?' asked David with a knowing smile.

'Ha! And there was me thinking I'd been discreet.' Michael was already smiling from David's insult of Raegan. 'He rides like a dream. I can arrange for you to ride him if you wish.'

'I'd love to, I would, but truth be known it's Cara who is enchanted by the beast. As soon as I can find something to give you in return, then I shall take you up on your generous offer.' David ran his hand across the horse.

'I don't want for anything sir' pleaded Michael. 'I've saved every penny I've ever earned and have lived from the land all my years. Ask Cara if she would be happy for me to teach her and then we can make it happen'.

'Very well...' David said gratefully. He was still intent on giving the young man something in return, and so decided to wait until he could see what it was the boy needed.

Carmel poked her head around the stable door. 'Master Alpin, I do believe you owe me the pleasure of a walk.' She smiled teasingly and nodded her acknowledgement to David.

David smiled and raised his eyebrows. He elbowed Michael in his side to kick him forward towards the pretty girl. Michael looked back to see David's encouraging expression.

'I shall ask my wife Michael', said David as the young man was leaving the stable. 'But it would appear you may have your hands full this evening,' he whispered to himself as he turned from the stable doors and looked back at Amador.

The sun was still soaring in the sky as the couple walked through the fields. The coastline was just up ahead and Carmel had insisted that they take a walk along the beach. The winds were cutting as they lashed out from the bitter Irish Sea. Carmel took Michael's arm and pulled herself into him to gather warmth as they strolled by the shore. He could see that dimples had risen on the milky skin of her bosom. He did not know how long he had been looking at them before she broke the silence.

'I like you Michael' said Carmel. She hugged him tighter as she delivered this message. 'You seem different from the other men in the village'.

'Is it because I'm still a boy?' Michael laughed.

'Don't be daft!' she slapped his arm playfully. 'You might be as tall as a pyramid, but you're certainly not as thick as one. I've seen you work. You're more of a man than I have ever seen out there. And look at you...' Her hands crept over his chest '...You have the body of a man.' She stood still and looked at him straight into his eyes. He could feel the tension between them. He knew she wanted to kiss him but he did not know how, or if he even wanted to. The second lingered in the air and passed. A wave broke at their feet and the chilling water shook them to their senses. Michael steered her from the tide and up upon the rock-pools that protected the cliff face.

He held her hand tightly as she stepped up onto the wet rock. The stone was slippery beneath their bare feet and the moss on top had become a slimy sludge. Carmel dipped her sand covered feet into one of the shallow rock pools, dusting the frothy water. Her bare feet looked so delicate to Michael. She lifted the hem of her skirt to expose the snowy flesh of her calf. The fire in his loins had come back. She was watching him the whole time. She patted his bum for them to walk on – leaving her hand in place for a few seconds longer than needed to feel the muscles tighten as Michael pressed forward.

Michael was no fool to the girl's games. He knew what she was doing but enjoyed the play anyway. He would be the envy of every hot blooded lad in the town if they were to see them now. Surprisingly, the thought pained Michael slightly. He felt as though he was losing something in looking at Carmel. She was full of life and raised more than a smile when she spoke of the world. But Michael felt like he had taken on the passions of all the other men in the town. If he wanted her, why had he not taken her when given the opportunity? Stopping himself from thinking, Michael pulled at Carmel's hips. He pulled her into him and brought his mouth forward.

The kiss took her completely by surprise and she sighed softly as their mouths were entwined. She threw her arms around his sides and filled her hands with him. One rummaged at his buttocks while the other climbed the muscles on his back, eventually hooking itself onto his shoulder. She pushed him back up onto the wall of the cliff face so that they did not fall. He was pinned beneath her. She grabbed at his hand and placed it firmly on her left breast. The fleshy mound melted under his palm as Michael dared not go beneath the fabric of her blouse.

Her body begged him to take her. She could feel that he was ready for her. With just the hint of intent from him, she would have lain naked with him on the shore for the entire world to see, as the waves would beat at their bare bodies. But he did not move. Instead he froze until the kiss became dull and the passion passed him by. She had never had a man not try anything before – and although she had not given into their efforts before, she had always loved the idea that she was wanted. Michael was the first man that she now wanted for not wanting her. The blood returned to his limbs and he looked nervously at his wanting mistress. He thought to himself that he should be celebrating. He should have been running through the fields declaring the news to everyone. But he felt empty in it. He saw the problem as his own. Any man would have been proud with such a beauty on their arm. She was gorgeous and moulded in the shape of Venus herself. Therefore, Michael concluded that the problem must be him, and for that he would give her time. Maybe time would make him wise to the woman and all her beauty. Maybe in time he would some feeling for her.

As they walked along the shore, Carmel did not feel rejected but instead resisted. She would have her reward in Michael and liked him all the more for making her wait. She had never acted on impulse like that before and was pleased that it had not been taken advantage of. Michael was a true gentleman and he surely held her best intentions in his heart. They turned off the beach before reaching the cove. She was blissfully unaware that Michael did not want her to see it.

✠✠✠

The following months played out like clockwork. Carmel could not be separated from Michael. His playful manner and the heart that he put into his labour endeared her to him completely. Each night they had walked through the vast fields, over every route possible until they would eventually and inevitably return to the door of her home. Michael would kiss her goodnight and pray that she slept well, as she would stand and watch as he walked away. He always grabbed a wild flower from her garden as he passed through. Carmel would look on lovingly at the man that he was becoming, until he was completely out of sight. She did not know that during his journey home, Michael would always sit by Lake Doriend at the same time every night, with the wild flower in his hand. After a short while, he would place the flower in the water and watch the flow of the lake carry the flower away towards the cove.

Chapter 13

It was the height of summer and David Irwin rolled off of his beautiful wife. He savoured the delight of making love to her in the sweltering summer afternoons. They were still trying for a child, and if it were not for the tremendous joy in the act the couple would have grown frustrated in the stubbornness of David's seed. Cara rose from the bed and sat near the porch of their house. She had clothed herself in nothing but the thin linen from their marital bed. Wrapped up tightly, she picked up her violin and began to play. David had never tired of hearing the piece she had played on the night that he had first seen her. Watching the sun rise, it was that very piece that she allowed her violin to cry out towards the land.

David arranged the room as if he was expecting a guest. He was extremely conscious of order and as a child had been well regimented to keep a tidy room by his father. Once he had everything in order, David stood by his bookshelf and found that he could not pick out a single book to read. He had read them all several times over, the spines broken and the pages tinged yellow with the many days they had sat in the shelf. None of them appealed to him anymore. It saddened him slightly that he could not escape into a book while listening to his wife play on the porch.

He was almost subservient as he spoke, 'Sorry to interrupt my love. But does your family have a library? I can't find a page to read in here.' Cara stopped playing and paused a moment.

'I'm afraid not my dearest. There's a large library in the town if you really need to get one. I think they pretty much have everything in there.' The truth was David was feeling lazy. He wanted to satisfy his passion but could not be bothered to scale great walls for it. The blistering day encouraged people to bask in its beauty and not busy themselves too much.

'Oh...' said Cara stopping herself as she was about to begin playing again. 'My sister has been tutored for some time now. I'm certain that she'll have a whole collection of books for you to choose from.'

'Fantastic. But forgive my ignorance... are we talking about Grace or young Imogen? You know I hate to pry into your family matters.'

'Grace dear' smiled Cara. 'Imogen is being educated at Eden. Father chose to educate Grace at home for whatever crazed idea he has for her.'

'Great' said David – despite being perplexed as to why Grace was kept under such a firm lock and key. 'I'll go over now and see what I can pinch.' David kissed his wife and left their home. His kiss made him want to stay with her but he knew that he was being wet and foolish. Even the greatest lovers required time apart.

The Darby estate was alive with colourful flowers. Great reams of ivy sprawled up the outer walls and the house itself was heavily decorated with freshly picked flowers from the fields. Fiona was a master at arranging them and would never let a maids hand be tasked with the duty of filling a single vase. David could see that Raegan's Panhard motor vehicle was not on the driveway. He remembered how his father-in-law had purchased one soon after the two military men had visited some years ago. David was also aware that he had never been invited to ride in it.

Glad that the master of the house was out, David made his way upstairs. Before their wedding day, David had often walked Cara back to her room and knew the route blindfolded. He counted aloud the seventeen steps that spiralled up to the first floor. Gentle memories of a love in blossom sprung to his mind as he looked on the door to Cara's old room. From inside he could hear the shrill of a stern woman drumming in facts as she punctuated her words with a loud bang against some sort of surface. He peered in to see Ms Ryann stamping a long piece of chalk onto the board as she studied young Grace to see if the information was registering.

'Good afternoon' announced David. His head floated several feet above the door handle. Slightly startled, Ms Ryann snapped her chalk upon the board.

'Oh…' she cried. 'Mr Irwin. To what do we owe this pleasure?'

'David!' screamed Grace excitedly. She stood from her desk and ran over to hug her brother-in-law tightly. They had not seen each other for months and David could see that Grace was growing into a fine young lady. Her chestnut hair cascaded down her shoulders and her youthful eyes were wide and bright above her buttoned nose. She was of a different mould to his Cara but astoundingly beautiful none the less. Though nature called for her to grow into a woman, her youthful face held her angelic features almost as tightly as the room she was trapped in.

'Grace…' smiled David. 'It has been too long. We live a stone's throw from you and yet we've not seen you for what seems like an age. You must visit us for dinner.' A cheeky smile flashed across his face. 'And despite thinking I'm completely brilliant, I'm certain Cara grows bored of me in your absence.' He was holding her hands and smiling without a hint of false nature.

'I'd love to David, I would,' she replied. He noticed that her soft lisp was replaced with a sharp lick of elocution. Ms Ryann had been busy after all.

'The only problem is…' Grace looked away and then back again. '…Father. He's awfully protective and I believe he would much rather have you visit us under his watchful eye then let me roam about the land meeting whom I wish.' She smiled sorrowfully. She was well aware of the inexcusable resentment her father held for David and an invite, despite their locality, was almost completely out of the question.

'Well, I fear it would not be until your wedding day that I would see you next if we wait on your father's decision,' said David. 'Nevertheless, I see you now and I must say you are beautiful. Ms Ryann, if you can reach… I advise you to pat yourself firmly on the back. Your student is a complete delight.' David altered his attention as it was Ms Ryann that he wanted to flatter somewhat.

'Ms Ryann' he said now walking over to the elderly lady that remained by the chalk board. 'I was much hoping that I could learn from you also. Not that it would take up any of your precious time, but more a little of your generosity.' He rested his hands on top of Grace's chair, who smiled as she could see her brother-in-law flirting hopelessly.

'Go on' said Ms Ryann beginning to thaw.

'Well, I'm informed that you're in possession of some of the finest literature the land has to offer. I'm afraid I've read all of mine so much that the words have been drained of all their meaning. I was, therefore, sort of hoping that you would be so kind as to offer me a few to soothe my minds demand for the written word.' He felt almost foolish in his declaration but hoped that Ms Ryann would see the humour in his request.

'Read this… read this!' screeched Grace. She rushed to her bedside and returned with a small claret coloured text book. She thrust the book into David's hands and clasped them tight with her own. 'It's a collection of poems by John Donne. You must read them to Cara.'

'That I shall' said David with true gratitude. 'Of course, if that is all fine with Ms Ryann of course?'

'Yes… very well' said Ms Ryann. 'Grace devoured the text quicker than I could teach it anyway. I am sure she could recite the work from memory if called to.'

'Then once more, I thank you both' declared David as he offered an animated bow. 'I bid you a good day. And Grace, visit us sometime.' David stopped turned and rested his hand like a spider on top of the book. 'Remember…the words written by these authors and poets are based on things found outside of these walls. Live within them rather than dream of them my sweetest sister.' David left the room with a triumphant smile.

✲✲✲

Michael was nervous. He had agreed to take Carmel into town that evening for a nice supper. It was in effect his first ever real date with her. For months now they had taken to just spending time together between their daily labours.

He knew that Carmel would want to talk. She would want to know what *they* were, where *they* were going and why the hell he had not jumped her bones by now. With no answers to mind, Michael intended to get out of his completely, hoping that maybe some answers would be at the bottom of a long tankard. He barely drank but felt the impending need to do so this evening. If he had to talk, then a slurred tongue is as good as a silent one he thought.

To take his mind off of it, he'd seized the opportunity to take Amador out. Raegan was out for the day and Connell could not be seen around the estate. So to hell with it, he was going for a ride.

Having been riding for half an hour, Michael was near the coastline. With so much on his mind he had not realised just how far away from the stables he had ridden. He looked out from the top of the cliff face. The sea was calm and the wind brushed at his hair.

Cautiously he took Amador down onto the beach front. There was a long stretch at low tide where the beach was nothing but fresh, clay-like sand. The rocks had been gradually pushed onto the cliff's base over time which opened up a superb track for Amador to gallop along.

The horse took to his new surroundings like he was raised upon it. He galloped full pelt with Michael sat on-top of him. The water lashed at his hooves as the sand clumped and kicked up around him. A gentle shower had begun to pour over them. Michael tried in vain to race the cloud above and break through the rainfall, but the water continued to beat at his face. The clouds were so low that Michael felt he could stretch out and touch heaven itself. The ocean was completely open with not a single boat upon it. The harbour and docklands were a few miles down the coast and Michael had no intentions of risking Amador being seen by the townspeople.

The rain became heavier and the waves begun to pound at the shore. Amador galloped in the shallow seafront as the waters broke beneath him. Michael held a hand to the great horse's neck and patted him. He was proud of how Amador had shown no fear to the ocean. Breaking down the beach, Michael raced the closing tide as the waves filled the sand behind them. They reached the shore moments before the high tide set in.

Having jumped off Amador, Michael held his head to his before walking him back up into the fields. He took a moment while stood at the top to look over at the cove. The closing showers had caused the waters to rage over the waterfall. He smiled to himself before making his way back to ready himself for the evening ahead.

Riding back towards the estate, Michael made a point of stopping off at Cara and David's house. He could hear the soft violin as he approached. Amador slowed his trot as if to match the beat of the violin. Seeing the great white horse outside, David stepped onto his porch.

'Master Alpin' said David. 'To what do we owe this pleasure? I take it you are aware that Raegan is out for the day.' David could see the flecks of sand up the legs of Amador. The bottoms of Michael's pants were soaking at the ankles.

'I thought I would stop by and advertise my services to your dear lady, sir.' Michael offered a half bow atop his horse.

'Well, Cara's more than happy to let you teach her Michael, but we're both not happy with you getting nothing in return.' David fished in his pockets foolishly trying to find something he could offer.

'To see this horse ride is enough for me, sir. I doubt I'll be able to hide him for much longer. Raegan will be sure to visit the stables soon.'

'Well let me speak with her' said David. 'Anyway, talking of women...'

Michael's ears pricked up hoping of news of Grace despite the fact he had never directly asked of any.

'What's happening with you and that fine lady Carmel I see you with?'

Michael sighed. 'Oh... yeah we have been courting for some six months now,' said Michael astonished at how long it felt when putting a number to it. 'I'm treating her to supper tonight in town.' A knot tightened in his stomach.

'Really?' said David with the tone of a proud older brother. 'Are you planning on shaving before you go?'

Michael had never shaved before and had recently begun to grow a rough thick beard. Carmel had stated that she liked the grizzly look that it gave him. However, Michael had never thought that it may appear untidy. He rubbed his palms over the stubbly sides of his face. The hair itched on his cheeks and neck. He had never been shown how to shave and did not really want to teach himself through trial and error. He had seen the way he buttered bread, and shuddered at the thought of the sliced loaf being his tender neck.

'Come on in' issued David. 'I'll show you how, and then we can get you cleaned up for your lady.' David opened the door to his house and walked inside. Michael tied Amador to the rear of the house – out of sight of the manor house. He followed David inside. Cara was stood by the stove preparing a hearty supper for them both. She turned and smiled at Michael. She had seen the boy grow over the years and remembered how her younger sister had been each time she could see him from her window.

'Good evening Ma'am' said Michael tipping his head forward. His long wet hair whipped forward and threw a splatter of salty water onto the wooden floorboards. 'I'm sorry' he said looking up at her. He looked like a stray dog. He ran his hands backwards through his hair. The water held it in place into a slick mould. Cara walked towards him and took his face in her hands.

'I'm sure there is a handsome man in their somewhere' she teased. 'I see you riding your horse most days. He is a stunning creature. I often play my music as I see you gallop through the meadows.'

'Thank you' said Michael. 'I can arrange for you to ride him if you wish miss?' He looked at her as she continued to cup his face. 'It would be no trouble at all.' His lips pursed slightly and made his speech muffled. He begged that it would not cause him to spit into her face.

'Well that would be most wonderful.' Cara released Michael's unkempt face. She had been reading his eyes as he spoke to her and she did not see a flicker of dishonesty in them. His eyes were deep dark swirls of black – just as she had heard them be described a thousand times by her sister. Among other things, her sister had favoured recalling them as deep pools in which to both escape and lose yourself completely. He flashed his signature smile, but his eyes remained cautious and a little terrified by Cara.

'Come now, Michael' said David. He was sat by a large armchair and had prepared a bowl of hot water and a towel. Michael sat down and had not as much rested his damp sodden bottom on the chair when David whisked a great white linen sheet over his chest and tied it behind his neck.

'I'll have you know I'm quite the hand with a blade Michael. It's almost the extension of my arm itself when I wield one.' David swept the shiny razor before Michael's eyes. His startled reflection bounced back at him upon the steel. Cara walked over and placed a large mirror upon the table where Michael was now sat. He could see the fun that filled David's face and relaxed into the moment.

'Have you read the *String of Pearls?*' asked David as he posed devilishly behind Michael.

'David… please,' said Cara in a 'behave now children' fashion.

'It's a Penny Dreadful publication… rotten load of tripe really,' said David until changing his voice into an eerie whisper. 'All that is, except the story of Sweeny Todd.' David leant in by Michael's ear as he held the razor by the side of his opposite cheek. 'Sweeny Todd was a barber… and a monster of a man. Regardless of its many versions, the fate of his customers was always the same. Depending only on what version you read depended on how his clientele were killed.' David began to slide the razor across the side of Michael's jaw line. The hair dropped off as smooth as a row of freshly scythed crops.

'You see…' said David as he tilted Michael's head to the side. 'They either had their necks broken first by tumbling through a trap door under the barber's chair' he banged his foot on the wooden floor in jest. 'Or they had their throats slit from ear to ear.'

David whipped the razor across Michael's throat. The soapy foam and loose hair came away with it, revealing the closest cut Michael had ever seen. 'Either way they all ended up as filling for London's infamous meat pies,' David said concluding his tale.

'Sounds grand' laughed Michael examining his neck in the mirror. 'At least it's only my appetite that's been butchered.'

David laughed as he turned to a large bookcase behind him. He pulled out a small paperback journal with a colourful illustration on the front. 'Here.' He held the pamphlet towards Michael, 'You can read it if you like?'

Michael was looking at him through the mirror still. He could see that his own expression was one of slight embarrassment – his cheeks were almost as red as his tendered neck line.

'I would love to, sir' said Michael. 'But the thing is… I'm not too good with words. I can get by reading and writing a little, but I was pulled out of school before I could master it. All those books behind you there, well they are just paper with print on them. There are no stories in there for me.'

David felt awful. He had overlooked his own privileged upbringing and like an arse had assumed that Michael had experienced the same. The young man spoke so well that it baffled David to think that he was partially illiterate. He placed his hands upon Michael's shoulders and smiled at him through the mirror.

'My boy...' said David. 'I think we may have found our means to barter. How about I teach you how to read and master the art of the written word, and in turn you can teach my wife Cara how to ride?'

'That would be grand sir' said Michael. 'But is there a need for a man like me to be able to write? What with what life has in store for me, all I need to know is the land and nothing more.'

'Michael' assured David. 'The pen is a fine weapon to have at your disposal. Any man can say the right words to those he states he loves... but not everyman can write them.' He looked at his wife Cara as she beamed back at him. 'Now let's finish this shave, you have a woman in waiting.'

David continued in a whirlwind of steel. The foamy soap suds flicked off Michael's face as the tender years were brought back to it. His smooth skin boasted the fine looks of a true gentleman. David splashed his two palms up the cheeks and neck of Michael. His palms were full of his favoured aftershave and the strong scent filled the room.

Michael bit at his lip as his face ignited. He curled his toes and held the curses back from Cara. They dangled on the very tip of his bitten tongue. His cheeks reddened for a while before soothing and gathering their usual complexion. David grabbed at a fine toothed comb from the back of his trouser pocket and ran it through Michael's hair. He flicked the grains of sand and water that collected on top of the comb as he pulled it from Michael's scalp. His hair was wild in its curls but David continued to comb and put some sense of order to it. Once he was finished, David admired his work. Sat in front of him was the finest boy that Orplow could boast of, and though it was more of a tampering than transformation, Michael looked his most handsome.

'Thank you' smiled Michael as he looked back at David.

'My pleasure' beamed David. 'Now go and get the girl...' David whipped the linen sheet from around Michael's neck. 'Oh, and remember our arrangement.'

'I will' said Michael, not sure which part of David's commands he was truly answering. He got up from his chair and noted the time. He was running late. He still had to put Amador back in the stables and would need to get his finest shirt, trousers and braces on.

'Oh bugger...' cried Michael as he shook David's hand, kissed Cara on the cheek and ran out of the door.

'...Thank you!' he shouted as he dragged his horse back to the stables. The kink in his hair fell forward a little and kissed at his brow. By the time Michael got home, he had about ten minutes to get ready. Carmel would be meeting him at the road into town in around twenty minutes and the road was a good ten minutes walk from Michael's cottage. Bursting through his front door he ran into his room.

'Hi Ma...' he shouted but got no reply. She must be still down the church he thought – wasting her time on that man. He had not told his mother of his plans tonight, but had told Oscar in hope that his chubby friend would most likely tell his mother Margaret who in turn would pass some elaborated form onto his own mother.

Allowing himself a moment of vanity, he admired himself for a second in the mirror. He felt quite the fool not to have kept on top of his appearance. His beard must have appeared pathetic. Although thick and full, it belonged on the face of a seasoned farmer and not some young man in old shoes.

Shaking the thought from his busy head, he found his favourite white shirt and trousers. He pulled the braces up over his shoulders and put on his waistcoat. Finding it draped over his bedside chair, he picked up his matching dark brown jacket. He had never worn his hair in this fashion before and liked how it aged him slightly. He placed a flat cap loosely on his head so to protect his hair from the elements, but not disturb the style. Once in place, his outfit was complete and still with a few minutes to spare. He peered under his bed and opened up a small wooden box. In it were the majority of his wages that he had saved over the years. He had saved as much as he could and only took enough to fill his and Carmel's bellies for the evening.

Getting to his feet, Michael's stomach was rumbled. He had worked up quite the appetite in the fields today, making sure not to eat at too many berries to keep his belly empty for the evening. Drink hit him harder on an empty stomach, and he wanted the option of escaping into intoxication if he needed to. He could feel the slight flicker of nerves in his stomach too. His belly growled a little when he thought of how Carmel would be waiting for him soon. Eyeing a loaf of thick bread on the kitchen table, Michael tore a chunk from the edge and plonked it into his mouth. He was still swinging his arms into his jacket as he left the cottage and headed out to meet his date for the evening.

Carmel had not been waiting long before Michael caught up with her at the first road that led into town. She was stood beneath a gas lamppost and was cloaked in a tinged yellow light. Michael stopped for a moment before she could see him, and admired the girl. She was as gorgeous as they came. Her hair was worn down and free, and she had a dark cotton wrap around her shoulders. She was full of figure and Michael was unsure whether she was wearing a corset or not, though her waist appeared thinner than usual and her breasts higher. What he did know was that she was a complete woman, and he prayed that she did see through his thin act to be a man.

'Good evening' said Michael. He had waited for her to face away before he had approached her. He did not want her to see him walk the awkward ten yards between them in silence. She turned and looked up to him. Carmel's wicked smile was worn in all its majesty. Michael smiled back and held out his right arm. His skin did not react at all to her touch. Once she had taken his arm, and pulled him in for a kiss, Michael walked her into town. The night was bitterly cold and Michael was desperately hoping that he would at some point begin to warm to the girl.

The Spread Eagle was a popular grog shop and public house in the centre of town. Its white painted stony walls stood out from the surrounding grey bricked houses and a huge green and gold sign — showing an Irish sea-eagle with its wings outstretched inside a golden wreath — swung from its doorway. Carmel had told Michael that she was not hungry and instead wanted only to go for a drink. Michael was grateful of the morsel of bread that now lined and rattled in his stomach, only muffling the rumbling slightly. His hand still shook with nerves, but he could always disguise that as the cold. He blew into his cupped palms as he showed Carmel to her seat.

Sat in an alcove by the lead-patterned window, Carmel watched Michael as he walked up to the patron at the bar and ordered their drinks. She sat in wonderment at how the young man walked with such conviction and presence. He seemed to fill the room and space that he walked in and always stood with purpose and place. The boy looked like he belonged to wherever he put himself.

Stood at the bar, amid the beer beaten men of the town, Michael felt out of place. Like a scorching sun in the blast of autumn – he felt a little foreign for his settings. Maybe he should have kept the beard. It aged him after all. He cleared his throat and hung his head slightly as he ordered the first round. The barkeep did not flinch at the order and poured the drinks out as he grunted for payment. Lighter in pocket, Michael returned to the table with two drinks. He placed Carmel's sweet cider down in front of her and raised his drink to his lips as he sat. He had opted for a long draft of Guinness. The drink was heavy and thick with iron. He hoped that the ale would fill his belly before the alcohol rushed into his veins.

'Cheers' he said as he chinked his glass with Carmel's. She raised her glass and took a hearty gulp.

'So, Michael' said Carmel as she placed her glass down onto the rickety table they were sat across. She took Michael's spare hand in hers and watched him take a shallow but long draw on his drink. 'Why have you not made a move on me yet?'

Michael almost refilled his glass as he coughed out what was in his mouth. He had expected the question but not so early into the night and not when he was sober enough to feel its impact. He had hoped the ale would have been given enough time to at least loosen his tongue a little. His mouth was dry and his mind was abstinent of any charming reply. He placed his drink on the table and took off his flat cap, resting it by the side of his glass. He opened his mouth slightly hoping an answer might fall out.

'Aren't we the handsome one?' said Carmel as she saw Michael's tightly combed hair. A soft curl still dangled down at the front. She ran her finger across the rogue curl but it bounced back defiantly.

'Well, I thought I should at least make the effort' smiled Michael. He was glad the conversation had steered away from his procrastination. He planned to talk about it later anyway. 'I couldn't be seen all ragged and rough when out with such a fine lass now, can I?' He took a long gulp at his drink. The smooth liquid poured down his throat. He looked around the pub. Everyone looked older and more tired. Men sat huddled in bunches, transfixed by an almost inaudible, indecipherable conversation. A pianist was playing old folk songs in the corner.

'You're quite the man Master Alpin.' Carmel leant forward across the table. Her heavy bosom rested upon the wood like two generous trifles ready for devouring. She knew that most of the men were looking at her and loved the fact she had a man in which to make them all jealous. Despite failing to feel close to her, Michael would allow her to keep the men's attentions but only at a distance.

Michael found that Carmel's curves did not rouse him like they used to. He had never allowed her to expose them to him but still they held no mystery. He sat and watched at how the older men ogled at her. Their lecherous tongues lapping at their drinks like dogs in the baking summer. He took a long draw on his drink and drained his glass.

'Another?' said Michael, half out of his chair.

'Why not?' said Carmel as she sat back into hers.

By the sixth round the barman began to remember Michael's order. He and Carmel had not moved from their alcove, but Carmel had shifted her chair around to be closer to Michael. She was full and tired of the cider and hollered the patron to pour them two selfish measures of whiskey. Michael's head was beginning to swim and he was glad he was seated as his legs felt like they were at sea. The pianist in the corner had begun to play louder and the atmosphere in the pub was merry along with its tenants. Carmel had her arm around Michael as she raised her shot glass and encouraged Michael to raise his. They chinked them together and drained them completely.

The whiskey burnt at Michael's throat but woke him from the heavy slumber the ale had been dragging him into. Before he could object, Carmel had ordered again and was raising her glass once more to Michael. The second shot held as much fire as the first. Michael's belly radiated as the drink found its way into the pit of his stomach. Carmel glowed beside him. He did not feel her hand ride up his leg at first until it came to rest in his lap. Her fingers rummaged and played a little. It was fortunate that she chose to kiss him as Michael was lost for words.

The kiss was wet and flavoured by the whiskey. They clattered teeth a couple of times before they both came up for air. The pub cheered to the young kissers as they surfaced. Michael's slick hair now stood at one end where Carmel had pulled at it. An elderly gent who had sat at the bar all night approached their table. His face was flush and his cheeks as rosy as freshly fallen apples. His speech was slurred and his back bent as he asked Michael if he could dance with Carmel. Looking at his date, Michael smiled and waved for the man to take her hand. Blushing back at him, Carmel stood up with the old man and began to dance. They shared a jolly jig to a series of folk songs that burst from the piano in the corner. The crowd of men began to stamp their feet and slap their thighs as Carmel interchanged with almost all of them in turn.

Watching the dance, Michael sat in his alcove and poured himself another shot of whiskey. He hated the taste but it served its purpose tonight. He knew that Carmel would return at some point and ask him again why he had not tried to take her, and he hoped that the drink would take his tongue before that time came.

Not distracted in her actions, Carmel was happily dancing for now and seemed to enjoy the men's attentions. She continued to look back at Michael who in turn would raise and drain his glass. She knew that he would soon not be fit for anything. It would be trying to play snooker with string. Her attempts to make him a little green eyed had failed and so she decided to return to her seat. She curtsied with little grace to her dancer and strolled back over to Michael. His eyes were beginning to roll.

'Come on you…' said Carmel. 'Let's get you some air.'

The cold night air hit Michael like another shot. The series of gas lights that lined the streets swirled like Catherine-wheels. He breathed deeply and hoped to find his land legs. He turned and smiled to Carmel.

'You're an awfully good dancer.' His tongue felt like it was made of lead.

'And you're an awful drunk Michael' scoffed Carmel. She could not be mad at the lad. There was no sign of aggression in him when with the drink and she had already seen her fair share of that. Her mother and father had often taken chunks out of each other when the drink was flowing, so much so that when the police arrived it was nearly impossible to distinguish between the wine and blood stains on the floor.

She held Michael up as they walked out of the town. Young couples paved the side roads and alleyways. Fits of giggles and the slow baser tones of encouragement filled the air. Michael began to come around and saw that they were walking near to the harbour. The moon was a sharp half crescent in the sky.

'So...' said Carmel as she saw that her young man was beginning to sober up. 'Where to now?' She turned Michael to face her and kissed him full on the mouth. She let her lips linger on his as they both closed their eyes. She felt all dreamy as her head began to fill with thoughts of finally seducing her man.

Michael on the other hand was on the edge of sleeping as the kiss drew on. His heavy eyes could not afford to be closed for so long without him dozing off. He shook his head and thinking of his home – and his own bed – he belatedly blurted the closest place to it.

'The farm' said Michael. 'We can go to the stables.'

The walk was long enough for Michael to shake off the sedating effects of the drink but was short enough to keep him remaining warm within his intoxication. Carmel was excited by the thought of the stables. She had loved to watch Michael tend to the horses and now she was hoping to ride her own stallion for the very first time. Her hands travelled along almost every inch of him as they walked. Taking it as a simple means to keep warm Michael held Carmel close also. His hands rubbed at her back and arms.

Reaching the farm, it was clear that the stables creaky doors were firmly shut. Michael knew that he would risk waking everyone if he pulled them open, so he led Carmel around to the back where a window was open near to the top of the building. Michael often left it open so that the horses could get plenty of fresh air throughout the night. It was large enough for them both to climb through, and led directly into the loft area where all the drying hay was stored. A long ladder lay by the side of the stable. Raising it up and resting it at the base of the window, Michael planted his foot on the bottom rung. The ladder was thick and stood firm against the wooden walls of the stable.

'Carmel...' whispered Michael. 'We'll have to go up this way'.

'You must be out of your fecking mind' cried Carmel. 'What if I fall?'

'I'll do my best to catch you,' laughed Michael. 'Anyway you will not. It's as easy as walking... only upwards'. He slapped her bottom as she climbed past him. Her legs wobbled slightly the higher she got but Michael held the ladder completely straight. Ever the gentleman he asked her to whistle once she was at the top so that she knew he was not looking up her dress the whole time. Her whistle came sooner than he expected and he looked up to find her clambering through the window. Realising that there was no one to hold the ladder for him, Michael stamped the base of the ladder as best he could into the soft earth. He kicked at the dirt around it to cram the soil into the holes as compact as possible, removed his shoes so that his steps would not be heard, placed them between his gritted teeth and began to climb. He had no idea what he was doing as he climbed up the ladder.

Once inside, he saw that Carmel had already lit one of the oil lanterns that hung from the high beams. They were too far to set fire to any of the hay and high enough not to wake the animals below. Carmel walked across to Michael and pushed him into a mound of loose hay. He lay there looking up at her as she stood astride him. She tossed her cotton wrap to the side as she swayed her hips slightly. The rocking motion made Michael's eyes glaze a little. Kneeling, she rested herself across Michael's lap. The drink was still in his legs and he could hardly feel her on top of him. She leant over and kissed him before letting his head drop back down into the thin layer of hay. It fell faster than expected and thudded on the wooden board beneath.

'Feck' slurred Michael. He stifled a laugh as he covered his mouth hoping not to wake the horses. Michael closed his eyes and ruffled the back of his head with his hand in a vain attempt to brush the pain away. Opening his eyes, he saw Carmel undoing her blouse. She lowered the cups on her corset and exposed her riotous breasts.

Michael almost lost his breath. His eyes bulged as he tried to focus on what rested before him. The two unmanageable mounds swung and crashed into his gawping face as Carmel leant forward to kiss him tenderly on the neck. She used her teeth as she nibbled a little beneath his jaw line, while her left hand was working the button on his trousers allowing the right one to slip beneath and take hold of Michael.

He shot to his feet.

Michael stood looking at the half naked Carmel. What was he doing? He could hear the encouragement from everyman from the town, screaming 'Take the girl for Christ's sake. Be a man and enjoy yourself'. He could almost feel the hearty pats on the back that the local men would give him on news of his conquest. Bedding Carmel would make him the man of the moment – the talk of the town. And, both capable yet unwilling, a deep conflict cursed him.

Eventually, his hesitation and indecision had decided for him. Carmel had turned from lustful to scornfully angry in the short time it had taken her to read Michael's expression. She stood to her feet and pulled up her blouse.

'What is your problem?' said Carmel as she barged past Michael. She was heading down the ladder inside the stables and down to the stable floor. 'Am I not good enough, is that it? I've given you enough time and still not a word from you.'

None came still. Michael's eyes were wide and blank. He tried to find a reason behind his hesitation. He demanded to know what stopped him from enjoying Carmel for all her glory. The girl was kind hearted, spirited and made for loving. He just did not have the words.

'I'm sorry Carmel' said Michael. But she was already out of the main stable doors.

They slammed firmly shut behind her. The oil lamp rocked on its hook above Michael's head, and he could hear Paco stir a little while Amador was completely oblivious and at rest.

Michael lay on the hay and let sleep take him before his confused state had chance to keep him awake all night. He would explain to Carmel in the morning. Maybe he just needed more time. She was a few years older than him and maybe she needed more than he did from a partner. But the truth of the matter was Michael did not know what he wanted. It puzzled him that, at this stage in his life where opportunities were open to him, all he knew were the things that he did not crave; all the options that he did not desire.

Mulling over what he truly needed in life, Michael lay still as the night drew to its close. Restless in his stagnation, Michael chose to say a prayer. God knows who it was for.

Chapter 14

She lit a candle and knelt by the altar. The candle stood alone as it began a fresh row on the stand. Those in front were half melted as the wax hung like solid tears at their side – the flames stumped, bearing little if any light. Until the next, Abigail Alpin's candle would shine the brightest of them all. Michael had not returned home the night before, and she could not help but wonder what the young man was up to. He had been acting strange lately. Though he had not told her himself, she had heard that he had become quite the smitten little kitten with his Carmel. Ever the protective mother, it worried Abigail slightly that the girl was a few years older than Michael, and she prayed that he did not rush into his feelings. She – more than anyone – knew how passionate her son could be, and how he'd give his all to anything he committed himself to.

But for the saintly statues and the weeping widow at the altar, the church was completely empty. Abigail could not hold the tears back whenever she prayed alone. She missed her match so much that it tore at her chest, a bitter acid grasping at her heart making it feel hot and thick as she breathed. She pulled at her rosary beads as she reeled off prayer after prayer. Her tears continued to pour from the cocktail of anguish, longing and bewilderment. No matter how often she had asked – whether in prayer or to herself – she could never find a reason as to why her Ferris had left her. They had everything to live for; a love that was felt more than it was said, and feelings that no words could capture.

Her time apart from him had left her numb, and often she would doubt what they had together. She would try to push and halt her feelings for fear of realising that his feelings may not have been true. How could they be if he had left her? How could he love her as much as he made her feel if he could simply stop it in an instant? And, where was he now?

It was these questions that busied Abigail's thoughts the most. They plagued every moment she missed him. Often she would try in vain to taint the memory so that it may dull her pain, so that it would ease her suffering. But in spite of all the unanswered questions, despite all the rotten thoughts that pricked at her memories like a crown of thorns, she knew how to forgive. True to her religion, Abigail knew she must forgive those that trespassed against her; that stepped upon her heart and stood within the pain-filled shadows of her darkest thoughts. Only forgiveness bore light upon her treasured memories, preventing her love from growing pale in the darkness. And so she believed most in the art of forgiveness. A belief that she begged her lord for each and every day.

The teaching towards suicide was a grey area in the transcripts. Nothing stated that it would either condemn a man to hell or bar him from the gates of heaven – so it was interpreted that these souls were lost among the countless stages of limbo; a lost plane where they rested for eternity. As a loyal friend to her faith, Abigail trusted it throughout its contradictions. She saw the differing stances in the testaments as two sides to the same coin. She recognised how the same god that declares an *eye for an eye* also stands to pardon those that repent. So, she reasoned that by giving her life to the church while praying for the absolution of her late husband, she would satisfy her god entirely. Her days were dedicated to the sole ambition of meeting her husband again in heaven, and she was more than willing to sacrifice a single lifetime to earn an eternity with the one person she truly loved.

Punctual as always, the dawn began to break through the windows of the church. The light of even the largest candle was now futile as the sunlight beamed in and banished every shadow. With the light of day firmly in its place, the working day would soon begin. The many chores ahead demanded that Abigail leave her grief behind for a while. Groaning, she got up from her knees. Her legs ached from the cold floor, and her joints had almost become set into the stone itself. Her body was no longer its youngest and the years of toil were beginning to take their toll. Wearily, Abigail genuflected to the altar, made the sign of the cross and walked down the centre aisle. Passing the marble font that stood at the end of the aisle, she dabbed her fingers into the holy water and blessed herself as she left the church.

The light outside was blinding. She felt like a cave dweller as her eyes struggled to adjust to the morning light. Squinting and covering her forehead with her palm, Abigail made her way towards the farm. Pausing, she thought briefly of her son – stranded somewhere and away from home. She wondered if he lay with the lustful Carmel, their limbs wrapped together. It was clear to see that the young lady was cut from the finest cloth that temptation could muster, and Michael was only a young man after all. Always dreading the worst when it came to her son, all she hoped for was that his heart would get it right when he made his choice. Maybe she was being old fashioned, she knew Michael was a handsome man and the majority of the town's girls would snap his arm off if he offered it. What's to say he hadn't notched a few bed posts already? Abigail knew she had to accept that while she was growing older, her young loyal son was becoming a man to his wretched world.

Down in the fields work had already begun. Abigail was late and grateful that the lingering Connell Locran was not at hand to observe the workers. The temperature was around seventy and the skies held a thin, almost intangible promise of rain. In time with the season the vast cereal crops – the likes of Irish victor and black oats – had begun to ripen, blanketing the fields in an assortment of sizes and colours. Impetuous as ever, following his takeover of the surrounding farms, Raegan Darby had ordered for many of the farmhouses and walls to be destroyed and completely flattened. As a result, the buried remains only encouraged the water to drain away from the soil, leaving pockets of weaker, smaller crops where the houses once stood. Like a weak ribbon, lines of discoloured wheat and barley boxed in the taller, thicker crop.

Abigail could see that the reaping of theses fuller crops had already begun. The wiser workers had taken all the cradle scythes from the wagon, halving their workload as it not only cut but caught the falling crop. All that remained on board for Abigail was a single sickle and a rusty old hay crook. Looking for strength, she wrapped her rosary beads around her right wrist and picked up her tools.

Placing the wrought iron sickle in her right hand, she gathered the hay crook – which was in effect a two foot piece of wood with a single barb on it – with her left. Once among the stronger crop, she pulled aside a thick bunch with the crook before slicing it off near to the ground with the sickle. Eventually, like a beaten boxer, the crop fell to the ground and lay flat. Within an hour she was sweating almost three times as much as the other workers, who appeared to glide through the field with the crops swooning at their sides. However, the cereal that Abigail harvested was as smooth as a blind cobblers thumb and took at least half a dozen hacks of her blade before it buckled.

Despite her handicap, Abigail completed as much as anyone else in the field. The sun had been beating down on her bent back and her dark clothing had held its heat. She was near exhaustion as she came to the end of her field. The cut crop was now being bound into sheaves and loaded onto the wagon before it was hauled into the barn. Abigail knew she had a moment to get some water before the threshing began. Heaving water bottles hung from the side of the wagon and she took the nearest one, only to drain the little drips of warm water that remained. Her throat was as dry as sand and she could have prayed for rain. Looking to the heavens, not a single cloud blocked her view.

The wagon carried the huge bundle of sheaves into the barn. Glad of the shade, she followed the wagon inside and gathered a staff and supple from the barn wall as the sheaves were laid onto the flooring of tightly packed earth. The tool was simply two pieces of wood attached by a leather strap. Abigail held the staff behind her head as she brought it down with a blunt slap onto the straw, decapitating every kernel of grain. Her back ached each time she brought the staff down to the ground. The dull thuds resonated up her spine and caused her to arch her shoulders. A farmer turned the straw with a hay fork for Abigail to repeat the process. He then gathered the spent hay and placed it in a crib to be used as soft bedding for the animals. Abigail breathed deeply.

Next came the winnowing. Abigail picked up the two handled winnowing scoop, bent down to the ground and gathered the grain from the floor. The task was intended to separate the grain from the chaff. The barn doors had been opened wide on both sides to allow the breeze of the meadow to flow through. A large sheet was placed onto the ground as Abigail climbed up into the loft. All the farmers inside the barn stood flat to the walls as if they had been pierced by invisible arrows – their arms and hands spread wide as if the ground beneath them had become a narrow ledge only a foot wide. With the many hulls and beards in the grain being lighter than the fine, heavier crop, the wind would carry these away from the sheet when dropped from the winnowing scoop. With everyone in position, Abigail emptied the heavy scoop and released the grain to the mercy of the passing winds.

✳✳✳

Moments before, Sergeant Howard Ende was enjoying a morning stroll. His pristine uniform clung proudly to the padding of his stout figure, and the sunlight bounced off the balled leather of his polished boots, kicking up a sharp glint from the tip of his toes. His moustache was combed perfectly and bobbed on his lip with each hearty stride. Despite the heat, he decided to complete his attire with his white gloves that shone like white sand beneath the sun.

In Orplow, nobody was a stranger to the next man and apart from a few drunk fuelled furies, Sergeant Ende had very little to deal with. Nevertheless, he knew his community. Every week he would visit every stall and store in the town and offer his sincerely selfless greetings and blessings. The truth that these stores would in turn reward his attention dutifully with gracious offerings was nothing but a sign of the generosity of the town to their loyal and brave Sergeant. He reasoned that those that did not cross his palm were most likely up to no good and would warrant his professional attention until their generosity returned. It was no coincidence that it would be around these times that the local vandals would stop smashing the store windows each and every night.

Today, however, there were no reports to take and Sergeant Ende was going to visit the Darby estate. The land looked its best in the summer light. The bright yellows of the land burst like flames across the meadows as the freshest, greenest lawns were freckled by the bright blues and whites of wild flowers. The Sergeant strolled down off the road to avoid the dust that would rise up from it. Instead, he brushed his boots through the long lush lawns. With crooked backs upon the bending horizon, he could see the farmers hard at work. The fields were flattened by their labour, and he grew hot just watching them graft. He removed his white handkerchief from his pocket and mopped at his watery brow. Salty water soaked the cloth as he folded it meticulously and placed it back into his pocket. Under the scrutiny of the sun, the Sergeant had grown thirsty and approached a wagon where the farmers toiled in the wheat field nearby. Finding a heavy flask brimming with cool water, he drenched his throat and quenched the thirst that lay on his pallid parched tongue. Seeing that his boots had gathered a speckle of dust, he poured the majority of the remaining water onto his shoe. Not trusting the nearby towels of the workers to be clean, he was almost aggrieved to have to dry the boot by rubbing it up the calf of his pressed pants.

It was the second week in July, and it struck the Sergeant that it had been sometime since he had gathered any grain from the estate. Not that the grain itself was much use to him, but he would make use of it as an empty gesture to the local baker who in turn would feign gratitude and exchange the useless seed for a range of freshly baked bloomers. After all, the cost of such bread was considerably less than a set of windows.

The Sergeant saw that the farmers had gathered in the barn and thought he would seize his chance to see what he could carry out with him. With both sides of the barn open wide, he chose to enter the opposite side to where the wagon had rolled up to. Stepping through into the barn, and opening his mouth to greet the farmers warmly, Sergeant Ende became peppered by the hulls and beards of the gust carried chaff.

✲✲✲

Michael was heading home for some well-deserved lunch. He had toiled all morning without any distractions. Not even Carmel had come down to the field to see him. She was probably still smarting from her rejection the night before. Not that it was a full rejection anyway — just a mere hesitation to act. He was sure that one day he would feel ready to be with her, but taking her while his legs were numb through drink didn't have much appeal to him. If he was ever to be with her then he wanted to feel and savour it. However, he was now only ravenous for a good meal.

Feeling the heat, Michael slung his jacket over his shoulder and walked up towards his cottage. The colours of the day were bold and bright — making the black smoky willow tree even more ghostly than usual. As he walked into his home, Michael saw his mother knelt in front of a half-naked man.

'What the F…' Michael dropped his jacket to the floor. His mother jumped to her feet and peered around the large frame of Sergeant Ende.

'Oh…' said Abigail slightly startled. 'Michael this is Sergeant Howard Ende. He got dirty this morning, and I said I'd help him get tidied up'.

'Looks like that filth carried on into the afternoon, eh Ma?' said Michael scornfully. He did not take his eyes off the Sergeant. 'And what the hell do you think you're doing in my house with your pants down by your ankles?'

'Look son…' said Howard. He changed his tone when he saw Michael's expression. 'This isn't as it appears. I got my uniform covered in grain and your mother said she'd dust me off. It's completely harmless.' He had pulled on most of his uniform now. His gloves rested on the small wooden dining table.

'I suppose…' said Michael not totally convinced. 'But if I hear of any boasts about my mother around town then they'll be blood spilt, do you hear me?' He took a drink of water from the table. He felt slightly awkward telling two grown adults off about their behaviour but he had never seen his mother so close to another man before. Before he could carry on his criticism, a panicked knock on the front door was followed by an excited farmer from the estate.

'Sergeant…' he said. His face was like a ripe tomato and he was as breathless as a drowned kitten. 'I'm glad I caught you here… can I have a word? We may need your help.' Duty bound, the Sergeant followed the man out into the garden to speak with him privately. Michael picked up the officers' gloves and turned to his mother.

'Seriously mother' said Michael in a role reversed tone. 'You have to be careful. The men in this town say the lewdest things about the women, and I don't want you to become some grog shop tale.'

'I know son, thank you' said Abigail. 'But hand on heart; I was simply dusting down his jacket. I had covered the poor soul in chaff this morning in the fields. You should've seen him… he looked like a startled scarecrow.'

'Ha!' roared Michael. 'You've got that right. Look at him… he looks like five pound of manure in a three pound sack.' They both laughed as they looked at the dishevelled, flustered officer through their kitchen window.

'Promise me something though mother' said Michael seriously.

'What's that son?'

'Just promise me…' repeated Michael. 'If his glaringly obvious charm does work on you, and eventually you bear a child together, if it's a girl, can you and Mr Ende call her Isabelle after her father?' Michael wore his wicked smile as he waited for his mother's reaction.

'Isabelle En… Behave,' said Abigail as the penny dropped. The officer came back into the cottage. His face was contorted and he looked perplexed.

'We have a slight situation in town' mumbled Howard. 'There is a girl threatening to jump out of the church bell tower.'

Michael was already running. He leaped over the wall that surrounded the small garden of his cottage. Close to stumbling, his feet quickened as the meadow sloped towards the town. Within two minutes he was by the gas lamppost where he had meet Carmel the previous night. His knees buckled slightly as the soft ground turned to hard tiles. His heart raced in his chest as he filled his lungs between each long stride. The sweat was pouring down his back and held his shirt tight to his skin. Sergeant Ende did not have any more information than he gave them back at the cottage, but Michael knew he had to help. Something in his bones told him that he needed to be there. The Sergeant was far too heavy and he'd not make it on foot for some time. The nearest car was at the Darby estate and even then it would take some pleading with Raegan for the keys to be handed over. So Michael trusted his legs instead, and, before the pain could slow his pace, he came to a stop outside the church gates.

Intrigued by the incident, a packed crowd had gathered around the church. Like a swarm of killer bees, they swayed within the haze of the blistering heat. With only hearsay to rely on, they all squinted towards the skies, looking for answers. At the front of the masses, Michael could not see if anyone was inside, and was not aware if the fire brigade had turned up.

The adrenaline was still pumping fast in his veins and he was not prepared to let it slow down. Jumping two at a time, Michael sprung up the church steps and burst through the main doors. Breaking into the church, he found the room to be almost silent. Broken shadows from the gathering crowds clawed at the great windows and shaded the aisle. Despite memory being an often deceiving friend, the church looked exactly as Michael had remembered it. Pausing only to dab his fingers into the font, he passed through and sprinted up to the stairwell that rested behind the grand altar.

Because one side of the stairwell had nothing to lean on, Michael held out his left hand and glided it along the church wall as he ascended. The noise of the curious crowd could be heard as he reached the top of the tower. The small loft area was filled by a central bell that showed its every side through four stone-framed lookouts. Like a telling trail, the thick rope that hung from the bell was taught and stretched out towards the alcove that sat left of where Michael stood. Tracing the rope, Michael saw that the heavy, knotted end was clasped in the shaking hands of Carmel Rhodes.

She was crying fiercely. He could not see her face but her shoulders shook in time with the sounds of her sobbing. Her wrists were red raw and her clothes were dirty and dishevelled. She still wore the same clothes from the night before. Sat upon the ledge of the bell tower, Carmel looked out over the town as her legs dangled towards the ground. Her thick frame cut the bright blue sky behind her. The coarse breeze pushed the gargled jabbering of the crowd below towards the heavens. Michael chose his words carefully.

'So…' he said as he approached Carmel slowly. 'Which is it to be?' he took a breath. 'Are you going to fall, or hang?'

'I don't know what I want any more Michael' said Carmel. She had not flinched when she heard his voice but was now getting to her feet.

'You're not alone in that feeling Carmel' said Michael as he held his hands out openly. 'But there are no answers up here… and definitely none down there either.' He was behind her, but she had not turned to face him. He wanted to see her safe; to wrap his arms around her and protect her. In that very moment he could only hate himself for pushing her away.

'You don't know my troubles Michael' cried Carmel. 'I've got demons too big for you to deal with.'

'I can try' said Michael. He stood upon the ledge with her. The crowd beneath them gasped. 'We won't fall together Carmel. I don't know about you, but when I fall I tend not to be able stop. But right now, we can… let's step back and turn away'. He took her hand in his. She gripped him tightly and the tears streamed down her face. Michael had no idea how she felt, but could not bear to see Carmel like this. He took a step back from the ledge onto the floorboards of the bell tower. With her arm stretched out behind her Carmel stepped back off the ledge. Michael could see the thick, dark bruises under her eyes as she turned to face him. Her mouth was bloodied and her top torn. She collapsed into his arms and brought Michael to his knees. Feeling safe and protected, Carmel lay in Michael's lap as she cried uncontrollably.

Chapter 15

A numbing hush lingered in the library. Muted and soft footed, people glided through the stalls as their heads hung towards the open pages before them. The air was thick and the humming of people breathing could just be heard above the buzzing silence of the building. Following the Public Libraries Act of 1850, a tradition of public provision was founded, and the *library* was now more about the people than the books themselves. Promoters of the public library believed that it must contain books that are attractive to the uneducated as well as those subservient to the studies of the clergyman, the merchant and the scholar. And so, Orplow's public library was a great house of utilitarian architecture. A looming portrait of the architect Harold Stickler hung over the reception desk on the north wall of the lobby. Ambitious in his design, Stickler drew his inspiration from a merger of the national library and the local church. With its Romanesque style, the library was a cross shaped structure with arcades of arches and squared windows. Stickler's 'cruciform basilica' provided excellent natural lighting from the thirty windows that filled the large reading room within its nave. On the day the ribbon was cut, Stickler had proudly declared the building to be his secular cathedral that was devoted to the books of the people.

Grace was in the reading room. It was the most commanding interior space and the floor dipped slightly as it was laid upon the natural slope of the land. Grace pushed a trolley in front of her and replaced all the returned books back onto their respective stalls. The wheels on the trolley squeaked as they turned. It could have proved irritating to those reading but on this particular afternoon there were very few people inside. The many rows of tables within the room lay empty and the wooden slates – that held the books up – were bare. At the south end of the building lay a gallery that overlooked the reading room, and Grace was observantly aware that she was without an audience as she went about her work. She had been working under the watchful eye of Miss Ryann for almost two years now. Having finished her tutoring, Grace still longed for the written word and her father had eventually, after months of persuading on his daughter's part, agreed to allow her to work with Ms Ryann at the library.

Ms Ryann had applied for the vacant manager role advertised in the parish paper and had been offered the role before she had even begun to argue her case. She was regarded as one of the most intellectual women in the town and had a sterling reputation from her days at Eden. For her, the library was a respite from the noise of the outside world. Society came with its loud demands and expectations – outside she could be considered as a shelved woman. Inside, however, she was a bride to every author. She would often escape inside a book and leave all her worries behind. Today, she sat and read as her young apprentice filled the stalls. She had gladly taken Grace on at the library as she found great delight in seeing another person love what she herself adored. After all, Grace had been her finest student and held an eternal fire for the written word, and so Ms Ryann could not think of a finer place for the young lady to spend her days. And such a fine young lady she was. It was no coincidence that the attendance from the local townsmen rocketed following Grace's arrival. She was a beauty that few words could ever capture, and over the years Ms Ryann had seen the young, mischievous cherub blossom into a heavenly creature. Slight in her frame and with hands so delicate and small that her fingers stroked the spines of the books as she placed them back into the stalls, Grace was beauty in its most fragile form.

Grace was used to the silence. Having spent most of her life inside the confines of her home, she had rarely felt the bustle and noise of a crowd. Instead she found her sound in the many volumes of the library. Her mind raced as her eyes scanned the books. Pictures of adventure and romance held her stare the most as she read countless romantic novels. However, the words were always written with someone else in mind; any line of beauty or purpose only saddened her as she knew not one line had been for her alone. She was now through most of her 17th year and could not recall the last time anyone had told her what she had meant to them. Her sister Cara was busy making her new life, and the attentions of her mother had passed onto Imogen who the doctors had declared to be a little slow in her development. Their mother catered to the young girl tirelessly, and within the walls of their home, was never seen far from her side.

Grace's father on the other hand had now become quite the figure in her life. He took a great and active interest in the course that Grace's life was taking and would guide – or more likely decide – her choices. But such advice came without compliment, and Grace had not forgotten the horror he held towards her mother.

Grace flicked on the light switches as the autumn evening drew away the natural glow of the day. Tones of stained light stretched weakly across the walls and only managed to colour varnished stalls. The card catalogues that lined the north and south walls were now completely shaded. Grace liked this time of the day. She found comfort in the shadows that cloaked her favourite stories. If Grace completed all her tasks then Ms Ryann would often allow her to take a few hours in the reading room. However, Grace still needed to tend to the returns and now made her way back to the service desk. If not making sure the stalls were in order, Grace would spend most of her time at this desk. It was here that the public would take out their books and also where they would place them into a basket to return them. When checking out the books, they would wait in line as Grace scribbled a return date and the keeper's details onto a card that rested in a paper pocket glued onto the inside cover. Once returned, Grace would simply open the book, check the dates and note them in the weighty journal on her desk. If anyone returned the book late then a fine could be imposed, but Grace could never scorn someone for enjoying literature, as she was often selfish with the text herself and was not a stranger to hiding her favourite books around the library to prevent other people from taking them out. This little misdemeanour was not known, however, by Ms Ryann.

Sat at the desk, Grace pulled at the short chain that dangled from her desk light. The light was stale and short. She opened the heavy journal as she placed the books from the returns basket onto the desk. Labouringly she trawled through the list and crossed off all the returns. There was no pattern in the favoured flavours from the town. The books varied from fact to fiction; rows of lustful fantasies lay on top of cook books as often as religious verse was spooned by ghostly thrillers. The chore was a necessary evil but was equally soul-destroying. Grace could only flirt with the titles as she had no time to read the books themselves – instead placing them to the side and moving onto the next on the list. Her eyes skimmed the surfaces of masterpieces that she would never have the time to get to know herself. As she ticked off the last book from the basket, Grace saw that Ms Ryann was closing up for the evening. Small pockets of light clicked to darkness as she passed the stalls. Soon it was only the light that fell short of Grace's hands that was left on. Ms Ryann stood before her.

'Time to go Grace' said Ms Ryann as she leant into the small halo that lined the desk. 'Very quiet today, was it not?'

'Yes' said Grace. 'Almost all the books have been returned now. We have very few outstanding. Maybe people have become tired of reading.'

'Well…' replied Ms Ryann, her voice just above a whisper. 'Life does leave people awfully busy. You should be grateful of the leisure and luxury that you have. I am sure someday you will miss it the moment you find that it has gone'.

'I dearly hope not. From what I know of outside, life seems terribly dull.' She looked around the place and smiled brightly. 'At least in here you can escape. You can live the life that you truly wish for.'

'True' said Ms Ryann, sharing the young girl's affectionate smile. 'But only if it has been written. I would not advise you to search for something in here that may already be waiting for you out there.'

'I seriously doubt it' laughed Grace. However, there was a slight flicker inside her; a memory curtained by falling water that always reminded her of the emotion captured within her favourite poem. Shaking herself, she saw Ms Ryann was still staring at her. 'Still… dream a dream eh?'

'Quite' smirked Ms Ryann. She had two books under her arm that she would no doubt be reading alone at home. 'Well the evening awaits young Grace. Do you have any plans?'

'My father has enough plans for the both of us Ms Ryann. I tend not to. I could not bear to meet with all the fruitless expectations.' She sighed as she stood from her chair. The evening held no plans at all. Following Ms Ryann through the tight corridor and through the main doors, Grace greeted the night alone. There was a chill in the air and hardly any sign of life lay on the street. The town was silent. Light emanated from the windows of all the houses, as the stores sat in darkness. At this hour, most of the families would be enjoying their supper together – eating hearty and stomach filling portions that were ultimately lacking in any true nutrition.

Walking over the bumpy cobbled streets, Grace made her way to the looming gates that stood at the first road leading out of town. She could already see her father's car parked up by the roadside. Each night he would meet her following her shift at the library. No doubt the journey home would be teaming with questions about the events of her day, but she always had very few answers for her father. His digging expeditions for any soiled exploits were ultimately empty as he failed to get his dirty hands on any scandal that involved, or even remotely surrounded, his daughter.

This was because there was none. If asked to report on what her day held, the report would be as tasty as a slice of bread without butter. Her days were wholesome but dry. She knew that it would not interest her father that her mind raced rampantly as she read the many volumes and stories contained within the walls of her work, for her dreams fell into the realm of fiction – a plane ignored by her father entirely. Raegan Darby worked on facts alone, and the facts were that his daughter was beautiful, desirable and ultimately valuable.

'Good evening young Grace' said Raegan as he leaned up against the bonnet of his motor vehicle. His dark pants blended into the cars body work so much that he looked like a modern day centaur, and his thick moustache acted like a fine mane upon his snarled lip. Grace knew the smile well and was well aware that it was as false and forced as the public affection that he showed his wife.

'Good evening father' said Grace as she approached the car. The door was already open and her father was getting into the rear passenger carriage. Connell sat at the wheel as the engine turned over.

'So, dearest Grace how was your day?' quizzed Raegan as the interview began.

'Not much different from most' said Grace. The car moved forward and started to make its way up the dusty road. 'But it is another one for me and for that I'm grateful.' Her lap lay empty of any books and she cursed herself for not bringing one home.

'Really?' said Raegan, his face bemused at his daughter's enjoyment of the mundane. 'Dear Grace, do you never get lonely?' The question shocked Grace. Her father had never shown this sort of consideration before. It unnerved her and her guard remained up.

'I have plenty to keep me occupied' she replied as she looked out across the passing fields. The thick night slumbered above the crops, squeezing them against the earth.

'Of course' said Raegan. 'And you have your family to thank for that. We have laboured tirelessly to provide you with the fittings that you have. But, my question is still unanswered. *I* feel that you're ready for the next step. You're a beautiful, intelligent girl, and the apple of my eye.' Grace noted how he wasn't even looking at her as he listed his superlatives. 'I think… rather… I know… that any man would be honoured to take your hand, and so I have begun my search for a suitor.' He raised his chin proudly to the sky. 'He will have to be of fine stock; tall, and handsome, and offer you the spoils of an empire that matches mine.'

Grace already hated him. Anyone that would be deemed fit in her father's eye would no doubt be a man cut from the same selfish cloth. Granted, David was a darling and Cara loved him completely, but even Grace knew that something was not right. Her father hardly mentioned the man's name anymore and never invited the couple for dinner. Somewhere her father's design had failed him, presenting David as a mistaken gift for Cara, and the fact that she in turn loved him made her father loathe the two of them collectively.

'I am not sure I am ready for that' said Grace softly. Her heartbeat flattened as she saw the still waters of Lake Doriend. The waters stretched out far in front of her and the dark night blended into the horizon. She thought of the cove and the waters that raged there.

'Nonsense' scoffed her father. 'I would not worry just yet. It's not like one will present themselves to you soon, and by the time I have found the right one you will think differently. It could take several months after all. But there is no waste in haste. You're at the spring of your life, and I recommend that you seize the season before you become a dry old prune like your employer Ms Ryann'.

'She made her own decisions father, and she is completely happy' said Grace. She would not usually speak up, but she feared she would have cut her tongue off if she had tried to bite it.

'Those are the words of the forgotten and abandoned. A lonely love bird will sing just as loudly, but the song is a bitter one.'

Connell laughed as he heard his master's venom. Grace decided not to argue. She found no bliss in her father's ignorance and did not want to play company to it this evening. Eventually, the car carried her up the road and back home.

The gates to the estate were already open and the car bumped its way up the steep driveway. Only a few lights peered out from the manor, and the excited barks of the dogs grew louder as the car crawled closer. Alone in her thoughts, Grace was resigned to an evening of longing for the sensation of belonging. Her home held no comfort for her. Making her way through the large doors she took a moment to look behind her. The fields before her held a secret that always gave her comfort.

***

David Irwin had kept his promise. In return for teaching Cara to ride, David had taught Michael how to read, and more importantly, write. Each evening the young man would make his last task tending to the stables. Once he had tended to the horses, he would bring his beautiful white stead Amador over to the Irwin house. Cara had been anxious initially but the beast had proved a calm host. Michael would hold the horse's head and whisper as Cara sat astride the saddle. It had begun with a slow canter as Michael held the reigns and walked in front of Amador. He knew the horse was ready and welcoming but waited until Cara was truly comfortable, and as planned the seeds of confidence grew over the following weeks and finally Michael handed Cara the reigns. She was not expecting to ride Amador alone that day, but Michael had asked her to hold the reigns while he tied up his boots. Bent over, staring at his tightened laces, Michael's playful slap on Amador's behind was enough instruction for the horse to carry its new rider. Screaming for the first dozen strides, Cara soon found ease in the endeavour, and her lungs flung laughter into the air.

Months on and she now rode the horse freely. She did not long for any sprints or gallops across the field, but instead savoured the gentle canter around the surrounding gardens of her home. Keeping behind the garden walls and hedges, she did not want her father to know of her latest talent, and furthermore would have never forgiven herself for showing him Amador. The love Michael held for the animal was as clear as the summer skies, and she would not be the one to darken them.

As Cara rode with confidence it freed time for Michael to meet with David. Though the young man had an appetite for learning, David almost felt selfish in teaching Michael. The act brought fresh life into the tired books on the shelf, for David had read them a hundred times over. But now, seeing them through the bright eyes of Michael, the words regained their original impact once more. It soon proved that the young man had been initially modest in his own review. David found that Michael could read quite capably. However, he did struggle with his writing. Michael had a peculiar way of holding his pencil and it would eventually cramp his hand if tasked for too long. His handwriting itself still had the appearance of a child's – being small and often unreadable. But the boy did not rush with it and his spelling was accurate at least.

David noted how Michael never took a book home to read. When asked about this he had replied that he simply wanted to be literate and that the stories told by others held no interest to him – he said that he barely knew his own mind and doubted he could grasp that of another's. David knew this to be a lie. He had heard of Michael's growing reputation in town among the men and, more particularly, the women. He was quite the social being come the weekends and was deemed – along with his pretty lady – to be the town's home grown firecracker. He danced and joked through the nights and so could not be seen to be a reader for he did not appear to have a life worth escaping.

Reputations aside, David still wanted the young man to acknowledge craft in his new tool. Often he stressed that while you could give a monkey a hammer and he'll use it to break a nut, if placed in the hands of someone skilled, the same tool can be used to build the most beautiful of homes. David engineered his lessons to this effect and, with shrewd intent he had introduced Michael to the works of all the romantic poets. It was then that David could see Michael's guard drop; his mask put aside so that he could truly see the words before him.

One lesson in particular rested in the memory. Versed almost to the brink of boredom, David handed Michael a small collection of poems from John Donne. Having borrowed it for some time, he had forgotten to take it back to Grace, and it was one of the few books that Michael had not been taught from. Selecting a poem at random, Michael was determined to scupper his teacher. He scanned the titles and chose the least attractive one he could see. He laughed to himself as he chose *The Flea*. Content with his choice and sitting at the dining table, Michael read aloud.

'Marke but this flea…' read Michael. His eyes enjoyed the poem as its silly scenario showed the actions of a hopeless lover using the flea as a tool for seduction. '… as this flea's death tooke life from thee.' Michael finished and looked up at the smug David.

'So, what do you think?'

'It's not bad… a little desperate maybe' smiled Michael.

'Ha!' laughed David. 'But it's more than that… it's genius. It's one of the finest arguments for seduction I have ever read.'

'They are arguing over a flea' said Michael. 'Hardly going to get the blood pumping is it? I've swatted loads.'

'That's exactly what it does… the blood is the key to it all' said David excitedly. 'Donne argues that he and his beloved are mixed inside the flea as it has bitten both of them. He states that she would not lose anything by giving into him as together they are already mixed in the *little* flea.'

'But she kills it' said Michael bluntly. He was re-reading the poem as David continued.

'That she does… but this just gives the speaker another angle. Quickly, he changes tact and argues that in killing the flea her fears are shown to be false as she would lose no more honour if she were to sleep with him. You see, in the flea, their *marriage bed and marriage temple* has already existed.'

'So you're saying that they had practically slept together by mixing their blood?' Michael shuddered animatedly.

'Please don't tell me you're the squeamish kind Michael' mocked David.

'No… not at all. You lose that the second you see the bloody birth of a horse, believe me. I'm just concerned. Oscar and I became blood brothers when we were younger!' He started laughing. 'I mean, the lad has a fine set of apples on him, but I hadn't envisaged him to be my first!'

'I think you make a fine couple' laughed David.

Michael wanted to move the conversation away from his relationship with Oscar. '…back to the poem. It seems to me that the parents don't really agree with the whole romance.'

'I would never worry about that Michael' said David with a knowing smile.

***

A few hours after the sun had set, Michael sat by the lake. The night was heavy upon him and his body ached from the day's toil. He needed to clear his mind but the waters that broke to his right distracted his thoughts. It had been two years since he had saved Carmel at the church and – although now from some distance – they were still together. The police had investigated the matter and found that her father had become violent that night, and had viciously assaulted Carmel for coming home late from the barn. He had seen her as a worthless unholy whore, as he tore at her clothes and blackened her eyes. Cruel though they werethey were, had resonated with his daughter as she had never known the difference between lust and love. Every man she had ever known had tried to take her – that is, all but one. She loved Michael for his hesitation. She saw it as a way of caring; as a way of showing that she meant more to him than just an object of physical affection. And though she had moved out of town to live with a distant aunt, she would still travel most weekends by train to come and visit her man.

The arrangement plagued Michael. His weeks were now consumed by his work and then the weekends brought with them a situation that he simply could not work out. He longed to write Carmel a letter. Sat by the side of the lake he had made a small fire upon the rocks. Fashioned only to burn for a while, the flames flicked away from the land, as they waited nervously in the knowledge that the lake would rise in the morning. The light cloaked Michael. His face was warmed by the fire and his hands itched with intent in front of him. The reeds sighed nearby as the gentle autumn wind brushed through.

The paper in front of Michael lay naked of any words. While he felt the need to write for Carmel, he had no idea what he wanted her to know. The words escaped him entirely – but then so did the message.

He knew he cared for Carmel. She was full of energy and life when they were out in public. She always stole the show as men gathered to gaze at her curves. And though Michael found no pride in this, he found himself by her side regardless. As most men wanted to decorate their arm with such a trophy, Michael knew it was more of an act of protecting her from such horny hoards than really stopping to enjoy her for himself. Sat alone, he found no answers upon the surface of the lake. Not even a ripple of thought had hinted at what he should write for her. Deep down, he wanted to write how he felt for her, to fish out feelings that he knew must be skulking in the very base if his being. But he could not scribble a single sentiment. Pausing to watch the moonlight shimmer across water, he thought of all the answers he had given to her, and could not even recognise the voice that had spoken them. Taking a deep breath, Michael stood up and looked back over the sweeping fields. A couple of lights stared back over the land from the manor. The pencil twitched in his hands. As the cold night held him, Michael knew it was time he spoke to Carmel.

Chapter 16

Connell had seen Cara riding the white horse. For weeks he had ordered his spies to watch her and the young Michael every time Raegan had left the estate. The information that trickled back to him made him salivate. However, Connell hesitated to tell his master until he had seen it with his own cynical eyes, and having bared witness to it himself, he could not have been prouder of his spies. Just as described, like clockwork, Cara would ride the horse, delivered to her by the ungrateful runt Michael, as soon as her father was away. Connell knew the information could be crippling to the two of them, and he could not wait to tell his master. Gushing through the manor doors, Connell made his way into Raegan's study – who was found perusing the morning news at his desk. Thick smoke rose from his pipe and his thin fingers twirled the dry tip of his moustache.

'Sorry to disturb you sir...' said Connell salivating. '... But I have news that you may wish to know.' Raegan looked up from his paper. He looked tired; wiry red veins held the edges of his eyes.

'Really?' replied Raegan, eventually. 'Go ahead then. I'm sure it will be riveting. What is it this time? Is one of the staff pregnant? Or have you found another one to your liking that you wish to be moved within your ravenous reach?'

Connell was fully aware that his master had been hard at it the previous night and knew not to take any personal offence to the venom he spat.

'It is about your daughter' said Connell in a tone as if he were delivering a death message.

'Which one?'

'Cara, sir.'

'And? Has she gone and found herself another fruitless partner, like that worthless husband of hers?'

'No sir. Unfortunately not. It appears we're still having to tolerate that polished turd of a son-in-law.' Connell lost himself in thought for a moment. 'But as for your daughter, well, of late she has been seen riding one of the stable horses.'

'What? Cara?' questioned Raegan. 'I was not aware she could even ride. Well good for her... it's quite the pointless talent anyway. Those wide hips of hers hardly lend themselves to winning any dressage competitions do they?' He shuffled his newspaper. 'Is that all? Or do you wish me to punish the daughter I have chosen to have no dealings with anymore?' Raegan looked back down at his paper as if to end the conversation.

'Well, sir' said Connell shyly. 'It was the horse itself that I thought you may have issue with. It would appear that your faithful stable boy has been hiding something of a secret from you.'

'Michael Alpin?' snorted Raegan. 'What has the young ruffian been up to now? I swear that lad is nothing but an obstacle.'

'True' replied Connell, his head nodded at the end of his master's every sentence. 'Well, it concerns one of the studs that he was tasked to raise...' He paused for effect, revelling in the drama. '... it is white sir.'

'White?'

'Yes sir. Now I know the young man did not choose the horse but he has had ample time to tell you of this.'

'White?' repeated Raegan.

'Blanco...' replied Connell with a feigned frown. 'I think that's what they call it. Or gray, I'm not sure. It stands out from your usual stock, sir.' Connell knew it was time to stoke the fire that was burning in his master's mind. 'It's almost an insult to your taste... a total disregard for your preference.' Connell could see Raegan's mind tick over.

'Very true indeed' he snarled. A white horse would serve no aesthetic purpose. Raegan's choice was black and nothing else. 'Well the animal will have to be sold. Seek out the next auction and have the horse taken away.'

'I will sir' smiled Connell. 'And what with your daughter and the stable boy... shall we punish them for their disrespect?'

'I think taking the horse from the boy will be enough... dock him a month's wage for good measure though.' Raegan mulled over his next decision. At least 12 ticks were heard from the golden pocket watch that he was staring at. 'As for my daughter, well, I would quite like to see her new talent in action. Does she ride any of the other animals?'

'Apart from that weasel David?' said Connell testing his parameters.

'Starve that tongue of his name please Connell' spat Raegan. 'Get the white horse over to the estate and have Michael ready the other stud. If Cara is boasting a new skill, then she will have to prove it to her father.'

'Gladly' said Connell. His meaty hands were clasped together like two sweaty skunks embracing.

✳✳✳

Cara was not feeling fantastic. The morning was dull, and the night had overstayed its welcome, and the tired sun failed to break through the unsightly mist. Cara's back ached and her head was thumping. It had been a few weeks since she had numbed her senses with her favourite wine, but still she felt like she was nursing the reward of a fine drinking session. The smell of the breakfast that crept in from the kitchen ridded her of any appetite as well as the contents of her stomach. Kneeling over the basin and retching violently, she could hear David humming from the next room. The thought of her man always made her smile and she felt awful for the mood she had been in with him for the last week. She smiled even more when she recalled how David had not once reacted badly to her mood swings. Instead he had laughed and gave her whatever she needed. He always seemed to know exactly what his wife required before she did, and she could not love her David more.

Whilst his wife was on her knees heaving in the bathroom, David was toasting thick cuts of bread in the kitchen, and had filled two cups from a fresh pot of tea. He already knew his wife would reject the food. Recently, she had lacked her appetite in all areas of the house. Even the bedroom had become a baron and fruitless table. The thought of the bedroom caused David to stop for a while and recall the last time he had taken his sweet wife. The thought of her rich body spread out in front of him gave him an excitement that he knew he would sadly have to temper, for now. Sighing to himself, David accepted the dry morning that lay ahead of him. Holding the tray with both hands, he made his way into the bedroom. Cara was where he had left her and was almost green in complexion.

'Are you alright, my love?' said David. 'Now, I know you're the stubborn kind, but I think we need to go and see a doctor. It's only a short ride over into town.' He placed the tray by the bedside and was surprised as she took a small sup from the tea cup.

'I am fine David' said Cara softly, but with emphasis on her pronunciation. 'I am just run down. The season has been heavy, and maybe I just need a little fresh air.'

'Well, let me walk with you,' replied David. 'Get some food inside that tender belly of yours and then we will take a walk into town. And I think you're right, the fresh air may do the trick.'

'I assure you I am fine,' said Cara with a bit more bite than she had intended. 'But very well, if we must, we can go for a walk. But get that toast away from me. Toss it to the birds or something.'

Patient towards his patient, David stayed like stone and waited for his wife to get ready. He would be best to move at her pace today and so took a step to the side. It was not before long that they were both ready, and wrapped up in their thick scarves and leather gloves they greeted the cold morning. The mist was low and thick – greying the land like a wide judicial wig. They could not see farther than the nearest field as they stepped inside the fog. David bravely put his arm around his wife's shoulder, leaving it there for a second to see how she reacted. Finding that she had not thrown it off her, he grasped her tighter and rubbed his hand down her arm. Feeling safe under his wing, Cara rested her head in his chest as they walked together.

The trotting of hooves could be heard amidst the mist. The gentle clip-clopping clicked in the air and grew louder as the couple came closer to the ménage. It was unusually early for Michael to be tending to the horses, but David would be glad to see him. The young man had become quite the friend, and Cara could not help but warm to his careless charm. Stepping deeper into the fog, David could hear the horse ahead clearer. He thought that the low mist must have been provoking Amador somewhat as the sound of the hooves was more erratic than usual.

Breaking through the grey hanging air, David saw that Raegan and Connell were inside the ménage. He could not see Michael nearby, nor could he see his beloved Amador. Struggling to stay still, Connell held the reigns to Paco. It was clear that the horse was not fond of the weather as he jerked and fidgeted like a flea on hot coals. The horse moved violently. There was a warning in his manner that David had never seen in Amador. Stepping towards the couple, Raegan held out his arms and coughed dryly before speaking.

'Dearest Cara' he said. Raegan did not acknowledge David, pretending that the mist had hidden him. 'My friends tell me that you have quite the new talent. How could you keep this from me?' He dramatically clasped at his chest as if an arrow had pierced his heart. 'I'm deeply hurt, that I assure you. You know how much I love to see my daughters parade their skills, and to think that this has been learnt by your own initiative just makes me keen to see it even more.' He patted the swaying side of Paco. The horse flinched forward.

'I don't know what you speak of father,' said Cara readying herself to leave.

'Oh come now…' barked Raegan. 'I know very well that you have been riding for some time. I just want to see it first-hand.' He opened his arms as if he wanted to hug the daughter he had kept at arm's length for so many years. 'Can a father not seek to be proud of his own daughter?'

Cara bit her lip. She did not know whether she wanted to run at him, or away from him. Connell, meanwhile, was enjoying the drama enormously. His greasy lips were pursed in a satanic smile. Seeing his wife's hesitation, David stepped forward.

'I have no idea what stick you may have picked up sir…' declared David. 'But you've certainly got the wrong end of it.' He held Cara's hand tightly. She could feel the gentle stream of nerves shake his arm. 'And even if she were to know how to ride, she is not well and in no condition to do so. Not for you or for any other man.'

'Be quiet' scoffed Raegan, spitting the words out like he had just inhaled a wasp. 'I can assure you that your wife's honour has been upheld by your weak declaration. However, I'm her father and I demand that she shows me. If you wish to live by someone else's rules then you are more than welcome to leave my land.' Raegan's nostrils flared and snorted out two balls of steam. 'But until that day, I deem it fair rent to allow me an interest in my own family. Now Cara, I ask as much as I demand… ride for me.'

Cara's belly turned over as she paused to think this through. Michael was clearly not nearby otherwise he would have made himself known, and her father had made no mention of him or Amador for that matter. In light of their absence, Cara knew it would be foolish to state that she rode on a different horse and hoped with her entirety that Michael had taken Amador from the stables before her father's visit. It would break her heart completely to see the boy without what he cherished the most. Nonetheless, she had never ridden Paco and had always found him to be a somewhat nervous creature. This morning, restless in company, Paco was remaining true to his character. He continued to move – never standing still under the uncomfortable grip of Connell. Completely ignorant of the regret she would soon hold for it, Cara made up her mind.

'If you must,' she snarled. 'Bring the horse over to me.'

'My darling,' pleaded David. 'You have nothing to prove to this man. Let us just go about our business.'

Connell brushed David to the side as he knocked his passing shoulder into the man's chest. A surly grunt was all that left his greasy lips as he barged past, and David was certain it held no apology. Slightly winded, David watched Cara take the reigns from Connell. She turned and smiled to him before stepping up onto the horse. Tracing the outline of her expression, David saw a hidden fear begin to surface. He thought he had seen every expression upon his wife's face, but today she offered one that he had no idea how to interpret. He felt hopeless as he failed to see what she needed. She mouthed something but the mist held the message from him.

Cara stroked at the neck of Paco. The horse calmed and began to canter forward. Cara's back was straight as her body bobbed lightly on top of the strange horse. She allowed herself a deep breath as Paco rode beautifully. Maybe she had been too anxious. Michael was young after all and maybe held a slight amount of bias towards his rebel stud.

'Very nice!' applauded Raegan. 'Why not raise the pace a little?'

'Don't,' blurted David. 'She has not been well of late. I don't think it would be healthy for her to push it this morning.'

'Nonsense' replied Raegan. 'Come now Cara, surely you can muster a little more out of the creature can't you?'

'Sir' pleaded David. 'I think it best that we just be satisfied with what we've seen. You've seen what you asked for? What more do you want?'

'For you to shut it,' spat Connell as he stood over David. David could smell the raw, musty sweat on his clothes. Connell reached forward and brought his heavy hand down onto Paco's firm rear as he passed. The horse bucked and kicked out. Completely rattled, Paco raced forward. His legs flicked out furiously. Raegan laughed loudly as he saw his daughter struggle on top of the bucking stud; her hands clung to the reins and her thighs clamped to its shuddering sides.

David was caught in two minds. He wanted to put his fist through to the very back of Connell's thick skull, but knew in his heart that he needed to help his Cara. Soon the decision was made for him. The force of Paco's defiant display threw Cara high into the air. Rider-less, the horse leapt over the fence and bolted through the fields as Cara's body crashed into the pitiless earth.

For what seemed an eternal moment, she lay completely still upon the ground. David was by her side in an instant.

'Cara!' He took her hand in his. 'Cara! Can you hear me?' He held her by her shoulders as he looked back towards her smirking audience. 'You cruel bastards... Go and get some help you fucking monsters!' His face turned from fury to fear as he looked back at his injured wife. She was breathing steadily but her legs were frozen beneath her. David's heart stalled as he saw the grim, red liquid that coloured his wife's hands.

'Cara!' he said. 'Cara, you are hurt my love. Where are you bleeding from?' David felt the dead weight in his arms as Cara lost consciousness. Her lap was a pool of thick, warm blood.

***

The yellow lights of the hospital ward stung Cara's eyes as she woke up. Her body was numb and she had been heavily strapped to her bed. She could not move her neck and darted her eyes across the little space that she was afforded. She could feel a warm hand holding hers.

'Cara...' David's voice was soft and tender. 'Cara... you took a nasty fall earlier my love. But you're going to be fine, I promise. I'm here for you.' David wiped the single tear that rolled down her face. The doctors had cleaned Cara as best they could without moving her. Her hair was still trodden with mud and her brow had become sweaty under the lights. She had been taken into surgery for several hours, and David had become unaware of the time. He was just delighted to see her open her eyes again. The moment she had closed them had been the most terrifying time of his entire life. The thought of losing her had caused his world to pause.

'What happened?' croaked Cara. Her throat was dry and her lips chapped. 'I can't remember how I fell.'

David did not know what to tell her. It would crush her to know that her father had caused this – that his faithful henchman had provoked the horse. But he knew his wife needed love and not hatred; he would bear that cross.

'It was an accident dear,' whispered David. His blood boiled at the thought of protecting those fiends, but he knew who it was ultimately protecting. 'The horse must have gotten spooked by something. It just went crazy. There was nothing you could have done.'

'How bad is it?' asked Cara. Her voice was longing for a casual answer – a breezy 'fine' or 'nothing to worry about' would have sufficed. Instead her heart shattered like a broken vase as

David offered nothing more than his most sincere smile. His eyes deceived his sweet intent as they were drowned in sadness. He struggled as he held the pity and sympathy back from his face – he held her hand as tightly as he could.

'We are waiting on the results from the doctors my love' said David softly. 'You were in surgery for some time. They have a lot to check on. But for now just get the rest your body craves. We'll cross any bridge we have to when it comes to it.'

Cara knew it was bad. She noticed how she was in an isolated ward – her single bed packed the tiny room. David filled the rest of the space as he leaned up the wall by the door – the narrow walls supporting him as he stood right by her side. Cara could hear the creak of the door opening and the polite voice of a stranger asking David if he could step outside for a moment. She saw David lean over her and kiss her on her forehead. His lips were light on her skin but his breathe was heavy and thick.

'I will just be a moment my love' said David. 'Your family are somewhere in the wing, so I'll let them know that you've woken up. That is, unless you want some space of course?' Cara did not answer but smiled back at her beloved husband. He always knew exactly what she wanted.

Out in the quiet hallway the doctor took David to one side. David could still see his wife through the frosty glassed window of the door and watched her as the doctor began to speak. There was no irritation in the young man's voice as he explained the situation to the seemingly inattentive David.

'Sir,' started the doctor. 'I am Doctor Anderson. I was the man who operated on your wife earlier today.' He need not have paused for a response; David was still staring through the window. 'I must tell you that your wife's condition is serious but manageable. We will keep her in for a few weeks, maybe a month to begin with.'

'A month?' questioned David. 'But I've just spoken with her. She's fine.'

'Her mind maybe' said Doctor Anderson. 'But I am afraid that her body is not so.' He cleared his throat. Bad news needed a full breathe. 'Mr Irwin, your wife suffered an acute injury to her spinal cord. In time, the bones surrounding it will heal and ease the pain but the chord itself is beyond repair.' David's attention switched to the doctor. He looked older than his voice had suggested as stark white strands flecked the fringe of his thin black hair.

'Beyond repair?' asked David. He lowered his voice so not to startle his wife. 'Tell me straight Doctor…what will she need from me?'

'Mr Irwin. Your wife will not be able to walk for the rest of her life. She is paralysed from the waist down – a paraplegic. She can be self-sufficient if stubborn enough, but could do with your help.' He saw a determined nod from David. 'Initially, we want her to stay with us until her bones heal. She will get all the support she needs, and in the meantime maybe we can offer her some counselling to cope with her loss.'

'She still has me doc' said David venting a little of his anger. 'I'll be all she needs, don't you worry about that.'

'Mr Irwin, I don't doubt your commitment at all' said Doctor Anderson. 'What we must remember is that your wife is very fortunate to be alive. But I must tell you… it is with my deepest sympathies that because of the severity of your wife's accident today and the huge loss of blood…' He paused to take a full breathe. '…We were unable to save your child.'

'What?' The corridor grew narrower around David. His chest was tight and his stomach knotted. Doctor Anderson could see the shock on David's face as the colour drained from his skin.

'Sir, Cara was six weeks pregnant. The fall today caused her to miscarry. I take it from your reaction that you did not know your wife was with child?'

'No' replied David. 'She didn't say.' He could not muster anymore words. Thoughts of her sickness over the past weeks flooded back to him, but he remembered how sad she had been within it. David knew his wife, and she would have rowed any storm with a smile if she had known that led to the motherland. Looking through the glass windows at his broken wife, David could see that she was not crying for herself or anyone else; she was not mourning a loss. The pain that was etched across her face was for her alone. David knew that he was the first to know.

Holding the door open slightly, he took a moment to get some composure. He filled his lungs before entering the shallow room. His heart bled and his hands trembled as he prepared to deliver the worst words he would ever utter to his cherished wife. He knew she would not want to hear it, but that she would want to know.

He took a deep breath.

Chapter 17

Michael had heard the news of the accident through his fellow farmhands. He hated himself for not being there for Cara. He would have never let her ride Paco and would have gladly taken the lashes from her father for it. He had a good mind to break the horse's leg but ultimately knew that the beast had only been true to its hostile nature. Cara would not want the horse to suffer anyway, and so Michael had let the rage drip from his body as he sweated out his grief in the fields. He had asked his mother to add a prayer to her list and light an extra candle at the church for Cara and David. He knew that they needed all the help they could get.

On hearing the tragic news Michael had felt selfish in his loss of Amador. Raegan had put the fine horse to the fate of the bidders at an out of town auction. The village was only a few miles from Orplow and Michael was almost ready to leave town. Ironically, he would have ridden Amador to his destination, but instead was now getting ready to enjoy his first ever journey on a steam engine. Crouched by his bed, Michael stretched his arm under to find the small box that contained his savings. Orplow had proved quite the privileged little kingdom, and – apart from the social distractions that he had placed on his relationship with Carmel – Michael had not needed to spend much of his wages. He did not care for coins and so would collect them until they were enough to exchange for a single bank note. The crisp clean notes lay in front of him now. Michael knew exactly how much was there and, after folding the notes into a fat bundle, he wrapped it with a strong string and placed it in his satchel. He had dressed in his best clobber and wanted to look as old as he could for the auction. He wore his hair in the fashion David Irwin had shown him. He sighed to himself as his reflection reminded him of the poor couple.

Greeting the morning with intent, Michael made his way across the fields and through the town. He was up before most of the workers had taken to the fields and the land was almost his own. No doubt his mother was already up and at the church. He saw very little of her these days – life simply kept them apart. Nevertheless, the times that he did see her were always remembered. He loved his mother and prayed that her efforts for his father were not fruitless. Looking up to the open sky, Michael considered his mother's plight. From what he knew of God, Michael hoped that the woman's sacrifice would be plenty for the mere exchange of his cowardly father's absolution. Michael wondered if it would aid his mother's endeavour if he could learn to forgive his father. It plagued him to think that his hatred was keeping his father suspended in limbo. Michael felt awful carrying such animosity towards a stranger but he could not ignore the pain his mother endured; any man that would cause such agony deserved his torture.

Michael was familiar with the station. He had met Carmel there on many a weekend over the last year. He recalled, with some regret, how the most peaceful and enjoyable times for him were not when the train had pulled up and Carmel had rushed out into his arms, but were the times that fell in between the arriving trains. In the gaps before the journeys started and ended, Michael would watch the people on the platform. He would guess their fates and their destinations. He saw the young women waiting silently for their travelling lover to return. He saw the cold businessman neatly wait for his carriage to carry him from the trappings of this town.

Despite seeing hoards of people leaving, Michael never thought that any of them would not return.

His return ticket was more expensive than he had thought it would be. However, it hardly put a dent into his bounty and he pulled off the top banknote from his bundle and slid it across to the ticket master. Michael felt like a bank robber on the run as the man eyed the note suspiciously. Michael enjoyed the fantasy a little and let the idea put a slight swagger in his walk. He found an empty bench on the platform and sat waiting for his train. His feet bounced in front of him excitedly. It would be a further thirty minutes until the train arrived. In the meantime, Michael watched the people.

The train journey was not as pleasant as he thought it would be. Michael was fortunate to get himself a seat by the window and had looked out upon the land that raced past him. Once outside the realm of his home town, Michael soon found that he could not read the land that flew by him. Each field blended and blurred into the next. He began to feel lost and had tried, unsuccessfully, to sleep several times. An hour passed before it was all over and having arrived at his destination, Michael was ready for the day ahead of him.

The 'Barn Abrumpo' was located on the rural borders of Dun Laoghaire. It was a farm just like any other and, if it were not for the crowds surrounding the main barn, it could have passed by completely unnoticed. However, the attending crowd gathered its own attention. The bloodstock auction attracted a variety of people. Equine professionals blended with the lay farmer and also those with no background in horsemanship whatsoever. Like a clown's eerie smile, a huge hanging yellow banner proudly declared the wide variety of horses that the auction was providing. Entering the barn Michael saw them all. There were those reared for dressage, a variety of cobs, all-rounders, mountain and moorland, warm-blood, show jumpers and, of course, young-stock. Michael felt at ease amongst the animals.

The farmers bumped and bustled between each other as they tried to gather a good look at all the stock. The musky smell of trodden hay and bedding filled the air. Michael almost got the urge to work, but instead he stood and watched the people pass him by. Amidst the grumblings of the farmers, Michael could hear the feint voice of a young child behind him. Turning towards the barn's entrance, Michael saw a young girl in a baby blue dress. Long blond ringlets twirled from her hair. She was stood next to a tall handsome middle-aged man who was dressed all in cream apart from his heavy green Wellington boots. Michael watched as he picked up his daughter and carried her into the barn. He clutched at her with one of his arms as the other gesticulated towards an auctioneer that had greeted him at the entrance. The auctioneer was a fast talker and was trying to do business well before the four-legged lots entered the ring. The gentleman, however, was in no rush to beat the gavel and had a keen eye for the animals. He walked past the pens and assessed each horse in turn.

'You see' said the gentleman. 'I am fully aware that the greatest strength of a horse is limited by its worst point. So, I am not here to be sold flaws.'

'Of course sir' rattled the auctioneer, his back bent slightly. 'Let me show you some of the finest you'll find. Maybe we can come to some agreement before the masses join in.' The auctioneer led the gentleman around the pens and through to a roped off area. There were very few people behind this and they practically had free reign to choose from the horses within. Michael slipped under as the auctioneer was distracted by the gentleman. He followed them casually, keeping them firmly in ear shot. The gentleman held his daughter tightly as he rejected the horses one by one.

'That has a big coarse head… he has a small sunken eye… he won't carry weight with that long slack back.' The rejections came thick and fast, not giving the auctioneer time to swing a single sales pitch. There was, however, no acid in the gentleman's tongue; just an assertive and sure manner.

'This one has a bad girth, he'll be light through the heart,' the gentleman continued. The auctioneer looked exhausted. 'Shallow chest… bent hocks and a goose-rump… my you have some ugly horses sir'. The auctioneer was drained of all argument until he brought the gentleman to the final horse. Michael's heart leapt as he saw Amador. The great white horse was in the largest pen. His coat glowed and he looked heavenly. Seeing his master, Amador became animated and displayed his finest pose as he stood on his rear hooves.

'I love him' said the gentleman. His daughter was laughing excitedly as the horse moved forwards to the front of the pen. 'I don't think I have seen a finer specimen. This horse is completely perfect.' His eyes traced every contour. 'Look at the lines on him. His mane, his coat… everything is immaculate.' The gentleman had made the auctioneer redundant in his self-assessment. His shrewd eye also picked up on the fact that Amador was transfixed with something behind him. The gentleman turned to see Michael stood smiling at the horse.

'Young man…' said the gentleman. 'What do you say of this horse? Is it not the most beautiful thing you have ever seen?'

'One of them sir…' replied Michael '…Most definitely.' He thought of Grace for a second. 'I believe he is of the bocado blood line… one of the proudest lines in Andalusia, Spain.'

'My Lord!' declared the gentleman. 'Finally, I find a man who knows his horses.' He took a step closer to Michael. 'I see I may have a little competition for this one.'

'Quite possibly, sir' smiled Michael. 'I have reared them since I was a child. I have never understood anything as much as I have these horses. They are my fondest distraction.'

'Very well' beamed the gentleman. 'Let battle commence!' His tone was jovial and Michael liked him instantly.

'Out of interest,' Michael began. 'What could you offer Amador?'

'You know the horse's name, and yet you do not have a program?' The gentleman eyed Michael with playful suspicion. 'Well young man, I own the largest estate outside of Dublin. My horses are left to the wild… within reason.' He flashed an *of course* expression that caused Michael to nod instinctively. 'They are reared and fed to a routine, but the days are their own, and the fields with them. What with you? What can you offer…' He checked his program. '…Amador?'

'Love sir…' said Michael, '… And little else.' It then struck Michael that it was only love, and that alone, that he could offer the animal. After all, the land was not his to give and he did not have the means to keep him to the level he deserved.

'You are the most intriguing character young man' said the gentleman as he patted Michael heartily on the back. 'But this is an auction after all. I hope your feelings can sing to the sweet tune of 200 punts.' The man watched for a reaction. He was certain a small smile crossed the young man's lips. 'A horse of this calibre is worth every bit of that value.'

'And more' laughed Michael. He felt like royalty knowing he could outbid the man. He had the means of getting Amador back and there was little else standing in his way now. That is apart from the slight doubt that had crept into his heart.

Sat in the main pit of the bloodstock auction, Michael waited as he watched the bidders do battle. He smiled to himself as he saw the rejected horses get snapped up by the unknowing punter. His hands clutched at his satchel that hung by his belly. His fingers rapped excitedly as he waited for Amador to take to the stage. Being the finest stock, Amador was inevitably the last to be shown. An exhilarated and rapturous silence filled the barn. Amador was clearly the prize animal. Michael scanned the room and saw the gentleman smiling back at him. He nodded his head before their dual.

'Next up is lot six one six' declared the auctioneer. 'This is a male adult Andalusian. He goes by the name of Amador and is of the finest bloodlines. Shall we start the bidding at 50 pounds?'

'Fifty' cried an anonymous bidder.

'Seventy five' boomed another.

'One hundred and fifty punts' declared a voice from the rear of the room. Michael looked behind to see the gentleman with his numbered panel lifted high into the air. His young daughter clapped excitedly by his side, her golden ringlets bouncing with joy. The gentleman caught Michael's eye and nodded for their dual to commence. The auction hall had been met with a sigh of resignation as the fellow bidders new they were beaten. Michael looked at Amador and felt nothing but love for the horse – the animal made him feel free from the world that surrounded him, and for that he was eternally grateful.

It was at that moment that Michael made his decision. Knowing he could love the horse completely, and that he could outbid the gentleman, Michael smiled at his rival and rose from his stool. Looking at Amador for the final time, Michael turned and left the barn. His heart dipped in his chest as he stepped out into the bright light of the afternoon. But his head told him that his horse was now going to a place where he could get the life he truly deserved. His satchel was almost as heavy as his heart as he slung it over his shoulder and made his way back to the train station. On the journey back to his home town, Michael told himself a thousand times that he had done the right thing in letting Amador go. He smiled painfully as he enjoyed the bitter triumph that was found in his good deed. Watching the foreign fields pass him by once more, Michael found comfort as the familiar horizon he knew so well drew ever closer.

That evening, Carmel was waiting by the first gas-lamp that led into town. The traffic lights that clung to the post were fixed in red. Michael had not had time to change since his travels and decided to meet Carmel straight from the station. He had previously envisaged his triumphant return into town, as he declared to the world that Amador was his and his alone; that nothing could keep them apart. He thought of Carmel running to him as her chest bounced in front of her and she lustfully embraced her returning hero. Watching her now, Michael saw a different picture. Carmel looked warm under the light and her arms rested firmly on her hips. She looked older to Michael as her clothes covered all but her face and cold, pale hands. She almost looked mournful as she waited for her man.

'I'm sorry for making you wait' said Michael as he made the token gesture to run the last few feet that separated them. 'The trains were not as scheduled and ran a little late.' Carmel smiled suspiciously and kicked out one of her hips to the side.

'I've grown used to waiting for you,' said Carmel with an rural twang to her voice. 'I think I would close my eyes and be greeted by angels if you were ever on time!' She laughed as she punched Michael playfully to the chest. Her arm kept Michael at a distance and he could feel the lack of intimacy in her touch. He tried to take a step closer but her arm did not budge from his chest – her elbow was locked in place. Her fingers spread out from a firm fist into an open palm. The tips hugged his chest as he saw Carmel take a deep breath.

'Where are we, Michael?' whispered Carmel. Her eyes had moistened and her smile was pleading. 'We've been together for some time now and still I feel... separate... I feel separate to you.'

'I don't know what to say' replied Michael sorrowfully.

'How about...' Carmel swallowed before she spoke. '...I love you.' Her voice was full of tender anguish more than red hot rage. 'I love you Michael. And all I have wanted during our time together is for you to tell me that you love me too.'

'I don't...' Michael sighed, 'I don't know what to say.' He put his hands on her shoulders and held her stare. 'I don't want to quit you. I want to look after you.' His brow furrowed as he said this and concern covered his soft face.

'But I don't need protecting,' said Carmel. 'I don't want a man to look after me. I want him to love me.' She kept her distance from Michael and watched him as his eyes met with the floor. His head hung down and his strong shoulders sagged.

'Carmel...' said Michael as he looked up. 'I fear I can only give you everything other than what you deserve.'

'I need you to *feel*, not *fear* for me' snarled Carmel. She had hoped her challenge would have shown her something that she did not already know. Michael's feelings, if not his words, were clear. He took her trembling hand from his heavy chest and held it in his. Her eyes raised up in line with his as he broke her heart completely.

'I can't promise you that I will ever love you.' Michael's words hung in the air like fireflies in a winter night. His tongue felt lighter, but still he stopped it from uttering thin words of reassurance and distraction. Carmel deserved nothing more than the truth. It was the thick cut of this that choked her as she tried to find the words to cloak her pain. It was true that she loved the man before her. Michael had come to represent everything that she relied on. He made her feel like she belonged and that one day she may have something that belonged to her and her alone. But in recent months her love for him had become a chore. An endless task to try to make a man feel something that he simply could not. She knew early on that Michael felt differently, but she had fooled herself into thinking that it was because of his age, or because he was a gentleman; that he had not once tried to take her. But the years had taken this excuse from her. He was now a man, and a man should know his feelings. Now that she knew them, it made her feel like a little girl again.

'Carmel, I am sorry' issued Michael. 'I did not want to waste your time. I prayed each night that the morning would bring me closer to you, but it never did. I wanted to love you... be sure of that. And you gave me every reason to. But what I know of it, I seem to understand that it is something that you shouldn't force.'

'Too right it's not,' said Carmel. Her anger had begun to flow from her tongue. 'I'm not some charity case that needs your sympathy Michael. I need a man and you are still just a boy!' She turned to walk away from him. She paused briefly awaiting his hand to stop her from going. But it never came. Michael held his tongue and his pride tightly. He wanted to argue his case – he wanted to show that he was not just a boy – that he knew his feelings and should not be sorry for them. However, his argument would hold no purpose or pleasure to Carmel, and so he let it slide.

He saw her hesitation as she walked away from him. He took a step back so that he could not reach her.

'Whenever you do find the person that you love Michael... don't be a fool; tell them.' Carmel did not turn around to say these words. Instead she walked on towards the town. It was not long

until she had walked out of his life completely.

Chapter 18

Grace was only working for half of the day. With the weekend approaching, her father had arranged with Ms Ryann for Grace to have the afternoon off from her work at the library. Grace had been spending more time at the library of late. Even when she was not expected to tend to the stalls, Grace would fill her day with meaningless chores. It was a welcomed distraction if nothing else; her home reminded her of her sister, Cara, and the loss she had suffered. Thinking it best for Cara to recover with her husband David, Grace had not visited recently but had sent her love with a bunch of flowers and a sweet card. The few lines she had scribbled inside had proved the most awkward of notes, seeing that she had never tried to capture so much feeling in so few words before. Knowing that it would be better to talk it through with her sister, Grace decided that she would have to visit her that evening.

The morning had brought no secrets with it; the beginning of the day had played out like any other. A handful of people had strolled into the library, browsed at several books and then left with a select few. No conversations were made and certainly no distractions were had. The human traffic just proceeded about its course and passed right on through. Shifting through aisles, with eyes keenly watching the few people that occupied them, it had not occurred to Grace that she did not read that often anymore, as the initial luxury and indulgence had soon been lost in the wide selection available. She no longer knew what she craved for, or what text would satisfy her the most. And for this reason, she chose nothing at all. After all, it was near impossible to please an appetite that did not know what it truly hungered for. So instead, with time, Grace's desires began to starve and the petals of her passion wilted and fell to the floor.

Ms Ryann had agreed to tend to the front desk for the afternoon, and Grace had made sure that all the returned books had been noted and placed back in their stalls. She smiled at Ms Ryann as she passed. The woman intrigued her. In all her time she had never seen the lady tire of any text. She was often found reading and always completely enthralled in whatever the book was. Granted, she had a shrewd and critical eye for any substandard work and was not shy with her scornful judgment, but even then she would just return to a book that had captured her heart before. It did not bother her that the pages held no mystery to her, that she knew what came next, as her emotions always surfaced as if she was reading the book for the very first time. Grace envied her tutor for that. Grace knew she was ripe for the picking and society - with its relentless demands - insisted that she be married soon. Society, however, was as foreign to Grace as a Camel are to snow. It never occurred to her that she had only had a fleeting relationship with society itself, and all that she knew about it had been tossed at her by her father. But why was she not to trust his review? The few scraps of life she had picked up – on the few times she had been left alone to her own devices – had not convinced her of any resemblance to the worlds she had read about in countless novels. The *real* world simply did not work out the way it so often did within the well-thumbed pages of romance and adventure. Every day she watched childhood friends grow older and settle down; she saw people marry for position rather than passion. Stood completely alone and among the timeless works of a thousand authors, Grace realised that maybe it had become time for her to settle her feud with society.

Passing through the heavy oak doors of the library, Grace entered the town. The sun was suspiciously low in the sky and a thick cloud hung overhead. Her hands clutched at a few books she had promised David she would deliver to him that evening, and it was then that she would take the opportunity to speak with her sister. But first she had to survive the lunchtime rush. Orplow was always busy in the afternoon and the markets came to life in that panicked hour where passing trade increased. The passing people remained polite in their rejection of the trader's keen attention and kept about their private business. Trying desperately not to lock eyes with any of the traders, everyone looked as if they had somewhere to go – somewhere they belonged – and were all in a rush to get there. Of the two sexes it was mostly the gentlemen that would cast their eye over Grace, drinking in the striking shape that she now inhabited. She was beautiful, but it was a beauty displayed more than it was realised as she always dressed with decorum rather than intent. She had the face of an angel; with the widest and most innocent pair of eyes that the town had ever witnessed. However, it was exactly these enchanting instruments of sight that failed to see the young man that had stopped dead in his tracks at the mere sight of her.

Pausing only to adjust her grip on the books she was carrying, Grace walked through the tide of destined people and made her way towards her father. As usual, he was stood near his car by the main gates of the town. Connell bumped and rattled in the driver's seat as the fiery engine struggled to turn over. By no mistake, Raegan Darby looked his finest as he walked the few steps that parted him and his daughter.

'Dear Grace' declared Raegan, his arms open wide. 'Well don't we have quite the afternoon planned for you?' His moustache raised at the tips as his lips cut a wild smile.

'Aren't I the lucky one' smiled Grace with mockingly, not making it clear whether she really needed an answer. She always hated being the centre of attention and grew uncomfortable when fussed over.

'Lucky?' blurted Raegan. 'I suppose you are… especially to have such a focussed father like me. You know I have your best interests at heart in all that I do, and I think I may have wielded my magic once more.' His smile was all-knowing and smug. It made Grace's skin crawl.

'And what would this great act be then father?' Grace had already made her way into the carriage of the car, not realising that she had shut the door firmly behind her.

'Oh… just you wait my dearest' said Raegan as he feigned a smile. He tugged at the door and stumbled into his chair. 'You will be grateful for my endeavours, I'm sure of it. But sit tight as the big reveal will come this evening.' He placed a heavy hand on her knee. Tenderness was never within his reach, or his voice for that matter. 'Dear Grace, I've felt that you've been missing something of late and I believe I may have solved your little problem. We can't be shy about this. Time and opportunity are nipping at our heels young Grace...' He looked at his pocket watch as if working to a deadline. '...Let's not allow them to pass us by.'

The car roared as Connell's fat foot hit the floor. The wheel shook in his hands as he locked his thick fingers around it.

'I can't wait' said Grace reluctantly as the car rolled on up towards the manor house. The cloud was lower now and a slight drizzle of rain began to peck at the carriage roof.

As the car rolled up to the manor house, the usual procession greeted them. The scullery maids, footmen, housekeeper and butler all graced the rain as it moulded their uniforms damply to their thin frames. Each wore a cold smile beneath squinted eyes as the master of the house walked past. Grace was almost embarrassed to warrant such attention and allowed her head to dip slightly as she entered the grand doorway. The hallway was warm and the crackle of a roaring fire could be heard from the lobby. The house was dark despite the hour, as the clouds loomed overhead and grey skylight broke through the windows and dressed the floors. But such shadows began to cower beneath the many lamps that were being lit by the housekeeper as she bustled past.

Grace placed the books down on the side table. The brown paper she had wrapped them in had become a knot of pulp from the rain. She flicked this into a nearby bin and dabbed at the books with a towel. The pages were fine and the covers had only the slightest hint of water marks.

'Come now, Grace' declared Raegan. 'Let us not waste time on those books. I have a guest arriving soon that you will be delighted to meet. Go upstairs and I will have the maids come and fix you up.'

'Who am I supposed to be meeting?' said Grace. Her voice did not hide the blend of nerves and discomfort.

'Don't you worry about that for now. I shall do the necessary introductions. Just be sure to look your finest.' Raegan issued Grace up the stairs and walked off into the lobby. The excited skip to his step concerned Grace. She despised his intentions and feared with all her soul what lay in wait for her that evening.

However, before preparing to meet her suitor, Grace decided to go and visit her dear sister Cara. She had been awfully shy of late and hated the fact that her sister may have felt let down by her absence. The truth of the matter was that Grace did not know what words she would need to comfort her sister, and so had left this chore to the one man who loved her more than anyone else. David had been Cara's rock in recent times and had not left her side for a moment. But his friendly face hid the true hatred that simmered beneath the surface of his silk like skin. In fear that the truth would cripple her further, David had never told Cara the exact events of that tragic day, and in turn shouldered the hatred of her father alone.

Cara was sat on the porch as Grace approached. She was in her wicker wheel-chair and sheltered from the rain that beat the earth before her. Grace's umbrella felt heavy in her delicate hands as the clouds drained themselves above her. The droplets were thick and fast – pounding on the thin canvas that tried in vain to protect her. Having re-wrapped the books for David, she now clutched them to her chest once more, and though he could not be seen, he was undoubtedly nearby.

'Good afternoon sister' Grace shouted. The rain was loud between them and greyed the air. 'I am sorry I haven't visited you recently. I do hope you are well.'

'Is that you Grace?' cried Cara. She struggled to see through the water that curtained her porch. 'What are you doing in the rain? You'll catch yourself a death of cold. Get inside you fool.' Her voice was cheerful and inviting. Grace saw her warm smile as she broke through the water and stood soaking wet on her porch.

'Just look at you' smiled Cara. 'What will your suitor think?' Cara's smile edged into a knowing smirk. She had heard the whispers of preparation from the staff and knew that her father must be up to his tricks once more.

'How did you know?' said Grace startled that people would be aware of her business before even she was. Always hating a fuss, she instantly felt nervous from the expectations of others. 'Do you really think that is what father has in store for me?'

'It wouldn't surprise me Grace' replied Cara as her eyes flickered towards the manor house. 'Although I haven't seen father since the accident, I seriously doubt that he has shed his coat in that time. He's driven by an agenda that is far from selfless, so don't be fooled by his charity... there's a personal gain in it for him mark my words. To a man like him, virtue is far from its own reward.' Her face framed the anger in her words. Grace had rarely seen her sister with such distaste before. The expression passed as quickly as a rain drop and soon enough Cara was wearing her sincerest of smiles.

'Enough about me' said Grace allowing her hand to touch Cara's. Her fingers were cold from the exposure and Grace knew she must have been sat outside for some time. 'How are you? Let's get you inside in the warm.' Grace winced at the taste of the patronising tone that had left her tongue. She tried a different tact. 'Come now, the cold has got my cockles pleading for a cup of your tea.'

'Of course' said Cara shaking her head. 'Where are my manners? Please, come inside we'll get you warm. David... put the kettle on my dear, we have a guest.' Cara placed her hands on the outer rim of her wheels but before she could move herself forward, David came out of the house and stood behind his wife.

'Good afternoon Grace' said David with a soft smile as he gripped the wheel chair firmly. 'Did you call, darling? Let's get you inside from the cold.' He did not wait for a reply before he wheeled Cara into their home. Her hands fell into her lap loosely.

Inside the house, Grace could see that the place was immaculate. David looked tired and had no doubt maintained the house to this impeccable standard. He placed Cara neatly to the dining table, and tended to the stove as he filled the kettle and prepared the tea cups. Grace took a seat next to her sister, shifting her chair to the side a little so that she could face her. The dry wood creaked and squealed on the tiles. The table was set for guests and Grace could not help but wonder when the last time the couple had entertained anyone. For a couple that had always been comfortable in each other's company, it concerned Grace that they remained so poised and in wait for guests.

'So...' said Cara as she patted Grace's lap excitedly. '... Are you excited about tonight? You may get to meet your prince charming!'

'Please' scoffed Grace. 'I seriously doubt father will get it right twice. He struck gold with David, and I fear his luck may have run dry.'

'But what if it hasn't? Are you ready for a man? I can tell you a few tricks if you wish.' Cara's voice was tainted by mock appetite. The truth was, since her accident she had not had the desire to lay with her husband at all. Her once ardent lust had been quashed as she found herself completely undesirable. Poor David had not the heart to force himself upon her despite the aching in his loins. Numbed and defeated, she failed to see just how much he still wanted her.

'Sister… honestly' said Grace as she blushed a deep crimson colour. 'I would not give myself to any man after one evening, so I'm sure I have plenty of time to master the arts. Anyway, I thought it was up to him to take the lead on such an event?'

'Ha…' Cara's laugh was partly in mockery. 'You're half right my sweet sister. You see, men are not different from any other animal. For instance, take a horse. Now they'll gladly visit any drinking hole to quench their thirst, but I assure you they will not return to it if the waters are not clean, crisp and full of life.' Confident in her metaphors but unable to hear the penny drop, Cara tried another. 'Remember, a laden sack of raw potatoes may boast the same fruit, but they will not be as inviting as those that are roasted properly.' Her laugh was playful and her eyes flashed with memories of her early years with David. Visions of his spent body strewn across the bed sheets filled her head; she could almost smell him. She smiled to herself as Grace held a face full of shock.

'Really?' said Grace. She was beginning to feel young and naïve. 'What do I do to keep him? That is if I want to keep him at all.'

'Ah, there in lays the rub my dear. I'm afraid any whore-house can equip a girl with the tricks to satisfy a man; to master his piece as it were. But the real art, my sweet sister, is causing him to make love to you. Sex is only a function, whereas love…' She looked at her husband preparing the tea. '…Well that's something that no one can invent.'

'Great' replied Grace as she rolled her eyes. 'So I just embrace the act until it feels real, do I?' Her voice held no anger but a hint of deflated realism.

'Not at all' said Cara softly, 'you never have to give yourself to anyone that you don't truly want. Remember, a true man would wait an eternity for you. Only the rampant rush, whereas a man in control knows how to time it just right.' The kettle began to whistle on the stove. 'Anyway, we ramble on. David, where is this bloody tea?'

✵✵✵

'Arnold Farrington, I presume?' Raegan held out his hand as the man took it firmly and shook it with executive intent. The man was the son of Lord Reginald Farrington – a great land owner and farmer known affectionately by friends as Reggie. Raegan Darby had been at loggerheads with Lord Farrington for decades as they had carved up the farmland of the southern counties. And while it was thought that both had similar kingdoms, Raegan was only too aware that it was dear old Reggie that had the means to continue his empire; he had a son, and heir. However, Lord Farrington was twenty years Raegan's senior and was famously seen to lack the hunger and appetite of his younger counterpart. Yet the tide was turning, and the young ambitious Arnold was poised to take over the mantle from his frail father. Raegan feared that with no apparent heir to his own kingdom, it would be wise to place a tainted olive branch into the soft delicate hands of his daughter Grace.

'It is a pleasure to meet with you, Mr Darby' replied Arnold. 'You appear exactly as my father described. And I must say, through all your venomous duels he did retain the utmost respect for you. In fact, he owes the last two decades of his life to you, for it was your apparent lust for competition that drove the old man to fight on for so long.' Arnold's voice was cold of any gratitude. He knew that he lay in wait to a fortune and had grown frustrated by his father's drawn out demise. Raegan watched the man stood with a rigid back and puffed out chest. There was no warmth in his face and his hair clung to his forehead as it receded sharply at the sides. His slight frame leant to the right, propped by a wooden cane that supported his damaged leg. It was widely known that Arnold had suffered an injury when he took to learning the tools of his father's trade too early. The exact details of the incident differed from each person telling it, but the result was always the same. Whether he had been bludgeoned by a rake he had blindly stepped on, or had felt the wrath of the whirring blades of the mill, Arnold had severed the muscles in his right leg and would now always walk with a limp, and aided by his cane.

'How is old Reggie these days?' smiled Raegan well aware of the old man's illness. 'I do hope he's fighting fit.'

'He is of good spirit sir… that is for sure' replied Arnold as his chin lowered slightly. 'However, I tend to speak for my father these days. Like any son, I have the best interests for the family at heart.'

'Don't we all' boasted Raegan with a hearty laugh and a distasteful pat to Arnold's shoulder. He was already turning and pouring two heavy sets of brandy into two glasses and failed to see his guest struggle to keep his balance behind him. 'Here…' said Raegan turning to greet his guest. 'Let us drink to the night ahead.'

'That we shall, sir' replied Arnold who was grateful of the fiery drink. It drowned the slight humiliation that had coloured his pale cheeks. 'But tell me Raegan' continued Arnold with a wheezy gasp, 'When do I get the pleasure of meeting your fine daughter? I've heard from many an old wife that she is most beautiful, and yet I can't find a man who can describe her at all. Have you kept her hidden for my eyes alone?'

'Ha…' Raegan drained his glass and poured another. 'Grace is quite the sight that is true. As for the absent reviews from the men of this town, I can assure you that that is to your benefit and nothing more. A lady's virtue can get tainted by the eyes of others; as whether green with envy or red with lust, they tend to cause the mouth to offer words and descriptions not befitting of what they see. No man has described my daughter, Mr Farrington, simply because no man has the words to.' He raised his glass triumphantly.

'Well Raegan, I don't know what to say' smiled Arnold as he chinked his glass with his host's. They filled their throats with the liquor and let its heat fill the pits of their empty stomachs. Raegan cast his arm around his guest tightly and poured out two more measures. Feeling the embrace, Arnold rocked slightly in Raegan's grip.

Upstairs, Grace felt the pull of the maids as they tugged and tightened the strings of her dress. She had no need to shave inches off her waist with a crippling garter and instead let the robes just fall and settle over her fine physique. The whirlwind of maids whooshed around her as her outfit began to take shape. Grace always hated the idea of making a targeted effort to look nice, but she took pride in her appearance and would have been much more at ease if she was allowed to dress herself. However, reminiscent of her childhood days, her father was most insistent that the maids be tasked with dressing her for that particular evening. No doubt the outfit would be to his design and would match the interests of the suitor perfectly, and Grace felt less than pretty when considering her father serving her up to her suitor like a choice piece of meat drizzled in his favourite dressing. With glazed eyes, she took to her dressing table and looked at herself in the large mirror. She did what little make up her pretty face required as her hair stood on end, balanced like a high haystack as a wild flower broached the side. She took a deep breath as she stared at the beautiful girl that filled the mirror. For a moment, she hardly recognised herself.

Downstairs the dinner was being laid out. The tables were being set and Fiona Darby was sitting with Imogen. The young girl still required a lot of attention, and Fiona had found herself to be the girl's permanent carer. They sat at each other's side and exchanged small talk and laughter, opposite two empty chairs where David and Cara could have sat if they had been invited. Like a proud bishop assessing his congregation, Raegan was stood by the head of the table and was deep in conversation with his guest. They were both seven sheets to the wind; now feeling the full effects of the bottle of brandy they had shared. Their mouths salivated in sync as they now craved the food that was being placed out in front of them. The growls of their stomachs were almost audible as their eyes feasted on the fine cuts of hot, roasted meat that sat before them.

'Grace should be joining us shortly' slurred Raegan as he rested his hand on the corner of the table. His legs were weak with the drink and his head grew heavier by the second; the pulse in his head boomed to the pace of the clock's second hand. Struggling to turn his head, Arnold had little time to offer a reply before the young lady entered the dining room. Seeing her, he drained a long glass of ice cold water in an attempt to cool his tongue and steady his eyes. Forcing his blurred eyes to focus, Arnold saw Grace for the first time. The walls and pictures around her were hazy, but her image was as clean as fresh winter snow. She was the purest present he had ever received, and he could not wait to unwrap it. Well aware that her beauty was leagues above his own and – while intimidated by it – it was in this instant that he decided he would not let her truly know it. After all, he could provide for her much more than any other man could, and for that alone she would be grateful. He steadied himself on his cane as he awaited the introduction.

Grace saw the man standing at the end of the table. He looked more like one of her father's business colleagues or advisors than the young buck she was expecting. He was dressed properly to the occasion and, while handsome, his face wore an age that was far older than her own; he looked tired and stood unevenly. His thin arm was outstretched in her direction as she approached.

'Dearest Grace...' said Raegan with a rehearsed amount of pride. 'Let me introduce you to Arnold Farrington.' Raegan gestured to the man and Grace took his hand obligingly. She curtsied as he bowed his head. Looking up from his bowed head, he had a sincere smile and Grace instantly felt safe with him. There was a sense of security and place about the man that he exuded like a warm fire. Glad not to feel any threat from him, she allowed herself to ease into the moment as her heart relaxed and her breathing steadied.

'It's a pleasure to meet you, sir' said Grace having taken a deep breath. Her nerves were settled and while her passion was not aflame, at least the man did not frighten her as much as she had feared.

'I assure you kind lady, I am wholly selfish in the act. For the fact of the matter is that the pleasure is entirely mine' replied Arnold with a candid smile. His mouth was thin and his upper lip was lined with a sharp moustache. Grace could feel the man's wrist grow limp in her hand and she placed her arm back by her side. The smell of brandy was prominent and no doubt the poor soul had been fuelled by her father. Given his intoxicated state, Grace knew she must be charitable with her judgement of him for his mind may not be completely his own this evening.

She looked around the dining hall for no other reason than to allow herself not to stare at the man who had grabbed her attention. She was sure she could feel his narrow, dark, insipid eyes burrowing into her blushing cheeks, but every time she looked he seemed occupied with something else. In time he would turn to look at her, but not for long.

Chapter 19

It looked like it was going to rain. The morning was grey and the land lay flat and damp from the sodden night before. Oscar could feel his chest as he wheezed his way up the hill. His fingers were sweating from the thick gloves his mother had insisted that he wear. It was Friday and he and Michael were heading into town for a day to remember. Or forget, given the amount they planned to drink. Once he had finally got to the cottage, he rapped his knuckles at the front door. A dull hollow thud bounced on the walls within. Impatiently, Oscar cupped his head with his clammy hands and peered through the window. The lights were off inside and there was no sign of life in the kitchen.

'Boo!'

Oscar almost blacked out as he banged his head onto the glass that had steamed under his heavy breath. He turned rubbing his brow to see Michael roaring laughing in front of him.

'You fecking prat!' boomed Oscar as he nursed his pride more than his bump.

'Oh come now you little girl' smiled Michael. 'You're late anyway.' Seeing his friend needed an explanation, Michael offered one. 'I just walked my mother to the end of the field over there. She's on her daily mission towards the church as usual.'

Eyeing an opportunity, Oscar tried to get his own back on his roguish friend. 'You know Michael...' He licked his lips and looked around in his best attempt to be casual. He played it like a wolf in sheep's clothing. '...People are starting to talk about your mother and her *relationship* with the church. What with all the time she's is spending down there, and with Father Daniel being so handsome and all.' Oscar was walking in front of his friend as they walked in the direction of the town.

'Shut up...' laughed Michael. 'By people, you mean you and your bloody mom. And anyway, Father Daniel is as appetising as a bowl full of dung on a full belly. My mother would rather starve to death than eat from that troth, believe me.' Michael always felt the need to protect his mother. It never occurred to him that, despite the hatred he held for his father, Michael had never pictured his mother with anyone else.

'She's like a moth to a flame Michael...' Oscar continued with a smirk. '...Every day she's drawn to the place.'

'Is that right? Well it's you that'll get burnt' taunted Michael. 'Especially if you keep making bad my mother's solid name. Anyway, we both know why she's always there. I've told you every time... she's praying for my father.'

'I know pal...' said Oscar. 'Or so she tells you!' He skipped a few steps ahead as Michael attempted to plant his right boot onto his buttocks. The young men laughed as the moment passed.

They walked through the fields towards town. The surrounding hills loomed overhead and leaned the land towards the travelling party. Michael held out his arms as the long grass brushed through his fingers – tiny droplets of water flicked at his hands. This was God's country.

On this rare occasion that both of the men found themselves with a day off from their labours, they had planned to fill it by emptying as many tankards as possible. It had been some time since the two friends had been able to chink glasses and catch up, as life came with its commitments and age itself brought with it less time for anything else.

'So... tell me' said Oscar. He was swinging a wet branch through the grass in front of him. 'What ever happened to that fine filly Carmel? You two looked great together.'

'It just didn't work pal' said Michael. It surprised him how talking about the girl failed to bring any sad memories or regret back to him.

'Work?' declared Oscar with mild shock. 'Work is what we do all day just so we may have the slightest sniff of lying with a lady like that.'

'Exactly' sighed Michael. 'Emotions come without effort right? And when they do, it's up to us to deal with them. Thing is, I'd none to deal with.'

'You had two massive ones to deal with more like' mocked Oscar. 'That lady has two of the biggest breasticles that I've ever seen.'

'Well, you'll never got to see them... so shut it' Michael allowed himself to gloat in is friend's envy.

'What were they like?' said Oscar. His voice had a trace of desperate pleading and his mouth hung open as if ready to cup a nipple.

'Are you bloody serious? I'm not fuelling your nightly fancies you grubby pervert.'

'Come on...' Oscar stood open armed, his hands cupped and outstretched. 'How did they fall? I bet they tumbled out of that bra. They were like boulders after all.' Oscar stretched his arms wider as if he was struggling to carry something. 'I'm guessing, based on the fact you didn't stay with her, they sagged right? I'm right aren't I? Like a pair of droopy fish eyes at her side!' Oscar bounced with excitement. Seeing his shift in balance, Michael nudged him down the hill. His laughter echoed through the valley as he watched his fat friend roll head first down the muddy hill. Water and dirt kicked up at his side as his well-fed frame ploughed down the hillside. His body flapped and bumped until it came to a final stop, punctuated by a firm splat.

'You fecking maniac' barked Oscar as he spat mud from his mouth. His pants were filthy and caked in soil. 'I thought we were heading into town? I look like my wife has left me and I've been living rough for a month.'

'You're not even married' smiled Michael.

'And it will stay that way if I present myself like this!'

'Calm down pal. It takes as much time to think as it does to panic. Let's think this through.' Michael smiled at his friend as he staggered to his feet and eventually stood drenched in front of him. 'Look, take them off and we'll get them cleaned up in town. I'll go and buy you a pair in the meantime as well. How does that sound?'

'A new pair?' beamed Oscar. 'God bless you Michael. Are you sure?'

'Of course… I've wrecked the ones you're wearing, so it's only fair. Here, give me those as you'll catch a death of cold.'

'I'll freeze my arse off before we even get close to town' said Oscar panicking.

'Come now' issued Michael. 'It is wet but it's not that cold. You used to run bare arsed through these fields as a child.'

'I had a little less to show off back then' boasted Oscar. Michael smiled widely as he wagged his little finger at his shy friend.

Michael held Oscar's pants as they walked into town, and as they were passing through the last field they reached the town wall. The lunchtime crowds had clustered in the streets and began to starburst on their own individual journeys. Among them the traders were on song and in full volume. Ambitiously, they reached out for passing trade despite the looming bad weather. The streets were still wet from the night's showers and the cobbles still housed small puddles of dank, dirty water in the gaps between them.

'Psst… Michael' the voice came from behind him. He turned, not realising his friend had not kept up the same pace.

'What are you doing now?' said Michael warmly. Oscar was crouched behind the wall and was clutching at his shirt trying to pull it over his bare knees.

'I can't go out there' snapped Oscar in a whispered rant. His face was flushed and his eyes flickered from left to right.

'Don't panic… the tailor's just one street away. No one will see.'

'Well I am panicking. We didn't think this through. I'll be a laughing stock, and you know how rumours spread in this bloody town.'

Michael smiled at the irony. 'Look, I'll take these pants to the tailors and get them to size you out a new pair.'

'Thank you… you're a top friend.' Oscar stood slightly to embrace his friend. The cold winds chilled and whipped at his behind.

Then Michael saw her. Panicking, he pushed his half naked friend back down behind the wall and stepped forward. Seeing the beautiful girl in front of him froze his feet to the ground. Despite the time they had spent apart. Despite the distance that had separated them. Michael knew he was looking at Grace. She stood by the doorway of the library and held a parcel close to her chest. Michael's chest was beating furiously, imploring his feet to rush to her and take her in his strong embrace. But instead he stood and watched her. Her hair was as brown as oak and framed the most wonderful of faces. Her cheeks were rosy from the gentle winds, but her eyes were wide and bright. Michael did not realise that his hand had floated up by his side and gently reached out for the beauty before him. He wanted to say that he had missed her, that he had waited for her each night by the lake. However, he stood still. He stood and admired the sight that blinded him.

And as quickly as she had stopped his heart, she was gone and the world around him started up again. The pace of the people seemed to have quickened. Their steps became thunderous and rained down on the cobbles. Michael had to steady his breathing. He turned to check on Oscar. He was sat hidden behind the wall — only his trembling goose pimpled thighs could be seen poking out. As he turned back to the town Michael could not see Grace anymore.

But he knew she had come from the library. Clutching at the pants that belonged to his bare-assed friend, Michael tipped his flat cap down over his brow and pushed through the crowd. A light shower had opened up and the water kissed at his hands as he patted the people that he passed. The doors to the library offered shelter from the rain as Michael stood and looked back to where he had left his friend. He could not see Oscar as the rain was pouring down now, but he could see that one of the bushes were shaking more that those surrounding it. Reasoning that it was simply the wind breaking from around the wall, Michael heaved open the library door and entered the hall. Shaking himself like a dog that had just came in from a storm, Michael looked about him. He did not know what he was looking for – yet he was certain that the girl was Grace. Visions of her at work flooded into his head, saturating the dry years they had spent apart. He allowed himself to see the young girl growing into the beauty that he had just seen. He saw the girl busied and distracted by life. He saw her walking home, and he saw how she had never chosen the path that led to the lake. Feeling the fool, Michael sighed deeply and left the library.

Outside the heavens sobbed. Thick droplets pelted at the ground and dampened the shoes of the passing tide of people. Michael felt like the air had been forced from his chest – he felt like he had been holding his breath for a dream that held no life in it. The thought of her living in wait for him was a nonsense – a nonsense that had allowed him to imagine them together. The thought of her had guided every decision he had ever made, every road he had taken, and every relationship he had allowed to fail. Michael felt as though he had paused for someone who had clearly moved on. Suddenly Michael remembered. Oscar; Michael had forgotten about him. He must be freezing he thought. Driven by guilt, Michael burst into a light sprint as he headed for the tailors.

Oscar was drenched by the time he saw Michael return through the town. Initially he had been glad of the rain as it soothed the stinging bite of the nettles that Michael had pushed him into. For minutes he had hidden in the bush and frantically rubbed the pulled damp grass onto his blistered buttocks, but they only satisfied as much as scratching an itch. Seeing his friend approach he noted how Michael's expression had an amused apology etched all over it. He was shaking his head and shrugging his shoulders as he walked across the town square, and he ran the last few yards as a token gesture of haste.

'I'm sorry pal' said Michael. He rapped his fingers on a parcel he was carrying. 'Here, I have a gift for you.' He tossed the parcel to Oscar, who – being forced to catch it – bravely exposed his genitals to the bitter elements.

'Sweet Jesus…' laughed Michael standing dead in his tracks. 'I didn't know button mushrooms were in season.'

'Feck off' scoffed Oscar as he tore at the paper parcel. He pulled at the string and threw it to the feet of Michael, who bent and picked up the wiry piece of fibre.

'Here you go,' smirked Michael. He hanged the string down in front of him and in line with Oscar's groin. 'And there was me wasting money on pants when this would suffice'.

'Very funny' said Oscar with a sting of ingratitude. 'But you're right. You may as well have saved your money. What the hell are these?' Oscar held up a pair of wide legged trousers that were part of a large one button sack suit. They were designed for the stout man and demanded the use of braces.

'What?' replied Michael, his arms open wide as if to catch something. 'The tailor said that these were at the height of fashion. To quote him… *we're swinging towards the conservative and these pants are the most fitting to the trend*' said Michael in a posh voice. 'He sounded *exactly* like that. And who am I to question a professional?'

'Well thanks for the fashion lesson… but these are not fitting anything!' Oscar held them aloft. The wind brushed through them and they expanded like a ship's main sail. Oscar did well not to take off. 'They need braces Michael… I don't have braces.'

'Well you'll just have to hold them up.' Michael turned and walked back into town. He knew his friend would crack eventually. The pants were fine, if in fact they were several sizes too big. But then Michael did order them that way. He had to stifle his laughter as he looked back to see his friend grabbing at the waist of the oversized pants. He skipped as the hems dragged under his shoes.

'Wait up!' shouted Oscar as he tried in vain to style out his predicament.

The Spread Eagle was almost full and about to add two more to its occupancy. Michael walked in first and went immediately to the bar, allowing Oscar to scurry over to a free table and shuffle his long trousers underneath. He grouped the surplus material into his crotch and clamped his legs together. The rain had drawn in a heavier crowd than usual, but the regulars still stood anchored to their chosen port of calls. Cocking an ear to the crowd, Oscar listened in hoping to grab some gossip to feed his mother with. However, only the murmur of light complaints surrounding the weather dominated most conversations – a slow drone humming through the grog shop like a dragged barrel. Michael thought his friend looked like he needed to relieve himself when he returned with the drinks. Oscar's legs were locked together and his knees bounced excitedly.

'Are you alright?' asked Michael as he sat at the table. 'It's just that you're squirming like an un-potty trained child. I can take you if you like, but I'm sure as hell not shaking it for you.' Michael took a long draw on his Guinness. It was probably the first afternoon drink he had had for months, and it hit the mark.

'Of course I'm not alright. I'm wearing a pair of pants the size of a bloody bed sheet, and now I'm sat amongst some of the roughest, violent men in town.' Oscar almost cleared half of his drink as he took his first gulp.

'Well don't worry' said Michael reassuringly. 'I'm here and I'll go to the bar all evening. These guys will be blind drunk before we've even had our third. Anyway, I have some news… guess who I saw today?'

'When?' asked Oscar. 'I've been with you the whole day.'

'When you were torturing the daisies with your pimpled ass…' laughed Michael. 'Go on, have a guess.'

'Jesus Mike, it could be anyone… any clues?'

'I'll just tell you. You're rate of drinking is far faster than your rate of thinking, and you'll probably fill those pants by the time you got it right.' Michael paused and saw that he friend was too keen on the answer to take any offence.

'It was Grace. I saw Grace today.'

'Who?' Oscar could not have looked less interested. He raised his glass and almost finished the remains.

'Grace… Grace Darby.' The mere sound of her name brought bumps to Michael's skin. He saw them freckle his thick forearm as he reached for his glass.

'Raegan Darby's daughter?' asked Oscar. He wiped his mouth with his sleeve. 'I've not heard anything about her for years.'

'More like your mother hasn't' scoffed Michael. He always enjoyed the flustered face of Oscar whenever anyone bad mouthed his mother.

'Either way…' Oscar avoided the bait. 'What was she up to? Did she look well?'

'Very well' replied Michael with his widest smile. His eyes lifted to the side as he recalled the image. 'She looked as well as life itself.'

'Given our surroundings Mike, and the life in these old boys, that's not a massively healthy image.'

'Well, maybe I'm as drunk on her as these boys are on the grog. But I have to say that she looked just like I had last seen her.'

'She looked like an eight year old girl?' Oscar was choosing to get his own back for the jibe against his mother. 'Either she has not grown at all, or you were eyeing up a midget.'

'Piss off' replied Michael. 'It was Grace.'

'How do you know for sure?' Oscar emptied his glass past his thick lips.

'You just know' replied Michael. His voice was hardly a whisper as he thought back onto the girl.

'Anyway,' Oscar broke the reflection. 'So what? What does it change?'

'Everything' smiled Michael. 'It means she has not been carted off to some cretin of a suitor and that she's still in town.'

'Michael, if that's the case then she's been in town for the last ten years or so. What does seeing her change?'

'I know she works in the library.' Michael was thinking out loud. 'I popped in earlier and saw on a cork board that she was listed as a librarian there. So, I was thinking of going inside to speak with her.'

'Go for it Romeo' beamed Oscar as he raised his empty glass. Michael saw that his friend was more interested in a refill. He stood up and made his way to the bar. Michael knew he had to make contact with Grace, and quickly. He had waited for too long. Returning to where Oscar was sat, Michael placed his empty hands firmly on the table.

'Come with me. I have a plan.' Michael's smile was at its deal-sealing best.

'What, now?' Oscar was far from keen on the idea of bracing the outside so soon. 'We've only just got in here. I thought we were going to spend the afternoon getting ourselves completely blotted?'

'There's plenty of time for that later,' Michael was stood up straight as if he was about to leave. 'Come on, we're heading back to the library.'

'But she's not even there Mike.' Oscar saw that his friend was already leaving the pub. Hoisting up his pants and holding his head down low, Oscar followed Michael back out into the storm.

They were soon stood outside the library and, given the weather, Oscar was grateful of the shelter the doorway offered. He was completely soaked through, but Michael was too excited to notice; he jigged and fretted as he pondered his next move. The weather was still beating down behind them and the street tiles were empty of any people. Even the market traders had retreated back to their store rooms as the rainfall was thunderous as it thrashed at the ground. Thick lines of dirt broke and shattered on the ground as the cobbles were cleaned by the shower.

'What next?' Oscar was clutching at his pants. His flat cap looked like it had melted on his head as it sagged down the sides of his dripping brow.

'One of us goes in' said Michael. He seemed breathless as he peered into the hallway through the main door.

'One of us?' barked Oscar. 'So what the hell do you need me for?'

'I didn't say which one,' replied Michael turning back from the door. His voice became a soft whisper and was barely audible over the rain. 'I'm not a member of this place. So, I need you to go in and get me some books.'

'I'm not a member either,' said Oscar pleased that his involvement may be over.

'Well that's grand as well' said Michael. 'I'll need you to steal the books. You see, if you got them out, then when they're returned Grace will know who had them.'

'Isn't that the whole point?' Oscar was not sharing his friend's enthusiasm.

'No... the whole point of a secret admirer is that they remain a secret. Initially at least.' Michael patted his friend on the shoulder. It slapped loudly on his soaked shirt. 'I saw that Ms Ryann works here as well. If she sees me in there, then there's a chance she may tell Grace and - if they notice books have been stolen - they won't need Scotland Yard to work out who pinched them.'

'I was in the same god damn class as you Michael, what's saying she won't recognise me?' Oscar was panicking a little. His face was flustered and his eyes fixed on Michael.

'Come now,' replied Michael with an attempt at reason. 'She doesn't even know you exist. When did you ever put your hand up in class?'

'She used to clip my ear twice a day' moaned Oscar. He could feel the sharp winds nipping at his earlobes.

'Well you're going in anyway. Make it a bit of payback for what she did to you all those years. You remember how she loved her books, so go in and spite her of a few.' Michael opened the heavy door. The air inside was no warmer than outside. Fretful that the sound of the rain from outside may bring someone to the doorway to check what was keeping the door ajar, Michael pushed Oscar inside, closing the door behind him. Knocking the glass slightly, Michael offered his friend a thumbs-up before running around the corner.

Skulking forward, Oscar made his way into the library. The building seemed enormous as the huge ceilings clung to the skies above. The sound of the rainfall was only a light patter from inside, and Oscar was worried that no one would understand why he was so wet. His feet squelched beneath him as he walked into the lobby. Seeing Ms Ryann walking back to the front desk, Oscar made a dash for the nearest stall, but flinging his arms in front of him caused his pants to fall to his ankles, which in turn tripped him up onto his face. Fearing his former teacher had heard the commotion, Oscar did not want to make any further racket. Instead he lay perfectly still with his pimpled buttocks staring up at the grand ceiling.

He allowed a few seconds to drag past before crawling forward. He peered through a book stand and saw that Ms Ryann was tending to a tray labelled 'Returns'. She looked occupied by her work and so Oscar felt more confident to move around. Crouching down and leaning up a wall, Oscar devised a plan. He tucked the soaked hems of the trousers into his socks. They bulged over his ankles in doughy bundles, making it look like his shoes were baking bread. He then stood up and grabbed at the first four books he could find. With not enough time to move around the library freely, he grabbed a group of books from the same shelf. Having no idea what texts he had taken, he dropped them into his pants, where his stuffed heels caught the books as they fell down his legs. Pausing to shake his pants a little, Oscar could feel some of the pages begin to cling to his sodden shins. All he needed to do now was to escape.

Oscar was nervous. It wasn't the first time he had stolen before, but usually it tended to be something edible and often scoffed before anyone could even notice it was gone. But he had no appetite for books and knew that there would be little means of excusing what he was up to if he were to be caught. Of course there was the truth but he did not always have time for that, and had no intention of paying the price attached to it. At the risk of feeling brave, he poked his head around the stall. Ms Ryann had left her desk and could be seen walking through towards the reading room. Seeing that her back was turned, Oscar clutched at the waist of his clown sized pants and made a dart for the door.

Michael was waiting patiently around the corner when he saw Oscar stumble down the steps. He was panting excitedly and looked extremely pleased with himself. Michael smirked at the sight of his friend as he waddled over to him.

'Did you do it?' Michael asked.

'Did you ever doubt me?' Oscar disappeared momentarily as he leaned into his pants. The chubby fingers of his left hand grasped the waistline of his trousers as he rummaged inside. 'Here's one...'

Michael grabbed the four books as Oscar pulled them from his pants like a magician producing a rabbit from his top hat. Oscar was smiling broadly as he enjoyed his victory.

'Travel books?' Michael was shuffling through the books as he saw the collection Oscar had gathered. Two of them discussed the artefacts of Egypt, one was a catalogue of photographs and maps from Europe and the last was an atlas.

'You didn't tell me what books to get Mike. You just told me to steal some books. Jesus, there's no pleasing you is there?' Oscar's face furrowed into a furious frown.

'No...' replied Michael looking the books over. 'They are grand, honestly. You delivered my friend, thank you.'

'That I did' smiled Oscar as he readjusted himself. 'What are you going to do with them anyway?'

Michael gazed up from the pages and smirked. 'Now that would be telling. Let's get back to the pub before those townsfolk run it dry. Come on, I owe you drink.' Michael wrapped his arm around his friend's shoulders. 'By the way, have you got a pen?'

Chapter 20

Arnold had been the complete gentleman. His manners at the table were precise and appropriate, while he only allowed himself to catch Grace's eye rather than to be seen to be staring at her. The pretty girl had been looking at him on occasion, and so he always chose the right thing to say when she was. He could see the smile on her face; it was one of gratification more than infatuation. But she was smiling nonetheless. In-between the shared glances with Grace, he had spent most of the evening nodding at her father's boisterous boasts of how the future held great times ahead for the both of them. While he did share the man's hunger, Arnold could not help but be distracted by the girl who now starred at him once more. Looking at her he nodded and cut a thin smile.

Following dinner, Arnold had asked Raegan if he would be allowed to take Grace for a walk, Raegan did not need much persuading as he practically forced the young lady's hand into that of his guests and pushed them outside into the night. The land sagged a little from the afternoon showers, and the slimy pebbles of the driveway shifted beneath their feet. Grace held her head down as she watched where she was treading. It was Arnold who broke the silence.

'You are most beautiful, young Grace.' He looked down at her as she peered up and offered a meek smile.

'Thank you Mr Farrington,' replied Grace. 'You must forgive me, as I don't know quite how to take to compliments. You see, I've not had much experience in the field of receiving them.'

'Balderdash. And please… call me Arnold.' His smile was warm. Hot enough to keep the cold at bay rather than banish it completely. 'I must apologise also. If I had known that I was to offer your first compliment, I would have tried a little harder.'

'There's no need to try at all,' issued Grace. 'A true compliment doesn't need craft or effort…' She looked out onto the fields. '…Just honesty.'

'Then honestly, Miss Darby, you are as cute as a button.' Arnold held her hand as he waited for her gratitude.

'Thank you' she muttered, slightly distracted. She had always hated the term 'cute'. It made her feel young and undesirable, and on this night it carried this exact impact when Arnold said it. However, Grace was surprised to find that in this instance she was neither angry nor upset by the remark. Instead she found a morsel of security in it. Arnold was, after all, significantly older than her and, by seeing her in this fashion, made her feel sheltered. They continued to walk until the night was thick and dull. Soon, only the sound of their own feet dragging through the lawn could be heard as Arnold walked Grace back home. Predictably, he chose not to make any rash moves and remained the perfect companion. He smiled as Grace turned and thanked him for the pleasant evening, before she retreated up the stairs to her room. Arnold watched her with intent as she made her way up to bed. Once she was out of sight he followed the sound of the roaring fire that was coming from inside the lobby. Inside, he found Raegan stood by the fireplace and was raising a glass with a member of his staff. The strange man had the posture of a bear and his grubby laugh came at the end of every sentence his master spat out.

'Raegan' declared Arnold with no concern as to who could hear his voice. His host looked at him with a victorious, if not off skew grin. 'I want to marry your daughter.'

'Then so you shall.' Raegan waved his hand as if to conjure up his magic.

***

Michael was riddled. He and Oscar had drunk almost their entire body weight in ale and were struggling to even stagger home. With one arm wrapped around his friend, Michael grasped at his books with the other. They both sang as they bounced through the fields. Singing like his next meal depended on it, Oscar sang the loudest as they reeled off an impressive repertoire of their favourite folk songs. Breaking from his friend, Michael danced and spun with his head turned to the heavens. High above them the stars pierced the thick blanket of night and shone like rebel diamonds in the sky. The land glistened under their light as the droplets of water that glazed the grass threw the stars glistening reflection back into the air.

'So,' burped Oscar, his tongue looked heavier than usual. 'What's your next move?' He punched his friend playfully on the shoulder before rolling his fists in front of his face. 'I mean with Grace?' He punched the air, and turned away not too interested in the answer. He continued to sing as he watched his friend mull over his reply.

'I'll write for her' beamed Michael.

'Write? I didn't even know you could read!' Oscar struggled to stand up straight. His legs were as stable as a sailor's stomach on their first day at sea.

'You'll see my friend. I'll do whatever it takes.'

They continued to stagger home as they reached the field that parted their paths. Michael embraced Oscar and could feel his friend's head rest tiredly on his shoulder. Oscar was practically sleepwalking and Michael realised he could not abandon him in this state so he walked his friend all the way back to his home. It was a considerable detour but at least – once inside his sanctuary – Oscar would rest peacefully. He would also be unable to see the alternate route home that Michael had now been taking for over ten years.

The extended walk sobered Michael a little. The cold air of the night had shaken him and shifted the drunken haze from his head. The great lake looked like it always had. With heavy legs, Michael slumped to the ground. The stolen books lay in his lap as he pondered his next move. The ale still raged through his veins, but his head seemed light and focussed. The waters before him sat peacefully as slight ripples burst from the reeds. A soft wind whispered through the night and all Michael could hear was his heart thumping at his chest. He emptied his head of the doubt that had clouded his thoughts earlier that day. He ignored the idea that Grace had never met with him at the lake since that fateful night, and like a man hanging on for dear life he stretched out his hands as if to push the fear of rejection away from his very fingertips.

Rustling inside his pocket, he found the pen that Oscar had pilfered from a slumbering patron back at the pub. Opening up the cover of the first book at hand, he took a deep breath and began to write. Not pausing to think of the words that flowed from his fingers, he scribbled them down as quickly as they flashed inside his mind. His hands were steady and his breath was caught by the moment. Concentrating only on her image, Michael's heart galloped away from him and carried him through the fields, over the garden walls, through the manor house, and finally up into her room. He pictured her sleeping peacefully, bathed in the brightest light. Breathing out, Michael finished and lay back onto the cold grass. He laughed excitedly as the drink flowed from his legs back into his head. It was not long until sleep was fast upon him. He did not move a muscle until the day broke at dawn.

***

The following morning Grace was late for work. Her father had insisted that, over breakfast, they discuss every detail of her evening with Arnold Farrington. Unable to speak for herself, she was unsure of what filled her mouth more; the thin slivers of warm toast or the countless words and opinions offered by her father. She sat there almost in complete silence as her father seemed to answer every question that he asked her.

'Do you like Arnold? Of course you do,' he had declared to all that were dining.

'What do you think of him? He is perfect for you isn't he? I thought so', was another of Raegan's redundant remarks. Despite not agreeing with her father completely, Grace did find a certain charm in the man. He was more worldly wise than she was used to and, with his age, a little more mature and set than the boys that still skipped and staggered through the town. He was ready for the bigger picture; for settling down and raising a family. And while Grace did not know if she was ready herself, she was fully aware what those around her expected. However, she would at least try to fall in love with the idea – if not in love with the man who was offering it.

Nevertheless, Grace did not have time for thoughts of fancy this morning as she was running late for work. She could already picture Ms Ryann's thunderous expression – the blood rushing to her pale cheeks like a simmering volcano. While Ms Ryann never shouted at Grace, she would always take the tact of showing her disappointment in a ferociously silent manner. Her cold shoulder would smoulder within Grace's moral fibre and would always set her sense of guilt ablaze. Knowing what to expect, Grace prayed for something different.

However, the library was just as she had imagined. Heaving herself through the main doors, Grace made a dash for the lobby and fell at her desk. She kicked her bag under the table and sat awaiting the scornful eye of Miss Ryann. She could see her now tending to the stalls. This was clearly one of Grace's tasks of the day, but having been late it would appear that Miss Ryann wanted to further highlight her poor punctuality by taking on her duties. Grace afforded herself a smile as she watched the woman thump the books back onto their respective shelves. It was clear to her that Ms Ryann was aware that Grace had arrived as her actions had increased in both volume and effort. Returning now, Grace had to admire how the woman had crafted the ability of not looking at someone, into a fine art.

'Ms Ryann, I'm so sorry.' Grace's apology was genuine. She could have further justified her lateness by running her father through the mud, but decided there was very little tact in that. She decided instead to take the bullet herself.

'Not a problem' fired Ms Ryann. She turned and wheeled her trolley to the end of the lobby. 'I was only replacing some of yesterday's returns anyway. Someone had soaked the floor last night and so I spent most of the blasted evening cleaning it up. I'm afraid I've not been able to look at today's returns.'

Grace held her tongue. She knew it was a trap. Quite clearly, Ms Ryann wanted Grace to make some sincere remark that detailed how it was hers and not Ms Ryann's task to deal with the returned books. Doing so would only serve to further condemn her lateness and in turn justify Ms Ryann's cold treatment of her for the entire day. Therefore, warm in her awareness, Grace remained shivering in silence.

Grace did not realise how coming into a familiar place at a different time brought with it a new energy. She had never been late before and so the days worked to a routine. However, by escaping this routine – if by only a few hours – Grace gazed on her surroundings with a fresh focus. She felt removed from the entire thing, as if she was looking on from outside. She took the time to watch the people as they passed and shared the most fleeting of exchanges. She wondered to herself if in such a swift meeting whether two people really could find love. Sighing at her desk, Grace thought of Arnold and, while she smiled to herself, her heart did not answer her call.

Confused by it all, Grace decided to acquiesce; to accept routine. She could no longer resist the allure of her chores and so she plonked the tray of returned books onto her desk. There was not many to deal with and so Grace went casually about her business. Firstly, she searched for the large log book that detailed all the books that had been issued out as well as who had taken them and when they were due back. The book was thick and old. The paper pages inside had yellowed at the edges and the leather on the spine was frayed and peeled. It met the table with a thud as Grace hauled the book open to the most recently earmarked page. With the tray of the returns to her right and the log book to her left, Grace began her first task of the day.

Gentle whispers of conversation could be heard in the reading room as Grace crossed the next book off the list. She feared for the poor chattering soul that was about to meet with the wrath of Ms Ryann in the reading room. She listened as the ripples of laughter and flirtation bluntly ceased with her intervention. Shaking her head at the comic scene, Grace leaned for the next book in her tray. She was still watching the young couple resist speaking to one another as they eyed up the overlooking Ms Ryann. Looking down at the book in front of her, Grace noted the title and referred to the log book. She scrutinized the log book four times over, but could not see any details regarding this atlas. She considered calling for Ms Ryann in case it was one of the books that had been returned the previous day and had somehow gotten muddled up with this morning's. But, seeing the expression on her employers face, Grace decided against bringing her renowned organisational skills into question.

Taking a final look at the log book and still finding nothing, Grace hoped that the paper pocket inside the cover might help her out. Opening up the thin cover, the plot thickened as Grace found that the pocket had been torn out. She knew that books were stolen from the library all the time, but it was what had replaced the paper pocket itself that made her feel that this book was always going to come back. Her stomach flipped a little as saw the rough, untidy makings of a poem. She melted into the words as she read them to herself.

The spring, and now the pole tilts towards the sun.
The ice does melt as new life's begun.
And as the gentle streams grow thick and rapid,
They break the damn my heart was trapped in.

For you're my light, its heat for one.
You are my love, my star, my sun.

Grace looked around her with the ill feeling that someone was waiting for a response. She poured her eyes onto every inch of the hall in front of her but found not a single soul looking back. She read the poem again and, unlike any other she had recently seen, she felt the raw impact of the words as she had the first time she read it. For once, she ignored her academic eye and refused to assess the rhyming structure or the flaws within. But instead she sat and celebrated the emotions captured between the lines. It soon dawned on her that this inscription was made for somebody specific. However, there was no way of discovering who. The book had no trace of where it had been and there were no names or signatures under or anywhere near the poem. In fact, there was nothing other than printed text within the whole book. Fearing she may have stumbled across the past message of two anonymous lovers, Grace took the book back to its stall.

The book was from the geography section of the library, which Grace knew to be near to the entrance – a perfect place for a thief to hide and scavenge. It was because of this that Ms Ryann had decided to place the less desirable texts near to the entrance. Nobody in Orplow had ever announced a great desire to travel, and so it was decided that all the maps, atlas' and travel guides be placed in this section. After all, Ms Ryann would never run the risk of losing any of her precious romantic texts. Standing in the stall, Grace ran her fine finger delicately along the shelves. She rolled her eyes over the numbers that had been taped to the spines of the books until she found where the atlas had been taken from. Placing the book on the shelf, she realised that there was a considerable gap either side of where the book should stand. Looking about the surrounding shelves, Grace could not see a single other travel book that had been taken out of the library, and yet in this specific spot there were at least another two or three missing. It was when she removed the atlas again that Grace saw the smudged remains of a dried water mark on the varnished wood.

Taking note of the numbers on the books either side of the atlas, Grace found that there were three more missing. Carrying the atlas, she hurried back to her desk. She scribbled down the three remaining numbers on the nearest piece of paper she could find and, checking the extensive filing cabinet, she found the titles that she was looking for. Returning to the log book, Grace found that none of these books were outstanding. To her sheer surprise she found that one of the books on Egypt had recently been taken out but returned a few days earlier – which was precisely a day after it had been taken out. Quite clearly nobody had a keen eye for these books, and even the first person to take one out for some time had only flirted with the idea of the world outside this town. Excited by the thought of finding another, Grace dug through the returns basket. Hitting the bare bottom of the basket, she felt defeated when she found that none of the other books had been returned.

Meanwhile, content that she had silenced the building, Miss Ryann had returned to the desk where Grace was stood burrowing through the returns basket. She smiled at the girl's enthusiasm to make amends for her lateness.

'I see you checked in the section where the water was last night. You didn't find any water damage did you?' Ms Ryann's voice could not hide the concern.

'What?' replied Grace as her head shot up from the basket.

'The water I mentioned from last night. It streamed from the stall you just came from. Masses of the stuff gathered in that section and then nearly a hundred drips led back outside.'

'From the geography section?' asked Grace.

'Yes dear, please keep up,' implored Ms Ryann. 'Not that I have any idea what anyone would be doing down there myself.'

'Nor I' replied Grace. Her smile was the widest Ms Ryann had seen on the girl since she was child.

Chapter 21

Three candles burned in the church. They sat from left to right like bright rising steps – the first having been burning for longer than the rest. Abigail had lit all three of them. The first, as always, had been lit for Ferris – fuelling the first of her prayers. The next burned for Michael. She only saw her son in passing these days but knew he was always there for her if she ever needed him. And though Michael was busy with his life and never tired from his work, Abigail sensed a loss within him.

The last candle burned for Cara Darby. The news of her accident had reached and touched everyone in the town. Some time had passed since that frightful morning, but the emotions were still raw among the staff at the estate. Cara had not been seen within a stone's throw of the manor house from the moment she had returned from the hospital and, in her absence, a piercing silence had replaced her. For all of Raegan's hot air and loud ambitions, there was no music anymore – no pure sounds of beauty pouring through the windows or cascading down the corridors. Abigail rose from her knees. The windows and doors had been opened invitingly and the passing talk of the people breezed through. It was beginning to gather the noise from the busy town outside.

Abigail had the making of a hearty stew in her basket. The steaks were lightly salted and rested thinly next to the carrots, potatoes and the flour for the dumplings. Michael had always loved dumplings. As a child, the impulsive rascal would always devour the doughy lumps first and then sit there with a glum face once they had gone. Abigail thought back fondly to the time she would watch her young son try in vain to fashion his own dumplings from thick clumps of bread. They always broke and limped off his fork. To Abigail, Michael's face was still set in that time. Despite his fatherly frame, and the raucous reputation he was gathering about town, Michael was still her little boy.

Leaving the church, Abigail skipped down the steps. Her basket hung over her arm as her hands held her rosary beads tightly. The weather was fair and the sky was skint of a single cloud. The townspeople passed in their droves as they roamed home to their lives away from work. A weary fatigue moved them as they travelled with tired strides. The flock fell through the many gates leading out of the town and broke amongst the pathways that would lead back to the lives that each of them worked tirelessly for. The sight of their sorrowful faces caused Abigail's heart to sink as she watched the people pass. The long demanding hours of the day had numbed them of any enthusiasm for their time off. Instead of rushing to the homes where their real lives rested, the people dragged their feet as if they were shackled to their trade. Between the work and the whiskey, the people allowed empty acts to fill their time. However, Abigail would never allow herself to forget what she worked for. She knew that a life free from her endeavour would only bring an eternity free from what she lived for.

'Good afternoon Mrs Alpin.' The voice greeted her at the bottom of the steps. Shaking herself from her thoughts of Ferris, Abigail saw Francis Morgan walking towards her. He was wrapped up warm and was carrying two bottles of wine.

'Francis, how are you? I haven't seen you for a while.' She noticed how the other women watched Francis. He was handsome in his neatness and always dressed with a European influence. Although pristine in his own presentation, his fair hair was wild and unkempt, hanging past his flat ears and kinking at the ends. He bunched the bottles under one arm as he ran his free hand through his curls.

'All's fine with me' replied Francis. 'I've been out of town for a few months. I've only just caught word of dear Cara and her ordeal, so I cut my travels short and returned to see if she was alright.'

'Well, I'm sure she'll be happy to see a kind face' said Abigail with a smile. 'I've been praying for her myself. Please send my blessings when you see her.'

'Bring them yourself' said Francis with a rush of excitement. 'Come on, we'll go and visit her together. I have a few bottles of wine and I'm sure she'll be grateful of some female company. The poor soul will have too many men around her with David and me, so come and balance it out for her. That is, unless you have plans of course.'

'Well, only those of every mother' said Abigail as she lifted up her basket.

'What? Is that grown lad of yours still having you make his supper?' Francis fired a cheeky grin towards Abigail. 'Tell the handsome lad to get himself his own woman.'

'I could say as much for you sir' replied Abigail. If she was flirting, it was without agenda.

'Oh come now' laughed Francis. 'We all know that I'm married only to my work.' Smiling, he held out the crook of his arm.

✺✺✺

Cara fed off her younger sister's smile. Grace had paid her a visit after work and was telling her of her recent adventure.

'So, I hear there is a man in your life now' said Cara with an inviting smile. David was tending to the tea and had left the ladies to catch up. 'Is he the one you were always looking for?' Cara knew her question was loaded and watched her sister's reaction intently.

'I think father has found quite the gentleman in Arnold Farrington,' said Grace. The dimples in her cheeks flattened a little as she mentioned his name. 'The man is set for life, and appears to know his manners and boundaries with a lady.'

'Any dog can be taught to sit' said Cara with a cock of her head. 'Are you sure father hasn't got his fingers in your affairs somehow?'

'I'm no fool sister,' Grace forced herself to sound a little more sensible than she felt. 'I'm aware of Arnold's family and why father would hold an interest. But still, it doesn't make Arnold a bad man. Father got it right with David didn't he?'

'Oh please,' laughed Cara. 'David is wonderful, but not through any fault of father's. That man had his eye on the land David's father was fighting for and nothing more. Why else would he cast us aside as soon as the news of David's father's death reached us? Father only did right by me by getting it wrong for himself.'

'He still found you love though,' scoffed Grace. She flinched at the thought of defending her father.

'No he didn't' scoffed Cara. 'Father found himself an opportunity. It was but fate and the heaven's work that brought David and I together. Please sister, if you think father found me love then you are sadly mistaken. And promise me you won't rely on him, or anyone else to offer you your feelings. Remember, others can only offer their own feelings... yours are yours alone.'

'I promise' said Grace with a sad smile. She knew she had not allowed herself to lose the feelings she had once held, but then she had not allowed herself to feel them recently either. They were emotions that she had never been able to understand – an infatuated impulse that had once controlled her had only just returned to her that afternoon. Recalling the poem she had read earlier, Grace felt the flutter of her heart force the hairs on the back of her neck to stand on end. She pulled the book from her bag.

'I found this today.' Grace placed the travel book into Cara's lap. David had brought the tea to the table and watched the excited girls in their exchange.

'A book?' posed Cara. 'Thank you for the gift but I've no designs on travelling the world.' She patted the sides of her wicker chair and looked puzzled.

'The inside of the cover...' said Grace quickly, having recognised the offence she may have caused her sister. '...It's been altered. The book was returned this morning but there was no record of it ever being taken out.' Seeing Grace's nod towards the book, Cara noted her cue and opened the book. There was a rectangular section of the page which was a paler, brighter white than the rest of the page. It was clear that something had been removed from this section, but then there was something added also. Cara saw the scribbled writing and began to read the poem. She could not feel her sister's eyes burning a hole into the side of her face as she read her reaction. Having allowed the words to fill her head, Cara sat back and smiled. She held the book to her chest as she breathed a sigh of pure pleasure.

'That's quite the sentiment' said Cara as she handed the book back to Grace.

'I know,' beamed Grace. 'Who do you think could have written it?'

'I have no idea at all' said Cara. 'But just as important as the question of who wrote it, is the question of whom it was written for?'

'I know. Lucky cow' barked Grace. The sisters laughed at her brief loss of decorum. Grace rarely cursed and while Cara saw the humour within it, she was not totally ignorant of the honest envy within it either.

'The thing is...' said Grace gathering herself. 'The book was only recently taken out, most likely last night. And moreover, it looks as if the same person took three other books from the same shelf.'

'But why?' said Cara. She was raising her tea cup to her mouth as she enjoyed watching her sister mull it over. Cara already had her own opinion, but wondered if Grace through all her innocence would find her way to the same spot.

'I have no idea.' She looked at her sister for a clue. 'It's free to take the books out of the library, and it seems as though this person has every intention of returning them. So it has to be all about the message in the poems, right?' Grace followed suit with her sister and took a drink of tea.

'Quite clearly' said Cara as she warmed her hands around the sides of her cup. Steam swirled skywards through the evening air. 'This person is well aware of the returns policy. Not only did they rip out the pocket that details who has taken the book, they placed the book into the returns basket.'

'So?' said Grace.

'So…' echoed Cara, '…Whoever took the book would have known that there would not be any record of them taking it and as such could have put the book back on the shelf without you ever seeing it. That is, if the message was not meant for you.'

'Me?' Grace almost spat out her tea.

'Think it through sister,' said Cara as she leaned forward and handed her sister a tissue. 'The book gets taken out one night, returned the next, and with it a poem. Anyone that goes into the library knows that you deal with the returns.'

'But I was not working that night, and anyone inside would have seen Ms Ryann tending to the returns.' Grace felt deflated when the fact she issued hit her.

'Well,' whispered Cara as she mulled it over. 'That may be the case. But we still have three books outstanding. Let's just see what they bring.'

'I can't wait' smiled Grace. 'And if the poem is for Ms Ryann… so be it. God knows the woman deserves love.' Grace placed the book back into her bag and stood as she made her way to the door. Night was drawing closer and dinner would be served up soon. Cara did not need Grace to remind her of the routines of the Darby house and was more than aware of the time. She clutched her sister's delicate fingers and stopped her for a moment.

'You may be right about the poem' said Cara with a gentle tone in her voice. 'But until you know for sure… enjoy the idea that it may be meant for you.'

'I daren't dream' said Grace with a sad smile. She kissed Cara's forehead tenderly and left for home. She held the bag within both her arms rather than letting it hang by her side. Cara watched the girl walk out into the thinly veiled night. Cara had always longed to protect her sister but, on seeing the controlling ways of their world, she knew that the greatest protection she could ever afford her sister was found in setting her free – free to feel in every gain or loss.

Francis and Abigail saw Grace leaving. She was walking the opposite way to them and so did not see them approach the house. Abigail held a soft spot for Grace. The young girl had the heart of a dreamer and the head of a romantic. She had admired the girl as she had blossomed into the finest flower to ever decorate the land. Francis had already entered the house and was creeping up behind Cara.

'Guess who?' said Francis as he cupped his hands over Cara's eyes. Fearing he would spoil the surprise, David contained his delight at seeing the man.

'A man's voice, but fingers as fine as any string' said Cara. She knew both the voice and touch. 'Francis, it has been far too long.'

'For that my dear, I'm forever sorry. If I'd known any earlier then I would not have made you wait a moment longer. I swear.'

'Oh…' scoffed Cara mockingly. 'So you only visit out of sympathy? Aren't I the lucky one?'

'It's true' braved Francis with a grin. 'I am sympathetic, but only for David. I have it from the highest authority that you haven't played any music for months.' Francis saw Cara throw a stern insinuating stare at her husband. 'Settle for a moment petal. David hasn't uttered a word of it to me. I have my spies.'

'It's true' replied Cara in a sad tone. She took David's hand and held it in her lap. He sat by her side smiling. 'I've not played any music since the accident. I always thought music was my movement. But now that my legs have been taken from beneath me, my heart breaks at the thought of playing.'

'That's enough of that' said Francis with his finest tone. 'The fall broke your legs… don't let it break your spirit as well.' He spun her around in her chair. 'Let music move you. Cara, your music was some of the finest I've ever heard. I see you have all the instruments from the house.'

'I do' replied Cara. 'Father had them all delivered over here once I moved out. He insisted it was a gift, but if you ask me I think he was just removing any reason for me to ever return.'

'Oh well, that may be true. But the dust on them is your fault,' said Francis. He ran his finger across the top of a fine harp. 'How about we dust them off? And come on, we'll play with such volume that your father has to listen.' Francis returned to the table and placed two bottles of wine in front of them. Cara's face warmed at the sight of the wine. She knew there was no point fighting it — Francis was bringing music back into her life.

'Agreed' said Cara. 'But what shall we play?'

'May I suggest something?' The voice came from behind Cara.

'Oh, where are my manners?' Francis spun Cara's chair around to face the doorway. 'I hope you don't mind me having company. Cara, I take it you know Abigail Alpin?'

'For as long as I can remember' smiled Cara. 'It's a pleasure to see you. I've grown quite close to your fine son and he often tells me of your kind prayers. I'm glad I can thank you in person.'

'Michael comes here?' Abigail felt distanced from her son.

'In passing,' replied Cara. 'David taught him how to read and write in exchange for Michael teaching me how to ride.'

'Oh, dear lord' said Abigail as she rolled her fingers across one of the beads on her rosary. 'No wonder he took the news of your accident so badly. I know he no longer tends to the horses.'

'Abigail,' said Cara with the sincerest of tones. 'I have nothing but gratitude for your son. He had nothing to do with what happened to me. The accident was exactly that, an accident.' David stirred at her side.

'Anyway' interrupted Francis. 'Enough talk of commiserations, we're here to celebrate. What were you going to suggest Abigail?'

'Well, I've always loved Turlough O'Carolan,' answered Abigail. She felt embarrassed to make suggestions to two classically trained musicians. 'I taught my son Michael to dance to his many songs, and it's one of my fondest memories of the boy as a child.'

'Then we shall play O'Carolan for you,' beamed Francis. The truth was he could not have picked a better suggestion himself. He plucked a guitar out from the corner and began to tune it. He could see Cara's violin resting atop the many instruments but refused to hand it to her. Instead he watched the hunger build inside the woman — he revelled in seeing the appetite return to the starving. It was but the work of a moment, but within it Cara took her bravest step. The violin was always only an arm's reach away from Cara and now she leaned for it. Francis smiled as he got his guitar ready. 'Anything in particular?' he asked Abigail.

'I think *Blind Mary* is a bit sorrowful for tonight,' she said as she lifted the glass of wine that David had poured for her. He was visibly excited and danced around the room tending to everyone's glass.

'Then we shall begin with this,' said Francis as his guitar roared into life. He played O'Carolan's concerto as freely as rainfall. The strings plucked and rang out as his fingers danced along the neck of his guitar. Abigail closed her eyes and fondly remembered carrying her son on her feet as they waltzed through the house.

Soon Cara had joined in. Once Francis had finished playing she burst through the pause and began with O'Carolan's *Butterfly*. The music hit David like a sledgehammer to his chest. He watched his wife play with the freedom that life had snatched from her. He saw the movement in her shoulders as her hand whipped up a blend of the most beautiful sounds. In that very moment, David loved his wife more than he ever had, and in turn he could have killed her father. Fearing his bitterness may burn the bridges that Francis had built that evening, David kissed his wife's head tenderly and left the house. Cara was lost in her craft and it would not be until the late hours of the night that she would even notice that David had gone. In his absence, Abigail sat and let her mind race as both Francis and Cara continued to pitch music out upon the evening breeze. The long grass swung like a conductor to the stars.

The midnight air cooled David's rage. He paced out his anger as he walked through the fields. The bright colours of the wild flowers were masked by the night's shade. The music that seeped from his house led him through the land. The long grass of the meadows whispered to him as they swayed to the sighs of the breeze. David let them distract him as he drifted away from his blood curdling hatred for Raegan and his lap dog Connell. Despite the darkness, the music brought life to the fields. The land hummed and the trees creaked. Right on cue, a barn owl added its call to the chorus. Carried by the choir, David pushed through towards the lake.

The moonlight skipped off the surface of the water as David stood gazing upon the great lake. He was an audience to the ambiance. The waters were still and framed the moon's reflection perfectly. The rocks stood firm at the water's side as the reeds rested against them. David could no longer hear the music from his house. He stood allowing the silence to fill his head and filter his thoughts. He forced the little fury that remained down into his fingers, as he bent and picked up a stone. Holding his breath, David hurled the stone high into the air. It felt as if the heavens held it for a moment as a pause gripped the land. A pause shattered as the stone crashed through the surface of the lake.

'What the...' shouted a voice at the lakeside. 'Who's there?'

'Sorry,' said David. 'I didn't know anyone was here.'

'Is that David Irwin?' said the voice. David recognised the voice of his concealed companion.

'The very same,' said David cheerfully as he walked towards the shadowy figure. David could see that he was still sat by the lake. 'What are you doing out here?'

'I could ask you the same thing,' deflected Michael. He slammed the covers of a book shut and stood to greet his friend. 'Well it's been some time since I last saw you sir. What's the story?'

'Oh... nothing really. Just clearing my head,' said David wearily. 'It gets hard sometimes you know? Believe me when I tell you Mike, I truly wish you never have to stand by and watch the one you love lose what they cherish the most.'

Michael thought only of his mother.

'Cara still has you David,' he replied as he rested his hand on his shoulder. 'So, she can't have lost what she holds the dearest, can she? She knows what love is because of you. So don't offend her with sympathy or regret of what you've lost...' He held his stare. '... Celebrate what you both have instead. After all, in you she's got all anyone ever needs.' Michael did not intend his words to sound passionate, so he tried to lighten the mood. 'Anyway, I'd ask you to send her all my love, but we can't be having her getting greedy now can we? If it's alright by you, I'll be saving mine for a special someone of my very own.'

'Really?' said David with mock surprise. 'The town's cad finally finds himself a match? I never had you down as the smitten kitten type?'

'Nah… just flattering myself with a fantasy that's all,' replied Michael as he bit the tip of his pen.

'I see you're writing. Good man.'

'Well, trying to,' said Michael. 'You know what? It's strange. When I first found I could write, I was so green and keen I put the finest spring morning to shame. But when I tried to pen something for someone so close to me…'

'Carmel?'

'Yeah… Carmel. I couldn't write a single word for her. The girl was everything a guy would want and was in touching distance of being mine for good, but I couldn't muster up a single feeling for her. And now, now that I've found someone I can't stop writing for, she couldn't be further from my reach.'

'If that's the case, why do you write at all?' asked David challengingly.

'For her…' smiled Michael. 'I write for her.'

'The pen never runs dry for the right person does it?' David nodded towards the pen Michael was gripping tightly. 'By the way… I saw your mother earlier.'

'My ma?' said Michael shaking his head. 'What was she doing over at yours?'

'Well she was with Francis Morgan paying my Cara a visit. I tell you what, there must be something in the air tonight as everyone has been passing through. Even young Grace has been around. Mind you, it was lovely to see her actually. You know what women are like; she had Cara all excited with gossip about some poem or other she had found in the library.' David was about to bid his farewells until he saw the question held in his friends face.

'Poem?' asked Michael. He was trying out his best 'distantly interested' expression. His fingers tapped on the side of the book he was holding.

'Yeah' replied David with a playful grin. 'I only came in at the end of the conversation, but from what I picked up it seems like Ms Ryann has herself an admirer.' David laughed as he nodded at the pen Michael was clutching. 'Hey, it's not you is it?'

'Ms Ryann you say?' asked Michael, feeling like he had just planted his finest seeds in the winter soil. 'How did she react when she found the poem? I bet she was livid.'

'To be honest, I've no idea' said David. 'I think Grace had the poem with her, so I don't think Ms Ryann has even seen it. Fancy hiding such emotions from someone hey?'

'Yeah…' Michael sighed. 'Quite the tragedy.'

Chapter 22

The following morning brought with it new words.

> *There is nothing quite as intimate,*
> *Or an emotion more infinite,*
> *As the one I have in place.*
> *As unknown as it is definite,*
> *And as simple as it is intricate;*
> *A love reserved for her, Grace.*

The poet could not have been clearer. Grace's heart raced and her hands grew warm as she held the book. The poem had been scribbled onto the inside cover of a book regarding ancient Egypt. It was one of the outstanding books she had been waiting for. Two more remained.

Sat alone at her desk, she had no idea how to feel. On the one hand she had words that had been written with her in mind, while on the other there was a passionate stranger out there who was making his statement clear. Part of her wished he would not hide behind his words – that he would burst through the doors and declare his love in person – but the rest of her knew that she would most likely crumble and die if she were to meet him. Puzzled by it all, she disappeared into the words once more.

✳✳✳

Raegan Darby was planning for the ball. Feeling triumphant in his match making abilities, he decided to address the tried and tested formula and have Arnold show his feelings to Grace at the annual New Year's Eve extravaganza. It always afforded Raegan the opportunity to display his finest colours and boast his wealth to his peers. As usual, the familiar faces of nearby affluent strangers would be rounded up and invited. The guest list read like a national rich list for the South East coast of Ireland, and Raegan always profited in the company of the well to do. Like a tactless hyena, the man knew exactly how to satisfy his seemingly ceaseless appetite.

Arnold Farrington sat at the table as he watched Raegan reel off his plans.

'My balls are showstoppers' he boasted as he raised a glass to cheer himself, and completely oblivious of any innuendo. 'Each year out-does the last, and this time around Arnold the stage will be set for you to steal the show.' He drained the glass and sat it down for another selfish measure.

'I'm glad you give your blessings Raegan,' said Arnold as he shifted in his seat. 'Once I've taken your daughter, she'll be in line to share all the land that I inherit from my father. Now, the old man isn't well at all, and we are talking months... hopefully. My only concern is Grace. Do you think she will agree to the arrangement?'

'Of course,' snorted Raegan. 'Don't you worry about that. When I'm asking, I'm not leaving it up to her... I'm saying you damn well better do as I say or I'll forget to put the chain on my dogs.' He laughed as he raised his glass triumphantly. Arnold clinked glasses with his business partner, unaware that they were playing to an audience.

'You won't drive another daughter out of this house,' spat Fiona as she walked over to the table. 'I've already lost one daughter to your ambitions and I refuse to lose Grace as well.' Her hand trembled from a cocktail of anger and fear.

'Oh behave woman,' scoffed Raegan. 'Grace will love Arnold, if that makes you sleep any easier.' He was already plotting her beating as he watched his wife grow uncomfortable in her defiance. 'Now leave us men.'

'Don't worry...' replied Fiona with a false smile plastered across her face. '...I left you to it a long time ago' she whispered as she turned and left the room. She paused outside and leaned her frail back against the corridor. A dull heat radiated in her chest as she thought of her husband and his laden gestures. She could not recall a time when his generosity did not come without a personal gain – regardless of the loss it may draw from others.

She crept up to Imogen's room. The young girl was almost a teenager but still had the innocence of a child half her age. Raegan hardly bothered with the girl, instead leaving her to her mother's constant attention. Fiona regretted the coldness she had first felt when Imogen was an infant. She had not felt the warmth from the child that she had with her older daughters, as Imogen had always appeared distant and distracted. It was not until the early years of her schooling that the teachers had noticed Imogen's slow progress. Initially, Raegan had challenged the observation, calling in specialists from across the country to confirm that his daughter was fine. However, each and every one of them had left with a scolding from Raegan after they delivered the same news – Imogen was retarded.

Fiona hated that term. Having never been asked to make use of her own mind, she saw academics as an unnecessary measure of a person. Her youngest daughter still had the same senses as anyone else, and so life could be just as sweet – or sour – for her as it was for the rest of us. On some level, Fiona actually envied Imogen's condition. She felt that there was a slight bliss in her daughter's ignorance. Her mental state meant that she neither longed nor missed the aspects of life that she could not understand – meaning Imogen would never feel the effect of her father's designs.

Watching her daughter at play in her bedroom, Fiona promised herself that she would not let this one slip through her fingers. She approached the young girl and picked up a book of fairy tales from the table. Sitting by her daughter's side, Fiona opened up the book and began to read. She was unaware of whether her daughter was even listening, but she continued to read to her regardless. Fiona held Imogen's hand as she turned the first page.

'An act for fools' blurted Raegan. 'Don't worry about making your proposal public. That act only serves to entertain the drooling masses who serve as spectators to the likes of us. No... you'll tell her of your intentions at the end of the ball, after you've shown to her just how desirable you are among the people, of course. All the local sycophants will be there, colouring their noses on you. When Grace sees this then she'll be grateful of you, I promise.'

'I hope so' replied Arnold as he fidgeted with his glass. He rolled the tumbler along the edge of its thick base nervously. 'I could not tolerate any form of rejection.'

'From Grace?' asked Raegan letting his guard drop slightly. To the focused eye, Raegan's trivial valuation of his daughter was clear, but Arnold was far too busy worrying about his own appearance. 'Grace has no right to turn you down sir. She's ready to be wed and so are you... that's all there is to it.'

'I hope so,' smiled Arnold wearily. He knew he had found a handsome lady in Grace. She had a beauty that was leagues above his own, and for what was probably the first time in his life Arnold was truly grateful for what he could offer her. He believed that every lady longed for a sense of security – a feeling of being protected. With all his wealth and trappings, Arnold was confident that Grace could find what every woman dreamed of. He raised his glass high in the air and made a toast.

'To partnerships,' he said.

'Indeed,' Raegan replied with a wry, snarling grin. The men drank and sat letting only the sound of the crackling fire break the silence. The logs smouldered as the smaller twigs snapped within the flames. Arnold's left leg was numb from his lack of movement and soon his whole body would join in as the alcohol etched into his bloodstream. Before long, his heart rate lowered as he began to feel his head swoon and grow heavier. He could see that Raegan was responding in a different manner. The man was getting redder in the face and his eyes became dark, soulless and as pitiless as a shark's. Raegan had clambered to his feet and zigzagged across the carpet that flowed towards the hallway. It was still only the afternoon but there was a frosty bite in the air. Arnold decided to try and sleep off the drink for a few hours and so slumped into his chair. His eyes darkened as each blink became drawn out. As his eyes shut for the last time, he was certain he saw Raegan loosening his belt as he made his way out into the hallway.

✻✻✻

Grace held the book as she finished work for the day and left the library. She was expected home that evening to prepare for the ball. She knew that her father was entertaining Arnold for the afternoon and was not surprised to only see Connell waiting for her by the gates. The man was growing thicker set with age, his greasy hands were hidden by his cracked and creased leather gloves, and his shoulders bulged and look set to burst through his dark green, waxed jacket.

'Miss Darby,' sneered Connell as his drew his sleeve across his damp mouth. The black wiry hairs on his face bunched and clutched at his skin. 'Your carriage awaits.'

'Thank you,' said Grace as she clambered into the car. She was still holding the book as she sat down. The pages were open inside her head as her mind's eye cast itself over the poem again. She wondered whether the words had come from Arnold. She had gotten the first poem around about the same time that he had arrived in town, and they had only been allowed a little time together since. Maybe this was a way for him to show how he felt away from the prying eyes of her father. He had not struck her as the type to be so romantic, as he appeared very formal in his approach to most things, but the idea of such a passionate side to the man excited her more than any aspect of his character so far.

Grace was glad to hear the engine turn over, and pour out its loud purr. She could not find the words inside her to make idle chit chat with Connell and had always felt soiled and spoilt in his presence. The man was a creep and she despised every moment she had to share with him. The car rolled through up the road towards the estate. The callous tyres bumped on the stones that rested on the road. Grace let her eyes breeze over the fields as her mind raced away. She did not focus on the workers that toiled in fields as the cold winds bit at their tired bodies. Instead, her eyes traced the beam of sunlight that broke through the clouds and punctured the ground like a golden arrow. Her eyes rested on where the light punctured the cornfield as the car pulled to a slow stop. She could see the manor in the distance and was aware that she was still far from her home.

She leaned forward to see that Connell was watching the woman who was approaching them. She was carrying a bundle and while she looked tired, there was a light in the lady's eyes that Grace recognised all too well. The sparkle of a day dream flickered – a feverish fire burning in her very soul. Grace wondered whether that was how she herself appeared when dreams took her from her surroundings. She prayed that her match had seen this and would free her from the trappings that tied her to her dull days.

'Good afternoon Mrs Alpin,' coughed Connell. He bore his toothy grin as he waved one of the meaty mallets that he called hands.

'Oh…' she replied, shaking herself from her thoughts. The bundle looked to gain weight in her arms as she came back around. 'You startled me there Connell. How are you?'

'I am very well Abigail,' said Connell. He was oblivious to the uncomfortable pauses that came once his mutterings had ceased. The dense silence was filled by his wandering eyes that devoured every inch of her body. He grew hard picturing taking her roughly up the side of the tree where her beloved husband had hanged. A sinister smile cut across his oily face and licked at his gristly ear lobes. Seeing how awkward Abigail had become within the grave gaze of Connell, Grace invited her to speak with her.

'Abigail, it's a pleasure to see you,' said Grace as she waved a hand from the side of her carriage. Over the years she had seen Abigail grow older by the side of her son Michael. Grace had watched how Michael would wait for his mother each day by the gateway that kept him from the manicured gardens of her home. Watching the woman approach the carriage, Grace wondered whether Abigail would recognise her.

'Miss Darby,' said Abigail with a kind smile. 'How have you been? I thought you had been locked away for good.' She shifted the bundle in her arms so that she could speak a little more freely.

'Father finally got bored of having me around, so I'm allowed out to experience the world now,' replied Grace. Despite the jest in her tone, the truth in her statement still hammered into her like a trusty nail.

'And aren't we all the better for it,' beamed Abigail. 'Having someone so pretty hidden from the world makes as much sense as storing your candles in a well.' Abigail leaned her head into the carriage a little as she made a token gesture of interest into what the young lady was carrying. 'So, what are we reading these days?'

'This?' asked Grace with more caution than the question required. 'It's just a book.' Her heart beat a little at the thought of anyone realising her childish fascination.

'They usually are,' said Abigail with a hint of jest about her. She stood back from the carriage as Connell had grown tired of the weary conversation and started up the engine. 'Ancient Egypt though… seems like everyone is reading that these days. Well take care anyway, have a great evening.'

'You to Mrs Alpin, send my love to the family.'

Abigail's words about the book did not register until the car had left her in the dusty distance. Grace looked back as if she could draw an answer from any knowing look or glance that Abigail offered, but the woman was walking the way she had been heading. Grace tormented herself with the idea that the town new of her admirer. She dreaded the thought of being the local punch-line. She pictured people grouped together, laughing and boasting lines of romance and promise as they scribbled them down inside the stolen books. Maybe she had become the victim of some boisterous wager. Maybe the glances she had been getting in town were from men trying to hoard material for their own offering.

Thinking back on the times she had seen Abigail, Grace saw the woman who tenderly held her son's hand every evening – the woman that warranted a fine man to protect her. Realising that this woman could not contain a poisonous bone in her body, Grace allowed the gust of paranoia to pass. Once more she settled on the exhilarating idea of having a shade of romance in her life.

***

Nobody waited to greet Grace as the car rolled up outside the manor. Raegan had put the staff to task on making arrangements for the ball, and so Grace was met with a cold carpet that crept up to the side of the car and fell through the main doors of the manor house like a limp tongue. Busy within its separate tasks, the household was quiet and focused as Grace walked inside. Her father had heard that Francis Morgan had returned to town and so he seized the opportunity to have the man aid his intentions. And so, Francis was waiting for Grace upstairs in her room. He had shifted the furniture to one side and opened up the floor to give room for movement. Grace was delighted to see him.

'Francis!' she ran and embraced him. He had grown thin from his travels and it surprised her to see that the man, who had once towered over her with stories of travel, now stood eye to eye with her. His eyes were almost silver as the grey of them glistened.

'My my my. Dear Grace, the rumours are true,' replied Francis as he held her at arm's length. Her heart skipped a little at the mention of rumours. 'I was told that Orplow possessed one of Europe's most precious pearls, and my Lord they were right. You are beautiful.' She knew there was no agenda hidden within his words, and felt comfort in the distance their ages gave them. Francis was the charmer without the snake – his words worked wonders but possessed no poison or bite in them.

'Please, you'll make a young lady blush' replied Grace with a trace of flirtation.

'Now that's not my intention,' declared Francis as he swept his jacket and scarf from his shoulders. 'I intend to make you dance, Grace.'

'Dance?' Grace grew nervous at the mere thought of it. She was always clumsy and was often finding herself in front of the school nurse back in Eden.

'As you know, the ball is coming up,' said Francis as he busied himself with his preparations. He pulled his violin out of its case and rested it on his shoulder. 'I won't deceive you with lies as I'm well aware that you know of your father's intentions, correct?'

'Not entirely,' said Grace coyly. She knew the man was plotting but never really allowed herself to realise exactly what he had in mind.

'Dear Grace,' whispered Francis as he checked whether he had an audience behind the bedroom door. 'Your father is as inventive as a bird with twigs. With all the options available to him, he'll only ever see how to build a nest for himself, and he only knows of one way to do it. Now he failed with Cara, and so you're next in line.' Francis was so cold in his matter-of-fact manner. The words made Grace feel inconsequential – as if her feelings were redundant and obsolete. 'I don't mean to upset you,' he continued. 'I'm just a messenger. Your father asked me to teach you how to dance for the ball, and I am assuming you won't be dancing on your own.'

'I guess not,' realised Grace. She did not know why the thought upset her, so she shook it from her head and embraced the task at hand. 'So, what will my fair tutor have me learn today?' She made an elaborate curtsy and smiled widely.

'Firstly,' said Francis as he ran his hands through his untamed hair. 'You'll need a partner. Allow me to introduce to you... for one afternoon only... Mr David Irwin.' David showed himself from behind the curtain that hung by the window near to Grace's bedside. She laughed heartily at the thought of her brother-in-law having been hiding there the whole time.

'Madam,' said David adopting a frightfully bad French accent. 'May, I have the eternal pleasure of this dance?'

'The pleasure would be all mine,' said Grace stifling her laughter.

'Hesitate please children,' interrupted Francis. 'Take a moment to familiarise yourself with the sound before throwing yourself into it.' He knew that they had both heard the piece countless times, but Francis could never forsake an opportunity to take centre stage. He played a series of concertos that would lend themselves to the simplest forms of the waltz. He had played to hundreds at a time in concert halls across the continent, but he still could not find a time more empowering than playing to such an intimate and small audience. He allowed himself a rapturous sigh as he drew his piece to a close. A gentle applause rained out from his friends. He opened his eyes to see that David had already begun to teach Grace a few steps. He held her hands in place and stood facing her. Francis admired the perfect lines of her posture as she stood ready for the music to carry her.

David stood away from her and nodded at Francis to begin, and so he played softly, as the strings whispered their muted melody. David assumed the stance of the lead and talked Grace through each of the steps he made.

'The waltz has the least steps of all the dances, as there are only three you really need to master,' explained David. 'Both the natural turn and the reverse turn cause you to turn to the right,' he skipped on the ground as he made an example of both steps. 'Then there is the change step. This allows us to move to the other foot if we need to.' The music continued as David mirrored his moves several times. 'See Grace, it's a simple straight and close, turn and close... and if you're feeling ambitious you can go from the turn into a straight and whisk.' Grace smiled as David pranced around like the puppeteer without the puppet.

'Also,' continued David. 'Remember if the dance leads you to a corner then the lead dancer will have to make a quarter turn to the left to allow the chasse that follows, and to move along the new line of the dance.' Grace was confused. Her face failed to hide as much when Francis interrupted.

'David,' he said while continuing to play. 'Maybe it will help if you took Grace and led her around with these moves. This is a practical lesson after all.' Francis offered Grace his most reassuring of smiles and nodded for her to stand with David.

'Fear not, I'll have you mastering the triple pivots and free spins in no time at all' boasted David in a low voice. He had intentionally failed to mention to Grace that he was the uninvited guest in the equation. Francis had sneaked him inside to help with the task at hand, despite Raegan's insistence that his daughter Cara had no part to play in the matter. Francis knew this gesture extended to David also, but he needed help and would achieve his task regardless.

'And so we dance,' declared Francis as he began to play once more. David held Grace's hand loosely for fear of being brutish with her delicate frame. He began to lead her around the room and had almost tackled his first change of step when Grace's shoe met bluntly with his shin.

'I'm so sorry,' said Grace letting go of his hands. She held hers to her face nervously.

'Not to worry,' smiled David as his shin throbbed beneath his trousers. He was sure he could feel the slight trickle of blood on his skin. 'Let us try again.'

It was not until the second reverse turn that Grace slammed the base of her heel into the toes of her leading man. David bit his lip as the pain screamed up his entire leg. He was certain that a bone had broken, but did not want to burden the young girl with worry. Francis stopped playing the music and, seeing the pain in his colleague's eyes, decided to take a separate tact.

'Grace, maybe we should have you dancing on your own for a moment to let you find your feet a little?' Francis did not want to patronise her but would have hated to cripple his dear friend any further.

'I'll try,' said Grace feeling foolish. She stood and danced a little as Francis played low enough for him to coach her over the music. However, despite her perfect posture and fine lines, Grace could not find the fluid movement that she required. She needed a lead. Francis was just fearful of the pain awaiting the man who chose to.

'Let's try a different song,' said Francis with an encouraging smile.

Chapter 23

Michael had plans for the turn of the New Year; he had promised Oscar that he would go into town and celebrate. They had both agreed that they would raise a toast to each memory they could recount from the past year, and in turn get so blind drunk that they would fail to remember the night itself. Michael smiled at the thought of carting the dead weight of his chubby friend home. As the evening drew to a close, Michael left the lake and walked up to the coastline. The winter air gripped him and his broad arms trembled as he held himself tightly. Birds chirped and called to one another across the land, while the sunset enticed the clouds together as they blanketed the stars behind them. A light shower had begun to rain down as Michael grew closer to the cliff face. Delicate rain drops pressed at the surface of the lake like light fingers across the keys of a grand piano. The sound of the shower's beat set the tempo of the tide as the ocean sighed and swept the waters to and fro from the shore.

Michael watched as the waters broke upon the rocks that guarded the cove. The deep blue of the lake burst into a whispery white haze as it fell into the streams beneath. The ceaseless flow of water seemed to take an eternity to reach the shore below – falling like snowflakes into the deep, unquenchable jaws of the pool. The rain had come too soon for Michael to write anything that evening. The heavens had spat at the paper pages before he could even begin to note his feelings. So he stuffed them in his satchel. Sheltered from the rain, the books dried in the satchel that Michael had cupped under his thick waxed jacket as an added measure.

Pausing for thought, Michael felt the falling water drain over his face as he closed his eyes and imagined himself dropping down over the cliff face. He could almost feel the wind race through his thick hair, forcing the curls back from his brow. Opening his eyes and recalling the night when first he fell, Michael smiled and nodded to the memory. He turned, patted his satchel and made his way back home. Above him, the rain clouds packed the sky and promised a storm.

Michael was soaked to the skin as he burst through his front doors. His mother had come home early from the church and was tending to the supper.

'Good evening son,' she said as she turned from the stove. 'Will I have the pleasure of your company tonight?'

'Of course,' said Michael slightly distracted. He pulled two books from his satchel and laid them out to dry. 'Something smells nice. What is it?' Michael embraced his mother as she eyed the books drying out behind him.

'Oh, just something warm and hearty, son. Thought it would match the romance that's in the air maybe?' said Abigail with a wry smile.

'What, in Orplow?' Michael tore himself from her. 'That'll be the day'. His face flinched as he spoke.

'Oh come now,' said Abigail teasingly. She paused a little to see if her nervous son would fill the empty air. Seeing that Michael had lost his tongue, Abigail threw him a lifeline. 'There are plenty of fine women in this little town of ours. When are you going to find yourself a nice slice of the pie?'

Michael was not stupid and had rarely heard his mother talk about romance so freely before. He also knew how much she frowned on the reputation that he had gained about town – regardless of how undeserving he was of it. And as for romance, what would his poor mother know of it? The idea must have died the second his father chose an eternity in limbo alone over a lifetime with her. Michael pulled up a chair and sat at the table, as he rustled a tough towel into his drenched hair.

'I see those books are popular,' said Abigail as she nodded to the one drying out. She looked for Michael's reaction and her heart stopped. Staring back at her with the widest eyes, she had never seen him look more like his father. She quickly turned back to the stove so to hide the single tear that streamed down her cheek.

'Erm...' Michael stalled. He was glad his mother had turned around as he knew he was an awful liar. 'These books you say? Well, I erm... I just thought I would take a look at the world outside this town. Who knows... maybe I'm missing out on something.'

'Maybe,' replied Abigail. She swallowed the ball of anguish that had clogged her throat. It felt like she was forcing a dusty dry cannon ball down her gullet; every sinew in her neck felt stretched. 'This town may not have it all for someone like you Michael. It's a big old rock that we live on, and don't ever feel like you have to stay here. Not for me, not for anyone.'

'I'll stay where love is mother,' smiled Michael. He stood behind her now and placed his hands on her shoulders. He could feel how tense she had become.

'Very well... just don't you get lost in it,' Abigail turned and saw Michael's concern at her glazed eyes. 'Pesky onions, they get me every time. Come on, let's eat.'

Michael insisted that his mother sit while he dished up their supper. It was his favourite and his nostrils flared as the scent of the stew tickled at his nose. Michael paused behind his mother, leant down and kissed her gently on her cheek. She clasped his hand to her shoulder tenderly before smiling up at him. Michael cut the moment with a wink and took his seat. For the first dozen mouthfuls Michael did not look up once from his bowl. Abigail hardly touched hers and instead sat admiring Michael's healthy appetite.

'I have some news,' said Abigail. Her tone sounded grave.

'Oh ay?' beamed Michael. 'I thought the stew was too much a treat to come without a cost. Is everything alright?'

'Yeah son,' replied Abigail. 'It's not a huge deal. It's just that we've been drafted in to work at the ball tomorrow night. Raegan wants all his staff on hand to manage what he insists will be his finest ever turn of the year bash. From what I've heard, it's supposed to be quite an important one.'

'Tomorrow night?' Michael's fork clunked into his bowl. 'Oscar will be livid. We had plans to head out.' He saw the timid expression on his mother's face. 'Never mind, I now get to spend it with you, so that's not all bad. Anyway, are you sure old Raegan wants me there? I heard he had a blunderbuss poised to blow my arse clean off if I even dared stepped near to his gardens, let alone inside the house itself.'

'I've not been told otherwise,' said Abigail sniggering at the image of her rascal son scampering away from his blundering boss. 'Apparently, he wants all his staff, and that includes you. I wouldn't get too excited though... he's having you carry a drinks tray amongst his guests. You will get to wear a suit though.'

'Great,' roared Michael. 'Me in a suit: Who would have thought it? So not only do I get to gate-crash the event itself, I also get to upstage every man inside as well.' He never played the arrogant card well, but he didn't want his mother to see his disappointment. He and Oscar had planned for the night to be one to remember. But now he was already trying to forget about it. Returning to his bowl Michael tore at a chunk of bread as he tried to fashion his own dumplings. He always regretted eating them first.

✷✷✷

With the news of his change of plans still ringing in his ears, Michael was feeling brave and almost exhilarated. The thought of seeing Grace the next night had thrilled him. Compelled to exhaust his excitement, he explained to his mother that he needed to go and break the bad news to Oscar. It slipped his mind that Oscar would most likely be at the ball himself and would already be sulking over his dinner as his mother delivered her embellished version of the circumstances. He could see the robust lady catering to her son's ego by feeding him some bull about being handpicked by the master himself. Michael laughed as he knew his apprehensive friend would eventually wobble to the flattery and accept it gladly as fact.

Once he had finished his dinner, Michael had made an elaborate scene of tidying up. He moved all his laundry to his room and had tried his best to bunch the books inside without his mother seeing. He placed one under his pillow while he tucked the other down the rear of his pants. The book's rigid spine caused him to arch his back and stand like a chicken. He tossed on his jacket to cover up his shirt and – despite having a bounty of pockets – Michael slipped his pencil under his flat cap. He seriously doubted his mother would pat him down before he left but he was not taking any chances. After all, she had been acting mightily suspicious recently, and Michael was not ready to declare his feelings to the world just yet – more as a matter of fear than pride.

Luckily, Abigail was cleaning the dishes as Michael headed out, and she did not have time to turn and see him before he had offered his goodbye and was out of the door. Outside, the night was boasting its finest shade of black. Michael took a moment to allow his eyes to adjust. Not even a single star cut the canvas of the sky and the moon cowered behind a thick smoggy set of clouds. Michael wondered where he would find the light in which he could write. Pouring his eyes across the land he could only see the distant lights of the Darby estate looking back at him. The narrow windows blazed like fierce flaming eyes in the distance. Knowing the way by heart, Michael made his way towards the house.

The night was warm beneath the cover of the clouds. The air was humid and the grass sagged from the roots. The unholy heat hauled the scents of all the flowers up from the earth. The porous evergreens glistened as droplets of dew rolled down their ample leaves. The nerves shook at Michael and his heart rattled in his chest. He pulled the book out from his shirt and began to run, holding one arm out by his side to guide him through the darkness. At the tips of his fingers the bushes turned to crops and then to rough walls – telling him that he was getting closer. He could see the house looming on the horizon as it began to stretch wider across the hilltop.

Coming to the final wall that separated the fields from the gardens, Michael ducked and took cover. He leaned his back against the smooth stone and scurried towards where the wall broke onto the pathway. The light from the house crept around the wall and paved the first few yards of the field. Pulling the pencil out from his hat, Michael stole some of the light as he allowed it to brighten the first pages of his book. He took a deep breath and braved a look up at the windows. The house looked tired as the lights from the windows began to go out. Like weary eyes, the curtains drew slowly across the windows and hid the light from the land. Before the darkness was upon him, Michael thought of her and started to write.

The final light went out in a flash. Michael sat in the dark and closed the book quietly. He peered around the wall – the house was in complete darkness. He quickly crept through the shadows and planted himself on the wall of the house. It wasn't long until he realised he had no idea how to get into the house itself. He naively toyed with the windows, hoping one had been left open – but the few he could reach were locked tight. Suddenly, a thin sliver of light leaked out onto the pebbled driveway. Seeing that the door was creeping open, Michael threw himself into the base of the ivy bush that climbed the walls of the house.

'Oh balls to him,' said the first man to leave the house. He had a thin ratted face and dressed like a member of the kitchen staff. He was lighting a cigarette as he stepped outside. His head was twisted to the side as he spoke to the man who walked behind him.

'But Connell said that we need to make sure all the food is ready,' warbled the stouter man that stood in the doorway with the door resting on his shoulder. He was dressed the same as his friend but was more full of face. His cheeks were flush and his nose had the stamp of a secret drinker.

'And it will be,' replied the smoker. His voice was more nasal as the smoke clogged his throat. 'Look, old donkey Darby is having us work tomorrow. I've done the New Year's Eve ball a dozen times now and he always finds fault, regardless of how good we deliver it.' He took a long draw on his cigarette and flicked the remains behind him. Michael watched as the ember burned on his chest. He bit his lip as the fire chewed at his skin.

'Anyway,' continued Ratty, he rustled under his apron. 'I have this, and I intend to finish it.' He produced a long bottle brimming with clear liquid and chugged back a greedy gulp. He gritted his teeth as the drink blazed inside his thin throat. 'Here, have a pull on that.'

'Oh, alright. Only one sip though,' smiled Fatty. His hefty hand gripped the bottle as his thick lips sucked at the neck like a greedy calf at his mother's teat. He wiped his sleeve across his mouth and raised the bottle once more.

'Hey!' snatched Ratty. 'Not here, we'll finish it in the gardens. And don't you worry about Connell. He can sit right on the end of my long finger for now.' Ratty raised his middle finger up and fired it back at the manor house, before stifling a laugh and pulling Fatty through the doorway. Seeing the door was closing, Michael grabbed the book and threw out his arm. His fingertips pinched at the pages as the book rested at the base of the doorframe. The door gripped it like a vice. Only the thinnest string of light broke through the frame. Michael lay outstretched and silent as he watched the shadows of Ratty and Fatty creep around the corner of the building.

Once they were out of sight, Michael crawled for the door. His back was damp, and he noticed that he had sat on a carpet of Windflowers. He saw the flattened white petals of the wild flower and decided to uproot the largest. Taking hold of the door with his spare hand, he pressed the flower inside his book and held it tightly. Cupping the book under his arm, Michael opened the door and made his way inside.

The hallway stretched out in front of him. The grand spiral staircase clambered up the wall to the left. During the years of his exile, Michael had shown an unhealthy interest in his mother's work – asking her daily to describe the layout of the manor house just so that he could place where Grace might be. And, if his memory served him correctly, she would be waiting for him behind the bedroom that rested to the right of the stairwell. The house slept as Michael made his move upstairs. His toes trod on their very tips as he paused on every step. The slightest of noises echoed throughout the darkness around him. The sighs of the night outside shook the walls and whispered for the household to wake up. Having held his breath the whole time, Michael knelt exhausted at the top of the stairs. He counted out the doors to his right and found what he was looking for. His hand trembled as he slid the book under the door. The pages dragged on the lush carpet inside.

Feeling victorious, Michael leaned against the door and breathed deeply. He was still smiling when he heard the noise from down stairs.

A man was awake and was pacing in the hallway. He had a slight lean to his stance and wore a thin moustache. Michael had not seen this man before, but was certainly not ready for an introduction. His heart raced knowing that he could not leave the same way he had come in – not while the new man was blocking his path. A window looked out over the driveway to Michael's right. He made a dash for it. He felt no need for silence anymore as he wrenched the bolt to the side and lifted up the glass. The window was not accustomed to being opened and let out a sharp screech. Abandoning his senses Michael lept through the open window and took hold of the first thing his fingers felt as he met with the night sky. The ivy tore at his hands as gravity pulled him to the ground. His knees buckled as his feet thudded at the earth. Excited and terrified by his adventure, Michael ran out into the land. He chose not to laugh and howl his heart out until he was some distance from the estate.

✳✳✳

Arnold Farrington was struggling to sleep. He was not one for grand gestures and was absolutely dreading the ball. Romance was a redundant notion for him; relationships were formalities and nothing more. There was no doubt that young Grace was beautiful and had looks that could conjure up passionate, if not impractical, feelings, but for Arnold matrimony was only a contract wherein a civil partnership was forged. Therefore, Grace would just be his partner and in turn they would offer one another vast wealth and security. In truth, the matter of her beauty was an aesthetic element that unsettled him. Having gained some Dutch courage from the bottom of a bottle of sherry, Arnold wanted to seal the deal as soon as possible. He had no time for taking the risk tomorrow in front of an audience and wanted to close the matter with Grace before he went to bed.

Leaving his bedroom, Arnold paced up and down the hallway. His leg was numbed by the alcohol and so he stood without his cane. He felt as if he was being watched through the darkness – as if the household was on edge waiting for him to move. Running the words through his head a hundred times, Arnold decided on his pitch. Above all, he would be blunt and forthright and hoped she would admire his straight talking. Leaning to the left a little, Arnold began to make his way upstairs. He stopped and looked behind him on hearing the terrible screech that scratched through the hallway. The sound had sobered him slightly and the strain returned to his injured leg. He held the wall as he hobbled up the remaining steps.

Breathing deeply and composing himself, Arnold cleared his throat and raised his clasped hand to knock at Grace's door. He stopped when he saw the window open to his right.

***

Grace was having a nervous night. Her sleep was broken by dreaded thoughts of the ball. She had a firm handle on her father's intentions, and – while not blown away by him – she had slowly come to appreciate the idea of settling with her suitor Arnold. Having seen what the town had to offer, Grace knew she could do a lot worse than him, and it was not like she had men queuing up at her door. Feeling hot in her anxiety, Grace turned her pillow to rest her head on the colder side. Hugging the cushion, her fingers glanced over the latest book that had been returned to her. She had kept it by her side ever since and, despite knowing the words by heart, she had chosen to read the poem a thousand times over. In spite of the darkness, Grace sat upon the edge of her bed and opened up the book. She traced her fine fingers across the shallow indents of the page where the words rested. Drifting deeply into the words, the thought of the poem allowed her to relax. She was about to let the dreams take her away when she heard something drag along the floor.

Her room was a den of darkness and at first she could not make out what was causing the sound. But it definitely came from her doorway. Moving cautiously through the room, Grace held out her arms to guide her. She remembered that her furniture had been moved to make room for her dancing, but she was not certain as to where everything lay. Bumping her way over to the cabinet that rested alongside the far wall, she fumbled around and found the small gas lantern on top of the cabinet. She switched it on. The light filled the room that had smothered her. It took a second for her eyes to adjust to the brightness before they rested on the book that lay at the base of her bedroom door.

She dropped to her knees and pulled the book towards her. The white petals of the Windflower clung to the pages as she opened it up. The page still held its crushed, sweet scent that climbed and teased at Grace's senses. The page came to life as she saw the words that fell from the centre of the page; the light from the lantern danced across the paper.

> *By night's closing light I think of thee,*
> *And as darkness grows, you're all I see.*
> *For true love can know no compromise,*
> *As it is blind when seen with open eyes.*

Grace held the book to her chest. She thought of who the writer may be. Fired by the thought that the author was still nearby, she leapt to her feet and flung her bedroom door wide open to find her match.

Her heart froze at the sight of Arnold Farrington standing before her.

Chapter 25

'Good morning,' said Abigail, giving her son a swift nudge. 'Today's a big day and we have lots to do.' Michael stirred more than he needed to. Truth was he had been wide awake; thoughts of Grace had not let him sleep a wink.

'Morning Ma',' he moaned. 'I thought you said I was just serving the drinks tonight?'

'That I did,' said Abigail perched on the edge of her son's bed. 'But, I've got to head to the church, and you still have your labour of love to attend to. Those fields won't look after themselves you know.'

Michael cursed as he clambered out of bed. The thought of the ball had made him forget about everything else. He still had a long arduous day of work to carry out. He had not changed from the night's adventures and was fully clothed as he kissed his mother on the head and ran out of the cottage.

'Tell God I'm sorry for cursing,' shouted Michael as the door closed behind him. 'Love you.'

'I love you too,' said Abigail in a soft whisper. She clutched the rosary beads in her hand and stood from her son's bed. The hard mattress had already begun to numb her bum and she wondered how the poor lad could get even the slightest of sleeps from it. Abiding to her maternal instinct, she neatly straightened out the bed and fluffed the thin pillow. The case was harder than she had expected as she shook and plumped out the pillow. Rummaging inside, Abigail found Michael's book. Deciding not to question the situation, she left it as she had found it. Thinking it through, she messed up his bed again so that Michael would not know what she had found.

Already dressed for the day in her mourning attire, Abigail took the cup of tea that Michael had not seen in his hurry and placed it by the sink. Prepared for the day ahead, she made her way outside. The morning held a crisp mist that guarded the earth from the skies above – a grey veil lingered lightly over the land. The first fingers of light from the day pushed back the remaining shadows of night. Pulling her cotton throw tightly around her shoulders, Abigail braved the elements and headed for the church. She could feel the chill of worry tap at her bones as she knew Michael was up to something. Not needing to know exactly what it was, she would still seek God's guidance for her son.

***

Grace had butterflies from the night before. She had fallen fast asleep once she had read the poem one last time. Arnold had stayed a moment after she had found him at her door.

She smiled at the thought of his nervous proposition. He had become straight talking and cold – expressing his desire to strike up a solid partnership and push things forward as a pair. Grace reasoned that he was simply embarrassed at being discovered so quickly; there was no way he would be expecting her to be up at that hour and must have thought he could have sneaked away before being found. Hearing him out, Grace had smiled knowingly, pressed the book to her chest, kissed him on his frosty cheek and bid him goodnight.

The windflower lay on her bedside cabinet. All the petals remained in place, and Grace had decided that she would incorporate it into her headwear for that evening. Like morning snow crowning the forests, the white petals blazed purely against the varnished oak. Her stomach jolted at the thought of seeing her admirer again that evening. She was intrigued how the conflict between security and sentiment seemed to have been settled within him.

The day ahead promised to stretch out into a montage of readying. Impatient in her excitement, Grace wanted the night to fall sooner. She looked from her window and pleaded for the day to pass. Ignorant of her demands, the morning birds continued to sing and welcome the day's break. The workers had already begun to taken to their labour. All, that was, apart from one. In his haste, a figure cut the horizon as he sprinted through the fields. The wind pulled at his body as he pounded the earth beneath him. He appeared to be gliding across the land as the long grass carried him swiftly. Grace's heart flipped at the sight of Michael as he broke through the gates that held the fields from the estate. He smiled to the people he passed, making sure he did not knock them down. Grace saw how the maids swooned and melted at his gentle and guiding touch. Oblivious to his admirers, Michael disappeared into the barn and out of Grace's sight. Sat high above the land in her bedroom, she cast her eyes onto the fields. They came to rest far in the distance where the blue of the sky kissed the lush green of the land. Today, this meeting of matters was concealed by a thin grey curtain of mist.

Down in the study, the fiery brandy lapped at the glass. He promised himself that he would only have the one to ignite his belly for the day ahead. Too much would always emphasise his frustration, and today was not a day of falling short. Today his daughter was to be engaged, and his empire extended. Raegan felt the drink bite at his empty stomach. His veins throbbed and he clenched his fists as his legs shivered; blood rushed to his head and his brain swam. He knew he needed to eat.

Entering the kitchen, Raegan was delighted to see his staff hard at work. Flurries of hands were delivering a feast of cold meats and biscuits. Oven doors clattered and clunked as countless joints of lamb filled their burning bellies. Connell stood beating the drum at the heart of it. He thrust his fleshy fingers in the air, directing the traffic. Chefs, maids and kitchen hands all wheezed and puffed past him – already fully aware of their tasks and ignorant of his orders. Raegan took on the role of sampler as he picked at a selection of breads and biscuits. The rustic rolls soaked up the acid that had gripped his gut. He raised a chunk appreciatively towards Connell and nodded his approval.

'Morning sir,' said Connell with a grubby grin. The workers swarmed around him regardless of his distraction. 'Everything is to schedule. We'll have quite the feast tonight.'

'Good,' replied Raegan. 'You'll be pleased to know that I've ordered all the staff to cater to our guests.' He picked a cold piece of meat from the nearest platter. 'That includes your chosen piece in particular.'

'Abigail?' said Connell as his wolfish eyes widened. His mouth salivated at the thought of having the woman within his grasp. 'Thank you, sir. You know we need all the hands we can get to ensure tonight is as memorable as you plan.'

'Of course,' said Raegan with amused mistrust. 'Are you sure there's no agenda in your insistence? I'm familiar with your appetite.'

'Ha!' laughed Connell. 'Every effort should be rewarded, don't you agree?'

'Well, bloody earn it,' smiled Raegan as he slapped his henchman's thick shoulder. He motioned for the man to get back to work and to not busy himself with distractions. Picking up a biscuit that was cooling on the table, Raegan tore a bite and tossed the remains into the bin as he left the kitchen.

The hallway was hectic as maids assisted contractors to line the walls with decorations. Raegan had been persuaded to run with a forest theme and so streams of imperial greens and purples flowed from wall to wall. A maid stood at the foot of a long ladder as the hall-boy nervously carried a heavy ring of flowers framed by ivy. They were using these to hold the cloth to the walls like wild broaches. The material cascaded and created a gorgeous gangway that flowed to the grand hall. Beneath them, designers measured out the walls for their showpiece. Dancers and contortionists had been hired to serve as a live wall – moving like animated statues as the guests filtered past. Flustered by the creative fuss, Raegan left the specialists to it.

He was met with good news as he stepped out into the driveway. His signature fireworks display had arrived. The large wooden imported crates were being hauled off a cart and dragged to the sides of the estate. Like clockwork they would explode at midnight – bringing in the New Year with a bang. Raegan stood and applauded the men that carted the crates. On first hearing the rave reviews some many years ago, Raegan had made use of fireworks every year since. Each year brought with it a more elaborate and explosive spectacle, and this year was to be no different. He wanted the estate to be swallowed by light and had ordered twice as many rockets as the year before. He beamed like a child as his ground began to boast the tightly packed fused décor.

Upstairs, the dresses had been picked and now the ladies were prepped for their final fittings. Fiona had been tasked by her husband to make sure Grace looked picture perfect. She had already made sure Imogen was ready and dressed, having picked out a deep green yoke bodice and long nine gored skirt for herself and a pretty lime green princess gown for her daughter. The outfit aged her incredibly and Fiona took great delight in seeing the rare sight of Imogen dressed so maturely. She had decorated both outfits with golden broaches and matching hairpins that held their elegant hair neatly. Seeing that Imogen was content and comfortable, Fiona left her for a moment to check on Grace.

Standing alone in front of a mirror that stretched from the floor to the ceiling, Grace was admiring her attire. Fiona almost wept at the sight of her beautiful daughter. The gown was stunning in its simplicity. Made from the finest silk, the golden white material hugged every fine contour of Grace's gorgeous frame. A single slit reached from the hem to the waist and was framed by an intricate thread of golden flowers. This pattern was mirrored by the slips that embraced her delicate shoulders in a blaze of colour. Fiona treasured her children, and tonight Grace was the brightest jewel that had ever shone on Orplow.

The girl looked nervous as she surveyed herself in the glass mirror. Her fingers patted at the side of her gown and soft tears kissed at her cheeks. In that moment Grace belonged to nothing other than her own nature – she savoured the final instance where her spirit was able to soar to dreamy planes. Framed by the glass, the girl within now knew her future and no amount of dreaming could change that. Her heart took flight at the thought of the poems that she had received. The words within them had set her free and, now that she had found the author, she could harness her desires and reign in her dreams.

Fiona watched as Grace tended to her hair. Some of her wild wavy locks were swept up to the top of her crown as the rest flowed past her shoulders in curling tendrils. The hair that gathered at the crown was being held by a stunning clasp wherein Grace had entwined the pressed windflower. A smile crossed her face once her outfit was complete. Focusing behind her, Grace saw her mother in the mirror.

'You look beautiful,' said Fiona draped against the frame of the doorway. 'I hope the man who receives you is ready to be judged; it seems he's going to meet heaven before he knows it.'

'Please mother. Do you think he'll like me?' Grace looked at her mother through the widest of eyes.

'He would be a fool not to love you,' replied Fiona as she held Grace for the first time in years. She could feel the slight tremble of tears as Grace lost out to her nerves.

Chapter 26

Down in the kitchen, orders were being offered in fast supply.

'Most of you already know the drill, but we have a few fresh faces and I want to make sure everything is clear.' Connell offered his best attempt at a gracious smile towards Abigail Alpin. His grizzly grimace made him look like a constipated bear. Dressed entirely in white as all the men were, Michael stood at his mother's side. The starched high collars of his shirt pinched at his broad neck and the bowtie choked a little. He tugged at his vest and was pulling on his white gloves as Connell continued.

'Firstly, when being spoken to by any of the guests you will stand still,' snarled Connell. His gaze clamped onto Oscar who stumbled forward following the swift nudge he received by Michael. Red faced and stifling a laugh, Oscar stood back in line.

'Prick,' he whispered through the side of his mouth to Michael.

'Furthermore,' barked Connell as he stood an inch from Oscar's grinning mug. 'Never let your voices be heard by the ladies and gentlemen of the household... including their guests.' Flecks of saliva fired from his meaty lips and crashed into Oscar's face. Michael felt as if he had done a thousand sit ups as his stomach clenched in an attempt to bury the laughter that gripped his gut.

'If...' continued Connell now turning to the group of servants that lined the kitchen walls. '... And this is a gigantic *if*. If any of you have the privilege of being spoken to, you will use the proper appropriate address. And I stress... that this is a response only. Never are any of you advised or granted permission to begin a conversation with the guests. Is that understood?' A chorus of agreement sounded out.

'Finally, never offer your opinion to anyone. And always give room...' said Connell. He elaborated on seeing the questioning stares from the fresher faces. '...By this, I mean if you encounter one of your betters in a corridor or stairwell, you are to make yourself as invisible as possible.'

'Who said that?' mocked Michael as he looked at Oscar. Seeing that Oscar was gaining attention, Connell mistook where the comment had come from. He charged up to Oscar and gripped his chubby cheeks and spun him around to face the wall. 'By invisible,' spat Connell, 'I mean you shall turn your heads to the walls and avert your eyes from your superiors.'

Michael stepped between the feuding couple and stared directly into Connell's eyes. His dark eyes glistened as they locked on the thin squinting slits of Connell's. Seeing the defiance in Michael's sight, Connell let go of Oscar and stepped back a little. Stumbling back he nudged at the kitchen table. A bundle of cutlery clattered onto the floor and rang out a trembling shiver of sound. Fearing the impact of his embarrassment, Connell deflected the attention masterfully.

'That reminds me,' coughed Connell as he cleared his choked throat. 'If any items are dropped by our guests they should be returned to them on a salver.' Connell bent down and placed a fork onto a silver tray. He brought his right arm forward in a gesture of offering as the fork rested on the salver. In a flash he slipped the sharpest knife he could find up his sleeve. The boy's defiance was going to cost him greatly.

***

Soon the ball was in full flow. A tide of the wealthiest tenants of neighbouring counties poured into the hallway. Raegan watched with wonderment as they responded positively to the décor. The guests often stopped and applauded as the live wall of performers reached out and postured like living branches of the forest that sprung from the walls. The hallway was a sea of greens and purples pebbled by red berries. Inside the grand hall an ocean of music saturated the room. The guests were drenched by a montage of the finest concertos as Francis Morgan had again been employed to steer the orchestra. Much to Raegan's stormy discontentment, Francis had implored his employer to invite Cara — insisting that if the ball was to be remembered for its music then it was appropriate that the very best be invited to play. A slave to his egotism, Raegan had agreed to the notion but only on the condition that his daughter come alone, and must play once unaccompanied. Francis accepted the compromise before even telling Cara that she was set to perform. Sat by his side on the stage, Cara played freely and wore the widest of smiles.

The floor was filled by dancers. Couples interchanged between songs after courteously thanking their previous partner. The slim silhouettes of the gowns and dresses streamed and surged on the floor, pivoted by the stable shadows of the gentlemen. The sight was a glorious one — Raegan had surpassed himself once again.

Dressed in his darkest tail coat, Arnold Farrington entered the hall. His jet black waistcoat blended into the lapels of his coat and the white winged collared shirt hung loosely to his slight frame. His pale bowtie condemned any colour from his pasty complexion, and looking exasperated Arnold leaned to the left as a decorated cane held him upright. Attached to his right arm was the most beautiful thing Michael had ever laid his eyes upon. Grace radiated as she entered the room. The guests that surrounded her stood and watched as the beautiful lady floated by. Her expression was one of reticence and shy acceptance as she peeked from under her brow. Michael watched as the world's rotation began to slow down, merging the whirlwind of colours into one single blaze of light that encased his desire.

'Oh Christ,' said Michael. He turned on the spot and faced the wall behind him. The tray of champagne flutes brimming with bubbles rested in his hands.

'What are you up to?' scoffed Oscar, keeping his voice to a whisper. 'There's nobody even near to you, so why are you turning?'

'It's Grace,' replied Michael. 'That man she is with, I saw him here last night.'

'Last night?' quizzed Oscar. 'What the hell are you talking about you tit? You're meant to be *serving* those drinks not supping them.'

'It doesn't matter,' said Michael. Ignoring his friend's advice, Michael drained a flute into his mouth. The bubbles tickled at his throat as the drink made its descent into his tight stomach. He passed one to Oscar who did not need a second invitation.

'I need to speak with her,' said Michael as he turned to look at Grace. She was taking a seat at the head table as her gentleman leaned above her. Michael prayed the man did not sit next to her – he hoped there was no intimacy in their relationship. However, his heart exploded as a sickly acid tore in his veins on seeing the gentleman stumble into the chair that sat next to Grace. Stood behind the man, Raegan planted him into the seat by landing his compelling hands onto the man's spindly shoulders.

'You must be mental,' said Oscar through the side of mouth. His attempt at being subtle lacked any tact and he stood their looking as if he was trying to bite an itch on his earlobe. 'She will be guarded for the entire evening. Mike, a girl like that can demand the earth off anyone. Just plant your eye on one of the waitresses. I'm sure you can steal a cheeky knee trembler from any of them after the ball.'

'Too late,' smiled Michael. 'I've already seen her, and I'll be damned if I lose sight of her again.'

'It's your suicide,' scoffed Oscar.

Meanwhile, at the head table, a union was being attempted.

'Any instructions for the music?' boasted Raegan feeling powerful in his success. Arnold squirmed in his grip and looked at Grace to reply. Seeing her expectant expression, he knew he would have to find some form of response. He rubbed his injured leg when thinking of the strain of dancing.

'I'm not much for movement,' squeaked Arnold. He saw Raegan shrug with disinterest.

'Very well,' said Raegan in a neutral tone. 'I'll leave you two love birds to your evening.' He bounced away, gripping hands with grateful strangers as he passed.

'So,' said Grace. 'You don't care much for dancing?'

'No,' replied Arnold bluntly. His tone was cold and unsavoury. Grace put it down to nerves and pressed on with bridging the clear gap between them.

'I must say,' she continued. 'I'm quite glad that you aren't enamoured by the whole dance process. I'm quite awful myself, and fear you may need two canes by the end of the evening.' Her smile was met by a frosty gaze as Arnold saw no humour in her sentiment. Dogged in her desire to fire up the passion side of her companion, Grace soldiered on.

'Have you seen this?' she said as she placed her delicate fingers onto the windflower that decorated her golden hair clasp. Her knowing smile invited a warm reply from Arnold.

'Yes,' he said flatly. 'I was wondering about that.'

'Really,' said Grace beaming. 'I'm ever so happy that you noticed.'

'Yes,' replied Arnold. 'While you do look angelic this evening, I did wonder why on earth you had that God awful flower in your hair.'

'What? I wore it as a symbol. To symbolise my acceptance of your offer.'

'Oh…' said Arnold. 'I see. Well yes, the flower *is* lovely. I just see it as a little unnecessary that's all. You are quite beautiful without it.'

'Thank you,' smiled Grace. She looked around as if to guard a secret. 'I adore your words by the way. They grip me every time I think of them. I have to say that they are the most romantic thing that has ever happened to me.'

'My words?' said Arnold puzzled by the girl's passion. 'Well, I do tend to be forthright and upfront when I talk. I see no reason in hiding intentions.'

'Yes, when you talk of course,' said Grace as she rested her hand onto his. 'But what about when you write? Is that when you prefer to show your passionate side?'

'Writing?' scoffed Arnold as he took a drink of his wine. 'What the devil are you talking about my dear? The only thing I have had to write in recent times is my signature on the various land contracts I have been sealing. I suppose I'm quite passionate about the content of them, if that's what you mean.'

Grace felt the fool in her delusion. In an instant, it was clear that Arnold had not written a single word for her. The side of her face flushed and burned as she felt like she held the sole, scornful and contemptuous stare of the crowd. She sat completely still as her heart shattered.

'Now, let's speak of us,' said Arnold with an assuming smile.

✿✿✿

The opportunity he had been waiting for had arrived. The blood rushed into his loins and pushed at his throbbing manhood that rose in his lap. Running his damp squalid tongue across his sordid lips, Connell watched Abigail break off from the herd. Alone, she headed down the corridor that divided the grand hall from the kitchen quarters. Thrilled at the prospect of seizing her among the shadows of the corridor, Connell stood from his table and made his way inside. He pulled at the bottom of his vest as the tip of his lustful offering threatened to break through the belt line of his pants.

Entering the corridor, Connell saw that Abigail had bent down to reach inside a cupboard where the kitchen linen was kept. Her ripe buttocks were raised to the heavens when Connell approached. The little light that staggered through from the ball behind them bounced off the steel of the knife that slipped into Connell's sweaty palm. Gripping the handle, Connell brought his spare hand down to land on top of Abigail's behind. Startled she leapt up but her back arched forward as she felt the sharp prod of the blade behind her. A thick palm slammed into the wall beside her face as she became pressed against it. The stale stench of Connell's breath bit at her nose as he whispered into her ear.

'Looks like you're going to have to pay the price for your son's insolence earlier,' snarled Connell as he dragged his slavering tongue across Abigail's tender cheek. The saliva stuck like a gooey slug's trail to her smooth skin. 'I'm going to enjoy this,' whispered Connell, 'You can look away if you like. I'm your superior after all.' He coughed as he stifled his wicked laugh.

Abigail fingered at her rosary beads and closed her eyes – the steel crucifix was pinched between her trembling thumb and forefinger. She could feel Connell rustling at his pants behind her. His breathing had escalated into a rampant panting.

'Brace yourself Mrs Alpin,' said Connell excitedly. 'You're about to find out what it feels like to have a real man inside you.' She could hear the sound of his zip lowering. 'A woman like you deserves to feel more than what that Ferris offered.'

Connell's pursed lips exploded in a flash of crimson as Abigail crashed the crucifix across his repulsive face. Blood splattered the walls as it spurted from his torn lip. Connell shrieked as he pawed at his face in a vain attempt to stem the blood flow. Thick rivers of red hot liquid seeped through his fingers. Connell fell to his knees as he tripped over his lowered belt. Abigail watched him squeal on the floor as his lip hung like a freshly carved joint of beef. A sliver of flesh drooped along his jaw line as his mouth was gaped wide open. Finding the man at her mercy, Abigail made the sign of the cross, kissed her beads and returned to the ball.

The direction of Connell's fall meant that Abigail remained clean from any spray of blood. Pristine in her appearance, she filtered into the proceedings unnoticed. Her hand shook under the linen that she was holding and she was glad that she was not tasked at holding any of the trays for the moment. Remembering her son, Abigail glanced across the crowd to find him. He was stood as still as a statue when she found him. People passed by and took a drink from his tray without him even flinching in acknowledgement. Tracing the direction of his fixed stare, Abigail found what had rooted her son to the spot. At the very tip of his focus was Grace. Abigail felt for her son as she watched him refuse to move. Feeling compelled to assist him, Abigail engineered her chores to bring her closer to the stage. She waited patiently for the opportunity to speak with Francis Morgan. The man danced as he rang out the most beautiful music the land could boast. Seeing that he was wanted, Francis made his way to Abigail and listened to her instructions intently.

Michael stood still and tried to read the words that danced off the lips of Grace's companion. He struggled to piece an entire sentence together as his view was momentarily broken by the passing crowds. They had grown thirsty through all their dancing and Michael's tray was becoming light. Grace looked unhappy as her ears were bombarded by her gentleman. Michael counted the seconds between the man's breathing – he did not pause for a moment as his lips rattled on at an alarming pace. It disturbed Michael that throughout the man's speech, he never once looked into Grace's eyes. Surely, if he had he could see the sadness etched into her stare – the lost look that kept her motionless in her chair. Even her head refused to nod politely at the end of her companion's sentences. This fact, however, had not gone unnoticed. Seeing that he had lost his audience, the gentleman became frustrated. His lips began to fire out words as his face contorted into a furious frown. Met with nothing but silence, the man stood to his feet. Michael almost rushed the man as he saw him clench his fist and begin to raise it. However, he was merely preparing to grip his cane before storming out of the ballroom. Raegan followed him as closely as a stitched on shadow.

Seeing their exit, Francis motioned to Cara. Seamlessly, they changed concertos. Dictated by the subliminal alteration, the dancers began to leave the floor. Abigail watched to see Michael's reaction. Sat in the centre of the stage, Cara plucked at a golden harp as her fingers rained out O'Carolan's concerto.

The music moved Michael. He began to head towards Grace's table, breezing past the crowds that tried to stop him so that he could serve them. His heart was pounding between his every step, and his mouth became dry as he drew closer. Plotting his move, Michael rustled in his pocket for something he had been keeping.

Grace sat alone. Her ears were numb from the words that Arnold had thrown at her. The bright future she had envisaged was now unclear as she tried to piece together the recent events. Her father had decided to follow Arnold out of the room rather than try and reason the situation with his own daughter. Having heard Arnold's every word, Grace found that she had no answers to his questions; she no longer shared his cold optimism or clear intent. He was not the man she had dreamt him to be, and so her answers were no longer the same. Sat still and listening to the music, Grace tried to find her answers. But before she could, she was asked another question.

'Ma'am' said the soothing voice from beside her. 'Did you drop this?'

Grace's heart clenched at the sight of Michael. He was knelt by her side and had in his hand a small silver salver. Her eyes welled up when she saw the pristine windflower that rested on top of the dish. Momentarily, her hand flashed up to her hair to check whether hers sat still in her hair clasp. Her fingers trembled as she felt the petals beneath them.

'I'm speechless,' whispered Grace as her heart held her breath from her.

'Then let me find the right words for you,' smiled Michael. Everything he had ever wanted stared back at him with the most breath-taking of eyes. He looked up at the stage and then back at Grace. 'This is my favourite piece of music. Will you dance with me?'

'I can't,' said Grace sadly. Her eyes stayed on Michael but her chin dipped a little into her chest.

'Because of the rules of the house?' asked Michael boldly. 'Don't worry. Let me answer to them.'

'No,' smiled Grace radiantly. 'I simply can't dance, as I don't know how to.'

'Ha!' Michael stood and held out his hand. 'Then take off your shoes and stand on mine. I'll take you around.'

Feeling defiant, Grace did as she was told. Slipping her feet from her slippers, she stood in front of Michael. He took the lead stance as Grace tentatively stepped onto his feet. Their mouths were millimetres apart as she stumbled slightly forward, sharing the same breath. Then Michael held her firmly. Soft music drifted out from the stage and the picked strings of the harp plucked the night air. Grace had never heard the song before but let it carry her as Michael began to dance. Together they glided across the floor as the crowd stood and watched them. No other pair dared to enter the floor as Grace and Michael danced their dance. Entwined in a bright white, their bodies dovetailed and moved harmoniously. Michael's eyes never left Grace's as he held her hands in his. Their chests were pressed together and their hearts raced to capture the other's beat. The desire inside them fired their movement as the passion burst from Michael's fleeting feet. His hands held Grace tightly and her head swam each time Michael smiled at her.

Hearing the music draw to a close, Michael stood from Grace and bowed. The ballroom was in complete silence; perplexed looks pictured the faces of the guests. Michael began to breathe deeply as the anxiety returned. His hand still rested in Grace's when Raegan burst furiously into the room. The old man's face was thunderous and his cheeks threatened to burst with the blood that boiled beneath them. He offered a startled look around him – gawping from guest to guest – struggling to work out what was going on. His head spun to the sound of a single pair of hands applauding loudly. Stood at the rear of the room, Oscar began to clap and cheer. Each pop that came from his chubby hands appeared to dictate Raegan's heart rate – his chest expanded and contracted as rapid as an untamed river.

Seeing her father's distraction, Grace pulled at Michael's arm and ran for the door. Together they pushed through the crowd, out through the hallway and into the night. Stood outside, Grace paused and looked up at Michael for guidance. Throwing his eyes across the fields and back at Grace, he gripped her hand as they continued to run through the fields. The long grass parted as the couple ploughed on – their feet beating at the ground that supported them.

The stars above dazzled like unruly treasures in the dark sky. They shone sporadically upon the land and lit the way for the young couple running beneath them. Oblivious to the confusion that they left behind, Grace and Michael pushed on and refused to pause. The darkness held the bright smiles they wore from one another, but their fingers felt the other's grip, making them feel safe in their escape. The great waters of Lake Doriend sat at their side and guided them to the coast, as the land began to rise beneath their eloping feet. The moon stood invitingly as it hung close to the horizon in front of them.

Running short of breath, they reached the cliff-face. Michael stood before Grace and his head whooshed as the momentum caught up with him and nudged him forward. Grace grabbed at his vest, stopping him from falling. He turned in her grip – her arm wrapped around his waist. So close to him, Michael could feel Grace's lungs fill with excited and baited breath. Their eyes met as they mirrored their smiles. Pulling Grace into him, Michael leaned his head and moved forward to kiss her.

In the distance a flash of light filled the land like an exploding star. It caused the couple to pause and look behind them. Far in the distance, the Darby estate was bathed in glittered fire that rose higher than the tallest wall. The New Year had arrived and Michael only had one intention. Resolute, he looked at Grace and spoke.

'Care to fall?'

Her light laughter was all the consent he needed. Swinging their clasped hands backwards towards the skies, Michael and Grace ran to the cliff's edge and jumped. For the slowest second they had ever experienced, Grace and Michael floated towards the line where the heavens met with the sea. Their hearts leapt in their chests as the cove pulled at them from below. The ocean winds cut at their bodies as it gushed through their hair. Feeling the chilling water crash around them, Michael pulled Grace in close and wrapped her in his arms. He thrashed out his powerful legs as the waters dragged them downwards. Above, like the brightest of lighthouses, the full moon shone through the surface of the pool.

Biting at the air, Grace and Michael broke through the surface. Their laughter echoed through the night and bounced off the sea kissed walls of the cove. Treading water, they clambered out of the pool and onto the side of the rocks. Their clothing clung to their bodies as they made their way around the side of the rocks. The waters surged above them as the waterfall pulverised the pool – pushing up crushed powdered jets of mist from the surface. Michael held Grace as he led her behind the pouring waters and into the cave where they had both hidden years before.

Sheltered from the cold, they enjoyed the heat that lay within the cave. The light of the moon illuminated the falling waters like clear glass before them. Moonlight danced at their feet as they stood facing one another, toe to toe. She ran her finger down the scar that kissed at Michael's brow. Michael could not wait a moment longer and brought his lips to meet with Grace's. He kissed her deeply and held her by her waist as they shared their stolen breath. Her stomach jolted at the thunder that roared out from her heart. Her hands ran through his thick hair, and she was cradled in his strong arms. Breaking from the kiss, Grace leaned into Michael's ear and whispered.

'I want you.'

The words both weakened and strengthened Michael. His knees buckled a little as his arms held her tighter. Terrified in his excitement, he kissed her again. Her hands raced over his body and pulled the shirt from his back. Drawing the flowered slips from her shoulders, Michael brought the gown to fall from Grace's frame. Her teeth bit gently at his neck as her hands danced at his belt. Soon, they were stood before each other as naked as the day they were first brought into the world.

Fired by his lust for love, Michael clutched at Grace's wrists and held them above her head as he rested hers against the stony walls of the cave. He entwined his fingers with hers as she wrapped her legs around his waist. Their lips crashed together as they felt their bodies join. Electricity surged inside Grace – her thighs clamped around Michael as she could feel him growing harder inside. Yearning to enjoy every inch of her, Michael slowly lowered Grace down onto him. The sensation stole her breath as she bit into his neck – locking her lips onto his tense throat. Michael released her hands and brought his to rest on her face. His eyes dived into hers as she gently rocked her hips – bringing him deeper inside her. His muscular legs trembled as she shuddered astride him. Her hands clasped at the back of his hair as her nails dug in a little. Tightening her thighs, Grace's toes curled as Michael brought her to the brink of ecstasy.

Outside a storm was brewing. The heavens had opened upon the land and fired down a torrent of of rainfall that fought the fireworks that burst from the land. The waves of the ocean rose, and the sands of the beach seized the rain tightly. Like kisses from heaven, the rain drops touched the tide that soon devoured each and every one of them. Protected behind the falling waters, Grace and Michael descended into the highest plane of passion. Guarded from the heavens, the couple basked in the love that they had made.

Chapter 27

'Where in Christ's name is she?' The vein in Raegan's temple throbbed like an irritated earth worm. He drank his whisky straight from the bottle.

'How am I supposed to know? I left her for a minute and now she's dropped off the face of the earth.' The cane dug into Arnold's palm as his tired legs pulled at him.

'Well, when I saw her last she was with that cretin Michael Alpin. But then she ran off.' Raegan rubbed his temple, massaging the worm. 'That boy has been trouble from the very first moment I knew of him. However, his father was no different. The smug shit.' Raegan drank to a more distant memory.

'I couldn't care less about some rogue's father,' barked Arnold. 'The pressing matter is that my fiancé is missing and if we want our partnership to work, it's pretty crucial that we find her.'

'Fiancé?' Raegan shook himself from his private memory. 'So you asked her? Good man.' He knocked Arnold's shoulder with the bottle of whiskey.

'Not as such. But it's agreed in principle with yourself, so I can't see there being any problems. Apart... of course... from the little matter of knowing where the hell she ran off to? If this Alpin fellow has stolen my lady, then I'll kill him.' His anger was unconvincing.

Raegan knew the feeling only too well. The fire in his eyes became shaded by his fatigue. The night was heavy upon the land and the household was being tidied around them. The ball had finished some hours ago and all the guests had parted merrily; their remains lay sprinkled and strewn across every surface of the hall. Tilted glasses rested on empty tables and ripped ribbons peppered the floors. Raegan had heard the whispers of the dance shared between Michael and his daughter, but nobody had braved him with the full story. His blood curdled at the thought of that small farm hand having the audacity to proposition his Grace. He strangled the neck of the bottle as he pulled it to his pursed lips. His eyes watered as the blistering drink drowned his tight throat.

'Come now,' issued Raegan patting Arnold on the shoulder. He ushered the unsteady man towards the door. 'Let's get some rest.'

'Shouldn't we go looking for Grace?'

'Not at all,' laughed Raegan. 'One night won't change a thing. Her future is set. And anyway, don't you worry about anyone else. If everyone just looks out for themselves, then everyone is happy, that's what I say. Those that care about the fates of others only risk missing out on their share of the action. By the way, you have signed the papers that I left you, haven't you?'

Arnold nodded as he digested his host's slurred advice.

'Good man,' said Raegan.

***

Grace rested her head on Michael's chest as she slept. Michael was awake – the song of the seagulls had stirred him over an hour ago. While the morning sun remained swallowed by the ocean, a thin grey light paved the seas. The falling waters drew a clear curtain between the cove and the cave. Michael held Grace's soft hand in his. He played with her fingers as he ran his thumb across her thin, dainty fingertips. His love for her was eternal: complete and infinite in design. He traced out the figure of eight in her palm with his forefinger, staying completely silent so not to wake her from her peaceful slumber. He kissed her gently on her head as his heaving chest cradled her. She moved as Michael wrote three simple words in her hand. Words he would never get to tell her.

Michael breathed in time with the waves that lapped at the rocks outside; their piercing teeth chewed the waters that broke upon them. Seeing a single ray of light break across the ocean, Michael woke Grace. She was wrapped in his shirt and perched up beside him.

'Good morning,' she managed before yawning widely. She rubbed at her eyes and blinked several times. Michael tilted her chin upwards and kissed her.

'The sun…' Michael nodded towards the curtain of water. 'It's rising.'

They both stood and walked past the waterfall. They sat on the drying rock-pools and watched the morning sun light up the world before them. Strands of light shot out across the land, piercing every shadow, in every corner of the day. The firelight burst on the blades of grass that swayed and cooled in the ocean's breeze. Michael gripped Grace as the blazing sphere emerged from its watery bed. A singed shade of orange coloured the muddied corners of the fields where night cowered and crept away. Filling the skies like the Lord's eye, the sun rose triumphantly before its intimate audience.

'That is the most beautiful thing I've ever seen,' said Grace as her heart melted at the scene.

'I couldn't agree more,' replied Michael with his eyes locked onto Grace. His smile blazed brightly when she faced him. Her hand ran tenderly down his strong jaw-line and came to rest on his shoulder. The words he wished to say teetered on the tip of his tongue as Grace kissed him fully. Her arms wrapped around his neck as he pulled her on top of him. The sun was completely in place before the lovers finished their embrace.

The Windflower twirled in Grace's fingers as she watched Michael get dressed. She held the flower in front of her, blocking her sight of him. His movement ran like a motion picture as broken glimpses of him could be stolen through the gaps of the spinning petals. Grace smiled as she toyed with her gift. Her gown remained a glorious white as it hugged her perfect frame. Her hair was tussled, as the golden hair clasp rested in her lap. She had both flowers in the palms of her hands.

'It was you…' said Grace staring at the flowers. '…The whole time. It was you?'

'It's always been me.' He stood before her and placed his hands over the flowers. Her smile crippled him – he had no defences against it. But then defences would be as senseless as a damned lake in a drought ridden landscape. Free in the fear that the woman could break his heart entirely, Michael savoured what he had found.

'And the poems… Did you make those also?'

'No,' Michael paused as he held her hands. 'I just wrote them. It was you that made them.'

The sea held the gaze of the sun above. The seals began to leave the cold waters and bathe in the warmth of the morning light. They lay out on the rocks and stared at the gulls that circled overhead. The morning was bright but came with a cold bite in the breeze. Grace clung to Michael as they walked out onto the sandy shores of the beach. The winds gripped them as they walked. Gentle waves lapped at their heels before the sea dragged them back to where they began. In the distance, just below the horizon, Dolphins broke the surface of the sea – dancing to the tempo of the gentle tide. Grace felt safe in Michael's arms. All her doubts drifted and he dreams soared when she was with him. The solitude she had endured had left her guarded and fretful; the love that had shrouded her childhood had always been accompanied by pain. Glimmers of hope had always come when she saw Michael – when her feelings felt true and justified. In his presence, Grace felt free in his protection; secure in her emotions. She walked on with the one man who meant everything to her.

The far fields stretched out before them. Meadows roamed for miles in search of the next. The valleys leaned the land back from the coastline. The hard Devonian-aged rock was quilted by carboniferous limestone – the pastures upon them fertile and lush. Michael stood and watched Grace walk in front of him. She held her arms out and leaned her head back as she swirled through the long grass. She hummed what she could recall of the song that she and Michael had danced to at the ball. She looked her most beautiful when she smiled, and she wore her brightest one of all as she spun through the meadow. Her gown lit up the land around her – the morning sun bounced from the white silk and ignited the golden flowers that decorated her dress.

Disabled by the distance between them, Michael ran to her. She jumped into his arms as he spun her around. The wind blew at her hair as Michael joined Grace in her song. Her legs swung out as Michael continued to spin. She closed her eyes and imagined taking flight – she felt like an angel that reigned over the land. Grace opened her eyes as she felt Michael beginning to slow down. Coming to a complete stop, Grace pressed herself into Michael's chest. His arms felt like they would never let her go.

'Stay with me,' whispered Michael as he held Grace tightly. The breeze carried the soft sound of birds singing.

'Leave with me.' Grace flashed a desperate glance towards the estate. Her brow furrowed pleadingly as she looked back at Michael.

'Leave? to where?'

'Who knows? But at least it's away from here. This town will never let us be together, you know that. There are too many obstacles.'

'Our fates are own Grace. Nothing can keep us apart.'

'Oh, I wish that were true, Michael. I really do. But certain people have great designs on my fate, and they'll stop at nothing to put them into action.' She paused for thought. 'Promise me that you'll never leave me.'

'I do. With all my heart, I do'

'I know, but just say it… please.'

'Alright, I promise.' Michael felt his feet become rooted to the spot. The pebbles that bordered the waters of the lake shifted beneath him. The wind whistled through the reeds and pulled towards the shore.

'Do you know something? Ever since the time I found you hiding by this lake, I've waited each night, at the very same spot, just in case you returned for me.'

Grace looked about her. She remembered how scared she had been that night. Flashes of her beaten mother filled her eyes. She could feel the intense fear that she had felt that evening – the complete dread of being lost forever. But standing by Michael, the land had changed. And now, the fields again became alive in their stillness – the soft melody of life furrowed beneath the crops, hidden and safe from the sun's spying eye.

'Will you wait for me tonight?' Grace pulled away from Michael and observed his reaction. He did not even flinch. He stepped closer to her.

'Let hell try and stop me.'

✳✳✳

The mourning continued inside the church. Knelt in front of a series of candles, Abigail once more prayed for her lost husband's soul. As usual, she begged the Lord for his redemption and their eternal reunion. Her hands clasped the rosary beads between them in prayer – the tips of her fingers reaching for the heavens and firing her words skywards. The passion that she witnessed the previous evening had brought her an equal amount of joy and anguish; the sight of her son in love fetched fond memories that were now forever tainted by tragedy.

The church windows remained closed at the break of day. The westerly breeze bled through the cracks and licked at the candlelight. Great greetings could be heard outside. The clattering of crates punched the gaps between the cries of the traders; the market was being braced for business. A dull din sounded within the walls of the church, accompanying Father Daniel's duties as he tiredly paced up the aisle, placing a generous and optimistic pile of prayer books on each and every stall. The priest was no fool, and he had witnessed the drop in attendance over the recent years. He reasoned that the new generation of folk worked all week and refused to forsake their weekends for some notion they cared not to believe – a notion that prevented them to enjoy what they had grown to regard so highly: their time. The rewarding principle of self-sacrifice was dead.

'Bless you my child, I didn't see you there' said Father Daniel as he tripped over the trailing heel of Abigail.

'I'm sorry father,' replied Abigail. She made the sign of the cross and stood to her feet. She embraced the priest and kissed him gently on the side of his face. His hand rose and patted at his rosy cheek in a vain attempt to disguise his unease. The physical boundary was one the church had chosen for him, and one he had adhered to vehemently. He knew Abigail's gesture was one of polite greeting rather than a lustful advance, but a prayer of forgiveness from temptation would be added to his list regardless. His fingers pressed at the prayer book in his hands.

'Father,' said Abigail with soft disquiet. 'I need your help.'

'What with my dear?' His breath was free from the communal wine and his tongue was his own.

'Answers…' She looked at the statue of Christ on the cross for the first time in years. 'I ask every day for the Lord's guidance. I even light a candle each time I pray, and yet all I have come to know is the darkness of my doubt.'

'And what is it that you seek? Wealth? A sound harvest, maybe? Or just good health?'

'My love, father. I seek my love.' A solitary tear washed over her eye.

'But it's clearly within you my child,' replied the priest. 'In all my time, I've never seen such commitment and sacrifice from another soul. Your prayers are generous in both their volume as well as purpose. Now, the Lord may seem silent at times, but he is never ignorant. Your efforts will be rewarded… but such a reward is not for me to measure.' His hands held her shoulders firmly. It was the first time Father Daniel had seen any hint of frailty in the woman. He had always admired and envied the lady for the strength that she drew from her very weakness – the clean and chaste commitment she had shown to the crippling vice that was her loyalty. The church had been Abigail's crutch, and Father Daniel was not intending to let her lean away from it.

'Have I wasted my time though Father? Have all my efforts to redeem my late husband been deemed selfish and futile?'

'My child, I can't answer that. But all I can say is that the moment Ferris took his own life he met with the answers that you now seek – leaving you with all the questions. I'm sorry to say that his act was selfish and would have been punished. That, I have no doubt about. But whether he can be saved… well that's just a matter of faith.'

'Thank you Father,' said Abigail. She genuflected towards the altar as she passed and made her way up the aisle. Her chest heaved as a dry, hearty cough ruptured the silent, dead air. Abigail cupped her hand to her mouth as she continued to cough loudly. Father Daniel turned away from the grave dusty sound of the cough. He saw Abigail raise her hand apologetically towards him. Facing the font, Abigail dropped her hands to dash them with holy water. Thick, bold droplets of crimson blood dripped from her fingers. She opened her palms to see the pool of blood that she was cupping. Suddenly, the light closed in around her as she turned to gather help. Stood in front of the altar, Father Daniel made the sign of the cross to his God. He did not see the lady collapse behind him.

✻✻✻

Michael felt alive. The love that he had realised invigorated him. His heart beat louder than it had ever done before, and his head dared to design dreams much clearer than he had ever allowed himself to imagine. The sweet scent of Grace lingered on his clothing, drawing him back to the moment he first kissed her. His arms felt light and empty without her. Thinking of the night that lay ahead, excitement gripped Michael. He had agreed to meet with Grace by the lake and together they were going to disappear. They had not spoken of how long they would go for, or exactly where to – only that it would be together. That was all that now mattered to them both – the harmony they had discovered in that fragile yet fixed moment.

Michael had enough money saved to let them travel. The thought of crossing the boundaries of the town had never appealed to him before – everything he had ever needed had been found within Orplow. But now everything that mattered was threatening to leave, and Michael could never abandon it. Like an old friend bidding farewell, the fields looked sad and downtrodden around him. The winds had picked up and floored the meadows. Rows of crops lay browbeaten to the ground as the breeze ploughed through them. The day had grown cold, and clouds drifted between the sun and the demanding land it embraced. Warmed only by thoughts of Grace, Michael was oblivious to the pressing chill in the air.

The cottage was empty. The front door creaked as Michael walked inside. Breakfast plates lay clean and dried out by the basin. Parched, Michael made a pot of tea and sat for a moment. Thinking of his evening, he drank in the memories. Flashes of Grace washed over him. The smile he wore tore at his ears. He ran his hands through his thick hair and gripped the back of it. He smirked as he recalled Grace pulling at it the night before – the sight of her gasping face calling to his very fibre.

Outside, the winds rapped at the windows. The shutters slammed and bulked at the storm that was brewing, but Michael could not care less. He was safe from the world outside and nothing that nature commanded was going to change his course now.

Changing for the day ahead, Michael put on his thick trousers and a clean shirt. The braces slapped at his shoulders as he pulled them on. Seeing that his bed was still unmade, Michael began to tuck the cover under the corners of the lean mattress. His fingers felt the book prodding out from within his pillowcase. Pulling the final book from the case, Michael laughed heartily. He had never needed to write a fourth or final poem as he had planned. Fate had already handed him Grace before he had time to tell her his true feelings. Shaking his head, Michael scoffed at the thought that one more poem would matter. He now had a lifetime to show her how he felt, and countless poems could never exhaust his emotions. Rewarded by impulses, Michael knew that no amount of writing would summarise what a single action could ever show her. Striving only to act, Michael decided he would leave with her tonight. But, first he would talk with his mother to show her the reason in what he feared she would surely deem madness.

The book twitched in his fingers. Despite its gratuity, Michael thought that maybe he should write another. After all, Grace *had* mentioned the impact that the poems had on her – the way they forced her heart to make decisions her head saw as mistaken. Picking up his pencil, Michael wanted to prove to Grace that he was the author – that the chance to fulfil her dreams lay in his hands. He lay back and drew inspiration from his muse. The night he had spent with her defined him entirely, and now he could never let go. Finding the words to write, Michael wrote one of the last poems Grace would ever read.

Satisfied by his labours, Michael rested on his bed. The mattress dug into his back and the pillows felt empty. He cupped his head as he rested in his hands. Exhausted in his excitement, Michael afforded himself the small luxury of an afternoon nap. He could not recall the last time that he had slept during the day as his years had been filled with countless distractions. Closing his eyes, Michael relaxed and let the darkness drift over him.

***

Sat up in his bed, Michael did not know if he was still dreaming. A heavy haze swirled around him – his head felt dazed and dizzy. The news Oscar was offering was hellish. He had shaken Michael from his slumber before he delivered his cannonball straight to Michael's gut. Michael rubbed his eyes. The fact they were dry made him again question if he was still dreaming – surely the news would have made him cry. Rocked by shock and racked with apprehension, Michael felt useless. The words had hit him hard and left him punch-drunk. Distracted and distressed, he did not realise that two other people stood around his bedside. Margaret was busy gathering Michael's coat as Maik stood by. He held open Michael's satchel and watched Margaret fill it with whatever her hands landed on – some spare clothing, money and the one remaining book. Maik could see that his wife was panicking, but he let her remain busy in her distraction. They both stayed silent as Oscar delivered the news.

Getting to his feet Michael felt his knees give way beneath him. Oscar grabbed his friend and held him upright.

'Come on pal,' said Oscar. 'I've got you.'

Michael had no idea where he was. He had lost track of the exact time; the date had completely escaped him. Having heard the news, Michael allowed himself to listen to it. The words Oscar had brought had frozen Michael to the spot, and left him little choice. Looking for guidance and powerless by its absence, Michael found himself completely lost without his mother.

Chapter 28

Grace waited alone. The evening was several hours old and Michael had not shown up. She had packed a small bag and was prepared for leaving the town. She had written a letter for each member of her family, and would post them once she was safely miles from home. Other than these letters, Grace carried very little. She wanted to start afresh with Michael – to build a life from the ground upwards. The thought had terrified her initially; she would be leaving a lifetime of security behind her. Resting by the lake, Grace suddenly felt vulnerable. The sun was setting. The birds had begun their long flight home, and the outstretched crops clung to the last strands of light that passed over them. The waters of the lake continued to flow ceaselessly to the coast – streaming tirelessly to the daunting depths of the ocean. A scented breeze kicked up hints of lavender and bid the day adieu. Stood between night and day, Grace continued to wait.

The clouds of doubt gathered with each passing moment. The fields teased as branches cracked and bushes rustled. Turning to every sound, Grace prayed that one would soon carry Michael to her. Her hands clasped the straps of her tiny bag tightly. Michael was pushing it. Grace had been seen returning home, and had so far successfully avoided her father, but it would not be long until his search party were put to task. Remaining where they had both agreed, Grace hoped Michael would find her. She was beginning to feel lost as the night drew closer.

The venom of the unknown began to set in. Images of Michael boasting of his conquest flashed before her – the town cheering as he provided every sordid and intimate detail. She shook the thought from her head; she knew him not to be that type of man. All the times she had watched him work, she had built up a story of a man loyal and true – a man who would not abandon whatever he loved. But maybe she had been mistaken. She'd heard the rumours of his past exploits and adventures – the tales of his triumphs throughout the town. Maybe she was just another notch on the bedpost? Maybe the night they shared amounted to nothing more than a one fingered salute to her father? Stood alone, she tried her best to stop her mind from releasing the crippling poison of paranoia.

She sought sanctuary in the memories of the night they had spent together. She recalled how all her doubts had drifted away at the very sight of him – how in his presence he made her feel like the world was theirs and theirs alone. Her stomach flipped at the thought of their first kiss. Flutters filled the pits of her belly. The soft dimples on his cheeks hugged the creases of his beautifully dark eyes when he smiled at her. Feeling the cold touch of the evening air, she longed for his arms – his strong embrace to carry her away. But instead she stood alone as the waters continued to pass towards the changing tide.

'I knew I would find you.'

Feeling her heart leap and clog her throat, Grace turned towards the man behind her. Stood facing her – with his arms open wide – Arnold Farrington wore his most welcoming of smiles.

***

'She needs to rest here for now,' said the doctor. His eyes were a bright blue and blazed beneath his jet black hair. Michael watched as he read from the flip board in his hands. He reeled off the conditions like a cheap check list.

'Mr Alpin, your mother has tuberculosis. The tests we've run show this to be very serious. You see, what we call *primary* tuberculosis is shown through a series of symptoms not uncommon to the flu. However, our results are showing that the infection has spread to multiple organs throughout your mother. In light of this, it's very likely that your mother is experiencing a reactivation of the infection – or what we call *secondary* tuberculosis.'

Michael was flummoxed by the jargon. All he'd gathered was that whatever was eating away at his mother it had begun to spread, and rapidly. The back of his head thumped at the wall as he let the thinly painted cold concrete carry his weight. The doctor continued with his report.

'Your mother has cavitary lesions on both of her lungs – this is what caused the massive haemoptysis she suffered earlier today.'

'What?'

'The bloody cough your mother experienced – it's a symptom of damage to the lungs caused by the infection. The fact that she collapsed is also a concern, and we are waiting on the results to see whether she is suffering further Potts disease.' He saw Michael's *cut the bull* expression. 'It's an infection in the vertebrae which can cause compression on the spinal-chord and paralysis.'

'Paralysis? Jesus! Is my mother paralysed doc?' Michael stood away from the wall.

'There is a chance... maybe. Firstly, we need to wait on the results. We may find that we can operate and drain the spinal abscesses that are applying pressure onto her spinal cord. But I'm afraid there are a few more pressing matters.'

Michael had seen the expression on the doctor's face a thousand times. The tense smile, the wincing eyes – it was not good news.

'How long?'

'We can't say for sure... a week at most.'

'Oh God...' Michael clasped his hands in front of his face. His lips pursed on the side of his forefingers as if he was kissing a silent prayer.

'The infection is no longer localised and has spread beyond repair. We advise that she stays with us. We have an iron-lung ward that can assist if her breathing weakens. But I must tell you that it's most likely that your mother will pass from respiratory failure. I truly am sorry.'

'But this iron lung... wont that keep her alive?'

'For a while longer, yes. But it only assists the patient with their breathing. It's a mechanical casement that surrounds them and covers the basic breathing functions. But it doesn't cure anything... it's merely a preservation tool.'

'Does my mother know?'

'Yes.'

'And what's her view on it? Does she want to stay here?'

'I think you may need to talk to her about that. But I strongly advise that we give her as much time for her to make her peace as we can, don't you?'

'That's not a problem. She's been doing that for as long as I've known her.'

Michael looked over to his mother. She was resting on her bed as Margaret made a fuss at her side. He could see how his mother still smiled and laughed at her flustered friend. Michael fought the tears that beat at his eyes. He took a drink of water to flush the ball of grief from his throat. He placed his satchel on the narrow cabinet that stood by his mother's bed. Margaret ushered her family away as she saw Michael staring at his mother. She smiled at Abigail before slapping Maik and Oscar into action. They scurried out of the ward like reluctant rats abandoning their sinking ship.

'I don't know what to say,' said Michael. He rested his hand onto his mother's. Her fingers felt cold beneath his.

'Don't worry Michael. Despite what those doctors say, I'm fine... believe me.'

'No, you're not,' shouted Michael. He shrugged shyly as his words lifted higher than the whispers that surrounded the neighbouring bedsides.

'Listen...' She swallowed tiredly. '... I'm happy Michael. If the Lord wants to take me, then that's his design. I can't change it, and I won't stop it.'

'What are you saying?'

'I know they have some contraption to postpone the inevitable. But son, death comes to us all... and I just have to accept it.'

'But, I don't want to lose you.'

'You won't. I'll always be with you... just have a little faith.'

Michael bit his lip. His heart had abandoned his religion the moment he found out the fate chosen by his father. Fearing losing his mother for an eternity, he knew that he would have to put his heart back into his faith – if only to keep her with him.

'Do you think father will be waiting for you?'

'I hope so Michael. But either way, I'll be waiting for you. Remember that always.'

'I'm not going anywhere,' whispered Michael as he offered his signature smile. Abigail saw the doubt flash across his beautiful eyes.

✱✱✱

Grace did not stay at home for long. She offered no answers for her disappearance and prompted no questions from Arnold. It settled her to see that he did not demand an explanation – instead showing an intense gratitude at finding her safe and sound. Walking her back from the fields, he had showered her with compliments dressed in concern – coloured by jealousy and territorial pride. Grace was destroyed when Michael had not turned up. He had broken her vision of a true love; a love where emotions echoed and words were worthless. She had dreamed of finding a man who did not need to tell her how he felt; a man who could make her feel it just by being near to her. This was the way Michael had made her feel, and it was exactly this that he had shattered the instance he left her alone. Confused and abandoned, Grace sought comfort in the words of Arnold. The plans he mapped out began to appeal in their simplicity. They were set to build an empire that would secure their families for generations. It was in his company that Grace's heart began to change.

Having hidden her bag and listened to the reasoning of Arnold, Grace visited her sister Cara. The house felt silent on approach, and only a solitary light shone from within. Grace had no need to knock as David and Cara beat her to opening the door.

'Oh... sister,' said Cara sadly. 'So you've heard the dreadful news?'

'What news?'

'It's the sweet Abigail Alpin,' replied David as he pulled on his long coat. 'She's fallen sick. She's up at the hospital, and we're set to go and visit her. Your father honoured us with the courtesy of ordering a car to take us up there.'

'Oh my...' Grace was stunned by the news. 'Would it be alright if I joined you?'

'Of course,' declared Cara. 'I'm sure Michael could do with seeing you. That's if he hasn't seen enough already?' She tried to add humour to the grave situation.

'My thoughts exactly,' said Grace sorrowfully.

✳✳✳

Connell had been sent to take them to the hospital. He chose to remain outside as his passengers made their way into the dreaded building. A small fire flicked in his hands as he lit a cigarette and watched them disappear inside the large main doors of the west wing. The large red bricks of the building loomed over him as he leant up against the nearest wall and took his first draw on his cigarette. The smoke bellowed from his dry chapped mouth, stinging the raw flesh that hung between the stitches. He hissed as he drew breath for his next puff, resting the damp paper of the butt on the gristle that he now called a lower lip.

The lights inside the wards bathed the room in a decayed yellow. Grace hung back as David and Cara went to Abigail's bedside. Grace could not believe her eyes. The way Abigail had aged over night was terrifying – the colour in her face had drained and her skin sagged like damp clay. She had been alive in all her beauty the night before but now she lay dying and looking her most grave. Grace scanned the room but could not see Michael. His jacket hanged on a chair next to the bedside cabinet. She felt nervous at the prospect of seeing him. While she was excited earlier by the prospect of spending the rest of his life with him, she now stood anxious in her tempered anger. Grace felt like she needed to apologise for the emotions she had experienced that day by the lake – to repent for feelings that Michael never knew she harboured. Coming closer to the bedside, Grace busied herself by tidying the items that rested on the cabinet. Clumsily she knocked a satchel to the floor. The items inside poured out. Feeling the fool, Grace rushed to gather the items that sprawled in front of her. She bundled the items of clothing back into the satchel until one item stopped her dead. Beneath a creased clean shirt, Grace found the final book. Her hands shook as she picked it up.

'How are you feeling Abigail?' Cara took hold of her hand.

'I'm fine, thank you.' She smiled brightly. 'How are you?'

'Oh... we're grand. Just wanted to come and show you that we're here for you if you need us.'

'That's very kind,' said Abigail as she tried to sit up a little. Her breathing became shallow and strained as the weight shifted in her chest. 'But don't worry about me, honestly.'

'You stubborn old mule,' smiled David.

'Too late for flattery Mr Irwin,' replied Abigail.

'I must say, you astonish me. How can you be so brave?' Cara clasped her cold hands tighter.

'In truth... I'm terrified,' replied Abigail with a sad grin. 'But I have faith and in that I suppose I'll find my strength. You see, throughout my life, the choices I made were my own, and I stayed true to them. If my faith is rewarded then I may be just moments from an eternity with my Ferris… and how can I scoff at that? But then, there is one concern of mine.'

'What?' asked Cara and David together.

'Michael.' Abigail's eyes fixed on Grace. 'Look after Michael.'

Cara and David glanced over their shoulders to see Grace standing behind them. Water trickled on her cheeks as she held a book in her hands.

Moments before, Grace had opened the book. Her heart began to pound as there on the inside of the cover lay an inscription. The conversation around her became muted and muffled as her eyes delved into the poem.

To her I owe my all, as I sit and watch her rest.
And deep within her beckon call, I chance to be my best.
For now I live the life of one, made and formed from two.
A life of love I could not live, if to live is without you.

The words tore at Grace. The simple expression tossed a whirlwind of conflict within her. Earlier that evening she had found herself prepared and ready to commit her life to Michael – to chance a life together. However, in the brief absence from him, Grace felt the fear crush her. Never before had one man held the capacity to destroy her as much as Michael did. The love she had for him was true and pure – a love vulnerable in its totality. Each moment she shared with him had given her more pleasure than she could ever imagine, and yet she feared it entirely. She feared a pleasure so full that to accept it and then lose it only promised a pain that would be unbearable. Grace knew if she was to give Michael her heart then she was also giving him licence to break it.

Grace felt selfish in hoarding the man's affection. She had always adored the love that Michael displayed for his mother. The way she had seen him wait for her each night by the fields – the way he promised to protect her. Grace felt sick at the thought that she had planned to steal the one lifeline that Abigail Alpin had. To take Michael from Abigail would be like tearing Christ from the cross itself – everything they had come to symbolise and represent would be incomplete in their separation. Tainted by her fears and confused by the clearest emotions she had ever felt, Grace ran from the room.

Michael saw Grace running. He stood at the doorway to the ward and – seeing his mother was with company – he went after Grace. She was outside in the cold night air when Michael found her. Her eyes were red and her cheeks damp. She flinched as he rested his hand on her shoulder.

'Grace, I'm so sorry I left you earlier. I had no choice you see? I couldn't leave my mother.' Michael looked her straight in the eye. He saw Grace drop his stare as she looked to the floor.

'I know Michael. Your mother needs you. I think you should stay with her. She'll need all the love you have right now.' Her heart dipped as she waited for his reply. Her desires were vacant and unknown as she stood hoping Michael would fulfil them. She realised that through all the guarded poems, all the hidden affection, he had not been straight in his words. She would have taken her words back and begged him to be hers in an instant if Michael was frank with how he felt for her. Three simple words would have eclipsed the bounty he had provided – to really know of his love for her rather than have it merely suggested.

However, Grace was fantastically unaware of the weakness that plagued Michael – of his endless and selfless strength to sacrifice. Michael was willing to lose everything he had if he thought it was for Grace's greater good. Listening to what Grace had said and failing to see what she truly wanted, Michael adhered to her wishes entirely.

'You're right, my Ma' will need me. I'm all she has. After my father decided to abandon her, she's only ever had me to support her. You know he killed himself right? He knew the repercussions; he knew he had married a strict catholic, and still he chose an eternity alone instead of one with the person he loved more than life itself. Imagine that? I really can't forgive the man for abandoning her the way that he did.'

'And that's why you shouldn't either, Michael.'

'But what about us? What about our plans? I'm ready to leave with you.'

'Forget that Michael. Maybe we were misplaced in the moment. There are bigger things right now that you need to deal with.' Grace looked at him with the widest of eyes. She hated the fact that she longed for him to correct her – to ignore his mother's needs and run with her. But deep in her heart she knew she could never ask that of Michael, and it was for this truth alone that she decided to tell her gravest lie.

'You and I can't work Michael. I just don't feel that we can make a go of things while we are both tied to this town. I need more than just words... I'm sorry.'

Michael felt his heart break as he listened to Grace. His reaching hand had been slapped back. His future no longer held her, and his arms felt weak and empty. The moment stunned him. All he had ever wanted and known to be true was stood before him and was definite in their rejection of him. His face stayed emotionless as all feeling drained from his body. Numb and bewildered, he could not find the words to say. Despite every fibre urging him to go after her, he stood completely still as Grace walked quickly away from him. Burdened by love, Michael did not know what else he could offer her.

'It's for the best.' The voice was nasal and gargled. Connell flicked the stub of his cigarette at the feet of Michael. 'She's too much of a lady for some field rat like you.'

'If I were you, I wouldn't dare come within the length of my arm you fucking beast.' Michael's fists clenched as he remained still.

'Oh, a bit of fight in you... I like it. You must take after your mother.'

'Fuck off.'

'Whoa there boy... you've got as much kick as that damned Paco. I was merely paying you a compliment. Come now... your mother is a fine woman, and totally undeserving of the weak man she ended up loving. I was just saying you should be glad to have her strength rather than that of your dear dead pa's.' Connell still felt the sting in his lip as he spoke. The stitches garrotted the exposed flesh that clumped between them.

'I'd be selfish to wish to have even half of that woman's strength. That'd be more than any man would need.' Michael let his hands relax. He didn't offer any gesture to Connell as he turned and made his way back into the hospital. His shoulders felt strained and heavy as he walked back down the tight narrow corridors. He gathered himself before entering his mother's ward. The stale light bit at his eyes and caused him to squint. Cara and David began their goodbyes as they saw Michael walking towards them. They kissed Abigail's head and wished her well before passing Michael.

'God bless you.' Michael looked between Cara and David.

'Don't let us distract him...' said Cara sweetly. 'He should be looking after his mother.'

'I'll be doing that, don't you worry.' Michael bent and kissed Cara and shook David's hand tightly. Waving as they left the ward, Michael stood at his mother's side.

'I'm here for you mother.'

She had never been so upset to see him on his own.

***

David helped Cara to the car. She was drained by her visit and had little strength to push her chair down the long cluttered halls of the hospital by herself. Grace stood shaking by the vehicle. Her shoulders shook as she sobbed into her hands. David saw the order in Cara's eyes as they met with one another. Leaving his wife to tend to her sister, he winked and walked back to the hospital. He peered over his shoulder as he walked away. He could see Cara reach out her hand and softly stroke the arm of Grace, who collapsed to the touch and embraced her older sister. No words appeared to be exchanged, just the scene of one sister supporting another.

'Bloody women.' The words spat at the side of David's neck. The stench of smoke rolled across his face.

'Excuse me?'

'Weak aren't they? Not like us guys, hey? You don't see us moaning about our injuries.' Connell spat a mouthful of bright blood to the dark floor. Green puss had begun to seep from between the stitches on his lip.

'I think they may have a little more to contend with than us.' David checked his shoes to see if they held the splatter of Connell's foul mouth.

'Oh bravo... quit the perfect dismount from your high horse their David. Which is more than I can say for that clumsy wife of yours. As for that cheap whore in there,' Connell nodded towards the hospital. 'What's coming to her is long overdue. She deserves every agonising bit of it. If you ask me there was enough room at the end of her husband's rope for her as well. She should have done us all a favour when she found him hanging.' Connell grimaced as he stifled a wide sinister grin.

David's fingers twitched at his jacket pocket. He would have given the world to have found his razor inside it. He stepped into Connell's face — he could feel his bloodied and baited breath.

'It's you that's on borrowed time, mark my words. Your master won't be around to protect you forever... and the very moment he isn't I'll be sure to reunite you both in hell just as quickly as it takes to tear a knife through that thick neck of yours.'

'Why wait?' Connell licked his lips.

'Oh don't worry — it's coming. I'm just giving the devil enough time to know your deeds first.' David turned and walked over to Cara. She was still comforting Grace as he made his way over. The girl looked devastated. David sighed; the impact of this fateful night had not ignored a single solitary soul.

Chapter 29

Raegan had no plans to visit the hospital. Abigail was no more than another member of staff, and had been just that for some time. Understandably, as a young man with a keen eye, Raegan had been no different from the rest of the town's folk. Each and every man had designs on the angel that was Abigail – her soft fair skin glowed almost as brightly as the stars themselves. Raegan remembered how she made him feel when he saw her working with her late mother. He'd even dared to ask his father what he made of people marrying from different classes.

'A horse may fuck a donkey, and the donkey will always be a donkey. But the horse, well the horse is shamed when they bear an ass for a child.' Raegan's father had always been blunt with his words. His message was clear; your reputation lives through your children, and Raegan had not taken any advice as strongly as this. Although Abigail was a forbidden fruit, her seed was rotten.

His father's words had come to fruition when Raegan saw who Abigail had settled for. He almost laughed when he found that she had chosen a life with a man who offered nothing more than the empty gesture that was that of affection. To Raegan, love was an empty and hollow vase, and only wealth could decorate it. The only thing the late 'great' Ferris had decorated the vessel – that was his wife – was with that of a son that proved almost as troublesome as his father. Raegan sympathised that the poor Abigail had been cursed with two of the most unpromising people the town had ever seen. He saw the irony in the fact that she had boasted of love and commitment and now at this very moment she lay alone and dying. From the sidelines, it was Raegan who had supported her with work and accommodation, who had funded her thankless child's brief and undue education. But now he would stand by and watch her die alone and without the support of those she truly required. But what did he care? She would soon be dust, and all her dreams with it. Preventing the dust from settling on his empire, he had already advertised her position in the local paper.

Nearby, the excited sound of a man packing emanated from the guest room. Arnold Farrington had filled his cases and had ordered for Grace's to be sent to her room. She had returned from her travels weary and upset and so he had given her some distance for the evening. However, he was not going to lose her to the world surrounding her again and so he prepared to take her home with him. The wedding could wait. Raegan had signed the agreement and their land would be divided accordingly. However, on the social surface Arnold could not bear the shame of having a fleet-footed fiancé, and so he proposed that she be allowed to bury her roots before they made things official. He had been frank with his intent but clouded in his design; she did not yet know of the move but was sure she would welcome it nonetheless. Anyway, she would have to. It was going to happen.

'Everything in order?' Raegan took a long puff on his pipe.

'As ready as we'll ever be. I take it you understand that I'll be taking your daughter for some-time. Surely in time she'll come around to the idea of us, and the importance it has on the future of our families.' Arnold grunted as he pulled his case, hoping his struggle would encourage some assistance from his host. None came.

'Oh God, yes of course. *Keep* her if you must. Just make sure that contract is on my desk before you go.'

'May I ask a question?' Arnold let gravity take hold of his case. It hit the ground louder than he had hoped.

'What, another one?' Raegan played the part of the smug smart arse perfectly.

'Well… yes. It's about Grace's disappearance the other night. I'm concerned about her behaviour. Has she done this sort of thing before?'

'No.' Reagan lied. He remembered the last time vividly, but saw no need to concern his future partner.

'Really? Well that is a relief. As you know, she'll find very little room for romance in a life like ours. I can't have her wasting her days on dreams of fancy and fable. I'm a busy man and will need a wife to manage and run the household. But what am I thinking? You've done it yourself for so long now. What's the secret?'

'Just wear a velvet glove on your iron fist.' Raegan clenched his. 'A horse doesn't know who their master is until it has been broken by him. Make them savour every gesture rather than hunger for the next, that's what I say. Now, I don't mean spoil them at all… just make sure they earn their place.'

Arnold was not entirely sure if he agreed with what Raegan was implying. He was certain in the man's stance that he was condoning, if not encouraging, physical violence towards his own daughter. Arnold had beaten plenty a servant in his time — the thrashings from his cane were legendary and the victims bore their branding for weeks — but he had yet to find cause to beat a peer, especially a female one. However, maybe relationships called for it? He knew he could not afford to have Grace leave him. His public reputation would be in tatters, and so he would have to shackle her somehow.

Her face was perplexed as she stood before the cases that lay packed on her bed.

'Dear Grace.' Arnold walked towards her, his cane digging at the lush carpet. 'We need to leave. This town is holding you back. When I found you by the lake last night, well you looked misplaced — lost even. I think it would be best if you came away with me for a while. I have great plans for the both of us, I swear. And I've been clear in my demands, and exactly what I want for us.'

'I want it also.' Grace shifted her feet. She felt off balance and pushed the thoughts of Michael from her head.

'Fantastic,' replied Arnold. 'I took the liberty of preparing a car for us. I had the maids tend to your cases — but we can just get you new clothes when we get there. This will be a fresh start for you. This place is too tired for someone as lively as yourself.'

'But won't half of this 'tired place' become yours soon?' Grace felt defensive for a moment.

'Ours actually… and we'll bring new life to it, just you wait and see.' Arnold rested his hand on Grace's stomach. His eyes were thin and his fine moustache creased as he smiled wearily.

'I need time Arnold.'

'Well we don't have long. The car will be here within the hour. I'll give you some-time once we have settled at home.'

Grace could not put meaning to the word *home*. She had never known any other place than that of this town – complete in its promises and trappings. All her life she had watched the sun set and rise upon the same fields, watched the winter return of the waders and gulls, and witnessed the ageless seasons arrive scarce of any secret. For as long as she could recall she had dreamed of a world outside of the town – of a world where dreams were not devised by anyone other than those that dared to follow them. But now, faced with the imminent prospect of leaving, Grace felt utterly defeated by disillusionment. Her dreams now held nothing more than disappointment. Knowing that Michael would always remain where he was required, Grace had to alter her want to her options – tailoring it to suit a different design to the one she had always dreamed of. She reasoned that given her standing, a match with Arnold was at least appropriate and would lend itself well to the needs of both families. She now had a future, and generations to come would be secure through their joining and, while not true to passion, her heart would remain intact throughout the whole affair. After all, she was of the age and society still expected.

***

The Irwin household were firm in their routine. Cara basked in the passion that had been reborn as David prepared dinner. The kitchen knife shimmered in his hands – the light of the lamps bouncing from the blade as David diced the raw meat. He tossed the cubed lumps into a dish and tended to the vegetables. The sweet scent of the casserole was hot in Grace's nostrils as she approached the front porch. Steam bellowed from the pot that David lay on the table. The sound of an unknown concerto filled the room. Grace envied her sister's talent – the freedom she found within it always reminded Grace of her restraints. Restricted by time, Grace knew her goodbyes needed to be swift.

'Sister, I have news.' Grace's face must have been grave when she saw the reaction from Cara.

'Oh Lord, is she gone?' Cara let the violin rest in her lap.

'What?' Grace looked at David to see if she had interrupted a conversation.

'Don't look at him,' said Cara. 'I'm talking to you, sister. Is Abigail alright? Is that what you came to inform us of?'

'No.' Grace felt the thunder drain from her news. 'I don't know how Abigail is coping, I'm afraid. The news is of me. I'm leaving.'

'Oh my,' Cara came closer to Grace. David had stopped serving up dinner and was an avid audience.

'Yes… I leave tonight. Well in a few hours actually.' Grace shifted her gaze between the two staring, slack-jawed observers. Cara shook her head and blinked to dampen her dry eyes.

'Well I must say… it's about time that man came to his senses. But his timing is awful.'

'It's somewhat sudden, I admit.' Grace's words held no excitement.

'Sudden? It's downright selfish and scandalous if you ask me. Fancy abandoning your mother in her time of need? And you missy, letting him do it. Can't it wait?'

'I'm not leaving with Michael if that's what you mean? I'm leaving town with Arnold Farrington.' Grace did not hear the bite she put into saying Michael's name, or how she had said the latter with a lot less conviction.

'The man from the ball? But I've hardly heard you mention his name.' Cara glanced at David for his intervention but he stood by in silence. His face was a breeding of anger and confusion.

'Exactly...' said Grace with no confidence in her impending argument. '...The man has not given me reason to speak of him. He's dependable, and solid. I need that. You may never hear me talk of him, but in turn you'll hear no complaints about him either.' Grace was justifying her decision to herself as much as she was to her sister. Her words were of twisted reason – weightless considerations used to compliment her cause.

'But what of Michael?' David finally spoke.

'He's needed here. As you said sister, I could never ask him to leave his mother. And I don't have it in my heart to rip Abigail's from her.'

'Have you asked Michael what he thinks?' Cara took the same line as her husband.

'I couldn't bring myself to ask him.'

'Then wait for him. It's senseless to run from it.' Cara's hands clutched at her violin. David rubbed his soothing fingers on her tense shoulders.

'The choice is no longer mine.' Grace was on the verge of crying. She rushed over to Cara and held her tightly. She could feel David's hand rest on her back. They continued the embrace until Grace was confident of hiding her distress. Pulling away, Grace looked her family in the eye and offered her weakest of goodbyes. She prayed that they would not be forever.

***

Michael had agreed to take his mother home. The doctors had been insistent that she stay in their care and were blunt with what the consequences would be. However, Abigail was set in her ways and had no intention of delaying the inevitable. The decayed lights of the lamps stained the walls of the corridor as the nurses escorted Abigail to her ambulance. She was unable to walk and remained in her bed as the gurney was rolled out and placed into the back of the vehicle. Michael held his mother's hand the entire time. He saw how she gripped her rosary beads with her free hand – rolling each bead through her fingers as she rattled off prayer after prayer. Not once did he hear her pray for herself.

Having returned home, Michael took his mother up to her room and lay her into her bed. She looked tiny on the mattress. A large, cold and untouched section lay beside her. The moonlight punctured the shadows that closed in around the room, and a white light broke upon the bed and bathed Abigail entirely. Minute flecks of black freckled the light as dense snowflakes sprinkled the skies outside. The falling snow had begun to set on the land. A pure crystal carpet blanketed the cold forlorn fields. Michael held his mother's hand – her fingers were as brittle as ice.

'Son, I love you.' Abigail still had strength to smile.

'You've never needed to say it mother. I've known it all my life.' Michael wanted to take hold of her.

'I just want to say that I'm sorry... I'm sorry for all the times you think I ignored or left you behind. I just could not tear myself away from the church. I have to confess that trying to save your father devoured me completely.'

'You did what your heart told you to mother. Nobody should have to apologise for that. And I promise you with all of my heart that not once did I feel as if I was without you... regardless of where you were.'

Michael felt his mother's fingers grip his. Tiny pebbles of shadow dashed across her face. Her eyes had never looked as dark as they did in this moment. They shone is stark contrast to her skin that remained a bright white throughout. The snow outside was creeping up the walls of the house as wayward snowflakes crashed and trickled down the windowpanes.

'I'm ready to go son.' Abigail's eyes became weary and heavy.

'No… I can't let you. I'll be lost without you mother.'

'Don't be. The world outside belongs to you Michael. Go and take it for all it's worth.'

'But you didn't. So why should I?'

'Because the only thing that ever mattered to me — other than you that is — was lost; it no longer belonged to this world. If you only learn one thing from me so, then don't ever allow yourself to lose a love. There's not a pain known that can compete with how that feels.'

'But I love you mother.'

'I know. But I'm not lost Michael. I'll live through you always… just like your father does. Now I know you hate to hear the mention of the man, but I must tell you that I saw him each day in you. Your heart, your desire, your loyalty… you took them from your father.'

Michael resented the memory his mother retained of his father. Every aspect of the man defied his actions. Watching his mother dying, Michael felt no desire to live — no call to capitalise on life's opportunities despite how much they moved him. Instead, he felt his feet begin to set beneath him.

'I want you to have these Michael.' Abigail passed him her rosary beads. Michael could almost see his mother's fingerprints on each individual bead as they had been worn down with her every aching prayer.

'I can't take these.'

'You will. I *need* you to take them. Michael, I've said my last prayer.' Michael's hand closed reluctantly. The cold steel crucifix hung from his grasp and swung gently.

'Son,' Abigail coughed as she tried to sit up. 'Promise me one thing. I've seen where your heart rests… promise me you'll follow it. Don't ever lose your life to love like me. You must live to love instead.' Shadows shaded her eyes.

Michael wanted to scream out. He wanted to implore his mother to stay with him — to continue to live. But he remained silent. He knew his next words would be the last his mother would ever hear and he would not let them be of defiance. Outside the winds escalated and encouraged the elements to do their worst. The billowing snowfall draped over the cottage and dressed the remains of the once smouldering willow tree. Seeing the light leave his mother's eyes as they closed for their final time, Michael held her hand and whispered.

'Go to him.' Her eyes closed and capped the finest smile he had ever seen.

✵✵✵

The journey was ready to be taken. The cases had been loaded into the brand new vehicle. Its fresh engine purred as the tyres bit into the cold ground. Wetted by the snowfall that broke upon its tough body, the black carriages of the car shone like a freshly cut onyx stone. The snow was settling fast and they would have to leave soon. Arnold offered Raegan a formal handshake.

'Have a swift journey, and give word that you have arrived safely.' Raegan draped his arm over the shoulders of Fiona who shivered at his touch. His frosty stare hid the fire that raged within him. The woman was still to learn from her misdeeds.

'I will,' said Grace as she embraced her mother. Her sister Imogen was upstairs in the warm — the weather was too much for the poor girl to bear.

'Please write to us. It will be awfully quiet without you around the house, and I'll miss you terribly.' Fiona pulled her daughter in for one last clinch.

'I shouldn't be gone for too long mother. Arnold insists that the move will be a good one for us, but I'll always consider this my home.' Grace could not tell if Fiona was crying or that snowflakes had melted on her face. Her cheeks blazed beneath a soft stream of water.

'Take a good look at the land at your new lodgings. Remember, that all that will become yours when you marry this fine gentleman.' Raegan patted Arnold heartily on the back. Thick balls of mist fired from his flared nostrils. Arnold stumbled as his cane slid on the iced driveway.

'Come now my darling. We can't afford to wait much longer. The weather will soon fence us in completely.' Arnold could feel the cold scratch up his injured leg. His bone felt brittle in the breeze.

'Coming,' said Grace. She took a moment to look around her. The gardens that she had looked upon for years were already changing before her. Like the final curtain drawing to a close, a veil of purest white dressed the fields and gardens. The petals and leaves of the evergreens became weighty cups full of fresh snow. The road ahead shimmered as the stones and gravel were glazed with a thin layer of ice. Stepping into the carriage, Grace gazed past Arnold – her eyes fixed on the land that began to pass her by. The carriage rocked and jolted as the hard tyres rubbed the stony road. Grace could feel every bump along the long road that lead out of town.

Chapter 30

The ceremony began at the entrance to the church. The whole town was in attendance – a sea of black suits lined the snow-capped streets. There was talk that because of the season the body of Abigail Alpin was to be stored in the receiving vault at the cemetery, as the ministers were concerned that they may need to allow the winter to pass and the ground to thaw. Michael, however, was insistent that the iron gates of the vault remain locked tight as he had assisted the reluctant gravediggers to brave the cold throughout the night. He was well aware of the spot where his mother had chosen for her final resting place. At the edge of the graveyard a single headstone sat alone and isolated. Crooked and facing south, the grave of Ferris Alpin rested outside of the church's sanctuary. Abigail had always been thankful of Father Daniel for interpreting the canon law accordingly – allowing Ferris to be buried inside the cemetery, if not outside the traditions of the church. The remaining headstones lay facing east to west upon the highest hill. Many a mother had scared their children at night with tales of how the eternal eyes of the town's elders watched out over every inch of the land. The view from the hill was spectacular.

The funeral mass had begun and fittingly Michael was dressed entirely in black. He had made use of the savings that he had stored to offer his mother the finest goodbye he could muster. He had paid for himself and Oscar to be suited out in the finest cloth for the occasion. It would be a suit that he would only ever wear one more time. Unlocked and welcoming, the church received the deceased with open arms. Father Daniel sprinkled the stained golden oak coffin with holy water before placing the pall, the book of gospels and the heavy gold platted cross on top. Beside the altar, the coffin rested by the large unlit paschal candle. The masses began to take their seats as Father Daniel led the ceremony.

'Today is a sad day for all – a day driven by loss and pain. But it is from this that we strive to draw our greatest strength of all. A loss as grave as this one can only follow a life so beautiful and pure. In memory we rejoice... for the past is a present to us all. Therefore, in light of what has passed, the community of our church celebrates today. It reaffirms in sign and symbol, word and gesture, that through baptism we all share in Christ's death and resurrection, and look forward to the day when we will be raised up and united in the kingdom of light and peace. Abigail Alpin is not lost. Her soul is at home amongst the angels of heaven.'

Michael felt alone in the company he kept. His neck trembled as the wells in his eyes threatened to break. Oscar sat beside his friend. He wanted to take hold of him, to show his support, but he knew that even the slightest of touches could cause Michael to crumble. So, he turned to his mother. Margaret wept at the side of her son. Her head was cushioned in the chest of her husband Maik, who held her tightly. Her tears poured and dampened his dark shirt, as she shook in his strong arms while the ceremony continued.

Music rained out from the organ that graced the grand altar, and the church sang with all their hearts before celebrating the liturgy of the word. Michael was numb. The mass played out around him like any other that he could remember as a child. He remembered how cold the benches made his backside, so he would always make a fuss and squirm in his seat. That was until he felt his mother's touch. However, she could no longer cause him to sit still and be quiet. Smiling at the memory, Michael was motionless.

The aisles started to fill once the act of communion had begun. Michael could not remember getting up or receiving the host, but now he sat in place as a stale flake of wafer grew wet on his dry tongue. The air was warm in the movement of the masses. Bodies pressed together as the building boasted its biggest congregation in years. The stalls bulged and many were forced to stand for the entire service. No doubt all of those present would tell Michael just how beautiful the mass was; how the stunning streams of lavender and lilies framed the aisles perfectly. But Michael would not be able to recall any of it. Present in body among the spirited occasion, Michael was absent in thought.

Father Daniel had asked Michael before the mass whether he wanted to say a few words. However, Michael had respectfully declined the offer. He explained to the priest how he had already said the words his mother needed to hear, and that today would be an occasion for all to speak their feelings, and he did not need the town to know his feelings for he was certain that his actions had always affirmed the love that he had for his mother. Finally, the mass drew to a close with a final prayer that concluded the rite of commendation. The body of Abigail Alpin was now ready for its final journey. The church sang the *Song of Farewell* while the coffin was prepared for its carriage.

Outside Michael stood and watched the tide of people pull away from the church. The familiar faces looked strange and drawn – an unseen sorrow etched across all of them. Placing himself by the church doors, Michael thanked each person that offered their blessings. The crowd gathered by the gates and broke only for the horse drawn carriage that awaited its dearly departed passenger. The carriage was a glass casket, framed by black varnished oak. The Friesian stallions were from the Darby stables. They stood firm and proud at the head of the carriage – their enormous hooves planted to the frosty pavement. Michael's keen eye could see the slight shiver on their skin. Their thick black coats sparkled in the light.

'God bless ya Mike. Do you need a hand with anything?' Oscar braved a hand on his friends shoulder.

'I should be fine,' replied Michael. He patted his friend's warm hand. 'Everything is being taken care of. Even Raegan offered the carriage as a gesture of his condolences. The money I had didn't stretch as far as I thought, so I took him up on his offer. He didn't need them anyway. The whole estate has been put on hold out of respect. Every worker is here to say their goodbyes. But like I say, it was a sweet gesture and I flattered his ego a little by letting him contribute.'

'I don't blame you pal. Abigail deserves the best... and she got it with you... I mean that.' Oscar wanted to wail into his mother's arms. He wanted to cry his heart out, but he knew Michael needed him. He let the cold crisp air cool his skin and check his nerves. Treading carefully, Oscar scanned the crowd. Every attending family was complete in its parts. He could not see a single absent soul – none that was except Grace. Oscar was wise to his friend's feelings, regardless of how well he guarded them. Seeing that Grace was not present, Oscar would try his best not to mention her. He had no intention of ever upsetting Michael, especially today.

'I love those animals,' whispered Michael. He distracted himself as the coffin was carried past him. 'You know, despite their size they move with such grace.'

'Grace?' asked Oscar lost in his own fears. 'Oh... I've not seen her. I don't think she's turned up.' He bit his lip when he realised he had dropped the ball.

'I was talking about the horses you clout.' Michael wore a wry smile. He could see Oscar was squirming. 'And don't worry about using her name. I already looked myself... I couldn't see her either.'

'Good. This day's for your mother... the rest can wait.' Oscar pulled on Michael's shoulder. 'Come on, the carriage is set to leave. We need to follow it.'

The coffin lay in the carriage as the horses pulled off from the crowd. Bright white flowers blazed at the side of the coffin where countless wreaths of lilies rested inside. Michael followed closely, setting the pace for the crowd behind him. The road up to the cemetery was paved in white snow. The path ahead looked uninhibited – the roads trodden only by the frost that hung heavily in the air. A tide of tender weeping seeped through the crowds. Margaret was still inconsolable. Beside her, David's hands gripped the cold handles of Cara's wicker chair. The Darby family stood nearby. Fiona gripped the hand of the thickly wrapped Imogen while Raegan's hand rested on the icy whisky flask that hugged his inside coat pocket. Established in the procession, they all followed Michael who stood ahead, his head hanging to his thick chest. In his hands he held the rosary beads his mother had given to him in her final moments. He could not recall an instance since that moment that he had been without them.

The hooves of the horses cut into the white carpet that paved the road. Resigned to their course, the coachman began to steer towards the gates of the graveyard. Two giant maple trees rested either side of the gateway. Stripped of any leaves, their bare branches reached out towards each other – draping the gates like two friends embracing. Rows of red fir trees, laden with bright shadows of snow, ran the entire stretch of the path that passed the countless headstones that faced one another along the open fields that poured out from the road. The wheels of the carriage creaked as they crept towards the entrance.

'Stop.' Michael ran to the carriage. 'No...' He looked from the carriage to the crowd and then back again. '... Not like this.' His head was shaking and his heart pounded. Oscar was beside him in an instant.

'Michael, come now... let's put your mother to rest.'

'I will...' Michael's hands were planted onto the window of the carriage. 'Who will help me?' He looked around the crowd quickly before walking to the rear of the carriage. The horseman had brought his beasts to a halt, and Michael began to open the doors at the rear of the casket.

'Come on... you heard the man. Who's going to help him?' Oscar knew instinctively what his friend wanted.

Three shadows broke from the crowd.

'It would be an honour.' Maik Sterrin stood by his son. Oscar smiled proudly at his father.

'Count me in.' David Irwin had asked Margaret to tend to Cara before stepping forward.

'If I can, then please let me help.' Francis Morgan looked his most handsome as he offered his assistance. His head was held in a gentle bow – hiding the tears he carried for his late friend.

Together, led by Michael, the five men carried the coffin from the carriage. Resting lightly on their broad shoulders, the coffin floated through the gateway. The snow crunched under their feet as they led the procession up the steep hillside. The cold air brought comfort as the men's heart's raced and burned at their chests. Proudly they continued up the hill, passing the countless rows of graves that mirrored the next. Michael's hands dug into the front of the coffin – he could feel the cold steel of the crucifix that hung from his beads.

Soon, the coffin was laid down at the very edge of the field. The plot looked out towards the coastline, with the town neatly cradled in the valleys behind. The scene was ghostly – ecclesiastical architecture adorned the fields. An ancient tombstone was nearby. It depicted a mourning woman embracing the heavy catholic cross – her hands, soiled and bloodied, clasped the robe that shrouded her face. The garish grey stone of the statue pierced the garlands of evergreens that circled the cemetery like a timeless wreath.

Michael could see the crooked headstone. While all the other graves reflected each other in almost perfect symmetry, the headstone of his father stared out towards the sea. The waves raged at the shore, pressing their tides onto the shifting sands beneath them.

The mourning crowd coiled around the open grave. Husbands held their wives, mothers held their children, and people held their tongue as the committal was commenced. Father Daniel wore his finest robes as he stood at the head of the grave. He had chosen to remain clear-headed out of respect for his most loyal of members, and was thankful that the winds were kind upon his sensitive, sober skin. Only a gentle breeze blew in from the ocean. Father Daniel broke the silence.

'Let us pray.' Despite his fluency, he opened up his bible and proceeded with the Lord's Prayer.

Michael's gaze was fixed on the grave as the coffin was lowered inside. His throat was frozen while his shivering hands warmed the beads within them. The sound of soft sobbing could be gathered on the breeze as the seas sighed tenderly. Oscar was by Michael's side throughout; braced to be leaned on at any moment. He knew he would have his time to mourn, to weep and pray for the kindest soul he had ever encountered, but this moment was for Michael. And it was for him that Oscar stood by.

'It's time to commit this body to rest.' Father Daniel stood forward and made the sign of the cross. 'Unto God's gracious mercy and protection we commit you. The Lord blesses you and keeps you. The Lord makes his face to shine upon you, and be gracious unto you. The Lord lifts up his countenance upon you, and gives you peace. Both now and for evermore. Amen.'

'Amen'. The crowd shuffled a little as they replied harmoniously. The dull monotones of the males muted the high cries of the women who struggled to hide their emotions. Before the priest begun his final prayers, Michael was invited to scatter the first handful of earth upon the coffin. The soil was dry between his hands. He paused, kissed his clench fist and then tossed the earth into the grave. The stained oak of the coffin lay dusted by the dirt.

'Unto Almighty God we commend the soul of our sister departed, and we commit her body to the ground; earth to earth, ashes to ashes, dust to dust.'

A basket breaking with long stemmed white lilies rested on a stand near to the grave. Each guest was invited to take a flower and toss it inside while Father Daniel drew the ceremony to a close. Oscar draped his arm around Michael's shoulders. He could feel the gentle trembles of the thick muscles beneath. Waiting for the final flower to fall, Father Daniel offered one final prayer.

'O God, whose mercies cannot be numbered; accept our prayers on behalf of the soul of thy servant departed and grant her an entrance into the land of light and joy, in the fellowship of thy saints; through Jesus Christ our Lord. Amen'

'*Amen.*'

Shrugging his shoulders and releasing Oscar's hand, Michael walked down to the edge of the grave. He had heard the words of the final prayer and felt compelled to offer one final gesture to his mother. Hanging the beads of the rosary in one hand, Michael dragged his free hand down the string that held them together. The beads broke like freshly plucked grapes and nestled in the thick plate of his palm. All that remained on the string was a small metal depiction of the Virgin Mary, and the steel crucifix.

'Michael, what the hell are you doing?' Oscar tugged lightly on Michael's jacket. The crowd watched on curiously – their critical eyes boring into Michael's broad back.

'These beads... they aren't my prayers.' He looked at what dangled from the string. 'I'll carry her cross, but these prayers belong to my mother. They should remain with her.'

Michael tossed the beads into the grave. The small varnished wooden droplets pebbled and bounced off the thick oak of the coffin. Leaving the prayers with her, Michael took the string that was once his mother's rosary, and wrapped it around his strong left wrist. He tied the ends tightly to form a bracelet. The depiction of the Virgin Mary rested on the inside of his arm while the crucifix dangled beneath.

Hours passed, but Michael remained. The congregation offered their individual prayers and made their way home. Father Daniel had waited for a while but he too was now gone, tending to his church in time for tomorrow's mass. Stuck between the afternoon and the dawn of evening, the day hung onto the last light of the winter sun. To its credit, the sun had stayed an extra few hours as of to honour the light that the departed had once brought to the world. Having paused for the service, the winds now begun to go about their usual course. The waves of the Irish Sea rose and smashed at the shore – bowing endlessly to its sturdy and powerful partner.

'The dead always get the best view, don't they?' Oscar had stayed with Michael.

'Depends what angle they're at.' Michael glanced at the headstone of his father. 'But you're right... a coastline like that. I don't think I could design a better place to rest.'

'The earth for an angel. That's all we can offer pal. I think your mother would be proud of you today.'

'Ha' smiled Michael. 'Her eyes will be elsewhere today... you can wager your life on that. I just pray that she found what she was looking for. But then, I suppose we'll never know.'

'Hey, you keep me out of it. I've mastered the art of asking for forgiveness, so I know I'll be sound when I meet my maker.'

Michael fired a look at his friend.

'I'm sorry.' Oscar smirked as he awaited his friend's judgement.

'You feckin eegit. Come on, let's go home.'

Chapter 31

On 28 June 1914, Grace was tending to the weeds that were spreading in her manicured garden. She was still struggling to adjust to life in Canndare, and was blissfully unaware that – at around the same time in Sarajevo – the Duchess of Hohenburg nursed the fatal bullet wound in her abdomen as her husband lay slain by her side. Armed with a garden fork and a pair of gloves, Grace tore at the rogue flora in her pavement at the precise moment when Gavrilo Princip approached the open topped automobile that carried the Archduke Franz Ferdinand and his wife Sophie, and proceeded to murder them. Situated at the crossroads between the counties of Wicklow, Dublin and Kildare, the town of Canndare was considered quite the political hot pocket – a great stage on which to declare and defend the entire world's conflicts. However, an entire day would perish before news of the Archduke's demise reached the angled ears of the townspeople.

It had been several months since Grace had moved into the town and still she was finding it difficult to settle. Unlike Orplow, the town buzzed with agenda and debate – clear sides were taken and friendships torn by political allegiances. Grace had only ever seen a blurring of cultures back home. Her father was the descendant of a Protestant family and was in turn inclined to agree with the unionists of the country – proclaiming the benefits of being governed by 'Mother England'. However, he had chosen to raise his daughters as Catholics and had entrusted them totally to the church. Grace had heard all of the whispers concerning her father's judgement – many agreeing that Raegan took the shrewd stance of an appeasing diplomat while also enjoying the position of opportunity. After all, his children were all women and could therefore be married and converted into whatever ideology her suitor followed. Leaving nothing to chance and everything to fortune, Raegan Darby was backing both sides of the Irish coin.

The borders of Canndare were a little clearer. While Arnold Farrington declared he could not afford time to practice, he had at least been raised in the Catholic Church. He was publicly a proud nationalist and determined to benefit from any form of independency the emerald isle could establish. However, having such land at his disposal, Arnold already enjoyed a certain amount of 'Home Rule'. While the town was urban in design, the surrounding lands that loaded the stores and lined the pavements were all Arnold's. His castle, however, was more modest than Grace's father's. Run more like an organisation than an autocratic empire, Arnold handled his territory in a small manor house in the centre of town. He had entrusted farmhands to occupy and run patches in a hands-on fashion, while he remained at home and managed the books. The affluent ball of the Farrington's had been rolling for decades and, with Arnold at the helm, shown no signs of slowing down.

In recent months political division had snowballed. Based at the epicentre of the debate, Grace had cupped an ear for both sides, if only to gather a rounded argument more than committing herself to the unionist ideal. After all, Grace had embraced the church entirely as a child regardless of her father's determination to keep her grasp loose and removable. She understood the teachings and traditions of Catholicism totally, and celebrated the community within it. It was for this reason mostly that she would support her peers in the drive for Home Rule.

Still a keen reader, Grace liked to keep her mind active. However, the only library in town was barren of any books – instead lending its readership to a coffee house filled with the daily papers. Brewley's was based at the cross junction between Market Street and Dublin Road. Heavy coffee-bean sacks lined the walls, casing the learned discussion that brewed within the store. It was one of Ireland's first 'Penny Universities', and established in 1648, Brewley's had housed the hottest and most scolding debates ever since.

The door to the store was found at the point of the building where the corners of both streets met. The viewpoints inside were almost as sharp as the rugged brickwork that framed the doorway. Although Brewley's only provided national newspapers, it was reading material nonetheless and Grace would escape into the broad-sheeted pages each morning. Despite the very same broadsheets being delivered to her breakfast table each and every day, Grace always opted to venture into town and peruse the well fingered copies that rested in the store like lazy, soiled linen. The short trip through the town was an occasion in itself for Grace. Passing by the markets and stalls, she enjoyed hearing the heated conversations amidst the masses – the strong blinkered and biased opinions of each side which were akin only in their refusal to find reason or resolve with the other. In Canndare, roads, streets and even houses were divided. Forever her father's deviant, Grace refused to walk the line.

Smoke poured from the fingers of the man sat next to her. The sooty scent of cigarettes flavoured the thin air inside the small store. Grace took a sip of her scolding hot coffee in a weak attempt to escape the wretched stench of cigarettes. She was growing to like the kick that her new drink offered her. She had always been familiar with all varieties of tea, but scarcely had she found a leaf with as much punch as the coffee bean. But this morning, the taste buds on her tongue burned as they licked hell's own fire. Her coffee was far too hot, and clearly the inept waitress had poured the milk in after the blistering water, scolding the coffee and leaving very little taste. The sheets of the *Irish Examiner* filled her table. Grace refrained from licking her thumb before turning the pages – as a smudged grimy black thumb-print already rested atop of each sheet. The paper was dampened by use. Its spine was broken and folded; the pages inside limp and wilted.

'Not fond of opinions then?' A cloud of smoke brushed past the page.

'Excuse me?' Grace placed her cup on the open pages. A thin brown moat ringed its base.

'That paper… it holds no real content.' The man stubbed his cigarette onto the thin ashtray. A thick black print remained on the upturned nub.

'You call a murder no content?' Grace held up the headline detailing the fate of the Archduke Franz Ferdinand and his late wife.

'That paper reports atrocities and international events, but only in a distilled fashion.' He lit up another cigarette. 'The editorials are watered down as the publisher sits on the fence and tries not to offend either side. It'll try to shock and awe you with concerns of survival... trying to mask the fact that it doesn't stand to support either the nationalist or the unionist alone.' His voice sounded squeezed before he exhaled a long line of smoke. 'The only survival it cares about is its own. Every conflict will in turn have a winner, and among the *victorious* will be readers. And papers like this will write for them, regardless of who they may be. Right now, it writes for everyone because nobody's winning.'

'But it's content nonetheless.' Grace raised her mug for a deep victory sip.

'Words without meaning or argument have no true *content*.' He stared until Grace put down her mug. Defeated, she did so. 'The only concern, or interest, that I have from that entire paper is the terminology it has chosen.' The man lit up another cigarette. He looked like he was going to stay.

'What do you mean?' Grace glanced at the article again. Everything seemed in order.

'Did you not notice how they've chosen to use the term 'assassination' rather than 'murder'?' He saw no reaction in Grace's expression. His mouth marched on. 'You see, in essence they are the same thing... the same act. But to make a murder an assassination is to make it a political act. That alteration is probably the only brave move this paper has made today, and I'm guessing it's for a very good reason.' He looked over his shoulders, almost paranoid. 'My dear, the best way to distract a nation from its conflicts is to focus them towards that of another's. Mark my words – this paper knows more than it is letting on.'

'Like what?' Grace felt dumb in her ignorance. 'I barely know what's going on in this town let alone any other nation. I'm kind of new to town you see.'

'Then I apologise Ma'am. I didn't mean to come across like a patronising ass. I'm not here to educate, just merely inform, I swear.' He mockingly placed his hand on his heart. 'Your opinions are your own, and I won't force them. But, I will say that there's a lot of trouble ahead. Over the continent there's a storm brewing...' He looked out of the window and into the far reaching skies. '... Let's just hope we don't get swept up in it.'

'I shall pray for it.' Grace touched the crucifix that hung from her necklace.

'A catholic girl? You stay true to that throughout, and you'll be fine. Well, I'll be seeing you.' And with that the man left the store. Grace had to admit she was slightly glad that he had not offered her his hand in greeting; his fingers were lined with thick, dark dirt. Looking at the thumbed paper in front of her, she smiled at the thought of the man berating a paper that he had clearly read from front to back. His prints grubbed up every page. Nonetheless, he *was* intriguing. She had not seen such a calm passion and belief in a man for some time; it was an attractive quality. The man was clear on what he wanted.

Having tracked the man's prints through the pages and drained her cup of all its perky content, Grace made her way back home. The house was still on her return. The bright sunshine washed the walls with a pale light, draining the colour from the hanging flower baskets. Beneath the sweltering dew of the day, her dress clung to her pressed body. The walk home had come with very little shade, and the sun had beaten down onto Grace's slight, delicate shoulders. Her head felt hazy and light once inside the cold dark hallway of her home. The room held a ghostly chill. Grace could feel the cold beads of sweat trickle down her spine.

Arnold was in his office. Since the overdue and eagerly awaited death of his father, he could always be found within these cramped four walls, slouched in the bulky leather chair that sat beneath a portrait of the late Lord Reginald Farrington. Stooped forward, Arnold's sallow skin was stark and pale next to the crimson colour of the leather. He had never spoken of his father's death since the funeral, and while suspicious of his absent emotion Grace was impressed by the manner in which Arnold had instantly taken the reigns and steered the family business forward. He had not missed a beat and had even taken great strides to continue the family traditions. It had never occurred to her naïve acceptance of her surroundings, that he had all his plans in place months before his frail father had met his timely fate.

'Good afternoon darling.' Grace forced the words from her dry lips.

'What? Oh… welcome back dear. Did you have a nice time in town?' Arnold's face flashed up at Grace and then back to his books. She was familiar with this pose and had begun to note daily how his crown grew increasingly through his thinning hair.

'It was pleasant. I just took a walk as usual. The town's alive at the moment, and there is *huge* news from abroad. There is talk of an international conflict.'

'Very nice dear.' Arnold thumbed the page of his paperwork.

'I met a man.' Grace watched for a reaction.

'Good for you.' Arnold fired out another empty reply. He was not even listening.

'He was quite the character, I must say. Such passion in his voice…'

'Sounds great.' Arnold was indifferent.

'I was thinking of having a child with him… I dream of his grimy fingers dirtying my night dress, and soiling my silk panties.' Grace watched intently. Arnold was passive and oblivious.

'If you must.' He raised his head. 'I'm very busy at the minute, is there anything that you need?'

'No…' She sighed. '…Nothing at all.' Grace painted on a smile and left the office. She could not believe she had married the man.

For the next two months she had continued to visit Brewley's coffee house. Unfortunately, the man she was hoping to see had always escaped her. Each and every morning, the edges of the *Irish Examiner* had remained dirty and thumbed. That was, until this morning. Grace could not sleep in her marital bed the previous night. She had already issued a thousand reasons for not sleeping with her husband, and she was now running thin on excuses. Fortunately, that evening Arnold had been worn out by his work and his routine nightly blast of whisky. As a result, all that had raged that night were the snores that thundered from his gaunt nostrils. Tired and in need of distraction, Grace entered the town much earlier than usual. The streets were screaming in their silence; a dull breeze bounced off the bricks and cobblestones. In the distance, the soft call of starlings whispered on the wind.

Bustling into the coffee house, Grace heard the bell on the door piercingly warn the shopkeeper of her arrival. Hearing the call, the shopkeeper came from the kitchens behind the counter. He looked as fresh as the dawn. His eyes flashed as he wiped a damp line of coffee from his lip.

'My my, aren't we the early bird Mrs Farrington? What brings you here so soon in the day? I didn't expect to fill your cup until around midday at least.'

'I couldn't sleep.' Grace felt exhausted.

'Then it won't be coffee that you're in need of. How about a fresh pot of tea and a cake? Maybe that'll help you drop off.'

'Honestly, my house is some walk from here. I wouldn't make it back if I got any more sleepy, and I doubt the market traders would celebrate an unconscious woman on their stalls.'

'Ha! Quite right. Although, I find you'd make quite the pretty scarecrow. Now, sit yourself down and I'll be with you soon.' The shopkeeper smiled widely and held out his arm for Grace to take a seat. She had the pick of all the stalls and tables. There was not a simmering cup in sight.

Grace slumped into the seat that she always took. It faced the large window that exposed the town outside. She had spent many an hour watching the world and had never grown tired of it. Ever since she was a child, Grace had attached a story to each person that passed her by – a background that gave them meaning and purpose. Scanning the room, and though it was now empty of anyone other than her and the shopkeeper, she saw that she had not been the first person in that morning. The papers had already been delivered and rested neatly in the rack. Their pages looked thick and firm. She picked up the Irish Examiner and took it to her table. The paper was clean of any print other than the text itself. Content in her privilege, Grace took to reading the paper before anybody else in town.

The man had been right. The paper was loaded with headlines concerning an outbreak of war in Europe. Nations were calling for others to unite against the oppressive Germany. Articles outlined how fate had offered Germany the opportunity to turn dreams into imperial reality; how they had granted a supposed 'blank cheque' to Austria for unconditional support against their enemies under any circumstances. Having already set a fast pace in the arms race, developing a naval fleet that only irritated the maritime nation of Great Britain, Kaiser Wilhelm II stepped away from the status quo and adopted a more aggressive political stance. If the paper was to be trusted, then blame was firmly at the feet of the German and Austro-Hungarian alliance for waging a deliberate and belligerent battle. Quite simply, the world was at war.

Excited in trepidation, Grace dropped the paper. A flash of colour caught her eye. Falling from the pages was a badge. Made from thin cloth, the small palm-sized badge had the bold incontestable image of the golden Irish harp stitched into the centre. Beneath the image was a date; today's. Etched beside it was a time and – more excitingly – an address. Unsure of her intentions, Grace pocketed the badge quickly. Regardless of the knowledge of being alone, she looked around the room in case she was being watched. Intently, she fixed her eyes on the people that passed by the windows in case any of them tossed their glances towards the newspaper rack. She felt as though she had fallen into one of their backgrounds, and now stood at the forefront of their secret world.

The hand that rested on her shoulder rose as she leapt from her chair. By some miracle, the shopkeeper was able to steady the hand that held Grace's coffee.

'Are you alright? Didn't drift off did you? I can't be having a scarecrow in my window, regardless of how pretty it may be.' He laughed as he placed the drink down on the table. 'Now rest a little, I'll go and get you some sponge cake. It looks like you need a little treat, and my wife's secret sponge recipe is as exciting as it gets from me I'm afraid.'

The shopkeeper returned from his kitchen with a thick slice of cake that nestled like a brick on the brightest of doilies. Soft crumbs had crumbled from the sides and flecked the white cloth that it rested on. Sweet cream layered the cake, glued by a sugary strawberry jam. However, in his haste the shopkeeper had not heard the jangle of the bell as the door was jerked open. The chair where Grace had sat was empty. The steam spiralling from the coffee had yet to even reach the ceiling. The newspaper lay flat – empty of its concealed content.

Later at home, Grace had not even needed to excuse her absence that evening. Following a quiet dinner – laden with muted exchanges between husband and wife – Arnold had retired into his office. He had begun to rest heavier on his cane of late, with his injured leg becoming more burdensome than before. Slipping out through the rear grounds of the estate, Grace braced herself for the night ahead. She had placed the stolen badge into a small purse that she carried with her. All day she had tried to work out what it meant and why it had been hidden inside the paper. She checked the paper that was delivered to her house, and there was nothing inside her copy. The badge had been placed in the copy at Brewley's for a reason, as a message to somebody. Her mind raced with visions of a secret society – a group hidden from the world, plotting tirelessly to make a difference. Yet in the cold light of day she reasoned that it had been simply misplaced; a meaningless bit of cloth belonging to someone proud enough to mark the date on which it was created. And while this may have answered as to why the cloth had an address attached, it still failed to explain the time that was woven into it.

The time referred to that evening, and Grace was minutes away from it. The summer sun still hung in the air, keeping any sign of the impending night away. The streets were empty as the kitchens filled with families taking to their supper. An air of quiet hummed through the streets. Grace was two streets away from the address noted on the badge. Her heart beat louder with every closing step. She was dressed discretely and had pulled her hooded wrap over her head. She peered through as she saw the gate in question. Located between a local grog shop and a locksmiths, a beaten cobbled path scuttled down towards a fortress of fawn and flora. A wall of thick evergreens encased a rusty gate.

Grace approached with caution. The sun blazed with all it's drama as it clung onto the remains of the day. Her palms felt damp and sweaty as she fingered her purse for the badge. The gate was locked from the inside. With trembling hands, Grace knocked on the gate. The dry, dank wood flaked at her touch. Eventually, the lock from inside heaved. The door dragged its stiff feet as the gateway opened. Stood before Grace was a nervous man, suspicious and questioning in his old age. He ran his tired eyes over her. The fingers he held out were no more than painted bone, hanging from a brittle hand on which Grace placed the badge. He appeared swallowed by the evergreens, and his hand snapped shut like a fly trap the instant the cloth rested in his sinewy palm. He leaned and looked beyond Grace before stepping aside. Not a word was exchanged before he seemed to sink back into the dark forest that was found behind the gate.

Grace entered without invitation; the old man no longer blocked her path. The gate slammed behind her once she was inside. The forest that stood before her bled with beauty. The landscape was sugar-coated by lichen and flowers, and standing like glittering guards to the gardens, huge bulking trees glistened beside the footpath that ran into the belly of the forest. Grace trod tepidly down the path; her hands still trembling. Daggers of sunlight slashed through the branches and cut into the dark path. Spears of light stabbed the earth. The stones upon the pathway were shaky – loosened and broken by time. Weeds and undergrowth tore at the path, pulling the stones further apart. Grace held her breath and kept her head down as she pushed on through the guarded garden.

The path then broke onto a wide lawn. The lush grass was barely sheltered from the sun, and a small pond sat still at the base of it. A small crowd had gathered by the waters, all facing a bricked gateway that had once housed the entrance to a tunnel beneath the pond. The soft grumblings of the people rippled among the crowds, and gentle waves of conversation flowed. Feeling out of her depth, Grace sunk at the back of the crowd and peered through the sea of people. One man stood at the head, facing towards them.

'The tide is about to change. But while the current concern for issues abroad will only serve to wash away the worries of this island, rest assured they will not cleanse this land. It will not drown out our cries… it will not dampen our ambitions.'

The man raised his hand into the air. His fingers were black and an unlit cigarette rested behind his ear. It was the same brand that he had smoked in Brewley's the day Grace had first met him. The doorway he stood in front of was framed by a flag emblazoned with the Irish Harp.

'My brothers, my sisters, stood together today we are torn; ripped apart by the promises and opportunities that our governing nation is granting. Our dream of Home Rule has been assured, but not delivered. The outbreak of war on the continent has put the matter on hold. But still we simmer and burn with ambition. And, through these tough times, a decision has been asked of us. There is talk that the unionists of Ulster will support Britain's plight – but we do not have to. Military conscription does not apply over here and so the choice remains our own. Do we stay and fight for what is ours, or do we show the world what we want by saving other nations from the fate we fear ourselves?'

Grace noted the silence that came when the man spoke. The school of people from all classes stood and stared intently. Nobody braved an answer to the question that the man posed. Answers divided people, and no one was yet ready, or brave enough, to split a group that shared one goal. Nevertheless, there were different paths that could lead to the same promised-land. On one hand they could chose to stay and force the issue of Home Rule while the momentum for change was rapidly increasing, or they could chose to succumb to the political blackmail that Britain had possibly placed upon them. To question Ireland's support was to reflect the crown's stance on the nationalist ideals, but to lean across and scratch their backs would in theory leave the nation indebted. However, it was the unionists whose itchy feet had already caused them to race to England's aid.

'I do not ask for answers tonight my friends.' The man continued to address the crowd. 'But what I will say is this… change will happen, and different roads will be taken. United in our desires, we may choose to answer to separate screams. The church asks us to do onto them as we wish to be done onto us – leading many to support the threatened catholic nations from invasion and destruction. But others will answer to their fatherland and remain to fight our own battles. All I ask is – regardless of or means – we remain united in our motive!'

The roar burst from the crowds. Grace felt carried by the energy that flowed through the people. Like Moses before the red sea, the ocean of people divided and allowed the man to pass through. The draining sunlight shimmered off the beaded rosary that hanged from his belt. The steel crucifix swung with his every stride and stroked the pistol that was holstered at his hip. He fired his gaze towards Grace as he walked by. She held his stare long enough to see the creases of a smile cut into his pallid cheeks.

The crowd broke and filtered through the forest among separate streams. A particular river of people followed the man the same way Grace had entered the gardens. The sluggish sunset painted the pool in an exquisite orange – the surface scorched like the skin of the fresh summer fruit. Stood alone at the water's edge, Grace did not know what path to take.

Chapter 32

Michael steadied the rifle in his hands. The 1910 Winchester 401 calibre self-loading weapon rested like a rock in his grip. He peered through the small hairline and lined up his shot. A box of two hundred soft-point bullets rested by his side. He was forty yards from his target, and well hidden within the crops. Catching his breath, he held it for just as long as it took for him to pull the trigger.

The recoil was punishing on his sturdy shoulders and the sunlight flashed upon the dark nickel barrel. The gunshot boomed across the fields, punching the air and causing the birds to burst from their trees. Looking up from his rifle, Michael saw that his shot had hit its mark. The herd of young red deer were startled by the bullet that whizzed past them, causing them to starburst across the meadows. Their hooves flicked and danced as they scattered far and wide upon the field. Michael sounded out one final shot for good measure.

Across the meadow lay a group of furiously frustrated hunters. With no natural predator in Ireland, the population of the red deer had flourished. Great herds could be found throughout the country, and it was only natural that they had grown quite partial to the lush pastures of Orplow. However, their growing numbers had recently begun to attract a more selfish and needless predator. The red deer were seen as fair game to the marauding hunters that travelled far and wide to try their anxious hand at execution. They prowled in packs and camped up beside the meadows both day and night; firing their guns during the day and then shooting off their mouths at night with boasts of their greatest kill and slaughter.

Michael loved his land. He knew that only the maternal instinct and influence of nature could hold claim to altering it. And while he accepted that men would kill to survive, to protect or to provide for their families, he felt that the needless culling of a species for sport alone served no natural purpose at all.

He lay hidden as the disgruntled hunters scanned the land to try and find the spoil-sport that had warned their game. The fields were now bare of any deer and they would surely not return until sunset. Michael watched the hunters gather their guns and satchels; their angry faces blazing brighter than the summer sun. He chuckled as many of the men hurled abuse to the skies and threatened the life of their hidden nemesis. With the rifle still and set in his hands, Michael shot his aim between all the men. They would have been easy pickings for any marksman, but having never fired at anything other than space, Michael did not know whether he could make the shot.

'Can I have a go now?' Oscar lay by Michael's side. His face was burnt by the sun and his fringe fell damp and flat to his clammy forehead.

'We need these men to leave first. Another shot might make them wise to our position, and God knows what they'll do to us if they found out.'

'Oh come on... just one shot?'

'Are you serious? If they see where we are, who do you think they are going to catch? I'd drag your bum as best I can but I seriously doubt we'd out run a bullet. And let's be honest... you offer a bigger target than me.'

'Don't be daft. They wouldn't shoot us.' Oscar flashed a glance to the hunters and back again. 'Would they?'

'Well, they've been out here all day and their trigger fingers are itching like your hairy arse on a hot summer's day. Personally, I wouldn't risk it. But if you want your head stuffed and hanging above some rich man's fireplace, then be my guest.' Michael handed Oscar the rifle.

Oscar's palms were dripping as he palmed the weapon. It was self loading and he knew a bullet was already poised and ready in the barrel. He squinted as he gaped down the rifle's sight. The hunters were still packing up their bags from under a large willow tree. It offered Oscar the perfect target for his first shot. He pictured the bark exploding as the bullet tore through the tree and left the men terrified. Filling his lungs, he steadied himself and lined up his shot.

'He's over here!' Michael jumped to his feet and was pointing down towards his friend.

'What the...' Oscar fired wildly into the air. He could not finish his sentence before Michael had dragged him to his feet.

'Run.'

Oscar slung the rifle over his shoulder and sprinted for it. Michael followed behind him, pushing him forward and constantly updating him on the hunter's movements.

'They are getting closer. Come on; move it or we're done for.'

Oscar did not have enough air in his lungs to berate his friend, nor fuel his scampering legs. His breaths were short and shallow. He felt like he could collapse.

'Come on, they're gaining on us!' Michael pushed Oscar on. The tubby lad stumbled with every nudge he received, struggling to keep his balance enough to stand upright. His lungs were on fire and the acid began to burn at the muscles in his whirring legs. Pain seeped into the searing sinews of his thighs. The unrelenting sun sweltered overhead.

'One's taking aim Oscar. He's lining up a shot! Zigzag – run from left to right. We'll be harder to hit if we don't stick to a straight line.'

The horizon crawled towards them as Oscar ran from left to right, ducking his head down as his feet flattened the dry grass. His lungs heaved as he slumped forward. The joints of his knees could no longer lock; his legs were like boiled string.

'Hit the ground.'

Oscar tasted dirt as his face blasted onto the earth. His chest caved as the ground pushed the air from his lungs. He was motionless, his legs glad of the rest, but still his heart raced and thumped at the floor. The dry dirt dusted his face. Wet and wide open, Oscar's lips were caked in damp muck. Unearthing the last ounce of energy within him, he rolled over to check on Michael. The man stood over him, his face decked with his signature smile.

'Ha ha! That was brilliant. You should've seen your little legs scurrying.'

'What the fuck?' Oscar hulked forward and sat upright. His breathing was still thin and brisk. 'But the hunters...' He took a breath. '...They'll catch us soon.'

'Come now... do you really think they would willingly run across a field towards a loaded gun?' Michael pointed towards where the hunters still sat. 'They didn't budge an inch.'

'You bastard, I almost died.'

'From what... exercise? I have to hand it to you though, you covered some distance. And let's be honest, it was bloody exciting.'

'Yeah Michael, I'm fucking thrilled. True, every guy takes a little bit of pride and pleasure in their morning dump, but *shitting* myself in a field in front of 30 blood thirsty men is not my idea of a great outing. Call me old fashioned, but I kind of enjoy the feeling of thinking I'm going to survive.'

'Ah, don't make a meal out of breadcrumbs Oscar. Also, did you say thirsty?' Michael was still smiling. 'What say I buy you a drink to calm those nerves of yours? I think I'll take that rifle from you first though.'

'Throw in a pot of stew and you might force my arm.'

'Done. Always a slave to your stomach, eh? Come on, we'll head into town.'

In town, there was a panicked composure about the place. People passed from one to another as they shared the news. Their bodies carried them about their daily business, but their faces wore an expression of distant concern. Michael watched them intently as he tried to gather what the great news was. Oscar was oblivious at his side – loudly listing the pros and mostly cons of each restaurant in town.

'The beef's too tough in there.'

'Ma said she found a rat in the ladies in *that* one.'

'I love the stew here, but the last time I ate there I put on about a stone.'

Michael had finished listening to him some quarter of a mile back, but now the town held his entire attention. The sun was searing above, forcing the folk to bask in the slim shadows of the stalls and stores. Asking no questions, Michael listened intently as he walked by. Various stories were bound together by the same common thread. Not aware of whether the accounts were embellished or accurate, Michael found that some sort of conflict was the theme of it all. There was a certain intensity in the people, a foreign ferocity, that Michael had rarely seen before.

'Michael, look at that.' Oscar was pointing to a news stand. The headline was all encompassing and yet totally unclear. The letters on the paper were bold and the sheet pinned back by a metal grill. The words 'World at War' filled the face of the stand.

'The world? Does that mean us? Mother hasn't told me of anything like this.' Oscar's stomach rumbled.

'Oscar, I'm as wise as you old pal. Surely we'd know about it if it involved us. I don't think it's that close to home just yet.'

'But what if it is? Would you fight? We've got a gun, maybe we can help.' Oscar's eagerness was endearing.

'Yeah... I'd fight, but only for something that was worth fighting for. You've heard the stories David told us about his father's battles. Each of them just smacked of greed to me. Anyway, I don't think we need to get carried away just yet.'

'David... of course. He'll know more about this than anyone. Let's go and pick his brains.'

'Very well, but let me get this first.' Michael strode up to a stall and bought the biggest and brightest apple he could find. Having paid the trader he turned and tossed the fruit to Oscar.

'I promised you a meal didn't I? Come on, let's go.'

David had devoured every paper he could get his hands on. His stomach rumbled and roared as he had overlooked his breakfast. Engrossed in the events from abroad, he had only an appetite for information. The nerves in the pit of his belly swirled and lashed at the sides. He had been kept updated by his old contacts in England of the coming conflict on the continent, but now that it was upon him he felt an awkward detachment from it. He was not shocked or awed by the outbreak. The event was expected, and dreaded entirely. Raised amidst the bloodshed and battles of his father, David was not adverse to the idea of countries waging war against one another. However, it was the mere magnitude of this conflict that alarmed him. Sides were fighting for more than just one reason, more than one motivation and purpose. Neither party were there through obligation or force; everybody had an eye on a prize of their own. The problem was, *everybody* stood between them.

'Sorry to invade your privacy David, just thought you could clear something up for me?' Michael was knocking on the already open door as he leaned into David's cottage.

'Michael. Good morning my good man. How the devil are you?'

'Very good, scared a few hunters earlier.' He smiled proudly.

'Yeah, and then put the bloody frighteners up me!' Oscar pushed past Michael only to see Cara sat staring at him. 'I'm so sorry ma'am. I didn't know a lady was present. My mom would cook my tongue if she knew I'd cursed in front of you.'

'Don't worry,' whispered Cara. She looked tired and drained. 'Come, sit and help us with this pot of tea. I fear I'd drown if I had another cup. Nice though it is dear.' Cara smiled at David who tossed her a mock frown.

'So, what brings you to my door today then gentlemen?' David poured Oscar a cup of tea. He was already sat at the table an eyeing up the tea cakes. Michael remained by the doorway.

'There's an awful lot of excitement in town. Some sort of concern in Europe. I wondered if you could shed a little light on it all? Are we being attacked or something?' Michael leaned up the door frame. The sun beat at his broad shoulders.

'Not quite,' said David. 'Unlike my fresh tea, this conflict has been brewing for some time now.' He flashed another smirk towards Cara who raised her cup and took an animated sip.

'Anyway, it's the countries of Europe that are at loggerheads. Germany mainly... seems they're reaching out and seeing what they can take hold of. You see, they've built up quite the army and so pose a huge threat to all. So, fearful of being knocked off its royal perch, Britannia has stepped in to tackle this Bavarian bully. But it isn't just these two nations going at it. Italy, France, Belgium... practically everyone in Europe is involved someway or other. And all the agendas together form a very tangled web indeed.'

'But what of Ireland? Do we fight or wait until we're attacked?'

'Who knows? For now, England will use its military, and rely on volunteers after that. Most of the articles I've read today, and word from abroad, are saying that this will all blow over in a year at the most. But, personally, I'm not so sure.'

'So, do we fight or what?' Michael ran his fingers through his hair. His neck was tense. Talk of the world outside of Orplow always made him edgy – all he knew was this town.

'For now, no. But just keep your guard up a little. This town is special somewhat – secure from the battles that rage across the borders. Ireland is torn as it is... and you may find that some may try to exploit the situation. You see, this town distances itself from the divide. People are united here... together. I'm English, born and raised in its church, and despite the fact I converted to marry Cara here, do you think that I would be seen as anything other than a unionist? In Orplow I'm not, but to all the towns surrounding us I would be. Now the unionists already have a sizeable paramilitary. No doubt the Ulster Voluntary Force – which violently opposes home rule – will seek to secure the union with Great Britain and fight alongside them from the start. With them distracted by this *great war*, we may just see the nationalists make a move.'

'But this town is nationalist right? I mean, I know very little granted. But from what I know, the nationalists are the Roman Catholics... well that's us right? So why should I worry, Orplow won't destroy itself surely?'

'Let's hope not. But division isn't black and white. There are grey areas within each side... areas of disagreement. Already nationalists are thinking of going to war.' David rustled through one of his papers to find the article. 'Here it is. You see, the Third Home Rule Bill was already agreed back in May, but has now been postponed for at least twelve months... exactly the same amount of time the crown thinks this war will last. The Bill only needed Royal Assent, a nod of approval, and then the nationalists would have had what they have always desired. But this war has caused a conundrum. Some feel that they should support Britain so to encourage the passing of the bill once the war is over. Others believe that Britain is bluffing and so will look to force its weakened hand.' David folded the paper. 'Michael, don't be surprised that the same sides begin to separate.'

'Well, I don't go for all that nonsense. I was raised to help those that were in need. If that's how I see it, then my decision is no longer mine to make. I'd have to help.'

'Yeah, me too,' said Oscar as he helped himself to a second teacake.

'Well, let's pray you won't have to. For all I know, this little skirmish could be done and dusted in a few months.'

✵✵✵

At the edge of the meadow, Connell gathered money from the travelling hunters. Employing a little of his master's entrepreneurial instinct, he had begun to charge men to access the land. He found the arrangement to be very profitable. The wealthy young bucks travelled from far and wide to enjoy the spoils of slaughtering a helpless animal. However, recently it was more than just the hunter's deep pockets that lay empty; for many had returned empty handed of any game. For weeks they had begun to whine about something startling the deer. At first, Connell had been met with disgruntled customers concerned that a hopeless hunter was constantly missing his shot before they even got a chance to take aim. Yet as the weeks brought with them similar incidents, Connell knew that sabotage was afoot. Still, he refused to act. The fact that the deer were being saved only meant that there would be more deer to hunt and, in turn, more game to trade with the hunters.

With bulging pockets, Connell wished his custom a happy return and made his way back to the estate. He laughed at the incompetence of them all. Crossing his palm with blood money from their dry hands, he took note of his surroundings. The day was as beautiful as they came. The sun clung to the heavens and showered the land in light. A brilliant and bright blue bounced in the breeze as the bluebells swayed from side to side. Chains of daises tied one field to the next, and songbirds filled the skies. Taken by his environment for a moment, Connell afforded himself the pleasure of a whistle as he walked through this harvest of haven. The notes rattled and rasped off his torn lips; spittle streamed from the jagged scar on his mouth. The chunk of flesh that had been ripped from his lips had never healed, and even as he closed his mouth, his sharp rotten teeth could be seen through the gristly gap. The man looked utterly repugnant.

Smiling at the sight before him, Connell's jagged teeth were on full display. Cut off from the herd, a lonely fawn grazed at the grass. Approaching the animal, Connell grasped a handful of ripe berries from the nearest bush and crushed them in his hand. The sweet scented juice dyed his grubby palm in a pulp of fleshy purple. Walking on the balls of his feet, Connell grew closer to the baby deer. Its eyes were like black marbles that rolled nervously; its legs thin and unsteady.

'Here boy,' whispered Connell as he held out his damp fist. The deer looked about it before taking an anxious step towards him. Connell was crouched, trying to look as small as he could. His arms were tight to his side, his knees bent crooked.

Seeing the juice that squelched upon Connell's hand, the fawn flicked out a testing tongue. Tasting the berries, it steadied itself and muzzled its mouth inside Connell's giant hand. The fawn's tongue lapped and licked at the lumpy liquid, unaware that Connell had begun to stand by its side. Feeling the fawn's tongue beginning to dry and drag in his hand, Connell raised his arm, causing the baby deer to stretch its neck to the skies. Holding the mouth tight, Connell drew his knife from his pocket and punched the blade into the deer's thin throat. The steel slid through the flesh with ease. Warm blood gushed as Connell pulled the blade through the fawn's quivering jugular. The muffled bleats soon became muted as the vocal chords were severed by the stained steel of Connell's knife. A cascade of hot crimson liquid covered his arm while the animal shook tiredly. With the head in Connell's hands, the body slumped beneath the slashed throat; only stretched strings of sinew and cartilage bound the two pieces together.

Wrenching the knife from out of the sturdy spinal cord that it had pierced, Connell ran the blade across his tongue. He stood over the lifeless carcass and began to laugh. Content with his kill, he left the body as it lay. He had no need for the flesh, and had no intention of making it into a trophy. Instead, he took a step back and admired his work. His heavy boots rested at the brink of the blood that soiled the ground. The sun began to bare down upon his shoulders and his body begged for the shade. Taking one last look at the defeated deer, Connell crashed his swinging boot into the face of the fawn – detaching the head completely from the body. His rasping whistle rattled in the air whilst he made his way home.

Chapter 33

The speech had moved Grace. It had ignited a deep burning passion to assist her countrymen. Her sense of duty smouldered inside her belly, imploring her to act – to do the right thing. However, like a hungry but empty handed fisherman, Grace had every intent and reason but not the means. All she needed was an opportunity; an avenue in which she could explore. She had heard of the volunteers, and how they assisted at the side lines – housing meetings and such. But Grace did not just want to accommodate the movement; she wanted to live within it. For her entire life – trapped in her own world – Grace had only her own concerns for company. Having been plucked away from her home, her horizons were stretched beyond recognition. The land of Canndare lay flat and far; unsheltered by hills or valleys. Roads splintered from the town centre, sprawling throughout the country like slender silvery veins, catering to the incessant human traffic and wit it carrying all its influence and ideals.

Back at home, stood before her husband, Grace found it difficult to convey her wishes.

'Arnold, I think we need to do something.'

'What?' He looked up from his papers. He looked annoyed by the distraction. 'What exactly do you have in mind dear? You can see I'm awfully busy. Whatever it is I am sure you can deal with the matter by yourself, right?' Arnold chewed his pen as he mulled over his finances.

'Well, that's the point. I don't think I can. I want to help so much, what with this outbreak in Europe, and with the problems at home. But I just don't know how to. I was hoping you could help me?'

'Gladly,' replied Arnold as he looked up from his desk. His eyes sunk beneath his furrowed brow.

'Firstly, I would tell you to forget about all this nonsense abroad. It's just some little spat that should not bear any threat to the likes of us. Let the dogged lower classes fight it out. After all, all of that god-awful labouring should have hardened their bodies to the task.'

Grace thought of Michael. She saw the body that had developed through his daily toil. She saw the strong arms that had held her that night. Unbinding herself from nostalgia, Grace looked to embrace what lay in front of her.

'But what if this war's more than just some brief affair? What if they drag *us* in? Will you fight?'

'Fight?' Arnold looked scared until he steadied himself. 'My dear, Ireland is under no obligation to fight.'

'Men don't need to be told to fight; they just need a reason to.'

'My sentiments exactly. Fools will bleed for a blinkered sense of commitment and duty. They'll lay down their lives for a loyalty that eventually abandons them. They'll fight for something that is out of sight, and they will die alone.'

'And you can't see the beauty in that?' Grace could not shake the image of Michael from her head. She thanked the stars that Ireland was out of reach of conscription.

'Darling Grace, you really do need to grow up. Romance is a concept shared between the bewildered. Wise men, like me, stand back from such nonsenses. Only the foolish find salvation in sacrifice.'

'But what if they need our help? What if the British army pulls us in, what will you do then?'

'I shall cater to my kingdom, and nothing else. Grace, even if this petty squabble abroad spreads out and flatters itself with some slight international importance, what good would I be? I'm injured, and it'd be unwise to send such a sharp mind to the slaughter. Don't you think?'

'I guess so.' Grace watched as Arnold feigned an ache in his leg. She knew he was terrified of confrontation. All his life he deflected his worries onto others, while he cowered behind his father's fortress. What once was a broadening empire and enterprise was now Arnold's asylum. While the world fought over a freedom barely tasted by those fighting for it, Arnold sought security and shelter in the trappings of his forefathers. Peering in from the outside, Grace tried to draw him out from under his rock.

'And what of the issues at home?'

Arnold sat back; the armchair seemed to swallow him.

'What issues at home my dear? This place has enjoyed its most profitable period in decades. Every store in town is stocked high with our crops, and you don't have to walk two tables in the market to find some of our produce crowning a stall.'

'Oh Arnold, look past your blasted work for a moment. This town – this country even – is on the brink of a defining divide. I've heard the nationalists in town talk of taking action against Britain. They want to stand up and seize what they have always hold claim to. Should we not help them?'

'Again... no. What good are we to some bunch of bandits that want nothing more than a title? A dog is still a dog, despite whatever breed it believes it is. Those people are barking for a state of mind rather than practice. It'll boast no difference to their standing in life; they'll simply continue to feed off the scraps that we toss from our table.'

Grace left the room without a word. Her legs felt heavy and her head swirled with argument and reason. She knew that what she felt was true and honest – that her desire to assist was not some flight of fancy but rather a calling to matter somehow. Passing through the cold corridor, she heard the call of the bells in the servant's quarters. A soft ringing carried the shuffling feet of the maid that scurried by. Her hands held a bright silver tray, topped by a crystal decanter heaving with whisky. Whistling by, the maid vanished through the doors of Arnold's study. Grace had become accustom to the sharp scent of the devil's water that bit into her husband's breath. Baited by its numbing virtues, Arnold drained a decanter each evening. He grew attached to the intrinsic quality that purged the pain from his wounded leg. Sitting at his desk for days at a time had weakened his body. His arms had become frail and struggled to support his weight, as the cane shook in his trembling hands whenever he tried to stand. He could no longer stand to be sober. Fortunately, the blurred books before him did not demand an accurate eye; his empire was entirely self-sufficient. Refusing to retire for the evening, Arnold rejected the fact that he was redundant. With every piece in place, and the mechanics mastered, the empire ran like clockwork. All that Arnold offered was the face that framed the fittings.

Kneeling at her bedside, Grace prayed for the first time in months. With her delicate fingers dovetailed, she begged that her purpose would become clear. She asked for guidance through the storm clouds that began to settle overhead. The world was braced for conflict, and Grace knew she could help somehow. She thought back upon the speech that she had heard in the secret garden. The words had urged her to follow a movement – to find meaning in motion. And yet she was still perplexed. Her heart wanted to help only those that called for it. She knew that the nation was on the brink of change; a time that would alter and separate the people. For years they had stood on different sides of the fence – savouring their private pastures – but now sides were beginning to take a stand and cross over into the battlefields. With her hands still entwined, Grace offered her strength to all those that needed it, and her love to those that truly felt it. Lastly, she thought of Michael and prayed that he would shy away from the all the world's troubles – that he would seek sanctuary in the secure secluded settings of Orlpow.

***

Michael had never signed his name before. Even as a child, there was never a need to sign his work. He was torn out of education years before any great essays were required, and even the poems he wrote for Grace had been anonymous in name if not nature. Looking at the line that he had scribbled on the form, Michael barely recognised his own name. The form itself was filled out by the recruitment officer – a general array of tick box questions and the occasional line that required some personal detail. Michael gave his date of birth, current occupation and home address. That and his full consent to be sent off to war as an Irish volunteer.

The physical tests would prove a mere formality. He stood way above the desired five foot three inches, and was at the lower end of the age limit. Oscar had joined him and was scratching his head at the invitation to sign his name. Like Michael he had never had reason or course to do so, and so hazarded at a rough ineligible squiggle. He nodded to the recruitment officer knowingly, suppressed his smug smirk and joined Michael in the line for the physical examination.

'We'll have that King's shilling in no time hey Mike?'

'He can keep his cash Oscar. What good will it do us over there? Hardly going to stop a bullet is it?' Michael felt anxious as he waited. The stream of people looked happier than he had seen them for some time. Carried on a wave of patriotism and propaganda, imposed by Field Marshall Lord Kitchener, the people stood tall and straight. One young recruit, however, looked completely crest fallen.

'Hey Oscar, take a look at that young lad over there. He doesn't look a day over 16.' Michael flashed a glance towards the young man. He was gaunt and his clothes were soiled and torn. His fine brown hair was damp on his brow, and crowned the shoulders so slight they struggled to keep his scraggy neck straight.

'Oh my god… you know who that is right? That's young Joshua Rhodes; the younger brother of your old shag piece.'

'Josh? But he's mustn't be far from fifteen.' Michael walked towards the boy. He could hear him whimpering in front of the suspicious recruitment officer.

'I'm sorry sir, but you look far too young for this draft. Maybe next time, hey?' The officer gave Joshua a dismissive glance. The emaciated boy turned and made his way for the door.

Michael could see the bruises that gripped his thin wrists; blackened bumps bulged beneath his eyes. Michael recalled how Carmel's father had been violent; how his battered children advertised his heartless handiwork. Stepping out of line, Michael made a pass for the young boy, wrapped his arm around his slight shoulders and spun him back towards the front of the queue.

'Josh, my old buddy, how the devil are you? I haven't seen you since school, and Lord you haven't changed at all. You hold onto those youthful looks my lad, you'll be the envy of all us aged and weathered folk for years to come.' Michael stepped closer to the officer and peered over at the form he had stopped writing for Joshua.

'So, sir, tell me… what regiment has my old pal gone for? Surely it's the 16th regiment like the rest of us?'

'Excuse me? Sir, are you vouching for this man's age? You understand that he looks quite the spring chicken compared to yourself.' The officer looked for a hint of hesitation from Michael. He didn't see any.

'Of course. A regular Peter Pan this one. If I knew his secret I'd bottle it and make my fortune, I promise you that.' Michael patted Joshua on the back. He could feel the bony contours of his ribs protruding through his thin sodden shirt. The look he offered the officer was one of pleading and persuasion.

'Very well. Sign this and join the queue. With a physique like that, I doubt you'll pass the physical anyhow.' Joshua gripped the pen and signed his name. Michael stood amazed at how clear the writing was. Flowing across the page, steady and complete, the name Joshua Rhodes filled the foot of the form.

Standing back by Oscar's side, Michael had re-joined the queue. He held Joshua in front of him and pulled him inside the tight line of volunteers.

'What's going on?' Oscar whispered through the side of his mouth.

'We're giving young Josh here a helping hand.'

'But he's too young Mike. You know that.'

'True, but he's old enough to know his own mind. If he wants to fight, who are we to stop him? Any finger can pull a trigger. If Josh thinks he's ready then he gets my support. Isn't that right Josh?' Michael gave the boy a gentle nudge.

'Erm… yeah. Whatever gets me out of here really.' The boy's voice had not risen from the weak whimper that Michael had heard earlier.

'So Josh, how's your sister doing these days?' Oscar leaned forward in order to hear the boy.

'She's fine. So I hear anyway. She doesn't have many dealings with us these days. Met some nice fella recently. She's all settled down now; four months pregnant last I heard.'

'Lucky guy.' Oscar offered his sincerest smile. 'Well tell her Michael and I asked after her. She was a fine looker that one.'

'Maybe not mention me there Josh,' said Michael. 'I don't think your sister and I left on the best of terms. I doubt it would brighten her day to hear of me.'

'Oh don't worry Mr Alpin,' said Josh with a thin smile. 'My sister asks after you every now and then. Not that I can offer much that is, but I know there are no hard feelings. She even mentioned the once how you'd *saved* her. Whatever the mad cow meant by that.'

Michael remembered the moment at the church. He could still see the pain and anguish in her eyes. This same pain now plagued young Joshua's eyes – a signal that beckoned salvation. Michael knew that this young man was looking to break from the realities of his home-life rather than support the plight of those abroad. In leaving Ireland itself, he would have ended his own battle. The war offered him an escape more than a mission.

The line was becoming smaller in front of Michael. People passed through the doors where young nurses sat waiting to examine them. Many of the men felt heroic as they waited in line. The words of the nationalist leader John Redmond still rang in their ears. They had agreed to fight for the freedom of the small nations; to tackle the militaristic aggressor that threatened the catholic nations of Serbia and Belgium. Rich in religious ideals, many nationalists thought that the good turn of defending their fellow Catholics would lead to the royal assent that they so desperately craved. Fixed in their determination, the men were strengthened by their beliefs. Each of them bursting through the medical doors as if the enemy lay in waiting on the other side.

'Look at him.' Oscar gawped at the sight of an older gentleman stripped down to his bare chest. He was leaving the examination room and was pulling on his shirt. Michael smiled as he looked back at his friend who had forgotten how to blink.

'He must be an old regular. I hear they raise the age limit if you've been in the army before.'

'Lowered it to the grave more like. That man looks ancient. Well his face anyway.' Oscar stood staring at the gentleman. His face was weathered; grounded by the callous sands of time.

'Looks like he's in shape though.' Michael found himself staring at the older gentleman. His creased skin was stretched out on top of a thick muscular chest.

'He must down brine by the pint load. Look at his skin... it's glistening.' Oscar patted his own pale stomach, and pulled Joshua to be before him in the queue. He was certainly not going to follow either the old boy or Michael.

Michael took a step forward and peered through the door. A young nurse was waiting for him. She shuffled a few papers as Michael entered. The room was small, but large enough for the task at hand. A hospital gurney had been rolled in and placed alongside the far wall. A piece of paper with a pyramid of differently sized letters hung above the bed. Michael coughed a little to get the busy nurse's attention.

'Hello,' said the nurse. Her golden hair was tied tightly in a bun, and she wore the traditional British nurse attire. A red cross blazed upon her breast.

'Hello... I'm Michael.'

'Well good afternoon Michael. Can you take your shirt off please?' She fingered a steel stethoscope and placed it over Michael's heart. The icy metal chilled his chest. Goosebumps bulged and surged to the surface. Michael could feel the nurse's nails scrape softly over his skin. His heart-rate climbed at the woman's touch. It was the first he had felt since Grace's warm embrace, and it was as cold as the Arctic Ocean. The nurse could hear the beats begin to quicken. She was flattered that she could have such an effect on this handsome man. Blood flushed her face, and her cheeks blushed brightly. Michael's eyes met hers as her hand brushed over his firm stomach. His abdomen rippled and tensed at her touch.

'Well your physical shape is not in question,' said the nurse as she reigned in her wandering hands. She questioned how creaky the gurney would be if she allowed the young man to take her right there and then.

'Thank you,' replied Michael. He felt embarrassed in the moment; a little lost in the lust that claimed him.

The rest of the examination was a formality. The nurse took a sample of blood, and reeled Michael through the conveyor belt of procedures. He was impressive on the eye test and was as flexible as a snake. Michael was about to leave when he thought of the young guy a few places behind him.

'Nurse, I was wondering if you could do me a favour. You see, there's a close friend of mine a few places back in the queue. He looks frightfully young, and frail with it, but he's one hell of a fighter. It's just that, by letting him pass you'll be helping him win his own war. He's as bright as a button and writes his signature perfectly. But as you'll see during his examination, though he wouldn't claim his father to be his greatest influence, the man certainly has left his mark on him.'

Michael tried to offer his usual dea-sealing smile, but he could feel the weight of sincerity upon his lips. To see such weakness in the strongest man she had seen all day, the nurse was almost drawn to tears. She had never known a man as beautiful as Michael Alpin.

He was buttoning up his shirt as he left the examination room. His cold bare chest clung to the cotton; his stiff nipples cut into the cloth. Seeing his nervous friend next in line, Michael offered him some support.

'Don't worry too much Oscar. It is a bit intimate though. If I had to go in again, I'd definitely go about it a little *differently*.' Michael cut Oscar a sincere look.

'Why? What happens in there?' Oscar's skin instantly became glossed in a nervous cold sweat.

'Oh don't worry. She sees hundreds of them every day. It's just another boring chore for her. But then I suppose she could be a little bit warmer with it. You see, she has an icy touch and… well… let's just say your little soldier will be at its shyest.'

'What? Seriously, I have to go naked in there?' Oscar's pores gave birth to a bucket load of sweat.

'Like the day that you were born. But if I were you, I'd get that part over and done with before she gets her freezing stethoscope out. Not unless you want to be known as Private Acorn anyway. My tip would be… just get in there, get it out and get it done.' Michael patted Oscar towards the door. The thin material of his shirt stuck to his clammy skin.

Heeding his friend's advice, Oscar walked towards the examination room. The door was ajar and so he nudged it open. He could see the pretty young nurse sat at her desk. She looked bored as she busied herself with some papers. The dim light hopped off the steel stethoscope. The room was muggy and Oscar was finding the air too thin for simple shallow breaths. He gulped deeply as the nurse's fingers flickered towards her emasculating apparatus. Sizing up his options, Oscar took the matter into his own hands; pulling at his belt and dropping his pants down to his ankles.

Michael beamed as the nurse's scream screeched down the walls of the tightly packed corridor.

Outside the young men felt relieved that their recruitment into the army had been completed. They had all opted for the 16th Regiment, which was a collection of Irish battalions, mainly made up of nationalists and Roman Catholics.

The day was torn between the summer and autumn; the bright sun shone like the sky's prized medal as the few fallen leaves began to brown on the floor. Anxious for their young ally, Michael and Oscar waited in the street for Joshua. They sat and leaned up a stone wall that offered modest shade from the morning heat.

'So, that's it then. Now we just wait for our travel warrant to arrive.' Oscar scraped a stick along the cobbled footpath.

'Yeah… it's just a matter of time. Soon we'll be regular Christopher Columbus'.' Michael was glad to be sitting down – his legs did not feel as strong as they usually did.

'But what about home? Won't you miss it a little?' Oscar leaned a look down into town. Everything was as it should be: the people remained stable in their routine.

'I suppose. But what's left for me here?' Michael twiddled the crucifix in-between his fore finger and thumb. The leather strap remained tight around his left wrist.

'Do you miss her?' Oscar rested a hand on his friend's slumped shoulders.

'Yes. But then, I hardly knew her. I suppose that's what makes it harder to deal with. Not only do I miss the little things that I know of her, I also long for every last detail that I don't.' He looked at the ground. 'Foolishly, I began to imagine a future with her. Now I have to mourn the loss of that as well.'

'Michael… who did you think I was asking about?' Oscar watched for his friend's reaction. He saw Michael's eyes flash over the Virgin Mary pendant on his bracelet.

'Oh… do you mean my mother? Mate, you never have to ask me if I miss her; she'll always be with me.' Like a dry desert kissed once by heavenly tears, Michael would always know what love was – even if only by its absence.

'Hey Mike, here comes Joshua. Come on, get up. We'll go see how he did.' Oscar pulled lightly on his friend's shirt. He felt like a dead weight beneath it.

'Joshua… over here lad. How did it go?' Oscar could see that Michael had gotten to his feet and was standing behind him. There was a shred of sadness in his voice.

'Ay, not bad. She wasn't a fan of you mind.' Joshua smiled and tossed a nod towards Oscar.

'Never mind that prude… did you pass?' Oscar shifted on his feet. He could still hear the nurse's chilling scream.

Michael looked at Joshua. The boy looked miniscule – his frail arms were yet to know the full labour of a man's working day. He was as thin as an autumn branch; his skin as white as the bone on which it lay, and the slight swell of starvation packed his belly. And yet there was a shimmer of light within his darkened eyes; a brightness between the bloodshot veins that sprawled from his sockets. One of his hands pawed at his pockets – the shallow sleeve almost swallowing his entire arm. He removed his clenched fist and held it out in front of him, with his clasped fingers pointed towards the skies. Joshua's eyes shimmered as he opened up his hand, parading the King's shilling that shone in his tiny palm.

Chapter 34

Steam spiralled from the cup; the rich scent of coffee crammed the small café. Watching the world outside, Grace longed to be a part of it. She was now a regular at Brewley's, and the shopkeeper knew her order off by heart. He was also wise to the usual time that Grace would visit, so it was not unknown for Grace to find her desired drink freshly poured out for her on arrival. She warmed her hands on the cup in front of her, wrapping them around the warm ceramic as if holding them in prayer. She had not been sleeping too well, and the coffee beans gave her the bounce that she needed to hide her fatigue from the freshly woken world. Back at her home, both sides of her marital bed lay cold and bare. The crisp creases in the corners of the linen felt only the touch of the chambermaid's fingers as she remade the unused bed each morning. Recently, Arnold had become totally consumed by his work and utterly devoured by the demon drink. Even his healthy leg was now unsteady, and so he chose to sit in his armchair for countless hours, calculating his fortune, and ignoring the losses that piled up around him.

Despite the warning signs from her warmed hands, Grace took a hearty gulp of her coffee. She would have to wait a while for the next as the tiny taste buds burned on her tongue – tiny blisters dried out her thirsty tongue. She patted her mouth with her handkerchief. Her tongue fastened itself to the cloth. It felt too big for her mouth; wider and thicker than her pursed thin lips. But at least the drink had shaken her from her slumber. Unknown to her distanced husband, Grace had been grateful of his absence. She could no longer imagine enduring the unmoving act of sex with him again. Arnold excelled in being inert and, while she had every intention of making their relationship work, he thrived in failure. There was no fire in his touch; there was no thunder in his heart. Allowing her tongue to cool down, Grace watched the storm that brewed within her coffee cup. The steam continued to swirl and spiral while the shop doorbell introduced another customer.

'It was good to see you there the other night.' The voice was whispered but familiar. Grace looked up to see the man from the secret garden. She looked around to see if she was being watched.

'I'm so sorry. I found the badge in the paper, and I was intrigued. I've not told anybody about what happened there, I promise.' Grace's voice was numbed by her drying tongue.

'And why not? What we spoke of was no secret... the whole nation is discussing it.'

'If that were so, then why do you need to recruit so secretly?' Grace shifted in her seat. She was now facing the man. He was cleaner than before, freshly shaven and spruced up. A feint smell of aftershave tickled her nose.

'It has been a tradition for some time. We're open in our beliefs, but it's not always wise to actually talk of them out in the open. Not now anyhow. With this sea of change, local ideologies could be swept away with it; our country may unite against one common enemy abroad, and in turn ignore the demon that already waits at our gates. You see, while the world is distracted, we must remain focused. England's extremity is Ireland's opportunity. So let's pick its pocket.' The man pinched a biscuit from Grace's saucer and took a bite. Thankfully, his hands were cleaner than usual.

'Shouldn't we help in the war effort?' Grace felt confident to take another sip of her coffee. The water had cooled and her body was grateful of the blast of caffeine.

'And which war is this? Just because there are louder cries from across the waters, doesn't mean that there are no problems at home. Out on the battlefield, if two men were gravely wounded... it would be the silent one that would be in more need of help. My dear, just because Ireland is silent does not mean that she is well.'

'But how can I help? I can't offer any experience, I have no money of my own. I'm just one woman.'

'But we're all just one person. That's why we must be together. As a collective we can move as one and march in mass. I've already decided to stay and fight for our nation's cause; a section of the nationalists are looking to make a difference at home. I think you should join us.'

'Join you? You sound like a rebellion... it may be too dangerous for the likes of me.' Grace hid her excitement at the prospect. There was an aroma of romance in the idea: a feeling of worth and honour.

'We'll only put into practice the words that we've already spoken. I'm sure you don't spit bullets, right?'

'No, of course not.'

'Then we'll be fine. Come back to the garden this evening. Say that Benjamin Griffin invited you. But who shall I say I'm expecting?'

'Grace Farrington, at your service.' She offered an animated wink and watched Benjamin leave the store. He pawed a copy of the Irish Examiner and potted it under his armpit before disappearing into the tide of townspeople. Finishing her coffee, Grace felt her pulse quicken. It was an intoxicating mix of caffeine and adrenaline.

The evening was upon her in moments. She had barely eaten a thing at supper, but then no-one had sat opposite her to even notice. Readying herself for the night ahead, Grace palmed a bible and said a soft silent prayer for those she loved. She missed her family terribly, and still longed for a certain someone's tender touch. The weather beat at the windows outside. Rain rattled against the thin windowpane, and the winds shook the few remaining leaves from their branches. Torn from the long leaves of their trees, the leaves scattered and fell inside the foreign fields, buried by the broken mounds of soaked soil.

The hallway inhaled as Grace opened the door. The frosty wind swept past her and pulled at her coat. The portraits clattered and clanked on the corridor walls; the gusts of wind lifted the frames before swiftly leaving them to fall back into place. The rain rumbled on the cap of Grace's umbrella; a crest of water poured around her. Cloaked by the shade of the night, she made her way into town. The night was thicker than usual. The deep darkness suppressed every shadow, shrouding the remains of the day, blanketing the pale light of the moon. A soft, sallow shade of blue flickered through the ceaseless rain. The soaked land shimmered beneath the showers.

The town was as quiet as a church. Only the rumbling of the rain could be heard as it pelted down upon the pebbled streets. The tips of Grace's shoes were drenched. Each stride jabbed her toes through the curtain of water that circled her. Her flat slippers were damp, and squelched with each step. She made her way into the town. Blurred light beat out from the bleary bulbs of the lampposts. Rows of tired lights lined the streets. Grace stuck to the shade – veiled in the night's silhouette. She took the turn that rolled down towards the garden gateway. A stream of water ran by her side; spooling towards the bed of the alleyway. A small muddied moat ringed the roots of the evergreens that draped the walls.

The gate was ajar. The same old man peered through the gap. His eyes shone like a wolf's – sharp slits that flickered like the final flames of a spent candle. Grace could not be heard the first time she spoke. Her voice was lost on the whistling wind.

'I am here to see Benjamin Griffin.' Grace shouted over the storm. Her throat trembled as she tried to be heard. The sharp eyes sank into the shadows as the gate swung open. The moat drained down the footpath that crept from the gateway. Once again, Grace stepped beyond the threshold and into the jaws of the garden.

A silence greeted her. Drips of rain stole through the branches that enclosed the garden from the skies. The swaying trees breathed like huge ribs, caged around the stony spine of the path. Small trenches had been dug beside the pathway. Slim channels laced with oil blazed brightly. Short flames danced on top of the trenches, leading the way into the gardens.

Breaking through the corridor of trees, Grace stood at the top of the lawn where she had witnessed Benjamin's speech. The patch of lush grass escaped the rainfall, and the dark clouds above had broken off, revealing the crescent moon and the few stars that dared to brave the bitter night. Fiery trenches spread from the base of the pathway – framing the lawn and lakeside in brilliantly bright flames. A crowd had gathered upon the grass, huddled and warming themselves from the wintry wind. Grace closed her umbrella and joined them. Greeted only by their backs, Grace could see that they all faced towards the small pool of water; towards a small stage that had been set. Two green flags, emblazoned with the golden Irish harp, stood either side.

'My brothers, welcome.' Benjamin stood between the flags. His long coat swept the stage. He eyed the men in blazers before him. He could see the woman at the back of the crowd. He smiled knowingly.

'My sisters, you are also welcome.' He nodded at Grace. 'People, tonight Ireland sleeps. It rests on a pillow of ignorance – content that the world's terrors are out of reach. But we're not safe in our slumber; there is no bliss in our ignorance. Together, we must reawaken the spirit of Irish nationalism; we must be militant as the military march abroad. This great nation is not an acquiescent arm of the United Kingdom; we're not some subordinate strand like our Celtic cousins. It's a fact that the government's resolution of every question we have posed to them has diluted our nationality. Must we really beg and plead to rule the land that is rightfully ours? My friends… I stand here today and declare that we do not. No longer do we ask; we will demand. No longer do we consider; we will act. And no longer will we suffer; for we will fight.'

A blood curdling roar rose from the crowd. Fists punched the air – shaking as if to loosen the shackles of a superfluous society. An energy soared through the people; fused by frustration, they began to believe. The people's pessimism passed over, and was soon replaced by an open aired optimism. Benjamin Griffin spoke to the people, but more importantly he spoke for them. His words were written on the tips of their tongues – etched out by years of disenchanted desires.

'We are gathered here tonight to take the first step towards the future we deserve. The time for talk has passed. There is a movement that is gaining pace in our closest regions. Our neighbours are plotting a motion that could shake this country to its very core, and I for one support them. For I would rather build from the ground up – to harvest the seeds that we ourselves have sown – than to live off the fallen fruits from our foreign fathers. In the following months, change will come; a change that we can cause or a chance that we can ignore. So I ask you all to walk with me – to where the grass is truly greener – to where the land is finally ours!'

Grace watched Benjamin as he roused the crowd. They looked ready to follow him into the pits of hell, and smiling all the way. His voice was cutting in its clarity. His aims were translucent and true. Ireland was for the Irish.

The flames in the trenches blazed brightly, casting a hopeful light amongst the people. Dejected, the darkness departed the lawn. A charge of inspired aspiration spiralled towards the skies. Baited, the people held their breath as Benjamin began to speak.

'In the months to come, we will aid *our* cause by uniting against our oppressors. Our target is Dublin, and we aim to take it back. You may hear the world scoff, condemning our timing. But be sure they will see the true measure of a man. And yes, they will call me Fenian; yes, they will call me a republican. Yet, they can never call me brother. For you are *my* people… and we are the I.R.B.'

The crowd cheered and clapped as Benjamin bowed. He stood for a moment and raised his fist to the air. Raindrops beat at his hand as the heavy clouds leaned towards the gardens. The fires fought the falling rain; punching through the torrent of water that thrashed and thumped at the ground. The flags flailed within the wind – wrapping themselves tightly to the flagpoles. Suddenly, the crowd dispersed into the shelter of the trees.

Grace stood still. She felt free as the rain washed over her. She raised her head to the heavens, forcing her eyes to remain open. She watched the individual droplets descend, each carrying a shred of moonlight with them. They twinkled as the clouds threw them down from the heavens towards God's country.

Staying long enough to feel the last tired drops drip from the sky, Grace decided to go home. She had read about the Irish Republican Brotherhood, and had to admit she was somewhat sympathetic to their cause. There had been countless articles on Tom Clarke and Sean McDermott, the leading names of the movement. She was aware of the slanderous reports linking them with Germany – allowing Europe's tormentor to arm them – but she was unsure as to how accurate the mud-slinging was to the mark. Walking back, Grace found that the streets were dry of anybody else. 'Pro-War' posters propped up every wall, declaring the need for everyone to enrol and aid the allies. The corpulent moustache that crowned Lord Kitchener's lip reminded Grace of her father. On the poster, the Secretary of State was thrusting his forefinger towards the reader, above the declaration 'Your Country Needs YOU'. The word 'You' was in full capitals and almost four times the size of the words that preceded it. She saw the steely stare of Lord Kitchener – his eyes direct and deadly – and prayed that her hometown was out of his sight. Staring through the pitted eyes on the poster, a wave of memories crashed over her. She saw the flying fists of her father thrash at her mother. She saw the closed windows of her chambers. She saw the finest sunrise she had ever encountered. Stood alone with only the cold night for company, Grace could almost feel Michael's arms around her. Every day since she had made the decision to leave him, she had questioned her own judgement. New to love, Grace had feared its control; she had chosen to lose the one thing that she had dreamed of, only in a bid to ensure that it could never hurt her. And so instead she lived fearless in her freedom as the new Mrs Farrington. In spite of the spark that was absent from his kiss — the ability to make her stomach skip at the mere sight of him — Grace was at least secure in her husband's commitment.

His desk light flickered. A weak light lit the papers that cluttered his study, tingeing the frayed and fingered edges. A crystal decanter laden with whiskey pinned the papers to the desk. A damp ring rested at its base. The window was ajar, and the cold wind leaked through into the room. Arnold's body was already numb. The heavy decanter was already on its third refill of the evening. An empty bottle of the finest whiskey teetered on the edge of the table. The alcohol had stolen the strength in Arnold's legs. He slumped in his chair and surveyed his finances scrupulously. He was set for life. The fortune secured by his father meant that he need not work another day. However, stubborn in his refusal to bask in his late father's shadow, Arnold was determined to make his mark. Admittedly, he had cut costs and overheads — slashing the worker's wages under the false mask of helping fund the war effort — but the profit was self-generating. His company owned the monopoly on the local trade, and would do so for years to come. The sudden outbreak of the war had doused any dreams a competitor may have had of rivalling him. Nobody was willing to invest in new enterprises. It was a time where risks were assessed, but rarely taken.

His fingers gripped his glass. The strong scent of whiskey filled his nostrils as he drenched his tongue. Having drowned his solemn sorrows for the past few hours, his throat was sedated, unable to feel the fire that coursed through it, while his stomach growled, ungrateful of another liquid supper. Barely a morsel of food had passed the man's lips in days. His skin was pallid, and pulled tightly around the brittle bones they housed.

He leaned back in his armchair. The leather creaked beneath his bony buttocks. A smaller, almost identical chair sat opposite his desk. He remembered the many meetings in which he had sat on that low chair, facing his elevated father. It was within these meetings that Arnold had first been taught the ways of running a successful business. Above all he had listed all the sacrifices involved; forcing home the necessity of running your own books.

'Although renowned for his acute eye, even the eagle has to feed from time to time.' His father had said this a thousand times. He had never trusted an accountant to oversee the books, fearful that their eye for business may lend itself too easily to swindling their employer.

Arnold could barely recall a time he shared with his father outside of his study. Every encounter was in itself a lesson; a constant schooling that was scant of any warmth or affection. His father's sole passion was profit, and not the pitfalls of individual goals or aspirations. And so Arnold had never been asked what he wanted to do in life, but rather implored to take up the reigns of the family business. All he was designed to understand was how to make the business work. Hunched over his desk, with his fingers sprawled around an empty crystal tumbler, Arnold knew he was no longer needed.

Chapter 35

The gravestone was simple. A small block of marble decorated only by the gold painted letters that were etched into it. Michael ran his finger across the two dates that sat beneath his mother's name. His heart sank at the small hyphen that stood between them – a thin line in which his mother's entire life was held. His finger slowed as it ran across the small shallow dash. He recalled the earliest memory of his mother, and then his last. The thought of his mother tending to him as a child – bandaging a ragged gash that had almost split his knee entirely – filtered into the final moments Michael had shared with her. He remembered the sweet smile that stretched across her face as death washed over her. She had looked completely at peace. Stood at her resting place, Michael was saying his goodbyes.

'I guess you already know this mother, but I thought I'd say it anyway. I've volunteered to help out with the trouble abroad. I think I can do some good over there. There's very little keeping me here anymore, and like you said... you'll always be with me right? I doubt old man Darby will be too fussed to have me out of the way. And, anyway, I'll be too far to hear him moan when he finds out that nobody can tend the fields like you taught me to. It's just, this town will always be my home, but it will never be the same now that you've gone.' He twiddled his bracelet. 'You'll be pleased to know that I decided to make my peace with God recently. Now don't blame me for being so bloody stubborn, I got that streak from you, but I'm sorry if being so negative ever made it harder for you to believe. You see, I never did give up believing... I just couldn't accept it. I felt that if I did, then my belief would somehow keep you from my father in heaven. I couldn't support something that would keep you two apart. Granted, I never knew him, and I doubt I'll ever understand why he left you the way he did... but if someone as wonderful as you loved him, then he must have been something special.' He paused for breath. 'As for me, well the truth is I miss you. But I suppose in losing you, heaven got the angel that it deserves.' Michael lay down some fresh wildflowers. The wind pulled several petals from the bunch and cast them into the breeze. Two fell onto the grave of Michael's father.

'I hope with all my heart you're not alone mother.' He tidied up the flowers. 'I love you.'

The afternoon came with a cutting chill; the breeze bit at Michael's skin. His hair waved from the whipping winds – whispering into his ears as they waltzed past. He could almost hear his mother's gentle hum. The songs she sang began to fill his thoughts, dragging him back to the times where she carried him across the kitchen floor. The dances they shared shone like a lighthouse within his stormy memories. Their past pleasures pained him, punching home the fact that such times – while not forgotten – were lost forever. Feeling his bracelet swing in the September wind, Michael left his mother's side, carrying her cross with him.

The fields were coated in a low hanging mist; a silver shadow set inches above the land. Michael made his usual stroll towards the horizon. His feet felt their way through the familiar path – on top of trodden steps that had grown larger and wider with time. Feeling the cold, Michael blew into his hands. Small streams of mist filtered through his fingers. The great lake swam beside him; the greying waters trailing his every step. Growing closer to the edge of the land, he could hear the thunder beneath him. The sun squatted above the sea, laboured by the long day it had watched over. Small waves broke upon the shore, crashing with the fresh waters that rolled out from the cove.

Michael stretched his arms out wide and imagined what it would feel like to fall again. The waters drew him closer – begging him to leap. He held his head back and closed his eyes. The ground rocked beneath his legs, beaten back by the waters that raged at his side. The sun light sprayed through the falling water, caught by the vapour of the vanishing stream that burst with rapturous applause into the air.

Embraced by the winds, Michael felt small droplets kiss at his face. He thought of Grace – he thought of the countless nights that he had waited – and of how he had fallen long before they had decided to leap together. However, now abandoned by opportunity, Michael picked himself up. On occasion he had found himself urged to write to her, to find the words that would bring her back to him, but no combination of sentiments and truths ever felt good enough. Once a foreigner to his faith, and forgotten by his own fate, Michael was also completely lost in his love.

Opening his eyes, he could see the sun shy away from the skies that held it. The deep depths of the Irish ocean lay below him with open arms. Bidding his favourite place in the world farewell, Michael turned and walked back towards the leaning valleys of the land. The waters waved behind him as he made his way home.

***

The house looked untouched. Each and every item rested in its rightful place. If it were not for the fresh flowers that filled the various vases, the house could be taken as utterly lifeless. Exhausted by the endless endeavour of maintaining his home, David lay out on his porch. His trailing leg rocked the swinging deck chair that he lazed in. Cara was out for the evening, having been invited to the town hall to teach music along with her mentor Francis. Yawning widely, David felt the silence stretch out over him. Of late he had not had the privilege of hearing his wife play. He knew by taking these classes she enjoyed escaping the rooted routine of daily life, and he would never invade her private space – no matter how many times she invited him. Since his wife's accident, David had been there to help her, but he knew more than most that sometimes it was his absence that aided her the most.

Forever for her, David lived to make Cara's life better. Yet he knew that it could only be achieved in moderation. On one hand he could not afford to become her carer, and on the other he could not allow her to feel alone. He could see that in love they had been blessed, but in life they had been torn apart.

On the cusp of consciousness, David's mind wandered. Lucid, poisonous lines drew out the day that he had seen his Cara fall. He could almost smell the musky sweat of the sniggering

Connell who stood by and watched as Cara lay bleeding on the ground. Thoughts of violence flashed in his mind, ferociously filtering the scene – trying in vain to change the outcome. David's mind wrapped his fingers around the thick throat of the sniggering coward, who choked beneath his closing grip. Connell's eyes bulged out of their sockets, as the veins in David's arms filled up and fuelled his fingertips with a fatal fury. Behind him, a motionless Raegan stood over his dying daughter.

Shuddering from his slumber, David felt the cold sweat trickle on his face. It took a moment for him to collect his thoughts – to divide the truth from his trance. His hands felt cold in the autumn evening. Having gathered his bearings, he sat up in his chair, planting both feet firmly onto the ground. He rubbed the balls of his palms over his eyes and breathed deeply. His mouth felt dry as he tried to swallow. The feeling of Connell's throat still throbbed on the tips of David's fingers. He did not flinch at the thought of seeing the last light of life leave the eyes of such a bastard. For years he had wished to have had his blade to hand – to have driven into Connell's neck. But in that fateful moment, David knew without instruction that his wife needed him. Haunted by his cravings, David remained completely committed to the wants of his wife. But, as hot and tempered as a volcanic spring, his lust for retribution simmered beneath his smooth skin.

David was beginning to doze when he heard the soft rapping of footsteps on his porch. A floorboard creaked slowly and then stopped.

'Hi David.' Michael's voice was hushed as if not to wake the man he addressed. David sat up and smiled drowsily.

'Mr Alpin. To what do I owe this pleasure? Cara's out, but I can put the kettle on if you want to wait for her.'

'That's quite alright. I was passing by anyway. I just wanted to let you know that I've decided to go and fight in the war. My travel warrant came through this morning, and I'll be heading out tomorrow for England.'

'Bloody hell. Are you sure you know what you're getting into Michael? It won't be some jolly around the continent you know?'

'If I'm honest, I have no idea what to expect. But then, if tomorrow wasn't a mystery what would be the point of living it?' Michael made a small unconvincing laugh. Abandoned by humour, he kept to the facts. 'All I know is that we'll be trained in England as part of the 16th Regiment and then shipped out to wherever we're needed.'

'We?' David ran his hands through his hair, unaware his was mirroring his friend.

'Oscar's coming too. Don't worry… I didn't ask him, he says he wants to do his bit as well. To be honest, there was quite a queue down town at the recruitment office the other week. It seems we're not the only ones who think we can help.' Michael did not mean his words to carry any attack in them. But still David got defensive.

'Well, more fool them. You may think I'm shying from it all, especially as I'm English as well. But I've spoken with my father's old friends and they're convinced I won't be needed. They say because I'm married, and what with Cara's disability, I'll be left out of the whole bloody mess.'

'Well I suppose it makes sense to have all the single men die alone first, right?' Michael smiled without a hint of malice.

'Michael, I didn't mean it like that.'

'I know. And I agree with you, honest I do. If there was a single reason for me to stay here then I would. But maybe *reason* left me some-time ago.'

David knew what Michael meant. He had watched from the side-lines as Michael and Grace had come together. He had known from the moment he saw Michael by the lake that it was him who had written those poems for Grace. Cara had even filled him in on the goings on at the ball. But now he was baffled as to why, almost a year on, they were not together. David was always drawn to Grace's boundless qualities – how endearing she was in the absence of inhibition. So to see that she had chosen a life to her father's design – one centred on enterprise more than emotion – seemed to defy her true nature. Seeing the remains of a lost romance stood before him, David knew Michael's motivation. He could see that the young man needed to escape the familiar fields with all their constant reminders and recollection. He knew that Michael wanted to discount his loss by gaining purpose – that he would sacrifice himself for the greater good. David knew all of this, and accepted it. He just regretted it.

'So you leave tomorrow?' David stood from his deck chair. It swung slightly behind him.

'First thing.' Michael's smile was sincere. A hint of resignation filled his eyes. There was no excitement for his adventure; there was no sense of heroic gesture. David opened his arms and embraced Michael. The friends felt the firm hug, and neither offered the customary pat on the back that demanded a release. Instead, their grips tightened for one last squeeze before they let go. David held Michael's stare.

'Michael, for whatever reasons you're going over there… promise me this. Promise that you'll return home. *For her* if nothing else.' Michael felt a pain stab at his chest.

'But she left me. And though I can see her reasons for it, I can't understand them. So if you ask me to return for her, you may be asking me to return for nothing at all.'

'Is love nothing?'

'No. I'd die for that.'

✳✳✳

The packed bags weighted the bedroom floor. The thin mattress of his bed pressed at his tense back. Michael was only a few hours away from leaving and yet none of his thoughts were of the future. Shrouded by a thin valiant veneer, Michael's decision to join the war was a selfish distraction. The political propaganda that peppered the papers was pointless to Michael. He had never taken the time to read the articles – accepting only that therein lay an opportunity for adventure. The countless motivations that tried to justify or reason the war were of no interest to him. He did not care for the intentions of strangers; he did not see his place as a mere pawn in the plans of faceless others. Nor did he ride on a wave of heroic optimism that promised to launder the oppressed. No, all he wanted was to help himself in the most selfless way possible. By laying his life on the line, he hoped to heal his own wounds, regardless of the price.

His body was tense as he tried to get some rest. The muscles in his arms ached a little. He had not eaten that day, and the tired fatigue that came with hunger had crept up on him. Beyond sleep, he lay awake and stared at his ceiling. He knew he would not be able to sleep that night. With little else to do, he knelt by his bed and began to pray. He held the small metal crucifix from his bracelet tightly, and whispered into his clenched fists like he had seen his mother do a thousand times. Taking a long breath, Michael addressed his prayers as he would a confidant.

'Dear Lord. What can I say? Maybe my decisions are clearer to you than they are to me right now. But, if it's true that we're part of some greater scheme, then I guess the decision was never mine to make. For I never decided to love either. And yet I'm ruled by it. So I guess fate does take a hold of us all. As for the goings-on abroad, I don't fear what awaits me... what's left to take from me? But you know I don't feel sorry for myself. And I won't wallow in pity. The fact is... I'm alive to feel it. Pain's only an emotion that lets us know that something is wrong; that something that was once right has been altered. But if this was meant to be – if this is some form of test – then please watch over me out there. Please give me a chance to tell *her* how I feel. For that I'll offer myself and all that I am. Amen.'

The remainder of the night slipped away. Brushed by the autumn breeze, the trees threw down the final leaves that remained on their branches. Crumpled and creased, they lay pressed upon the stone walls that grilled the fields. Swarms of stars stole through the night's canvas, breaking shards of light upon the land. Shadows danced in the moonlight as the night held back the day. Feeling the tender touch of the night air creep over him, Michael lay wide awake, but not alone in the company of his thoughts.

Chapter 36

On 2 August 1915, the headlines of the *Irish Examiner* were dominated by the funeral of Jeremiah O'Donovan Rossa. Born in Rosscarbery to a family of tenant farmers, he grew up to father what became the basis for the Irish Republican Brotherhood. Charged in 1865 with plotting a Fenian uprising, Rossa was put on trial for high treason and sentenced to life imprisonment. Having been exiled to the United States in 1870 – as part of the Fenian Amnesty – he took up residency in New York City. Despite his foreign residence, Rossa was still a force in Ireland and his infamous 'dynamite campaign' was the first ever bombings of English cities organised by the Irish Republicans. Having survived being shot in 1885 – some suggest for his 'Skirmishing Fund', which supported the arming of those who stood to fight the British – Rossa survived for two more decades before passing away in a hospital bed in St Vincent's Hospital. A fruitful man, having raised 18 children, Rossa's legacy was the template for change in Ireland; his seed was planted deeply into the public consciousness.

Grace's cold coffee mug pinned the paper to the café table. She had read the paper from front to back, engrossed by the reaction from the funeral of O'Donovan Rosso. His remains had been taken to the Pro-Cathedral and lay before the High Altar until they were later lay in state in Dublin's City Hall. Hundreds of Irish Volunteers had stood guard, while droves lined the route to the Glasnevin Cemetary where he was finally laid to rest. Befittingly, a ceremony of such magnitude demanded none other than the foremost orator of the time; a certain Patrick Pearse. A barrister and school teacher, Pearse delivered the inspirational graveside oration. His words stood to move the nation.

Benjamin Griffin burst into the coffee house. His fingers were wrapped around a copy of the *Irish Examiner*. Despite the intensity of his entrance, he still spoke in a whisper as he sat next to Grace. Exhausted in his excitement, he panted like a spent dog.

'Have you seen this?' Benjamin flashed the paper towards Grace before secreting it under his armpit. He was oblivious to the one that lay like a slain spread eagle on Grace's table. He continued without an answer.

'We've crossed the line Grace. There's no need to shy away from public scrutiny anymore. Now we can declare our desires, and to hell with the consequences. It's a clear call for us to stand together, as one, for the freedom of Ireland.'

Grace zoned out from Benjamin's enthusiasm. She had read the speech and was fully aware of the message within it. Pearse had hardly made it encrypted, instead choosing to make a clear, concise declaration. The article quoted him as speaking 'On behalf of a new generation that has been re-baptised in the Fenian Faith'. It emphasised how all the founding fathers of the movement all held one definition of freedom – a definition surmised by Pearse in his closing statement that *'Ireland unfree shall never be at peace'*.

Shaking herself back into the room, Grace caught the final few words of Benjamin's sentence.

'I said… an uprising is being planned. Obviously, I can't speak right now about it, but rest assured its happening. And I want you to be a part of it Grace.' Benjamin laid his hand on Grace's knee. She flinched at his touch.

'How can someone like me help? I've no idea what such a thing would even involve.'

'Numbers. Nothing more than numbers.' Benjamin smiled widely.

***

The next few months were a blur. Grace's days had been swallowed by countless secret meetings and speeches. Always remaining on the fringes, she watched from the sides as the tempered talk became written proposals, written proposals became physical acts; acts that were hell bent on nothing other than a single end product. Home 'Rule or Ruin' was the ethos, and every man, woman and child was committed to the cause.

The means, however, was still unclear to Grace. She wasn't entirely sure what Benjamin's intentions were with her, and she had not wanted to appear foolish in asking him. The secret garden brimmed with boxes and crates. Recently, the speeches had been replaced with shipments, and Grace did not know where to stand.

It was not until one cold December evening that Grace finally got to see what the crates contained. Creeping into the gardens, she was set to challenge Benjamin on what role she had to play. The wave of public euphoria was beginning to wane and Grace wanted answers. The usual crowd had gathered – clustered and busy in their unity. Groups of young men cheered as the crates cracked open. Grace stood at the edge of the lawn watching them. Bundles of hay were pulled out of the crates, lining the trodden ground as they were strewn in all directions. The men peered inside and looked at one another with delight. They looked invincible as they began to stand taller and widen their shoulders.

Grace walked towards them. The sweeping breeze brushed strands of hay onto her slippers. She scanned the crowd for Benjamin. He had been shy of late – rarely found reading in Brewley's and very reticent when he was. Grace was stood staring when she heard his voice.

'Anything caught your eye Mrs Farrington?' A small pocket of smoke poured over her shoulder. She turned to see Benjamin stood before her. He walked past and turned to face her. His body shielded the men that scurried busily behind him.

'How committed are you Grace?' Benjamin took a draw on his cigarette. The recent weeks had aged his tired face.

'What's going on Benjamin? I feel like the last few months have left me behind. I'm off the pace and have no idea what I'm a part of anymore.' The words seemed silly when she said them; Grace wondered if she had ever been a part of it.

'You're a number Grace… and so you're as important as the next. It's just our next step may be a little bit out of your stride. We all want the same thing, but there's more ways than one to skin a cat. I doubt you want to get your hands dirty, right?' He raised his fingers for another draw on his cigarette. The small burning amber that brightened as he pulled on the butt lit the leather glove that covered his hand.

'What would you have me do? I'll support as best I can.' Grace was angered by the arrogance of the man. He hardly knew her and yet he passed judgement like he was her father. She thought back on her times with her father, and could only remember one man who would dare defy him. If she had any at all, then such heroic thoughts of her husband doing the same sat as idle in her mind as his drunken body did in his study. Bored of the security that suffocated her; Grace's thoughts travelled to a hidden place where waters fell and lovers leaped.

'In a few months we'll be ready to make our move. Now Grace, I leave it up to you to decide what part you play. Britain is busy letting our brave fools rush to their deaths on stranger's fields. So we mustn't let them forget our fight, and we'll demand their focus. Even if we have to bore their ignorant eyes through the back of their thick skulls, then so be it. But we *will* have our day; where the green flags fly in Dublin and the golden harps sound out for *our* Ireland.' Benjamin walked over to an open crate. He leaned his long arm inside and pulled out a small object. The dark winter night cloaked it.

Walking over to Grace, he took hold of her hand and placed the cold metal object into her upturned palm.

'This is your fight as well. But how you fight it is up to you.' Benjamin glanced down at Grace's hand. The pistol fell from her frail fingers.

Chapter 37

Stood on the foreign sands of France, Michael bent down and picked up his rifle. Under the command of Major-General William Hickie, the 16th Irish Division was preparing to make its way to war. The crisp sea air clung to their chests, filling their lungs with a salty blast. Thousands of footsteps were already etched into the sand. Freshly formed dunes lined the edges of the beach, strengthened by the freshly pressed sand pushed up from the passing armoured trucks. Recovering his land legs, Michael marched on behind.

The training in England had been drawn out and intense. Michael's already hardened body ached from the months of toil and tutoring. He had slaughtered countless sandbags with his bayonet, not once seeing them as the enemy when his strong arm punctured their bellies and split them in two. The force he had hit them with had almost lifted them off the hooks on which they hung, and such power was only matched by the noise made by Theodore Brown. Known as Teddy to his friends, Theodore Brown was the brawny old boy that Oscar had admired in the medical suite. Having already served in the army as a young man, his mature years were appreciated and the age restrictions on the recruits ignored. The silver hair on his head shone almost as brightly as his white sands of the shores.

Emptying his guts onto the damp sands of the beach, Oscar dried his mouth on his dry sleeve. The cross over from England had been short but rough. The ship had shaken the soldiers like grains in an offbeat maraca. With the remains of his breakfast being pondered by the passing gulls, Oscar ran to catch up his friend. The sand beneath his feet was hard and flat, feeling more like concrete than the soft sands of his home town. Michael was only a few yards away. His shoulders bulged as he hauled the large satchel that held his kit. Despite being praised in training for his sharp shooting, it did not require Oscar's eagle-eye to spot that Josh's bag was half the size of Michael's. No doubt, Michael had helped the young boy out.

Defiant to the season, the sun shone brightly in the skies. The 16th Division was at its full strength. Almost a thousand men, separated into four platoons – each with their own four sections – lined the beach. A sea of olive green uniforms drowned the coast completely. Like a wicked seaweed that had washed over the shores, the troops tangled together and trawled towards the battlefields. Their target was the Somme. Stretching out from the fateful sight, miles of trenches threaded the French fields. In an effort to bind the efforts of the British troops, the 16th Division were recruited as reinforcements; to add their revered ferocity to the proceedings.

Even in training, the division had already built up a reputation for their gritted toothed approach to combat. For hours they marched that morning; each step inching them closer to the beastly battles that lay ahead. Michael was walking behind Josh when Oscar caught him up. Teddy was not far behind.

'Alright pal… so this is it. We're finally here.' Oscar's mouth still held slivers of spittle in the corners.

'I have a strange feeling we're not even halfway there yet b'hoy.' Teddy's voice rasped out from behind Oscar.

'Amen to that… I'm in no rush for what's ahead.' Michael pulled the straps of his satchel upon his shoulders. They dug into him deeply.

'Yeah, well I don't need to be close enough to smell them to shoot them.' Oscar patted his rifle. He saw how nervous Josh looked as he eyes flirted with every inch of the road ahead. If he had excelled in anything in training, then it was probably effort. His small frame lacked the strength to wield the bayonet and his hand shook whenever his rifle rested in it.

Hours passed by but the sound of the shells still fell far from their travelling feet. The heat of the day was swiftly replaced by the bitter bite of the winter night. The troops – tired and massed together – stayed warm on top of their marching legs. With all their kit hanging heavy on their backs, it was still a few fields further before they found their resting place.

The grand châteaux sat far behind the British lines. Once used as a large guest house for travellers, it now catered to tired soldiers who found themselves half way between the shores of the ocean and the front line. The rooms had been pulled of all their furnishings – opening up their bare floorboards to the many bodies that clutched at as much rest as they could force into the few hours before daybreak. Every inch of the châteaux was utilised. Makeshift stables had been made in the gardens to house the fine horses of the cavalry, while the infantry huddled around small fires that sat like fiery freckles on the marble floors of the hallway. The orange light licked at the soldier's faces, exposing them from the deep sleeves of the châteaux's shadows.

'What's he up to?' Sat by the smallest fire, Teddy nodded towards Michael.

'Just praying.' Oscar watched his friend sat on the windowsill at the bay window. The moonlight flashed off the crucifix that spun at the end of his bracelet. His thick hands were held together – propping up his lowered brow.

'So, is he the religious type then?' Teddy ran his knife through an apple. The thick wedge filled one side of his mouth, as he began to slice another.

'Roman Catholic; born and raised. We both are actually.' Oscar looked for a reaction. Teddy sat like ice through the flames.

'Well he can pray to his Lord as much as he likes. I have my saviour right here.' Teddy wiped the blade of his bayonet.

'I don't plan to use mine. My bullets will keep far from the filthy Hun's reach.' Oscar looked for his rifle. It rested on top of his packed satchel. He had removed a small saucepan from the side and was now warming some coffee. He dipped his hardtack biscuit inside to soften it. Once the coffee had begun to boil on the small fire, he offered the softened biscuit to Josh. The boy lay on the brink of sleep, kept awake only by the rumblings of his empty stomach.

'Here, Josh… eat up. That stomach of yours might give us away if you don't muffle it.' Oscar tossed Josh a wink as he passed him a cup of coffee. He broke the biscuit in half and handed it over. Josh took a bite. It dried his mouth out like a sand-based cracker. Oscar held the remains out towards Teddy.

'No thanks. You can keep those tooth-dullers to yourself. Mine won't be for eating – I cracked a molar on the first bleeder I ever bit. So from now on, I'll be keeping those little squares of sheet iron close to my chest. I doubt even a bullet could break through those bloody things.' Teddy tapped his palm on his chest. The shadows sagged under the raised veins in his hands; tired skin cradled his bones.

Sat away from his friends, Michael looked out over the land. The foreign fields lay in waiting, resting beneath the night's cold quilt. None of the prayers that he had whispered into his hands had been for him. Several were always reserved for his mother, but mostly he prayed for *her*. Despite the distraction that he had filled his days with, Grace was never far from his thoughts. The final prayer had asked for her protection above all. He felt it unfair to pray for his own protection – instead, he opted to allow fate to play its part on the battlefields.

'Asking for a miracle?' Oscar looked past Michael and through the huge bay window.

'Are you kidding? I think I've just witnessed one. Did I just see you give your food away?' Michael smiled.

'Fuck off.' Oscar mirrored the smile. 'Granted it was a courtesy offer to Teddy as he was staring at me, but Josh needs all the strength he can get. We're not even a day in and he looks as spent as the first ever penny.'

'True. We'll keep an eye on him you and me. But at a distance mind, we don't want to make him feel any less than the rest of us. He's a good kid – let's keep him on our side.' Michael turned and faced the hallway.

'Well his heart's in it… even if his legs aren't.' Oscar handed Michael a small cup of coffee. Silver steam spiralled in the shadows.

'Cheers.' Michael took a long sip.

'Mike, what do you make of Teddy?' Oscar spoke with the familiar tones of his gossiping mother. The nature of it encouraged scrutiny but did not commit to it. Oscar would see what flag Michael was waving before deciding on showing his own colours.

'He seems fine. A little old in the tooth with it all, but he's been here before. You can't expect to eat all the cake and not get fat. He's been in most battles so he's going to be a little beaten. Just take it with a pinch of salt.'

'On these rations? I'll be clean out of salt by sun up.' Oscar smiled widely. The truth was that the man scared him. To think that there may be a thousand Teddy's waiting for him on the other side was a case for living a lifetime without sleep. Looking at the man's tough snake like skin, Oscar doubted his bayonet was sharp enough to shed a single layer of it. If he was to say a single prayer tonight, it would be to thank the Lord for his ability with a rifle.

'Who are you writing to?' Oscar saw his friend rustling for his pen in his jacket pocket. The piece of paper was already laid out on the windowsill.

'It's more of a *for* than *to*.' Michael rubbed his jaw. His fingers told him he could do with a shave.

'For… to… whatever. Just make sure you get some rest for God's sake. I've got a feeling these days are going to get a whole lot longer.' Oscar picked up Michael's empty coffee cup and walked back to the fire. He did a final check on Josh before resting his head down on his satchel.

Alone in his wakeful state, Michael looked at his sleeping friend. Oscar hugged his rifle as if it were a teddy. Twiddling his pen within his thumb and forefinger, Michael pondered what it should write.

Chapter 38

His signature settled at the pit of another contract. Old age, and a trembling hand, had drawn the lines of his name out longer. Thin lines of ink stretched out at the bottom of the page. He ran his fingers through his dampened moustache. It held the scorching scent of his morning whiskey. The wiry bristles bent over the bridge of his pale blue lips like a soggy broom. Forever dressed in his finest attire, Raegan tried to persuade the day of his importance. He had not bothered himself with the distresses abroad, instead preferring to ponder the more immediate opportunities the situation provided. His business head was as healthy as ever. In spite of a number of his workforce upping arms and rushing to tend to bloodier fields, Raegan had been masterful in his delegation. Having already seen through the Boer War without incident – apart from losing part of his stock to that fruitless David Irwin – Raegan was confident of his means to increase production with fewer staff. Finding peace in his profit, he had begun to equip the British army with supplies at a higher price than what the local traders could dare offer. In turn, the produce his fields provided was making a killing.

Having married off all of his viable family, he no longer had a need to hold onto their inheritance and so he invested heavily into transporting his stock directly to the front line. Within a matter of weeks scores of trucks, vans and cargo ships delivered the Darby goods throughout the continent while the government lined his pockets at a sizeable profit. Now, soldiers all across Europe could enjoy the bounty of Raegan's generous land. Pausing to fill his own belly with another dram of his finest whiskey, he mulled over the day's proceedings.

Feeling the warm weight of the whiskey ride inside his gut, Raegan stood from his desk and walked out of his study. In spite of the war being in its infancy it had already given birth to such a sizeable opportunity that Raegan in turn had almost ignored the local trade entirely. Within eighteen months of the war's outbreak, he had forgotten to sustain the town that he once had fought so hard to be loved by. The crops from his fields now fled to foreign soils while the local townspeople stood by and starved. Though at his wealthiest, a time of subsistence surrounded Raegan.

Passing through the hallway, he saw a portrait of his pretty wife shift uneasily. Fiona was standing between the priceless paintings that pinned the walls, combing her hair as she faced the large mirror. She was tidying herself for the day that lay ahead. The shades of springtime had begun to tint the land, and a quilt of vibrant colour warmed the fields; gorgeous greens melted behind the blues and reds that burst from the bushes. Mounded in makeup, Fiona softened the shade of the black bruise that dwelled beneath her bright eyes. Although growing frail and flaccid, Raegan still had enough strength to beat his wife – if not the decency to decorate her in less pronounced areas. Of late, her face had often been seen to show her husband's proud signature. The thin bony knuckles of his hand always came sharp at the front of his cowardly fist.

Standing behind her, she could feel Raegan's fingers fondle at her waist. Fiona shook silently as the violent flinch shuddered at her core.

'Good morning, my love.' Raegan's brewed breath stained the air. 'I was wondering what your plans were today? It seems I'm free later, and so a spot of afternoon tea could be in order.'

'I'm afraid I shall be out with Imogen all day. I've promised her a walk into town to see the market.' Fiona continued to smear foundation onto her face. Rough flakes rose as she rubbed across the broken skin.

'Oh, bollocks to all that.' Raegan brought himself closer to his wife. His fingertips were like ice and his cold crotch pressed against her. 'The young girl wouldn't have a clue if you backed down on your promise. She's as retentive as a sieve.'

'How dare you? That girl is our flesh and blood, and if you see anything rotten in her, then I'd question the seed she sprung from.' Fiona spat the words out. Her fingers trembled slightly – furious within the cause and yet fearful of the consequences.

'Well maybe there's a fault with the oven the bun was kept in. She's half-baked at the best of times.' Raegan's fist planted itself into the small of his wife's back. Her knees buckled a little, but her feet stayed firm. She gripped the makeup brush in her hand – the base shimmered like a steel stiletto. She imagined punching it through her husband's sunken chest. She could almost smell the death drain from him as his cold blood bolted away from his poisonous heart. But in her own sweet heart, she knew that she could not do it. Regardless of Raegan's faults, he was the father of her daughters, and she could never remove him from them. She thought of this right up until the very moment he knocked her unconscious.

Upstairs Imogen was getting dressed. Having grown into the body of a young lady, her mind remained as young and optimistic as the break of day. Pretty in her sprightly manner, her ignorance of the world endeared those closest to her. Her hair was fair and long – a fine frame to the sharp contours of her bony cheeks. Her body fitted perfectly into her tight dress. Her shoulders were slight and thin, and – though fully formed – she still cut the look of a young girl on the cusp of adulthood.

Lingering on the landing, Connell admired the young girl's small breasts as he peered through a crack in the door. Often he had ignored the brainless child, suiting his master's opinion that she was of very little use to the family. However, the years had crept up on Connell and now he was met with a ripe young cherry that he could not wait to pluck. He widened his lecherous eyelids as the young girl continued to dress. Stood before a long mirror she raised her foot onto a stool and leaned down to buckle her slipper. The shadows veiled the girl's modesty but did little from keeping Connell's foul fingers from rummaging into his underpants. With his fat heart thumping at his chest, he could feel himself bulge inside his fist.

Imogen had been looking forward to her day out with her mother. It confused her as to why – despite all the fun times they shared – her mother always had an air of sadness about her. Blind to the bullying of her cruel father, Imogen naively put it down to the fact that her mother missed her other daughters. It had not gone unnoticed that Fiona spent far more time with young Imogen than she had ever done with Cara or Grace, with such names now rarely uttered at all within the walls of the estate. Finding her finest brush, Imogen began to run the thin teeth through her long hair. She failed to hear the hand that punched the wall outside.

It was Connell's plump palm that pushed at the wall. His toes had tightened and curled at the very point of climax. Throbbing intensely but spent of lust, he began to grow flaccid in his fist. Removing his hand from the squalid depths of his pants, Connell tightened his belt. He could feel the damp cotton cling to his crotch as he closed his belt buckle. He tossed the young girl a scornful scowl and made his way down the stairs. With each step, his toes stretched out within his shoes; the leather creaked as he ambled down the stairwell. Apart from a small makeup brush that rested on the floor under the grand mirror, the hallway was completely empty. He looked around for a maid so that he could make use of his authority and order her to bend down and pick it up. He paused to think of it. The mere thought of a maid's raised buttocks revived his loins a little. However, fate proved fruitless and there were none available. Feeling the bones in his joints grind and pop, Connell bent his knees and picked up the small brush himself. The cartilage cracked like firewood as he rose to stand, holding the brush which appeared like a fragile twig in his bulky hands. Seeing if there was anybody watching, he slid it into the long pocket of his waxed jacket. Maybe, if he could get her alone, he would give it to the girl as a gift.

'Morning sir, is Mr Darby at home?' Connell turned to see Arnold Farrington at the doorway. His elbow was locked as he leaned on his cane.

'Mr Farrington. What a pleasure it is to see you here.' His attempt at posh was as convincing as a wolf dressed as a lamb. 'Master's around somewhere. Come on in.' Connell offered his moist mitt for Arnold to shake.

'I'm afraid I'd fall if I took your hand,' said Arnold raising his right palm up. 'Not so steady on the feet as I used to be. Shall I wait for him in the lobby? Maybe you could bring us in a bottle of the devil's water as well.'

'Very well, sir. Make yourself at home. I'll see that Master knows you're here.' Connell watched Arnold limp and lean his way over to the chair. The man looked weaker than he had ever seen him – his tired limbs flushed of any hint of strength.

Having informed Raegan, Connell prepared the drinks. The two gentlemen were sat in the lobby discussing business matters, perched on the edge of their seats in anticipation for their selfish measures of whiskey. Connell's grey eyes grew green as he heard the hearty laughter that rang out from the room. Stopping for a moment, he rested the silver tray on a table in the hall and raised one goblet to his mouth. The crystal glistened as he ran his slimy tongue around the rim. Thick reams of saliva slid down the inside of the glass.

'Come now Connell, what *is* the wait?' Raegan could see the tails of Connell's coat in the doorway.

'Sorry sir. Coming right up.' Connell's throat was dry and croaky. He laid the tray on the small table that sat between his two parched patrons. Heavy with whiskey, he handed the goblets to each of them. Beneath his sharp smile, he ran his tongue over his jagged teeth.

'Cheers.' Arnold chinked his goblet with Raegan's and took a long gulp before resting his glass on the table. The remains of his whiskey ran slower than Raegan's as it seeped through the spit on the inside of his glass.

'So, what brings you here?' Raegan was pleased to have a drinking partner now that his wife slept upstairs.

'A change of scenery more than anything. My walls are growing awfully tired.' Arnold sank into his chair.

'But what of business? Surely that hasn't died down?'

'Not at all. In fact the family business has never been in such health.' Arnold was reluctant to call it *his* business now that he played no real part in it.

'Good. I wouldn't have any extension of my arm coming to any harm, so I'm glad to hear that business is booming. And if I may say, the Darby Empire is doing particularly well also. Those fools in government are so blinkered by this bloody war that they must have sacked their accountants. I mean, they're practically haemorrhaging cash with me, and I for one won't stem the flow. Keep it pouring I say.' Raegan raised his glass and drained it entirely.

'Here, here.' Arnold mirrored his host. 'On another matter entirely… while I am without her… I must say that I am somewhat concerned about your daughter.'

Until it was announced, Raegan had not even noticed Grace's absence.

***

Over at the guesthouse, the letters arrived few and far between. But still they came. The blade of his letter-opener tore through the thin envelope, sounding out a satisfying note as the sealed paper ripped apart. The letter was addressed as always:

Mr & Mrs Irwin (plus one for her).

David knew the handwriting by now. He had been receiving letters from the front line for a while, and was always delighted to hear from Michael. The post marks were always severely delayed, and sometimes the letters took weeks to reach their destinations, but some solace was savoured by David for he knew that Michael had survived up until that date at least. The letters themselves were always very matter of fact. With no trace of complaint or compliment, Michael would simply detail how he was. He never gave any specific details as to what he had been up to or where he was heading. Instead, he filled his letters with questions and concerns as to how David and Cara were – sending remarks of hope and good wishes. Despite the gesture, David knew the real reason as to why Michael sent his letters.

He took a drink of his morning tea before moving his cup to the side of the table. He brushed the toasted breadcrumbs off the table top, and opened the envelope. Tucked away in the corner, folded into a tiny square, was another piece of paper. David picked this out and placed it in a metal tin with the others. There were three so far, but David hoped there would be many more to come. The small tin was labelled *'For Her'*, and was placed on the sideboard in the kitchen. The first letter had ended with strict instructions as to what to do with these letters if Michael were never to make it home. And though there were no details on whether David or Cara could read them, David chose not to out of respect for his friend's privacy. However, he was pretty certain what they were. Forever happy to hear from his friend, David placed the tin back onto the side.

'Another letter?' Despite being fully dressed and having been up for four hours already, Cara yawned as if she was greeting the day for the first time. Her hand stretched for the tin. David pulled it away playfully.

'Those letters are addressed to the both of us, you know?' Cara shot a mocking scowl over to her husband.

'That they are, but it's not our letter that you're interested in is it?' David teasingly placed the tin on the top shelf and way out of his wife's reach.

'Spoil sport.' Cara sulked in her chair.

'Have you heard from Grace lately?' David began to boil the kettle.

'Not for a week or so. I've tried calling her house but she's never in, or so that's what I'm told. Last I heard she was planning a trip to Dublin. Not that I heard any mention of Arnold's name in all the preparations.'

'Dublin? What the devil would Grace be doing there?' David kept an ear out for the whistle of the kettle.

'I have no idea. But she's out an awful lot these days. Even when I speak with her, it's almost as if she has something to say but can't say it; as if she wants me to guess what she's up to.'

'Well it's strange times we're living in. Maybe we should go up and visit soon? You must miss each other. And don't you worry I'll endeavour the boredom of Arnold gladly if it means you catching up with your sister. Though that man is as colourful as a rose bush in winter.'

'But not quite as sharp,' said Cara with a smile.

'True. Maybe I'd better cram up on my business jargon just in case he even bothers to speak to me.' David could hear Cara's sweet laughter between the kettle's sharp whistle.

Together, they chose to sit and enjoy the sunshine that sprung through their open windows. Small choruses of birds could be heard on the softly distanced breeze. With one arm around his wife, David closed his eyes and pictured their first night together. His heart still raced at the sight of her naked frame – making him feel as terrified in his excitement as it had done in that initial intimate encounter. With a smile so wide it could swallow his ears, he could feel the sunlight on his face, warming his cheeks.

'So, what news does Michael bring?' Cara peered up from under her husband's arm.

'Nothing more than the fact he was still alive at the beginning of March. You know how guarded he must be.'

'Was the letter *plus one?*' Cara's playful smile crept over her face. David kissed her deeply to distract her. She saw the fire in his eyes as she pulled away from him. Feeling the sun's heat cover her body, Cara leaned and kissed her husband the way she always did. Her hands ran through his hair, clamping him to her. Her body had ached for her husband for some time and had longed for his tender touch. Forever together, it was the tedious trials of life that had kept them apart from one another. Inhibitions had been reinforced by self reservation; building obstacles between them – obstacles that were broken by this simple kiss. They shared the same single breath as David stood and lifted her from her chair. Cradled in his arms, Cara was carried to their bed where they made love for hours.

As the afternoon attached itself to the day, Cara crept out of bed. David lay content in his exhaustion, smiling as he snored softly. Slow and cautious in her movements, Cara wheeled her way into the kitchen as quietly as a mouse wearing slippers. And though her wheels creaked with every turn, none were loud enough to wake David. The playful smile returned to her face as she came to the kitchen sideboard. Having already piled several thick towels on the sideboard beneath the shelf, Cara reached for the kitchen broom. She held the head of it and poked the tin with the long thin end of the broom handle. The tin scraped along the shelf, dragged by the excited push of the broom. Tilting on the edge of the shelf, the tin eventually fell into the bed of towels with the softest of thuds.

Cara pulled open the lid and found the freshest note inside. Thick in its many folds, Cara picked at the corner and opened up the page. The paper was bare but for the few words that beat at the heart of it.

On the brink of battle I think of thee,
In all your light and security.
And with you in mind I feel protected
From the hurt of pain, as love's selected.
And though apart, with words untold,
I give my heart for you to hold.
For as I fight until the light creeps through,
I walk through death, and live for you.

Chapter 39

Monday had begun a little more relaxed than the usual begrudged start of the working week. The River Liffey lay calm and uncut by the standard ships that chugged along on their way to Cork. Closer to the horizon, the morning sun bounced off the copper dome of the Custom House, blinding the masses that crossed the Ha'Penny Bridge on their way to the seaside. In other areas of the city, eager punters rose early and headed to the Fairyhouse Racecourse for the Grand National; keen to gamble their entire wage packets on the hotly tipped horse *All Sorts*. With everyone set for the plans they had made, the Easter Bank Holiday had begun with all the promise of a bright and memorable day in Dublin.

Familiar to the sight of armed men marching through the town, the Dubliners were not startled by the one hundred and fifty men that strutted from Liberty Hall towards the General Post Office. Led by Patrick Pearse – and armed only with rifles and pick axes – these men casually stormed Dublin's General Post Office, claiming it as the seat of the provisional government, which they had now declared. With very little resistance, other than the helpless British Officer caught buying stamps at the counter, the men begun to fortify the building. The ground floor windows had been smashed, while heavy ledgers were piled high in anticipation of an imminent and aggressive counter attack. As symbolic as it was strategic, snipers took up their positions under the highest points of the building, perched beneath the two freshly hoisted flags. One was a tricolour of green, white and gold. The other was a great green flag adorned with bright white letters that were shadowed by a golden rim. Between the heavens and earth, the words *Irish Republic* swung in the balance of the breeze.

Grace watched as a crowd gathered around the base of Nelson's Pillar – their faces a mix of intent and amusement. Stood at the front of the column they all stared down at the ground. Leaning through the crowd, Grace saw the papered Proclamation. The bold black headline declared a republic had been established for the people of Ireland. The paper expressed the clear hopes and plans of the uprising, laying claim to the provisional government that was made up of seven members of the council – including that of Patrick Pearse and James Connolly. Grace's eyes drank in every last sentiment of the proclamation; her eyes beginning to well at the conflict that lay within the words themselves. Here were men who strived for social and economic change – who held a vision of a free Irish state that would oversee the welfare of all its citizens, cherishing all its children as equals in light of religious and civil liberty. They proclaimed that '*Ireland through us summons her children to her flag*'. These were men who prayed for peace so much that they were now willing to die for it.

Initially Grace had only come to Dublin to take part in the Easter marches. Mustering support from surrounding counties, the marches condemned the passage of the National Service Act which threatened national conscription being imposed in Ireland for the war. And so Grace's motivation was simple; she feared that her friends and loved ones, however far and distanced from her, would be dragged into a war that they neither supported nor cared for. With all the struggles at home, Grace wished that those she loved would remain and fight for what they truly desired. However, having found that the marches had been cancelled, Grace stayed in Dublin overnight.

Suggestive in his secrecy, Benjamin Griffin had informed Grace of the potential that the capital held that weekend, and so she decided to stay, if only to see what Monday held. Having attended many of the secret meetings back in Canndare, she was already well versed on the general movements of the day. Assisted by the Irish Citizen Army, the IRB had selected to command the main routes into the capital. By the time that the General Post Office had been seized, the volunteers would also have captured strongpoints at the Four Courts, the College of Surgeons and Stephen's Green. Looking to assist only by supplying the troops with food and water, Grace would soon make her way to the Mount St Bridge where Benjamin and his men lay in waiting. Having refused to take up arms herself, Grace was assured by Benjamin that the profit of the protests would be peace and not bloodshed.

Stepping back from the crowd, Grace heard the rapping of hooves upon the street. With unfazed expressions, the faces of the small cavalry sat astride their cantering horses. Their uniforms blazed in the bright spring sunshine as they headed up the street towards the General Post Office. Without a sense of urgency in their hooves, the horses casually carried the soldiers to their execution. Grace could not tell whether the cavalry were countering the uprising or obliviously patrolling, but the outcome was as bold as the hot blood that soon paved the cold streets. The racket of the rifles rang out from the windows of the Post Office, cutting the soldiers from their mounted seats. Startled, the horses sprinted away from the soldiers who lay dying on the dusty stone paths of Dublin's town centre.

Fired by the thunderous gunshots, Grace ran. Her heart raced forward, leaving her legs and breath far behind her. Cries from the crowd banged off the walls, as the people burst out in all directions. The gunfire had ceased, but it was now replaced by the rumbling of panicked feet upon the stretched streets. Unguarded by cloud, the sun threw down a smoke screen of sheer light that left Grace unsighted as she ran blindly towards it. Slamming herself against the shaded wall of an unknown alleyway, Grace caught her breath. Her lungs heaved and the balls of her feet throbbed. She could feel the blood burn in her veins as her heart pounded at her taut chest.

The streets were quiet and still. The air felt thin and tired, as if forced from the last silent scream of the slain soldiers. Refusing to look behind her, Grace straightened her back and marched away. A small basket of supplies hanged in her tightened hands. She knew that Mount St Bridge was not far, but she prayed it would be a lot safer.

The following day was one of uncertainty. Rumours had begun to fuel the fires on both sides of the conflict. Warm whispers of a German invasion were countered by talk of a grand assault by the British Army. With General Lowe at the helm, nearly five thousand soldiers were readied from Carragh as a further thousand polished their rifles in Belfast. Both sets of soldiers were soon mobilised and by the afternoon the rebels were already outnumbered in Dublin by four to one. And to the ill fate of the volunteers, the odds had no intention of closing.

Along the streets of the city centre, shards of glass lay bedded on the ground among upturned bins and tossed bricks. With the declaration of martial law at 11:30am that morning, the looters had snatched their fill from almost every store before it was time for tea. Shop windows were smashed and the stores gutted like the carcass of a crippled fish; their unwanted remains sprawled across the sodden streets. In a bid to stem the spree, Patrick Pearse published a small paper entitled *Irish War News* that called for an end to the looting. However, its importance lacked impact as the only other paper to filter through the city's blockades was the heavily Pro Unionist *Irish Times*. This valued the importance of the uprising to a mere three lines. If the uprising was being taken seriously, nobody was letting on.

As the sun began to descend, doors on every house and home slammed shut. Parents dragged their children indoors, and workmen raced home before it turned dark. Having taken a stand to tackle the volunteers, General Lowe had made it clear that any movement outside the hours of daylight would be deemed part of the uprising and in turn was punishable. Defiant to the threat and shrouded by the night, the volunteers at Stephen's Green sat blindly to the hundred soldiers that held them in the sights of their rifles from the high windows of the Shelbourne Hotel; the morning was to be blessed with blood.

Far from the gunfire, Grace prepared a morning coffee. The kitchen of the Old Clanwilliam House was just beneath the bedroom where Benjamin had sat guard. Having held his heavy eyelids open for the entire night, Benjamin had requested that his coffee be as black as a panther and twice as strong. Grace passed the dented tin lid of the flask to Benjamin. Her thumb caressed the groove on the side of the hot tin. Benjamin was on edge through his exhaustion. Polite in tongue, his eyes told a different tale. The whites of them were a stained yellow that surrounded small pin sized pupils. Purple bags bunkered his eyeballs and pressed his face down onto his gaunt chin bones. He had not shaved in days, and stubs of rough dark hair pricked his cheeks and jaw.

'Thank you Grace,' said Benjamin. He supped on the drink like a thirsty tramp. His raised arm had been wrapped with a tri coloured cloth. Stripes of green, white and gold circled his tightened bicep. The house was filled with volunteers. The thin barrels of rifles slid through the cracks of windowsills that overlooked the roadside. More armed men lay in waiting within the gorgeous Georgian houses that lay either side of the road that passed over the bridge. A couple scoped the road from the front windows of a house on Northumberland Road, while a further four could be found in both Roberts Yard and the Parochial Hall a few doors down. Their positions were engineered from intent, as the road that they all overlooked led into the centre of Dublin, and was likely to be used by any attacking infantry.

'I thought you said there would be no fighting?' Grace whispered as other volunteers were both in ear shot and an arm's reach. Tired muffled mumblings marred the tense air.

'I said we were here to promote peace, not practice it.' Benjamin leaned his head back onto the wall. The cold slab offered comfort to the creak in his neck. He took a shallow breath; his lungs pushed slightly at his heavy dark jacket.

'But how can we expect to get anything by attacking those that we need to help us? Is it not these men that guide the government?'

'Because bullies only respond to a show of strength. Not many of us expect to return from this Grace. We all know what could possibly lie on the other side of all this, but we don't simply do it for the sake of hurting those that have hurt us. We do it so that our friends and families are no longer pained by it all.' He received a nod of agreement from a nearby volunteer. 'If my sacrifice saves a single person from those bastards abroad, then it'll be worth every agonising moment of it.' He took another drink of his coffee. Colour began to return to his tired eyes.

'And what of those you kill in the meantime? They only fight because you've forced their hand.' Grace's tone bordered on a shout. In a flash, Benjamin's palm was pressed against her mouth; the forefinger of his other hand pointed upwards across his pursed lips.

'They chose their sides.' His voice was little more than a whisper. He looked about him. 'And yeah, you're right. We are forcing their hand. And I for one am willing to break every finger on it until it points towards what we are after.' He took a quick look out from his window. 'If I'm forced to crush what stands before me and my dream, then let hell hold a spot for me because I'm willing to do whatever it takes.' Fire flashed in his eyes. Looking over Grace's shoulder, something snatched his focus. He pushed her to the floor and took up his rifle.

***

There was a sense of confusion among the regiment. Green but keen, the Sherwood Foresters had arrived in Ireland that morning. A band of young volunteers recruited from the towns and villages of Nottinghamshire, they had heard Kitchener's call and dreamed of fighting for their nation in the tough trenches of Belgium and France. However, their loyal services were requested for a dispute a little closer to home. Stood by the still shores of Kingstown, they held their new rifles in their raw hands. The three months military training they had all received had yet to toughen the skin of their tender palms.

Overwhelmed by occasion, Timothy Tate was on the brink of embarrassment. Having joined the army to make a man out of himself, the young boy felt like it was his first day at school all over again. The officers tugged at his uniform, straightening his jacket and palming his fringe flat to his forehead. He could feel the curious and concerned eyes of the crowd claw into him as the officers insisted the young man point his rifle towards the sea when he was first loading it. The truth was none of the Sherwood Foresters had trained with live ammunition before. Having been handed live rounds for the first time only moments ago, they were as much a danger to themselves as they were the rebels they had been sent to tackle.

Leaning up the wall of St George's Harbourside Yacht Club, Timothy pulled open a small tin of bully beef. His legs were tired from the travel and so he craved the strength the stale salted meat could offer. A tight thirst also gripped his tongue, but he had very little other than dry biscuits to whet his appetite. The march ahead was long and he would need to ration the fresh water that filled his heavy canister. He treated his tongue to a splash before sealing the screw-top tightly. Leaning back against the wall, he could hear the plum throated roars of the officers inside the club. All from a public school background, they shared a hearty and full breakfast before they plotted their men's course. Meanwhile, in the scorching sun and dusted streets of Kingstown, the infantry sat starved of orders.

The huge guns of the warship Helga had already flattened Liberty Hall. Edged on by days of public expectation, the military had begun to step up their attacks. Corners of the city had been plundered and ransacked while bullets pattered the windows where rebel rifles were potted. Allowing the particular to reflect the general, the press had focused on Kelly's Fishing Tackle Shop, on the corner of O'Connell Street. The small, indifferent shop was hammered by heavy artillery. Huge shells were hurled into the windows as clouds of throaty red dust fell from the thumped walls.

Streets away, Timothy knelt as he tied the laces on his boots. He was a stranger to many of his regiment, having been too shy to make an impression during the few months of training. Standing to his small feet, he clutched at his Lee-Enfield Rifle. With little else to do than prepare, he had already cautiously attached his sparkling bayonet to the barrel of his rifle. With the weapon leaning against his slim shoulder, he struggled to stand at ease under its sharp shining blade. Surrounded by the rest of his regiment, Timothy tried his hardest to cut an unassuming shadow.

'France isn't how I expected it.' One member of the infantry squinted around – looking too scared to touch a thing for fear that the town would shatter under his shaking fingers. Blinkered by it all he had failed to see either the posters or store signs written in clear English, nor hear the soft Irish accent sweeten the words of his mother tongue upon the locals. Disillusioned and unapprised, many of the men had no idea where they were. Like the hand grenades that were absent from their arsenal, the men were ill-equipped with any tangible intelligence from their supervisors. Having signed up to hunt the Hun and batter the Bosch, most of the Sherwood Foresters had not foreseen a fight in Ireland, for they had dreamed of glorious battles abroad where the enemy's blood was shed in the name of their nation. To think that they may have to spill their own on neighbouring soil had never been part of the plan. Nevertheless, they would be patriotic to their end.

Hearing the guns of Helga sound out, Timothy was beginning to miss the one friend he had made during his time in the regiment. Louie was the nickname for one of the Lewis Machine Guns that he had been fortunate enough to see in action. Having sat and watched a demonstration on the weapon, Timothy had dreamed of having hands strong enough to hold it. A fearsome, drum fed weapon capable of firing large calibre bullets at a rate of ten rounds per second, Timothy knew that this would be his best friend in any battle. Together with Louie, he had imagined himself playing the part of the hero as he tackled the overwhelming enemy head on, as he remained the last man standing. The imagined rapturous applause of the hero's welcome already rang in his tiny ears.

However, Louie would play no part in Timothy's war. An overzealous loading officer – drunk on a deluded measure of self importance – insisted that the Sherwood Foresters leave their Lewis Machine Guns at Liverpool. And so without Louie, Timothy could not help but feel light handed.

Bright and full of cheer, the spring sunlight was almost as welcoming as the people themselves. Not knowing what to expect, it still surprised the small regiment to see people line the streets and welcome them with open arms. Having received the order to march from Kingstown to the centre of Dublin, the troops made their way forward. The wide streets were lined with trees, offering soothing shade from the enthusiastic sun. Seeing the smiles stretched out upon the faces of the locals, Timothy begun to feel at ease. Drifting deeper into the most affluent of suburbs, a rich sense of security blanketed the young boys.

'I say, this is nice.'

'I could get use to this battle.'

'War zone? You should see where I grew up.'

Guarded by gawping men, Timothy marched on. The atmosphere was intoxicating. Surrounded by people who greeted the soldiers like heroes, the young men were loaded with invitations to dinner whilst tea and cakes were thrust upon them. Not wanting to offend, Timothy accepted a small sandwich from an old dear – winking as he pocketed the treat for later. Others had even accepted generous offerings of field goggles and maps. Accepted by their important visitors, cheers rang out from between the leafy trees – the crowd incessant in their welcoming.

Timothy had not known a place quite like it. Usually reserved in nature, he found himself smiling and waving to the pretty girls that had gathered. In an instant the weight of his adolescence had been lifted – his chest felt bigger and his hands stronger. Feeling triumphant, he had never been prouder to wear his uniform. Organised amid the cheery chaos, the men marched onwards.

Towards the end of the road, the soft shade began to break. Light broke through the last leaves of the tall trees and brightened the dusty road ahead. Battalion scouts rode forward on their bicycles; the screeching of their wheels whistled as they went. Stood near to the front of the regiment, Timothy could see the scouts go about their business. With the roads baron of any public, they resorted to peering through the windows that they passed by. Flashing past the expensive buildings of the suburb, they returned with less than a bounty of information. The only food for thought was the scrap of insight that the centre of Dublin lay across the Mount St Bridge.

A host of stunning buildings sat on the other side of the canal. Near the edge of the bridge was a gorgeous three storey Georgian town house; its long gracious windows had a commanding view of the bridge and the Northumberland Road. Terraced houses faced this town house, which was also guarded by a yard and a grand hall. Satisfied with their route, the officers at the front of the regiment approached the canal bridge with more cause than caution.

As they grew closer to the quiet waters of the canal, a stream of gunfire spat out from one of the buildings. Blasts of blood burst from the officer's bodies as at least 10 of them fell to the ground. Timothy ducked behind a small brick wall only 300 yards away from the canal. Fierce gunshots punched through the windows and tore at the chests of the soldiers. The automatic machine guns held by the enemy proved too quick for the Sherwood Foresters – the bullets tearing them apart before they could even take aim. Timothy could hear the whistles of the officers blowing in front of him. The shrilling sound was a clear order for the men to press forward. Having only been trained to attack the enemy head on, Timothy stood and readied himself.

The rows of boys before him fell like crushed autumn leaves. Their bleeding bodies stacked heavily upon one another. Timothy could see two rebels firing towards him from number 'Twenty Five'. Their weapons were quicker and more lethal than the single-shot rifles that the regiment gripped. Dropping to his knees, Timothy looked for the nearest officer. A man in his mid-twenties was running back from the bloodshed. His uniform was clotted by deep crimson stains. The whistle in his mouth screamed beneath his soiled moustache.

'Sir,' cried Timothy. 'The men are in number twenty-five. They have us pinned down. Shouldn't we try and go around them?' The officer did not have time to register his request. Instead he spun his head from side to side, trying to address as many men as he could.

'Press on men… at all costs… press on.' The officer turned and drew his long sword. The sun twinkled at the tip of the blade as it was held high. Followed by a roar of infantry, the officer ran across the bridge and towards the house Timothy had mentioned. His legs bent as shots met with his thighs, but still he pressed on. Finally reaching the front of the building the officer turned and beckoned his men forward. Returning to face the building, the officer sunk to his knees when one of the rebels stepped from the doorway and shot him point blank in his face. His sword clattered onto the cold ground.

Behind the fallen officer, the boys were left to the slaughter. Bullets rained out from either side of the street, cutting them in two. Timothy raised his rifle and took aim. His bullet split the wood on a windowsill, but the single shot was not enough to drop the heads of the rebels. Soon enough, bullets poured out once more. With few men in front of him, it was Timothy's turn to make a stand.

Holding his rifle as tightly as he could, and flanked by men either side, he charged forward. Among the cries and gunshots, he could hear a deep splash as one of the men's bulleted bodies crashed into the canal – the momentum of his charging legs carrying him a few yards further from where his head had been hit.

Faster than the troops beside him, Timothy came to the end of the bridge first. Stones kicked up around him as bullets bit at the walls. Windows from both sides of the street were firing at him. Caught in a cacophony of crossfire, Timothy held his breath and ran. His sight was tunnelled. Adrenaline beat at his brain. Cutting through his fallen friends, he found himself further down the road than any other. He paused to gather where his enemies lay, losing his breath entirely as a dead weight landed upon him.

Stood completely still, Timothy could feel the warm blood seep from his neck. The bullet had come from the Georgian building above him, and had torn through his neck and down into his lungs. Blood bubbled from where the bullet had left his body – cracking a rib as it turned his lung into a sunken sack. The blade of his bayonet scraped the slabs in front of him, jamming between two tiles of the road. His soft lips opened and his knuckles grew pale. Circles of black closed around his sight as the final bullet broke through his skull.

***

'Got him.' Benjamin cheered as he watched the young soldier fall. His last bullet had hit the boy directly in the head. 'His lights were out before his body even hit the ground.'

Benjamin cocked his rifle and took aim. His shoulder jolted back as he fired on the soldiers once more. A grim grin began to sit on his tight lips; a lust for life flashed in his dark eyes. He wiped his mouth on the small flag that was wrapped around his arm, never for a moment taking his eyes from the road. The sound of gunfire rattled through the air as the pretty streets of the splendid suburb were seduced by an orgy of violence. Speechless within all the mayhem, Grace sat in shock.

Camped up in the front bedroom of the Clanwilliam House, a handful of volunteers held back an army. Hundreds of British soldiers fell as the hours raced by. Absent of any element of surprise or ambush, the screams of a whistle sounded every twenty minutes, bringing with it a fresh wave of men to wound. British bodies crashed to the ground whilst the volunteers held their positions. Benjamin had lost count of the number of kills he had collected, averaging at least two bullets to every boy that approached. At least thirty empty shells surrounded his feet.

Grace ached inside. The bloodshed was too much for her to bare witness to, and far away from the means that she desired. Her tears tried to wash the images from her eyes; to cleanse the memories that would soon haunt her. She flinched at the sound of every gunshot – her back arching with every thunderous retort from the republic.

'Shit...' said Benjamin as he stood for the first time in hours. He moved down the room to the next window and took up his position. Grace glanced out of the window from where so many soldiers had been slain. Across the bridge she could see a garrison gather with heavier guns. The Dublin Military Garrison had brought with them crates full of grenades and Lewis Machine Guns, and it would not be long before their bullets pounded at the houses.

First came the grenades. With pins plucked, dozens were tossed into each window, timed to explode within seconds. Shards of shrapnel splintered the rooms, spiking the floral wallpaper like metallic thorns. Small fires spread within the buildings; the tiles on the roofs cracking before they collapsed in on themselves.

Then the machine guns whirred into action, slicing through the buildings like a hot razor through flesh. Streams of bloodthirsty troops poured in after the heavy tirade of bullets. Watching on, Grace knew it would not be long before they would turn their attention to the Clanwilliam house. She began to fill her basket with supplies. Hundreds of innocent people had already suffered within the crossfire and Grace was not ready to add herself to that tally. Turning, she screamed at Benjamin.

'Come on Benjamin. We need to leave. You don't have enough bullets for all of them… come on.' Benjamin's head did not turn. Crouched by the window, he continued to take pot shots at the troops that crossed the bridge. Seeing the small flash from the rifle, the machine guns turned towards the Georgian building. Chunks of brickwork began to break from the beaten walls. The rooms shook and the stairways lit up under the first grenade. One volunteer took the full force and proceeded to decorate the walls with his ruptured remains.

'Benjamin, if we stay here we're as good as dead.' Grace took the slightest step towards him. Small droplets of blood dripped from his shoulder. He had been hit, but not halted. He offered her the briefest of glances, but not a word. His fingers returned to the rifle's trigger.

Grace ran from the room. Fires had begun to consume the corridors. Smoke bellowed from the street beneath. Passing by the other bedroom, she could not see any other volunteers left within the house. It seemed Benjamin would be the last. The dull thudding of single shots still punched out from his room, each time answered by a gale of gunfire and grenades.

The back door led onto a garden that was guarded by a small gate. Sprinting through, Grace slammed the gate firmly behind her and hid behind the fence. A flood of footsteps rumbled through the garden. British accents barked orders between the gunshots. Looking back, she saw how smoke continued to seep through the windows of the Clanwilliam house as dozens of soldiers poured in. Running from the house, Grace heard a familiar voice scream out before three single shots silenced it. A ghostly stillness shrouded the burning building. Soon, soldiers begun to stream out of the doors and move on up the road. Thick soot charred the rubble remains of the rooms, as Grace ran deeper into the heart of the city.

Chapter 40

Oscar's feet stunk. The sticky climate congealed with the damp clay of the trenches; the sun tanning the soldier's faces as their feet stood planted inside muddy puddles. The walls within the trenches were dry and cracked. Lines of railway sleepers held back the earth like gaping ribs. Small, thin duck boards were placed on the ground to offer some form of flooring. It didn't work. The travelling feet of the troops would tread the boards into the deep, dug soil, forcing any moisture out of the ground like a flattened sponge. Sat away from the thin mucky puddles, Oscar had taken off his shoe.

'It's not trench foot you big girl.' Michael held his nose, turning his head as he inhaled. The stale stench of his friend's foot stung his tongue as he breathed.

'But look at it... it's wrecked.' Oscar held his ankle with both hands and pointed his foot closer to Michael's face. Young Josh emptied his stomach lining in the corner.

'Does it hurt?' Michael tucked his mouth and nose into his sleeve.

'It stings a little.'

'It stings my eyes more like. Your foot is fine, but I can't say as much for your socks. I've got a fresh pair you can have. Hopefully that should hold back the stink for a while.'

'But how do you know it's alright? You're not a doctor.' Oscar looked up at his friend. Holding his breath Michael took hold of Oscar's exposed foot.

'Does that hurt at all?' He shook the foot.

'No... not really.'

'Then it is fine you bloody baby. Just keep it clean.' Seeing Oscar was off balance, Michael pushed his foot downwards. It made a dull splat as it rooted itself deep within a brown puddle.

'You bastard.' Oscar's anger did not last for long and he was soon laughing along with his friends.

Keeping a strong spirit was crucial during these times. The war had demanded everything from the men. The days dragged by with little punctuation, bleeding tirelessly into the next. Nothing but the light stopped at night. Listening posts were guarded on the front line, angling an ear over the small field of 'no man's land'. Officer patrols were carried out half an hour before dawn – calling the entire front line to 'Stand to' throughout the trenches in wait for a morning raid. Only at the break of dawn would the order 'Stand down' be sounded out. During the night, for eight straight hours in the pitch black, Michael had held an ear to the land that lay between the French towns of Loos and Hulluch. Farms and football fields surrounded the British and German trenches that ran like viscous violent veins within the land. Half a mile either side of them, civilisation went about its daily business. However, the battle fields that lay between were governed by slightly greyer rules of engagement.

With sleep threatening to shut his eyes, Michael began to scribble on a scrap of paper. The conditions in the camp had started to deteriorate quickly, and simple luxuries were as common as manure from a rocking horse. However, one of the officers had been kind enough to spare Michael some paper, and had promised to have any letters he wrote dispatched along with his own. This pleasure, however, had a price and Michael now found himself standing guard more often than the rest of his regiment. Sitting for the first time in what felt like days, Michael let his mind drift through his razor-wired surroundings. Closing his eyes and clasping his small cross, he thought of her.

Down by the small cabin that they called a toilet, Oscar was tending to his foot. Thankfully, his nostrils were now numb to the stale stench that surrounded what the men had nicely entitled the 'shit pit', and so he scraped the sopping sludge from his soiled foot before the sun had had chance to dry it. He opened his water canister and began to pour the mildly warmed contents over his foot.

'Hey, that's damn wasteful that lad. Surely you can find a better way of washing those rotten toes of yours?' Teddy snatched the canister from Oscar's hands and took a hearty sup from it.

'Piss off. What do you expect me to do? Wave it over the trench and hope the Hun hose it down with one of their machine guns? Now give that back you old git.' Oscar grabbed the canister back from Teddy. He wiped the rim with his soiled sleeve and continued to pour the water onto his foot.

'Bloody hell. What chance do we have of winning with idiots like you? That'll only get filthy again the second you step down onto the floor.' Teddy spat onto the ground. He had been digging all morning and dirt had dug into the pores of his skin. The thick hairs on his chest were kinked with mud.

'What the hell are you talking about? I'm washing my foot not my boot.'

'Exactly... what's the point of washing your dick if you only plan to stick it into a filthy whore? Make sure your socks are fine and your feet won't be a problem. Like my old pa' used to say – look after your bed and your socks, because if you're not in one you'll be in the other.'

'And what about the whore? Is she in this bed of yours?'

'You stay out of them young man. Women are nothing but trouble. Even the purest have a poison that'll crush your cock.' Teddy wiped his dry mouth with his dirty forearm.

'I'll bear it in mind. Good talk Teddy. Thanks,' said Oscar sarcastically with a fake smirk. He walked off down the trench. He prayed that Teddy and his pep talks were not following him.

At the end of the front-line was the listening point. Having had the night to himself, it was Josh's turn to take up post. The lookout was a small square that had been cut out from the boards that stretched a few feet above the tip of the trench. A brown cloth hung like a curtain on the inside of the cut frame. This was never opened during daylight as the scopes of enemy snipers were set upon it. Occasionally, shots would fire through, flicking the curtain as if kissed by a cutting breeze. Just to the side of the post, a small flag sagged. This monitored the direction of the wind – something the sentries were ordered to keep a keen eye on.

Josh took a drink from his canister. Having arrived in petrol cans, and then disinfected by lime chloride, the liquid tasted rank. A small portion of sick greeted the water in his throat as

Josh tried to stop his sensitive gag reflex. Leaning against the wall he could see the small corridors that lined the trenches. The walls zigzagged throughout, never letting themselves be straight for too long – the idea being that a single bullet could pass through a straight line more deadly than it could a wall. Fingering the old periscope, Josh took a look across no man's land; beyond the parapet of sandbags, and through the bed of barbed wire, rested a battered and broken field. The daily shelling from both sides had sown the seeds for this iron harvest. Rows of bombs and explosives had fallen short of their target and now lay buried within fresh smoking craters. Like raw measles scratched on the face of Mother Nature itself, deep pits and ditches scarred the land. Counting down the minutes, Josh was certain that the show was about to begin.

***

Discipline was tough in the trenches. Rumours ran between the men quicker than the army of rats that slalomed through their feet, and now talk of troops being shot for falling asleep at their post was the latest panic to push its way through the front-line. Although nobody had seen it firsthand, everybody seemed to know a friend of a friend who had suffered the fate of a British bullet simply because they had failed to fulfil their duty. Michael sniggered as Oscar continued to tell his tale.

'I'm serious. A close friend of mine told me that some guy in his regiment was shot, because – after being sentry for the entire night – he dozed off during 'Stand to'. Apparently he had 'endangered the entire army'... can you believe that?'

'No... I can't,' laughed Michael as he patted Oscar on the back. They were taking a well-earned break from repairing the trenches and had begun playing cards at their dugout.

'Shut up Mike. What do you know anyway?' Oscar put his next card down.

'Granted, not a lot. But I do know that you don't know anyone other than these guys around you, and none of them are backing your story up.' He smiled as he placed a card on top of Oscar's.

'Well that's where you're wrong mucker. They don't call that the communication trench for nothing, you know.' Oscar nodded to the long trench that linked the front line to the fire bay and support trenches.

'What are you talking about? We all know that there's a bloody one way system on that corridor. Supplies and mail come up the line, as injured soldiers go the other way. And – unless you've been wounded recently – I can't remember any mail coming your way either.' Michael's tone was all in jest, but he could see a scowl crossing his friend's brow.

'I get as much mail as you pal.'

'Well, I've got nobody back home. So who's going to write to me?'

'Exactly. But don't think I don't know about these letters you've been passing to the officers. After all, they don't call me Eagle Eye Oscar for nothing.' Feeling triumphant, he took a small victory sip from his canister.

'No, they call you that because you paid them. Probably with that pert ass of yours. And anyway, if you must know I don't write to get a reply.' Michael felt the hard clay of the dugout begin to numb his own behind.

'So why do you do it then?' Oscar feigned interest in his hand. He swapped two cards around for no reason at all.

'Like I always say; for her. I only write for her.' Michael became tired at the thought of Grace.

'For her? Are you out of your mind? You spend your days in this shit tip, with shells firing inches from your thick skull, and you worry yourself with the thoughts of some girl who left you high and dry back home? She is a grain of sand Michael, a tiny grain of sand.' Oscar slammed his card down.

'A grain of sand? She sounds more like a *beach* if you ask me.' Teddy laughed at his own joke. His rough accent lent itself well to the delivery.

'I wouldn't bother cleaning that gun of yours if you're looking to make more comments like that Teddy. They'll be fishing pieces of it from your colon for a week if you think you can lay into my friend here.' Despite Oscar's anger at Michael, he was not opening a firing range for everyone else. He stretched his middle finger to the skies and fired it towards Teddy.

'Keep that dirty digit away from me you chubby git. Who knows how many dirty pies you've fingered with it?' Teddy continued to clean pieces of the Vickers machine gun that rested in his lap. The oily rag he was using was almost as filthy as his hands.

'Hey now, ease up,' said Michael playing the peacemaker. 'This place is hard enough as it is without a pair of tits swinging for each other.'

'Well he's the only one with tits around here.' Teddy nodded towards Oscar.

'That's it.' Oscar sprung to his feet and made a move towards Teddy. Michael was on him in a flash, holding him back far enough for his flailing arms to fall short of their mark.

'That's right… get your boyfriend to look after you, you tubby little girl.' Teddy felt brave behind Michael's blockade. Hearing the words, Michael sat Oscar down and turned to face Teddy.

'Now listen hear. I've done you a favour today. So don't go pissing me off as well, because I can't see anyone close enough to hold me back.'

'Jesus Mike, I was just joking.' Teddy held up his hands. It was the first time Oscar had seen fear in the old man's eyes.

'Oscar,' Michael turned to his fallen friend. 'If any of that nonsense is true about falling asleep at the post, maybe we should go and look after Josh? I'm on sentry tonight anyway and I could do with some company if you want to play sniper?'

'Josh?' Oscar took a moment to remember the lad. 'Oh… Yeah, of course. Poor sod must me bored to death. Though I suppose that'd be fate better than dysentery, and there's been an awful lot of shit flying about here recently.' Oscar flashed a look at Teddy but he was busy cleaning. Michael ignored the insult.

'Well let's take him up some tucker. He'll need the strength.' Michael grabbed his satchel and filled it with a few tins.

Josh was beginning to wane when he saw Michael pop his head around the corner. He was too tall for that part of the shallow trench and walked with his back bent forwards. A small satchel swung from his hands – the straps skimming the puddles that had swallowed and dragged the duck board beneath them. Oscar followed closely behind, crouching a lot more than was necessary.

'Ay up Son.' Michael whispered and took a seat on top of the firing step. It was a small ledge that the soldiers had dug out from the earth. At night snipers would stand there and guard the sentries.

'Budge up.' Oscar nudged Michael. A heavy Vickers machine gun sat centre stage on the step, taking up most of the room. Like Michael, Oscar had his satchel with him.

'Aren't I glad to see you two? There's no life in those fields out there,' said Josh with a wry tired grin. The periscope hung heavily in his hands. Michael began to speak.

'Well, keep looking lad. Those boys out there don't keep to a timetable like us. I mean, I'm *sure* they'll be shaken and surprise by our daily artillery attacks from two 'til four tomorrow.'

'And the day after that,' scoffed Oscar as he rummaged through his bag. 'Anyways, we brought you up some grub.' He pulled out a tin of stewed meat and vegetables and tossed it to Josh who caught it against his chest with his free hand. Michael took the periscope and passed it to Oscar.

'Here, take hold of that while the young lad gets himself fed.' Michael pulled out a thick wedge of bread from his bag and passed it to Josh. He took a large bite of the loaf before opening the tinned food.

'Thanks guys,' spat Josh with a thick lump in the side of his mouth. He looked like a starving squirrel storing his food for the winter. Michael raised his nose a little. Oscar was peering through the periscope.

'Josh, is that food alright?' He sniffed around. 'I'm getting an awful whiff of something. Oscar, you didn't give him rotten stock did you?' Michael had a glance at the stewed meat.

'Are you joking? Some of that stuff will out-live all of us.' Oscar continued looking through the periscope.

'Well what the hell is that smell then?' Michael looked around him, but the dry walls offered no answers. Looking up he saw the small curtain on the looking post sway. The flag beside it began to flicker towards the back of the trench. It was then that Michael knew what the smell was. The wind that blew towards them had carried the stench of the rotten corpses with it from no man's land. The warm smell of putrefied flesh filled the air and clung to the soldier's lungs. Josh gulped down as much food as he could before his gag reflex kicked in. Oscar stood rooted to the spot.

'Oh shit,' screamed Oscar as he jumped for his satchel.

Seeing Oscar root through his bag, Michael knew what was happening. He tossed Josh his own satchel from the floor and turned to empty the one he had brought with him.

'Smoke attack!' Oscar pulled on his gas mask. The phenate-hexamine goggle helmets had been dipped in glycerine and held the stale scent of a hospital. Oscar gritted his teeth against the small exhaust valve that fed from the mask into his mouth. He saw that Michael and Josh were pulling their masks on also. The wind could be a useful ally or fearsome foe depending on which way it blew. And with it blowing towards the British trenches today, the enemy had sprung a gas attack. Thick jets of fog hovered above the fields, edging ever closer to the trenches.

Michael took hold of the heavy machine gun, raised it above the firing step, and onto the tip of no man's land. Oscar was soon by his side.

'Josh, head back and warn the front line.' Michael had not heard the alarms sounding out from the trenches yet and was worried that the men were unaware of the attack. He watched Josh sprint with his head ducked down. The snouted sack over his face gave the impression of a metallic mouse. The thick rimmed goggles steamed up under his panicked breath.

'Here Mike; it's ready.' Oscar's voice was muffled beneath his mask. He had prepared the machine gun and had fed the drum with long heavy rounds. Taking hold of the weapon, Michael sprayed gunfire through the smoke that cloaked the landscape.

Like two satanic scarecrows, the young men stood firm against the approaching enemy. Not even a shadow could be seen through the spiralling smoke, but still they fired on. Michael's muscular arms swung the gun from left to right as if it were a huge claymore sword. The bullets sliced through the air, threatening to cut the horizon itself in two. Huge shells leaped over Michael's shoulder; chipped into the air from the gun's heavy recoil. It pounded and pressed into Michael's forearms as he fired on. Oscar continued to feed the drum, in what seemed an endless tide of gunfire.

Pausing for a moment, Michael did not hear a single gunshot fired in reply to his assault, nor did he see any red clouds dust the fog as the bullets passed through the advancing enemy. Nevertheless, he and Oscar stood guard for the longest hour of their lives. Peppered by the smoke, the young men peered above no man's land in hope to catch any attack as early as possible. With their heads high above the trenches, they prayed that the fog blinded the snipers as much as it did them.

Oscar gripped his rifle in his hand and trained it upon the land. He struggled to see past the barrel of the gun, and his bayonet punctured the grey smoke.

'Something's not right.' Despite the thick sack covering his entire head, Michael kept his voice close to a whisper.

'Tell me about it. I know you have to make use of the wind, but that seemed wasteful.' Oscar lay as low as he could to the land.

'It's still on their side though, look.' Michael nodded towards the cocked flag.

'I suppose they hadn't hoped on us spotting it so early eh? Those fools will be hard pushed to pull the wool over our eyes.' Oscar was ignorant in his irony.

Half an hour passed and the fog began to clear. No man's land began to open up in front of Michael. He thought it wise to step down from the firing step. Oscar followed suit. Behind him, Michael could hear the approach of light footsteps. He turned to face the corner of the listening post. A small boy popped his head around the corner. It was Josh.

'You can take those off now lads. The officers are saying we're quite safe.'

Michael pulled off his mask. The chalky taste of the smoke clung to his tongue. He took a long drink from his canister. Behind him, Oscar was doing the same.

'Well thank God for that. Can't say I couldn't have spent some of those rounds a bit more wisely, but what were we to know?' Michael stretched his aching shoulders.

'Exactly. For all we know, they may have been pocking their heads out from their trenches before you guys unleashed hell onto them. It could've been a lot worse for all of us.' Josh had lost many a night's sleep to the stories that filtered from the Somme. Despite the disease and squalor, he would have welcomed seeing out the war from inside the trenches. He had no intention of stepping out onto no man's land, not unless he was ordered to do so at least.

'Well head on back and get some supper inside you. Oscar and I have drawn the short straw on the night shift, so think of us when you're saying grace.' Michael winked at the young boy as he darted off back towards the front line. He hardly had to duck down as he passed through the shallow trench.

'Well that shows us,' said Oscar as he mopped his sweaty brow. He had been too busy clearing his face to look at Josh. 'All that grub we gave him and he didn't even think to offer us any of that fruit he had. I mean, where did he get that from?'

'What are you talking about?' Michael turned to see Oscar was busy tucking his mask inside his satchel.

'That smell. It kind of smells like sweet fruit. Did he have a tin of fruit in syrup or something?'

'He didn't have a thing on him Oscar.' Seeing the flag pointing towards him, Michael smelt the air. Having taken off his mask, he had been too busy gulping in gallons of air through his open mouth and had not bothered to use his nose. With his nose raised, he could smell it. The sickly scent of over ripe fruit had flavoured the thin air. His wide eyes opened to their edges when he saw Oscar's hand.

'How have you done that?' Michael pointed to the red skin that stretched across the back of Oscar's fleshy hand. Small blisters had begun to bubble on the surface.

'Oh dear God... put your mask back on!' Michael sprinted off towards the front line.

Across the field, the enemy had released over seven thousand cylinders of chlorine gas. Stretched across three kilometres, the gas clawed its way through no man's land. Hanging heavier than air, the condense gas was perfect for packing low lying areas. Carried by the pressing winds, it began to settle at the rim of the British trenches. Thick lines of deep greens and dank yellows skulked past the idle sandbags and rooted razor wire. Brimming on the tip of the trench, the lethal gas seeped in over the top.

Michael was pulling on his mask as he screamed down the trench. No longer concerned about the snipers, he sprinted as fast as he could. His arms fired him forwards as he pushed through the falling vapour. Seeing Josh making his way back to the trench, Michael spat the exhaust valve from his mouth and yelled his name. However, Josh could not hear him. Oblivious to the gas cloud that hung above him, Josh walked on.

Within yards of the boy, Michael jumped on top of him. His huge frame covered the thin bones of Josh, who lay winded and breathless beneath him. Michael saw the terror in his eyes as he turned the boy around and grabbed at his satchel. Without hesitating to instruct him, Michael pulled the mask out and threw it over Josh's face. The young man was frozen by fear. Dragging him to his feet, Michael took hold of Josh's trembling arm and continued to run towards the front line.

Then he saw Teddy. Caught within the crippling clouds, the old man had fallen to his knees. Thrashing on the floor, he began to cough violently. His vision was blurred and he could not make out where Michael's calls came from. He crashed into the side of the trench – the dry walls forcing the air from his tight lungs. Instinctively, he inhaled. His eyes washed with tears as fear gripped him by the throat. Thick clots of blood coloured the vomit that sprayed from his mouth. He waved his arms about him, desperate to take hold of anything that he could find. Touched by the reaper's hand, Teddy sank to his knees one final time. Staring directly at Michael, he began to die. The gas had turned every drop of water within his throat to acid. Within moments, he had drowned under the dry wave of the lethal wind.

Chapter 41

The journey home had been awful. Fighting had framed the streets of Dublin as the British army closed in. Bullets passed from building to building, showing no mercy for those caught in-between. Civilian casualties were common, and the public began to despise the rising. Outnumbered and out-muscled, the volunteers were destined to succeed only in their failure.

There was no car waiting for Grace at the city walls; nobody had arranged for her safe return. The train stations were clotted with people keen to quit the bloodshed. The platforms were peppered by families looking to distance themselves from the plight back home. Suitcases sprawled along the station, surrounded by their tired owners. Equally exhausted, Grace lost herself within the crowd. She overheard conversations that berated the actions of the brotherhood – declaring that their selfish acts would now be paid for by the peaceful law abiding public. Dubliners welcomed change, but the venomous tone of the people implied that the volunteers were the uninvited guest to the party that nobody had wanted. Fire had only been met with by fire. Caught at the seat of the battle, it was ultimately Dublin that got burnt. Buildings had been flattened only to find them empty of any volunteers, as shops and stalls were riddled by gunfire in the attempt to flush out a faceless foe. Because the British army was uncertain on where their enemies were, they approached the matter as if they were everywhere.

Stood in the stations, people began to lose hope. Because of the British blockade, no trains were scheduled to leave the stations for some time. Only military trains came and went, bringing more soldiers to aid the British cause. Officers from the Royal Irish Constabulary weaved among the crowds, hoping to harvest any volunteers that hid within. Trying her hardest not to overreact, Grace bowed her head and followed the stream of disheartened people that left the platform. There was no need for a ticket master, and so the people passed through the turnstiles freely. Soldiers stood either side and scoped the faces that skulked past. Grace filed past the men and pressed on. Despite her delight, there was no reason to smile. She was still no further from the capital, and she was still a long way from home.

In the late hours of the evening, Grace finally made it back to Canndare. Her feet throbbed from the journey. With no other option available, Grace was driven to walk the entire trip home. Stopping only to hide from the droves of military trucks that passed, Grace was now exhausted. Her stomach growled above her hollow legs. She felt fit to devour an entire deer in one sitting. Creeping into her kitchen, she removed a block of cheese from the cupboard and grabbed a crusty loaf from the breadbasket. Dry crumbs flaked down the sides of the bread as she cut two thick slices. It only took half of the sandwich she had made to fill her tiny stomach, so she took the other half into the study. Not finding her husband slumped in his usual spot; Grace left the sandwich on his desk for him. No doubt he would return to his books later.

The house was quiet and dimly lit. The moon had greeted the starlit skies and bid farewell to the remains of the day. The songbirds were nestled in for the night, and the crickets took up their chorus. Too tired to sleep, Grace walked outside and took a seat on the steps that led into the gardens. She could still make out the bright colours of the flower beds as they rested beneath the dark sheet of night. Dimmed plots of red roses and bluebells decorated the edges.

With no pets or animals allowed in the estate, the place always lacked a sense of life. Sat in the silence, she found herself missing her hometown. She could picture the wild deer bounding across the fields, and even her father's dogs chasing the cars that came and went. Grace could also see the horses at play, and the young man that had set them free. For years she had watched Michael raise the horses, always finding herself almost hypnotised by the freedom he shared with them. Never once had she seen him take a firm hand with them, nor find cause to discipline them in anyway. Instead they simply responded to the soft touch of his strong hands. Thinking back to a time when she felt most alive, Grace missed Michael more than anything she had ever known. In the briefest of moments that they had shared together, he had given her more joy than she could ever imagine possible. Staring at the bed of white lilies that lay at the bottom of the lawn, she prayed that Michael was safe.

Since arriving in her new town, Grace had lost touch with life at home. Regularly she had forgotten to return calls from her sister, and had never written as often as she had promised. The truth was she had found the new town exciting. There was a buzz about the streets that she had never experienced before; people's interests were on a national scale. Here, people were fighting for the greater good and, for once, Grace had felt allowed to take a stand. Back home her private education had taught her all the skills she needed to be a marketable product for her father's empire, but nothing of how to achieve what she really wanted. Her new surroundings had brought with it a fresh approach to attaining all that you could dream of. And yet, her stomach knotted at the thought of how she had settled for a life that promised little surprise. The taste of security that she had craved for had grown stale. Not once had a hint of romance threatened to enter her relationship with Arnold, and if she had to be honest she could not really commit to knowing whether he loved her or not.

Knowing her own feelings, Grace was compelled to act. Stooping to the side of the steps, she picked a single flower from the bush. On moving to the estate, she had insisted that two bushes, bursting with wildflowers be planted at the base of the steps. Bringing the chosen one to her nose, she smelt the sweet scent of the white windflower. Her hands wrapped around the stem as if in prayer, as she made her way back inside.

***

The police had begun to sweep the nation. Buildings were raided and homes were plagued by the authorities looking for sympathisers of the Easter Uprising. Having taken back the capital from the volunteers, the ring leaders had been rounded up and arrested by the police. Patrick Pearse was among the men that were marched from prison to prison, suffering the jeers and abuse of the public as he passed. The date for their trials had been set and the wheels were now in motion to halt any reaction from their supporters.

Within days, close to two thousand people had been rounded up by the army and the police. The Commander in Chief, Sir John Maxwell was pushing for the death penalty, and it was yet to be seen how many were to get a bullet as a reward for their bold defiance. Having rounded up more volunteers than most, Sergeant William Stewart had arrived in town. Supported by his most trusted officer – Constable John Cox – Sergeant Stewart had followed a tip off on the whereabouts of a certain Fenian sympathiser. Having hopped onto one of the travelling military trains, he had arranged for Constable Cox to meet him at the city gates. As ordered the old officer had been waiting with a police wagon when Sergeant Stewart arrived.

'Good evening John' said Stewart. His dark tunic hung from his thin shoulders.

'Oh, hello there Sarge. Just getting this thing ready.' Cox was brushing down the inside of the police wagon. A small cell was located at the back of the vehicle – a meshed grill would separate the officers from the detained.

'Don't bother cleaning that. They'll be a fresh piece of shit in it soon enough.' Stewart could never carry off the tough man approach. His frame was too thin and his face too young for it to sound convincing.

'Right you are boss.' Cox stifled a snigger. He had been in the job over two decades longer than his supervisor and had met enough characters to know Sergeant Stewart wasn't tough. However, always the obedient, Cox played along.

'The tipoff said that the person should be hiding nearby. We got the first call a few days ago, started off as a bit of a missing person's enquiry, but then with all the shenanigans in Dublin our informant was certain that this one was involved.' He continued to brush down the car seats. 'We got another call earlier this evening to say that they'd returned home.' Stewart cracked his knuckles. The leather of his new gloves creaked on his fingers.

'So, is our guy meeting us here or do we have directions?' Cox played along with the over excited warm up. He removed his revolver and began to spin the barrels. Having heard of the job in store for them, he had not bothered to load it. Snapping it shut with a flick of the wrist, he holstered the gun.

'That's right. Get prepared. If this one plays up, be ready to do whatever it takes.' Stewart spoke with a forced rasp in his voice. He found it easier to feign the gravelled sound when forcing a lower tone to his voice.

'Very well.' Cox ignored the humour in his supervisor's voice. He knew, more than most, that people had been hurt recently – innocent people. Distant friends of his had been mowed down during the uprising, and he found it hard to have any sympathy for the sympathisers. What troubled him was that he could not be sure who had killed the most – the rebels or the army. Either way, blood had been shed and someone needed to be held accountable.

The two officers made their way into town. The unstable wagon felt every bump of the cobbled road beneath it. Pot holes played hell with the suspension, sending short sharp shocks into the officer's buttocks. The road ahead was long and baron. Staggered street lamps lit the way. Stretching deep into the centre of the town, the officers had the road all to themselves. Soon the well farmed fields became replaced with row upon row of stores and townhouses. Every corner of every road was utilised. Stores faced houses, sometimes even supporting them as shopkeepers took up lodgings in the space upstairs. The dimly lit streets were clear of any ramblers; Stewart's keen eye could not see a drunk in sight for miles. It was like a ghost town.

'This place gives me the creeps.' Cox broke the silence.

'Really? This place… it's nothing but a tired little town. There's no secrets in a place like this, believe me.' Stewart peered out of the window, desperate to find someone to harass and trouble.

'Well, it must have had some secrets to end up housing a sympathiser, that's for sure.' Cox held the wheel. It jerked with every bump in the road.

'Not a secret no more though is it? We'll root out the weeds in no time – let these people enjoy their town without the rotten few that threaten to spoil it.' Stewart looked for something to drink but could not find anything.

'But surely, this one wouldn't have been alone in all of this. There must be others in this town that encouraged it all. I mean, it's awfully rare that you'd just get the one.'

'Exactly. You might have a good old Roman nose on you Constable, but it's nice to see that you can see beyond it. This one may be the tip of the iceberg. If we manage to crack them, then the whole bloody lot might surface.' Stewart hoped Cox could hear his low tones. His throat was drying out from all the husky emphasis.

'But we're just to take this one in, right? It's not up to us to interrogate them?' Cox could see his Sergeant had already drawn his wooden baton. It was almost as thick as the scrawny leg it rested on.

The informant was waiting at the end of the road. Seeing the lights of the police wagon approach, he waved his hand high in the air. Rain had begun to fall, and thick droplets pelted down from the skies. The man held himself tightly. His slight physique was drowned by a long trench coat. Thin eyes peered from beneath the peek of his flat cap.

'Is that our man?' Cox could not miss the silhouette that waved within the tainted yellow light of the wagon's headlights.

'I believe it is.' Stewart shifted in his chair. The man looked uneasy on his feet. Stewart guessed that he had been drinking.

✵✵✵

Cases were sprawled out across her bed. Knowing that there was nothing she would really need, Grace could not decide what to pack. She randomly chucked dresses, coats, and skirts into cases. Without looking at what her hands held, she crammed the clothes in and forced the lids shut. The shiny silver clasps threatened to snap open at any time. With four cases full, Grace still had countless wardrobes brimming with clothes for every season. Some she had never even seen, let alone worn. Pulling the cases from the bed, Grace noticed that she had packed more than her small hands could carry. Not knowing what any truly contained, she picked two at random and placed them by the door. She could always send for the rest.

Turning frantically about her room, Grace rummaged through her drawers. Tucked beneath a pile of freshly laundered bed sheets, she found what she was after. A small thick fold of paper sat in the corner of the drawer. Several pages had been folded over and formed a solid square. Some of the edges were torn, where Grace had ripped them from the books that they had originally been in. Her hand began to shake as her heart raced at the sight of them. Opening up the stolen pages, Grace saw Michael's handwriting. Having forced herself not to read the poems for months, the words hit her like the first time she had seen them. Letting the words cover her, her head swam with images of their naked bodies entwined beneath the raging waters of the cove.

Outside, rain was tapping on the windowsill. A harsh wind entered the house, almost filling the bedroom with a cold blast. Goosebumps raised on Grace's milky skin. Placing the pages into her pocket, she made her way to the door. Her feet were no longer tired; she felt as though she could run a hundred miles and more if necessary. She now knew that she would go to the end of the earth for love. Thoughts of seeing Michael empowered her. She tried not to think of what may have passed within the time they had been apart; Cara had never told her of news of Michael marrying or moving on. In fact, she had told her nothing of Michael whatsoever, even when she had asked. Trying not to worry herself with possibilities, Grace could not imagine the man in any other way than how she had seen him throughout her confined years. She had always pictured him free within the fields, catering to the town and keeping it safe from all the worries of the world outside.

Pulling on her heavy coat, Grace walked down the stairs. A strong breeze was blowing through the front door. Only the light of the moon mixed with the streetlights lit the ice cold hallway. A pale white light tinted the cold marble tiles of the floor, as the netting behind the open curtains hung hauntingly in the air. Even the common cries of the crickets could no longer be heard beneath the wailing of the passing winds. Stopping before the door to Arnold's study, Grace gathered her words. It felt almost needless to find any that would end a relationship that had never really begun. Despite the years they had spent together, they had never truly been one. Like a conductor without an orchestra, there had been no music in this arrangement, only a silly man with a stick. Being an affair more for business than of love, Grace was excited to bring it to a close. However, she was not heartless and so she would be careful not to hurt Arnold. He was after all an honest man, and he had provided for her just as he had promised. Swallowing her pride, Grace knew that if there was anyone who was untrue in the relationship then it had been her; she had cowardly chosen a life of precautions rather than passion. Despite giving her hand to Arnold, her heart had always belonged to Michael.

Taking a deep breath, Grace opened the door to the study and walked inside. Stood facing Arnold's desk, she was again met with an empty chair. Her chest sank at the thought of not being able to say goodbye in person, but her heart was set on leaving. She walked over to the large oak desk and pulled open the drawers. Half empty bottles of brandy and whiskey rattled within them. Looking for a single sheet of paper, Grace rustled through the business accounts that lined the desk. Finding what she needed, she began to write down her farewells. The letter was short, detailing how she would rather pass the message in person if he would ever give her the opportunity to explain herself. The message, however, was clear. She was leaving him.

Making sure her note would not be lost among the many papers, Grace stood back from the desk. She pulled on the small chain that swung from the desk light and placed the note under it. Checking the desk, Grace noticed the light reflect off the empty plate that had once held the sandwich she had left. Hearing the door of the study creak open, she saw Arnold stood before her. His clothes were drenched. Two policemen stood beside him.

Chapter 42

The 185th Division and the machine gun company of the 88th Bavarian Division were ready. Crouched down in the network of tunnels and dugouts under the ruins of the village, they were determined to sell their lives dearly. The heavy British bombardments had flattened the soil of the Somme, and an imminent attack was expected. However, the Bavarian army felt well guarded within their concrete bunkers. Having anticipated the war to last a little longer than their naïve enemies had, they had established an intricate network of reinforced underground cabins and tunnels. Snipers looked out from loopholes that ran level to the ground. High above them, observation posts stood tall over the captured village of Ginchy – a small farming village just north from Guillemont. Together, they held the entire battlefield within their sights. Any attack from the British would be seen long before their bayonets could reach the enemy. Like clockwork, the shells from the British army began to thump at the land.

'Stand to.' The officer shouted with a bit more purpose than usual. Michael could hear the moaning-minnies roar in the skies above them. Dull thuds rang out in the distance. Ladders leaned against the walls of the front line, dusted by soft layers of September mist which lay on the splintered wooden steps. Michael's cold hand gripped at his rifle.

The 16th Division had not been at the Somme for long and already they had been called into battle. Preceded by the savage reputation they had earned in Hulluch, they were now set the task of recapturing a small French farming village on the other side of no man's land. Having heard of the horrors that had met many of their brothers in arms, Michael had sent David his most heartfelt poem to date. The letter was accompanied by the strict instruction of only reading it to Grace at a time when Michael could never do so. Thousands of men had already died at the Somme, and Michael was not arrogant enough to believe he would not fall. He held the small crucifix from his bracelet to his mouth and kissed it. Only fate now kept him from the two women he had ever loved. One he lived for, the other he would die for.

Oscar was silent at the side of his friend. Small balls of frost fired from his nostrils. His chest raised and fell in beat with his shallow breaths. The order was only moments away and every man knew what was coming to them. The heavy artillery pulsated behind them, tossing shells laden with shrapnel high into the skies. Hot iron rained down as they exploded short of the enemy trenches. Packed tightly together, Oscar kept his eyes straight ahead. At his side, he could feel Josh flinch with every explosion. The young man's shoulders juddered and twitched as the shells beat down in front of them.

'This could be it.' Oscar whispered through the side of his mouth. The sound of the shells exploding ceased. A still quiet gripped the land.

'I think you may be right pal. Let's just get each other home.' Michael looked at his friend and smiled. The officer's whistle shrieked at the end of the front line.

'I'll meet you there.' Oscar nodded as he filled his lungs.

One by one the men climbed the ladders. No man's land awaited them with arrested anticipation. The muddy fields were covered in water; smoke spiralled from fresh pot holes. Heavily, Michael dragged his feet through the bog. The cold September winds were not enough to freeze the land. The soil was damp and trodden. Standing like ducks in a shooting gallery, the men lined up along the top of the trench. Several struggled with carrying the Stokes mortar cannon as the legs of the tripod, on which it rested, continued to drag through the damp dirt. The men knew they were a key target for the enemy snipers, and tried to hide their nerves under their tilted helmets. Areas of the barbed wire had been cut in advance for the attack. The sandbags slumped in the soil in front of the razor sharp steel.

The enemy trenches stretched out across the land, and cut through two thick areas of woodland. The targeted town sat centre stage between the leafy curtains of the forests. The late afternoon light shone over the small stretch of land that stood between Michael and his target. A thin mist hung overhead. The blade of Michael's bayonet cut through the lip of the mist as the officer's order pierced the deathly silence.

'Advance!'

A surge of bullets swept the ground. Funnelled through small gaps in the razor wire, the machine guns of the enemy rested their sights upon the single file of falling soldiers. Four waves of men in open order from the south, with fifty yards between them, marched on. Michael saw how few made it through the gaps in the wire. He pulled at his jacket and called to his friends.

'This way men; follow me.' Chucking his thick khaki jacket over the barbed wire, Michael clambered across. Among others, Oscar and Josh followed him. On the other side they continued to advance. The Irish soldiers that approached from the right were checked by three machine guns. Blood burst from their bullet ridden chests. Their knees sunk into the mud as their flailing arms soon fell still at their sides. Michael knew the machine guns needed to be taken out. Falling into the prone position, he pulled Oscar down next to him.

'I need you to fire on those machine guns. I'll sweep around and try to get them from closer in.' Michael pointed towards a small concreted wall that was potted by three gun turrets.

'Are you insane?' Oscar wriggled his rifle from beneath him. He had been lucky not to puncture himself on his own blade. The bayonet was caked in mud.

'Here, Mike… take these.' Josh fumbled at his side and handed Michael two grenades. The small explosives were as large as the boy's trembling palms.

'Thanks. I'll tell the Hun you said hello.' Michael placed the grenades in the pockets of his trousers. Bullets flew by overhead, clattering into every limb of the approaching soldiers. Michael listened to the bursts of gunfire, counting the seconds between each round. Hoping he had got the timing right, he got to his feet and ran towards the trenches. He could feel the bullets from Oscar's rifle brush past him, puncturing the concrete pits in front of him. Michael prayed that the gunners would be too distracted with trying to take out the mortar cannons that they would not see the crazy man running directly towards them. Gaining ground, he could see the barrels of the guns pointing out towards the wave of soldiers that marched forward. None were facing him.

Oscar continued to fire on the turrets. Small chips of concrete skipped into the air off the edge of the potholes. Seeing the men duck their heads from the bullets, Michael pressed on. His heart was racing as he got within a stone's throw of the enemy. Trying to keep his body close to the ground, Michael's feet became buried in the mire. The force that brought him to his knees, tossed the rifle from his hands. His palms planted themselves flat onto the muddy field and dirt splashed into his face, covering one of his eyes completely. Smearing the soil from his face, Michael saw the one thing he had hoped he would not. One of the guns began to swing towards him. Bullets erupted on the ground on a course that crept towards Michael's fallen body. The earth clung to his legs, stopping him from standing. His fingertips stretched out in front of him, falling inches short of his rifle. Gunfire peppered the puddles that sat only a few feet from Michael. His muscles bugled in his arms as he pulled himself free from the mud. Rejecting this fate, Michael grabbed the grenades from out of his soiled pockets, pulled out the pins and began to count. Beside him the bullets crept closer. With all the energy he could find, he ran, leapt forward and tossed the grenades towards the gun turrets. His body crashed against the concrete side of the wall as the other side rocked within the explosion. Inside, shrapnel tore through the huddled bodies of the enemy, and the guns went quiet.

Gathering his breath, Michael picked up his rifle and sprinted back towards Oscar and Josh. Covering fire passed him as he grew closer to Oscar's prone body.

'Come on. We need to move.' Michael dragged Josh to his feet and headed back towards the wave of soldiers that marched past their fallen friends. Bodies became buried in the mud, planted to the spot by the blasts of gunfire. Mortars raced ahead of the Irishmen, dropping down onto the enemy line. Feeling closed in, German snipers began to crawl out into the fresh craters left by the bombardment. The very best of them kept count of their kills as each shot brought another man to his end. They sat flanking a set of soldiers armed with heavy machine guns.

Michael joined the rear of the wave, watching as the left side of the right wing swept around the field and attacked the machine guns from the flanks. Surrounded by soldiers attacking from the north and the west, the German troops broke out of their line, and ran directly into the approaching enemy. Blood bathed the ground as bayonets crashed into chests. Screams of agony punched through the air, and the last remains of life poured out of the beaten men. Hundreds lay dying as the rest fought on above them.

Michael ran forward and dived behind a fallen tree. Josh and Oscar were with him in seconds. They were all caked in dirt and barely recognisable to each other. Together they crouched beneath the thick tree; bullets prodded and poked the other side. Beyond them lay the remains of a ruined farm. Snipers and riflemen remained in the northern half of the village, hidden within their concreted loopholes.

'We need to take this place. The enemy are hidden in one of those buildings. From what I saw, there's a barn to the left and a farmhouse straight ahead. I'm going to need to draw them out somehow.' Michael looked back at his two friends. Other troops had begun to gather. Two men clambered through the mud holding a mortar cannon. They dropped to the ground as shots flashed above their heads.

'Someone get those mortars ready, I'm going to flush them out. Oscar you cover me with your rifle. If any of them dare show their heads, take it from their shoulders.' Michael shouted above the explosions. He saw the men ready the cannon upon the tripod. The end of the thick barrel poked above the fallen tree.

'Why don't we just storm the place? Some of us are bound to get through.' Oscar looked back at the waves of men approaching.

'At the cost of how many lives? This way, only one of us could die.'

'Michael, let me come with you.' Josh pulled on Michael's arm.

'No. I doubt I'll be coming back Josh. I think you should stay here and rush the barn. Guys, have you got that barrel pointed at the farmhouse?' The men nodded as they continued to angle the barrel. Oscar had crawled beneath the tree and was almost invisible.

'Michael, I'm coming with you. I can't let you go alone.' Josh's expression burned through the dirt that was drying on his pale cheeks. Michael knew there would be no convincing the man otherwise.

'Alright, but keep low. If you hear a shot, hit the ground. Hopefully these guys will take care of the rest.'

'You've got it Mike.' Josh flashed a bright smile. His teeth were a stark white against his muddy mask. Setting himself for battle, Josh wiped the end of his bayonet, cleaning the soil from his blade.

'Everyone set? Josh and I will make for the barn. Oscar, if you can hear me keep an eye out for the windows. If you see even a hint of something, give it hell.' Michael planted his hand on Josh's shoulder and nodded. The battle raged either side of them. Mounds of earth blasted from the grounds as shells whirred in the skies, crashing down and smashing into the earth. They were surrounded by death; men continued to kill one another, covering themselves in the blood of the beaten. Only the village ahead had the slightest pretence of peace; it sat quietly as the two young men charged towards it.

Michael held his rifle low. He did not envisage getting close enough to use his bayonet, and doubted he would have time to take aim. He leaned forward and sprinted for a small stone wall that ran parallel to the front of the farm house. Parts of the wall were crushed and broken. Empty shells lay scattered on the ground. Still the village remained silent. Josh was breathing heavily behind Michael. Taking hold of a stone, Michael tossed it into the centre square of the village. It was greeted by nothing; not a sound or a hint of movement came.

'The barn is just across to the left. If we run for that, it's likely they'll start shooting from the farmhouse. Chances are we could get cut up between the two. Get your rifle ready Josh. We may need to go hands on if we get too close.' Michael rolled onto his stomach and peered around the wall. The place was lifeless.

'Remember... hit the deck if they start firing. Our boys will have our backs. Are you ready?' Josh nodded.

'Then let's go.' Michael stood to the lowest point that his knees would bend and made a run for it.

Josh followed closely behind. The huge hulking wooden barn was a hundred yards away to their left. The doors were wide open, and large bails of hay were piled at the sides. A small village square with a fountain separated the barn from the farmhouse. The mermaid of the fountain no longer threw water from her vase; the base was dry and choked by rubble.

Shots fired out towards them as they approached the barn. Machine guns rattled from the windows of the farmhouse, spitting their bullets across the square. Tiles erupted on the pavement, cutting the ground like hot rain through snow.

'Get down.' Michael dropped to the prone position and Josh fell by his side. Michael placed one hand on his helmet and the other over Josh's back, keeping him pinned to the floor. Gunfire blasted above them. Incessant streams of bullets sprang out, relentless in their attempts to find their mark. The ground was pebbled by gunshots yards from where Michael lay. The sound of the shots whistled in the wind, beating at the weak breeze. One had sounded more muffled than the rest.

Looking up, Michael saw movement in the windows of the farmhouse. Nothing was coming from the barn. The enemy were tucked away beneath the hanging curtains; poking the barrels of their weapons out of the small slits between. He gestured to the men behind him. A dull pumping thud sounded out from the battlefield. Hearing the whine of the rocket, Michael glanced back at the farmhouse. The front walls exploded in a mass of broken brick and clay. Another mortar hit its mark, destroying the front wall entirely. Bodies banged against the walls, blown from their feet. The few that could still stand stumbled forwards only to be sat down by the precise shots from Oscar's rifle.

Bullets now began to burst out from the barn. Loose and unsteady shots headed in Michael's direction. The enemy had begun to flank them.

'Josh, we've been dragged into this, come on.' He pulled at the boy's jacket as he jumped to his feet. Josh's body rolled over and stared at the heavens. A thick pool of blood poured from his eye socket. His jaw opened slightly, and his tongue was dusted by the ground. For a moment, Michael stood still. His body was upright and his shoulders wide. There was nothing he could do to help his friend. Josh was already gone.

With tears washing his cheeks, Michael ran for the barn. Shells continued to pound the farmhouse, and Oscar remained hidden. Screaming as loud as he could, Michael burst through the barn doors. A soldier stood before him with agony etched across his face. The sharp blade of Michael's bayonet was already tearing through his gut. The soldier raised his pistol and shot Michael directly into his chest. Feeling the bullet break through the back of his shoulder blade, Michael pulled the trigger of his rifle. Warm blood splattered over him. Raising his free hand, he pushed the man to the floor and climbed up into the loft of the barn. A sniper, who had hidden himself in the hay, jumped out onto Michael's back. He was as heavy as a horse, and brought Michael to his knees. They crashed onto the thick wooden floorboards; their weapons falling from their hands. Michael stood to face his foe. He looked the same age as him. His arms were long and stretched. Two darks dots for eyes sat either side of a large bridged nose. The man swung first; his fist crashed into Michael's jaw. Pain exploded across Michael's face. The man swung again, this time with his left. Michael ducked and ran at the man, thumping his wounded shoulder into the man's stomach. The wind left the man's lungs on impact and they fell into a mound of hay. The man's fingers wrapped themselves around Michael's throat. His elbows were locked, and he held Michael outstretched. Michael reached forward but he could not take hold of the man. Blood pounded at Michael's brain as the man's thumbs pressed harder into his throat.

The sides of Michael's sight began to darken. Shadows closed in around the snarling face of his enemy. Michael's arms grew tired, and fell to his side. A small handle was felt by his fingertips. Taking hold of it, Michael swung his arm towards the man's face. The lamp he was holding fractured into his forehead. Shards of glass shredded his skin. Instinctively, the man pulled his hands over his face, screaming in agony. Pulling the knife from his belt, Michael plunged the blade deep under his enemy's chin. His head jerked back and blood seeped out onto the straw beneath him. Hearing footsteps enter the barn, Michael held his hand over the dying man's mouth.

Feeling the last breath cross his palm, he let go and crawled over to the edge of the loft. Pain pulled at his chest. A layer of blood lined his shirt. Beneath him, two German soldiers readied their rifles. They whispered and pointed out towards the village square. Michael watched as one of the soldiers set their sight onto the fallen tree where Oscar lay hidden. Pulling the pin from his last grenade, Michael counted to three. On the third count, he rolled the grenade off the side of the loft. It landed with a muted clunk inside a small mound of hay. Not caring for the noise he now made, Michael ran and jumped into the opposite corner of the loft. He felt the thump of the explosion against the base of the boards as his body hit it. The soldiers did not have time to scream before the shrapnel cut them in two.

Outside the 16th Division swarmed the village. The enemy had begun to hide in dugouts and shadowed corners of the ruined houses. Within an hour they all lay dead on the ground. The Irish soldiers had slaughtered them entirely. The German troops had proved no match for the grit and determination that the young Irish men had shown. Dozens of soldiers at a time poured into the concrete dugouts that had fenced the village, putting their bayonet to deadly use on anyone that stood in their way. The Irish Rifle regiment remained to hold the captured ground as many men continued to charge ahead through the village.

Walking from the barn, Michael could hear a piper playing. The Celtic song was laden with lament for those that would never return home. Hazy from the fight, Michael stumbled towards the fallen body of Josh. The clouded skies above began to grey the light. The sun was tired and shone dimly upon the village. The cold September winds whisked the dust of the ruins into the air. Beneath the ghostly cloud lay the dead body of a young man.

Oscar was already out from under the tree when he saw Michael. His friend's face was now whiter than the shirt that he wore upon his beaten back. Deep shades of crimson coloured his chest. His tired legs had enough to carry him towards the small lifeless body that had once housed their young friend. However, he could not stand for long. Oscar sprinted towards Michael, still too far away to catch him as he fell. Michael's body lay at Josh's side. His fingers stretched across the young man's chest; his eyes completely closed.

Chapter 43

Originally built as an institution for young offenders, HMP Reading was rebuilt and completed on 1 July 1844. Based on the Pentonville model, each cell had gas lighting – set behind a glazed panel – and was charmed with a hand basin and toilet. The prison itself was divided into four wings, labelled A to D alphabetically. The layout rested like a fallen crucifix and the wardens followed the 'separate system' as if it were their bible. The only time a prisoner was to interact with any other inmate would be during the brief exercise period they had each day. Every other hour was spent alone in their cell.

Renowned for housing Oscar Wilde in 1895, the prison was not afraid of taking in those that had gathered huge public attention. Reducing the inmate to nothing but the number of their cell, Grace Farrington soon became known as D3.4. The number, however, did not define the woman for long. Having served her sentence for being a sympathiser to the Easter Uprising, Grace was one of the last people to be set free by the British Government. Her verdict was shrouded and greyer than others. There was very little proof, other than the testimony of her husband, which had linked Grace to the IRB. Nobody could put a smoking pistol in her hand, and so her case was dealt with as an unwelcome aside to the entire episode. But she was guilty by association and, therefore, she would pay a price.

In spite of her ill-fate, Grace remained grateful. Her stretch amounted to a mere few month's imprisonment, while many others suffered a sentence from which there was no release date. In May of the same year – ill advised and lacking in foresight – the British Government executed the 15 leaders of the uprising. Having had the people on their side, the government changed public opinion quicker than it took the bullets of the firing squad to kill the leaders of the Fenian movement. Those punished soon became martyrs, and what was meant to cripple the movement had only granted it fresh legs. The second wind had come and the nationalists remained standing.

Part of her conditional release was that Grace remained in England. She was forbidden to return to her homeland, and were it not for the generosity of David Irwin she would have been completely lost. David had made arrangements for Grace to stay with friends from his father's old regiment. The many wars that had busied the British Isles did not come without their widows, and it was with an elderly war widow by the name of Marian Brown that David had arranged for Grace to stay.

The small terraced house was set in a small village just outside of the county of Berkshire. With a population that struggled to break two-hundred, the village of Bourneville was a welcome break to Grace. Fed by the river Bourne on the fringe of the county, Bourneville was a quiet and peaceful site. Following national conscription, the village was baron of young men and only a few elderly gentlemen could be found in the few watering holes that remained open. Although distanced from the fight, the women of Bourneville still played their part in the nation's struggle. Commuting every morning to work in local factories, they filled the roles left by the conscripted men and strived to keep the economy afloat. Despite the shrewd factory owners and their exceptional ability to circumvent the wartime equal pay regulations, the women of Bourneville soldiered on and worked every hour their bodies allowed them.

Drinking in the clean country air, Grace felt fresh as she arrived at her new address. She was without any bags and had only that which she wore on her back. Stood in the small porch on the doorstep of the house, a small woman waited to greet Grace. Her back was stooped slightly and her hands showed the work of old age. The silver hair that was worn in a tight bun rested atop a youthful and smiling face.

'Welcome. You must be Grace. David has told me everything about you.' She ushered Grace inside. 'Come now, you must remind me to have stern words with the man because he didn't mention anything about how beautiful you were. Damn it, I'll have to reinforce the front door when the soldiers return. They'll be beating it clean off its hinges when they know a face like yours sleeps inside.' The old lady flashed a bright smile. She was clearly happy to have made Grace blush.

'Well I don't intend to be any trouble. It's so nice that you let me stay. You are Mrs Brown I assume?' Grace held her hand out. It was taken firmly by her hostess.

'Now please, you know what they say happens when you assume? And I assure you I am more than capable of making an ass out of myself on my own. Especially after a few sherries.' Marian winked as she nudged Grace in the side. She was dressed as if she were set for a ball. Her finest pearls hung from her neck upon a stunning black dress. She led Grace inside and shut the door.

'No bags? Well I suppose we'll have to get the lustful men to spoil you on their return.' Marian laughed boisterously and walked towards a table already set for tea.

'I'm not quite sure what my husband would say to that Mrs Brown.' Grace questioned herself for bringing him into the conversation.

'Oh… married? I'm so sorry my dear but I didn't see a ring on your finger. See, what did I tell you about assuming?' Marian made an uncomfortable smile.

'Ha! Please don't worry on my part. The truth is I don't believe he would care one jot for my wellbeing. After all, he had no qualms with calling the police to arrest me in the first place, and I haven't heard word of him since.' Grace looked at the table.

'My dear, please sit. It sounds like you've had a right old time of it. Have a cup of tea. Soothe your worries for a while. I'll get the bath on soon and we can get you all sorted out by supper time.' Marian sat opposite Grace and poured out two cups of tea.

'I really must thank you for all of this. Taking in a stranger like me from the streets, it's not everyday someone would do such a thing.' Grace took a small sip from her cup. The drink was like nectar on her tongue.

'Well we're living in strange times now Grace. I can call you Grace can't I?' Grace nodded to Marian's request. 'Since losing my Charlie to the Boer War, I prayed we wouldn't have another.

But here we are again, bearing witness to another load of cobblers that men see it fit to die for. It really does break my heart to see all the lonely women this world creates. So, when David told me of your tale, I had little choice but to help. I must say, he did omit the detail about your husband though. Do you think you two will survive all this?' Marian's deep brown eyes peered over her raised teacup.

'No, I'm afraid the little love we shared would not have survived through any times – peaceful or otherwise. Rest assured, this war can't claim another victim in my husband and me, Mrs Brown. What we had died long before all this began.' Grace felt cold at the thought of her relationship with Arnold. There was no anger, no bitterness; just nothing at all.

'Then it wasn't love at all.' Marian saddled the saucer with her teacup.

'Excuse me?' Grace liked the woman's nerve.

'Love doesn't just pass, my dear. Not through time, not through death, not through anything whatsoever. If you say that what you had with your husband has gone, then what you *had* was not love.' Marian gave a knowing smile.

'And you know this after ten minutes in my company?' Grace began to smile.

'Only if what you're saying is true. Do you think that you have truly loved anyone else?' Marian asked the question in an open way. Her expression was one of wonder and not knowing.

'No,' said Grace sadly. Marian watched her carefully.

'There's something you're not telling me, and that's quite alright. But I do run a house of honesty, and I shall answer any question you may ask me with the complete truth if you would do me such the honour also.' Marian took a small sip from her teacup. The faded autumn light filtered through her netted curtains.

'I did tell you the truth.' Grace offered a cheeky smile.

'David warned me that you were quite the bright little button. Alright, I'll ask it differently this time. Do you *know* that you have truly loved anyone else?'

'But I thought you said love was a constant. To have *loved* someone means that it has stopped, and if it has stopped then it never was, right?' Grace took a small sip for her small victory.

'Very well… let me rephrase the question. Are you in love with someone?' Marian had taken to Grace's playful nature.

'With all my heart; yes.' Grace's face flushed and her heart fluttered when she heard her utter the words. It shocked her how hearing what she had always known still made her stomach tingle.

'Bravo. Honesty it is!' Marian applauded as if she had sat through an entire west-end production.

'And now for my question,' said Grace with her most serious of scowls. 'Do you have anymore of this lovely tea?'

Following her bath, and the wonderful supper Mrs Brown had laid on for her, Grace settled into her new bedroom for the night. Her hostess had gone to bed and had left a small glass of warm milk on Grace's bedside cabinet. The bedroom was makeshift – a basic guest room with a single bed and wardrobe. Other than the small cabinet, there was very little room for anything else. Grace noticed how there had been no pictures of any children inside the house. The unlit fireplace sat cold beneath a baron mantelpiece. The house itself had only another master bedroom and a bathroom on the top floor. No signs of anyone other than Mrs Brown and her memories could be found within the tight walls of the terraced house.

Finding the bible in the draw of the cabinet, Grace thought it right to pray. Kneeling at her bedside, she gave thanks to her friends and loved ones. She praised the Lord for blessing her with a woman as kind as Mrs Brown — for leading her to someone so sweet and honest in her nature that Grace had known within minutes that she need not be anyone other than herself. Lastly, she prayed for the one person she missed more than anyone else. Ignoring the fact that once again fate had kept her from him, Grace gave thanks for being blessed with knowing how true love felt. For this, she gave thanks for Michael.

The next morning, Grace was awoken by a commotion in the kitchen. The morning songs of the sparrows were muffled by the clattering of pots and pans. Rising from her slumber, Grace pulled on the dressing gown that had been left for her and headed downstairs. Waiting for her at the bottom was a frantic Mrs Brown.

'Come now Grace; let's get you ready for the day. We've a good few hours of work ahead of us and the day won't wait for the idle.' She waved her hand as if wafting the heat from her flushed face. 'I've taken the liberty of sending your clothes to the laundrette. Don't worry, later today, we'll head into town and get you a whole batch of new dresses and what not. Until then, you'll find a selection on my bed that you can choose from.' Marian's dress was dusted in flour and small flecks of dough.

'What the devil are you up to?' Grace had a tired but warm smile.

'Just doing my bit, you'll see. Now, despite me being opposed to this blasted war, I still like to do my bit and support our men as best I can. We are the nurturing sex after all and what would a woman be if she didn't look out for her boys? Also, I must warn you that there are an awful lot of women in this village who fear that this war has put their social influence and political — shall we say — advancement at risk. I for one like to separate myself from the sordid world of money making and life taking, but you can't help but admire these women who strive to be more than mere Madonnas and handmaidens. As for me? Well I'd be *made* if I was ever handled again, and as for the Virgin Mary, if you ask me I'm not too mad on 'er.' Marian looked to see if Grace had grabbed her loose joke.

'Awful.' Grace laughed. 'Truly awful.'

'Well it's early in the morning, so be gentle. Anyway, go and get yourself dressed. We've got food to deliver.' Marian spun on her heels and headed for the kitchen. Woken by the woman's energy, Grace skipped upstairs.

The village hall was hosting a small festival to the men on leave from the army. Most had been injured slightly and would return to the war as soon as they were fit. However, those fit enough to fight had not been granted leave — leaving their wives to cook for the injured husbands of their friends while they fought tirelessly on the frontline.

Most of the village had gathered in the main hall. The fresh smell of varnish filled the large room. Economically astute, the cleaner had chosen to smear a small amount on the radiators rather than cleaning the entire wooden floor. Once the hall was full of muddy wellingtons and boots, the heating had been put on — warming the varnish and releasing its strong scent. Stood behind a stall laden with crusty loaves, Grace smiled at the villagers that walked by. Many stopped and spoke with her — keen to check the young lady's account against the gossip that had already attached itself to her name. Without telling her, many of the women were shocked to see such a petite and pretty little thing — not quite the aggressive militant they were expecting.

Meanwhile, Marian was at the top of a ladder that had been stacked next to the stage. The corner of a banner was pinned under her fingertips as she hammered in a thick tack. The blue and white banner welcomed everyone to the Bourneville village hall, advertising their fine local produce and imploring people to show their support for the boys of Britain. Those few that had returned walked slowly through the hall, draped by their partner who kissed them each time another woman caught their eye. Many of the men wore an expression of sad inevitability – resigned to the simple fact that they were soon set to leave for war once more. Weighted by the worries of what lay ahead, the soldiers failed to feel the highs of freedom.

'How are people finding the bread?' Marian rummaged through the basket that sat on the table.

'I think they are all fond of it Mrs Brown. It smells delicious and is a welcome break from that stink of varnish that's in the air. I'm almost dizzy from the fumes.' Grace feigned a feint as she slapped the back of her wrist onto her brow.

'Good. Mrs Stokes over there is forever bragging about her blasted buns, but I think we may have outdone her this time. With a pretty face like yours on the stall we're bound to give ours away first.' Marian rushed off and busied herself at other tables. Grace watched as the old lady spoke with everyone in the hall, leaving almost all of them laughing.

'So, how's the bread? Warm enough to melt a knob of butter I hope.' A young soldier was stood in front of Grace. His front teeth bucked beneath a thin upturned lip. A goofy smile sat on his pale face.

'Yes it's all freshly baked today. Please feel free to take as much as you wish. That's what it was made for.' Grace opened her hands towards the basket.

'An Irish girl I see? What brings you to Bourneville?' The soldier was already wrist deep in the loaves of bread. He did not look at Grace for an answer.

'Just circumstance. There's many a fellow finding themselves far from home at the minute.' Grace watched the soldier raise his head.

'Very true. Sadly, I for one will be re-joining them shortly. Took a nasty scratch from a grenade and got treated to a few weeks leave. No doubt I'll be back in the thick of it soon enough.' He took a bite of a bun. His stuffed mouth did not stop him from talking. 'Do you have anyone over there? Maybe I could pass a message on when I return? Can't promise it'll get there though.' The soldier let out a short giggle. His large Adam's apple slid up and down his throat.

'No, I'm afraid I don't know anybody who's out there. From what I gather the boys back home have managed to avoid conscription so far.'

'Doesn't stop the volunteers though. But I suppose if you don't know anyone out there from home, you should count yourself lucky. I hear most of the Irish divisions have been near enough wiped out. Bloody good soldiers I must say, but there are only so many battles you can take before the enemy gets the better of you.' The soldier nodded as he bit into a fresh bun and walked on to the next stall.

Grace felt a cold shiver up her spine. She began to worry for Michael. Cara had never offered her word of him, and Grace wondered if it was to protect her from any bad news. Maybe Cara knew something that she could not bare to have her sister suffer? There were few telephones that crossed the waters from England to Ireland and Grace was sure a small village such as Bourneville would have no need for one. She wondered whether it would be worth writing to her sister and asking her directly. No doubt she could still mask any bad news in writing – sugar coating her account or even ignoring it entirely. Nevertheless, she would have asked the question at least. Stood watching the young men adorned by their doting partners, Grace realised how lost and alone she suddenly was.

After dinner Grace had to be honest.

'Mrs Brown, I need to get home.'

'My my, but you've only just arrived here. Bourneville isn't such a bad place is it? Have I already scared you off? Don't tell me Mrs Stokes gave you a mouthful after we thrashed her today? I'd be in a right mind to shove her French sticks right back up her fat oven if she has.' She gestured with a clenched fist.

'No, it's not that, honestly. This place seems wonderful it really does, and you've been too much, you really have. But this is not my home.' Grace looked out of the kitchen window.

'Quite right my dear… but *you're* not allowed to be where your heart is. Not according to your criminal record anyway.' Marian rummaged through her phonebook as Grace began to wash the dishes.

'I know, but then I'm not sure if he's there anyway. This damn war has shaken the world like a bloody dice; letting folk fall wherever their number came up. But I have to start my search somewhere.'

'Well there's no rush at the minute my dear. If he is out fighting then he won't be back until this darn thing is over. And if he didn't go, well he'll be waiting for you when you return.' She ran her wrinkled finger over a tired old page in a phonebook.

'But that's just it… like you said… I can't go back.' Grace jumped back from the sink. A small cut bled on her finger where she had sliced herself on a knife that had escaped her in the soapy water.

'Oh for God's sake.' Grace sucked her forefinger then examined the small cut.

'Now now, don't you worry about that. I'll take care of it for you.' Marian took Graces hand in hers. The other held a torn page from the phonebook.

Chapter 44

'Welcome back soldier.' The nurse busied herself at Michael's bedside.

His head was pounding and his chest felt like an anvil was resting on it. He tried to move but a long wire anchored him to the bed.

'Easy there young man, you're not fit for much at the minute. Just give your body what it's after and get some rest. You've been in a grand old battle by the looks of it.' The nurse was middle-aged, her face worn and the early signs of greying tinted her tightly pulled hair.

'Where am I?' Michael felt the anvil hit his chest again.

'You're in a field hospital, and you have Lewisohn and Robertson to thank for your recovery.' The nurse tucked Michael in, she smelt like humbugs.

'Are they the soldiers that carried me in?' Michael could not remember much after he fell in Ginchy. He did not feel like he had recovered at all. Surrounding him, doctors flocked around beds that filled the tent. New soldiers filled the beds as soon as they were emptied.

'No, not at all. You can't expect me to make a note of the thousands of men that pass through here. No, Lewisohn and Robertson are two of the finest doctors around. It was these two that discovered the best means to get that needle into your arm there.' The nurse nodded towards a small needle that was in Michael's forearm. It was connected to a large rubber bung that plugged a conical flask. The delivery tube passed through and sat within the blood that filled the glass container. A side tube held a rubber bellows with a cannula that formed an air lock to the apparatus.

'Is that my blood?' Michael's eyes opened wide at the sight of the flask.

'Nope. Wrong again. Oh my, we aren't sending the brightest boys out to fight now are we?' She had a sense of jest in her voice. 'That right there is a kind donor's blood that your body is greedily devouring. You see…' She adopted the tone of a teacher. '…While Dr Lewisohn found a safe concentration at which citrated blood can be transferred – using sodium to prevent clotting I think – it was Dr Robertson who thought of introducing its use into the army. If you ask me, I think it's the finest method amongst all this madness. Luckily this blood can even be stored for weeks if chilled properly. They use something called anticoagulants, but what they are, well even that escapes me.' The nurse smiled as she fluffed Michael's pillow.

'Easy there nurse. He won't understand a word you're saying.' Oscar entered the tent from the opposite side from where the nurse stood. 'Talk like that will have him think that he's been captured by the tongue twisted Hun.' Michael's bed was near the entrance to the field hospital, and the large tent doors had been opened to shine some light into the makeshift ward.

'Oscar my pal, how did all this happen? I don't recall much after leaving that barn.'

'You collapsed Mike. It gave me one hell of a fright; you were in a right state. I blame the training. Somebody should have told you not to get shot. It's not good for your health you know?' Oscar patted Michael's arm.

'He's not wrong,' said the nurse staring at Michael like a disappointed head mistress. 'The fact is most of our donors have an O blood type. Usually, just in case, we do a small sample to check how your body reacts to the blood before doing a full transfusion. But I'm afraid you had quite a reaction to it. So, we ran some tests and I'm not sure if you're aware but you have a very rare blood type. It's a CO type and not always compatible with what the docs call the 'universal' type. So your tubby friend is quite right... you shouldn't have gotten yourself shot.'

'A little late for that, but I'll keep it in mind.' Michael looked at the transfusion needle in his arm.

'But he's going to be alright isn't he nurse?' Oscar made a note of her insult and decided he would come back to it later.

'Yes. Fortunately, his type is rare but not impossible to find.' The nurse turned her forearm towards Michael. A large bruise surrounded a tiny pin prick below her elbow joint.

'So that's why you look like death warmed up.' Oscar smiled at how quick he had struck back.

'Shut it Oscar,' said Michael. 'Nurse, for what it's worth... thank you. It seems you top those two docs on the 'saving my life' list.' He tried a laugh but his chest ached.

'All in a day's work my dear. But you were touch and go; for a while we did it directly – with me sat by your side and one tube leading from my arm to yours. But soon my hands were needed elsewhere so I made a few donations after my shift finished. And to think all I got for it was a biscuit.' The nurse placed her hand on Michael's. He took hold of her warm fingers.

'You've got my eternal thanks also.' Michael managed a smile.

'I bet you guys didn't have much trouble finding a vein, the way he was brought in? His chest all open like that, I guess you were spoilt for choice.' Oscar remembered the pools of blood that bathed his friend as he lay fighting for life on the stretcher. He had scrubbed his hands a hundred times and still he could feel the blood pumping through his fingers as they had pressed against Michael's chest.

'On the contrary tubs,' said the nurse tallying up her score as two to one. 'His body was collapsed. During the surgery, we left his arm in a bath of hot water. We knew he'd need a whole lot of blood, and had no time to waste looking for a vein. The water brought one up to the surface straight away. It's the media basilica if you must know.'

'Smart arse,' whispered Oscar.

Having flashbacks from the tricks he used to play on Oscar when they were young, Michael remembered the results of leaving his friend's greedy little hands in a bowl of water as he slept. He looked down at his lap as he spoke to the nurse.

'With my hand in that water, I didn't – you know – did I?' Michael flashed his eyes from his lap to the nurse.

'What? Wet yourself? No don't worry... your little soldier stayed dry in his barracks I promise. Anyway, what with being shot and all, that's the least of your worries. You Irish boys must have a guardian angel or something, because the way that bullet passed through your body,

I still can't see how it missed you're major organs. Granted it's left its mark in your left shoulder muscle, but that's it.'

'But he shot me point blank in the chest. How did he miss?' Michael remembered the soldier's face as he squeezed the trigger.

'Beats me… but let's hope they all have an aim like his. We'll be done with the lot of them in no time.' The nurse winked as she left Michael's bedside. Despite saving his life she cared not for sharing names; simply moving on to help the next soldier in need. Sadly, most that greeted her were far beyond it.

'Well that's you done for now. No more trench food for you Mike, you lucky swine.' Oscar stood directly in front of the tent entrance. Michael had to squint as the sunlight bounced over his friend's shoulders. Stretcher bearers streamed in and out of the entrance.

'What? I'll be right as rain in no time, I won't quit.' Michael tried to sit up.

'Don't be daft. If I had a ticket out of this shit tip I'd take it. You were a hero back there Mike, *and* you survived it all. Only a fool would want to go back.' Oscar knew his stubborn friend would not want to return without seeing the whole war out.

'And why would I want to go back Oscar? Tell me that. There's sod all left for me. You saw young Josh. He came here to get away, not so he could go back to that damn place. There's nothing left for me there. At least here I have something to fight for.' His mouth felt dry.

'And what would that be? Everyman out there is fighting for something… most are doing it so they can go home. If you reckon you don't want to, then you didn't deserve that bullet Mike. For Christ's sake, it sounds like you would have rather it killed you. Is that why you've been writing those letters? Are you too much of a coward that you would rather die in some white light over here than face rejection from that girl on your return? Is that it? Damn it Michael, she left you. She had the choice, and she left you. What good would dying do you? Go home. Because going back out there is a pointless suicide.'

'You're right.' Michael thought of his cowardly father. 'I guess I don't have a choice do I?'

'Amen to that.' Oscar smiled as the bodies continued to flow in behind him.

❃❃❃

It took Michael nearly a week to get back to Orplow. After a series of boat and train journeys, the last had left him on the platform at his home station. There was no heroes welcome, no banners to greet his return and nobody waiting for him. The platform was bare of familiar faces. Michael lugged his bag onto his good shoulder and headed for home. His left arm was wrapped in a sling – although Michael could not really see what good it did his shoulder. The doctors had prescribed him enough painkillers to slay a rhino, but Michael had refused to take any. His reasoning was that if he could not feel his arm then he would have no idea if he was doing anything wrong with it. Pain was a precursor to a problem. Removing it only stopped the warning.

The evening was warm beneath a cover of clouds. The air was close and muggy. Within it, the sun shone sorrowfully and the skies were preparing for the night. Birds chirped in the trees bidding farewell to the day, as the familiar fields sat slumped and untouched by any breeze. A small trail of sweat trickled down Michael's back. He felt it gather at the base of his spine; the salty liquid soaking into his shirt.

Looking out over the farmyards and fields, Michael felt uneasy. He felt as though he had returned home having failed to make a life for himself away from it all. He had never imagined returning from the war, believing that he had seen his home for the last time. Stood before it all once more, Michael felt unworthy.

The roads were in need of repair, and Michael almost twisted his ankle completely off as he hobbled up the stony boulevards. The crops in the fields looked drab and withered. Several deer pranced by, their slim stomachs folded tightly over their brittle bones. The bushes were bare of any berries and even the evergreens looked drained of colour. As the sun passed finally over the land, a final stream of orange light hugged the meadows and offered one last warm embrace.

It was the dead of night by the time Michael reached his cottage. Both his shoulders screamed and the balls of his feet throbbed. Despite the darkness, Michael had no problem in finding his way home. Opening the front door, he entered enough to drop his bags to the floor before shutting it again in front of him. The sight of the door alone was enough to bring back a shower of memories, each poisoned by the pain of loss. Michael knew he was not ready to face the rain just yet, and so he decided to visit an old friend.

David was still up when Michael arrived at the Irwin household. Seeing the soldier walking towards the house, he had shouted for his wife and ran out to meet him. The two men embraced; Michael bit his lip to stem the pain in his shoulder. David stood back and slapped Michael on the tops of his arms before looking sheepish as he saw the sling.

'Michael I'm so sorry,' said David.

'Don't worry. I've felt worse.' Michael smiled. His eyes were heavy and his smile lacked its usual sparkle.

'I'm sure you have my friend. Come in, we'll have a drink. I can't believe you didn't tell us you were coming back. We would have made preparations.' David guided Michael into his house.

'You know me David, not one for a fuss. Just seeing you in good health is enough for me.' Michael led the way inside.

'Well, that's more than I can say for you. Are you alright? Maybe you should get some rest.' David saw how wearily Michael walked.

'I'm just drained from the journey David, honestly. There's plenty of time for me to rest tomorrow. Did you get my letters?' Michael looked about the house as if he expected to see them all laid out on a table.

'Depends how many you sent. We have quite a few though. I've not read the parts that aren't meant for me, I promise.' David walked to his small drinks cabinet. A large bottle of brandy rested under an inch of dust.

'I bet your Cara has.' Michael's smile regained its magic.

'Well, I couldn't really say Mike. You have to admit, there's an air of mystery to it all. Women like that.' David pulled open the bottle and carried it to the table. He was already holding two small tumblers.

'David, don't worry. I sort of hope she has. Does she know the purpose of them?' David nodded. 'Good. They seem pointless now though. Now that I'm back, I mean. Maybe they won't be put to any use at all.' Michael raised his glass and took a sip.

'So, do you want me to destroy them? Or give you them back?' David followed suit and took a drink from his tumbler.

'No. Keep hold of them. I still doubt I'd be able to allow myself to tell Grace how I feel. The woman's married. Who am I to break that up?'

'Do you really believe that?' David took another drink.

'Well she is isn't she?' Michael rolled the base of his tumbler on the table.

'Lord knows. Apart from the scraps she sends in telegrams, we've hardly heard word from her for nigh on two years. Last we know she was up at the Farrington estate planning some trip to Dublin. Then the whole place goes crazy with the uprising and all.' David spoke as if Michael had been away for few days and not years.

'The what?' Michael drained his glass.

'Of course, forgive me. There's plenty of news to fill you in on my friend. Get yourself comfortable while I fill your glass. Mike…' David turned and looked at his friend. 'It's good to have you back.' David poured a large measure into both glasses.

Having had David fill him in on the recent events, Michael's head was swimming. Maybe it was the brandy or maybe the overload of information that had left him a little lightheaded, but Michael felt different. His tired legs were ready to roam once more and, after bidding his friend goodnight, Michael got lost among the meadows. While his feet knew where they stood, Michael's head did not. Despite David's thorough update, he did not know exactly what the extent of the matters in Ireland amounted to. But he did know they were serious. David rarely bothered himself with trivial matters and he had seemed well versed on the situation. Stuck in the centre of the war, Michael could not believe how little he knew of it compared to David. But then, the spectator does get to see more of the match than the player. For Michael, it was all too much to absorb in one sitting, especially as most of his brain had already soaked up the brandy like a sponge. As a child he had never worried about matters outside of his hometown, but now all that he cared for was no longer at home.

Walking on, his feet felt their way along the known nooks and ditches of the meadows. The shadow of the midnight wind comforted Michael as he walked through the dark valleys that guarded the countryside. The heat of the night stirred the sweet scents of the few remaining flowers, igniting the tired soldier's senses. Reaching the great lake – where waters shimmered beneath the moonlight – Michael decided to wait for the dawn.

For hours he cast his eyes across the waters. Motionless, he sat and watched the small ripples that weakened as they spread further from the reeds. He thought of those lost on foreign fields, too far from home. The few clouds overhead cried small teardrops that pattered on the surface of the lake. The rain fell onto Michael's body, soothing his tense skin. For no reason other than to find reason itself, he started to measure the meaning in his return. Grace was not here and was most probably happy in the choices she had made. As for himself, well he had no family to care for and even his best friend was still out fighting for the luxury of one day returning to a place where Michael could find no purpose to be.

Despite leaving, Michael found it hard to escape the war. The faces of the men he had killed had begun to fill every shadow that he saw. He saw the moment death claimed them; the moment that the light left their frightened eyes. Shaken by the shadows of his memories, Michael washed his hands in the lake. The water looked dirty in his palms, as the white light of the moon remained on the lake, brightening the waters that fell from his dark hands. Michael thought of the families he had torn apart – of the histories he had altered. They had all been damned by fate, and had died for a purpose they deemed worth fighting for. With no real reason to fight at all, Michael wondered why he had survived. Foreign to his fate, he pondered whether everything did happen for a reason – whether every pattern had already been woven by God's hand. Michael concluded that with no reason to his life, he had nothing to die for.

As the new light of day broke upon the dark waters, Michael stood and walked to the one place he hoped could save him.

Chapter 45

'Sweet Jesus,' said Marian as she slammed down the phone. The phone lines were only connected to surrounding villages, and she had near enough called everyone who was in a one mile radius to one.

'No joy?' Grace had become used to the rejection by now. It had so far been over a year of trying.

'Do not despair my child, we'll get you home eventually. Given our approach though, it might be in our favour to wait for this war to be over with.' Marian thumbed her phonebook. She had torn most of the pages out and had scribbled thick lines across the names that had refused to help. Unbeknown to them, many had removed themselves from Marian Brown's illustrious Christmas card list.

'How many more names do we have left?' Grace hated putting pressure on her hostess.

'Oh don't you worry about that. The bitter beauty of this war is that the list keeps on growing. We'll strike lucky soon.' Marian paused for breath and decided she needed a cup of tea.

Grace joined her for a drink. Her body had begun to relax. For the first few months she had been so tense; forever poised at the prospect that she could be going home at any minute. Time, however, had forced her to wait. She thought it best not to alert anyone in Ireland to her proposed return as it was far from lawful, and she would hate herself if a loved one paid a price for her acts. Moreover, even the means of the return was illegal, let alone the fact that she had been exiled. Given the grim circumstances that would bring success, Grace had wished she would find what she needed, but had refused to pray for it. The list of war widows was ever growing, and Marian wanted to find one that would be willing to sell their passport. Tied to the lives they built and the families they had formed, it was unlikely that any widow would have a mind to travel. However, many refused to sell them, feeling it was immoral and would be seeking reward in letting go of something that bore the family name of their husband. Initially, Marian had tried her friends who had lost their husbands in the Boer war, as they had grown accustom to their loss. However, Grace questioned the likelihood of her passing for an elderly Englishwoman and, therefore, it was agreed that the donor would have to be someone of a similar age; an age that was finding death to be a fresh figure within the family.

'Give it time.' This was becoming Marian's catchphrase.

'I will,' said Grace unable to hide her pessimism. 'I just feel awful waiting on some poor soul to lose their life so that I have the chance to live the life I want.'

'Well don't.' Marian pushed a plate of biscuits towards her guest. 'Those young men out there would die anyway. It's not like we're loading the gun that kills them. Think of it as making a wine only from the berries that have fallen from the bush. We're not plucking them ourselves dear, nor tearing them off the branches before they are ripe. War kills people darling. God knows I'm aware of that. But – and I say this with no intention to soothe you – if I knew that my Charlie's death could help another then I would never hold that person responsible for my loss. That list will grow Grace, whether you want it to or not.' Marian nodded at the torn piece of paper on the table. Thick lines of lead striped it like the battered back of a zebra.

'Give it time.' Marian smiled.

'I will,' repeated Grace. She still felt awful. 'Let's see what tomorrow brings with it.'

***

The next day was the 11th of November 1918. At 6am the leaders of the war's armies met in Ferdinand Froch's carriage headquarters in Compiegne. They were set to change the world forever. Soon an armistice was signed that came into force five hours later, and on the 11th hour of the same day, all parties were ordered to stand down. Britain and her allies had claimed victory; the war was over. However, it was not in time to stop the death of Canadian soldier George Lawrence Price who was shot by a German sniper a mere two minutes before the ceasefire, but at least not a single shot was fired after. Together, soldiers dropped their arms and raised their hands in celebration. They had survived and would be returning home.

Michael was delighted to have heard from Oscar. The news was that the few remaining officers from the 16th Division were set to return home that evening, and Oscar's train was scheduled hours before the bells would ring for last orders in the local pub. Michael could not wait to drag his friend out for a drink. For almost a year now, the only alcohol to have passed his lips had been the sour communion wine served at church. Troubled and in search of answers, Michael had chosen to commit himself to the holy place – more for salvation than to offer worship. There, Father Daniel remained the chaplain. Old age had met him early and, but for the darker stains on his teeth, he looked the same as when Michael had first met him. Granted, time had allowed a few unruly hairs to sprout from small boils on his neck, but other than that Father Daniel remained the rosy nosed priest Michael had always remembered him to be.

Sat in the stalls, Michael twirled the small crucifix that swung from his bracelet. Oscar's train was due shortly, and there was still time for one final prayer. Not sticking to the conventional forms, Michael offered his own words to the heavens. His troubles were his alone, and so he failed to find the words in any parable or psalm to address them.

'Here again I see.' Father Daniel was collecting the small song books from the edges of the stalls. 'Making quite a second home of this place aren't we? I might have to up the rent a little.'

'Isn't my life enough,' said Michael with a cheeky smile. The priest knew there was a slight mockery in his words.

'We don't ask anyone to do that Michael. We're here as a guide to God's will, that's all. The fact that people commit themselves totally is usually because of something they lack, or seek. Loyalty to the church is not often selfless I'm afraid.'

'But isn't that what faith is all about; reward?' Michael liked to challenge his priest.

'Sacrifices are repaid if that's what you mean?' The priest smiled and continued on his miniature mission of rounding up the songbooks.

'And what if the sacrifice is death, father? There's no offer of life is there? For those lost I mean.' Michael saw the dying faces of his enemies.

'Is eternal life not enough?' The priest grinned. Touché to him he thought.

'Only for those that get it. To me, it's all circumstantial. What about those who die at war? Surely they had no belief they could survive it… so is that not deemed suicide? And we know all too well how *they* don't get rewarded at all.' Michael thought of his cowardly father. He began to miss his mother.

'But you survived it Michael. Did you not think you would? Just because the odds are stacked against you, doesn't mean there is no hope. After all, why do you believe religion is so often called faith? We must have it always if nothing else.'

'They didn't die for their religion father. They died for their lives, for selfish reasons regardless of whatever form they took. And true, many died for others but those *others* were faceless leaders who could not run a bath let alone a battle.' His own anger surprised him. 'These men, who you say will be rewarded, died to gain a land only others wanted – regardless how stained by blood it may be.'

'You shouldn't separate religion from life Michael. Rest assured, the greedy that you so bitterly condemn will be judged when their time comes. However, towards those that die for their own reasons, well we – the church – don't encourage these people to die as much as we encourage them to fight for what they believe in. Out there, people fought for the life they loved. If religion was part of that, then they shall be rewarded.'

'And what about those that killed them?' Michael's face was full of guilt. His skin crackled under a nervous breeze that swam down his spine. The priest sensed the young man's plight. Still shy of twenty-five, the man looked as if he carried the worries of thousand lifetimes upon his shoulders.

'Michael, mankind is its own monster. The horrors it invents and the troubles it makes for itself are not the Lord's plan. But they are part of our makeup. If we are designed in his image, then he gave us the choice to act in our own interests. So often, like many find in times of war, *that* choice has been removed.'

'But father, I've killed. No amount of confession can clean my hands of that. So, should I not die for my sins? An eye for an eye seems fair.'

'If that were the case Michael, then we would all be blind. The importance is that you now see the light. And sometimes it takes the darkness to set in before people see the light. The Lord will forgive you Michael.'

'Well I won't.' Michael clutched his crucifix. 'Goodnight father.' He stood to his feet and nodded. Making the sign of the cross, he made his way down the aisle, not pausing as he passed the holy font. He did not want his fingers to taint the water.

Maik and Margaret Sterrin were stood at the platform. The train was running a little late, luckily giving Michael enough time to sprint down from the church. He apologised as he stood panting next to the nervous parents.

'I'm sorry Maggie.' Michael felt too old to keep addressing her as Mrs Sterrin.

'Oh don't be daft. You're here, that's the important thing.' Maggie had a small basket in her arms. Like a pelican's bill brimming with food, the lid was lifted by the many cakes and sandwiches that filled it to the brink of bursting.

'As she said Mike, at least you're here. And, hopefully soon, so will our son be.' Maik took a short nip on his steel flask. Michael smelt the scent of cheap whiskey in the breeze.

Anxious and excited, the three of them stood at the side of the tired railway; the tracks had begun to rust beneath the fallen rotting leaves. Like the few remaining scattered leaves of autumn, only a few other families shared the platform. Michael did not fail to see the sharp contrast to the heroic parade and send off that they enjoyed on their way to war. Gone were the banners and lines of well-wishers, replaced by a handful of close family – all terrified of what might return. None of them dared say it, but the families were nervous. Having heard of the atrocities that men had met on the frontline, many of them feared that a stranger would return home in place of their son. Whether they had been altered physically or mentally by the war, every man had been dented by it. With the train pulling into the station, it was now Margaret and Maik Sterrin's turn to see how damaged their most cherished possession had become.

'There he is.' Michael shouted as he saw Oscar step down onto the platform. Weighted by all his kit upon his back, Oscar barely made it across the gap between the platform and the train. Watching him, Michael wanted to run over and greet his friend but dared not steal Margaret's thunder. Instead he placed himself just behind the women who stormed forward.

'Oscar.' Maggie yelled at the top of her voice. She waved wildly with one hand before returning it quickly to the handle of the heavy basket. Maik took another swig from his flask. His shaking hand settled with the drink. Seeing his welcoming party, Oscar's face was torn by the widest smile. Dropping his bags he sprinted over to his parents and embraced them with such force he almost lifted them both clean from the ground.

'Look at my boy! He's so darn strong.' Margaret smiled and handed him the basket. She patted him down affectionately, hiding the fact she was stock checking his limbs. He felt like he was in one piece.

'You look great son. Have you lost weight?' In the absence of finding the right words to say, Maik thought that a lazy compliment was best.

'Nah, the green uniform is slimming that's all,' said Michael with a laugh.

'How would you know? You weren't bloody in it long enough!' Oscar laughed, hoping to gain the upper hand.

'What can I say; bullet holes don't make good accessories.' Michael walked forward and hugged his friend. Holding him at arm's length, he pulled him in for one more. Margaret and Maik joined in. They could all feel the heat of Oscar's embarrassment as his red cheeks flared up.

'Come on, it's just me. Get a grip people.' Oscar had an eye on the sandwich basket. Despite the bear hug his mother had locked on, he had still managed to swipe one and was now stuffing it in his mouth.

'I bet you've missed your mom's cooking son?' Margaret had worried about his diet the whole time he had been gone.

'Are you joking? Of course I did. Just one of your stews is worth more than a thousand portions of the tripe they were serving out there. To be honest, it was the thought of your cooking that helped me drift off to sleep at night.'

'Not me though,' said Michael. 'His growling stomach was louder than the bloody shells sometimes.' Michael jabbed Oscar in the arm.

'Well, you'll be glad to know that I've got a meal sorted for you back home. I can put it on the pot if you like. I guess you'll want to head out for a while.' Margaret had seen how polished Michael's shoes were. He had even worn his hair in his most handsome fashion.

'Are you sure? I wouldn't want to seem ungrateful.' Truth was Oscar was completely parched and could not wait to down his first Guinness.

'Of course I'm sure. Go and get yourself well and truly tanked up. God knows you deserve it.' Margaret opened the lid of the basket and handed the men some sandwiches. Michael gave her a soft kiss on the cheek for payment.

'Are you joining us Maik?' Michael thought he must have nearly emptied his flask by now.

'What? Me? Nah boys, you go on ahead without me.' He took a gulp on his flask. 'Son, I'll be at home waiting with your mother for when you get back. I'm so pleased to have you home boy.' Maik was almost emotional. Michael could not recall the last time he had seen him so caught up in the moment.

'That'll be grand, father. Well, get your questions ready as I'll answer them all gladly in the morning. When I get my strength back that is.' Oscar helped his father with the bags he had dropped.

'Will you bollocks. You won't be fit for shaking after he's finished with you.' Maik nodded towards Michael, and gave his son a tender smile as he heaved the bags onto his thin back.

'Come on then soldier. You've heard your orders; we're on a mission tonight.' Michael placed his hand onto Oscar's shoulder. 'There's a bar full of glorious black gold just ready for the taking.'

'Good, because I've got a thirst on that would shame a camel.' The boys laughed together.

Oscar kissed his family before marching into town with his best friend. They stood and watched their boy proudly; he was in one piece – for the meantime at least.

At the pub, Oscar sat at the nearest table to the door. The Spread Eagle was half full and, though most were locals, years sat in the trenches had taught Oscar to stay facing his enemy at all times. He could not bear to have anyone behind him. The mere thought of it made him flinch violently. Scanning the room, he saw Michael return from the bar with two pints laden with Guinness.

'Home sweet home,' said Oscar as he raised his glass. His taste buds exploded on impact with the drink.

'Glad to be back?' Michael drank the thick frothy head first. A small moustache of foam lined his lip.

'What's not to like? Granted this place has its faults, but at least we're not getting shot at all day.' Oscar gulped his Guinness. 'Having visited hell Mike, this place is as close to heaven as we've been.'

'Maybe.' Michael thought of Grace's naked body, but quickly took a drink to drown the memory. 'Sorry about the small welcome back pal. Not quite the parade you had in mind, I bet?'

'I didn't go out there for glory Michael.' Oscar lied. 'Returning is enough reward for me.'

'True, many would kill to be where we are right now.'

'Many *did* Mike, they just didn't get the rub of the green like us. Look here, the war's over for all of us now. Let's start trying to forget it.' Oscar raised his glass. 'To us.'

'To us.' Michael completed the toast.

'To tell the truth – I thought you would have at least laid on a lady for me tonight. Surely you've not been short of admirers since your return. I mean, the market's certainly opened up a little recently.' Oscar new his joke was in bad taste.

'Fear not you horny shit. The night's still young my friend. But I must warn you, we're not the most popular of people at the minute.'

'What? Two strapping young men like us? Nonsense.'

'I mean soldiers. Not all the public have taken to us.'

'Yeah I know. I caught wind of it on the way back; men getting pelted with turnips instead of flowers as they arrived home. It's not right Mike. It's not right at all. For instance, soon after you left, we started to see little signs out on the fields. The pesky Germans had decided to place boards on no man's land declaring *'The British are killing your people'*, and *'You fight for an army that is murdering your family'*. We had no idea what they were talking about, simply putting it down to bullshit mind-games. Turns out there were real bits of corn in the shit they were feeding us.'

'I know. I spoke to David about it all. Turns out, the nationalists have been staging uprisings all over Ireland. So much so that the British army had to assist the police in calming it all down. By the sounds of it, it was a bloody mess. And with it came casualties – most of them innocent to it all. After tonight, if I were you, I'd think about putting that uniform away for good.'

The eyes that stared at Oscar began to make sense. At first he thought they belonged to tired drunks who glared at the terrible hand life had dealt them. Now he knew he had given them a channel for their hatred – an ace card for them all to unite against. One young joker caught his eye. A fresh puddle of ale was drying on his shirt.

'What you looking at?' The man slurred and stood from his stool. His large green eyes swivelled in their small sockets.

'Are you looking at me pal?' Oscar looked from Michael to the man.

'Yeah, I'm looking at you. You piece of scum.' The man took two staggered steps towards Oscar's table and spat on the floor. Michael began to stand but Oscar took his arm.

'So, what's the problem? Apart from the fact you're talking out your arse that is. I mean, I'm still trying to work out if that's spit or shit that stains your shirt.'

'Me? I'm talking arse?' The man came closer. 'Well at least I've not got my lips planted on the British army's arse, you fucking prostitute.' He spat the final word out as if his tongue couldn't stand the taste of it.

'Apologise now.' Michael's voice was rattled.

'Alright, alright. I'm sorry. I apologise; I do the whores a disservice. You see, the difference is… between you and the whores I mean… is that you get paid while it's the rest of us at home that gets royally fucked.'

'Sit down and shut up.' Oscar stood from his table.

'Make me.' The man began to clench his fists. He waved them in front of his face like a cat toying with a ball of wool.

'Behave.' Michael's voice was louder than he expected.

'Me behave? It aint me that's been misbehavin' mate. Tell your bitch here that he's a dirty traitor.' Spittle flew from his lip. 'Those nationalists that got shot in Dublin, they're the real martyrs to the cause. His kind, well they're just bloody bitches to the British army, aren't they?' His feet shuffled from side to side.

'Look here.' Oscar got the man's attention. 'I don't know where you get off playing some kind of weekend warrior with me, maybe it's the beer muscles or something, but I'd close that trap before you force me to do it for you.' Oscar stepped closer to his foe. 'My friend and I didn't spend years with our faces towards the fire to come back and get our names burnt by no-marks like you. So take my advice. Find the rock you crawled out from under, pick it up, and use it to bash a bit of sense into that shit bucket you use as a skull.'

'Oh, so you're friend is a soldier as well is he? No wonder you're being the brave boy tonight. Well he gets added to my list of local traitors too.' The man pretended to lick an imaginary pencil and write on an invisible pad he held in his swaying hand. 'And what would your name be sir?'

'Michael.'

'Mr Michael?' The drunk look bemused.

'Michael Alpin.'

'Alpin? Really? Well, I see you're not wearing your uniform tonight *Mr Alpin*. Clearly not as brave as your friend here. But then cowardice runs in the family doesn't it?'

'Look here you prick. We're all nationalists, and Catholic's to boot. We're on the same bloody side. *We* just chose a different fight that's all. So let's not chose another tonight.' For the sake of avoiding bloodshed, Michael was willing to ignore the insult about his father.

'And what if I want to? Fight that is.' He dropped his invisible pencil and clenched his fists.

'Then you'll lose.'

The man had hardly begun to swing his arm before Michael's knuckles crashed into the side of his skull. His brain rattled inside his head like a wasp on heat. The punch was so hard; the guy was knocked out well before his feet had even begun to leave the ground. The sound of Michael and Oscar's scampering feet were muffled by the sound of the table breaking under the man's tumbling body.

Oscar was home, and already the young men were in trouble.

Chapter 46

Fate sometimes leaves itself to chance. When two independent acts share the same impeccable timing, the fate of an entire nation can be sealed. Following the 1918 landslide in the General Election, wherein Sinn Fein claimed seventy per cent of the Irish seats, they pledged not to sit in Westminster and so set up their own Irish parliament. Known as the First Dail, they held a meeting on 21th January 1919 at Mansion House where they issued the Declaration of Independence to – what they called – the free nations of the world. They publicly announced that, though the Great War was done, there was still an 'existing state of war, between Ireland and England'. Although not an aggressive declaration, merely opting to ignore the parliament of the United Kingdom while establishing their own, the members of the First Dail were to find that fate was a conniving and canny mistress. When Sean Treacy and Dan Breen, members of the re-badged Irish Republican Army, took it upon themselves to shoot and murder two officers of the Royal Irish Constabulary an aggressive stance was interpreted by the British government. With tactical interpretation on the agenda, the acts of Treacy and Breen were tied into the First Dail's declaration. Soon, the War of Independence had begun.

Properties belonging to the British government were targeted, while prominent members of the British administration were tracked down and killed. As Director of Intelligence for the IRA, Michael Collins established an effective network of moles to unearth members of the Dublin Metropolitan Police's 'G' Division. A small but relentless group, the 'G' Division threatened the republican movement by identifying volunteers who would usually escape the radar of the British soldiers and the Royal Irish Constabulary. Political sabotage was rife on both sides; Ireland was shrouded by the war's cloak, and bleeding from its dagger.

So far untouched by the hands of the war, Orplow was not without its devious predators. Having proven she could be allowed some freedom from the nest, Imogen had begun to take strolls in the forests that neighboured the sanctuary of her family estate. For the last few months, Fiona had granted her daughter one afternoon each week to herself. Accustom to the routine of daily life, Imogen had at first found her new freedom unsettling – not knowing exactly what to do or even what was expected of her. While housed in the innocent frame of such a sweet young girl, her mind still remained in a childlike state. Schooled at home and never more than two rooms away from her mother, Imogen was not accustomed to time alone. For the first few afternoons she had spent alone she chose to remain within the confines of her gardens. However, with time her confidence began to blossom, and by the season of spring the bright wildflowers that adorned the small forest drew her away from her nest. For hours she would wander through the trees enjoying the soft scents of the flowers, often stopping to pick a few for her ever-grateful mother.

Today, it was the bulging fruit of a blackberry bush that had snatched her attention. Her long fine hair flowed down her back – the ends kinked by the gentle rain that was falling. Around her, fresh water weighted the tips of the grass, bending each blade towards the dampened ground. The softer berries burst inside Imogen's small hands as she squeezed them from their branches. Dark juices inked her fingertips. With no hint of sexual suggestion, she licked her fingers. However, small stains of sweetly scented purple remained. Enjoying the moment, Imogen smiled as the bittersweet taste touched her tongue.

Hidden by a large oak tree, Imogen's admirer waited. He watched as the young girl skipped from bush to bush, bursting berries as she passed. His groin throbbed and the ends of his fingers twitched with poisonous anticipation. Sliding his tongue across his broken and leathered lip, Connell stepped out from behind his hiding place. His heavy boots brushed through the wet grass silently. His old knees cracked as he stooped down beneath the level of the bushes and drew closer to his prey.

The beat of Imogen's heart paused as her soft, tender lips became covered by a soiled palm. The stench of dirt and sweat rose into her flared nostrils. Her legs froze with panic, before being completely taken from beneath her. The moist grass dampened her chest as she was pushed to the floor. Crawling, she began to cry as a crushing weight pinned her to the ground. Thick hands gripped her tiny waist and spun her onto her back. Facing her attacker, Imogen saw the devil's eyes staring back at her above a dark cloth that had been wrapped around his mouth and nose. Long strands of greasy hair were slapped flat against his thick brow. He pressed his hand against her mouth once more and held both her wrists with the other. Her arms were stretched above her head, and he was now wriggling his legs to get between her frozen thighs. The dead breath of her muted scream heated the dank palm of his hot hand. Releasing it from her mouth, he lifted his mask and spat into her eyes.

Then his body fell onto hers. His chest squashed her to the ground and he released his grip. Imogen turned her face away from her attacker as his head fell by the side of her slender neck; his lips just the length of a kiss away from her skin. Waiting for him to strike, the bite from his gnarled teeth never came. His breathing was slow.

'Come on,' a man's voice came from above the heavy body. Two hands grabbed the beast's shoulders and pulled it from off the young girl. Still frozen by fear Imogen saw her saviour. He held out his hand.

'Imogen, come quickly.' David kept his hand outstretched. The other held a large rock that had a small blooded stain on its base. He took hold of the young girl's hand and pulled her to her feet. Her knees gave in a little and she stumbled forward. Her entire body had been drained by terror. Tossing the rock to the side, David bent down and picked her up. Her head nestled into his chest as she began to cry. Her tears soon added to the rain that had already dampened David's shirt. With her in his arms, he moved as quickly as he could through the trees, and towards his home.

Lying on the ground, with dirt dressing his crooked teeth, the beast rolled over. His chest heaved as he lay staring at the clouds that spat down on him. Though he had woken earlier and heard the voice of his attacker, he had remained completely still. Connell could feel the blood dripping from his crown. Drops of rain washed over the exposed flesh, biting into the wound like acid.

'English bastard,' snarled Connell. His poisoned mind began to plot his vengeance.

✳✳✳

Wrapped in a blanket and cupping a mug of tea, Imogen rocked in her chair.

'Cara, I thought it best to bring her back here. I don't know why, but I panicked.' David was still in shock.

'Don't worry my love. You did right by bringing her here. The main thing is that Imogen is safe. I don't want her anywhere near that monster. Who knows what he's capable of?' The thought of Connell beating Paco flashed in David's mind. He could still see his wife's slow descent to the ground.

'We'll need to get the police around. We can't let him get away with this.' David was trying to regain a little order to the chaos.

'Are you sure that's wise? I thought you said you may have caved his skull in? If that's true, then for all we know Connell could be dead. Regardless of the reason, the police won't ignore that David. So, let's just concentrate on getting Imogen safe first. Then we can face the music together.'

Cara was by her sister's side. She had not seen her for some time and was proud of the beautiful young girl she had grown into. The girl looked so delicate, like a wilted rose, as she rocked on her chair. Still spinning from the event, Imogen had not taken a single sip of her tea, preferring to warm her shaking hands around the cup.

'Imogen, everything is going to get better soon. Do you hear me? What happened today, none of it was your fault.' Cara rested her hand on Imogen's knee. She flinched violently.

'I'm sorry,' whispered Imogen.

'For what?' Cara mirrored her sister's tone.

'For that man. I didn't mean to hurt him. I can't remember it all. I saw his blood... he was hurt.' She closed her eyes to try to forget but all she could see was the monster's staring back at her.

'No, my love. He was going to hurt you, so don't ever be sorry for him. Beasts like that don't deserve your sympathy.' Cara looked at David. He was pacing the room.

'What was he going to do to me? He didn't want me to speak. I tried to scream but no sound came out.' Imogen was beginning to see the event. Her eyes were fixed on Connell's face. His eyes burned with a dark dingy fire.

'Don't worry about that. You're safe now, remember that. I'm here for you sister. I'll look after you.' Cara felt responsible. Someone should have been looking out for Imogen. She made a note to add a prayer of thanks for her David's afternoon stroll. If it were not for him, it may be Imogen's body and not Connell's that remained lost among the trees.

Running all the best courses of action to take through his head, David continued to pace from wall to wall. But time brought with it its own decision.

Within hours a crowd had gathered around the house. Massed together as if to flush out an ogre, the people heckled and jeered. Stones pelted the walls, crashing through the windows and spreading glass across the kitchen table. Inside, Imogen cradled herself – pulling her knees tightly into her chest. She heard the noise from outside, but could not make out what they were calling for. Nobody knocked the door. Instead they stood at the porch, waiting like hell's own carol singers. Many had wooden bats, some even iron bars. The others just had clenched fists and faces of fury. The man at the front held a large wooden plank that was pierced by a long rusty nail.

'Come out Englishman, we know you're in there.' Connell swung his weapon in the air. Jeers followed his cry.

Rocks began to thunder against the house. Imogen flinched at every thump. Cara was by her side.

'David what are we to do? You can't go out there.'

'I don't know my love. How the devil has he got a crowd together? I've got to tell them what he did. Maybe they'll turn on him?' David ran his hands through his hair. His head felt tense.

'But why would he be after you?' Cara put her arm around her shivering sister.

'Because I left him for dead. I'm the only witness to what he did today. He's just throwing the first punch, hoping to scare me off.' David placed his hands on the kitchen table. A small shard of glass dug into his fingers.

'David, call the police. Let them deal with him.'

'No. Will you call them for me? I'm going outside. If I don't, at this rate they'll have destroyed the place before anyone comes to help us.' David kissed his wife tenderly on the head and made for the door. She held his hand tightly until he was completely out of reach.

'There he is.' Connell spat on the floor. He stood at the front of the crowd, drenched by the pouring rain.

'Connell, what is it you want from me? Why are all these people at my house?' David remained dry beneath his porch.

'They're here for you David! Pinching a young girl from the woods like you did... doesn't rest well with us my friend. Give her back to us.' The water streamed down Connell's face, skipping over his butchered lip.

'To you? Never. And to all you lot as well...' said David casting his eyes over the crowd. '...I don't know what tale this creature has fed you but it's rotten, believe me.' David pointed his finger at Connell.

'What did I tell you?' Connell turned and opened his arms to his crowd. 'The coward won't even admit it, despite the fact that we *know* the young girl is inside.'

'She's inside with her sister you animal. Some bastard tried to rape her today.' David stepped down from the porch. He was face to face with Connell; their feet shared the same puddle. The crowd backed away, giving them room.

'We know what you are.' The rain flicked off Connell's split lip. 'We've been watching you since the first day you brought your pale English arse into this town.'

'What?' David could not grasp Connell's altered angle.

'We know David.' Connell's thick lips struggled to hold back a sinister smile. 'We've had spies in this country long before you were even a tadpole in your dead daddy's testicle. And we know how to sniff them out. You wreak my friend.'

'A spy? That's absurd. I know where an animal like you keeps his brains Connell. And you really are thinking like a prize prick right now.' David could see that the mob behind no longer cared for reason. Together they had found an enemy – regardless of the form he took.

'Yeah, a fucking spy! Tell me Mr Irwin, although you're English, why didn't you go off to war with everyone else? Now, many would say that you were a deserter or even a coward. But that's not it is it? No embarrassment came your way did it? Instead, you stayed here and kept an eye on this little town of ours didn't you? The government must have found it real handy to have one of their own in the thick of it – watching to see if this town gives in to the republicans. Tell me, how many names have you sold out?' Connell did not wait for an answer. The crowd cheered as he planted his thick fist into David's stomach.

Kneeling in the puddle, David saw Connell raise the wooden plank. He brought his arm across his face to protect himself as it came crashing down. He tried not to scream as the rusty nail punched through his forearm. Without pause, the steal toecaps of Connell's boot thumped into

David's chest. He collapsed into the muddy water, blood trickling from his arm.

'You see… we're peaceful people around here David.' Connell kicked him once more. 'We can't abide to the likes of you… coming here and stirring up trouble.' The third kick broke David's ribs.

'You're a monster.' David almost choked on the water from the puddle.

'Come now… is that all you have?' Connell grabbed David by the hair and dunked his face into the muddy water. He pulled his head up out of the puddle.

Cara had come out onto the porch. She screamed as she saw Connell crouched over her husband.

'Oh… look.' Connell raised David's head and faced him towards his crying wife. 'Your wife seems upset. It must hurt to find out that your husband is a snivelling coward.' Connell forced David's head under the puddle again. The brown water began to mix with the blood from his arm. David's tired hands pushed up on the ground, only to slip on the wet mud.

'Go inside princess. I don't think you could *stand* what I'm about to do here.' Connell fired his smile at Cara. She screamed for someone to help her husband, but nobody moved. They all stood stunned by what they were witnessing.

'Look at what you've done? You've upset your dear disabled wife.' Connell's lips were close to David's ear. 'Let that burn into your eyes for a minute. I want you to take that image with you.'

David felt the knife enter his back. His chest sagged as he felt the blade twist inside. A pure pain raged up his spine, like a crippling charge of electricity. Discreetly, Connell palmed the blade into the cuff of his jacket, hiding his act from the masses.

'Won't someone stop this beast? He tried to rape my sister!' Cara was crying. Her tears rivalled the rainfall. A figure stepped from the crowd and pulled Connell to his feet. The man was unknown to Cara — just a faceless figure from within a crowd of strangers. His body slumped to the ground as Connell instinctively crashed the back of his fist across the man's face. David felt the weight lift from him. He rolled out of the water and onto his back. His blood blended with the mud beneath him. Rummaging inside his trouser pocket, his fingers found what they searched for.

Connell stood over the fallen man. His thick fists clenched — hanging from his arms like wide slabs of meat.

'What are you doing you fool? I'll deal with you after I send this English bastard to his grave.' Connell turned to face David.

'I'll race you. there.' David's razor flashed across Connell's throat. He stood motionless for a second before the thin red line began to tear his neck apart. As the flesh parted, buckets of blood burst from the wound. Defeated, Connell dropped to his knees and thrust his hands around his own throat. The fresh blood flowed through his thick, clutching fingers. David stood by his side; his razor shimmering in the rain.

'David.' Cara called out to her husband. She could not see the wound that was already killing him. Next to David, Connell's body splashed into the muddy ground. His neck continued to drain his veins like a slashed bag of grain. Blood pumped from Connell's throat as his heart became cold and dry.

David stumbled over to his wife. The crowd behind him stood watching in complete silence. Sat beneath the porch, Cara held out her hands for David to take. The mud beneath him shifted, causing him to fall onto his knees. As the rain continued to pour down, David began to crawl. He reached the first step of the porch before he fell onto his chest. His legs were numb and his pulse could only ring out a dull muted note. The final beat of his heart skipped as he saw his wife for the last time. Her fingers were inches away from his.

David knew he would always miss her.

Chapter 47

Her husband never returned. She could still see how proud he had looked as he marched through the town, waved on by thousands of well-wishers. With only a few photographs and letters to remember him by, Janet Turner savoured every memory of her husband. For nearly two years she had ignored his absence, believing that one day he would return. Even the official letter that had declared his death in action did little to stem her hope. But the countless nights alone finally began to set in. The thousands of possibilities that she had pondered no longer convinced her. Her husband was dead, and he was never coming back.

Having received a phone call from the meddlesome Marian Brown, Janet agreed to meet her for lunch. The pretty widow sat across Marian's kitchen table as a young lady poured them all a fresh cup of tea.

'Janet, honestly… thank you so much for coming today.' Marian sounded quite business-like in her hospitality.

'That's quite alright, really. It's not like I had anything planned today. Sunday used to be stew night, but cooking a whole pot just for one these days seems a waste now.' Janet twiddled her fingers and smiled shyly.

'It's hard isn't it?' Marian locked her eyes onto Janet's. They were filled with sincerity. 'You must feel so alone in your loss, but you're not my dear. Sadly, there are so many women in your position, and we should stick together. And we should help one another.'

'I suppose.' Janet noticed the young lady with the teapot shift uneasily.

'Janet, this is my dearest friend Grace.' Marian opened her hand towards her lodger.

'How do you do Mrs Turner. I'm so sorry to hear of your loss.' Grace dropped her head a little as she spoke.

'And you're the one who wants the favour from me?' Janet looked from Grace to Marian.

'She is,' interrupted Marian. 'You see, while you and I have lost our loved ones, young Grace here has a chance of saving hers. All she needs is your help.'

'Why me?' Janet asked.

'Because you know what it's like to love someone. And sadly, you also know what it's like to lose them. You see, Grace here needs your help to get back to Ireland. We'll offer a handsome sum for your documents, and rest assured we'll cry forgery if caught. Nothing will come back on you.' Marian watched the young woman as she took a sip from her teacup. She wasn't thirsty, but wanted to bring a pause to the conversation.

'And that's all you wish for? My passport documents. Nothing more?'

'That's all she needs, other than your help that is. Just think if the roles were reversed, how much you too would hope that someone came to your aid.' Marian's eyes implored Janet to do the right thing.

'Very well, you can have them. Little good they'll do me anyway.' Janet could not help but see the delight that burst from Grace's teary eyes.

***

That night Marian had helped pack Grace's bags and escorted her to the nearest port. Stood on the docks she had chosen to hide within the many shadows that the cold night had brought with it. The calls of the seagulls were muffled by the sounds of preparation. The huge ship was being readied for boarding. Grace had already said her goodbyes in the car, and was nervous about making a scene near to any members of the crew. She wanted as little attention as possible, planning only to interact enough to show her documents and then step on-board. Fortunately, Janet was only a few years older than Grace and so she was comfortable that she would not have to try too hard to fool anyone. Nevertheless, she had revised Janet's date of birth religiously – so much so that it dangled so heavily on the tip of her tongue it threatened to leap off at the nearest hint of a question. Her false details tipped her tongue as her teeth tried to keep it bitten.

Butterflies began to do battle in her stomach as she drew closer to the front of the line. There were few individuals boarding the ship, and Grace was worried that she would begin to stand out. Her feet jittered a little while she had to stop her mind from racing ahead of her. The mere thought of going home both terrified and excited her at the same time. Above all the concerns, like a batch of fresh endorphins, she wanted to let her mind flood with thoughts of Michael and how she would feel when she saw him. However, she hesitated. Until she was aboard that ship, and safely on her way back home, Grace knew that every dream could still be taken from her. Not allowing herself to be in a position where she could lose everything that she loved, Grace tried her hardest not to think about it.

Her cold hands began to tremble. She was next in the queue and the boarding master was awaiting her documents. The papers shook slightly in her pinched fingers – the slight breeze helping to disguise her nerves.

'Very well madam. Have a nice trip.' The boarding master offered the same smile as he did to all the passengers. A polite *'let's get on with it'* coloured his wide, teeth clenched smile.

Wanting to turn and scream out her thanks to Marian until her lungs ached; Grace simply stooped her head, and walked on-board. Thoughts of Michael began to wash over her.

***

Among the public clamour and disputes, Ireland still had its secrets. Very little was made of the deaths of Connell Locran and David Irwin. The local papers reduced it to a heated argument that had simply boiled over, and so decided not to run a story at all. The police, on the other hand, busy with bigger issues and with nobody to arrest, saw no profit in an investigation. Politically, both parties were scared in case the story became national. The bloody battle between an Englishman and a republican was the last thing the nation needed right now, especially while the War of Independence raged on. Within their deaths, both sides would have gained another martyr and so with it a fresh piece of firewood with which to further stoke the flames of the conflict. So, with peace in mind, the police closed the case without putting pen to paper and the reporters saved the names of David and Connell for the obituary pages only.

The funerals themselves were also small affairs, reserved for friends and family only. However, there was no surprise which coffin had gathered the greater of the crowds. Despite Raegan ordering his staff to attend Connell's funeral, he still found himself standing alone as the slain body of his chief of staff was dropped into the ground. Raegan was growing visibly weaker by the day and the townspeople had openly reserved all their sorrow for David alone. Putting the bodies to rest, the town prayed that there would be peace within it.

In the long months that passed very little had changed; Cara never gave up mourning her husband, the staff continued to ignore Raegan's orders, and Michael added another prayer of regret to his ever growing rosary. The hands of time had pulled Michael to the church, and he used every minute to reflect on the decisions he had made so far. But never once did he pray for himself; he knew firmly that his fate lay far outside of the churches reach. Only he would decide the outcome.

Having seen the months turn into a year, the town still did not see any change. The high hills and valleys guarded them from the political pressures of the duelling regions nearby. Keeping a distance from the nation's troubles, the people of Orplow focused on matters much closer to home. Survival in its simplest definition was the key concern. The Darby Empire had begun to falter. Petulant and short-sighted, Raegan had chosen to severe his nose to spite his haggard face. Without Michael, the fields no longer thrived. The townspeople had written letters and often visited the estate to beg Raegan to employ Michael so that the fields would once again bear a fruitful harvest to feed the land.

However, Raegan had decided to do nothing. As his ageing body grew weaker and more dependent on others, he fired the majority of his staff and sat idle as his fields rotted around him. People still had the bounty of the market stalls and shops to gather their stock from, but without an income they no longer had the means to buy them. Like a possessive parent and so desperate for the town's affection, Raegan had made it completely dependent upon him. No longer interested in how he was perceived, Raegan abandoned his parental duties entirely.

Dipping a small cloth into the font, Michael dabbed the holy water upon the small silver pendant on his bracelet. The image of the Holy Mother shimmered as Michael scrubbed it. Looking back towards the altar, he saw the large crucifix that hung above it. He examined the statue of Christ that was nailed to the cross. Blood poured from his wrists and brow, and his ribs could be seen pressed up through his sunken chest. The man looked defeated. Often, Michael would lose himself as he stared into the statue's eyes. The look of sadness and sorrow that shone from them haunted him. Though his sacrifice was to be rejoiced and celebrated for an eternity, Christ hung to the cross with a look of pure loss and sadness. Michael knew that even the most selfless of acts came at a cost. Eternity had its price.

Flustered and with a look of despair, Father Daniel rushed into the church. His pace was no faster than a brisk walk, but there was huge effort and emphasis in his movement.

'Michael, thank God that I've found you here.' The old priest was out of breath.

'What is it Father? Are you alright?' Michael rested his hand on the priest's bent back.

'Me? Oh, I'm fine.' He took a sharp breath. 'I've just been called to issue a dying man his last rites. But the thing is; I was half way over there when I was informed of the strangest of requests. I went straight to your place first and when I couldn't find you, I thought you might be here.' The priest was regaining his breath.

'And what can I do for you?' Michael was puzzled.

'I have no idea. It's just that one of the man's last wishes was to speak with you, before it was too late. He said he could not have his last rites read to him before he had a chance to speak with you.' Father Daniel was straightening himself out. A bible was in his right hand.

'Bizarre. And who might this old chap be?'

The priest's expression was almost as peculiar as his answer.

***

A stillness gripped the building. The once buzzing corridors and chambers were now empty. Dust veiled the frames of the family portraits and priceless vases sat empty of any flowers. The home looked tired and unkempt. Most of the curtains had been drawn and only a small bead of light filtered through. The hallway was cold as a crypt and Michael could feel the hairs rise on his forearms. He had seen the estate in a thousand ways – each time decorated and bursting with life. For years he had pictured every room just how his mother had detailed them to him; he had seen the fine cutlery shimmering on the grand table, the host of parties that celebrated and advertised the family wealth. And he had seen the children, adorned by the pressures of their father, grow into adults dressed by dreams of breaking free of their roots. However, not once had his mother described the place as he now found it.

Up past the spiral staircase, upon an Edwardian four poster bed, Raegan Darby lay dying. The room was a little lighter than most. A single curtain had been opened, and the brilliant light from the crisp afternoon blazed like fire upon Raegan's bed. The seasons had begun to blend. Winter was ending and the land, on the cusp of spring, lay in eager anticipation. Most of the snow had thawed and the small amounts that remained were spiked by the greenest of grass. Above the land, the chilling winds fought back the sun that had regained its mighty glare.

A chain of colour rained through the glass of the window, shredding the sunlight into a string of reds, yellows and greens. Beneath the light, Raegan was as pale as ice.

Without a word, Fiona ushered Michael into the room. Imogen was being cared for by Cara, who remained downstairs. Michael thought how cruel Raegan's placement was. The bastard had decided to die upstairs, away from his daughter's reach. Maybe the coward feared she would strike him down before the reaper had chance to. Hating the man, Michael was stood in the darkness when Raegan spoke.

'Is that you Michael?' His voice was slurred. He spoke through the side of his mouth, as one side of his face hung lower than usual. Michael said nothing. Raegan began to cough.

'Tell me boy, is that you?' He spluttered.

'Yes.' Michael stood still.

'Good. I need to talk to you.'

'Is this about the fields? Why leave it so late? So many lives are already crushed.' Michael felt nothing of showing anger to a dying man.

'It's not. It shouldn't surprise you that I couldn't care less for those damned fields. One will bury me and that's the last I'll have to do with them.'

'Then what is it?'

'Tell me…' Raegan tried to move but his body relented. '…If you saw what you cherished more than anything, being possessed by something so undeserving, would you do anything to get it?' Raegan could not see Michael's face. Hidden in the shadows, Michael thought of Grace and Arnold. He knew he cherished her, but had no idea how undeserving Arnold was.

'It depends,' said Michael.

'On what, exactly?'

'Whether what I cherish is better off without me.'

'And what if it wasn't?' Raegan traced pain in Michael's tone.

'I could only offer them all that I am. I suppose, it then rests on them to decide what's best for them. Does all this have a point?' Michael rushed the man.

'It does. You see, the lion doesn't only roar to win his mate Michael – he does it to destroy any threats to his territory. In that sense, we're quite alike you and I.' Raegan forced a half-smile.

'I'm nothing like you.'

'Really? Did you not try to steal my daughter? That was hardly fair play now was it? You saw that she was with a suitor that night, a man whose feathers were brighter than yours, and still you tried to take her for yourself. You roared Michael, but... like me... you lost.'

'The moment we shared was enough for me.' Michael's voice was low.

'But not for her,' laughed Raegan. 'Know this Michael... you will never have my blessing for my daughter's hand. Not now, not ever.'

'Her hand has been out of your reach for some time now old man.'

'True, but nowhere near yours either.' Raegan's laugh descended into a fit of coughs.

'So that's it? You called me here to tell me something that I already know? You're not in a position to mock anyone you twisted old fool.'

'No. Patience Michael, that isn't it. I called you here to offer one thing; a single truth.' Raegan sounded his most serious.

'About what?' Michael's voice rose within the shadows.

'When Connell died last year, so too did the only man who knew of my darkest hour. An hour that has held me for every second of my life since. You see... like you... I once truly loved a girl. And it's not that awful baby maker stood outside.' Michael saw Raegan's eyes flash with fire as he stared into the hallway where his wife was standing.

After a second, he addressed the shadow once more.

'Michael, as a small child I was given everything by my parents – land, riches, all of which had once belonged to someone else. When my father planted the first seed from which our estate would grow, he told me of a farmer that lived on a plot of land that he had never been able to gain. It would not be until late after the farmer's death that I was able to gain the land for my family, and every field around it for that matter. However, as a child I saw that this farmer had a daughter; a girl so sweet she put sugar to shame. Through the years I watched her grow into the finest of flowers, and I knew that I had to have her. But, even when my only obstacle was removed and she was mine for the taking, something else came that kept her from me.' Raegan's eyes searched the shadow. 'That *thing* Michael... was you.'

The hair on Michael's neck stood on end. The thought of Raegan with his mother nearly crippled him inside.

'The fact is Michael, your mother loved you completely. She loved you as much, if not more than that weasel father of yours.' Raegan wheezed as his anger increased. He took a sip of water.

'My mother would never be with a man like you.'

'Quite right. But I was always going to try wasn't I? Just like you.'

'Bullshit. Grace and I shared something... something you can't invent or force. But I let her go because I knew that Arnold could provide for her better than I ever could. My mother was dying, and Grace deserved someone who could give her their full attention and affection. To try and compare what I have with your daughter to the selfish lust you held for my mother is sinful and delusional. Old man, like night and day, you and I might share the same land but we see it in a completely different light.'

'Me being the darkness, I assume? You may be right there. You see, despite the wealth and opportunities I could offer your mother, she chose a man who couldn't offer her a thing. Every day I was forced to watch her toil in fields while he spent countless hours away from her. And yet, just like all the ungrateful people of this town, your mother would celebrate the efforts of a lowly farmhand rather than enjoy the spoils and riches that I offered.'

'But even he left her.' Michael thought of his mother – pregnant and abandoned.

'I know. I was there when he did.' Raegan waited for Michael to step forward, but he remained in the shade.

'What?' The words were said through gritted teeth.

'I grew sick of your mother's foolish choices Michael, so I had to intervene. I remember, it was 1889 and the sun was as hot as hell's own fire. Like always, your mother and father were apart, working in different parts of my land. Knowing that your father, Ferris, would be coming to the end of his working day, Connell and I decided to pay him a visit. We knocked on the door to your cottage and there, in all his revered handsome glory, came your father. Always accommodating, he invited us in for a drink, seeming a little surprised to see us if I'm honest. You see, your father and I had never seen eye to eye on most things, and... if I have to give the man one thing... I'd agree that he was far more reserved in his hatred for me than I was for him. So, in spite, we declined his casual invite. We were there for business, and I told him that I had a proposition I wanted him to consider. I offered him a life of luxury in exchange for his wife.'

'You foul bastard.'

'Oh don't worry. Your father was honourable to the end. He declined my generous offer – stating that in his wife he had all that he would ever need. Connell and I almost gagged at the sentiment. Here was a man struggling to put food on the table and yet he would rather, selfishly, watch his wife starve than know she was being looked after. I mean, what kind of a man does that? You didn't. Right?'

Raegan didn't get a reaction. So he continued.

'We told him what a fool he was, your father that is, and boy did he get angry; furious in fact. He slammed the door so hard I thought I felt the earth shift a little. Connell wanted to call it a day, but I wasn't through. I thought to hell with him, and all his sentiments. So, I asked Connell to knock on the door once more while I went around the corner of the cottage. Well, when your father answered again he was done with words. Instead he flew at Connell in a blind rage. The strength he had was marvellous – tossing my strongest henchman around like a bear with a rag doll. Now surely you understand, I *had* to do something. So I picked up a rock. And I mean one hell of a rock. Even with both hands, I could hardly lift it above my head. It was that heavy. And Michael, to this day, the sound it made when it thumped into the back of your father still rings in my ears.'

'You fucking coward. Couldn't you face the man eye to eye?'

'Oh, I did... listen. Michael, the best is yet to come. The impact of the rock knocked your father clean out. He was finally at my mercy. With adrenaline coursing through my veins, I'd like to say that I panicked. But now is not a time for lies; I knew exactly what I was doing. Ferris was a dead weight – his hulking arms were like tree trunks. So I ordered Connell to help me, forced him in fact. Together we dragged your father to the willow tree that stood outside of your house. And there we hanged him.'

Michael stepped into the light. His face was reddened by the blood that boiled beneath his skin.

'Ha! There's your father's fury alright. Now let me finish. This is the best part. Connell and I tied the rope around your father's thick neck and lynched him up over the tallest branch. But, as the noose tightened around his throat, your father suddenly woke up. He began to thrash around, intent in killing us. So… bravely… we hung onto his arms, keeping him as still as possible as the rope continued to choke at his throat. Seeing that he was on his last breath, I whispered in his ear all the intentions I had for his wife, and then watched him die. You should have seen the sadness on his face.'

'You'll burn in hell for what you've done.' Michael's fists were clenched so tight that his fingertips cut into his palms.

'Come now. You would have done the same.'

'Nobody would. For years, you let my mother think that my father killed himself. She prayed every day for his salvation. And all the time you knew! Well they're together now, where they both belong, and there's nothing your damned soul can do about it.' Michael snarled. His fingers twitched. He wanted to wrap them around Raegan's thin, pale throat.

'Don't you think I know that?' Raegan sat up in his bed. 'That's why I want you to kill me. Before the chance to do so is forever removed from you.'

'And give up an eternity in heaven with my parents? You're not worth it.'

'Heaven? You? Don't fool yourself man! With all the people you've killed in battle? Hell has a seat all set for you my son. We'll both dine with the devil.'

'Maybe. And yes, my actions will be judged, I know that. But be sure that you'll have nothing to do with my fate. And don't worry, when you die, rest assured that all of the town will gather to dig your grave. We'll dig it so deep that we can hand deliver you to Satan himself.' Michael stood over Raegan. He saw that the man was close to death. Leaning close to his cold ear, Michael tilted his head and whispered his intentions. Raegan's face became weighted with sadness. Fingers of darkness closed in around his eyes.

'He's all yours father,' said Michael as he left the room. The priest walked past clutching his bible.

Stood in the hallway, Michael's heart was racing. Part of him wanted to kill Raegan; he wanted to see pain in the old man's eyes. But what good would that have done? Michael knew that the man was dying and would soon be gone. With his parents already dead – sharing an eternity together in heaven – there was no pride to be restored; no need to save face. Fighting his impulses, Michael decided to let the man live for the last lonely seconds of his life. Hell would have an infinite amount of pain and torture lined up for Raegan, and Michael's act would have only been a selfish one. Collecting his thoughts, he began to plan the rest of his day. Part of him wanted to sprint to his mother's grave and speak with her – to tell her the news – but he imagined that she already knew. So, instead he wanted to apologise to her. For years, Michael had made life awkward for his mother. He had displayed openly his distaste at how she would pray daily for someone who had abandoned her. And so, he knew he had made her life more difficult. And for that, he was truly sorry.

Saddened by the thought of hurting the one woman who had always been there for him, Michael walked down the spiral staircase. The house remained silent and still. Shadows had moved in and masked the portraits that clung to the walls. A light breeze brushed past Michael as he descended. His trembling hand ran down the dark varnished banister. Beneath him, he could hear soft whispers in the room that sat closest to the bottom of the stairs. Inside, Cara was comforting her younger sister; offering her the sugar coated version of death. Michael could not help but feel that Cara's words sounded cold and generic – none of them held any personal tones of loss or emotion. This was a woman so numbed by death that it no longer could hurt her. Nevertheless, the kind words helped Imogen hold back the tears. She stood silent next to her sister, her face solemn and distant.

'Hello.' Michael turned away to face the voice.

The doors at the end of the hallway were wide open, and sunlight burst through, devouring the darkness. The marbled floor shimmered as if stepped on by angels. Cutting through the heavenly rays that blinded Michael stood a single silhouette. The light that broke past it warmed his face. Upon it, he could feel his lips begin to smile, and his legs trembled as his heart stood still.

Grace was home.

Chapter 48

Arnold's nose was broken. The ropes were beginning to cut into his wrists. Raw and bloody, he tried to wriggle them free but it was no good; he was stuck. Twisted and tied behind his large leather chair, Arnold's arms were at the brink of popping from their shoulders. He could taste fresh blood on his tongue as the two soldiers continued to ask their questions.

'Where is she?' Dill was the bigger of the two. A raw, recent tattoo of Christ on the cross decorated his thick forearm.

'Yeah, just tell us.' Birdy spat a shell on the floor before Arnold's feet. His mouth was full of sesame seeds.

'I told you everything.' Arnold was light-headed. Dill slapped him around the face.

'Obviously not. We're still here aren't we?' Dill stood nearly six foot two inches tall. He towered over Arnold's slumped body like a child torturing an ant.

'Yeah, obviously not.' Birdy planted his boot into Arnold's shin. He was certain he could feel the bone splinter inside. The man screamed in agony.

'I told you… I don't know where she is. I had her arrested. Surely your friends would have the details of what happened to her after that.' Speaking exhausted Arnold. He wanted to wake up; to realise he was dreaming. However, the crippling pain reminded him that he wasn't.

'You see, we checked that.' Dill brought his face down in front of Arnold's. His hair was as dark as his eyes. 'Turns out that your wife was released, and that's the last *we've* heard from her. You see, we're supposed to keep a check on her; to see if she stays true to her conditional release. Now, you know she's not allowed back in Ireland right?' Though Dill's question was rhetoric, he still did not give Arnold time to offer answer before blowing his fist straight across the man's trembling jaw.

'Your dumb fuck of a wife's quite the trouble maker it seems, and it wouldn't look good on you if she were to come back to you.' Birdy was almost cackling as he danced excitedly around his partner.

'To me?' Arnold raised his head. It felt heavier than usual. 'Why would she come back to me?' Blood poured from his mouth.

'We ask the questions.' Birdy spat a shell into Arnold's face. 'You just answer them.' The desk light flickered off his blonde hair. A demonic smile sat on his boyish face.

'Well she isn't here. Look around.' Arnold's tongue could feel the torn gums where his teeth used to be.

'Oh we will. And if we find her, rest assured your precious farm will burn to the ground… with you in it.' Dill lit a cigarette. His large hand cupped the tip, guarding the small flame on his lighter from the winds. Beside him, Birdy had opened the windows in case he could hear someone clambering down the drainpipe.

'Something's missing here. You're not telling us something.' Dill took a draw on his cigarette before planting the end onto Arnold's exposed leg. The small ember scolded Arnold's bare leg. A small circle of ash sat atop the burnt skin. Arnold chose to grit his few remaining teeth rather than scream. He saved his energy; nobody had come to his previous cries for help.

'Shall I start on his fingers?' Birdy chomped on his mouthful of seeds.

'Shortly. We'll give him another chance to tell us something useful.' Dill planted his heavy hands on Arnold's shoulders. 'Where is Grace Farrington?'

'Darby,' spluttered Arnold.

'The city?' Birdy continued to chomp. A grey mush filled the side of his mouth.

'No…' he struggled for breath. 'Her name; Grace's maiden name is Darby.'

'There we are. That wasn't so bad now was it? And to think you were one bad answer away from causing my mate Birdy here to pull the nails from your fingers. But don't get too comfortable. Tell me, what use is that name to me?' Dill tightened his grip on Arnold's shoulders. His thumbs screwed tightly into the pressure points.

'Because… her family own a huge estate back in a small town called Orplow. Her father is a huge trader. Maybe they've heard from her.' Blood trickled from his wrists.

'And so we have it… a lead at last. You must be a sucker for punishment Mr Farrington. Why not just tell us that in the first place?' Dill walked in front of Arnold's chair. He had lit another cigarette.

'Now we'll leave you in peace Mr Farrington. You've been quite helpful. But, if our paths were to cross once more don't dare waste my time again, or I'll fucking end yours.' Dill flicked his cigarette into Arnold's lap. A few seconds past before smoke began to smoulder from the chair. Arnold's weak breath could only alter the smoke's path to the ceiling, as the cigarette continued to burn and bite at his groin.

'We'll be seeing you.' Dill and Birdy left the room. Hopefully not, prayed Arnold.

Outside, the walls of Canndare were ablaze. Windows were smashed and the sound of doors being forced open cracked between the crackles of the fires. Nearly a hundred men were at work – aggressively routing out members of the Irish Republican Army.

The Auxiliary Division – commonly known as the Auxies – were recruited by the Royal Irish Constabulary to assist the police. Under the command of Brigadier-General F P Crozier, a former officer of the Ulster Volunteer Force, their main objectives were to root out and suppress all leads to the IRA. Divided into companies, they mainly operated in rural areas and independent to the RIC. This was often to the benefit of the constables, as the Auxies soon developed a reputation that no peace keeping side would ever desire.

Lighting another cigarette, Dill admired the view. Back home, his English family would call him Philip James Cooper. However, having spent years in the trenches, his brother's in arms had for some reason, unknown to him, begun to call him Dill. The name had stuck like the thick clay that clung to the trench walls, and now he would answer to nothing else. After the war, his return home had brought nothing but disappointment. Having been promoted from rank rather than through it, Dill's uniform was decorated by two medals; the small common soldier's Military Medal sat aside the revered officer's Military Cross. However, the spoils of being an officer no longer existed within civilian life, and now he found it hard to adjust to the loss of the status and pay. On seeing the advert for volunteers to assist in Ireland, Dill had jumped at the chance. The fact he was paid twice as much as a constable helped a little, and the contract promised to last for at least a year. However temporary, he was determined to regain his gentleman status.

Stood by his side, Birdy continued to smile as he chomped on a fresh mouthful of seeds. His Tam-O-Shanter cap lay lopsided on his head, and the small woollen bobble on top bounced with every enthusiastic chomp of his overactive jaw. The habit had initially disgusted Dill, but he soon grew used to it. What bothered him more was the question as to why the man did it? His name was Mark Thomas Bird, and naturally, through playground punch-lines, he developed his nickname Birdy. Dill just wondered whether it was for pleasure or mainly for namesake that his friend feasted entirely on sesame seeds. Turning to face his ally, Dill brushed off a shell that had fallen on his friend's jacket. But for Dill's medals, they wore identical uniforms.

'So, it would appear we're off to Orplow.' Dill raised his chest a little, filling his lungs. Around him, heavily armed Auxies were throwing tired men into the back of vans, landing the occasional punch before the van doors slammed shut.

'May God help them.' Birdy laughed. His wide mouth cupped a mushy grey lump.

'Ha! They'll need more than that, I'm afraid. That old boy is on our side.' Dill opened up his forearm – the face of Christ stared back at him.

The following journey was arduous. Having interrogated a host of suspects, the division had handed the majority of them over to the Royal Irish Constabulary. And so, now on their way to Orplow, Dill's knuckles throbbed as he gripped the steering wheel. His dark eyes were heavy and the lack of turns in the road made it hard for him to stay awake. However, adamant he had the nocturnal instincts of an owl, Birdy was wide awake. Sat at the back of the van, he rallied the troops with songs from the trenches. Exhausted, Dill hated everyone and everything. He mumbled to himself as his hands rocked and jerked on the wheel. It was the bumpiest road Dill had ever driven upon, and like a heavily armoured caterpillar, a large convoy of trucks followed behind, bouncing in unison. Bumper to bumper along the tight strip of road, several headlights had already smashed following Dill's heavy use of the breaks. Often he did it on purpose just to keep himself awake, as every thump and smash had brought a wry smile across his face. Meanwhile, Birdy crowed with every bump.

'For fuck's sake Dill, you drive like a tart.'

'Shut your beak Birdy, or I'll cut you in half just so I can beat you twice, you tit.' Dill jerked the wheel violently from left to right. He laughed loudly, if only to drown out the squawks from his furious friend.

With only a few miles to go, Dill parked up suddenly. Smiling, he could hear the trucks clatter behind him. Finding the nearest tree, he emptied his bladder on its thick trunk. A stream of steam rose from the ground. Not needing anymore than to pee, Dill almost drained his bowels when an explosion split the cornfields in front of him. High pitched laughter rattled behind him. Turning, with his dick still in his hand, Dill saw Birdy. He was stood on top of the van, jumping up and down as he laughed hysterically. A small grenade pin swung around his forefinger.

'You fucking arsehole.' Dill's Midland's accent was broad when he was angry.

'Maybe. But it was you that nearly shit yourself.' Birdy slid down from the roof. He tried his best to reason his madness. 'Come on mate. I could see you were shattered, and thought this might shake you up a bit. You can always let me drive if you like?' Birdy was still spinning the grenade pin on his forefinger as he held out his other hand for the keys.

'With those limp wrists? No chance. I'm lucky you were able to throw past me you bloody girl. So, I doubt you'd be able to handle a road like this.' Dill slapped his friend's outstretched hand as he passed him. The impact made a loud popping sound that echoed across the fields.

'Well at least let me ride shotgun?' Birdy steadied an imaginary gun in his hand as he scoped the horizon, picking off invisible targets.

'Hell no.' Dill frowned.

'Jesus Christ.' Birdy chucked seeds into his mouth.

'Yup. He'll be riding up front with me.' Dill flashed his forearm. 'Now get in the back with the rest of the flock.'

It was only another hour until the trucks arrived at the small walls of Orplow. In the dead of night the small farmhouses and cottages looked completely at peace. The air was cold and cutting, and the fields whistled in the wind beneath the half-crescent moon. Most of the men inside the van were asleep; their snoring pelted on the metal walls as if a storm was contained within.

'We'll eat first.' Dill was thinking out loud. He turned and shook some of the sleeping men behind him.

'Yeah, can't pillage on an empty stomach.' Birdy was as excitable as ever. Dill wondered if it was more than just seeds that he chewed.

Getting out of the van first, Dill set up a small fire. Living off his friend's importance, Birdy ordered some of the men to get the pans out and to gather some food from the supply trucks. Two cadets sprinted towards the convoy behind them, entering the back of a large military truck. They soon returned with arms brimming with tins. Dill watched as a line of fires soon spotted the roadside. Having seen the first fire, the troops followed suit and began to cook their supper. Within minutes, circles of men wreathed the small scattered fires. All of them spoke in hushed voices – whispering so not to wake the town. Surprise was to be the key. After that, complete carnage.

The light from the fire flickered. Dill crouched at the fireside and studied the photograph. A bloody fingerprint blotted one corner – the thin red thumbprint of Arnold Farrington had smudged slightly when Dill had ripped the picture from the man's fingers. And despite his initial reluctance to help them, Dill was baffled by how the man had shown no pain towards his wife's fate. At first, Dill had thought that Arnold was going to be a tough nut to crack – a man who would never offer up his wife for an end to the torture. But instead, they had found a man who knew very little of the one woman he had spent most of his days with. All that he did know he had offered to violent strangers within a heartbeat. Looking at the picture, Dill studied the woman's face. Her features were of true beauty – totally angelic and untouched. A deep sadness was captured in her eyes.

Steel forks began to scratch on the bottoms of tins. The men's bellies were now full and the fires had warmed their travelling legs. Excitedly, Birdy fidgeted at Dill's side. His shoulders sprung up and down as he crouched on the balls of his feet. There was a deadly spring in his enthusiasm, and his impatience was potent as much as it was contagious. Soon, the many fires that lined the roads were being trodden on and doubted. Together, the Auxies replaced their forks with rifles, and the shrilling sound of cocked weapons popped in the night. Dill looked at the picture once again. The woman was sat alone in the gardens of her family home. Her eyes stared away from the camera's lens.

Seeing the many men that were sent to flush her out of her sleepy hollow, Dill could not help but feel that they were heavy handed. However, experience had taught him that trouble rarely keeps its own company. No doubt there would be others helping, and Dill's experience in the trenches taught him that it could only take a few to stop so many.

Having swapped the trenches for towns, the guerrilla tactics that Dill had already encountered were a lot more strategic than the blinkered approach he knew from his time in the trenches. What his new enemy lacked in numbers, they more than made up for in intelligence. That's why surprise was the key. Like a plague of locusts, his men were to swarm the town and devour all before them. Pulling a piece of paper from his pocket, Dill saw his first port of call – the home address of Grace Darby.

Chapter 49

Michael was stood outside the estate. A wash of pale blue coloured the skies. Despite the hour, a ribbon of light tied the night-sky to the land. Warmed by the words he was about to utter, Michael could not feel the chill of the breeze. The first buds of spring danced in the air, carried by the final winds of winter. It had been several hours since Michael had seen Grace stood in the doorway of her home. Given the fact that her father lay dying upstairs, Michael had been brief with his greetings — simply asking whether she would wait for him later that night. She could see that his eyes held intentions that he had yet to voice. Without hesitation, Grace had agreed to meet him.

Close to the hour, Michael waited by the nearest wall to the house. It had been years since he had hidden beneath this wall, where he wrote the last poem he had knowingly passed to Grace. Tonight — with no reason to hide — he stood tall beside it. Rolling his thumb across his bracelet, Michael found that not a single bead was upon it; no prayers were present for him to call on anymore. Feeling the small cross beneath his finger, he pondered whether his intentions were true and pure. The last he knew of her, Grace was married. Her return home could simply be that of a daughter visiting her ill father. Beginning to question his right to romance, nerves began to make him sweat. He took off his jacket and hung it over his broad shoulder. A buckle on his braces pressed against the scar on his chest. He could feel it rub against the raised rugged skin.

Waiting with only the answer to one question, Michael wondered what Grace would ask of him. The sound of small hooves pattered the fields behind him. Deer raced through the meadows, seeing no reason to fear the night. For a moment, Michael closed his eyes and listened to the land. The trees hummed and the soft trace of falling waters could be heard in the distance. His ear was angled to the sweet calls of two owls when he heard the creaking of a door.

Opening his eyes, Michael saw Grace. Stood by the doorway to her estate, she was wrapped in a red woollen cloth. The blaze of colour upon her shoulders flashed beneath her milky skin. Michael's heart rapped at his chest. His tongue felt heavy with the words he had longed to say. A barrage of pulled petals spiralled in the wind, carpeting her path as she walked towards him. Her small, delicate hands held the red cloth tight to her.

'Hello,' Michael said with a smile. Grace could hear the happiness in his voice.

'Michael.' Grace called his name softly. He was stood before her within an instant. He looked at her lips, eager to kiss them.

'How are you?' Michael found his hands holding her shoulders.

'I don't know anymore. It has been so long since I have been home, and so much has changed. That is, apart from one thing.' Grace looked up at Michael. She wanted to feel his kiss. To know whether the electricity she remembered was true. A small bolt of lightning struck in her stomach. Her heart jolted.

Michael felt tense. Nervously he changed the subject.

'And what of your father?'

'Gone.'

Grace dropped her head. She felt Michael's hands hold her tighter. She was ready to fall into them forever when he spoke again.

'So much has happened Grace. Ever since the night you left, I've regretted letting you. Everything that stopped me from being true to myself has now left me. But then, my very reason left me the moment that you did.' Michael's breath was held by the winter breeze.

'What are you saying?' Grace wanted a clear answer.

'Walk with me.' Michael took Grace by the hand and led her through the gardens. Her hand felt cold, and he took it in both of his and blew upon it. Holding it again in a single hand, Michael ran his forefinger across her palm. He made the mark of a cross in her upturned hand.

Grace asked questions about the war. She wanted to know everything that Michael had experienced since the day she had left him. He spared her the grizzly parts, making the whole effort seem so easy and passive. He had also told of his joy at finding out about his father's fate. Although, he intentionally omitted – for Grace's sake – who the killer had been. At first she had found it odd how a young man could celebrate such an unholy act, but Michael explained how he now knew that his mother was not alone in heaven, and how he could move on with his own life away from the constant prayers for redemption.

As the winds began to rise, he wrapped his arm around her and pulled her into his chest. She could feel his heart beating. He could feel her breath against his body. They both wanted each other more than anything they had ever known. Knowing what he wanted to say, Michael again chose the wrong words.

'How is your husband?' Grace sank away from his grasp. Her shoulders folded slightly.

'I don't know. It has been so long since I heard anything from him.' Grace looked at her hands. She could not remember when she had stopped wearing Arnold's ring.

'I'm sorry to hear that Grace.'

'Don't be…' She looked back at Michael. 'I'm not.' His sincere smile weakened her. The gentle rain that began to fall had kinked the ends of his tussled dark hair. It softened the features of his face.

'What happened?' Michael held out his hand once more. Soon they were walking back through the gardens. A tinged scent swept across the air from the town behind them. The bottom of the skies had turned a faint shade of orange. Finding themselves at the door to the estate, Grace had run out of words. She had told Michael everything about her adventures; her time in Canndare, her loveless marriage to Arnold, the events in Dublin, and her eventual exile in England. He had not flinched to a single one of them. Instead, his eyes had held hers as tightly as their hands were entwined. Dovetailed, their fingers were wrapped together.

'Grace,' Michael whispered into her ear. His lips could almost taste her skin.

'Yes?' She looked up at him.

'Stop me if I talk out of line, but I have to tell you something.' He looked away, hoping to find the words behind her beautiful face. He held her stare again as the words came to him.

'Grace, for all my life I've lived for someone else. The actions of others have shaded my own desires, causing me to take paths away from those I wanted to follow. And yet, through it all – through the staggered steps and wrong turns – there has been one bright part of my life that I have always been led by. If I stood here and said that it was only now that I knew what this was then I'd have you standing before a liar. The truth is, I have always known. I've always known the one thing that I lived for – the one thing that I had no choice but to love with every fibre of my body. Now, I don't know about fate, and I don't know how to measure what any man deserves... but I know what I love. Grace, with all my heart it's...'

'You!' The man barked behind Michael. Turning he saw two men dressed in police uniforms. They wore different hats than the usual officers, and Michael recognised the military medals that decorated one of their breasts.

'Miss Darby, let me introduce myself.' The larger of the two began speaking. His accent was English but slightly slurred. 'My friend's call me Dill, and this is my colleague Birdy. Beings though I'm hoping that we can get along, I doubt you will need to address us in any other way.' Dill passed a small photograph to Birdy who held it up to Grace's face.

'She's as pretty as a picture.' Birdy chomped on his seeds. His jaw slackened as Michael gripped him by the throat. Birdy was stood on the very tips of his toes when Michael spoke.

'What's going on?' He looked at Dill. The shade of orange that had coloured the horizon had now altered into large towers of fire. Thick, spiralling smoke screened the light of the moon.

'We're looking for trouble.' Dill smiled as he nodded towards Grace. She had shied behind Michael. Several other cadets had grouped behind Dill. It was clear he was in charge. Meanwhile, the one they called Birdy was growing a deathly shade of blue within Michael's fierce grip.

'I think you should go.' Michael's voice was close to a growl.

'We have no intentions of staying. But then, we can't let your friend stay either.' Dill raised his gun. 'I think you need to let go of my colleague now.'

Michael had already pulled the gun from Birdy's holster. He dug it into the man's back as he released his grip. He placed his free hand on the man's shoulder, pulling him into gun's cold barrel.

'What do you want with Grace?' Michael addressed Dill, but kept an eye on the men behind him.

'She shouldn't be here. She needs to come with us.' Dill opened his hand and held it out to Michael. 'We have no issue with you sir. Just give the woman to us.'

'Never.'

'Now, that puts us in an awkward position doesn't it? That is, I'm afraid, awkward only for you.' Dill smiled. 'My good man, what you must realise is that you don't have a fair trade there. Kill him if you must, but we'll still get the girl.'

'You won't get her cheaply.' Michael seemed to grow in size. Every muscle in his body was tense. Dill knew not to call the man's bluff. The cold stare of death flashed in his golden brown eyes.

'Alright you win. Just give us our colleague back and we'll be on our way.' Dill took a step closer to Michael. Birdy's jaw was locked at its lowest point.

'You must think I'm a fool. You'll kill us both the second you have him back. Call your men off, and let us be.' Michael could feel Grace hold onto the back of his shirt.

'You have my word.' Dill held out his arm again. Michael saw the tattoo.

'Then I have nothing at all.' Michael pushed Birdy to the ground and fired his gun above the heads of the cadets. They hit the deck. Without pause, Michael planted the butt of his pistol into the shoulder of Dill who sunk to his knees.

'Run!' Michael took Grace's hand and sprinted through the small woodland that surrounded the estate. A gale of bullets burst behind them. Gunfire crackled in the air. Michael continued to run. His strength carried Grace with him. Twisting through the trees, they grew closer to the flames that had begun to consume the town. Bark splintered beside them as bullets missed their mark.

'The cove… why don't we head for the cove?' Grace was shouting above the thunder that followed them.

'We'd never make it.' Michael looked at the town in front of him. Gunshots echoed through the streets, greeted often by screams of agony and fear. The men Dill had brought with him were ravaging the town. Windows either exploded from the bricks that were tossed through them or from the fires that burned within. Spirals of smoke roofed every house and store in sight. People had run out into the streets, leaving all that possessed to the fire.

Sat within the heart of all the fighting, the spire of the church cut through the thick blanket of smoke.

'There, the church. Follow me.' Michael pulled on Grace's hand. They made a sprint for it. Lost within the crowds of people, Dill and his cadets lost sight of their target. Some fired blindly into the crowd, bringing innocent men to the ground, and Dill gave no order for them to stop.

Passing through the church gates, Michael crouched down as he led Grace up the steps and through the main doors. He scanned the crowd to see if he had been followed. Turning, Michael entered the church. He had failed to see the slack-jawed cadet who stood nursing his throat, and staring straight at him.

Securing the door behind them, Michael paused and pulled Grace into him. Pausing, she ran her finger across the scar on his brow as her eyes locked into his. Michael planted his hand firmly on the wall behind them as he leaned in and kissed her. Her knees buckled and her arms draped around his neck. Running her hand across his skin, she could feel the scar upon his chest. She kissed his neck tenderly as she rested her hand upon his heart.

'Father!' Michael called out into the empty church. The fires that glowed outside caused a tainted light to filter through the stained glass windows. Like a burnt rainbow, the spoilt colour carpeted the aisles.

'Father Daniel, are you here?' Michael shouted again, but got no reply. Grace followed Michael as he searched the church. Looking inside the small quarters behind the altar, all he could find was an empty room. A few bottles of wine had fallen from the shelves; the stains of crushed grapes began to dry on the floor. The priest was nowhere to be seen.

'Father… where are you?' Michael took Grace's hand and ran up the stairwell that led to the bell-tower. The narrow steps almost took Michael's footing as he staggered to the top. Pausing for breath, they looked out upon the town. Through the alcoves of the bell-tower, they could see the terror that was spreading almost as fast as the fires that closed in on the church. Exhausted and frozen by fear, the people had no fight left in them. Empowered by the weakness of the people, the Auxies continued to drag countless men away from their families and into the back of trucks. Some would never return.

Many houses had completely collapsed, crushing all that remained inside. All that was left was the smoke that spun from their ashes.

'Look.' Grace pointed down towards the entrance of the church. A group of men, led by Dill had gathered by the steps. The excitable Birdy bounced by his side as he thrust his finger in the direction of the church doors.

'What shall we do?' Grace looked at Michael for answers.

'There's no time for praying, that's for sure.' Michael watched the men's initial efforts to break down the door. Fortunately, they held out.

'Oh no...' said Grace in a breathless whisper. The church had become surrounded. At least a dozen men had begun to smash the windows. Several others carried large wooden planks that smouldered at the edges. Dipped within the flames, they had now been tossed inside the church. Confined in the tower, the fire roared out below Michael and Grace. The fine drapes and carpets of the church lit up like dry hay. Michael knew they were trapped.

'Let's split up.' Grace was looking around her.

'Not a chance.' Michael held her still. 'They only want you; they won't come after me. And you need me. Grace, for most of my life I've believed that my father abandoned my mother – that in killing himself he sacrificed an eternity in heaven with her. I would never do that to you. I would never abandon you.'

'Nor I you.' A small tear burned upon Grace's soft cheek.

Michael tucked his shirt into his trousers. Birdy's pistol was still nestled in behind his leather belt. Michael did not know how many bullets remained, but he had no intentions of firing them. Running the situation through his mind, he knew that they would have to move from the bell-tower, and there were only two ways out of it; the stairs or a hundred foot drop to the ground. If they left it any longer to decide, even the stairs would no longer be an option. Michael could hear the fires burning in the church. Soon it would eat away at the wooden beams and weaken the doors. It was only a matter of time before Dill and his men were inside.

Seeing the rope hanging from the church bell, Michael had an idea. He handed Grace the pistol and made his way down the steps that led back into the church.

'Wait for me. I'll be back soon.' Michael smiled before sprinting down the stairwell. The gun shook in Grace's small hands. She placed it on the floor where she had begun to kneel. Clasping her hands together, she began to pray.

The church below was like the devil's chamber. Decorated by hellish fire, the hall was almost completely ablaze. The air boiled and the heat stole the breath from Michael's open mouth. Running towards the main door, Michael took hold of the remains of a stall and propped it against the lock. Turning back to face the altar, he dipped the sleeves of his shirt in the font and placed the drenched cloth around his mouth. The holy water was still ice cold.

Only a small corner of the hall remained untouched from the flames. A huge bay window, draped by a large purple cloth, stood at the opposite end to where Michael stood. Pressing his damp sleeve to his mouth, he charged across the church. The flames failed to burn his skin as he brushed through them like a morning breeze did the meadows. Countless bricks fell behind him. Support beams began to topple to the floor. Reaching the window, Michael pulled at the huge drape that hung from the ceiling. His arms bulged as he tore the cloth from the rails above. Behind the glass, silhouettes had begun to gather – their arms extended by a mixture of bats, blades and rifles.

Rolling the drape up into his chest, Michael ran towards the altar. He was already tying one end around his stomach as he bounded up the steps. Breathless, he passed the final step and found Grace on her knees. The smoke was yet to reach her, but still her eyes were closed tight and dampened in the corners. Shaking her by the shoulders, Michael found that she was praying.

'Grace, we have to go. Come on.' Michael handed her the opposite end of the drape. The cloth was enormous; the middle section sagged and trailed down the first few steps of the stairwell. Seeing that one end was tied to Michael, Grace knew what she had to do. Only needing a little to belt her waist, Michael came in close to her and pulled the cloth tightly around her slight hips.

'Now what?' Grace looked at Michael for an answer.

'We fall.' Michael glanced at the window. A smile flashed across his face.

'Together?' Grace knew they would not survive.

'No. You first. But don't worry, we're tied together. I'll stay here and let you down gradually.' Michael held Grace's gaze. 'Don't worry. I'm bound to you.'

Grace looked out over the town. The ground below her was clear. Every cadet was busy trying to smash down the front doors. Stepping onto the stone balcony, she could feel the heat of the town that burned beneath her. Michael stood behind her. His hands were planted to the sides of the walls. A thick line of cloth was wrapped around his right wrist. Looking into his eyes, she saw him nod. It was time.

Lowering her feet from the stones, Grace felt nothing but air beneath them. She hung inches below the edge as Michael's arms gripped the purple drape. Leaning back, he dug his feet into the base of the wall and allowed the cloth to run slowly through his hands. The cloth tightened around Grace's waist as she gradually became closer to the ground. Looking up, she could no longer see Michael in the alcove. Only a thread of cloth that poured over the edge could be seen. Panicking slightly, her fingertips dragged along the church walls, feeling each brick as she passed. She was certain she could feel them warmed by the fire that burned within them.

Soon, the cloth stopped coming, and Grace's feet felt the ground beneath them. Untying the cloth from her waist, she called for Michael. But the sounds that cried out from a town in turmoil muffled Michael's name. Grace continued to scream but knew she could not be heard. Remembering her instructions, she pulled three times on the cloth, and soon it began to make its way back up into the tower. Suddenly alone, Grace looked around. Nobody had seen her.

She sunk into a shadow and waited for Michael.

Reeling the cloth in, Michael gathered the loose end. The gaps between the alcoves were too wide for Michael to wrap the cloth around, and so he needed somewhere on which to anchor himself. With no other option, he tied the loose end to the rafter on which the church-bell hung. It was several feet above the floor and further from the alcove than Michael would have wished. He wondered how far he would have to drop to the ground if it failed to reach. Clutching a clump of cloth, Michael pulled with all his might. The rafter shifted a little, before a huge crash came from below him.

Standing still, Michael could hear footsteps within the fire. A gust of wind flew up into the tower. The main door had been breached. Twisting around, Michael saw the pistol on the floor. He leaned over to take hold of it.

'I wouldn't if I were you.' Dill was already stood at the top of the stairwell. He pointed the barrel of his pistol at Michael's head.

'Do it.' Michael held his stare. His arm was still outstretched.

'Where is she?' Dill took a step forward. More men had joined him on the stairway. Michael did his best not to look at the alcove. Instead, he stood straight and shifted his step to the middle of the room. A sheer drop onto the floor of the church was an inch from his foot.

'You must have passed her on your way up.' Michael nodded towards the stairwell.

'Don't play games with me.' Dill fired a bullet into the floor between Michael's feet. The bullet punched clean through the thin wooden panels. Michael jumped back, the tips of his toes rested on the edge of the floorboards. He gripped the cloth tightly. His back tilted the large bell behind him.

'It's too late. You've lost her.' Michael steadied himself.

'Then what do I need you for?' Dill raised his gun and fired.

The bullet flew past Michael's falling body. Anticipating the man's reaction, Michael had already jumped. The bullet tore through the tightening drape that tied Michael to the rafters above. Falling, the cloth burned in Michael's palms as he hurtled towards the ground. Certain death lay in wait for him.

However, only a few feet from the ground, the large drape that tied Michael to the rafters above snapped tight. Pain shot up Michael's back, and his lungs were emptied. He inhaled but the air inside the church was too hot to breathe. His eyes became watered as he hung facing the ceiling; the bell above him was completely blurred. Focusing on the drape, Michael untied himself. His fingers fumbled over the knot until it released him onto the hot tiles below. Pain returned to his back. Winded, Michael got to his feet. The sound of metal hitting the floor grabbed his attention.

Bobbling upon the tiles of the church floor, three grenades rolled past him. Michael knew the pins had been pulled. Frozen, he watched as they rested at the base of the stairwell. Michael was sure he could hear the men above screaming something. He turned and ran as fast as his beaten legs would carry him. Nothing but fire faced him now. Like a forest of flames, every inch of the church was alight. Leaping through it all, Michael felt the explosion press at his back. Shrapnel splintered the statues, and the grenades cut into the wooden base of the stairwell like the final blow from Lucifer's lumberjack.

The tower began to lean towards the aisle. Turning, Michael saw the cadets scramble down the stairs. Dill pushed past every one of them and was half way up the aisle already. Seeing Michael, he stopped and raised his pistol towards him. However, the falling bricks from the tower crushed him just as his finger cupped the trigger.

***

Outside, a cloud of dust filled the skies as the roof began to fall. The statue of Christ fell from the walls and into the fire; the crucifix burned brightly upon the altar. Not even Christ had survived the explosion.

Grace had run from the crumbling building. The church had now been pulled to the ground. Like an ancient ruin, only the doorway and one bay window remained standing. A mound of rock and marble crushed the shattered glass beneath it. Together, they glowed like hot coals upon the land. Flames still licked at the air as they crept through the cracks of the rubble.

Seeing her running from the wreckage, Oscar had taken hold of Grace. His mother and father had shielded her from any prying eyes. Devoured by anguish, she cried uncontrollably into Oscar's warm chest. His chubby arms held her tightly. He could feel his shirt dampen beneath her sunken eyes.

With the collapse of the church, the town had grown silent. Hundreds of people had gathered around the ruins. Only the hush of the rising dust from the debris could be heard. Oscar muffled the sobbing cries of Grace. He could feel her shake in his arms. Consumed in grief, she could not take in what surrounded her, or feel the racing heartbeat of the man that held her. Nor could she feel the soft tears that rained onto her crown. Oscar bit his lip so tight it almost bled.

Mountains of ash smouldered on the ground; falling rain passed the rising smoke. Not a single body could be seen beneath the stones, but nobody had yet tried to remove them. As the ground seized the rain that fell from the heavens, a cloud mixed of mist and dust began to screen the scene. The crowd stood still as the waters covered them.

With the flames still fighting back the water, a damp light shone behind the cloud. A light obscured only by the shape of a man.

'Michael.' Oscar screamed at the top of his lungs. The first syllable screeched from his dry throat.

Raising her face from Oscar's chest, Grace stared towards the figure within the haze. Her eyes were blurred and glazed over. Adjusting to the scene, she saw the frame of a man. A man who staggered and fell as he tried to pull himself away from the burning ruins. A man who's face she knew and loved.

'Michael!' Grace called out as she ran towards him. Her legs slipped upon the soaked ground, but still she ran. Rain was beating down upon her outstretched arms and smiling face.

Seeing her run towards him, Michael held out his aching arms. It took all his strength just to stand, but he knew he would find what it took to carry her. He heard her call his name, and was about to call hers when the bullet passed clean through Grace's side and deep into his hand.

Ignoring the agony, Michael saw Birdy standing behind the falling body of Grace. Smoke spiralled from the barrel of his pistol. No longer capable of baring witness, the crowd – led by an outraged Oscar – swarmed over Birdy. His body was pulled to the ground and was never to be seen again.

Running to her, Michael knelt by Grace's side. He pulled her into his arms and raised her head. He pushed his hand onto her side in an effort to stem the bleeding. Her pulse was slowing and her body was growing colder.

Chapter 50

The medical staff could not work miracles. Surrounded by doctors and nurses, Grace had been resuscitated and was now lying in a private ward in the trauma wing of the hospital. Wires and tubes pierced her sleeping body. Michael could not take his eyes off of her. One of his hands held hers – Cara held his other. Grace's hand was still cold, but some colour had come back to her face. Her lungs lifted with each shallow breath. The ward window was open, and the swaying curtain cast a shadow that danced over Grace's skin. The stillness of the room itself was deafening apart from the extractor fan that hummed and spluttered on the wall. Silent and still, the quiet was interrupted by the sound of the bustling corridor outside. The door was opened. A doctor entered with a clipboard in hand.

'Are you her family?' The doctor peered at his clipboard as if to find the answer.

'Yes,' said Cara. Her voice was whispered as if not to wake her sister. She clutched a small biscuit tin on her lap. The doctor looked at Michael for a response.

'How's it looking doc?' Michael could feel eyes boring into his head. He had not taken his gaze from Grace. The doctor's hesitation said it all. Michael had heard the pause before. It was never good.

'Can we talk outside for a moment?' The doctor looked shy. Whatever he had to say, he did not want his patient to hear it just yet.

'You go Michael. I'll watch over my sister.' Cara pulled on his hand. He placed Cara's hand inside Grace's, kissed Cara on her forehead and left the room.

Outside, the corridor was far from private. Countless nurses rushed past, tired doctors consulted on complicated medical procedures before an audience of bewildered visitors, while families sat by in the hope of good news. A mixture of medicines scented the stale air, and the sticky floors were lacquered with bleach and chlorine. Michael wanted answers.

'How is she?' Michael watched the doctor's reaction. The smile on his lips was not mirrored by his eyes. If it was meant to offer empathy, it was not working. If anything, the smile looked more like a grimace.

'Not good. I'm afraid the bullet tore most of her liver to pieces. There's very little of the organ left. We also didn't recover the bullet.' The doctor saw Michael raise his bandaged hand.

'Don't worry. I caught that.' Michael had wrapped a cloth around his palm to stop the bleeding. The bullet had not passed completely through, and it was still inside, tucked between the broken bones. 'So, the liver – it will heal itself, right?'

'Usually it would. The organ has fantastic healing capabilities, but in this case there isn't enough left to regenerate itself. I'm sorry to say that very soon, your friend will be in an excruciating amount of pain.'

'Soon?'

'Well, yes. As I said, there's still a little of the liver remaining. And for now at least, it's able to take the painkillers that we've administered, and even the small sedative that has put her to sleep. But any more than that, I'm afraid, could kill her.'

'So that's it? We wait for her to wake up and then just watch her die in agony?' Michael looked back at Grace. She looked so peaceful, so unaware of her fate.

'It's a miracle her body has taken to the drugs so far. You see, without a liver to filter what the body takes in, her defences will eventually collapse and her body will begin to poison itself. Your friend needs an entirely new liver, and well, that's not going to happen.' The doctor examined his clipboard. He hoped there were no more questions. But there were.

'A new liver?' Michael rubbed his clean hand through his hair. Bits of rubble still dusted his scalp. 'Can't we just get her a new liver? I mean, there were plenty of guys back in that church that don't need theirs anymore.' Michael thought of the fallen Auxies.

'Impossible.'

'Or just improbable?' Michael's eyes locked onto the doctor. There was something he wasn't saying.

'It's called an allograft transplant – one that involves the transfer of organ or tissue matter between two genetically non-identical members of the same species. But it's just talk; it's never been done here before. Not successfully anyway.'

'Why not?' Michael had hope.

'Because it's all just research so far; work that has come from the back of Alexis Carret's findings.'

Michael looked blankly at the doctor. He shrugged his shoulders.

'He's a famous French surgeon, even won the Nobel Prize for his work in Physiology and Medicine.'

'He's not here though, is he?' Michael was growing impatient. The love of his life lay dying in the room next to them.

'My point is… he established new techniques. In turn these techniques laid the groundwork for the future of transplant surgery. So far, on the basis of Carret's findings, we've had surgical successes with kidneys, hearts and even spleens.'

'But not livers?'

'Yes livers also. But not on *humans*.' The doctor mopped his brow. 'All the operations have been on dogs. We've never worked on a human, and even if we did there's still the problem of rejection.'

'Go on.' Michael twirled the crucifix in his fingers.

'Even if we went ahead with the procedure, we'd still need to find a match for our patient. Variables such as similar age groups and the like are desirable, but matching blood type is essential. Otherwise, her body will just reject it. Sir, I think we have to face the facts that Ms Darby is circling the drain.' The doctor regretted his harsh tone, but was surprised by Michael's reaction. There was no fury or anger, just a sunken sadness to his powerful frame.

'I'm so sorry.' The doctor placed a hand on Michael's shoulder, before passing him by and entering the ward. Michael could see him deliver the news to Cara. Her expression was polite and reserved. She would cry her tears alone at home. The doctor offered his most sincere of expressions and hung his clipboard on the end of Grace's bed. He passed Michael in the corridor before leaving. Michael made note of his name.

'Did he tell you also?' Cara asked Michael. He was stood at the end of the bed.

'Yeah. Do you think she could hear him?' Michael nodded at Grace. She had not moved since he had left her side.

'He says she's in a deep sleep at the minute. I hope he's right, as he was far from shy with the details.' Cara dabbed her eye. Her throat was croaky.

'There's still hope Cara. I'm not giving up, and if you can hear me Grace, don't you give up just yet either.'

'What do you mean?' Cara blew her nose into her handkerchief.

'He mentioned a transplant. All I need to do is find her a liver.' Michael new his task was impossible.

'And what if we don't? I don't want to take the shine off your apple Michael, but it does look bleak for her.' Cara did not want Michael to lose himself in false hope.

'We don't end like this. Me and her, I mean.' Michael's face was a blend of hope and resignation.

'You've always loved her, haven't you?'

Michael nodded. His fingers wrapped around the rails at the base of Grace's bed. The hanging clipboard brushed against his hand. Michael picked it up and began to read. Condensed to a single side of paper were all the details of the one thing he truly loved. It listed Grace's age, her gender, her condition, and even her blood type. Seeing the scribbled letters that filled the last box, Michael looked to the heavens and laughed. God had one sick sense of humour.

'We have a chance.' Michael had found his killer smile. Cara had never questioned why her sister could fall so deeply for Michael. He was beautiful. She smiled to mirror Michael's. However, it was one she had never seen before. Cara could not copy how Michael smiled so brightly while his eyes were on the brink of crying.

He stood between her and Grace and took Grace's hand.

'Grace…' Michael could not find the words. Instead he opened up her hand and drew a cross onto her palm. With his forefinger, he then traced the three words her had always longed to tell her.

Removing the bracelet from his wrist, he placed it into Grace's open hand and closed her fingers. Holding the clenched fist, Michael ran Grace's forefinger along the scar on his face. He trembled at her touch. Turning, Michael nodded to Cara and left the room. He could not see the tears that streamed down Grace's face – he would never know that she had heard every word, and that she had read his touch.

Chapter 51

The call to the emergency services was brief. Only the location and what was to be found had been made clear. Chilled by the night, the waters of the Irish Sea raged at the sunken shores. Waves crashed into the sharp teeth of the cove, foaming at the mouth of the ragged rocks. A mixture of rain and spray from the falling waters washed over Michael's face. A light shower shimmered through the moonlight, drying almost as quickly as it fell onto his skin. Raising his chin, he stared at the skies. The white cotton clouds shifted slowly within the deep blue of the horizon. Michael looked down at where the waters fell. He saw the cave nestled in behind the waterfall. A wash of memories poured over him, so strong and vivid, they helped him ignore the calls from the people down below him. The memories helped him block out the flashing lights of the ambulances that had gathered on the shore. All he knew now was that he was stood in the only place that the world had ever allowed him and Grace to be together. Fate, design and circumstance had always held them at a distance from one another since that night. But now it was love's turn. The one thing that had always joined them was now going to keep them apart forever.

Wind held him now. His arms were outstretched, and his feet were flat on the firm ground. As if God himself had sat upon his heart, a huge weight bore down on Michael's chest. A single memory flashed in his mind. He saw the fallen statue of Christ in the church – the fire creeping over his saddened eyes. Feeling the wind wrap around him, Michael breathed deeply. His head began to dance to the tune of his charging heart. Pounding and pulsating, the beats thudded at his chest. As if angels had begun to rain down from the skies, the heavens opened up. In a show of bittersweet reflection, all of Michael's senses exploded. His dry lips could still taste Grace's kiss, his empty arms could still feel her entwined within them, and his closed eyes could finally see what he needed to do.

For as long as he could recall, he had begged God for a reason. He had always longed to know how someone could choose to abandon those that they truly loved the most. Tirelessly, he had searched in-between the lines of fate and faith, and only found a dim grey light within. But in this moment, stood at the end of the land – overlooking his favourite place on earth – Michael found his answer. And with arms wide open, he embraced his fate.

Knowing that he would sacrifice an eternity with her, Michael stepped from the cliff's edge and fell for Grace.

Falling, his eyes escaped into images of the life he was leaving behind. Realising his mother was not alone in heaven, all Michael saw was Grace. He saw her smile, her delicate hands, her awkward steps as she danced, and her piercing eyes. And above all else, he saw his sweetest friend; the love of his life. Feeling the air rush beneath him, all Michael could see was Grace in all her beauty. Right up until the moment he could see nothing at all.

***

The cadaver was rushed to the hospital. Michael's phone-call had made it crystal clear that the remains were to be brought to the attention of one doctor in particular. Once the doctor had seen the body of the young man he had broken such bad news to only an hour before, he knew immediately what he was facing. Within minutes, the operating room was prepped and ready to make history.

Cara had been asked to officially identify the deceased. Seeing Michael, cold and bruised, she had not been able to suppress her grief. Tears burst from her eyes, as her fist beat at the cold slab in the morgue. Composing herself, she had returned to her sister's ward. Grace was awake now, and the painkillers were beginning to wear off. Having felt the full effects of the day, Cara had taken some of her own painkillers, placing the rest inside her purse.

'I say sis, you look worse than I do.' Grace smiled as she saw Cara's sullen face. She almost broke down completely at the sight of Michael's bracelet in Grace's hand.

'I'll be fine. Don't you dare worry about me.' Cara's voice was cracked; her throat was choked.

'Oh, don't hide all the news from me sis. I know what's happening. I could hear the doctor talking to you earlier.'

'Really?'

'Yes. I just hope that it's quick. Where's Michael? I have so much to tell him.' Cara began to cry once more.

'Grace, they may be able to save you.' She tried her hardest to sound her most hopeful.

'What? But, how? I heard the doctor earlier.' Grace's face was a mixture of hope and anger. 'Don't mess with me sister. Not now of all times.' Grace felt a fire sting at her side.

'It's only a chance, but it's more than we had.'

'What is?'

'They've found you a liver. So the doctor is going to try to swap it with your damaged one.' Grace mulled over her sister's words. They were of sorrow rather than optimism.

'Who's liver exactly? If it's one of those wretched soldiers then I refuse to take it. I'd welcome my fate a thousand times over before I'd carry a part of them with me.' The pain was increasing by the second.

'No. It's not one of the soldiers.' Cara looked into her lap. She was still carrying the small biscuit tin from her house.

'What aren't you telling me?' Grace's heart-rate wasn't helping matters.

'Dear sister it's complicated. The doctor says that, to have any chance of this procedure being successful, the organ has to be as near a perfect match as possible. Well, the soldiers back at the church, their bodies were not fresh enough and their organs had already died. Also, we would not have had time to blood test all of them, before...'

'I died?' Grace was more in pain than angry. 'Come on sis, don't sugar the pill. Just tell me what's going on.'

'Michael must have seen your blood-type on your file.' Cara nodded to the flipchart on the end of the bed. 'Grace... it matched his.'

'What?' Grace lost her breath. Her hand clasped the bracelet so hard the bones in her fingers almost shattered.

'They say it was an accident; out at the cove.' Cara came closer to her sister. The wheels on her chair rubbed against the bed post. 'They found Michael's body at the bottom. I'm so sorry Grace.'

'An accident?' Grace wanted to get up but her legs failed her. 'He knew that place like no other. There's no way he would have fallen.' The look on Cara's face said it all. Michael's fate was no accident. He had chosen it.

'No. He wouldn't.' Grace began to cry. 'Why?'

'For you... Grace. To give you a chance.'

'But I don't want one without him.'

'I don't think he could live without you either.'

Pain covered Grace's body. She knew that taking any more painkillers could prove fatal, and so she chose to close her eyes and try to ride it out. Ignoring her agony, all her thoughts became targeted on Michael. In all his beauty, she had often seen true flashes of passionate anger whenever he heard the mention of his father. Having loved his mother so much – and so strong in his beliefs – Michael had been bewildered by his father's suicide. The act had seemed so selfish and cowardly – so short sighted. Michael had stressed over how his father could choose to toss his soul into limbo forever, knowing that he would never be reunited with his mother in heaven. From the moment he had first told Grace this story, he had vowed never to leave the one that he loved. She remembered how he had held her hand each time he wanted to tell her something. She remembered the words he had traced into her palm with his finger. The words he had never had chance to say to her. And now he was gone forever – cast into limbo by his own hand.

'Michael wanted you to have these.' Grace opened her damp eyes to the sound of her sister's voice. She was holding a small biscuit tin in her hands.

'What are they?' Grace sat up a little.

'His feelings. Every last one of them.' Cara placed her tin and purse onto the side table. 'I'll give you a moment alone with them. The doctors will be in shortly to take you to surgery. I'm hoping Michael's words will strengthen you for what's ahead.' Cara kissed her sister's hand before heading towards the door.

'Cara...' Grace whispered.

'Yes?'

'I love you.' Cara smiled at the sound of the words. It had been a while since she had heard them.

Moving the purse, Grace picked up the tin and placed it in her lap. The pain was beginning to weaken her, and she even found it difficult to pop open the lid. Once she had, what lay inside took her breath away. Tiny pieces of paper, folded and dated, filled the tin. Rummaging through the pile, Grace started at the beginning.

The words numbed her physical agony, but tortured her emotions. Each poem was more beautiful than the last. Exhausted, she did not tire of the words that were written down, but read on as she began to truly understand the feelings within them. Her eyes streamed as she found the final piece of paper. The date was closer to the present time than all of the rest. It was Michael's final poem.

Opening up the small, stained piece of paper, Grace read the words that would seal her fate.

If the heaven should decide that they need me more,
Then you'll lose the words I should have said before.
The ones that could never leave love behind,
Are those that would keep you always, by my side.

Tonight sits in darkness, tomorrow brings new light,
And with it comes chances to put our hearts in line.
So I offer my forever, and a love that's pure and true.
In life I give my soul, and in words I love you.

She held the poem to her breast. Her pulse was weakening beneath her hands. Feeling the soft air of the dawn creep into the room, Grace looked towards the door. Bodies filtered past the small window. Doctors and nurses were preparing for her surgery. The atmosphere was tense and tight. Knowing they were on the brink of making history, all the staff teetered on the edge of their nerves. Frantic and working against the clock, they rushed past one another like colliding tides.

Assessing both outcomes of the surgery, Grace had no interest in either of them. She knew that if she would survive it, then she faced a lifetime away from Michael. However, in the likelihood that she would die, she then stood to endure eternal life without him. Alive or dead, both outcomes left her alone. Now only words were all she had, but these were no longer enough. All she wanted was Michael.

As the day broke upon the land, a light shone through the window. It warmed Grace's face and blinded her. Shading her eyes, she put the tin back onto the side table. Not being able to see properly, she knocked over Cara's purse, causing the contents to spill out. Among the tissues and a small mirror sat a plastic bottle full apart from the two tablets Cara had taken earlier.

Finding the strength to open the lid, Grace emptied the container into her trembling hand. Filling her palm, the bundle of painkillers nested on top of Michael's bracelet — only the silver face of the Madonna stared through the centre of the pile. Clenching her fist, Grace brought her hand to her mouth and whispered a prayer. It asked not for forgiveness, but for understanding.

The soft whisper of *Amen* was followed by an unholy consumption.

Swallowing the painkillers, Grace could feel their dry descent down her throat. Taking a final sip of water, she lay back, rested her head upon her pillow, and closed her eyes for the last time. The pain she felt was masked by the light that shone through the window. Her lungs became shallow and her chest sank. Hearing the morning cry of the birds — singing in peaceful harmony — Grace listened to her slowing heart. As the darkness closed in around her thoughts, a single light shone within the centre. No angels stood waiting to carry her, nor were there heavenly steps upon her path. Instead she saw a solitary face; a face with which she would spend her forever.

Having taken its final breath, Grace's body became still. Her hand fell by her side and released the bracelet within. With nobody left to carry it, Michael's cross fell to the ground.

Breaking in through the window, the light of a new day shone upon the silver faces of the pendant and the crucifix.

-Epilogue-

He had picked the most beautiful flowers he could find. Admiring his selection, he adjusted the huge sunflower that rested in the middle of a bunch of wildflowers. Having heard Michael mention them a thousand times, he made sure to add a handful of white windflowers to the bunch. God, he missed his friend so much. He no longer drank as often as used to – finding that drinking to forget only brought back more memories. And despite months of mourning, every memory still hit him like a bullet. However, time had made him able to smile through the pain. Within the brief time that they had shared together lay a life worth celebrating, and a friendship like no other.

Passing through the town, Oscar drank in the scenery. The day was held between morning and afternoon, and the traders were preparing for their peak hour. Business beat on as usual. Shaded only by the lightest of cloud, the sun embraced the land like a returning relative. It shone over every face in the town, forcing warm smiles upon squinted expressions.

Near the centre of the town sat a flat plot of land. There were plans to rebuild the church, and countless fêtes and fairs had been held to raise funds. Even Oscar had been dragged into running a sponsored five miles to contribute, and still the balls of his feet throbbed above the burst blistered skin. Everyone had paid up though, and it was rumoured that the first brick was due to be placed by Father Daniel on Sunday. Not ready to make his peace with God, however, Oscar planned to keep his distance. The brutal and blunt end that he had brought to the cadet who had shot Grace still haunted every blink of his eyes. From that moment on, Oscar had not found an inch of darkness without the man's bloody, beaten face hanging within it.

Letting the sun lead the way, Oscar headed for the horizon. Colour had returned to the land, and the farmland looked its most fruitful. Having inherited a large proportion of the estate, Cara had returned it to all the independent farmers, letting them feed their own families and build their own legacy. But her generosity did not end there. With full consent from her mother Fiona, Cara had renovated half of the manor house into a school where she taught music to the children who could not afford the tuition fees of the surrounding colleges. Such was her talent that many families hid their fortunes so that their children could enjoy the teachings of Cara. Even when these were found out, she never had the heart to refuse a child of music.

Passing by the estate for the last time, Oscar could hear the sound of one of Cara's classes carry out upon the whispering winds. He removed his camera – a Kodak No.2 Folding Brownie

— from his satchel. It had been a Christmas gift from an American soldier he had met in the trenches, and still worked perfectly. The ball bearing shutters were in fine working order as Oscar clicked away merrily. The imitation leather of the Brownie sparkled in his hand, looking like a small purse if seen from a distance.

Finally reaching the final site, Oscar picked the flowers out from his satchel and laid them onto the ground. Bunched and tightly bound by string, they sat perched between two gravestones.

Sat outside of the cemetery fences, while those buried within looked out from east to west, the gravestones of Michael and Grace faced each other, with the coastline by their side.

'What did I tell you?' Oscar stood looking at Michael's humble gravestone. 'The dead do get the best views.'

He chuckled to hold back the lump that blocked his throat.

'Anyway, I've come to bid my farewells.' Oscar found his voice. 'Well my old chum, I'm finally leaving this town. There's very little here keeping me now, and I need to find what's out there for me.' He took a breath. 'I miss you Michael... and you too Grace, don't you get jealous now. But the fact is, I'm not getting any younger, and I want to find for myself what the two of you had. Anyway, I think mother's growing sick of me and my ears can't take any more of her blasted tales.'

Standing back, Oscar admired the view. The heavens seemed to wink as a cloud passed over the sun. Gulls glided above the gentle tide of the sea, and children played freely upon the shores.

Focusing his camera, Oscar took his final shot of Orplow. It captured where the coast met with the horizon, and where the blue skies were cut by the bright white fence of the cemetery. And most of all, it captured the two gravestones that broke away from tradition and faced each other forever.

'Goodbye old friend.' Oscar smiled as he turned his back for the last time. Home was no longer here for him.

ND - #0244 - 270225 - C0 - 234/156/26 - PB - 9781780911601 - Matt Lamination